THE YEAR IS 1327.

Franciscans in a wealthy Italian abbey are suspected of heresy, and an English Brother, William of Baskerville, is sent to investigate. His delicate mission is suddenly overshadowed by seven bizarre murders that take place in seven days and nights of apocalyptic terror. One monk is found dead in a cask of pig's blood; another is discovered floating in a bathhouse; still another has been crushed to death after falling from a window. Rumors hum throughout the abbey, and people piously cover their tracks, hiding clues. Brother William turns detective, and a uniquely deft one at that. His tools are the logic of Aristotle, the theology of Aquinas, the empirical insights of Roger Bacon—all sharpened to a glistening edge by wry humor and ferocious curiosity. He collects evidence, deciphers secret symbols and coded manuscripts, and digs into the eerie secret labyrinth of abbey life. Before his task is completed, Brother William witnesses crimes beyond his imaginings and meets an enemy with the awesome features of the Antichrist...

"An alchemical marriage of murder mystery and Christian mystery. It conveys remarkably the desperation of a dying culture, while at the same time touching on perennial issues of love, religion, scholarship and politics . . . prodigious necromancy."

—*Washington Post Book World*

"A kind of novel that changes our mind, replaces our reality with its own. We live in a new world . . . a time of multiple popes and multiple anti-Christs, a time when a man would trade sexual favors for a book, when the papal palace in Avignon displayed 'crucifixes where Christ is nailed by a single hand while the other touches a purse hanging from his belt, to indicate that he authorizes the use of money for religious ends . . .' The plot is as neat as Conan Doyle or Christie . . . We accept the tale as Eco submits it, 'for sheer narrative pleasure': 'For it is a tale of books, not of everyday worries.'"

—*Los Angeles Times*

"Eco has written a long, rich, multilayered novel about murder, dogma, heresy and the pursuit of knowledge, both sacred and profane, in 14th century Italy. And he has given us that rare gift, a truly popular novel that has been accepted by critics as well . . . The mystery in itself is intriguing, but the real pleasure is in the richness of context and character. Eco has written a novel that celebrates imagination and skepticism, faint but important lights in dark times. He also makes it clear that such qualities are needed just as much now, in our own times."

—*Philadelphia Inquirer*

"This splendid book from Italy deserves to be read and treasured all over America . . . an exciting detective story, a colorful evocation of medieval life and a lively morality tale on fanaticism, books and the search for truth . . . Eco is a superb practitioner of the art of creating character, dialogue, setting and plot. And for all its erudition, the book moves with the pace of a thriller."

—*Newsday*

"A puzzling, scary detective story...a picture of the dark side of 14th century monasticism...rich in philosophical and theological arguments...demanding...gripping...(not) easily forgotten."

—*The Wall Street Journal*

"Absorbing and provocative...one begins to understand how medieval clerics reasoned. Then one begins to think in the same way. Finally, with a certain discomfort, one realizes that these antique habits of thought are still present and active, working under modern aliases. This is the real purpose of Mr. Eco's novel—to make the reader see the similarities between the fourteenth century and today. The mystery, while not irrelevant, is frosting on a rather rich cake."

—*Atlantic Monthly*

"Irresistible...explodes with pyrotechnic inventions, literally as well as figuratively."

—*The New York Times Book Review*

"This rose is a many-petaled contraption, as much history as mystery...Eco's learning is prodigious. Fortunately, it does not interfere with his keen satiric sense...THE NAME OF THE ROSE is a first-class mystery, but it does have higher claims as well. Eco asserts these by using the genre itself as a trope; the mystery is a figure for all epistemological questioning—how do we know things, what can we know?"

—*The New Republic*

"Amazingly complex, richly textured and unapologetically intelligent ...ambitious, creative, thought-provoking. Like the best books from any age, it opens up a new world and helps us understand our old one—and ourselves—a little better."

—*Atlanta Journal-Constitution*

"Wholly engrossing as a mystery. It also gives a brilliant picture of the late Middle Ages...Wonderful passages describe the physical realities of those times, while others reflect the dazzling testaments and debates that later would lead both to the Renaissance and to the Reformation."

—*Boston Ledger*

"Through Eco's brilliant use of the language, the 14th century comes alive . . . You are transported effortlessly back in time to an era of doubts, suspicions, upheaval and madness. You feel, taste, touch and become a part of one of the most colorful and frightening periods of history. This beautifully written, philosophical as well as intriguing investigation is no mere detective tale, it is a many-faceted gem of a novel, well worth the reading."

—*Worcester, Mass. Telegram*

"THE NAME OF THE ROSE follows the Sherlock Holmes form: a series of baffling crimes which can only be solved through the intervention of a master detective who opposes his scientific methods to the prevailing emotionalism and superstition . . . But was there ever a mystery story like this? Eco demonstrates what many fans of the genre have always suspected, that sometimes a 'low' form of literature can provide the best solution to the labyrinth of the human heart."

—*Rochester, NY Times-Union*

"A brilliant match of method and material, THE NAME OF THE ROSE is that rarest of literary blossoms: a page-turner about ideas."

—*The Pittsburgh Press*

"What Eco has given us beneath the fascinating guise of a complex murder mystery, is a moral, intellectual, and spiritual guided tour of a time in human history that seems, for all its crudity of creature comforts, more richly textured than our own . . . We come away enriched by seeing contemporary questions unraveled through a parallel, but distinctive, historical period."

—*Seattle Weekly*

"A masterwork by a scholar who knows how to play . . . dazzling . . . delightful . . . masterful."

—*Houston Chronicle*

"It has both a sense of humor and a sense of excitement, a combination of qualities that is quite rare. But it also has moral and philosophical implications about liberty and tolerance."

—*Newark Star-Ledger*

"Eco's novel reads like Arthur Conan Doyle and Thomas Mann combined forces... THE NAME OF THE ROSE meets the ancient formula of enlightening as it entertains. Once you begin it, you will certainly finish it."

—*Greensboro, NC News*

"A brilliantly conceived adventure into another time, an intelligent and complex novel and a lively and well-plotted mystery."

—*San Francisco Chronicle*

"An extraordinarily fascinating novel with numerous levels of interest... Mystery enthusiasts will love its unusual setting and medievalists will breathe a sigh of pleasure at its convivial rendering of life in the early part of the 14th century."

—*Santa Cruz Sentinel*

"A richly textured portrait of the times; the pungent foods, herbal medicines, sexual mores. This masterful, far-ranging novel—narrated with elegance, spirit, and wit—has won top literary awards in Europe."

—*Mystery News*

"A remarkable reading experience... a novel that reeks of the spicy magic of an illuminated manuscript recovered from a well-sealed treasure chest."

—*Portland Oregonian*

"Wonderful... magnificent... well-written, well-conceived, an extremely intelligent book. Readers who enjoyed Barbara Tuchman's *A Distant Mirror* will also enjoy this."

—*Tulsa, OK World*

"Both an entertaining detective story and a tour-de-force of medieval scholarship... both an entertaining puzzle and a richly detailed portrait of another world."

—*The Grand Rapids, Iowa Press*

Translated from the Italian by
William Weaver

U M B E R T O   E C O

THE
NAME
OF THE
ROSE

WARNER BOOKS

A Warner Communications Company

NATURALLY, A MANUSCRIPT

On August 16, 1968, I was handed a book written by a certain Abbé Vallet, *Le Manuscrit de Dom Adson de Melk, traduit en français d'après l'édition de Dom J. Mabillon* (Aux Presses de l'Abbaye de la Source, Paris, 1842). Supplemented by historical information that was actually quite scant, the book claimed to reproduce faithfully a fourteenth-century manuscript that, in its turn, had been found in the monastery of Melk by the great eighteenth-century man of learning, to whom we owe so much information about the history of the Benedictine order. The scholarly discovery (I mean mine, the third in chronological order) entertained me while I was in Prague, waiting for a dear friend. Six days later Soviet troops invaded that unhappy city. I managed, not without adventure, to reach the Austrian border at Linz, and from there I journeyed to Vienna, where I met my beloved, and together we sailed up the Danube.

In a state of intellectual excitement, I read with fascination the terrible story of Adso of Melk, and I allowed myself to be so absorbed by it that, almost in a single burst of energy, I completed a translation, using some of those large notebooks from the Papeterie Joseph Gibert in which it is so pleasant to write if you use a felt-tip pen. And as I was writing, we reached the vicinity of Melk, where, perched over a bend in the river, the handsome Stift stands to this day, after several restorations during the course of the centuries. As the reader must have guessed, in the monastery library I found no trace of Adso's manuscript.

Before we reached Salzburg, one tragic night in a little hotel on the shores of the Mondsee, my traveling-companionship was abruptly interrupted, and the person with whom I was traveling disappeared—taking Abbé Vallet's book, not out of spite, but because of the abrupt and untidy way in which our relationship ended. And so I was left with a number of manuscript notebooks in my hand, and a great emptiness in my heart.

A few months later, in Paris, I decided to get to the bottom of my research. Among the few pieces of information I had derived from the French book, I still had the reference to its source, exceptionally detailed and precise:

Vetera analecta, sive *collectio veterum aliquot operum* & opusculorum omnis generis, carminum, epistolarum, diplomaton, epitaphiorum, &, *cum itinere germanico*, adnotationibus & aliquot disquisitionibus R.P.D. Joannis Mabillon, Presbiteri ac Monachi Ord. Sancti Benedicti e Congregatione S. Mauri—*Nova Editio* cui accessere *Mabilonii* vita & aliquot opuscula, scilicet Dissertatio de *Pane Eucharistico, Azymo et Fermentato* ad Eminentiss. Cardinalem *Bona*. Subiungitur opusculum *Eldefonsi* Hispaniensis Episcopi de eodem argumento *Et Eusebii* Romani ad *Theophilum* Gallum epistola, *De cultu sanctorum ignotorum*, Parisiis, apud Levesque, ad Pontem S. Michaelis, MDCCXXI, cum privilegio Regis.

I quickly found the *Vetera analecta* at the Bibliothèque Sainte Geneviève, but to my great surprise the edition I came upon differed from the description in two details: first, the publisher, who was given here as "Montalant, ad Ripam P.P. Augustinianorum (prope Pontem S. Michaelis)," and also the date, which was two years later. I needn't add that these analecta did not comprehend any manuscript of Adso or Adson of Melk; on the contrary, as anyone interested can check, they are a collection of brief or medium-length texts, whereas the story transcribed by Vallet ran to several hundred pages. At the same time, I consulted illustrious medievalists such as the dear and unforgettable Étienne Gilson, but it was evident that the only *Vetera analecta* were those I had seen at Sainte Geneviève. A quick trip to the Abbaye de la Source, in the vicinity of Passy, and a conversation with my friend Dom Arne Lahnestedt further convinced me that no Abbé Vallet had published books on the abbey's presses (for that matter, nonexistent). French scholars are notoriously careless about furnishing reliable bibliographical information, but this case went beyond all reasonable pessimism. I began to think I had encountered a forgery. By now the Vallet volume itself could not be recovered (or at least I didn't dare go and ask it back from the person who had taken it from me). I had only my notes left, and I was beginning to have doubts about them.

There are magic moments, involving great physical fatigue and intense motor excitement, that produce visions of people known in the past ("en me retraçant ces détails, j'en suis à me demander s'ils sont réels, ou bien si je les ai rêvés"). As I learned later from the delightful little book of the Abbé de Bucquoy, there are also visions of books as yet unwritten.

If something new had not occurred, I would still be wondering where the story of Adso of Melk originated; but then, in 1970, in Buenos Aires, as I was browsing among the shelves of a little antiquarian bookseller on Corrientes, not far from the more illustrious Patio del Tango of that great street, I came upon the Castilian version of a little work by Milo Temesvar, *On the Use of Mirrors in the Game of Chess*. It was an Italian translation of the original, which, now impossible to find, was in Georgian (Tbilisi, 1934); and here, to my great surprise, I read copious quotations from Adso's manuscript, though the source was neither Vallet nor Mabillon; it was Father Athanasius Kircher (but which work?). A scholar—whom I prefer not to name—later assured me that (and he quoted indexes from memory) the great Jesuit never mentioned Adso of Melk. But Temesvar's pages were before my eyes, and the episodes he cited were the same as those of the Vallet manuscript (the description of the labyrinth in particular left no room for doubt).

I concluded that Adso's memoirs appropriately share the nature of the events he narrates: shrouded in many, shadowy mysteries, beginning with the identity of the author and ending with the abbey's location, about which Adso is stubbornly, scrupulously silent. Conjecture allows us to designate a vague area between Pomposa and Conques, with reasonable likelihood that the community was somewhere along the central ridge of the Apennines, between Piedmont, Liguria, and France. As for the period in which the events described take place, we are at the end of November 1327; the date of the author's writing, on the other hand, is uncertain. Inasmuch as he describes himself as a novice in 1327 and says he is close to death as he writes his memoirs, we can calculate roughly that the manuscript was written in the last or next-to-last decade of the fourteenth century.

On sober reflection, I find few reasons for publishing my Italian version of an obscure, neo-Gothic French version of a seventeenth-century Latin edition of a work written in Latin by a German monk toward the end of the fourteenth century.

First of all, what style should I employ? The temptation to follow Italian models of the period had to be rejected as totally unjustified: not only does Adso write in Latin, but it is also clear from the whole development of the text that his culture (or the culture of the abbey, which clearly influences him) dates back even further; it is manifestly a summation, over several centuries, of learning and stylistic quirks that can be linked with the late-medieval Latin tradition. Adso thinks and writes like a monk who has remained impervious to the revolution of the vernacular, still bound to the pages housed in the library he tells about, educated on patristic-scholastic texts; and his story (apart from the fourteenth-century references and events, which Adso reports with countless perplexities and always by hearsay) could have been written, as far as the language and the learned quotations go, in the twelfth or thirteenth century.

On the other hand, there is no doubt that, in translating Adso's Latin into his own neo-Gothic French, Vallet took some liberties, and not only stylistic liberties. For example, the characters speak sometimes of the properties of herbs, clearly referring to the book of secrets attributed to Albertus Magnus, which underwent countless revisions over the centuries. It is certain that Adso knew the work, but the fact remains that passages he quotes from it echo too literally both formulas of Paracelsus and obvious interpolations from an edition of Albertus unquestionably dating from the Tudor period.[1] However, I discovered later that during the time when Vallet was transcribing (?) the manuscript of

[1] *Liber aggregationis seu liber secretorum Alberti Magni*, Londinium, juxta pontem qui vulgariter dicitur Flete brigge, MCCCC-LXXXV.

Adso, there was circulating in Paris an eighteenth-century edition of the *Grand* and the *Petit Albert*,[2] now irreparably corrupt. In any case, how could I be sure that the text known to Adso or the monks whose discussions he recorded did not also contain, among glosses, scholia, and various appendices, annotations that would go on to enrich subsequent scholarship?

Finally, was I to retain in Latin the passages that Abbé Vallet himself did not feel it opportune to translate, perhaps to preserve the ambience of the period? There were no particular reasons to do so, except a perhaps misplaced sense of fidelity to my source....I have eliminated excesses, but I have retained a certain amount. And I fear that I have imitated those bad novelists who, introducing a French character, make him exclaim "Parbleu!" and "La femme, ah! la femme!"

In short, I am full of doubts. I really don't know why I have decided to pluck up my courage and present, as if it were authentic, the manuscript of Adso of Melk. Let us say it is an act of love. Or, if you like, a way of ridding myself of numerous, persistent obsessions.

I transcribe my text with no concern for timeliness. In the years when I discovered the Abbé Vallet volume, there was a widespread conviction that one should write only out of a commitment to the present, in order to change the world. Now, after ten years or more, the man of letters (restored to his loftiest dignity) can happily write out of pure love of writing. And so I now feel free to tell, for sheer narrative pleasure, the story of Adso of Melk, and I am comforted and consoled in finding it immeasurably remote in time (now that the waking of reason has dispelled all the monsters that its

[2]*Les Admirables Secrets d'Albert le Grand,* A Lyon, Chez les Héritiers Beringos, Fratres, à l'Enseigne d'Agrippa, MDCCLXXV; *Secrets merveilleux de la magie naturelle et cabalistique du Petit Albert*, A Lyon, Chez les Héritiers Beringos, Fratres, à l'Enseigne d'Agrippa, MDCCXXIX.

sleep had generated), gloriously lacking in any relevance for our day, atemporally alien to our hopes and our certainties.

For it is a tale of books, not of everyday worries, and reading it can lead us to recite, with à Kempis, the great imitator: "In omnibus requiem quaesivi, et nusquam inveni nisi in angulo cum libro."

January 5, 1980

NOTE

ADSO'S MANUSCRIPT IS DIVIDED INTO SEVEN DAYS, AND each day into periods corresponding to the liturgical hours. The subtitles, in the third person, were probably added by Vallet. But since they are helpful in orienting the reader, and since this usage is also not unknown to much of the vernacular literature of the period, I did not feel it necessary to eliminate them.

Adso's references to the canonical hours caused me some puzzlement, because their meaning varied according to the place and the season; moreover, it is entirely probable that in the fourteenth century the instructions given by Saint Benedict in the Rule were not observed with absolute precision.

Nevertheless, as a guide to the reader, the following schedule is, I believe, credible. It is partly deduced from the text and partly based on a comparison of the original Rule with the description of monastic life given by Édouard Schneider in *Les Heures bénédictines* (Paris, Grasset, 1925).

Matins   (which Adso sometimes refers to by the older expression "Vigiliae") Between 2:30 and 3:00 in the morning.

Lauds   (which in the most ancient tradition were called "Matutini" or "Matins") Between 5:00 and 6:00 in the morning, in order to end at dawn.

Prime   Around 7:30, shortly before daybreak.

Terce   Around 9:00.

Sext   Noon (in a monastery where the monks did not work in the fields, it was also the hour of the midday meal in winter).

Nones   Between 2:00 and 3:00 in the afternoon.

Vespers   Around 4:30, at sunset (the Rule prescribes eating supper before dark).

Compline   Around 6:00 (before 7:00, the monks go to bed).

The calculation is based on the fact that in northern Italy at the end of November, the sun rises around 7:30 A.M. and sets around 4:40 P.M.

THE ABBEY

A Aedificium J Balneary
B Church   K Infirmary
D Cloister   M Pigsties
F Dormitory N Stables
H Chapter house R Smithy

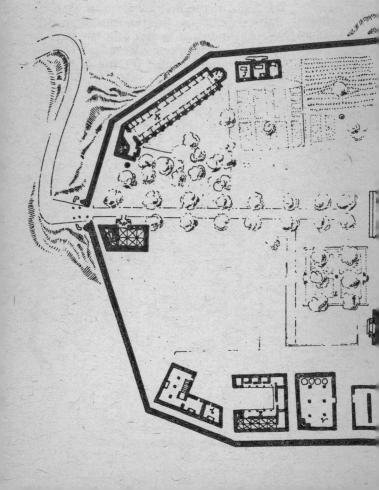

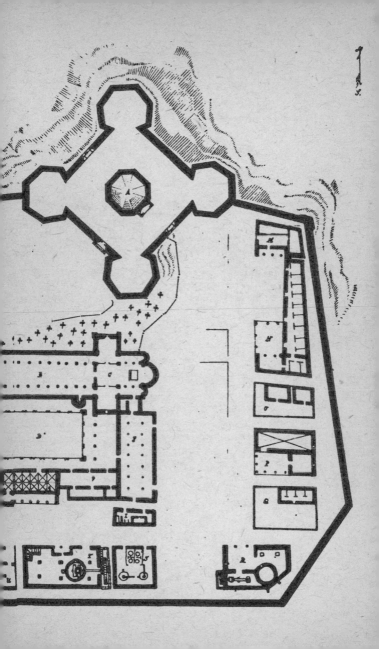

THE
NAME
OF THE
ROSE

PROLOGUE

In the beginning was the Word and the Word was with God, and the Word was God. This was beginning with God and the duty of every faithful monk would be to repeat every day with chanting humility the one never-changing event whose incontrovertible truth can be asserted. But we see now through a glass darkly, and the truth, before it is revealed to all, face to face, we see in fragments (alas, how illegible) in the error of the world, so we must spell out its faithful signals even when they seem obscure to us and as if amalgamated with a will wholly bent on evil.

Having reached the end of my poor sinner's life, my hair now white, I grow old as the world does, waiting to be lost in the bottomless pit of silent and deserted divinity, sharing in the light of angelic intelligences; confined now with my heavy, ailing body in this cell in the dear monastery of Melk, I prepare to leave on this parchment my testimony as to the wondrous and terrible events that I happened to observe in my youth, now

3

repeating verbatim all I saw and heard, without venturing to seek a design, as if to leave to those who will come after (if the Antichrist has not come first) signs of signs, so that the prayer of deciphering may be exercised on them.

May the Lord grant me the grace to be the transparent witness of the happenings that took place in the abbey whose name it is only right and pious now to omit, toward the end of the year of our Lord 1327, when the Emperor Louis came down into Italy to restore the dignity of the Holy Roman Empire, in keeping with the designs of the Almighty and to the confusion of the wicked usurper, simoniac, and heresiarch who in Avignon brought shame on the holy name of the apostle (I refer to the sinful soul of Jacques of Cahors, whom the impious revered as John XXII).

Perhaps, to make more comprehensible the events in which I found myself involved, I should recall what was happening in those last years of the century, as I understood it then, living through it, and as I remember it now, complemented by other stories I heard afterward—if my memory still proves capable of connecting the threads of happenings so many and confused.

In the early years of that century Pope Clement V had moved the apostolic seat to Avignon, leaving Rome prey to the ambitions of the local overlords: and gradually the holy city of Christianity had been transformed into a circus, or into a brothel, riven by the struggles among its leaders; though called a republic, it was not one, and it was assailed by armed bands, subjected to violence and looting. Ecclesiastics, eluding secular jurisdiction, commanded groups of malefactors and robbed, sword in hand, transgressing and organizing evil commerce. How was it possible to prevent the Caput Mundi from becoming again, and rightly, the goal of the man who wanted to assume the crown of the Holy Roman Empire and restore the dignity of that temporal dominion that had belonged to the Caesars?

Thus in 1314 five German princes in Frankfurt elected Louis the Bavarian supreme ruler of the empire. But that same day, on the opposite shore of the Main, the Count Palatine of the Rhine and the Archbishop of Cologne elected Frederick of Austria to the same high rank. Two emperors for a single throne and a single pope for two: a situation that, truly, fomented great disorder....

Two years later, in Avignon, the new Pope was elected, Jacques of Cahors, an old man of seventy-two who took, as I have said, the name of John XXII, and heaven grant that no pontiff take again a name now so distasteful to the righteous. A Frenchman, devoted to the King of France (the men of that corrupt land are always inclined to foster the interests of their own people, and are unable to look upon the whole world as their spiritual home), he had supported Philip the Fair against the Knights Templars, whom the King accused (I believe unjustly) of the most shameful crimes so that he could seize their possessions with the complicity of that renegade ecclesiastic.

In 1322 Louis the Bavarian defeated his rival Frederick. Fearing a single emperor even more than he had feared two, John excommunicated the victor, who in return denounced the Pope as a heretic. I must also recall how, that very year, the chapter of the Franciscans was convened in Perugia, and the minister general, Michael of Cesena, accepting the entreaties of the Spirituals (of whom I will have occasion to speak), proclaimed as a matter of faith and doctrine the poverty of Christ, who, if he owned something with his apostles, possessed it only as usus facti. A worthy resolution, meant to safeguard the virtue and purity of the order, it highly displeased the Pope, who perhaps discerned in it a principle that would jeopardize the very claims that he, as head of the church, had made, denying the empire the right to elect bishops, and asserting on the contrary that the papal throne had the right to invest the emperor.

Moved by these or other reasons, John condemned the Franciscan propositions in 1323 with the decretal *Cum inter nonnullos*.

It was at this point, I imagine, that Louis saw the Franciscans, now the Pope's enemies, as his potential allies. By affirming the poverty of Christ, they were somehow strengthening the ideas of the imperial theologians, namely Marsilius of Padua and John of Jandun. And finally, not many months before the events I am narrating, Louis came to an agreement with the defeated Frederick, descended into Italy, and was crowned in Milan.

This was the situation when I—a young Benedictine novice in the monastery of Melk—was removed from the peace of the cloister by my father, fighting in Louis's train, not least among his barons. He thought it wise to take me with him so that I might know the wonders of Italy and be present when the Emperor was crowned in Rome. But the siege of Pisa then absorbed him in military concerns. Left to myself, I roamed among the cities of Tuscany, partly out of idleness and partly out of a desire to learn. But this undisciplined freedom, my parents thought, was not suitable for an adolescent devoted to a contemplative life. And on the advice of Marsilius, who had taken a liking to me, they decided to place me under the direction of a learned Franciscan, Brother William of Baskerville, about to undertake a mission that would lead him to famous cities and ancient abbeys. Thus I became William's scribe and disciple at the same time, nor did I ever regret it, because with him I was witness to events worthy of being handed down, as I am now doing, to those who will come after us.

I did not then know what Brother William was seeking, and to tell the truth, I still do not know today, and I presume he himself did not know, moved as he was solely by the desire for truth, and by the suspicion—

which I could see he always harbored—that the truth was not what was appearing to him at any given moment. And perhaps during those years he had been distracted from his beloved studies by secular duties. The mission with which William had been charged remained unknown to me while we were on our journey, or, rather, he never spoke to me about it. It was only by overhearing bits of his conversations with the abbots of the monasteries where we stopped along the way that I formed some idea of the nature of this assignment. But I did not understand it fully until we reached our destination, as I will tell presently. Our destination was to the north, but our journey did not follow a straight line, and we rested at various abbeys. Thus it happened that we turned westward when our final goal was to the east, almost following the line of mountains that from Pisa leads in the direction of the pilgrim's way to Santiago, pausing in a place which the terrible events that took place there dissuade me from identifying more closely now, but whose lords were liege to the empire, and where the abbots of our order, all in agreement, opposed the heretical, corrupt Pope. Our journey lasted two weeks, amid various vicissitudes, and during that time I had the opportunity to know (never enough, I remain convinced) my new master.

In the pages to follow I shall not indulge in descriptions of persons—except when a facial expression, or a gesture, appears as a sign of a mute but eloquent language—because, as Boethius says, nothing is more fleeting than external form, which withers and alters like the flowers of the field at the appearance of autumn; and what would be the point of saying today that the abbot Abo had a stern eye and pale cheeks, when by now he and those around him are dust and their bodies have the mortal grayness of dust (only their souls, God grant, shining with a light that will never be extinguished)? But I would like to describe William at least once, because his singular features struck me, and it is charac-

7

teristic of the young to become bound to an older and wiser man not only by the spell of his words and the sharpness of his mind, but also by the superficial form of his body, which proves very dear, like the figure of a father, whose gestures we study and whose frowns, whose smile we observe—without a shadow of lust to pollute this form (perhaps the only that is truly pure) of corporal love.

In the past men were handsome and great (now they are children and dwarfs), but this is merely one of the many facts that demonstrate the disaster of an aging world. The young no longer want to study anything, learning is in decline, the whole world walks on its head, blind men lead others equally blind and cause them to plunge into the abyss, birds leave the nest before they can fly, the jackass plays the lyre, oxen dance. Mary no longer loves the contemplative life and Martha no longer loves the active life, Leah is sterile, Rachel has a carnal eye, Cato visits brothels, Lucretius becomes a woman. Everything is on the wrong path. In those days, thank God, I acquired from my master the desire to learn and a sense of the straight way, which remains even when the path is tortuous.

Brother William's physical appearance was at that time such as to attract the attention of the most inattentive observer. His height surpassed that of a normal man and he was so thin that he seemed still taller. His eyes were sharp and penetrating; his thin and slightly beaky nose gave his countenance the expression of a man on the lookout, save in certain moments of sluggishness of which I shall speak. His chin also denoted a firm will, though the long face covered with freckles—such as I often saw among those born between Hibernia and Northumbria—could occasionally express hesitation and puzzlement. In time I realized that what seemed a lack of confidence was only curiosity, but at the beginning I knew little of this virtue, which I thought, rather, a passion of the covetous spirit. I believed instead that the rational spirit should not indulge such passion, but feed only on the Truth, which (I thought) one knows from the outset.

Boy that I was, I was first, and most deeply, struck by some clumps of yellowish hair that protruded from his ears, and by his thick blond eyebrows. He had perhaps seen fifty springs and was therefore already very old, but his tireless body moved with an agility I myself often lacked. His energy seemed inexhaustible when a burst of activity overwhelmed him. But from time to time, as if his vital spirit had something of the crayfish, he moved backward in moments of inertia, and I watched him lie for hours on my pallet in my cell, uttering barely a few monosyllables, without contracting a single muscle of his face. On those occasions a vacant, absent expression appeared in his eyes, and I would have suspected he was in the power of some vegetal substance capable of producing visions if the obvious temperance of his life had not led me to reject this thought. I will not deny, however, that in the course of the journey, he sometimes stopped at the edge of a meadow, at the entrance to a forest, to gather some herb (always the same one, I believe): and he would then chew it with an absorbed look. He kept some of it with him, and ate it in the moments of greatest tension (and we had a number of them at the abbey!). Once, when I asked him what it was, he said laughing that a good Christian can sometimes learn also from the infidels, and when I asked him to let me taste it, he replied that herbs that are good for an old Franciscan are not good for a young Benedictine.

During our time together we did not have occasion to lead a very regular life: even at the abbey we remained up at night and collapsed wearily during the day, nor did we take part regularly in the holy offices. On our journey, however, he seldom stayed awake after compline, and his habits were frugal. Sometimes, also at the abbey, he would spend the whole day walking in the vegetable garden, examining the plants as if they were chrysoprases or emeralds; and I saw him roaming about the treasure crypt, looking at a coffer studded with emeralds and chrysoprases as if it were a clump of thorn apple. At other times he would pass an entire day in the great hall of the library, leafing through manuscripts as if seeking nothing but his own enjoyment (while, around us, the corpses of monks, horribly murdered, were multiplying). One day I found him strolling in the flower garden without any apparent aim, as if he did not have to account to God for his works. In my order they had taught me quite a different way of expending my time, and I said so to him. And he answered that the beauty of the cosmos derives not only from unity in variety, but also from variety in unity. This seemed to me an answer dictated by crude common sense, but I learned subsequently that the men of his land often define things in ways in which it seems that the enlightening power of reason has scant function.

During our period at the abbey his hands were always covered with the dust of books, the gold of still-fresh illumination, or with yellowish substances he touched in Severinus's infirmary. He seemed unable to think save with his hands, an attribute I considered then worthier of a mechanic: but even when his hands touched the most fragile things, such as certain freshly illuminated codices, or pages worn by time and friable as unleavened bread, he possessed, it seemed to me, an extraordinarily delicate touch, the same that he used in handling his machines. I will tell, in fact, how this strange man carried with him, in his bag, instruments that I had never seen before then, which he called his wondrous machines. Machines, he said, are an effect of art, which is nature's ape, and they reproduce not its forms but the operation itself. He explained to me thus the wonders of the clock, the astrolabe, and the magnet.

But at the beginning I feared it was witchcraft, and I pretended to sleep on certain clear nights when he (with a strange triangle in his hand) stood watching the stars. The Franciscans I had known in Italy and in my own land were simple men, often illiterate, and I expressed to him my amazement at his learning. But he said to me, smiling, that the Franciscans of his island were cast in another mold: "Roger Bacon, whom I venerate as my master, teaches that the divine plan will one day encompass the science of machines, which is natural and healthy magic. And one day it will be possible, by exploiting the power of nature, to create instruments of navigation by which ships will proceed *unico homine regente*, and far more rapid than those propelled by sails or oars; and there will be self-propelled wagons 'and flying apparatuses of such form that a man seated in them, by turning a device, can flap artificial wings, *ad modum avis volantis*.' And tiny instruments will lift huge weights and vehicles will allow travel on the bottom of the sea."

When I asked him where these machines were, he told me that they had already been made in ancient times, and some even in our own time: "Except the flying instrument, which I have never seen or known anyone who has seen, but I know of a learned man who has conceived it. And bridges can be built across rivers without columns or other support, and other unheard-of machines are possible. But you must not worry if they do not yet exist, because that does not mean they will not exist later. And I say to you that God wishes them to be, and certainly they already are in His mind, even if my friend from Occam denies that ideas exist in such a way; and I do not say this because we can determine the divine nature but precisely because we cannot set any limit to it." Nor was this the only contradictory proposition I heard him utter; but even now, when I am old and wiser than I was then, I have not completely understood how he could have such faith in

11

his friend from Occam and at the same time swear by the words of Bacon, as he was accustomed to doing. It is also true that in those dark times a wise man had to believe things that were in contradiction among themselves.

There, of Brother William I have perhaps said things without sense, as if to collect from the very beginning the disjointed impressions of him that I had then. Who he was, and what he was doing, my good reader, you will perhaps deduce better from the actions he performed in the days we spent in the abbey. Nor do I promise you an accomplished design, but, rather, a tale of events (those, yes) wondrous and awful.

And so, after I had come to know my master day by day, and spent the many hours of our journey in long conversations which, when appropriate, I will relate little by little, we reached the foot of the hill on which the abbey stood. And it is time for my story to approach it, as we did then, and may my hand remain steady as I prepare to tell what happened.

FIRST DAY

PRIME

*In which the foot of the abbey is reached,
and William demonstrates his great acumen.*

It was a beautiful morning at the end of November.
During the night it had snowed, but only a little, and
the earth was covered with a cool blanket no more than
three fingers high. In the darkness, immediately after
lauds, we heard Mass in a village in the valley. Then we
set off toward the mountain, as the sun first appeared.

While we toiled up the steep path that wound around
the mountain, I saw the abbey. I was amazed, not by the
walls that girded it on every side, similar to others to be
seen in all the Christian world, but by the bulk of what
I later learned was the Aedificium. This was an octagonal construction that from a distance seemed a tetragon
(a perfect form, which expresses the sturdiness and
impregnability of the City of God), whose southern
sides stood on the plateau of the abbey, while the
northern ones seemed to grow from the steep side of
the mountain, a sheer drop, to which they were bound.
I might say that from below, at certain points, the cliff
seemed to extend, reaching up toward the heavens,

UMBERTO ECO

with the rock's same colors and material, which at a certain point became keep and tower (work of giants who had great familiarity with earth and sky). Three rows of windows proclaimed the triune rhythm of its elevation, so that what was physically squared on the earth was spiritually triangular in the sky. As we came closer, we realized that the quadrangular form included, at each of its corners, a heptagonal tower, five sides of which were visible on the outside—four of the eight sides, then, of the greater octagon producing four minor heptagons, which from the outside appeared as pentagons. And thus anyone can see the admirable concord of so many holy numbers, each revealing a subtle spiritual significance. Eight, the number of perfection for every tetragon; four, the number of the Gospels; five, the number of the zones of the world; seven, the number of the gifts of the Holy Ghost. In its bulk and in its form, the Aedificium resembled Castel Ursino or Castel del Monte, which I was to see later in the south of the Italian peninsula, but its inaccessible position made it more awesome than those, and capable of inspiring fear in the traveler who approached it gradually. And it was fortunate that, since it was a very clear winter morning, I did not first see the building as it appears on stormy days.

I will not say, in any case, that it prompted feelings of jollity. I felt fear, and a subtle uneasiness. God knows these were not phantoms of my immature spirit, and I was rightly interpreting indubitable omens inscribed in the stone the day that the giants began their work, and before the deluded determination of the monks dared consecrate the building to the preservation of the divine word.

As our little mules strove up the last curve of the mountain, where the main path divided into three, producing two side paths, my master stopped for a while, to look around: at the sides of the road, at the road itself, and above the road, where, for a brief stretch, a series of evergreen pines formed a natural roof, white with snow.

"A rich abbey," he said. "The abbot likes a great display on public occasions."

Accustomed as I was to hear him make the most unusual declarations, I did not question him. This was also because, after another bit of road, we heard some noises, and at the next turn an agitated band of monks and servants appeared. One of them, seeing us, came toward us with great cordiality. "Welcome, sir," he said, "and do not be surprised if I can guess who you are, because we have been advised of your visit. I am Remigio of Varagine, the cellarer of the monastery. And if you, as I believe, are Brother William of Baskerville, the abbot must be informed. You"—he commanded one of his party—"go up and tell them that our visitor is about to come inside the walls."

"I thank you, Brother Cellarer," my master replied politely, "and I appreciate your courtesy all the more since, in order to greet me, you have interrupted your search. But don't worry. The horse came this way and took the path to the right. He will not get far, because he will have to stop when he reaches the dungheap. He is too intelligent to plunge down that precipitous slope...."

"When did you see him?" the cellarer asked.

"We haven't seen him at all, have we, Adso?" William said, turning toward me with an amused look. "But if you are hunting for Brunellus, the horse can only be where I have said."

The cellarer hesitated. He looked at William, then at the path, and finally asked, "Brunellus? How did you know?"

"Come, come," William said, "it is obvious you are hunting for Brunellus, the abbot's favorite horse, fifteen hands, the fastest in your stables, with a dark coat, a full tail, small round hoofs, but a very steady gait; small head, sharp ears, big eyes. He went to the right, as I said, but you should hurry, in any càse."

The cellarer hesitated for a moment longer, then gestured to his men and rushed off along the path to the right, while our mules resumed their climb. My curiosity aroused, I was about to question William, but he motioned me to wait: in fact, a few minutes later we heard cries of rejoicing, and at the turn of the path, monks and servants reappeared, leading the horse by its halter. They passed by us, all glancing at us with some amazement, then preceded us toward the abbey. I believe William also slowed the pace of his mount to give them time to tell what had happened. I had already realized that my master, in every respect a man of the highest virtue, succumbed to the vice of vanity when it was a matter of demonstrating his acumen; and having learned to appreciate his gifts as a subtle diplomatist, I understood that he wanted to reach his destination preceded by a firm reputation as a man of knowledge.

"And now tell me"—in the end I could not restrain myself—"how did you manage to know?"

"My good Adso," my master said, "during our whole journey I have been teaching you to recognize the evidence through which the world speaks to us like a great book. Alanus de Insulis said that

> *omnis mundi creatura*
> *quasi liber et pictura*
> *nobis est in speculum*

and he was thinking of the endless array of symbols with which God, through His creatures, speaks to us of the eternal life. But the universe is even more talkative than Alanus thought, and it speaks not only of the ultimate things (which it does always in an obscure fashion) but also of closer things, and then it speaks quite clearly. I am almost embarrassed to repeat to you

what you should know. At the crossroads, on the still-fresh snow, a horse's hoofprints stood out very neatly, heading for the path to our left. Neatly spaced, those marks said that the hoof was small and round, and the gallop quite regular—and so I deduced the nature of the horse, and the fact that it was not running wildly like a crazed animal. At the point where the pines formed a natural roof, some twigs had been freshly broken off at a height of five feet. One of the blackberry bushes where the animal must have turned to take the path to his right, proudly switching his handsome tail, still held some long black horsehairs in its brambles.
... You will not say, finally, that you do not know that path leads to the dungheap, because as we passed the lower curve we saw the spill of waste down the sheer cliff below the great east tower, staining the snow; and from the situation of the crossroads, the path could only lead in that direction."

"Yes," I said, "but what about the small head, the sharp ears, the big eyes...?"

"I am not sure he has those features, but no doubt the monks firmly believe he does. As Isidore of Seville said, the beauty of a horse requires 'that the head be small, siccum prope pelle ossibus adhaerente, short and pointed ears, big eyes, flaring nostrils, erect neck, thick mane and tail, round and solid hoofs.' If the horse whose passing I inferred had not really been the finest of the stables, stableboys would have been out chasing him, but instead, the cellarer in person had undertaken the search. And a monk who considers a horse excellent, whatever his natural forms, can only see him as the auctoritates have described him, especially if" —and here he smiled slyly in my direction—"the describer is a learned Benedictine."

"All right," I said, "but why Brunellus?"

"May the Holy Ghost sharpen your mind, son!" my master exclaimed. "What other name could he possibly have? Why, even the great Buridan, who is about to become rector in Paris, when he wants to use a horse in one of his logical examples, always calls it Brunellus."

This was my master's way. He not only knew how to read the great book of nature, but also knew the way monks read the books of Scripture, and how they thought through them. A gift that, as we shall see, was to prove useful to him in the days to follow. His explanation, moreover, seemed to me at that point so obvious that my humiliation at not having discovered it by myself was surpassed only by my pride at now being a sharer in it, and I was almost congratulating myself on my insight. Such is the power of the truth that, like good, it is its own propagator. And praised be the holy name of our Lord Jesus Christ for this splendid revelation I was granted.

But resume your course, O my story, for this aging monk is lingering too long over marginalia. Tell, rather, how we arrived at the great gate of the abbey, and on the threshold stood the abbot, beside whom two novices held a golden basin filled with water. When we had dismounted, he washed William's hands, then embraced him, kissing him on the mouth and giving him a holy welcome.

"Thank you, Abo," William said. "It is a great joy for me to set foot in Your Magnificence's monastery, whose fame has traveled beyond these mountains. I come as a pilgrim in the name of our Lord, and as such you have honored me. But I come also in the name of our lord on this earth, as the letter I now give you will tell you, and in his name also I thank you for your welcome."

The abbot accepted the letter with the imperial seals and replied that William's arrival had in any event been preceded by other missives from his brothers (it is difficult, I said to myself with a certain pride, to take a Benedictine abbot by surprise); then he asked the cellarer to take us to our lodgings, as the grooms led our mules away. The abbot was looking forward to visiting us later, when we were refreshed, and we entered the great courtyard where the abbey buildings extended all about the gentle plain that blunted in a soft bowl—or alp—the peak of the mountain.

I shall have occasion to discuss the layout of the abbey more than once, and in greater detail. After the gate (which was the only opening in the outer walls) a tree-lined avenue led to the abbatial church. To the left of the avenue there stretched a vast area of vegetable gardens and, as I later learned, the botanical garden, around the two buildings of the balneary and the infirmary and herbarium, following the curve of the walls. Behind, to the left of the church, rose the Aedificium, separated from the church by a yard scattered with graves. The north door of the church faced the south tower of the Aedificium, which offered, frontally, its west tower to the arriving visitor's eyes; then, to the left, the building joined the walls and seemed to plunge, from its towers, toward the abyss, over which the north tower, seen obliquely, projected. To the right of the church there were some buildings, sheltering in its lee, and others around the cloister: the dormitory, no doubt, the abbot's house, and the pilgrims' hospice, where we were heading. We reached it after crossing a handsome flower garden. On the right side, beyond a broad lawn, along the south walls and continuing eastward behind the church, a series of peasants' quarters, stables, mills, oil presses, granaries, and cellars, and what seemed to me to be the novices' house. The regular terrain, only slightly rolling, had allowed the ancient builders of that holy place to respect the rules of orientation, better than Honorius Augustoduniensis or Guillaume Durant could have demanded. From the position of the sun at that hour of the day, I noticed that the main church door opened perfectly westward, so choir and altar were facing east; and the good morning sun, in rising, could directly wake the monks in the dormitory and the animals in the stables. I never saw an abbey more beautiful or better oriented, even though subsequently I saw St. Gall, and Cluny, and Fontenay, and others still, perhaps larger but less well proportioned. Unlike the others, this one was remarkable for the exceptional size of the Aedificium. I did not possess the experience of a master builder, but I immediately realized it was much older than the buildings surrounding it. Perhaps it had originated for some other purposes, and the abbey's compound had been laid out around it at a later time, but in such a way that the orientation of the huge building should conform with that of the church, and the church's with its. For architecture, among all the arts, is the one that most boldly tries to reproduce in its rhythm the order of the universe, which the ancients called "kosmos," that is to say ornate, since it is like a great animal on whom there shine the perfection and the proportion of all its members. And praised be our Creator, who has decreed all things, in their number, weight, and measure.

TERCE

In which William has an instructive conversation with the abbot.

The cellarer was a stout man, vulgar in appearance but jolly, white-haired but still strong, small but quick. He led us to our cells in the pilgrims' hospice. Or, rather, he led us to the cell assigned to my master, promising me that by the next day he would have cleared one for me also, since, though a novice, I was their guest and therefore to be treated with all honor. For that night I could sleep in a long and wide niche in the wall of the cell, in which he had had some nice fresh straw prepared.

Then the monks brought us wine, cheese, olives, bread, and excellent raisins, and left us to our refreshment. We ate and drank heartily. My master did not share the austere habits of the Benedictines and did not like to eat in silence. For that matter, he spoke always of things so good and wise that it was as if a monk were reading to us the lives of the saints.

That day I could not refrain from questioning him further about the matter of the horse.

"All the same," I said, "when you read the prints in

the snow and the evidence of the branches, you did not yet know Brunellus. In a certain sense those prints spoke of all horses, or at least all horses of that breed. Mustn't we say, then, that the book of nature speaks to us only of essences, as many distinguished theologians teach?"

"Not entirely, dear Adso," my master replied. "True, that kind of print expressed to me, if you like, the idea of 'horse,' the verbum mentis, and would have expressed the same to me wherever I might have found it. But the print in that place and at that hour of the day told me that at least one of all possible horses had passed that way. So I found myself halfway between the perception of the concept 'horse' and the knowledge of an individual horse. And in any case, what I knew of the universal horse had been given me by those traces, which were singular. I could say I was caught at that moment between the singularity of the traces and my ignorance, which assumed the quite diaphanous form of a universal idea. If you see something from a distance, and you do not understand what it is, you will be content with defining it as a body of some dimension. When you come closer, you will then define it as an animal, even if you do not yet know whether it is a horse or an ass. And finally, when it is still closer, you will be able to say it is a horse even if you do not yet know whether it is Brunellus or Niger. And only when you are at the proper distance will you see that it is Brunellus (or, rather, that horse and not another, however you decide to call it). And that will be full knowledge, the learning of the singular. So an hour ago I could expect all horses, but not because of the vastness of my intellect, but because of the paucity of my deduction. And my intellect's hunger was sated only when I saw the single horse that the monks were leading by the halter. Only then did I truly know that my previous reasoning had brought me close to the truth. And so the ideas, which I was using earlier to imagine a horse I had not yet seen, were pure signs, as the hoofprints in the snow were signs of the idea of 'horse'; and signs and the signs of signs are used only when we are lacking things."

On other occasions I had heard him speak with great skepticism about universal ideas and with great respect about individual things; and afterward, too, I thought this tendency came to him from his being both a Briton and a Franciscan. But that day he did not have the strength to face theological disputes, so I curled up in the space allotted me, wrapped myself in a blanket, and fell sound asleep.

Anyone coming in could have mistaken me for a bundle. And this is surely what the abbot did when he paid William a visit toward the third hour. So it was that I could listen, unnoticed, to their first conversation.

And so Abo arrived. He apologized for the intrusion, repeated his welcome, and said that he had to speak with William privately, about a very serious matter.

He began by congratulating his guest on the skill demonstrated in the business of the horse, and asked how he had been able to give such confident information about an animal he had never seen. William explained to him briefly and with detachment the path he had followed, and the abbot complimented him highly on his acumen. He said he would have expected nothing less from a man preceded by a reputation for great wisdom. He said he had received a letter from the abbot of Farfa that not only spoke of William's mission for the Emperor (which they would discuss in the coming days) but also added that in England and in Italy my master had acted as inquisitor in some trials, where he had distinguished himself by his perspicacity, along with a great humility.

"I was very pleased to learn," the abbot continued, "that in numerous cases you decided the accused was innocent. I believe, and never more than during these sad days, in the constant presence of the Evil One in human affairs"—and he looked around, imperceptibly, as if the enemy were lurking within those walls—"but I believe also that often the Evil One works through second causes. And I know that he can impel his victims to do evil in such a way that the blame falls on a righteous man, and the Evil One rejoices then as the righteous man is burned in the place of his succubus. Inquisitors often, to demonstrate their zeal, wrest a confession from the accused at all costs, thinking that the only good inquisitor is one who concludes the trial by finding a scapegoat...."

"An inquisitor, too, can be impelled by the Devil," William said.

"That is possible," the abbot admitted with great circumspection, "because the designs of the Almighty are inscrutable, and far be it from me to cast any shadow of suspicion on such worthy men. Indeed, it is as one of them that I need you today. In this abbey something has happened that requires the attention and counsel of an acute and prudent man such as you are. Acute in uncovering, and prudent (if necessary) in covering. If a shepherd errs, he must be isolated from other shepherds, but woe unto us if the sheep begin to distrust shepherds."

"I see your point," William said. I had already had occasion to observe that when he expressed himself so promptly and politely he was usually concealing, in an honest way, his dissent or puzzlement.

"For this reason," the abbot continued, "I consider that any case involving the error of a shepherd can be entrusted only to men like you, who can distinguish not only good from evil, but also what is expedient from what is not. I like to think you pronounced a sentence of guilty only when..."

"...the accused were guilty of criminal acts, of poisoning, of the corruption of innocent youths, or other abominations my mouth dares not utter..."

"...that you pronounced sentence only when," the abbot continued, not heeding the interruption, "the presence of the Devil was so evident to all eyes that it was impossible to act otherwise without the clemency's being more scandalous than the crime itself."

"When I found someone guilty," William explained, "he had really committed crimes of such gravity that in all conscience I could hand him over to the secular arm."

The abbot was bewildered for a moment. "Why," he asked, "do you insist on speaking of criminal acts without referring to their diabolical cause?"

"Because reasoning about causes and effects is a very difficult thing, and I believe the only judge of that can be God. We are already hard put to establish a relationship between such an obvious effect as a charred tree and the lightning bolt that set fire to it, so to trace sometimes endless chains of causes and effects seems to me as foolish as trying to build a tower that will touch the sky.

"Let us suppose a man has been killed by poisoning. This is a given fact. It is possible for me to imagine, in the face of certain undeniable signs, that the poisoner is a second man. On such simple chains of causes my mind can act with a certain confidence in its power. But how can I complicate the chain, imagining that, to cause the evil deed, there was yet another intervention, not human this time, but diabolical? I do not say it is impossible: the Devil, like your horse Brunellus, also indicates his passage through clear signs. But why must I hunt for these proofs? Is it not already enough for me to know that the guilty party is that man and for me to turn him over to the secular arm? In any case his punishment will be death, God forgive him."

"But I have heard that in a trial held at Kilkenny three years ago, in which certain persons were accused of having committed loathsome crimes, you did not deny diabolical intervention, once the guilty parties had been identified."

"Nor did I affirm it openly, in so many words. I did

27

not deny it, true. Who am I to express judgments on the plots of the Evil One, especially," he added, and seemed to want to insist on this reason, "in cases where those who had initiated the inquisition, the bishop, the city magistrates, and the whole populace, perhaps the accused themselves, truly wanted to feel the presence of the Devil? There, perhaps the only real proof of the presence of the Devil was the intensity with which everyone at that moment desired to know he was at work...."

"Are you telling me, then," the abbot said in a worried tone, "that in many trials the Devil does not act only within the guilty one but perhaps and above all in the judges?"

"Could I make such a statement?" William asked, and I noticed that the question was formulated in such a way that the abbot was unable to affirm that he could; so William took advantage of his silence to change the direction of their dialogue. "But these, after all, are remote things. I have abandoned that noble activity and if I did so, it was because the Lord wished it..."

"No doubt," the abbot admitted.

"...and now," William continued, "I concern myself with other delicate questions. And I would like to deal with the one that distresses you, if you will speak to me about it."

I felt the abbot was pleased to be able to conclude that discussion and return to his problem. He then began telling, with very careful choice of words and with long paraphrases, about an unusual event that had taken place a few days before and had left in its wake great distress among the monks. He was speaking of the matter with William, he said, because, since William had great knowledge both of the human spirit and of the wiles of the Evil One, Abo hoped his guest would be able to devote a part of his valuable time to shedding light on a painful enigma. What had happened, then, was this: Adelmo of Otranto, a monk still young though already famous as a master illuminator, who had been decorating the manuscripts of the library with the most beautiful images, had been found one morning by a goatherd at the bottom of the cliff below the Aedificium. Since he had been seen by other monks in choir during compline but had not reappeared at matins, he had probably fallen there during the darkest hours of the night. The night of a great snowstorm, in which flakes as sharp as blades fell, almost like hail, driven by a furious south wind. Soaked by that snow, which had first melted and then frozen into shards of ice, the body had been discovered at the foot of the sheer drop, torn by the rocks it had struck on the way down. Poor, fragile, mortal thing, God have mercy on him. Thanks to the battering the body had suffered in its broken fall, determining from which precise spot it had fallen was not easy: certainly from one of the windows that opened in rows on the three stories on the three sides of the tower exposed to the abyss.

"Where have you buried the poor body?" William asked.

"In the cemetery, naturally," the abbot replied. "Perhaps you noticed it: it lies between the north side of the church, the Aedificium, and the vegetable garden."

"I see," William said, "and I see that your problem is the following. If that unhappy youth, God forbid, committed suicide, the next day you would have found one of those windows open, whereas you found them all closed, and with no sign of water at the foot of any of them."

The abbot, as I have said, was a man of great and diplomatic composure, but this time he made a movement of surprise that robbed him totally of that decorum suited to a grave and magnanimous person, as Aristotle has it. "Who told you?"

"You told me," William said. "If the window had been open, you would immediately have thought he had thrown himself out of it. From what I could tell from the outside, they are large windows of opaque glass, and windows of that sort are not usually placed, in buildings of this size, at a man's height. So even if a window had been open, it would have been impossible for the unfortunate man to lean out and lose his balance; thus suicide would have been the only conceivable explanation. In which case you would not have allowed him to be buried in consecrated ground. But since you gave him Christian burial, the windows must have been closed. And if they were closed—for I have never encountered, not even in witchcraft trials, a dead man whom God or the Devil allowed to climb up from the abyss to erase the evidence of his misdeed—then obviously the presumed suicide was, on the contrary, pushed, either by human hand or by diabolical force. And you are wondering who was capable, I will not say of pushing him into the abyss, but of hoisting him to the sill; and you are distressed because an evil force, whether natural or supernatural, is at work in the abbey."

"That is it . . ." the abbot said, and it was not clear whether he was confirming William's words or accepting the reasons William had so admirably and reasonably expounded. "But how can you know there was no water at the foot of any window?"

"Because you told me a south wind was blowing, and the water could not be driven against windows that open to the east."

"They had not told me enough about your talents," the abbot said. "And you are right, there was no water, and now I know why. It was all as you say. And now you understand my anxiety. It would already be serious enough if one of my monks had stained his soul with the hateful sin of suicide. But I have reason to think that another of them has stained himself with an equally terrible sin. And if that were all . . ."

"In the first place, why one of the monks? In the

abbey there are many other persons, grooms, goatherds, servants...."

"To be sure, the abbey is small but rich," the abbot agreed smugly. "One hundred fifty servants for sixty monks. But everything happened in the Aedificium. There, as perhaps you already know, although on the ground floor are the kitchen and the refectory, on the two upper floors are the scriptorium and the library. After the evening meal the Aedificium is locked, and a very strict rule forbids anyone to enter." He guessed William's next question and added at once, though clearly with reluctance, "Including, naturally, the monks, but...."

"But?"

"But I reject absolutely—absolutely, you understand—the possibility that a servant would have had the courage to enter there at night." There was a kind of defiant smile in his eyes, albeit brief as a flash, or a falling star. "Let us say they would have been afraid, you know...sometimes orders given to the simpleminded have to be reinforced with a threat, a suggestion that something terrible will happen to the disobedient, perforce something supernatural. A monk, on the contrary...."

"I understand."

"Furthermore, a monk could have other reasons for venturing into a forbidden place. I mean reasons that are...reasonable, even if contrary to the rule...."

William noticed the abbot's uneasiness and asked a question perhaps intended to change the subject, though it produced an even greater uneasiness.

"Speaking of a possible murder, you said, 'And if that were all.' What did you mean?"

"Did I say that? Well, no one commits murder without a reason, however perverse. And I tremble to think of the perversity of the reasons that could have driven a monk to kill a brother monk. There. That is it."

"Nothing else?"

"Nothing else that I can say to you."

"You mean that there is nothing else you have the power to say?"

"Please, Brother William, Brother William," and the abbot underlined "Brother" both times.

William blushed violently and remarked, "Eris sacerdos in aeternum."

"Thank you," the abbot said.

O Lord God, what a terrible mystery my imprudent superiors were broaching at that moment, the one driven by anxiety and the other by curiosity. Because, a novice approaching the mysteries of the holy priesthood of God, humble youth that I was, I, too, understood that the abbot knew something but had learned it under the seal of confession. He must have heard from someone's lips a sinful detail that could have a bearing on the tragic end of Adelmo. Perhaps for this reason he was begging Brother William to uncover a secret he himself suspected, though he was unable to reveal to anyone—and he hoped that my master, with the powers of his intellect, would cast light on—what he, the abbot, had to shroud in shadows because of the sublime law of charity.

"Very well," William said then, "may I question the monks?"

"You may."

"May I move freely about the abbey?"

"I grant you that power."

"Will you assign me this mission coram monachis?"

"This very evening."

"I shall begin, however, today, before the monks know what you have charged me to do. Besides, I already had a great desire—not the least reason for my sojourn here—to visit your library, which is spoken of with admiration in all the abbeys of Christendom."

The abbot rose, almost starting, with a very tense face. "You can move freely through the whole abbey, as

I have said. But not, to be sure, on the top floor of the Aedificium, the library."

"Why not?"

"I would have explained to you before, but I thought you knew. You see, our library is not like others...."

"I know it has more books than any other Christian library. I know that in comparison with your cases, those of Bobbio or Pomposa, of Cluny or Fleury, seem the room of a boy barely being introduced to the abacus. I know that the six thousand codices that were the boast of Novalesa a hundred or more years ago are few compared to yours, and perhaps many of those are now here. I know your abbey is the only light that Christianity can oppose to the thirty-six libraries of Baghdad, to the ten thousand codices of the Vizir Ibn al-Alkami, that the number of your Bibles equals the two thousand four hundred Korans that are the pride of Cairo, and that the reality of your cases is luminous evidence against the proud legend of the infidels who years ago claimed (intimates as they are of the Prince of Falsehood) the library of Tripoli was rich in six million volumes and inhabited by eighty thousand commentators and two hundred scribes."

"You are right, heaven be praised."

"I know that many of the monks living in your midst come from other abbeys scattered all over the world. Some stay here a short time, to copy manuscripts to be found nowhere else and to carry them back then to their own house, not without having brought you in exchange some other unavailable manuscript that you will copy and add to your treasure; and others stay for a very long time, occasionally remaining here till death, because only here can they find the works that enlighten their research. And so you have among you Germans, Dacians, Spaniards, Frenchmen, Greeks. I know that the Emperor Frederick, many and many years ago, asked you to compile for him a book of the prophecies of Merlin and then to translate it into Arabic, to be sent as a gift to the Sultan of Egypt. I know, finally, that such a glorious abbey as Murbach in these very sad times no longer has a single scribe, that at St. Gall only a few monks are left who know how to write, that now in the cities corporations and guilds arise, made up of laymen who work for the universities, and only your abbey day after day renews, or—what am I saying?—it exalts to ever greater heights the glories of your order...."

"Monasterium sine libris," the abbot recited, pensively, "est sicut civitas sine opibus, castrum sine numeris, coquina sine suppellectili, mensa sine cibis, hortus sine herbis, pratum sine floribus, arbor sine foliis.... And our order, growing up under the double command of work and prayer, was light to the whole known world, depository of knowledge, salvation of an ancient learning that threatened to disappear in fires, sacks, earthquakes, forge of new writing and increase of the ancient.... Oh, as you well know, we live now in very dark times, and I blush to tell you that not many years ago the Council of Vienne had to reaffirm that every monk is under obligation to take orders.... How many of our abbeys, which two hundred years ago were resplendent with grandeur and sanctity, are now the refuge of the slothful? The order is still powerful, but the stink of the cities is encroaching upon our holy places, the people of God are now inclined to commerce and wars of faction; down below in the great settlements, where the spirit of sanctity can find no lodging, not only do they speak (of laymen, nothing else could be expected) in the vulgar tongue, but they are already writing in it, though none of these volumes will ever come within our walls—fomenter of heresies as those volumes inevitably become! Because of mankind's sins the world is teetering on the brink of the abyss, permeated by the very abyss that the abyss invokes. And tomorrow, as Honorius would have it, men's bodies will be smaller than ours, just as ours are smaller than those of the ancients. Mundus senescit. If God has now given our order a mission, it is to oppose this race to the abyss, by preserving, repeating, and defending the treasure of wisdom our fathers entrusted to us. Divine Providence has ordered that the universal government, which at the beginning of the world was in the East, should gradually, as the time was nearing fulfillment, move westward to warn us that the end of the world is approaching, because the course of events has already reached the confines of the universe. But until the millennium occurs definitively, until the triumph, however brief, of the foul beast that is the Antichrist, it is up to us to defend the treasure of the Christian world, and the very word of God, as he dictated it to the prophets and to the apostles, as the fathers repeated it without changing a syllable, as the schools have tried to gloss it, even if today in the schools themselves the serpent of pride, envy, folly is nesting. In this sunset we are still torches and light, high on the horizon. And as long as these walls stand, we shall be the custodians of the divine Word."

"Amen," William said in a devout tone. "But what does this have to do with the fact that the library may not be visited?"

"You see, Brother William," the abbot said, "to achieve the immense and holy task that enriches those walls" —and he nodded toward the bulk of the Aedificium, which could be glimpsed from the cell's windows, towering above the abbatial church itself—"devout men have toiled for centuries, observing iron rules. The library was laid out on a plan which has remained obscure to all over the centuries, and which none of the monks is called upon to know. Only the librarian has received the secret, from the librarian who preceded him, and he communicates it, while still alive, to the assistant librarian, so that death will not take him by surprise and rob the community of that knowledge. And the secret seals the lips of both men. Only the librarian has, in addition to that knowledge, the right to move through the labyrinth of the books, he alone knows where to find them and where to replace them, he alone is responsible for their safekeeping. The other monks work in the scriptorium and may know the list of the volumes that the library houses. But a list of titles often tells very little; only the librarian knows, from the collocation of the volume, from its degree of inaccessibility, what secrets, what truths or falsehoods, the volume contains. Only he decides how, when, and whether to give it to the monk who requests it; sometimes he first consults me. Because not all truths are for all ears, not all falsehoods can be recognized as such by a pious soul; and the monks, finally, are in the scriptorium to carry out a precise task, which requires them to read certain volumes and not others, and not to pursue every foolish curiosity that seizes them, whether through weakness of intellect or through pride or through diabolical prompting."

"So in the library there are also books containing falsehoods...."

"Monsters exist because they are part of the divine plan, and in the horrible features of those same monsters the power of the Creator is revealed. And by divine plan, too, there exist also books by wizards, the cabalas of the Jews, the fables of pagan poets, the lies of the infidels. It was the firm and holy conviction of those who founded the abbey and sustained it over the centuries that even in books of falsehood, to the eyes of the sage reader, a pale reflection of the divine wisdom can shine. And therefore the library is a vessel of these, too. But for this very reason, you understand, it cannot be visited by just anyone. And furthermore," the abbot added, as if to apologize for the weakness of this last argument, "a book is a fragile creature, it suffers the wear of time, it fears rodents, the elements, clumsy hands. If for a hundred and a hundred years everyone had been able freely to handle our codices, the majority of them would no longer exist. So the librarian protects them not only against mankind but also against nature, and devotes his life to this war with the forces of oblivion, the enemy of truth."

"And so no one, except for two people, enters the top floor of the Aedificium...."

The abbot smiled. "No one should. No one can. No one, even if he wished, would succeed. The library defends itself, immeasurable as the truth it houses, deceitful as the falsehood it preserves. A spiritual labyrinth, it is also a terrestrial labyrinth. You might enter and you might not emerge. And having said this, I would like you to conform to the rules of the abbey."

"But you have not dismissed the possibility that Adelmo fell from one of the windows of the library. And how can I study his death if I do not see the place where the story of his death may have begun?"

"Brother William," the abbot said, in a conciliatory tone, "a man who described my horse Brunellus without seeing him, and the death of Adelmo though knowing virtually nothing of it, will have no difficulty studying places to which he does not have access."

William bowed. "You are wise also when you are severe. It shall be as you wish."

"If ever I were wise, it would be because I know how to be severe," the abbot answered.

"One last thing," William asked. "Ubertino?"

"He is here. He is expecting you. You will find him in church."

"When?"

"Always," the abbot said, and smiled. "You must know that, although very learned, he is not a man to appreciate the library. He considers it a secular lure.... For the most part he stays in church, meditating, praying...."

"Is he old?" William asked, hesitating.

"How long has it been since you saw him?"

"Many years."

"He is weary. Very detached from the things of this world. He is sixty-eight. But I believe he still possesses the spirit of his youth."

"I will seek him out at once. Thank you."

The abbot asked him whether he wanted to join the community for the midday refection, after sext. William said he had only just eaten—very well, too—and he would prefer to see Ubertino at once. The abbot took his leave.

He was going out of the cell when from the courtyard a heartrending cry arose, like that of someone mortally wounded, followed by other, equally horrible cries. "What is that?" William asked, disconcerted. "Nothing," the abbot answered, smiling. "At this time of year they slaughter the pigs. A job for the swineherds. This is not the blood that should concern you."

He went out, and he did a disservice to his reputation as a clever man. Because the next morning... But curb your impatience, garrulous tongue of mine. For on the day of which I am telling, and before its night, many more things happened that it would be best to narrate.

SEXT

In which Adso admires the door of the church, and William meets Ubertino of Casale again.

The church was not majestic like others I saw later at Strasbourg, Chartres, Bamberg, and Paris. It resembled, rather, those I had already seen in Italy, with scant inclination to soar dizzyingly toward the heavens, indeed firmly set on the earth, often broader than they were high; but at the first level this one was surmounted, like a fortress, by a sequence of square battlements, and above this story another construction rose, not so much a tower as a solid, second church, capped by a pitched roof and pierced by severe windows. A robust abbatial church such as our forefathers built in Provence and Languedoc, far from the audacity and the excessive tracery characteristic of the modern style, which only in more recent times has been enriched, I believe, above the choir, with a pinnacle boldly pointed toward the roof of the heavens.

Two straight and unadorned columns stood on either side of the entrance, which opened, at first sight, like a single great arch; but from the columns began two embrasures that, surmounted by other, multiple arches, led the gaze, as if into the heart of an abyss, toward the doorway itself, crowned by a great tympanum, supported on the sides by two imposts and in the center by a carved pillar, which divided the entrance into two apertures protected by oak doors reinforced in metal. At that hour of the day the weak sun was beating almost straight down on the roof and the light fell obliquely on the façade without illuminating the tympanum; so after passing the two columns, we found ourselves abruptly under the almost sylvan vault of the arches that sprang from the series of lesser columns that proportionally reinforced the embrasures. When our eyes had finally grown accustomed to the gloom, the silent speech of the carved stone, accessible as it immediately was to the gaze and the imagination of anyone (for images are the literature of the layman), dazzled my eyes and plunged me into a vision that even today my tongue can hardly describe.

I saw a throne set in the sky and a figure seated on the throne. The face of the Seated One was stern and impassive, the eyes wide and glaring over a terrestrial humankind that had reached the end of its story; majestic hair and beard flowed around the face and over the chest like the waters of a river, in streams all equal, symmetrically divided in two. The crown on his head was rich in enamels and jewels, the purple imperial tunic was arranged in broad folds over the knees, woven with embroideries and laces of gold and silver thread. The left hand, resting on one knee, held a sealed book, the right was uplifted in an attitude of blessing or—I could not tell—of admonition. The face was illuminated by the tremendous beauty of a halo, containing a cross and bedecked with flowers, while around the throne and above the face of the Seated One I saw an emerald rainbow glittering. Before the throne, beneath the feet of the Seated One, a sea of crystal flowed, and around the Seated One, beside and above the throne, I saw four awful creatures—awful for me, as I looked at them, transported, but docile and dear for the Seated One, whose praises they sang without cease.

Or, rather, not all could be called awful, because one seemed to me handsome and kindly, the man to my left (and to the right of the Seated One), who held out a book. But on the other side there was an eagle I found horrifying, its beak agape, its thick feathers arranged like a cuirass, powerful talons, great wings outstretched. And at the feet of the Seated One, under the first two figures, there were the other two, a bull and a lion, each monster clutching a book between talons or hoofs, the body turned away from the throne, but the head toward the throne, as if shoulders and neck twisted in a fierce impulse, flanks tensed, the limbs those of a dying animal, maw open, serpentlike tails coiled and writhing, culminating, at the top, in tongues of flame. Both monsters were winged, both crowned by haloes; despite their formidable appearance, they were creatures not of hell, but of heaven, and if they seemed fearsome it was because they were roaring in adoration of One Who Is to Come and who would judge the quick and the dead.

Around the throne, beside the four creatures and under the feet of the Seated One, as if seen through the transparent waters of the crystal sea, as if to fill the whole space of the vision, arranged according to the triangular frame of the tympanum, rising from a base of seven plus seven, then to three plus three and then to two plus two, at either side of the great throne, on twenty-four little thrones, there were twenty-four ancients, wearing white garments and crowned in gold. Some held lutes in their hands, one a vase of perfumes, and only one was playing an instrument, all the others were in ecstasy, faces turned to the Seated One, whose praises they were singing, their limbs also twisted like the creatures', so that all could see the Seated One, not in wild fashion, however, but with movements of ecstatic dance—as David must have danced before the Ark—so that wherever their pupils were, against the law governing the stature of bodies, they converged on the same radiant spot. Oh, what a harmony of abandonment and impulse, of unnatural and yet graceful postures, in that mystical language of limbs miraculously freed from the weight of corporeal matter, marked quantity infused with new substantial form, as if the holy band were struck by an impetuous wind, breath of life, frenzy of delight, rejoicing song of praise miraculously transformed, from the sound that it was, into image.

Bodies inhabited in every part by the Spirit, illuminated by revelation, faces overcome with amazement, eyes shining with enthusiasm, cheeks flushed with love, pupils dilated with joy: this one thunderstruck by a pleasurable consternation, that one pierced by a consternated pleasure, some transfigured by wonder, some rejuvenated by bliss, there they all were, singing with the expression of their faces, the drapery of their tunics, the position and tension of their limbs, singing a new song, lips parted in a smile of perennial praise. And beneath the feet of the ancients, and arched over them and over the throne and over the tetramorphic group, arranged in symmetrical bands, barely distinguishable one from another because the artist's skill had made them all so mutually proportionate, united in their variety and varied in their unity, unique in their diversity and diverse in their apt assembly, in wondrous congruency of the parts with the delightful sweetness of hues, miracle of consonance and concord of voices among themselves dissimilar, a company arrayed like the strings of the zither, consentient and conspiring continued cognition through deep and interior force suited to perform univocally in the same alternating play of the equivocal, decoration and collage of creatures beyond reduction to vicissitudes and to vicissitudes reduced, work of amorous connecting sustained by a law at once heavenly and worldly (bond and stable nexus of peace, love, virtue, regimen, power, order, origin, life, light, splendor, species, and figure), numerous and resplendent equality through the shining of the form over the proportionate parts of the material—there, all the flowers and leaves and vines and bushes and corymbs were entwined, of all the grasses that adorn the gardens of earth and heaven, violet, cystus, thyme, lily, privet, narcissus, taro, acanthus, mallow, myrrh, and Mecca balsam.

But as my soul was carried away by that concert of terrestrial beauty and majestic supernatural signals, and was about to burst forth in a psalm of joy, my eye, accompanying the proportioned rhythm of the rose windows that bloomed at the ancients' feet, lighted on the interwoven figures of the central pillar, which supported the tympanum. What were they and what symbolic message did they communicate, those three crisscrossed pairs of lions rampant, like arches, each with hind paws planted on the ground, forepaws on the back of his companion, mane in serpentine curls, mouth taut in a threatening snarl, bound to the very body of the pillar by a paste, or a nest, of tendrils? To calm my spirit, as they had perhaps been meant also to tame the diabolical nature of the lion and to transform it into a symbolic allusion to higher things, on the sides of the pillar there were two human figures, unnaturally tall as the column itself and twins to two others facing them on either side from the decorated imposts, where each of the oak doors had its jamb. These figures, then, were four old men, from whose paraphernalia I recognized Peter and Paul, Jeremiah and Isaiah, also twisted as if in a dance step, their long bony hands raised, the fingers splayed like wings, and like wings were their beards and hair stirred by a prophetic wind, the folds of the very long garments stirred by the long legs giving life to waves and scrolls, opposed to the lions but of the same stuff as the lions. And as I withdrew my

fascinated eye from that enigmatic polyphony of sainted limbs and infernal sinews, I saw beside the door,
under the deep arches, sometimes depicted on the
embrasures in the space between the slender columns
that supported and adorned them, and again on the
thick foliage of the capital of each column, and from
there ramifying toward the sylvan vault of the multiple
arches, other visions horrible to contemplate, and justified in that place only by their parabolic and allegorical
power or by the moral lesson that they conveyed. I saw
a voluptuous woman, naked and fleshless, gnawed by
foul toads, sucked by serpents, coupled with a fat-
bellied satyr whose gryphon legs were covered with
wiry hairs, howling its own damnation from an obscene
throat; and I saw a miser, stiff in the stiffness of death
on his sumptuously columned bed, now helpless prey
of a cohort of demons, one of whom tore from the
dying man's mouth his soul in the form of an infant
(alas, never to be again born to eternal life); and I saw a
proud man with a devil clinging to his shoulders and
thrusting his claws into the man's eyes, while two gluttons tore each other apart in a repulsive hand-to-hand
struggle, and other creatures as well, goat head and
lion fur, panther's jaws, all prisoners in a forest of
flames whose searing breath I could almost feel. And
around them, mingled with them, above their heads
and below their feet, more faces and more limbs: a man
and a woman clutching each other by the hair, two asps
sucking the eyes of one of the damned, a grinning man
whose hooked hands parted the maw of a hydra, and
all the animals of Satan's bestiary, assembled in a consistory and set as guard and crown of the throne that
faced them, singing its glory in their defeat, fauns,
beings of double sex, brutes with six-fingered hands,
sirens, hippocentaurs, gorgons, harpies, incubi, drago-
pods, minotaurs, lynxes, pards, chimeras, cynophales
who darted fire from their nostrils, crocodiles, polycau-
date, hairy serpents, salamanders, horned vipers, tortoises,

snakes, two-headed creatures whose backs were armed with teeth, hyenas, otters, crows, hydrophora with saw-tooth horns, frogs, gryphons, monkeys, dog-heads, leucrota, manticores, vultures, paranders, weasels, dragons, hoopoes, owls, basilisks, hypnales, presters, spectafici, scorpions, saurians, whales, scitales, amphis-benae, iaculi, dipsases, green lizards, pilot fish, octopi, morays, and sea turtles. The whole population of the nether world seemed to have gathered to act as vestibule, dark forest, desperate wasteland of exclusion, at the apparition of the Seated One in the tympanum, at his face promising and threatening, they, the defeated of Armageddon, facing Him who will come at last to separate the quick from the dead. And stunned (almost) by that sight, uncertain at this point whether I was in a friendly place or in the valley of the last judgment, I was terrified and could hardly restrain my tears, and I seemed to hear (or did I really hear?) that voice and I saw those visions that had accompanied my youth as a novice, my first reading of the sacred books, and my nights of meditation in the choir of Melk, and in the delirium of my weak and weakened senses I heard a voice mighty as a trumpet that said, "Write in a book what you now see" (and this is what I am doing), and I saw seven golden candlesticks and in the midst of the candlesticks One like unto the son of man, his breast girt with a golden girdle, his head and hair white as purest wool, his eyes as a flame of fire, his feet like unto fine brass, as if they burned in a furnace, his voice as the sound of many waters, and he had in his right hand seven stars and out of his mouth went a two-edged sword. And I saw a door open in heaven and He who was seated appeared to me like a jasper and a sardonyx, and there was a rainbow round about the throne and out of the throne proceeded thunder and lightning. And the Seated One took in His hands a sharp sickle and cried: "Thrust in thy sickle and reap, for the time is come for thee to reap; for the harvest of the earth is ripe"; and He that sat on the cloud thrust His sickle on the earth; and the earth was reaped.

It was at this point that I realized the vision was speaking precisely of what was happening in the abbey, of what we had learned from the abbot's reticent lips—and how many times in the following days did I return to contemplate the doorway, convinced I was experiencing the very events that it narrated. And I knew we had made our way up there in order to witness a great and celestial massacre.

I trembled, as if I were drenched by the icy winter rain. And I heard yet another voice, but this time it came from behind me and was a different voice, because it came from the earth and not from the blinding core of my vision; and indeed it shattered the vision, because William (I became aware again of his presence), also lost until then in contemplation, turned as I did.

The creature behind us was apparently a monk, though his torn and dirty habit made him look like a vagabond, and his face bore a resemblance to those of the monsters I had just seen on the capitals. Unlike many of my brothers, I have never in my whole life been visited by the Devil; but I believe that if he were to appear to me one day, prevented by divine decree from concealing completely his nature even though he chose to resemble a man, he would have the very features our interlocutor presented to me at this moment. His head was hairless, not shaved in penance but as the result of the past action of some viscid eczema; the brow was so low that if he had had hair on his head it would have mingled with his eyebrows (which were thick and shaggy); the eyes were round, with tiny mobile pupils, and whether the gaze was innocent or malign I could not tell: perhaps it was both, in different moods, in flashes. The nose could not be called a nose, for it was only a bone that began between the eyes, but as it rose from the face it immediately sank again, transforming itself only into two dark holes, broad nostrils thick with hair. The mouth, joined to the nose by a scar, was wide and ill-made, stretching more to the right than to the left, and between the upper lip, nonexistent, and the lower, prominent and fleshy, there protruded, in an irregular pattern, black teeth sharp as a dog's.

The man smiled (or at least so I believed) and, holding up one finger as if in admonition, he said:

"Penitenziagite! Watch out for the draco who cometh in futurum to gnaw your anima! Death is super nos! Pray the Santo Pater come to liberar nos a malo and all our sin! Ha ha, you like this negromanzia de Domini Nostri Jesu Christi! Et anco jois m'es dols e plazer m'es dolors. . . . Cave el diabolo! Semper lying in wait for me in some angulum to snap at my heels. But Salvatore is not stupidus! Bonum monasterium, and aquí refectorium and pray to dominum nostrum. And the resto is not worth merda. Amen. No?"

As this story continues, I shall have to speak again, and at length, of this creature and record his speech. I confess I find it very difficult to do so because I could not say now, as I could never understand then, what language he spoke. It was not Latin, in which the lettered men of the monastery expressed themselves, it was not the vulgar tongue of those parts, or any other I had ever heard. I believe I have given a faint idea of his manner of speech, reporting just now (as I remember them) the first words of his I heard. When I learned later about his adventurous life and about the various places where he had lived, putting down roots in none of them, I realized Salvatore spoke all languages, and no language. Or, rather, he had invented for himself a language which used the sinews of the languages to which he had been exposed—and once I thought that his was, not the Adamic language that a happy mankind had spoken, all united by a single tongue from the origin of the world to the Tower of Babel, or one of the languages that arose after the dire event of their division, but precisely the Babelish language of the first day after the divine chastisement, the language of primeval confusion. Nor, for that matter, could I call Salvatore's speech a language, because in every human language there are rules and every term signifies ad placitum a thing, according to a law that does not change, for man cannot call the dog once dog and once cat, or utter sounds to which a consensus of people has not assigned a definite meaning, as would happen if someone said the word "blitiri." And yet, one way or another, I did understand what Salvatore meant, and so did the others. Proof that he spoke not one, but all languages, none correctly, taking words sometimes from one and sometimes from another. I also noticed afterward that he might refer to something first in Latin and later in Provençal, and I realized that he was not so much inventing his own sentences as using the disiecta membra of other sentences, heard some time in the past, according to the present situation and the things he wanted to say, as if he could speak of a food, for instance, only with the words of the people among whom he had eaten that food, and express his joy only with sentences that he had heard uttered by joyful people the day when he had similarly experienced joy. His speech was somehow like his face, put together with pieces from other people's faces, or like some precious reliquaries I have seen (si licet magnis componere parva, if I may link diabolical things with the divine), fabricated from the shards of other holy objects. At that moment, when I met him for the first time, Salvatore seemed to me, because of both his face and his way of speaking, a creature not unlike the hairy and hoofed hybrids I had just seen under the portal. Later I realized that the man was probably good-hearted and humorous. Later still . . . But we must not get ahead of our story. Particularly since, the moment he had spoken, my master questioned him with great curiosity.

"Why did you say Penitenziagite?" he asked.

"Domine frate magnificentissimo," Salvatore answered, with a kind of bow, "Jesus venturus est and les hommes must do penitenzia. No?"

William gave him a hard look. "Did you come here from a convent of Minorites?"

"Non comprends."

"I am asking if you have lived among the friars of Saint Francis; I ask if you have known the so-called apostles...."

Salvatore blanched, or, rather, his tanned and savage face turned gray. He made a deep bow, muttered through half-closed lips a "vade retro," devoutly blessed himself, and fled, looking back at us every now and then.

"What did you ask him?" I said to William.

He was thoughtful for a moment. "It is of no matter; I will tell you later. Let us go inside now. I want to find Ubertino."

It was just after the sixth hour. The pale sun entered from the west, and therefore through only a few, narrow windows, into the interior of the church. A fine strip of light still touched the main altar, whose frontal seemed to glow with a golden radiance. The side naves were immersed in gloom.

Near the last chapel before the altar, in the left nave, stood a slender column on which a stone Virgin was set, carved in the modern fashion, with an ineffable smile and prominent abdomen, wearing a pretty dress with a small bodice, the child on her arm. At the foot of the Virgin, in prayer, almost prostrate, there was a man in the habit of the Cluniac order.

We approached. The man, hearing the sound of our footsteps, raised his head. He was old, bald, with a glabrous face, large pale-blue eyes, a thin red mouth, white complexion, a bony skull to which the skin clung like that of a mummy preserved in milk. The hands were white, with long tapering fingers. He resembled a maiden withered by premature death. He cast on us a gaze at first bewildered, as if we had disturbed him

49

during an ecstatic vision; then his face brightened with joy.

"William!" he exclaimed. "My dearest brother!" He rose with some effort and came toward my master, embraced him, and kissed him on the mouth. "William!" he repeated, and his eyes became moist with tears. "How long it has been! But I recognize you still! Such a long time, so many things have happened! So many trials sent by the Lord!" He wept. William returned his embrace, clearly moved. We were in the presence of Ubertino of Casale.

I had already heard much talk about him, even before I came to Italy, and more still as I frequented the Franciscans of the imperial court. Someone had told me that the greatest poet of those days, Dante Alighieri of Florence, dead only a few years, had composed a poem (which I could not read, since it was written in vulgar Tuscan) of which many verses were nothing but a paraphrase of passages written by Ubertino in his *Arbor vitae crucifixae*. Nor was this the famous man's only claim to merit. But to permit my reader better to understand the importance of this meeting, I must try to reconstruct the events of those years, as I understood them both during my brief stay in central Italy and from listening to the many conversations William had had with abbots and monks in the course of our journey.

I will try to tell what I understood of these matters, even if I am not sure I can explain them properly. My masters at Melk had often told me that it is very difficult for a Northerner to form any clear idea of the religious and political vicissitudes of Italy.

The peninsula, where the power of the clergy was more evident than in any other country, and where more than in any other country the clergy made a display of power and wealth, for at least two centuries had generated movements of men bent on a poorer life, in protest against the corrupt priests, from whom they even refused the sacraments. They gathered in independent communities, hated equally by the feudal lords, the empire, and the city magistrates.

Finally Saint Francis had appeared, spreading a love of poverty that did not contradict the precepts of the church; and after his efforts the church had accepted the summons to severe behavior of those older movements and had purified them of the elements of disruption that lurked in them. There should have followed a period of meekness and holiness, but as the Franciscan order grew and attracted the finest men, it became too powerful, too bound to earthly matters, and many Franciscans wanted to restore it to its early purity. A very difficult matter for an order that at the time when I was at the abbey already numbered more than thirty thousand members scattered throughout the whole world. But so it was, and many of those monks of Saint Francis were opposed to the Rule that the order had established, and they said the order had by now assumed the character of those ecclesiastical institutions it had come into the world to reform. And this, they said, had already happened in the days when Saint Francis was alive, and his words and his aims had been betrayed. Many of them rediscovered then a book written at the beginning of the twelfth century of our era, by a Cistercian monk named Joachim, to whom the spirit of prophecy was attributed. He had in fact foreseen the advent of a new age, in which the spirit of Christ, long corrupted through the actions of his false apostles, would again be achieved on earth. And he had announced certain future events in a way that made it seem clear to all that, unawares, he was speaking of the Franciscan order. And therefore many Franciscans had greatly rejoiced, even excessively, it seems, because then, around the middle of the century, the doctors of the Sorbonne condemned the teachings of that abbot Joachim. Apparently they did so because the Franciscans (and the Dominicans) were becoming too powerful, too learned, at the University of Paris; and those Sorbonne doctors wanted to eliminate them as heretics. But this scheme was not carried out, happily for the church, which then allowed the dissemination of the works of Thomas Aquinas and Bonaventure of Bagnoregio, certainly not heretics. Whence it is clear that in Paris, too, there was a confusion of ideas or someone who wished to confuse them for his own purposes. And this is the evil that heresy inflicts on the Christian people, obfuscating ideas and inciting all to become inquisitors to their personal benefit. For what I saw at the abbey then (and will now recount) caused me to think that often inquisitors create heretics. And not only in the sense that they imagine heretics where these do not exist, but also that inquisitors repress the heretical putrefaction so vehemently that many are driven to share in it, in their hatred for the judges. Truly, a circle conceived by the Devil. God preserve us.

But I was speaking of the heresy (if such it was) of the Joachimites. And in Tuscany there was a Franciscan, Gerard of Borgo San Donnino, who repeated the predictions of Joachim and made a deep impression on the Minorites. Thus there arose among them a band of supporters of the old Rule, against the reorganization of the order attempted by the great Bonaventure, who had become general of the order. In the final thirty years of the last century, the Council of Lyons rescued the Franciscan order from its enemies, who wanted to abolish it, and allowed it ownership of all property in its use (already the law for older orders). But some monks in the Marches rebelled, because they believed that the spirit of the Rule had been forever betrayed, since Franciscans must own nothing, personally or as a convent or as an order. These rebels were put in prison for life. It does not seem to me that they were preaching things contrary to the Gospel, but when the possession of earthly things is in question, it is difficult for men to reason justly. I was told that years later, the new general of the order, Raymond Gaufredi, found these prisoners in Ancona and, on freeing them, said: "Would God that all of us and the whole order were stained by such a sin." A sign that what the heretics say is not true, and there are still men of great virtue living in the church.

Among these freed prisoners there was one, Angelus Clarenus, who then met a monk from Provence, Pierre Olieu, who preached the prophecies of Joachim, and then he met Ubertino of Casale, and in this way the movement of the Spirituals originated. In those years, a most holy hermit rose to the papal throne, Peter of Murrone, who reigned as Celestine V; and he was welcomed with relief by the Spirituals. "A saint will appear," it had been said, "and he will follow the teachings of Christ, he will live an angelic life: tremble, ye corrupt priests." Perhaps Celestine's life was too angelic, or the prelates around him were too corrupt, or he could not bear the strain of the interminable conflict with the Emperor and with the other kings of Europe. The fact is that Celestine renounced his throne and retired to a hermitage. But in the brief period of his reign, less than a year, the hopes of the Spirituals were all fulfilled. They went to Celestine, who founded with them the community known as that of the fratres et pauperes heremitae domini Celestini. On the other hand, while the Pope was to act as mediator among the most powerful cardinals of Rome, there were some, like a Colonna and an Orsini, who secretly supported the new poverty movement, a truly curious choice for powerful men who lived in vast wealth and luxury; and I have never understood whether they simply exploited the Spirituals for their own political ends or whether in some way they felt they justified their carnal life by supporting the Spiritual trend. Perhaps both things were true, to judge by the little I can understand of Italian affairs. But to give an example, Ubertino had been taken on as chaplain by Cardinal Orsini when, having become the most respected among the Spirituals, he risked being accused as a heretic. And the cardinal himself had protected Ubertino in Avignon.

As happens, however, in such cases, on the one hand Angelus and Ubertino preached according to doctrine, on the other, great masses of simple people accepted this preaching of theirs and spread through the country, beyond all control. So Italy was invaded by these Fraticelli or Friars of the Poor Life, whom many considered dangerous. At this point it was difficult to distinguish the spiritual masters, who maintained contact with the ecclesiastical authorities, from their simpler followers, who now lived outside the order, begging for alms and existing from day to day by the labor of their hands, holding no property of any kind. And these the populace now called Fraticelli, not unlike the French Beghards, who drew their inspiration from Pierre Olieu.

Celestine V was succeeded by Boniface VIII, and this Pope promptly demonstrated scant indulgence for Spirituals and Fraticelli in general: in the last years of the dying century he signed a bull, *Firma cautela*, in which with one stroke he condemned bizochi, vagabond mendicants who roamed about at the far edge of the Franciscan order, and the Spirituals themselves, who had left the life of the order and retired to a hermitage.

After the death of Boniface VIII, the Spirituals tried to obtain from certain of his successors, among them Clement V, permission to leave the order peaceably. I believe they would have succeeded, but the advent of John XXII robbed them of all hope. When he was elected in 1316, he wrote to the King of Sicily telling him to expel those monks from his lands, where many had taken refuge; and John had Angelus Clarenus and the Spirituals of Provence put in chains.

All cannot have proceeded smoothly, and many in the curia resisted. The fact is that Ubertino and Clarenus managed to obtain permission to leave the order, and the former was received by the Benedictines, the latter by the Celestinians. But for those who continued to lead their free life John was merciless, and he had them persecuted by the Inquisition, and many were burned at the stake.

He realized, however, that to destroy the weed of the Fraticelli, who threatened the very foundation of the church's authority, he would need to condemn the notions on which their faith was based. They claimed that Christ and the apostles had owned no property, individually or in common; and the Pope condemned this idea as heretical. An amazing position, because there is no evident reason why a pope should consider perverse the notion that Christ was poor: but only a year before, a general chapter of the Franciscans in Perugia had sustained this opinion, and in condemning the one, the Pope was condemning also the other. As I have already said, the chapter was a great reverse in his struggle against the Emperor; this is the fact of the matter. So after that, many Fraticelli, who knew nothing of empire or of Perugia, were burned to death.

These thoughts were in my mind as I gazed on the legendary figure of Ubertino. My master introduced me, and the old man stroked my cheek, with a warm, almost burning hand. At the touch of his hand I understood many of the things I had heard about that holy man and others I had read in the pages of his *Arbor vitae crucifixae;* I understood the mystic fire that had consumed him from his youth, when, though studying in Paris, he had withdrawn from theological speculation and had imagined himself transformed into the penitent Magdalen; and then his intense association with Saint Angela of Foligno, who had initiated him into the riches of the mystic life and the adoration of the cross; and why his superiors, one day, alarmed by the ardor of his preaching, had sent him in retreat to La Verna.

I studied that face, its features sweet as those of the sainted woman with whom he had fraternally exchanged profound spiritual thoughts. I sensed he must have been able to assume a far harsher expression when, in 1311, the Council of Vienne, with the decretal *Exivi de paradiso*, had deposed Franciscan superiors hostile to the Spirituals, but had charged the latter to live in peace within the order; and this champion of renunciation had not accepted that shrewd compromise and had fought for the institution of a separate order, based on principles of maximum strictness. This great warrior then lost his battle, for in those years John XXII was advocating a crusade against the followers of Pierre Olieu (among whom Ubertino himself was numbered), and he condemned the monks of Narbonne and Béziers. But Ubertino had not hesitated to defend his friend's memory against the Pope, and, outdone by his sanctity, John had not dared condemn him (though he then condemned the others). On that occasion, indeed, he offered Ubertino a way of saving himself, first advising him and then commanding him to enter the Cluniac order. Ubertino, apparently so disarmed and fragile, must have been equally skillful in gaining protectors and allies in the papal courts, and, in fact, he agreed to enter the monastery of Gemblach in Flanders, but I believe he never even went there, and he remained in Avignon, under the banner of Cardinal Orsini, to defend the Franciscans' cause.

Only in recent times (and the rumors I had heard were vague) his star at court had waned, he had had to leave Avignon, and the Pope had this indomitable man pursued as a heretic who per mundum discurrit vagabundus. Then, it was said, all trace of him was lost. That afternoon I had learned, from the dialogue between William and the abbot, that he was hidden here in this abbey. And now I saw him before me.

"William," he was saying, "they were on the point of killing me, you know. I had to flee in the dead of night."

"Who wanted to kill you? John?"

"No. John has never been fond of me, but he has never ceased to respect me. After all, he was the one who offered me a way of avoiding a trial ten years ago, commanding me to enter the Benedictines, and so silencing my enemies. They muttered for a long time, they waxed ironical on the fact that a champion of poverty should enter such a rich order and live at the court of Cardinal Orsini.... William, you know my contempt for the things of this earth! But it was the way to remain in Avignon and defend my brothers. The Pope is afraid of Orsini, he would never have harmed a hair of my head. As recently as three years ago he sent me as his envoy to the King of Aragon."

"Then who wished you ill?"

"All of them. The curia. They tried to assassinate me twice. They tried to silence me. You know what happened five years ago. The Beghards of Narbonne had been condemned two years before, and Berengar Talloni, though he was one of the judges, had appealed to the Pope. Those were difficult moments. John had already issued two bulls against the Spirituals, and even Michael of Cesena had given up—by the way, when does he arrive?"

"He will be here in two days' time."

"Michael...I have not seen him for so long. Now he has come around, he understands what we wanted, the Perugia chapter asserted that we were right. But then, still in 1318, he gave in to the Pope and turned over to him five Spirituals of Provence who were resisting submission. Burned, William...Oh, it is horrible!" He hid his face in his hands.

"But what exactly happened after Talloni's appeal?" William asked.

"John had to reopen the debate, you understand? He had to do it, because in the curia, too, there were men seized with doubt, even the Franciscans in the curia— pharisees, whited sepulchers, ready to sell themselves for a prebend, but they were seized with doubt. It was then that John asked me to draw up a memorial on poverty. It was a fine work, William, may God forgive my pride...."

"I have read it. Michael showed it to me."

"There were the hesitant, even among our own men, the Provincial of Aquitaine, the Cardinal of San Vitale, the Bishop of Kaffa...."

"An idiot," William said.

"Rest in peace. He was gathered to God two years ago."

"God was not so compassionate. That was a false report that arrived from Constantinople. He is still in our midst, and I am told he will be a member of the legation. God protect us!"

"But he is favorable to the chapter of Perugia," Ubertino said.

"Exactly. He belongs to that race of men who are always their adversary's best champions."

"To tell the truth," Ubertino said, "even then he was no great help to the cause. And it all came to nothing, but at least the idea was not declared heretical, and this was important. And so the others have never forgiven me. They have tried to harm me in every way, they have said that I was at Sachsenhausen three years ago, when Louis proclaimed John a heretic. And yet they all knew I was in Avignon that July with Orsini.... They found that parts of the Emperor's declaration reflected my ideas. What madness."

"Not all that mad," William said. "I had given him the ideas, taking them from your Declaration of Avignon, and from some pages of Olieu."

"You?" Ubertino exclaimed, between amazement and joy. "But then you agree with me!"

William seemed embarrassed. "They were the right ideas for the Emperor, at that moment," he said evasively.

Ubertino looked at him suspiciously. "Ah, but you don't really believe them, do you?"

"Tell me," William said, "tell me how you saved yourself from those dogs."

"Ah, dogs indeed, William. Rabid dogs. I found myself even in conflict with Bonagratia, you know?"

"But Bonagratia is on our side!"

"Now he is, after I spoke at length with him. Then he was convinced, and he protested against the *Ad conditorem canonum*. And the Pope imprisoned him for a year."

"I have heard he is now close to a friend of mine in the curia, William of Occam."

"I knew him only slightly. I don't like him. A man without fervor, all head, no heart."

"But the head is beautiful."

"Perhaps, and it will take him to hell."

"Then I will see him again down there, and we will argue logic."

"Hush, William," Ubertino said, smiling with deep affection, "you are better than your philosophers. If only you had wanted..."

"What?"

"When we saw each other the last time in Umbria—remember?—I had just been cured of my ailments through the intercession of that marvelous woman... Clare of Montefalco..." he murmured, his face radiant. "Clare... When female nature, naturally so perverse, becomes sublime through holiness, then it can be the noblest vehicle of grace. You know how my life has been inspired by the purest chastity, William"—he grasped my master's arm, convulsively—"you know with what... fierce—yes, that's the word—with what fierce thirst for penance I have tried to mortify in myself the throbbing of the flesh, and make myself wholly transparent to the love of Jesus Crucified.... And yet, three women in my life have been three celestial messengers for me. Angela of Foligno, Margaret of Città di Castello (who revealed the end of my book to me when I had written only a third of it), and finally Clare of Montefalco. It was a

59

reward from heaven that I, yes, I, should investigate her miracles and proclaim her sainthood to the crowds, before Holy Mother Church moved. And you were there, William, and you could have helped me in that holy endeavor, and you would not—"

"But the holy endeavor that you invited me to share was sending Bentivenga, Jacomo, and Giovannuccio to the stake," William said softly.

"They were besmirching her memory with their perversions. And you were an inquisitor!"

"And that was precisely why I asked to be relieved of that position. I did not like the business. Nor did I like—I shall be frank—the way you induced Bentivenga to confess his errors. You pretended you wished to enter his sect, if sect it was; you stole his secrets from him, and you had him arrested."

"But that is the way to proceed against the enemies of Christ! They were heretics, they were Pseudo Apostles, they reeked of the sulphur of Fra Dolcino!"

"They were Clare's friends."

"No, William, you must not cast even the hint of a shadow on Clare's memory."

"But they were associated with her."

"They were Minorites, they called themselves Spirituals, and instead they were monks of the community! But you know it emerged clearly at the trial that Bentivenga of Gubbio proclaimed himself an apostle, and then he and Giovannuccio of Bevagna seduced nuns, telling them hell does not exist, that carnal desires can be satisfied without offending God, that the body of Christ (Lord, forgive me!) can be received after a man has lain with a nun, that the Magdalen found more favor in the Lord's sight than the virgin Agnes, that what the vulgar call the Devil is God Himself, because the Devil is knowledge and God is by definition knowledge! And it was the blessed Clare, after hearing this talk, who had the vision in which God Himself told her they were wicked followers of the Spiritus Libertatis!"

"They were Minorites whose minds were aflame with the same visions as Clare's, and often the step between ecstatic vision and sinful frenzy is very brief," William said.

Ubertino wrung his hands and his eyes were again veiled with tears. "Don't say that, William. How can you confound the moment of ecstatic love, which burns the viscera with the perfume of incense, and the disorder of the senses, which reeks of sulphur? Bentivenga urged others to touch a body's naked limbs; he declared this was the only way to freedom from the dominion of the senses, homo nudus cum nuda iacebat, 'naked they lay together, man and woman....'"

"Et non commiscebantur ad invicem, but there was no conjunction."

"Lies! They were seeking pleasure, and they found it. If carnal stimulus was felt, they did not consider it a sin if, to satisfy it, man and woman lay together, and the one touched and kissed the other in every part, and naked belly was joined to naked belly!"

I confess that the way Ubertino stigmatized the vice of others did not inspire virtuous thoughts in me. My master must have realized I was agitated, and he interrupted the holy man.

"Yours is an ardent spirit, Ubertino, both in love of God and in hatred of evil. What I meant is that there is little difference between the ardor of the seraphim and the ardor of Lucifer, because they are always born from an extreme igniting of the will."

"Oh, there is a difference, and I know it!" Ubertino said, inspired. "You mean that between desiring good and desiring evil there is a brief step, because it is always a matter of directing the will. This is true. But the difference lies in the object, and the object is clearly recognizable. God on this side, the Devil on that."

"And I fear I no longer know how to distinguish, Ubertino. Wasn't it your Angela of Foligno who told of that day when her spirit was transported and she found herself in the sepulcher of Christ? Didn't she tell how first she kissed his breast and saw him lying with his eyes closed, then she kissed his mouth, and there rose from those lips an ineffable sweetness, and after a brief pause she lay her cheek against the cheek of Christ and Christ put his hand to her cheek and pressed her to him and—as she said—her happiness became sublime?..."

"What does this have to do with the urge of the senses?" Ubertino asked. "It was a mystical experience, and the body was our Lord's."

"Perhaps I am accustomed to Oxford," William said, "where even mystical experience was of another sort...."

"All in the head." Ubertino smiled.

"Or in the eyes. God perceived as light, in the rays of the sun, the images of mirrors, the diffusion of colors over the parts of ordered matter, in the reflections of daylight on wet leaves... Isn't this love closer to Francis's when he praises God in His creatures, flowers, grass, water, air? I don't believe this type of love can produce any snare. Whereas I'm suspicious of a love that transmutes into a colloquy with the Almighty the shudders felt in fleshly contacts...."

"You blaspheme, William! It is not the same thing. There is an immense abyss between the high ecstasy of the heart loving Christ Crucified and the base, corrupt ecstasy of the Pseudo Apostles of Montefalco...."

"They were not Pseudo Apostles, they were Brothers of the Free Spirit; you said as much yourself."

"What difference is there? You haven't heard everything about that trial, I myself never dared record certain confessions, for fear of casting, if only for a moment, the shadow of the Devil on the atmosphere of sanctity Clare had created in that place. But I learned certain things, certain things, William! They gathered at night in a cellar, they took a newborn boy, they threw him from one to another until he died, of blows... or other causes.... And he who caught him alive for the last time, and held him as he died, became the leader of the sect.... And the child's body was torn to pieces and mixed with flour, to make blasphemous hosts!"

"Ubertino," William said firmly, "these things were said, many centuries ago, by the Armenian bishops, about the sect of the Paulicians. And about the Bogomils."

"What does that matter? The Devil is stubborn, he follows a pattern in his snares and his seductions, he repeats his rituals at a distance of millennia, he is always the same, this is precisely why he is recognized as the enemy! I swear to you: They lighted candles on Easter night and took maidens into the cellar. Then they extinguished the candles and threw themselves on the maidens, even if they were bound to them by ties of blood.... And if from this conjunction a baby was born, the infernal rite was resumed, all around a little jar of wine, which they called the keg, and they became drunk and would cut the baby to pieces, and pour its blood into the goblet, and they threw babies on the fire, still alive, and they mixed the baby's ashes and his blood, and drank!"

"But Michael Psellus wrote this in his book on the workings of devils three hundred years ago! Who told you these things?"

"They did. Bentivenga and the others, and under torture!"

"There is only one thing that arouses animals more than pleasure, and that is pain. Under torture you are as if under the dominion of those grasses that produce visions. Everything you have heard told, everything you have read returns to your mind, as if you were being transported, not toward heaven, but toward hell. Under torture you say not only what the inquisitor wants, but also what you imagine might please him, because a bond (this, truly, diabolical) is established between you and him.... These things I know, Ubertino; I also have belonged to those groups of men who believe they can produce the truth with white-hot iron. Well, let me tell you, the white heat of truth comes from another flame.

Under torture Bentivenga may have told the most absurd lies, because it was no longer himself speaking, but his lust, the devils of his soul."

"Lust?"

"Yes, there is a lust for pain, as there is a lust for adoration, and even a lust for humility. If it took so little to make the rebellious angels direct their ardor away from worship and humility toward pride and revolt, what can we expect of a human being? There, now you know: this was the thought that struck me in the course of my inquisitions. And this is why I gave up that activity. I lacked the courage to investigate the weaknesses of the wicked, because I discovered they are the same as the weaknesses of the saintly."

Ubertino had listened to William's last words as if not understanding them. From the old man's expression, as it became filled with affectionate commiseration, I realized he considered William prey to culpable sentiments, which he forgave because he loved my master greatly. Ubertino interrupted him and said in a very bitter voice, "It does not matter. If that was how you felt, you were right to stop. Temptations must be fought. Still, I lacked your support; with it, we could have routed that band. And instead, you know what happened, I myself was accused of being weak toward them, and I was suspected of heresy. You were weak also, in fighting evil. Evil, William! Will this condemnation never cease, this shadow, this mire that prevents us from arriving at the holy source?" He moved still closer to William, as if he were afraid someone might overhear.

"Here, too, even among these walls consecrated to prayer, you know?"

"I know. The abbot has spoken to me; in fact, he asked me to help him shed light on it."

"Then observe, investigate, look with a lynx's eye in both directions: lust and pride...."

"Lust?"

"Yes, lust. There was something…feminine, and therefore diabolical, about that young man who is dead. He had the eyes of a maiden seeking commerce with an incubus. But I said 'pride' also, the pride of the intellect, in this monastery consecrated to the pride of the word, to the illusion of wisdom."

"If you know something, help me."

"I know nothing. There is nothing that I *know*. But the heart senses certain things. Let your heart speak, question faces, do not listen to tongues.…But come, why must we talk of these sad things and frighten this young friend of ours?" He looked at me with his pale-blue eyes, grazing my cheek with his long white fingers, and I instinctively almost withdrew; I controlled myself and was right to do so, because I would have offended him, and his intention was pure. "Tell me of yourself instead," he said, turning again to William. "What have you done since then? It has been—"

"Eighteen years. I went back to my country. I resumed studying at Oxford. I studied nature."

"Nature is good because she is the daughter of God," Ubertino said.

"And God must be good, since He generated nature," William said with a smile. "I studied, I met some very wise friends. Then I came to know Marsilius, I was attracted by his ideas about empire, the people, about a new law for the kingdoms of the earth, and so I ended up in that group of our brothers who are advising the Emperor. But you know these things: I wrote you. I rejoiced at Bobbio when they told me you were here. We believed you were lost. But now that you are with us you can be of great help in a few days, when Michael also arrives. It will be a harsh conflict with Berengar Talloni. I really believe we will have some amusement."

Ubertino looked at him with a tentative smile. "I can never tell when you Englishmen are speaking seriously. There is nothing amusing about such a serious question.

At stake is the survival of the order, which is your order; and in my heart it is mine, too. But I shall implore Michael not to go to Avignon. John wants him, seeks him, invites him too insistently. Don't trust that old Frenchman. O Lord, into what hands has Thy church fallen!" He turned his head toward the altar. "Transformed into harlot, weakened by luxury, she roils in lust like a snake in heat! From the naked purity of the stable of Bethlehem, made of wood as the lignum vitae of the cross was wood, to the bacchanalia of gold and stone! Look, look here: you have seen the doorway! There is no escaping the pride of images! The days of the Antichrist are finally at hand, and I am afraid, William!" He looked around, staring wide-eyed among the dark naves, as if the Antichrist were going to appear any moment, and I actually expected to glimpse him. "His lieutenants are already here, dispatched as Christ dispatched the apostles into the world! They are trampling on the City of God, seducing through deceit, hypocrisy, violence. It will be then that God will have to send His servants, Elijah and Enoch, whom He maintained alive in the earthly paradise so that one day they may confound the Antichrist, and they will come to prophesy clad in sackcloth, and they will preach penance by word and by example. . . ."

"They have already come, Ubertino," William said, indicating his Franciscan habit.

"But they have not yet triumphed; this is the moment when the Antichrist, filled with rage, will command the killing of Enoch and Elijah and the exposure of their bodies for all to see and thus be afraid of imitating them. Just as they wanted to kill me. . . ."

At that moment, terrified, I thought Ubertino was in the power of a kind of holy frenzy, and I feared for his reason. Now, with the distance of time, knowing what I know—namely, that two years later he would be mysteriously killed in a German city by a murderer never discovered—I am all the more terrified, because obviously that evening Ubertino was prophesying.

"The abbot Joachim spoke the truth, you know. We have reached the sixth era of human history, when two Antichrists will appear, the mystic Antichrist and the Antichrist proper. This is happening now, in the sixth era, after Francis appeared to receive in his own flesh the five wounds of Jesus Crucified. Boniface was the mystic Antichrist, and the abdication of Celestine was not valid. Boniface was the beast that rises up from the sea whose seven heads represent the offenses to the deadly sins and whose ten horns the offenses to the commandments, and the cardinals who surrounded him were the locusts, whose body is Apollyon! But the number of the beast, if you read the name in Greek letters, is *Benedicti!*" He stared at me to see whether I had understood, and he raised a finger, cautioning me: "Benedict XI was the Antichrist proper, the beast that rises up from the earth! God allowed such a monster of vice and iniquity to govern His church so that his successor's virtues would blaze with glory!"

"But, Sainted Father," I replied in a faint voice, summoning my courage, "his successor is John!"

Ubertino put a hand to his brow as if to dispel a troublesome dream. He was breathing with difficulty; he was tired. "True, the calculations were wrong, we are still awaiting the Angelic Pope....But meanwhile Francis and Dominic have appeared." He raised his eyes to heaven and said, as if praying (but I was sure he was quoting a page of his great book on the tree of life): "Quorum primus seraphico calculo purgatus et ardore celico inflammatus totum incendere videbatur. Secundus vero verbo predicationis fecundus super mundi tenebras clarius radiavit....Yes, these were the promises: the Angelic Pope must come."

"And so be it, Ubertino," William said. "Meanwhile, I am here to prevent the human Emperor from being deposed. Your Angelic Pope was also preached by Fra Dolcino...."

"Never utter again the name of that serpent!" Ubertino cried, and for the first time I saw his sorrow turn into rage. "He has befouled the words of Joachim of Calabria, and has made them bringers of death and filth! Messenger of the Antichrist if ever there was one! But you, William, speak like this because you do not really believe in the advent of the Antichrist, and your masters at Oxford have taught you to idolize reason, drying up the prophetic capacities of your heart!"

"You are mistaken, Ubertino," William answered very seriously. "You know that among my masters I venerate Roger Bacon more than any other...."

"Who raved of flying machines," Ubertino muttered bitterly.

"Who spoke clearly and calmly of the Antichrist, and was aware of the import of the corruption of the world and the decline of learning. He taught, however, that there is only one way to prepare against his coming: study the secrets of nature, use knowledge to better the human race. We can prepare to fight the Antichrist by studying the curative properties of herbs, the nature of stones, and even by planning those flying machines that make you smile."

"Your Bacon's Antichrist was a pretext for cultivating intellectual pride."

"A holy pretext."

"Nothing pretextual is holy. William, you know I love you. You know I have great faith in you. Mortify your intelligence, learn to weep over the wounds of the Lord, throw away your books."

"I will devote myself only to yours." William smiled.

Ubertino also smiled and waved a threatening finger at him. "Foolish Englishman. Do not laugh too much at your fellows. Those whom you cannot love you should, rather, fear. And be on your guard here at the abbey. I do not like this place."

"I want to know it better, in fact," William said, taking his leave. "Come, Adso."

"I tell you it is not good, and you reply that you want to know it better. Ah!" Ubertino said, shaking his head.

"By the way," William said, already halfway down the nave, "who is that monk who looks like an animal and speaks the language of Babel?"

"Salvatore?" Ubertino, who had already knelt down, turned. "I believe he was a gift of mine to this abbey...along with the cellarer. When I put aside the Franciscan habit I returned for a while to my old convent at Casale, and there I found other monks in difficulty, because the community accused them of being Spirituals of my sect...as they put it. I exerted myself in their favor, procuring permission for them to follow my example. And two, Salvatore and Remigio, I found here when I arrived last year. Salvatore...he does indeed look like an animal. But he is obliging."

William hesitated a moment. "I heard him say Penitenziagite."

Ubertino was silent. He waved one hand, as if to drive off a bothersome thought. "No, I don't believe so. You know how these lay brothers are. Country people, who have perhaps heard some wandering preacher and don't know what they are saying. I would have other reproaches to make to Salvatore: he is a greedy animal and lustful. But nothing, nothing against orthodoxy. No, the sickness of the abbey is something else: seek it among those who know too much, not in those who know nothing. Don't build a castle of suspicions on one word."

"I would never do that," William answered. "I gave up being an inquisitor precisely to avoid doing that. But I like also to listen to words, and then I think about them."

"You think too much. Boy," he said, addressing me, "don't learn too many bad examples from your master.

The only thing that must be pondered—and I realize this at the end of my life—is death. Mors est quies viatoris—finis est omnis laboris. Let me pray now."

TOWARD NONES

In which William has a very erudite conversation with Severinus the herbalist.

We walked again down the central nave and came out through the door by which we had entered. I could still hear Ubertino's words, all of them, buzzing in my head.

"That man is . . . odd," I dared say to William.

"He is, or has been, in many ways a great man. But for this very reason he is odd. It is only petty men who seem normal. Ubertino could have become one of the heretics he helped burn, or a cardinal of the holy Roman church. He came very close to both perversions. When I talk with Ubertino I have the impression that hell is heaven seen from the other side."

I did not grasp his meaning. "From what side?" I asked.

"Ah, true," William acknowledged the problem. "It is a matter of knowing whether there are sides and whether there is a whole. But pay no attention to me. And stop looking at that doorway," he said, striking me lightly on the nape as I was turning, attracted by the

sculptures I had seen on entering. "They have frightened you enough for today. All of them."

As I turned back to the exit, I saw in front of me
another monk. He could have been William's age. He
smiled and greeted us cordially. He said he was Severinus
of Sankt Wendel, and he was the brother herbalist, in
charge of the balneary, the infirmary, the gardens, and
he was ours to command if we would like to learn our
way better around the abbey compound.

William thanked him and said he had already
remarked, on coming in, the very fine vegetable garden,
where it looked to him as if not only edible plants were
grown, but also medicinal ones, from what he could
tell, given the snow.

"In summer or spring, through the variety of its
plants, each then adorned with its flowers, this garden
sings better the praises of the Creator," Severinus said,
somewhat apologetically. "But even now, in winter, the
herbalist's eye sees through the dry branches the plants
that will come, and he can tell you that this garden is
richer than any herbal ever was, and more varicolored,
beautiful as the illuminations are in those volumes.
Furthermore, good herbs grow also in winter, and I
preserve others gathered and ready in the pots in my
laboratory. And so with the roots of the wood sorrel I
treat catarrhs, and with the decoction of althea roots I
make plasters for skin diseases; burrs cicatrize eczemas;
by chopping and grinding the snakeroot rhizome I
treat diarrheas and certain female complaints; pepper
is a fine digestive; coltsfoot eases the cough; and we
have good gentian also for the digestion, and I have
glycyrrhiza, and juniper for making excellent infusions,
and elder bark with which I make a decoction for the
liver, soapwort, whose roots are macerated in cold
water for catarrh, and valerian, whose properties you
surely know."

"You have widely varied herbs, and suited to different climates. How do you manage that?"

"On the one hand, I owe it to the mercy of the Lord, who set our high plain between a range that overlooks the sea to the south and receives its warm winds, and the higher mountain to the north whose sylvan balsams we receive. And on the other hand, I owe it to my art, which, unworthily, I learned at the wish of my masters. Certain plants will grow even in an adverse climate if you take care of the terrain around them, and their nourishment, and their growth."

"But you also have plants that are good only to eat?" I asked.

"Ah, my hungry young colt, there are no plants good for food that are not good for treating the body, too, provided they are taken in the right quantity. Only excess makes them cause illness. Consider the pumpkin. It is cold and damp by nature and slakes thirst, but if you eat it when rotten it gives you diarrhea and you must bind your viscera with a paste of brine and mustard. And onions? Warm and damp, in small quantities they enhance coitus (for those who have not taken our vows, naturally), but too many bring on a heaviness of the head, to be combatted with milk and vinegar. A good reason," he added slyly, "why a young monk should always eat them sparingly. Eat garlic instead. Warm and dry, it is good against poisons. But do not use it to excess, for it causes too many humors to be expelled from the brain. Beans, on the contrary, produce urine and are fattening, two very good things. But they induce bad dreams. Far less, however, than certain other herbs. There are some that actually provoke evil visions."

"Which?" I asked.

"Aha, our novice wants to know too much. These are things that only the herbalist must know; otherwise any thoughtless person could go about distributing visions: in other words, lying with herbs."

"But you need only a bit of nettle," William said then, "or roybra or olieribus to be protected against such visions. I hope you have some of these good herbs."

Severinus gave my master a sidelong glance. "You are interested in herbalism?"

"Just a little," William said modestly, "since I came upon the *Theatrum Sanitatis* of Ububchasym de Baldach..."

"Abul Asan al-Muchtar ibn-Botlan."

"Or Ellucasim Elimittar: as you prefer. I wonder whether a copy is to be found here."

"One of the most beautiful. With many rich illustrations."

"Heaven be praised. And the *De virtutibus herbarum* of Platearius?"

"That, too. And the *De plantis* of Aristotle, translated by Alfred of Sareshel."

"I have heard it said that Aristotle did not really write that work," William remarked, "just as he was not the author of the *De causis*, it has been discovered."

"In any event it is a great book," Severinus observed, and my master agreed most readily, not asking whether the herbalist was speaking of the *De plantis* or of the *De causis*, both works that I did not know but which, from that conversation, I deduced must be very great.

"I shall be happy," Severinus concluded, "to have some frank conversation with you about herbs."

"I shall be still happier," William said, "but would we not be breaking the rule of silence, which I believe obtains in your order?"

"The Rule," Severinus said, "has been adapted over the centuries to the requirements of the different communities. The Rule prescribed the lectio divina but not study, and yet you know how much our order has developed inquiry into divine and human affairs. Also, the Rule prescribes a common dormitory, but at times it is right that the monks have, as we do here, chances to meditate also during the night, and so each of them is given his own cell. The Rule is very rigid on the question of silence, and here with us, not only the monk who performs manual labor but also those who write or read must not converse with their brothers. But the abbey is first and foremost a community of scholars, and often it is useful for monks to exchange the accumulated treasures of their learning. All conversation regarding our studies is considered legitimate and profitable, provided it does not take place in the refectory or during the hours of the holy offices."

"Had you much occasion to talk with Adelmo of Otranto?" William asked abruptly.

Severinus did not seem surprised. "I see the abbot has already spoken with you," he said. "No. I did not converse with him often. He spent his time illuminating. I did hear him on occasion talking with other monks, Venantius of Salvemec, or Jorge of Burgos, about the nature of his work. Besides, I don't spend my day in the scriptorium, but in my laboratory." And he nodded toward the infirmary building.

"I understand," William said. "So you don't know whether Adelmo had visions."

"Visions?"

"Like the ones your herbs induce, for example."

Severinus stiffened. "I told you: I store the dangerous herbs with great care."

"That is not what I meant," William hastened to clarify. "I was speaking of visions in general."

"I don't understand," Severinus insisted.

"I was thinking that a monk who wanders at night about the Aedificium, where, by the abbot's admission ...terrible things can happen...to those who enter during forbidden hours—well, as I say, I was thinking he might have had diabolical visions that drove him to the precipice."

"I told you: I don't visit the scriptorium, except when I need a book; but as a rule I have my own herbaria, which I keep in the infirmary. As I said, Adelmo was very close to Jorge, Venantius, and ... naturally, Berengar."

Even I sensed the slight hesitation in Severinus's

voice. Nor did it escape my master. "Berengar? And why 'naturally'?"

"Berengar of Arundel, the assistant librarian. They were of an age, they had been novices together, it was normal for them to have things to talk about. That is what I meant."

"Ah, that is what you meant," William repeated. And to my surprise he did not pursue the matter. In fact, he promptly changed the subject. "But perhaps it is time for us to visit the Aedificium. Will you act as our guide?"

"Gladly," Severinus said, with all-too-evident relief. He led us along the side of the garden and brought us to the west façade of the Aedificium.

"Facing the garden is the door leading to the kitchen," he said, "but the kitchen occupies only the western half of the ground floor; in the other half is the refectory. And at the south entrance, which you reach from behind the choir in the church, there are two other doors leading to the kitchen and the refectory. But we can go in here, because from the kitchen we can then go on through to the refectory."

As I entered the vast kitchen, I realized that the entire height of the Aedificium enclosed an octagonal court; I understood later that this was a kind of huge well, without any access, onto which, at each floor, opened broad windows, like the ones on the exterior. The kitchen was a vast smoke-filled entrance hall, where many servants were already busy preparing the food for supper. On a great table two of them were making a pie of greens, barley, oats, and rye, chopping turnips, cress, radishes, and carrots. Nearby, another cook had just finished poaching some fish in a mixture of wine and water, and was covering them with a sauce of sage, parsley, thyme, garlic, pepper, and salt.

Beneath the west tower an enormous oven opened, for baking bread; it was already flashing with reddish flames. In the south tower there was an immense fireplace, where great pots were boiling and spits were turning. Through the door that opened onto the barnyard behind the church, the swineherds were entering at that moment, carrying the meat of the slaughtered pigs. We went out through that same door and found ourselves in the yard, at the far eastern end of the plain, against the walls, where there were many buildings. Severinus explained to me that the first was the series of barns, then there stood the horses' stables, then those for the oxen, and then chicken coops, and the covered yard for the sheep. Outside the pigpens, swineherds were stirring a great jarful of the blood of the freshly slaughtered pigs, to keep it from coagulating. If it was stirred properly and promptly, it would remain liquid for the next few days, thanks to the cold climate, and then they would make blood puddings from it.

We re-entered the Aedificium and cast a quick glance at the refectory as we crossed it, heading toward the east tower. Of the two towers between which the refectory extended, the northern one housed a fireplace, the other a circular staircase that led to the scriptorium, on the floor above. By this staircase the monks went up to their work every day, or else they used the other two staircases, less comfortable but well heated, which rose in spirals inside the fireplace here and inside the oven in the kitchen.

William asked whether we would find anyone in the scriptorium, since it was Sunday. Severinus smiled and said that work, for the Benedictine monk, *is* prayer. On Sunday offices lasted longer, but the monks assigned to work on books still spent some hours up there, usually engaged in fruitful exchanges of learned observations, counsel, reflections on Holy Scripture.

AFTER NONES

In which there is a visit to the scriptorium, and a meeting with many scholars, copyists, and rubricators, as well as an old blind man who is expecting the Antichrist.

As we climbed up I saw my master observing the windows that gave light to the stairway. I was probably becoming as clever as he, because I immediately noticed that their position would make it difficult for a person to reach them. On the other hand, the windows of the refectory (the only ones on the ground floor that overlooked the cliff face) did not seem easily reached, either, since below them there was no furniture of any kind.

When we reached the top of the stairs, we went through the east tower into the scriptorium, and there I could not suppress a cry of wonder. This floor was not divided in two like the one below, and therefore it appeared to my eyes in all its spacious immensity. The ceilings, curved and not too high (lower than in a church, but still higher than in any chapter house I ever saw), supported by sturdy pillars, enclosed a space suffused with the most beautiful light, because three enormous windows opened on each of the longer sides, whereas a smaller window pierced each of the five external sides of each tower; eight high, narrow windows, finally, allowed light to enter from the octagonal central well.

The abundance of windows meant that the great room was cheered by a constant diffused light, even on a winter afternoon. The panes were not colored like church windows, and the lead-framed squares of clear glass allowed the light to enter in the purest possible fashion, not modulated by human art, and thus to serve its purpose, which was to illuminate the work of reading and writing. I have seen at other times and in other places many scriptoria, but none where there shone so luminously, in the outpouring of physical light which made the room glow, the spiritual principle that light incarnates, radiance, source of all beauty and learning, inseparable attribute of that proportion the room embodied. For three things concur in creating beauty: first of all integrity or perfection, and for this reason we consider ugly all incomplete things; then proper proportion or consonance; and finally clarity and light, and in fact we call beautiful those things of definite color. And since the sight of the beautiful implies peace, and since our appetite is calmed similarly by peacefulness, by the good, and by the beautiful, I felt myself filled with a great consolation and I thought how pleasant it must be to work in that place.

As it appeared to my eyes, at that afternoon hour, it seemed to me a joyous workshop of learning. I saw later at St. Gall a scriptorium of similar proportions, also separated from the library (in other convents the monks worked in the same place where the books were kept), but not so beautifully arranged as this one. Antiquarians, librarians, rubricators, and scholars were seated, each at his own desk, and there was a desk under each of the windows. And since there were forty windows (a number truly perfect, derived from the decupling of the quadragon, as if the Ten Commandments had been multiplied by the four cardinal virtues), forty monks could work at the same time, though at that moment there were perhaps thirty. Severinus explained to us that monks working in the scriptorium were exempted from the offices of terce, sext, and nones so they would not have to leave their work during the hours of daylight, and they stopped their activity only at sunset, for vespers.

The brightest places were reserved for the antiquarians, the most expert illuminators, the rubricators, and the copyists. Each desk had everything required for illuminating and copying: inkhorns, fine quills which some monks were sharpening with a thin knife, pumice stone for smoothing the parchment, rulers for drawing the lines that the writing would follow. Next to each scribe, or at the top of the sloping desk, there was a lectern, on which the codex to be copied was placed, the page covered by a sheet with a cut-out window which framed the line being copied at that moment. And some had inks of gold and various colors. Other monks were simply reading books, and they wrote down their annotations in their personal notebooks or on tablets.

I did not have time, however, to observe their work, because the librarian came to us. We already knew he was Malachi of Hildesheim. His face was trying to assume an expression of welcome, but I could not help shuddering at the sight of such a singular countenance. He was tall and extremely thin, with large and awkward limbs. As he took his great strides, cloaked in the black habit of the order, there was something upsetting about his appearance. The hood, which was still raised since he had come in from outside, cast a shadow on the pallor of his face and gave a certain suffering quality to his large melancholy eyes. In his physiognomy there were what seemed traces of many passions which his will had disciplined but which seemed to have frozen those features they had now ceased to animate. Sadness and severity predominated in the lines of his face, and his eyes were so intense that with one glance they could penetrate the heart of the person speaking to him, and read the secret thoughts, so it was difficult to tolerate their inquiry and one was not tempted to meet them a second time.

The librarian introduced us to many of the monks who were working at that moment. Of each, Malachi also told us what task he was performing, and I admired the deep devotion of all to knowledge and to the study of the divine word. Thus I met Venantius of Salvemec, translator from the Greek and the Arabic, devoted to that Aristotle who surely was the wisest of all men. Benno of Uppsala, a young Scandinavian monk who was studying rhetoric. Aymaro of Alessandria, who had been copying works on loan to the library for a few months only, and then a group of illuminators from various countries, Patrick of Clonmacnois, Rabano of Toledo, Magnus of Iona, Waldo of Hereford.

The list could surely go on, and there is nothing more wonderful than a list, instrument of wondrous hypotyposis. But I must come to the subject of our discussion, from which emerged many useful indications as to the nature of the subtle uneasiness among the monks, and some concerns, not expressed, that still weighed on all our conversations.

My master began speaking with Malachi, praising the beauty and the industry of the scriptorium and asking him for information about the procedure for the work done there, because, he said very acutely, he had heard this library spoken of everywhere and would like to examine many of the books. Malachi explained to him what the abbot had already said: the monk asked the librarian for the work he wished to consult and the librarian then went to fetch it from the library above, if the request was justified and devout. William asked how he could find out the names of the books kept in the cases upstairs, and Malachi showed him, fixed by a little gold chain to his own desk, a voluminous codex covered with very thickly written lists.

William slipped his hands inside his habit, at the point where it billowed over his chest to make a kind of sack, and he drew from it an object that I had already seen in his hands, and on his face, in the course of our journey. It was a forked pin, so constructed that it could stay on a man's nose (or at least on his, so prominent and aquiline) as a rider remains astride his horse or as a bird clings to its perch. And, one on either side of the fork, before the eyes, there were two ovals of metal, which held two almonds of glass, thick as the bottom of a tumbler. William preferred to read with these before his eyes, and he said they made his vision better than what nature had endowed him with or than his advanced age, especially as the daylight failed, would permit. They did not serve him to see from a distance, for then his eyes were, on the contrary, quite sharp, but to see close up. With these lenses he could read manuscripts penned in very faint letters, which even I had some trouble deciphering. He explained to me that, when a man had passed the middle point of his life, even if his sight had always been excellent, the eye hardened and the pupil became recalcitrant, so that many learned men had virtually died, as far as reading and writing were concerned, after their fiftieth summer. A grave misfortune for men who could have given the best fruits of their intellect for many more years. So the Lord was to be praised since someone had devised and constructed this instrument. And he told me this in support of the ideas of his Roger Bacon, who had said that the aim of learning was also to prolong human life.

The other monks looked at William with great curiosity but did not dare ask him questions. And I noticed that, even in a place so zealously and proudly dedicated to reading and writing, that wondrous instrument had not yet arrived. I felt proud to be at the side of a man who had something with which to dumbfound other men famous in the world for their wisdom.

With those objects on his eyes William bent over the lists inscribed in the codex. I looked, too, and we found titles of books we had never before heard of, and others most famous, that the library possessed.

"*De pentagono Salomonis, Ars loquendi et intelligendi in lingua hebraica, De rebus metallicis* by Roger of Hereford, *Algebra* by Al-Kuwarizmi, translated into Latin by Robertus Anglicus, the *Punica* of Silius Italicus, the *Gesta francorum, De laudibus sanctae crucis* by Rabanus Maurus, and *Flavii Claudii Giordani de aetate mundi et hominis reservatis singulis litteris per singulos libros ab A usque ad Z,*" my master read. "Splendid works. But in what order are they listed?" He quoted from a text I did not know but which was certainly familiar to Malachi: "'The librarian must have a list of all books, carefully ordered by subjects and authors, and they must be classified on the shelves with numerical indications.' How do you know the collocation of each book?"

Malachi showed him some annotations beside each title. I read: "iii, IV gradus, V in prima graecorum"; "ii, V gradus, VII in tertia anglorum," and so on. I understood that the first number indicated the position of the book on the shelf or *gradus*, which was in turn indicated by the second number, while the case was indicated by the third number; and I understood also that the other phrases designated a room or a corridor of the library, and I made bold to ask further information about these last distinctions. Malachi looked at me sternly: "Perhaps you do not know, or have forgotten, that only the librarian is allowed access to the library. It is therefore right and sufficient that only the librarian know how to decipher these things."

"But in what order are the books recorded in this list?" William asked. "Not by subject, it seems to me." He did not suggest an order by author, following the same sequence as the letters of the alphabet, for this is a system I have seen adopted only in recent years, and at that time it was rarely used.

"The library dates back to the earliest times," Malachi said, "and the books are registered in order of their acquisition, donation, or entrance within our walls."

"They are difficult to find, then," William observed.

"It is enough for the librarian to know them by heart and know when each book came here. As for the other monks, they can rely on his memory." He spoke as if discussing someone other than himself, and I realized he was speaking of the office that at that moment he unworthily held, but which had been held by a hundred others, now deceased, who had handed down their knowledge from one to the other.

"I understand," William said. "If I were then to seek something, not knowing what, on the pentagon of Solomon, you would be able to tell me that there exists the book whose title I have just read, and you could identify its location on the floor above."

"If you really had to learn something about the pentagon of Solomon," Malachi said. "But before giving you that book, I would prefer to ask the abbot's advice."

"I have been told that one of your best illuminators died recently," William said then. "The abbot has spoken to me a great deal of his art. Could I see the codices he was illuminating?"

"Because of his youth, Adelmo of Otranto," Malachi said, looking at William suspiciously, "worked only on marginalia. He had a very lively imagination and from known things he was able to compose unknown and surprising things, as one might join a human body to an equine neck. His books are over there. Nobody has yet touched his desk."

We approached what had been Adelmo's working place, where the pages of a richly illuminated psalter still lay. They were folios of the finest vellum—that queen among parchments—and the last was still fixed to the desk. Just scraped with pumice stone and softened with chalk, it had been smoothed with the plane, and, from the tiny holes made on the sides with a fine stylus, all the lines that were to have guided the artist's hand had been traced. The first half had already been covered with writing, and the monk had begun to sketch the illustrations in the margins. The other pages, on the contrary, were already finished, and as we looked at them, neither I nor William could suppress a cry of wonder. This was a psalter in whose margins was delineated a world reversed with respect to the one to which our senses have accustomed us. As if at the border of a discourse that is by definition the discourse of truth, there proceeded, closely linked to it, through wondrous allusions in aenigmate, a discourse of falsehood on a topsy-turvy universe, in which dogs flee before the hare, and deer hunt the lion. Little bird-feet heads, animals with human hands on their back, hirsute pates from which feet sprout, zebra-striped dragons, quadrupeds with serpentine necks twisted in a thousand inextricable knots, monkeys with stags' horns, sirens in the form of fowl with membranous wings, armless men with other human bodies emerging from their backs like humps, and figures with tooth-filled mouths on the belly, humans with horses' heads, and horses with human legs, fish with birds' wings and birds with fishtails, monsters with single bodies and double heads or single heads and double bodies, cows with cocks' tails and butterfly wings, women with heads scaly as a fish's back, two-headed chimeras interlaced with dragonflies with lizard snouts, centaurs, dragons, elephants, manticores stretched out on tree branches, gryphons whose tails turned into an archer in battle array, diabolical creatures with endless necks, sequences of anthropomorphic animals and zoomorphic dwarfs joined, sometimes on the same page, with scenes of rustic life in which you saw, depicted with such impressive vivacity that the figures seemed alive, all the life of the fields, plowmen, fruit gatherers, harvesters, spinning-women, sowers alongside foxes, and martens armed with crossbows who were scaling the walls of a towered city defended by monkeys. Here an initial letter, bent into an *L*, in the lower part generated a dragon; there a great *V*, which began the word "verba," produced as a natural shoot from its trunk a serpent with a thousand coils, which in turn begot other serpents as leaves and clusters.

Next to the psalter there was, apparently finished only a short time before, an exquisite book of hours, so incredibly small that it would fit into the palm of the hand. The writing was tiny; the marginal illuminations, barely visible at first sight, demanded that the eye examine them closely to reveal all their beauty (and you asked yourself with what superhuman instrument the artist had drawn them to achieve such vivid effects in a space so reduced). The entire margins of the book were invaded by minuscule forms that generated one another, as if by natural expansion, from the terminal scrolls of the splendidly drawn letters: sea sirens, stags in flight, chimeras, armless human torsos that emerged like slugs from the very body of the verses. At one point, as if to continue the triple "Sanctus, Sanctus, Sanctus" repeated on three different lines, you saw three ferocious figures with human heads, two of which were bent, one downward and one upward, to join in a kiss you would not have hesitated to call immodest if you were not persuaded that a profound, even if not evident, spiritual meaning must surely have justified that illustration at that point.

As I followed those pages I was torn between silent admiration and laughter, because the illustrations naturally inspired merriment, though they were commenting on holy pages. And Brother William examined them smiling and remarked, "Babewyn: so they are called in my islands."

"Babouins: that is what they call them in Gaul," Malachi said. "Adelmo learned his art in your country, although he studied also in France. Baboons, that is to say: monkeys from Africa. Figures of an inverted world, where houses stand on the tip of a steeple and the earth is above the sky."

I recalled some verses I had heard in the vernacular of my country, and I could not refrain from repeating them:

> *Aller wunder si geswigen,*
> *das erde himel hât überstigen,*
> *daz sult ir vür ein wunder wigen*

And Malachi continued, quoting from the same text:

> *Erd ob un himel unter,*
> *das sult ir hân besunder*
> *vür aller wunder ein wunder.*

"Good for you, Adso," the librarian continued. "In fact, these images tell of that country where you arrive mounted on a blue goose, where hawks are found that catch fish in a stream, bears that pursue falcons in the sky, lobsters that fly with the doves, and three giants are caught in a trap and bitten by a cock."

And a pale smile brightened his lips. Then the other monks, who had followed the conversation a bit shyly, laughed heartily, as if they had been awaiting the librarian's consent. He frowned as the others continued laughing, praising the skill of poor Adelmo and pointing out to one another the more fantastic figures. And it was while all were still laughing that we heard, at our backs, a solemn and stern voice.

"Verba vana aut risui apta non loqui."

We turned. The speaker was a monk bent under the weight of his years, an old man white as snow, not only his skin, but also his face and his pupils. I saw he was blind. The voice was still majestic and the limbs powerful, even if the body was withered by age. He stared at us as if he could see us, and always thereafter I saw him move and speak as if he still possessed the gift of sight. But the tone of his voice was that of one possessing only the gift of prophecy.

"The man whom you see, venerable in age and wisdom," Malachi said to William, pointing out the newcomer, "is Jorge of Burgos. Older than anyone else living in the monastery save Alinardo of Grottaferrata, he is the one to whom many monks here confide the burden of their sins in the secret of confession." Then, turning to the old man, he said, "The man standing before you is Brother William of Baskerville, our guest."

"I hope my words did not anger you," the old man said in a curt tone. "I heard persons laughing at laughable things and I reminded them of one of the principles of our Rule. And as the psalmist says, if the monk must refrain from good speech because of his vow of silence, all the more reason why he should avoid bad speech. And as there is bad speech there are also bad images. And they are those that lie about the form of creation and show the world as the opposite of what it should be, has always been, and always will be throughout the centuries until the end of time. But you come from another order, where I am told that merriment, even the most inopportune sort, is viewed with indulgence." He was repeating what the Benedictines said about the eccentricities of Saint Francis of Assisi, and perhaps also the bizarre whims attributed to those friars and Spirituals of every kind who were the most recent and embarrassing offshoots of the Franciscan order. But William gave no sign of understanding the insinuation.

"Marginal images often provoke smiles, but to edifying ends," he replied. "As in sermons, to touch the imagination of devout throngs it is necessary to introduce exempla, not infrequently jocular, so also the discourse of images must indulge in these trivia. For every virtue and for every sin there is an example drawn from bestiaries, and animals exemplify the human world."

"Ah, yes," the old man said mockingly, but without smiling, "any image is good for inspiring virtue, provided the masterpiece of creation, turned with his head down, becomes the subject of laughter. And so the word of God is illustrated by the ass playing a lyre, the owl plowing with a shield, oxen yoking themselves to the plow, rivers flowing upstream, the sea catching fire, the wolf turning hermit! Go hunting for hares with oxen, have owls teach you grammar, have dogs bite fleas, the one-eyed guard the dumb, and the dumb ask for bread, the ant give birth to a calf, roast chickens fly, cakes grow on rooftops, parrots hold rhetoric lessons, hens fertilize cocks, make the cart go before the oxen, the dog sleep in a bed, and all walk with their heads on the ground! What is the aim of this nonsense? A world that is the reverse and the opposite of that established by God, under the pretext of teaching divine precepts!"

"But as the Areopagite teaches," William said humbly, "God can be named only through the most distorted things. And Hugh of St. Victor reminded us that the more the simile becomes dissimilar, the more the truth is revealed to us under the guise of horrible and indecorous figures, the less the imagination is sated in carnal enjoyment, and is thus obliged to perceive the mysteries hidden under the turpitude of the images. . . ."

"I know that line of reasoning! And I confess with shame that it was the chief argument of our order when the Cluniac abbots combatted the Cistercians. But Saint Bernard was right: little by little the man who depicts monsters and portents of nature to reveal the things of God per speculum et in aenigmate, comes to enjoy the very nature of the monstrosities he creates and to delight in them, and as a result he no longer sees except through them. You have only to look, you who still have your sight, at the capitals of your cloister." And he motioned with his hand beyond the window, toward the church. "Before the eyes of monks intent on meditation, what is the meaning of those ridiculous grotesques, those monstrous shapes and shapely monsters? Those sordid apes? Those lions, those centaurs, those half-human creatures, with mouths in their bellies, with single feet, ears like sails? Those spotted tigers, those fighting warriors, those hunters blowing their horns, and those many bodies with single heads and many heads with single bodies? Quadrupeds with serpents' tails, and fish with quadrupeds' faces, and here an animal who seems a horse in front and a ram behind, and there a horse with horns, and so on; by now it is more pleasurable for a monk to read marble than manuscript, and to admire the works of man than to meditate on the law of God. Shame! For the desire of your eyes and for your smiles!"

The old man stopped, out of breath. And I admired the vivid memory thanks to which, blind perhaps for many years, he could still recall the images whose wickedness he decried. I was led to suspect they had greatly seduced him when he had seen them, since he could yet describe them with such passion. But it has often happened that I have found the most seductive depictions of sin in the pages of those very men of incorruptible virtue who condemned their spell and their effects. A sign that these men are impelled by such eagerness to bear witness to the truth that they do not hesitate, out of love of God, to confer on evil all the seductions in which it cloaks itself; thus the writers inform men better of the ways through which the Evil One enchants them. And, in fact, Jorge's words filled me with a great desire to see the tigers and monkeys of the cloister, which I had not yet admired. But Jorge interrupted the flow of my thoughts because he resumed speaking, in a much calmer tone.

"Our Lord did not have to employ such foolish things to point out the strait and narrow path to us. Nothing in his parables arouses laughter, or fear. Adelmo, on the contrary, whose death you now mourn, took such pleasure in the monsters he painted that he lost sight of the ultimate things which they were to illustrate. And he followed all, I say all"—his voice became solemn and ominous—"the paths of monstrosity. Which God knows how to punish."

A heavy silence fell. Venantius of Salvemec dared break it.

"Venerable Jorge," he said, "your virtue makes you unjust. Two days before Adelmo died, you were present at a learned debate right here in the scriptorium. Adelmo took care that his art, indulging in bizarre and fantastic images, was directed nevertheless to the glory of God, as an instrument of the knowledge of celestial things. Brother William mentioned just now the Areopagite, who spoke of learning through distortion. And Adelmo that day quoted another lofty authority, the doctor of Aquino, when he said that divine things should be expounded more properly in figures of vile bodies than of noble bodies. First because the human spirit is more easily freed from error; it is obvious, in fact, that certain properties cannot be attributed to divine things, and become uncertain if portrayed by noble corporeal things. In the second place because this humbler depiction is more suited to the knowledge that we have of God on this earth: He shows Himself here more in that which is not than in that which is, and therefore the similitudes of those things furthest from God lead us to a more exact notion of Him, for thus we know that He is above what we say and think. And in the third place because in this way the things of God are better hidden from unworthy persons. In other words, that day we were discussing the question of understanding how the truth can be revealed through surprising expressions, both shrewd and enigmatic. And I reminded him that in the work of the great Aristotle I had found very clear words on this score...."

"I do not remember," Jorge interrupted sharply, "I

am very old. I do not remember. I may have been excessively severe. Now it is late, I must go."

"It is strange you should not remember," Venantius insisted; "it was a very learned and fine discussion, in which Benno and Berengar also took part. The question, in fact, was whether metaphors and puns and riddles, which also seem conceived by poets for sheer pleasure, do not lead us to speculate on things in a new and surprising way, and I said that this is also a virtue demanded of the wise man.... And Malachi was also there...."

"If the venerable Jorge does not remember, respect his age and the weariness of his mind...otherwise always so lively," one of the monks following the discussion said. The sentence was uttered in an agitated tone—at least at the beginning, because the speaker, once realizing that in urging respect for the old man he was actually calling attention to a weakness, had slowed the pace of his own interjection, ending almost in a whisper of apology. It was Berengar of Arundel who had spoken, the assistant librarian. He was a pale-faced young man, and, observing him, I remembered Ubertino's description of Adelmo: his eyes seemed those of a lascivious woman. Made shy, for everyone was now looking at him, he held the fingers of both hands enlaced like one wishing to suppress an internal tension.

Venantius's reaction was unusual. He gave Berengar a look that made him lower his eyes. "Very well, Brother," he said, "if memory is a gift of God, then the ability to forget can also be good, and must be respected. I respect it in the elderly brother to whom I was speaking. But from you I expected a sharper recollection of the things that happened when we were here with a dear friend of yours...."

I could not say whether Venantius underlined with his tone the word "dear." The fact is that I sensed an embarrassment among those present. Each looked in a different direction, and no one looked at Berengar, who had blushed violently. Malachi promptly spoke up, with authority: "Come, Brother William," he said, "I will show you other interesting books."

The group dispersed. I saw Berengar give Venantius a look charged with animosity, and Venantius return the look, silent and defiant. Seeing that old Jorge was leaving, I was moved by a feeling of respectful reverence, and bowed to kiss his hand. The old man received the kiss, put his hand on my head, and asked who I was. When I told him my name, his face brightened.

"You bear a great and very beautiful name," he said. "Do you know who Adso of Montier-en-Der was?" he asked. I did not know, I confess. So Jorge added, "He was the author of a great and awful book, the *Libellus de Antichristo,* in which he foresaw things that were to happen; but he was not sufficiently heeded."

"The book was written before the millennium," William said, "and those things did not come to pass...."

"For those who lack eyes to see," the blind man said. "The ways of the Antichrist are slow and tortuous. He arrives when we do not expect him: not because the calculation suggested by the apostle was mistaken, but because we have not learned the art." Then he cried, in a very loud voice, his face turned toward the hall, making the ceiling of the scriptorium re-echo: "He is coming! Do not waste your last days laughing at little monsters with spotted skins and twisted tails! Do not squander the last seven days!"

Vespers

In which the rest of the abbey is visited, William comes to some conclusions about Adelmo's death, there is a conversation with the brother glazier about glasses for reading and about phantoms for those who seek to read too much.

At that point the bell rang for vespers and the monks prepared to leave their desks. Malachi made it clear to us that we, too, should leave. He would remain with his assistant, Berengar, to put things back in order (those were his words) and arrange the library for the night. William asked him whether he would be locking the doors.

"There are no doors that forbid access to the scriptorium from the kitchen and the refectory, or to the library from the scriptorium. Stronger than any door must be the abbot's prohibition. And the monks need both the kitchen and the refectory until compline. At that point, to prevent entry into the Aedificium by outsiders or animals, for whom the interdiction is not valid, I myself lock the outside doors, which open into the kitchen and the refectory, and from that hour on the Aedificium remains isolated."

We went down. As the monks headed toward the

choir, my master decided the Lord would forgive us if we did not attend holy office (the Lord had a great deal to forgive us in the days that followed!), and he suggested I walk a bit with him over the grounds, so that we might familiarize ourselves with the place.

The weather was turning bad. A cold wind had risen and the sky was becoming foggy. The sun could be sensed, setting beyond the vegetable gardens; and toward the east it was already growing dark as we proceeded in that direction, flanking the choir of the church and reaching the rear part of the grounds. There, almost against the outside wall, where it joined the east tower of the Aedificium, were the stables; the swincherds were covering the jar containing the pigs' blood. We noticed that behind the stables the outside wall was lower, so that one could look over it. Beyond the sheer drop of the walls, the terrain that sloped dizzyingly down was covered with loose dirt that the snow could not completely hide. I realized this was the pile of old straw, which was thrown over the wall at that point and extended down to the curve where the path taken by the fugitive Brunellus began.

In the stalls nearby, the grooms were leading the animals to the manger. We followed the path along which, toward the wall, the various stalls were located; to the right, against the choir, were the dormitory of the monks and the latrines. Then, as the east wall turned northward, at the angle of the stone girdle, was the smithy. The last smiths were putting down their tools and extinguishing the fires, about to head for the holy office. William moved with curiosity toward one part of the smithy, almost separated from the rest of the workshop, where one monk was putting away his things. On his table was a very beautiful collection of multicolored pieces of glass, of tiny dimensions, but larger panes were set against the wall. In front of him there was a still-unfinished reliquary of which only the silver

95

skeleton existed, but on it he had obviously been setting bits of glass and stones, which his instruments had reduced to the dimensions of gems.

Thus we met Nicholas of Morimondo, master glazier of the abbey. He explained to us that in the rear part of the forge they also blew glass, whereas in this front part, where the smiths worked, the glass was fixed to the leads, to make windows. But, he added, the great works of stained glass that adorned the church and the Aedificium had been completed at least two centuries before. Now he and the others confined themselves to minor tasks, and to repairing the damage of time.

"And with great difficulty," he added, "because it's impossible now to find the colors of the old days, especially the remarkable blue you can still see in the choir, so limpid that, when the sun is high, it pours a light of paradise into the nave. The glass on the west side of the nave, restored not long ago, is not of the same quality, and you can tell, on summer days. It's hopeless," he went on. "We no longer have the learning of the ancients, the age of giants is past!"

"We are dwarfs," William admitted, "but dwarfs who stand on the shoulders of those giants, and small though we are, we sometimes manage to see farther on the horizon than they."

"Tell me what we can do better than they were able to do," Nicholas exclaimed. "If you go down to the crypt of the church, where the abbey's treasure is kept, you will find reliquaries of such exquisite craftsmanship that the little monstrosity I am now cobbling up"—he nodded toward his own work on the table—"will seem a mockery of those!"

"It is not written that master glaziers must go on making windows, and goldsmiths reliquaries, since the masters of the past were able to produce such beautiful ones, destined to last over the centuries. Otherwise, the earth would become filled with reliquaries in a time when saints from whom to take relics are so rare,"

William jested. "Nor will windows have to be soldered forever. But in various countries I have seen new works made of glass which suggest a future world where glass will serve not only for holy purposes but also as a help for man's weakness. I want to show you a creation of our own times, of which I am honored to own a very useful example." He dug inside his habit and drew out the lenses, which dumbfounded our interlocutor.

With great interest, Nicholas took the forked instrument William held out to him. "Oculi de vitro cum capsula!" he cried. "I had heard tell of them from a Brother Jordan I met in Pisa! He said it was less than twenty years since they had been invented. But I spoke with him more than twenty years ago."

"I believe they were invented much earlier," William said, "but they are difficult to make, and require highly expert master glaziers. They cost time and labor. Ten years ago a pair of these glasses ab oculis ad legendum were sold for six Bolognese crowns. I was given a pair of them by a great master, Salvinus of the Armati, more than ten years ago, and I have jealously preserved them all this time, as if they were—as they now are—a part of my very body."

"I hope you will allow me to examine them one of these days; I would be happy to produce some similar ones," Nicholas said, with emotion.

"Of course," William agreed, "but mind you, the thickness of the glass must vary according to the eye it is to serve, and you must test many of these lenses, trying them on the person until the suitable thickness is found."

"What a wonder!" Nicholas continued. "And yet many would speak of witchcraft and diabolical machination...."

"You can certainly speak of magic in this device," William allowed. "But there are two forms of magic. There is a magic that is the work of the Devil and which aims at man's downfall through artifices of which it is not licit to speak. But there is a magic that is divine, where God's knowledge is made manifest through the knowledge of man, and it serves to transform nature, and one of its ends is to prolong man's very life. And this is holy magic, to which the learned must devote themselves more and more, not only to discover new things but also to rediscover many secrets of nature that divine wisdom had revealed to the Hebrews, the Greeks, to other ancient peoples, and even, today, to the infidels (and I cannot tell you all the wonderful things on optics and the science of vision to be read in the books of the infidels!). And of all this learning Christian knowledge must regain possession, taking it from the pagans and the infidels tamquam ab iniustis possessoribus."

"But why don't those who possess this learning communicate it to all the people of God?"

"Because not all the people of God are ready to accept so many secrets, and it has often happened that the possessors of this learning have been mistaken for necromancers in league with the Devil, and they have paid with their lives for their wish to share with others their store of knowledge. I myself, during trials in which someone was suspected of dealings with the Devil, have had to take care not to use these lenses, resorting to eager secretaries who would read to me the writings I required. Otherwise, in a moment when the Devil's presence was so widespread, and everyone could smell, so to speak, the odor of sulphur, I myself would have been considered a friend of the accused. And finally, as the great Roger Bacon warned, the secrets of science must not always pass into the hands of all, for some could use them to evil ends. Often the learned man must make seem magic certain books that are not magic, but simply good science, in order to protect them from indiscreet eyes."

"You fear the simple can make evil use of these secrets, then?" Nicholas asked.

"As far as simple people are concerned, my only fear is that they may be terrified by them, confusing them with those works of the Devil of which their preachers speak too often. You see, I have happened to know very skilled physicians who had distilled medicines capable of curing a disease immediately. But when they gave their unguent or their infusion to the simple, they accompanied it with holy words and chanted phrases that sounded like prayers: not because these prayers had the power to heal, but because, believing that the cure came from the prayers, the simple would swallow the infusion or cover themselves with the unguent, and so they would be cured, while paying little attention to the effective power of the medicine. Also, the spirit, aroused by faith in the pious formula, would be better prepared for the corporal action of the medication. But often the treasures of learning must be defended, not against the simple but, rather, against other learned men. Wondrous machines are now made, of which I shall speak to you one day, with which the course of nature can truly be predicted. But woe if they should fall into the hands of men who would use them to extend their earthly power and satisfy their craving for possession. I am told that in Cathay a sage has compounded a powder that, on contact with fire, can produce a great rumble and a great flame, destroying everything for many yards around. A wondrous device, if it were used to shift the beds of streams or shatter rock when ground is being broken for cultivation. But if someone were to use it to bring harm to his personal enemies?"

"Perhaps it would be good, if they were enemies of the people of God," Nicholas said piously.

"Perhaps," William admitted. "But who today is the enemy of the people of God? Louis the Emperor or John the Pope?"

"Oh, my Lord!" Nicholas said, quite frightened. "I really wouldn't like to decide such a painful question!"

"You see?" William said. "Sometimes it is better for certain secrets to remain veiled by arcane words. The secrets of nature are not transmitted on skins of goat or sheep. Aristotle says in the book of secrets that communicating too many arcana of nature and art breaks a celestial seal and many evils can ensue. Which does not mean that secrets must not be revealed, but that the learned must decide when and how."

"Wherefore it is best that in places like this," Nicholas said, "not all books be within the reach of all."

"This is another question," William said. "Excess of loquacity can be a sin, and so can excess of reticence. I didn't mean that it is necessary to conceal the sources of knowledge. On the contrary, this seems to me a great evil. I meant that, since these are arcana from which both good and evil can derive, the learned man has the right and the duty to use an obscure language, comprehensible only to his fellows. The life of learning is difficult, and it is difficult to distinguish good from evil. And often the learned men of our time are only dwarfs on the shoulders of dwarfs."

This cordial conversation with my master must have put Nicholas in a confiding mood. For he winked at William (as if to say: You and I understand each other because we speak of the same things) and he hinted: "But over there"—he nodded toward the Aedificium— "the secrets of learning are well defended by works of magic...."

"Really?" William said, with a show of indifference. "Barred doors, stern prohibitions, threats, I suppose."

"Oh, no. More than that..."

"What, for example?"

"Well, I don't know exactly; I am concerned with glass, not books. But in the abbey there are rumors... strange rumors...."

"Of what sort?"

"Strange. Let us say, rumors about a monk who decided to venture into the library during the night, to look for something Malachi had refused to give him, and he saw serpents, headless men, and men with two heads. He was nearly crazy when he emerged from the labyrinth...."

"Why do you speak of magic rather than diabolical apparitions?"

"Because even if I am only a poor master glazier I am not so ignorant. The Devil (God save us!) does not tempt a monk with serpents and two-headed men. If anything, with lascivious visions, as he tempted the fathers in the desert. And besides, if it is evil to handle certain books, why would the Devil distract a monk from committing evil?"

"That seems to me a good enthymeme," my master admitted.

"And finally, when I was repairing the windows of the infirmary, I amused myself by leafing through some of Severinus's books. There was a book of secrets written, I believe, by Albertus Magnus; I was attracted by some curious illustrations, and I read some pages about how you can grease the wick of an oil lamp, and the fumes produced then provoke visions. You must have noticed—or, rather, you cannot have noticed yet, because you have not yet spent a night in the abbey—that during the hours of darkness the upper floor of the Aedificium is illuminated. At certain points there is a dim glow from the windows. Many have wondered what it is, and there has been talk of will-o'-the-wisps, or souls of dead librarians who return to visit their realm. Many here believe these tales. I think those are lamps prepared for visions. You know, if you take the wax from a dog's ear and grease a wick, anyone breathing the smoke of that lamp will believe he has a dog's head, and if he is with someone else, the other will see a dog's head. And there is another unguent that makes those near the lamp feel big as elephants. And with the eyes of a bat and of two fish whose names I cannot recall, and the venom of a wolf, you make a wick that, as it burns, will cause you to see the animals whose fat you have taken. And with a lizard's tail you make everything around you seem of silver, and with the fat of a black snake and a scrap of a shroud, the room will appear filled with serpents. I know this. Someone in the library is very clever...."

"But couldn't it be the souls of the dead librarians who perform these feats of magic?"

Nicholas remained puzzled and uneasy. "I hadn't thought of that. Perhaps. God protect us. It's late. Vespers have already begun. Farewell." And he headed for the church.

We continued along the south side: to our right the hospice for pilgrims and the chapter house with its gardens, to the left the olive presses, the mill, the granaries, the cellars, the novices' house. And everyone was hurrying toward the church.

"What do you think of what Nicholas said?" I asked.

"I don't know. There is something in the library, and I don't believe it is the souls of dead librarians...."

"Why not?"

"Because I imagine they were so virtuous that today they remain in the kingdom of heaven to contemplate the divine countenance, if this answer will satisfy you. As for the lamps, we shall see if they are there. And as for the unguents our glazier spoke of, there are easier ways to provoke visions, and Severinus knows them very well, as you realized today. What is certain is that in the abbey they want no one to enter the library at night and that many, on the contrary, have tried or are trying to do so."

"And what does our crime have to do with this business?"

"Crime. The more I think about it, the more I am convinced that Adelmo killed himself."

"Why is that?"

"You remember this morning when I remarked the heap of dirty straw? As we were climbing up the curve beneath the east tower I had noticed at that point the traces left by a landslide: or, rather, a part of the terrain had given way below the tower, more or less there where the waste collects, and had slipped. And that is why this evening, when we looked down from above, the straw seemed to have little snow covering it; it was covered only by the latest fall, yesterday's snow, and not by that of the past few days. As for Adelmo's corpse, the abbot told us that it had been lacerated by the rocks, and beneath the east tower, where the building joins a sheer drop, there are pines growing. The rocks, however, are directly under the point where the wall ends, forming a kind of step, and afterward the straw dump begins."

"And so?"

"And so, think whether it is not less—how shall I say it?—less costly for our minds to believe that Adelmo, for reasons yet to be ascertained, threw himself of his own will from the parapet of the wall, struck the rocks, and, dead or wounded as he may have been, sank into the straw. Then the landslide, caused by the storm that night, carried the straw and part of the terrain and the poor young man's body down below the east tower."

"Why do you say this solution is less costly for our minds?"

"Dear Adso, one should not multiply explanations and causes unless it is strictly necessary. If Adelmo fell from the east tower, he must have got into the library, someone must have first struck him so he would offer no resistance, and then this person must have found a way of climbing up to the window with a lifeless body on his back, opening it, and pitching the hapless monk down. But with my hypothesis we need only Adelmo, his decision, and a shift of some land. Everything is explained, using a smaller number of causes."

"But why would he have killed himself?"

"But why would anyone have killed him? In either case reasons have to be found. And it seems to me beyond doubt that they existed. In the Aedificium there is an atmosphere of reticence; they are all keeping something quiet. Meanwhile, we have already collected a few insinuations—quite vague, to be sure—about some strange relationship between Adelmo and Berengar. That means we will keep an eye on the assistant librarian."

While we were talking in this fashion, the office of vespers ended. The servants were going back to their tasks before retiring for supper, the monks were heading for the refectory. The sky was now dark and it was beginning to snow. A light snow, in soft little flakes, which must have continued, I believe, for most of the night, because the next morning all the grounds were covered with a white blanket, as I shall tell.

I was hungry and welcomed with relief the idea of going to table.

COMPLINE

In which William and Adso enjoy the jolly hospitality of the abbot and the angry conversation of Jorge.

The refectory was illuminated by great torches. The monks sat at a row of tables dominated by the abbot's table, set perpendicularly to theirs on a broad dais. On the opposite side there was a pulpit, where the monk who would read during supper had already taken his place. The abbot was waiting for us next to a little fountain, with a white cloth to wipe our hands after the lavabo, following the ancient counsels of Saint Pachomius.

The abbot invited William to his table and said that for this evening, since I was also a new guest, I would enjoy the same privilege, even though I was a Benedictine novice. In the following days, he said to me paternally, I could sit at table with the monks, or, if I were employed in some task for my master, I could stop in the kitchen before or after meals, and there the cooks would take care of me.

The monks were now standing at the tables, motionless, their cowls lowered over their faces, their hands under their scapulars. The abbot approached his table and pronounced the "Benedicite." From the pulpit the precentor intoned the "Edent pauperes." The abbot imparted his benediction and everyone sat down.

Our founder's Rule prescribes a frugal meal but allows the abbot to determine how much food the monks actually need. In our abbeys now, however, there is greater indulgence in the pleasures of the table. I will not speak of those that, unfortunately, have been transformed into dens of gluttony; but even those that follow standards of penance and virtue provide the monks, almost always engaged in taxing intellectual labors, with a nourishment not effete but substantial. On the other hand, the abbot's table is always favored, not least because honored guests frequently sit there, and the abbeys take pride in the produce of their lands and their barns, and in the skill of their cooks.

The monks' meal proceeded in silence, as is customary; they communicated among themselves with the usual alphabet of fingers. The novices and younger monks were served first, immediately after the dishes meant for all had been passed at the abbot's table.

With us at the abbot's table sat Malachi, the cellarer, and the two oldest monks, Jorge of Burgos, the venerable blind man I had met in the scriptorium, and Alinardo of Grottaferrata: ancient, almost a centenarian, lame, and fragile-looking, and—it seemed to me—addled. The abbot told us that, having come to the abbey as a novice, Alinardo had lived there always and recalled almost eighty years of its events. The abbot told us these things in a whisper at the beginning, because afterward he observed the custom of our order and followed the reading in silence. But, as I said, certain liberties were taken at the abbot's table, and we praised the dishes we were offered as the abbot extolled the quality of his olive oil, or of his wine. Indeed, once, as he poured some for us, he recalled for us that passage in the Rule where the holy founder observed that wine, to be sure, is not proper for monks, but since the monks of our time cannot be persuaded not to drink, they should at least not drink their fill, because wine induces even the wise to apostasy, as Ecclesiastes reminds us. Benedict said "of our time" referring to his own day, now very remote: you can imagine the time in which we were supping at the abbey, after such decadence of behavior (and I will not speak of my time, in which I write, except to say that here at Melk there is greater indulgence in beer!): in short, we drank without excess but not without enjoyment.

We ate meat cooked on the spit, freshly slaughtered pigs, and I realized that in cooking other foods they did not use animal fats or rape oil but good olive oil, which came from lands the abbey owned at the foot of the mountain toward the sea. The abbot made us taste (reserved for his table) the chicken I had seen being prepared in the kitchen. I saw that he also possessed a metal fork, a great rarity, whose form reminded me of my master's glasses. A man of noble extraction, our host did not want to soil his hands with food, and indeed offered us his implement, at least to take the meat from the large plate and put it in our bowls. I refused, but I saw that William accepted gladly and made nonchalant use of that instrument of great gentlemen, perhaps to show the abbot that not all Franciscans were men of scant education or humble birth.

In my enthusiasm for all these fine foods (after several days of travel in which we had eaten what we could find), I had been distracted from the reading, which meanwhile continued devoutly. I was reminded of it by a vigorous grunt of assent from Jorge, and I realized we had reached the point at which a chapter of the Rule is always read. I understood why Jorge was so content, since I had listened to him that afternoon. The reader was saying, "Let us imitate the example of the prophet, who says: I have decided, I shall watch over my way so as not to sin with my tongue, I have put a curb upon my mouth, I have fallen dumb, humbling myself, I have refrained from speaking even of honest things. And if in this passage the prophet teaches us that sometimes our love of silence should cause us to refrain from speaking-even of licit things, how much more should we refrain from illicit talk, to avoid the chastisement of this sin!" And then he continued: "But vulgarities, nonsense, and jests we condemn to perpetual imprisonment, in every place, and we do not allow the disciple to open his mouth for speech of this sort."

"And this goes for the marginalia we were discussing today," Jorge could not keep from commenting in a low voice. "John Chrysostom said that Christ never laughed."

"Nothing in his human nature forbade it," William remarked, "because laughter, as the theologians teach, is proper to man."

"The son of man could laugh, but it is not written that he did so," Jorge said sharply, quoting Petrus Cantor.

"Manduca, iam coctum est," William murmured. "Eat, for it is well done."

"What?" asked Jorge, thinking he referred to some dish that was being brought to him.

"Those are the words that, according to Ambrose, were uttered by Saint Lawrence on the gridiron, when he invited his executioners to turn him over, as Prudentius also recalls in the *Peristephanon*," William said with a saintly air. "Saint Lawrence therefore knew how to laugh and say ridiculous things, even if it was to humiliate his enemies."

"Which proves that laughter is something very close to death and to the corruption of the body," Jorge replied with a snarl; and I must admit that he spoke like a good logician.

At this point the abbot good-naturedly invited us to be silent. The meal was ending, in any case. The abbot stood up and introduced William to the monks. He praised his wisdom, expounded his fame, and informed them that the visitor had been asked to investigate Adelmo's death; and the abbot also urged the monks to answer any questions and to instruct their underlings, throughout the abbey, to do the same.

Supper over, the monks prepared to go off to the choir for the office of compline. They again lowered their cowls over their faces and formed a line at the door. Then they moved in a long file, crossing the cemetery and entering the choir through the north doorway.

We went off with the abbot. "Is this the hour when the doors of the Aedificium are locked?" William asked.

"As soon as the servants have finished cleaning the refectory and the kitchens, the librarian will personally close all the doors, barring them on the inside."

"On the inside? And where does he come out?"

The abbot glared at William for a moment. "Obviously he does not sleep in the kitchen," he said brusquely. And he began to walk faster.

"Very well," William whispered to me, "so another door does exist, but we are not to know about it." I smiled, proud of his deduction, and he scolded me: "And don't laugh. As you have seen, within these walls laughter doesn't enjoy a good reputation."

We entered the choir. A single lamp was burning on a heavy bronze tripod, tall as two men. The monks silently took their places in the stalls.

Then the abbot gave a signal, and the precentor intoned, "Tu autem Domine miserere nobis." The abbot replied, "Adiutorium nostrum in nomine Domini"; and all continued, in chorus, with "Qui fecit coelum et terram." Then the chanting of the psalms began: "When I call Thee answer me O God of my justice"; "I shall thank Thee Lord with all my heart"; "Come bless the Lord, all ye servants of the Lord." We had not sat in the stalls, but had withdrawn into the main nave. From there, we suddenly glimpsed Malachi emerging from the darkness of a side chapel.

"Keep your eye on that spot," William said to me. "There could be a passage leading to the Aedificium."

"Under the cemetery?"

"And why not? In fact, now that I think about it, there must be an ossarium somewhere; they can't possibly have buried all their monks for centuries in that patch of ground."

"But do you really want to enter the library at night?" I asked, terrified.

"Where there are dead monks and serpents and mysterious lights, my good Adso? No, my boy. I was thinking about it today, and not from curiosity but because I was pondering the question of how Adelmo died. Now, as I told you, I tend toward a more logical explanation, and, all things considered, I would prefer to respect the customs of this place."

"Then why do you want to know?"

"Because learning does not consist only of knowing what we must or we can do, but also of knowing what we could do and perhaps should not do."

SECOND DAY

MATINS

In which a few hours of mystic happiness are interrupted by a most bloody occurrence.

Symbol sometimes of the Devil, sometimes of the Risen Christ, no animal is more untrustworthy than the cock. Our order knew some slothful ones who never crowed at sunrise. On the other hand, especially in winter, the office of matins takes place when night is still total and all nature is asleep, for the monk must rise in darkness and pray at length in darkness, waiting for day and illuminating the shadows with the flame of devotion. Therefore, custom wisely provided for some wakers, who were not to go to bed when their brothers did, but would spend the night reciting in cadence the exact number of psalms that would allow them to measure the time passed, so that, at the conclusion of the hours of sleep granted the others, they would give the signal to wake.

So that night we were waked by those who moved through the dormitory and the pilgrims' house ringing a bell, as one monk went from cell to cell shouting,

"Benedicamus Domino," to which each answered, "Deo gratias."

William and I followed the Benedictine custom: in less than half an hour we prepared to greet the new day, then we went down into the choir, where the monks, prostrate on the floor, reciting the first fifteen psalms, were waiting until the novices entered led by their master. Then each sat in his regular stall and the choir chanted, "Domine labia mea aperies et os meum annuntiabit laudem tuam." The cry rose toward the vaulted ceiling of the church like a child's plea. Two monks climbed to the pulpit and intoned the ninety-fourth psalm, "Venite exultemus," which was followed by the others prescribed. And I felt the warmth of renewed faith.

The monks were in the stalls, sixty figures made indistinguishable by their habits and cowls, sixty shadows barely illuminated by the fire from the great tripod, sixty voices joined in praise of the Almighty. And, hearing this moving harmony, vestibule of the delights of paradise, I asked myself whether the abbey were truly a place of concealed mysteries, of illicit attempts to reveal them, and of grim threats. Because it now seemed to me, on the contrary, the dwelling of sainted men, cenacle of virtue, vessel of learning, ark of prudence, tower of wisdom, domain of meekness, bastion of strength, thurible of sanctity.

After six psalms, the reading of Holy Scripture began. Some monks were nodding with sleepiness, and one of the night wakers wandered among the stalls with a little lamp to wake any who had dozed off again. If a monk succumbed to drowsiness, as penance he would take the lamp and continue the round. The chanting of another six psalms continued. Then the abbot gave his benediction, the hebdomadary said the prayers, all bowed toward the altar in a moment of meditation whose sweetness no one can comprehend who has not experienced those hours of mystic ardor and intense inner peace. Finally, cowls again over their faces, all sat and solemnly intoned the "Te Deum." I, too, praised the Lord because He had released me from my doubts and freed me from the feeling of uneasiness with which my first day at the abbey had filled me. We are fragile creatures, I said to myself; even among these learned and devout monks the Evil One spreads petty envies, foments subtle hostilities, but all these are as smoke then dispersed by the strong wind of faith, the moment all gather in the name of the Father, and Christ descends into their midst.

Between matins and lauds the monk does not return to his cell, even if the night is still dark. The novices followed their master into the chapter house to study the psalms; some of the monks remained in church to tend to the church ornaments, but the majority strolled in the cloister in silent meditation, as did William and I. The servants were asleep and they went on sleeping when, the sky still dark, we returned to the choir for lauds.

The chanting of the psalms resumed, and one in particular, among those prescribed for Mondays, plunged me again into my earlier fears: "The transgression of the wicked saith within my heart, that there is no fear of God before his eyes. The words of his mouth are iniquity." It seemed to me an ill omen that the Rule should have set for that very day such a terrible admonition. Nor were my pangs of uneasiness eased, after the psalms of praise, by the usual reading of the Apocalypse; the figures of the doorway returned to my mind, the carvings that had so overwhelmed my heart and eyes the day before. But after the responsory, the hymn, and the versicle, as the chanting of the Gospel began, I glimpsed just above the altar, beyond the windows of the choir, a pale glow that was already making the panes shine in their various colors, subdued till then by the darkness. It was not yet dawn, which would triumph during Prime, just as we would be singing "Deus qui est sanctorum splendor mirabilis" and "Iam lucis orto sidere." It was barely the first faint herald of a winter daybreak, but it was enough, and the dim penumbra now replacing the night's darkness in the nave was enough to relieve my heart.

We sang the words of the divine book and, as we were bearing witness to the Word come to enlighten all peoples, it was as if the daystar in all its splendor were invading the temple. The light, still absent, seemed to me to shine in the words of the canticle, mystic, scented lily that opened among the arches of the vaults. "I thank Thee, O Lord, for this moment of ineffable joy," I prayed silently, and said to my heart, "Foolish heart, what do you fear?"

Suddenly some noises were heard from the direction of the north door. I wondered why the servants, preparing for their work, disturbed the sacred functions in this way. At that moment three swineherds came in, terror on their faces; they went to the abbot and whispered something to him. The abbot first calmed them with a gesture, as if he did not want to interrupt the office; but other servants entered, and the shouts became louder. "A man! A dead man!" some were saying. And others: "A monk. You saw the sandals?"

Prayers stopped, and the abbot rushed out, motioning the cellarer to follow him. William went after them, but by now the other monks were also leaving their stalls and hurrying outside.

The sky was now light, and the snow on the ground made the compound even more luminous. Behind the choir, in front of the pens, where the day before had stood the great jar with the pigs' blood, a strange object, almost cruciform, protruded above the edge of the vessel, as if two stakes had been driven into the ground, to be covered with rags for scaring off birds.

But they were human legs, the legs of a man thrust head down into the vessel of blood.

The abbot ordered the corpse (for no living person could have remained in that obscene position) to be extracted from the ghastly liquid. The hesitant swineherds approached the edge and, staining themselves with blood, drew out the poor, bloody thing. As had been explained to me, the blood, having been properly stirred immediately after it was shed, and then left out in the cold, had not clotted, but the layer covering the corpse was now beginning to solidify; it soaked the habit, made the face unrecognizable. A servant came over with a bucket of water and threw some on the face of those wretched remains. Another bent down with a cloth to wipe the features. And before our eyes appeared the white face of Venantius of Salvemec, the Greek scholar with whom we had talked that afternoon by Adelmo's codices.

The abbot came over. "Brother William, as you see, something is afoot in this abbey, something that demands all your wisdom. But I beseech you: act quickly!"

"Was he present in choir during the office?" William asked, pointing to the corpse.

"No," the abbot said. "I saw his stall was empty."

"No one else was absent?"

"It did not seem so. I noticed nothing."

William hesitated before asking the next question, and he did so in a whisper, taking care that the others could not hear: "Berengar was in his stall?"

The abbot looked at him with uneasy amazement, as if to signify that he was struck to see my master harbor a suspicion that he himself had briefly harbored, for more comprehensible reasons. He said then rapidly, "He was there. He sits in the first row, almost at my right hand."

"Naturally," William said, "all this means nothing. I

don't believe anyone entering the choir passed behind the apse, and therefore the corpse could have been here for several hours, at least since the time when everyone had gone to bed."

"To be sure, the first servants rise at dawn, and that is why they discovered him only now."

William bent over the corpse, as if he were used to dealing with dead bodies. He dipped the cloth lying nearby into the water of the bucket and further cleansed Venantius's face. Meanwhile, the other monks crowded around, frightened, forming a talkative circle on which the abbot imposed silence. Among the others, now making his way forward, came Severinus, who saw to matters of physical health in the abbey; and he bent down next to my master. To hear their dialogue, and to help William, who needed a new clean cloth soaked in the water, I joined them, overcoming my terror and my revulsion.

"Have you ever seen a drowned man?" William asked.

"Many times," Severinus said. "And if I guess what you imply, they do not have this face: the features are swollen."

"Then the man was already dead when someone threw the body into the jar."

"Why would he have done that?"

"Why would he have killed him? We are dealing with the work of a twisted mind. But now we must see whether there are wounds or bruises on the body. I suggest it be carried to the balneary, stripped, washed, and examined. I will join you there at once."

And while Severinus, receiving permission from the abbot, was having the body carried away by the swineherds, my master asked that the monks be told to return to the choir by the path they had taken before, and that the servants retire in the same way, so the ground would remain deserted. Thus we remained alone, beside the vessel, from which blood had spilled during the macabre operation of the body's recovery.

The snow all around was red, melting in several puddles where the water had been thrown; and there was a great dark stain where the corpse had been stretched out.

"A fine mess," William said, nodding toward the complex pattern of footprints left all around by the monks and the servants. "Snow, dear Adso, is an admirable parchment on which men's bodies leave very legible writing. But this palimpsest is badly scraped, and perhaps we will read nothing interesting on it. Between here and the church there has been a great bustle of monks, between here and the barn and the stables the servants have moved in droves. The only intact space is between the barns and the Aedificium. Let us see if we can find something of interest."

"What do you expect to find?" I asked.

"If he didn't throw himself into the vessel on his own, someone carried him there, already dead, I imagine. And a man carrying another man's body leaves deep tracks in snow. So look and see if you find around here some prints that seem different to you from the prints of those noisy monks who have ruined our parchment for us."

And we did. And I will say immediately that I was the one, God preserve me from all vanity, who discovered something between the jar and the Aedificium. They were human footprints, fairly deep, in a zone where no one had yet passed, and, as my master remarked at once, fainter than those left by the monks and the servants, a sign that more snow had fallen and thus they had been made some time before. But what seemed to us most noteworthy was that among those prints there was a more continuous trail, as of something dragged by the one leaving the prints. In short, a spoor that went from the jar to the door of the refectory, on the side of the Aedificium between the south tower and the east tower.

"Refectory, scriptorium, library," William said. "Once

again, the library. Venantius died in the Aedificium, and most probably in the library."

"And why in the library exactly?"

"I am trying to put myself in the murderer's place. If Venantius had died, been killed, in the refectory, in the kitchen, or in the scriptorium, why not leave him there? But if he died in the library, then he had to be carried elsewhere, both because in the library the body would never have been discovered (and perhaps the murderer was particularly interested in its being discovered) and because the murderer probably does not want attention to be concentrated on the library."

"And why should the murderer be interested in the body's being discovered?"

"I don't know. I can suggest some hypotheses. How do we know that the murderer killed Venantius because he hated Venantius? He could have killed him, rather than another, to leave a sign, to signify something else."

"Omnis mundi creatura, quasi liber et scriptura . . ." I murmured. "But what would that sign be?"

"This is what I do not know. But let us not forget that there are also signs that seem such and are instead without meaning, like blitiri or bu-ba-baff. . . ."

"It would be atrocious," I said, "to kill a man in order to say bu-ba-baff!"

"It would be atrocious," William remarked, "to kill a man even to say 'Credo in unum Deum.' . . ."

At that moment Severinus joined us. The corpse had been washed and examined carefully. No wound, no bruise on the head.

"Do you have poisons in your laboratory?" William asked, as we headed for the infirmary.

"Among the other things. But that depends on what you mean by poison. There are substances that in small doses are healthful and in excessive doses cause death. Like every good herbalist I keep them, and I use them with discretion. In my garden I grow, for example, valerian. A few drops in an infusion of other herbs calms the heart if it is beating irregularly. An exaggerated dose brings on drowsiness and death."

"And you noticed no signs of any particular poison on the corpse?"

"None. But many poisons leave no trace."

We had reached the infirmary. Venantius's body, washed in the balneary, had been brought there and was lying on the great table in Severinus's laboratory; alembics and other instruments of glass and earthenware made me think of an alchemist's shop (though I knew of such things only by indirect accounts). On some long shelves against the wall by the door was arrayed a vast series of cruets, ampoules, jugs, pots, filled with substances of different colors.

"A fine collection of simples," William said. "All products of your garden?"

"No," Severinus said, "many substances, rare, or impossible to grow in this climate, have been brought to me over the years by monks arriving from every part of the world. I have many precious things that cannot be found readily, along with substances easily obtained from the local flora. You see . . . aghalingho pesto comes from Cathay: I received it from a learned Arab. Indian aloe, excellent cicatricizant. Live arient revives the dead, or, rather, wakes those who have lost their senses. Arsenacho: very dangerous, a mortal poison for anyone who swallows it. Borage, a plant good for ailing lungs. Betony, good for fractures of the head. Mastic: calms pulmonary fluxions and troublesome catarrhs. Myrrh . . ."

"The gift of the Magi?" I asked.

"The same. But now used to prevent miscarriage, gathered from a tree called Balsamodendron myrra. And this is mumia, very rare, produced by the decomposition of mummified cadavers; it is used in the preparation of many almost miraculous medicines. Mandragora officinalis, good for sleep . . ."

"And to stir desires of the flesh," my master remarked.

"So they say, but here it is not used for that purpose, as you can imagine." Severinus smiled. "And look at this," he said, taking down an ampoule. "Tutty, miraculous for the eyes."

"And what is this?" William asked in a bright voice, touching a stone lying on a shelf.

"That? It was given to me some time ago. It apparently has therapeutic virtues, but I have not yet discovered what they are. Do you know it?"

"Yes," William said, "but not as a medicine." He took from his habit a little knife and slowly held it toward the stone. As the knife, moved by his hand with extreme delicacy, came close to the stone, I saw that the blade made an abrupt movement, as if William had shifted his wrist, which was, however, absolutely still. And the blade stuck to the stone, making a faint metallic sound.

"You see," William said to me, "it attracts iron."

"And what is its use?" I asked.

"It has various uses, of which I will tell you. But for the present I would like to know, Severinus, if there is anything here that could kill a man."

Severinus reflected a moment—too long, I would have said, considering the clarity of his answer: "Many things. As I said, the line between poison and medicine is very fine; the Greeks used the word 'pharmacon' for both."

"And there is nothing that has been removed recently?"

Severinus reflected again, then, as if weighing his words: "Nothing recently."

"And in the past?"

"Who knows? I don't recall. I have been in this abbey thirty years, and twenty-five in the infirmary."

"Too long for a human memory," William admitted. Then, abruptly, he said, "We were speaking yesterday of plants that can induce visions. Which ones are they?"

Severinus's actions and the expression on his face

indicated an intense desire to avoid that subject. "I would have to think, you know. I have so many miraculous substances here. But let us speak, rather, of Venantius's death. What do you say about it?"

"I would have to think," William answered.

PRIME

In which Benno of Uppsala confides certain things, others are confided by Berengar of Arundel, and Adso learns the meaning of true penitence.

The horrible event had upset the life of the community. The confusion caused by the discovery of the corpse had interrupted the holy office. The abbot promptly sent the monks back to the choir, to pray for the soul of their brother.

The monks' voices were broken. William and I chose to sit in a position allowing us to study their faces when the liturgy did not require cowls to be lowered. Immediately we saw Berengar's face. Pale, drawn, glistening with sweat.

Next to him we noticed Malachi. Dark, frowning, impassive. Beside Malachi, equally impassive, was the face of the blind Jorge. We observed, on the other hand, the nervous movements of Benno of Uppsala, the rhetoric scholar we had met the previous day in the scriptorium; and we caught his rapid glance at Malachi. "Benno is nervous, Berengar is frightened," William remarked. "They must be questioned right away."

"Why?" I asked ingenuously.

"Ours is a hard task," William said. "A hard task, that of the inquisitor, who must strike the weakest, and at their moment of greatest weakness."

In fact, as soon as the office was over, we caught up with Benno, who was heading for the library. The young man seemed vexed at hearing William call him, and he muttered some faint pretext about work to be done. He seemed in a hurry to get to the scriptorium. But my master reminded him that he was carrying out an inquiry at the abbot's behest, and led Benno into the cloister. We sat on the inner wall, between two columns. Looking from time to time toward the Aedificium, Benno waited for William to speak.

"Well, then," William asked, "what was said that day when you were discussing Adelmo's marginalia with Berengar, Venantius, Malachi, and Jorge?"

"You heard it yesterday. Jorge was saying that it is not licit to use ridiculous images to decorate books that contain the truth. And Venantius observed that Aristotle himself had spoken of witticisms and plays on words as instruments better to reveal the truth, and hence laughter could not be such a bad thing if it could become a vehicle of the truth. Jorge said that, as far as he could recall, Aristotle had spoken of these things in his *Poetics*, when discussing metaphor. And these were in themselves two disturbing circumstances, first because the book of the *Poetics*, unknown to the Christian world for such a long time, which was perhaps by divine decree, had come to us through the infidel Moors...."

"But it was translated into Latin by a friend of the angelic doctor of Aquino," William said.

"That's what I said to him," Benno replied, immediately heartened. "I read Greek badly and I could study that great book only, in fact, through the translation of William of Moerbeke. Yes, that's what I said. But Jorge added that the second cause for uneasiness is that in the book the Stagirite was speaking of poetry, which is

125

infima doctrina and which exists on figments. And Venantius said that the psalms, too, are works of poetry and use metaphors; and Jorge became enraged because he said the psalms are works of divine inspiration and use metaphors to convey the truth, while the works of the pagan poets use metaphors to convey falsehood and for purposes of mere pleasure, a remark that greatly offended me...."

"Why?"

"Because I am a student of rhetoric, and I read many pagan poets, and I know... or I believe that their words have conveyed also truths naturaliter Christian.... In short, at that point, if I recall correctly, Venantius spoke of other books and Jorge became very angry."

"Which books?"

Benno hesitated. "I don't remember. What does it matter which books were spoken of?"

"It matters a great deal, because here we are trying to understand what has happened among men who live among books, with books, from books, and so their words on books are also important."

"It's true," Benno said, smiling for the first time, his face growing almost radiant. "We live for books. A sweet mission in this world dominated by disorder and decay. Perhaps, then, you will understand what happened on that occasion. Venantius, who knows... who knew Greek very well, said that Aristotle had dedicated the second book of the *Poetics* specifically to laughter, and that if a philosopher of such greatness had devoted a whole book to laughter, then laughter must be important. Jorge said that many fathers had devoted entire books to sin, which is an important thing, but evil; and Venantius said that as far as he knew, Aristotle had spoken of laughter as something good and an instrument of truth; and then Jorge asked him contemptuously whether by any chance he had read this book of Aristotle; and Venantius said that no one could have read it, because it has never been found and is perhaps lost forever. And, in fact, William of Moerbeke never had it in his hands. Then Jorge said that if it had not been found, this was because it had never been written, because Providence did not want futile things glorified. I wanted to calm everyone's spirit, because Jorge is easily angered and Venantius was speaking deliberately to provoke him, and so I said that in the part of the *Poetics* that we do know, and in the *Rhetoric*, there are to be found many wise observations on witty riddles, and Venantius agreed with me. Now, with us was Pacificus of Tivoli, who knows the pagan poets very well, and he said that when it comes to these witty riddles, no one surpasses the African poets. He quoted, in fact, the riddle of the fish, of Symphosius:

> *Est domus in terris, clara quae voce resultat.*
> *Ipsa domus resonat, tacitus sed non sonat hospes.*
> *Ambo tamen currunt, hospes simul et domus una.*

"At this point Jorge said that Jesus had urged our speech to be yes or no, for anything further came from the Evil One; and that to mention fish it was enough to say 'fish,' without concealing the notion under lying sounds. And he added that it did not seem to him wise to take the Africans as models.... And then..."

"Then?"

"Then something happened that I didn't understand. Berengar began to laugh. Jorge reproached him, and he said he was laughing because it had occurred to him that if one sought carefully among the Africans, quite different riddles would be found, and not so easy as the one about the fish. Malachi, who was present, became furious, took Berengar by the cowl, and sent him off to his tasks.... Berengar, you know, is his assistant...."

"And after that?"

"After that, Jorge put an end to the argument by going away. We all went off to our occupations, but as I was working, I saw first Venantius, then Adelmo approach Berengar and ask him something. From the

127

distance I saw he was parrying their questions, but in the course of the day both went back to him. And then that evening I saw Berengar and Adelmo confabulating in the cloister before entering the refectory. There, that's all I know."

"You know, in fact, that the two persons who have recently died in mysterious circumstances had asked something of Berengar," William said.

Benno answered uncomfortably, "I didn't say that! I told you what happened that day, because you asked me...." He reflected a moment, then hastily added, "But if you want to know my opinion, Berengar spoke to them of something in the library, and that is where you should search."

"Why do you think of the library? What did Berengar mean about seeking among the Africans? Didn't he mean that the African poets should be more widely read?"

"Perhaps. So it seemed. But then why should Malachi have become furious? After all, he's the one who decides whether or not a volume of African poets is given out to be read. But I know one thing: anyone leafing through the catalogue of books will often find, among the collocations that only the librarian understands, one that says 'Africa,' and I have even found one that said 'finis Africae,' the end of Africa. Once I asked for a book that bore that indication, I can't recall which book, though the title had aroused my curiosity; and Malachi told me the books with that indication had been lost. This is what I know. And this is why I say you're right, check on Berengar, and check when he goes up into the library. You never can tell."

"You never can tell," William concluded, dismissing him. Then he began strolling with me in the cloister and remarked that, first of all, Berengar had once again been the subject of his brothers' murmuring; second, Benno seemed eager to direct us to the library. I observed that perhaps he wanted us to discover there things he, too, wanted to know; and William said this was probably the case, but it was also possible that in directing us toward the library he wanted to keep us away from some other place. Which? I asked. And William said he did not know, perhaps the scriptorium, perhaps the kitchen, or the choir, or the dormitory, or the infirmary. I remarked that the previous day it was he, William, who had been fascinated by the library, and his answer was that he wanted to be fascinated by the things he chose and not as others advised him. But the library should be kept under observation, he went on, and at this point it would not be a bad idea to try to get into it somehow. Circumstances now authorized his curiosity, within the bounds of politeness and respect for the customs and laws of the abbey.

We left the cloister. Servants and novices were coming from the church after Mass. And as we walked along the west side of the church, we glimpsed Berengar coming out of the transept door and crossing the cemetery toward the Aedificium. William called him, he stopped, and we overtook him. He was even more distraught than when we had seen him in choir, and William obviously decided to exploit, as he had with Benno, this state of his spirit.

"So it seems that you were the last to see Adelmo alive," he said.

Berengar staggered, as if he were about to fall in a faint. "I?" he asked in a weak voice. William had dropped his question as if by chance, perhaps because Benno had told him of seeing the two conferring in the cloister after vespers. But it must have struck home, and clearly Berengar was thinking of another, really final meeting, because he began to speak in a halting voice.

"How can you say that? I saw him before going off to bed, like everyone else!"

Then William decided it might be worthwhile to press him without respite. "No, you saw him again, and you know more things than you wish to admit. But there are two deaths involved here, and you can no longer be silent. You know very well there are many ways to make a person speak!"

William had often said to me that, even when he had been an inquisitor, he had always avoided torture; but Berengar misunderstood him (or William wanted to be misunderstood). In any case, the move was effective.

"Yes, yes," Berengar said, bursting into a flood of tears, "I saw Adelmo that evening, but I saw him already dead!"

"How?" William asked. "At the foot of the hill?"

"No, no, I saw him here in the cemetery, he was moving among the graves, a ghost among ghosts. I met him and realized at once that I did not have a living man before me: his face was a corpse's, his eyes already beheld the eternal punishment. Naturally, it was only the next morning, when I learned of his death, that I understood I had encountered his ghost, but even at that moment I realized I was having a vision and that there was a damned soul before me, one of the lemures....Oh, Lord, what a gravelike voice he had as he spoke to me!"

"And what did he say?"

"'I am damned!' That is what he said to me. 'As you see me here, you see one returned from hell, and to hell I must go back.' So he said to me. And I cried to him, 'Adelmo, have you really come from hell? What are the pains of hell like?' And I was trembling, because I had just left the office of compline where I had heard read the terrible pages on the wrath of the Lord. And he said to me, 'The pains of hell are infinitely greater than our tongue can say. You see,' he said, 'this cape of sophisms in which I have been dressed till today? It oppresses me and weighs on me as if I had the highest tower of Paris or the mountain of the world on my back, and nevermore shall I be able to set it down. And this pain was given me by divine justice for my vainglory, for having believed my body a place of pleasures, and for having thought to know more than others, and for having enjoyed monstrous things, which, cherished in my imagination, have produced far more monstrous things within my soul—and now I must live with them in eternity. You see the lining of this cloak? It is as if it were all coals and ardent fire, and it is the fire that burns my body, and this punishment is given me for the dishonest sin of the flesh, whose vice I knew and cultivated, and this fire now unceasingly blazes and burns me! Give me your hand, my beautiful master,' he said to me further, 'that my meeting with you may be a useful lesson, in exchange for many of the lessons you gave me. Your hand, my beautiful master!' And he shook the finger of his burning hand, and on my hand there fell a little drop of his sweat and it seemed to pierce my hand. For many days I bore the sign, only I hid it from all. Then he disappeared among the graves, and the next morning I learned that his body, which had so terrified me, was now dead at the foot of the cliff."

Berengar was breathless, weeping. William asked him, "And why did he call you his beautiful master? You were the same age. Had you perhaps taught him something?"

Berengar hid his head, pulling his cowl over his face, and sank to his knees, embracing William's legs. "I don't know why he addressed me like that. I never taught him anything!" And he burst into sobs. "I am afraid, Father. I want to confess myself to you. Have mercy, a devil is devouring my bowels!"

William thrust him away and held out a hand to draw him to his feet. "No, Berengar," he said to him, "do not ask me to confess you. Do not seal my lips by opening yours. What I want to know from you, you will tell me in another way. And if you will not tell me, I will discover it on my own. Ask me for mercy, if you like, but do not ask silence of me. Too many are silent in this abbey. Tell me, rather, how you saw his pale face if it was darkest night, how he could burn your hand if it was a night of rain and hail and snow, and what you were doing in the cemetery. Come"—and he shook him brutally by the shoulders—"tell me this at least!"

Berengar was trembling in every limb. "I don't know what I was doing in the cemetery, I don't remember, I don't know how I saw his face, perhaps I had a light, no . . . he had a light, he was carrying a light, perhaps I saw his face in the light of the flame. . . ."

"How could he carry a light if it was raining and snowing?"

"It was after compline, immediately after compline, it was not snowing yet, the snow began later. . . . I remember that the first flurries began as I was fleeing toward the dormitory. I was fleeing toward the dormitory as the ghost went in the opposite direction. . . . And after that I know nothing more; please, question me no further, if you will not confess me."

"Very well," William said, "go now, go into the choir, go to speak with the Lord, since you will not speak with men, or go and find a monk who will hear your confession, because if you have not confessed your sins since then, you have approached the sacraments sacrilegiously. Go. We shall see each other again."

Berengar ran off and vanished. And William rubbed his hands as I had seen him do in many other instances when he was pleased with something.

"Good," he said. "Now many things become clear."

"Clear, master?" I asked him. "Clear now that we also have Adelmo's ghost?"

"My dear Adso," William said, "that ghost does not seem very ghostly to me, and in any case he was reciting a page I have already read in some book conceived for the use of preachers. These monks read perhaps too much, and when they are excited they relive visions they learned from books. I don't know whether Adelmo really said those things or whether

Berengar simply heard them because he needed to hear them. The fact remains that this story confirms a series of my suppositions. For example: Adelmo died a suicide, and Berengar's story tells us that, before dying, he went around in the grip of a great agitation, and in remorse for some act he had committed. He was agitated and frightened about his sin because someone had frightened him, and perhaps had told him the very episode of the infernal apparition that he recited to Berengar with such hallucinated mastery. And he was going through the cemetery because he was leaving the choir, where he had confided (or confessed) to someone who had filled him with terror and remorse. And from the cemetery he was heading, as Berengar informed us, in the opposite direction from the dormitory. Toward the Aedificium, then, but also (it is possible) toward the outside wall behind the stables, from where I have deduced he must have thrown himself into the chasm. And he threw himself down before the storm came, he died at the foot of the wall, and only later did the landslide carry his corpse between the north tower and the eastern one."

"But what about the drop of burning sweat?"

"It was already part of the story he heard and repeated, or that Berengar imagined, in his agitation and his remorse. Because there is, as antistrophe to Adelmo's remorse, a remorse of Berengar's: you heard it. And if Adelmo came from the choir, he was perhaps carrying a taper, and the drop on his friend's hand was only a drop of wax. But Berengar felt it burn much deeper because Adelmo surely called him his master. A sign, then, that Adelmo was reproaching him for having taught him something that now caused him to despair unto death. And Berengar knows it, he suffers because he knows he drove Adelmo to death by making him do something he should not have done. And it is not difficult to imagine what, my poor Adso, after what we have heard about our assistant librarian."

"I believe I understand what happened between the two," I said, embarrassed by my own wisdom, "but don't all of us believe in a God of mercy? Adelmo, you say, had probably confessed; why did he seek to punish his first sin with a sin surely greater still, or at least of equal gravity?"

"Because someone said words of desperation to him. As I said, a page of a modern preacher must have prompted someone to repeat the words that frightened Adelmo and with which Adelmo frightened Berengar. In these last few years, as never before, to stimulate piety and terror and fervor in the populace, and obedience to human and divine law, preachers have used distressing words, macabre threats. Never before, as in our days, amid processions of flagellants, were sacred lauds heard inspired by the sorrows of Christ and of the Virgin, never has there been such insistence as there is today on strengthening the faith of the simple through the depiction of infernal torments."

"Perhaps it is the need for penitence," I said.

"Adso, I have never heard so many calls to penitence as today, in a period when, by now, neither preachers nor bishops nor even my brothers the Spirituals are any longer capable of inspiring true repentance. . . ."

"But the third age, the Angelic Pope, the chapter of Perugia . . ." I said, bewildered.

"Nostalgia. The great age of penitence is over, and for this reason even the general chapter of the order can speak of penitence. There was, one hundred, two hundred years ago, a great wind of renewal. There was a time when those who spoke of it were burned, saint or heretic as they may have been. Now all speak of it. In a certain sense even the Pope discusses it. Don't trust renewals of the human race when curias and courts speak of them."

"But Fra Dolcino," I ventured, curious to know more about that name I had heard uttered several times the day before.

"He died, and died dreadfully, as he lived, because he also came too late. And, anyway, what do you know of him?"

"Nothing. That is why I ask you...."

"I would prefer never to speak of him. I have had to deal with some of the so-called Apostles, and I have observed them closely. A sad story. It would upset you. In any case, it upset me, and you would be all the more upset by my inability to judge. It's the story of a man who did insane things because he put into practice what many saints had preached. At a certain point I could no longer understand whose fault it was, I was as if... as if dazed by an air of kinship that wafted over the two opposing camps, of saints who preached penitence and sinners who put it into practice, often at the expense of others.... But I was speaking of something else. Or perhaps not. I was speaking really of this: when the epoch of penitence was over, for penitents the need for penance became a need for death. And they who killed the crazed penitents, repaying death with death, to defeat true penitence, which produced death, replaced the penitence of the soul with a penitence of the imagination, a summons to supernatural visions of suffering and blood, calling them the 'mirror' of true penitence. A mirror that brings to life, for the imagination of the simple and sometimes even of the learned, the torments of hell. So that—it is said—no one shall sin. They hope to keep souls from sin through fear, and trust to replace rebellion with fear."

"But won't they truly sin then?" I asked anxiously.

"It depends on what you mean by sinning, Adso," my master said. "I would not like to be unjust toward the people of this country where I have been living for some years, but it seems to me typical of the scant virtue of the Italian peoples to abstain from sin out of their fear of some idol, though they may give it the name of a saint. They are more afraid of Saint Sebastian or Saint Anthony than of Christ. If you wish to keep a place clean here, to prevent anyone from pissing on it, which the Italians do as freely as dogs do, you paint on it an image of Saint Anthony with a wooden tip, and this will drive away those about to piss. So the Italians, thanks to their preachers, risk returning to the ancient superstitions; and they no longer believe in the resurrection of the flesh, but have only a great fear of bodily injuries and misfortunes, and therefore they are more afraid of Saint Anthony than of Christ."

"But Berengar isn't Italian," I pointed out.

"It makes no difference. I am speaking of the atmosphere that the church and the preaching orders have spread over this peninsula, and which from here spreads everywhere. And it reaches even a venerable abbey of learned monks, like these."

"But if only they didn't sin," I insisted, because I was prepared to be satisfied with this alone.

"If this abbey were a speculum mundi, you would already have the answer."

"But is it?" I asked.

"In order for there to be a mirror of the world, it is necessary that the world have a form," concluded William, who was too much of a philosopher for my adolescent mind.

TERCE

In which the visitors witness a brawl among vulgar persons, Aymaro of Alessandria makes some allusions, and Adso meditates on saintliness and on the dung of the Devil. Subsequently William and Adso go back to the scriptorium, William sees something interesting, has a third conversation on the licitness of laughter, but in the end is unable to look where he wishes.

Before climbing up to the scriptorium, we stopped by the kitchen to refresh ourselves, for we had partaken of nothing since rising. I drank a bowl of warm milk and was heartened at once. The great south fireplace was already blazing like a forge while the day's bread baked in the oven. Two herdsmen were setting down the body of a freshly slaughtered sheep. Among the cooks I saw Salvatore, who smiled at me with his wolf's mouth. And I saw that he was taking from a table a scrap of chicken left over from the night before and stealthily passing it to the herdsmen, who hid the food in their sheepskin jerkins with pleased grins. But the chief cook noticed and scolded Salvatore. "Cellarer, cellarer," he said, "you must look after the goods of the abbey, not squander them!"

"Filii Dei they are," said Salvatore, "Jesus has said that you do for him what you do for one of these pueri!"

"Filthy Fraticello, fart of a Minorite!" the cook shouted

at him. "You're not among those louse-bitten friars of yours any more! The abbot's charity will see to the feeding of the children of God!"

Salvatore's face turned grim and he swung around, in a rage: "I am not a Minorite friar! I am a monk Sancti Benedicti! Merdre à toy, Bogomil de merdre!"

"Call Bogomil that whore you screw at night, with your heretic cock, you pig!" the cook cried.

Salvatore thrust the herdsmen through the door and, passing close to us, looked at us, worried. "Brother," he said to William, "you defend the order that is not mine; tell him the filii de Francesco non sunt hereticos!" Then he whispered into an ear, "Ille menteur, puah!" and he spat on the ground.

The cook came over and roughly pushed him out, shutting the door after him. "Brother," he said to William with respect, "I was not speaking ill of your order or of the most holy men who belong to it. I was speaking to that false Minorite and false Benedictine who is neither flesh nor fowl."

"I know where he came from," William said, conciliatory. "But now he is a monk as you are and you owe him fraternal respect."

"But he sticks his nose in where he has no business only because he is under the cellarer's protection and believes himself the cellarer. He uses the abbey as if it belonged to him, day and night."

"How at night?" William asked. The cook made a gesture as if to say he was unwilling to speak of things that were not virtuous. William questioned him no further and finished drinking his milk.

My curiosity was becoming more and more aroused. The meeting with Ubertino, the muttering about the past of Salvatore and his cellarer, the more and more frequent references to the Fraticelli and the heretic Minorites I had heard in those days, my master's reluctance to speak to me about Fra Dolcino . . . A series of images began to return to my mind. For example, in the course of our journey we had at least twice come upon a procession of flagellants. Once the local populace was looking at them as if they were saints; the other time there was murmuring that these were heretics. And yet they were the same people. They walked in procession two by two, through the streets of the city, only their pudenda covered, as they had gone beyond any sense of shame. Each carried a leather lash in his hand and hit himself on the shoulders till blood came; and they were shedding abundant tears as if they saw with their own eyes the Passion of the Saviour; in a mournful chant they implored the Lord's mercy and the intercession of the Mother of God. Not only during the day but also at night, with lighted tapers, in the harsh winter, they went in a great throng from church to church, prostrating themselves humbly before the altars, preceded by priests with candles and banners, and they were not only men and women of the populace, but also noble ladies and merchants. . . . And then great acts of penance were to be seen: those who had stolen gave back their loot, others confessed their crimes. . . .

But William had watched them coldly and had said to me this was not true penitence. He spoke then much as he had only a short while ago, this very morning: the period of the great penitential cleansing was finished, and these were the ways preachers now organized the devotion of the mobs, precisely so that they would not succumb to a desire for penance that—in this case— really was heretical and frightened all. But I was unable to understand the difference, if there actually was any. It seemed to me that the difference did not lie in the actions of the one or the other, but in the church's attitude when she judged this act or that.

I remembered the discussion with Ubertino. William had undoubtedly been insinuating, had tried to say to him, that there was little difference between his mystic (and orthodox) faith and the distorted faith of the heretics. Ubertino had taken offense, as one who saw the difference clearly. My own impression was that he was different precisely because he was the one who could see the difference. William had renounced the duties of inquisitor because he could no longer see it. For this reason he was unable to speak to me of that mysterious Fra Dolcino. But then, obviously (I said to myself), William has lost the assistance of the Lord, who not only teaches how to see the difference, but also invests his elect with this capacity for discrimination. Ubertino and Clare of Montefalco (who was, however, surrounded by sinners) had remained saints precisely because they knew how to discriminate. This and only this is sanctity.

But why did William not know how to discriminate? He was such an acute man, and as far as the facts of nature went, he could perceive the slightest discrepancy or the slightest kinship between things....

I was immersed in these thoughts, and William was finishing his milk, when we heard someone greet us. It was Aymaro of Alessandria, whom we had met in the scriptorium, and who had struck me by the expression of his face, a perpetual sneer, as if he could never reconcile himself to the fatuousness of all human beings and yet did not attach great importance to this cosmic tragedy. "Well, Brother William, have you already become accustomed to this den of madmen?"

"It seems to me a place of men admirable in sanctity and learning," William said cautiously.

"It was. When abbots acted as abbots and librarians as librarians. Now you have seen, up there"—and he nodded toward the floor above—"that half-dead German with a blind man's eyes, listening devoutly to the ravings of that blind Spaniard with a dead man's eyes; it would seem as though the Antichrist were to arrive every morning. They scrape their parchments, but few new books come in.... We are up here, and down below in the city they act. Once our abbeys ruled the world. Today you see the situation: the Emperor uses us, sending his friends here to meet his enemies (I know something of your mission, monks talk and talk, they have nothing else to do); but if he wants to control the affairs of this country, he remains in the city. We are busy gathering grain and raising fowl, and down there they trade lengths of silk for pieces of linen, and pieces of linen for sacks of spices, and all of them for good money. We guard our treasure, but down there they pile up treasures. And also books. More beautiful than ours, too."

"In the world many new things are happening, to be sure. But why do you think the abbot is to blame?"

"Because he has handed the library over to foreigners and directs the abbey like a citadel erected to defend the library. A Benedictine abbey in this Italian region should be a place where Italians decide Italian questions. What are the Italians doing today, when they no longer have even a pope? They are trafficking, and manufacturing, and they are richer than the King of France. So, then, let us do the same; since we know how to make beautiful books, we should make them for the universities and concern ourselves with what is happening down in the valley—I do not mean with the Emperor, with all due respect for your mission, Brother William, but with what the Bolognese or the Florentines are doing. From here we could control the route of pilgrims and merchants who go from Italy to Provence and vice versa. We should open the library to texts in the vernacular, and those who no longer write in Latin will also come up here. But instead we are controlled by a group of foreigners who continue to manage the library as if the good Odo of Cluny were still abbot. . . ."

"But your abbot is Italian," William said.

"The abbot here counts for nothing," Aymaro said, still sneering. "In the place of his head he has a bookcase. Wormeaten. To spite the Pope he allows the abbey to be invaded by Fraticelli. . . . I mean the heretical ones, Brother, those who have abandoned your

141

most holy order . . . and to please the Emperor he invites monks from all the monasteries of the North, as if we did not have fine copyists and men who know Greek and Arabic in our country, and as if in Florence or Pisa there were not sons of merchants, rich and generous, who would gladly enter the order, if the order offered the possibility of enhancing their fathers' prestige and power. But here indulgence in secular matters is recognized only when the Germans are allowed to . . . O good Lord, strike my tongue, for I am about to say improper things!"

"Do improper things take place in the abbey?" William asked absently, pouring himself a bit more milk.

"A monk is also human," Aymaro declared. Then he added, "But here they are less human than elsewhere. And what I have said: remember that I did not say it."

"Very interesting," William said. "And are these your personal opinions, or are there many who think as you do?"

"Many, many. Many who now mourn the loss of poor Adelmo, but if another had fallen into the abyss, someone who moves about the library more than he should, they would not have been displeased."

"What do you mean?"

"I have talked too much. Here we talk too much, as you must have noticed already. Here, on the one hand, nobody respects silence any more. On the other, it is respected too much. Here, instead of talking or remaining silent, we should act. In the golden age of our order, if an abbot did not have the temper of an abbot, a nice goblet of poisoned wine would make way for a successor. I have said these things to you, Brother William, obviously not to gossip about the abbot or other brothers. God save me, fortunately I do not have the nasty habit of gossiping. But I would be displeased if the abbot had asked you to investigate me or some others like Pacificus of Tivoli or Peter of Sant'Albano. We have no say in the affairs of the library. But we would like to have a bit of say. So uncover this nest of serpents, you who have burned so many heretics."

"I have never burned anyone," William replied sharply.

"It was just a figure of speech," Aymaro confessed with a broad smile. "Good hunting, Brother William, but be careful at night."

"Why not during the day?"

"Because during the day here the body is tended with good herbs, but at night the mind falls ill with bad herbs. Do not believe that Adelmo was pushed into the abyss by someone's hands or that someone's hands put Venantius in the blood. Here someone does not want the monks to decide for themselves where to go, what to do, and what to read. And the powers of hell are employed, or the powers of the necromancers, friends of hell, to derange the minds of the curious...."

"Are you speaking of the father herbalist?"

"Severinus of Sankt Wendel is a good person. Of course, he is also a German, as Malachi is a German...." And, having shown once again his aversion to gossip, Aymaro went up to work.

"What did he want to tell us?" I asked.

"Everything and nothing. An abbey is always a place where monks are in conflict among themselves to gain control of the community. At Melk, too, but perhaps as a novice you were not able to realize it. But in your country, gaining control of an abbey means winning a position in which you deal directly with the Emperor. In this country, on the other hand, the situation is different; the Emperor is far away, even when he comes all the way down to Rome. There is no court, not even the papal court now. There are the cities, as you will have seen."

"Certainly, and I was impressed by them. A city in Italy is something different from one in my land.... It is not only a place to live, it is also a place to decide, the people are always in the square, the city magistrates count far more than the Emperor or the Pope. The cities are like...so many kingdoms...."

"And the kings are the merchants. And their weapon is money. Money, in Italy, has a different function from what it has in your country, or in mine. Money circulates everywhere, but much of life elsewhere is still dominated and regulated by the bartering of goods, chickens or sheaves of wheat, or a scythe, or a wagon, and money serves only to procure these goods. In the Italian city, on the contrary, you must have noticed that goods serve to procure money. And even priests, bishops, even religious orders have to take money into account. This is why, naturally, rebellion against power takes the form of a call to poverty. The rebels against power are those denied any connection with money, and so every call to poverty provokes great tension and argument, and the whole city, from bishop to magistrate, considers a personal enemy the one who preaches poverty too much. The inquisitors smell the stink of the Devil where someone has reacted to the stink of the Devil's dung. And now you can understand also what Aymaro is thinking about. A Benedictine abbey, in the golden period of the order, was the place from which shepherds controlled the flock of the faithful. Aymaro wants a return to the tradition. Only the life of the flock has changed, and the abbey can return to the tradition (to its glory, to its former power) only if it accepts the new ways of the flock, becoming different itself. And since today the flock here is dominated, not with weapons or the splendor of ritual, but with the control of money, Aymaro wants the whole fabric of the abbey, and the library itself, to become a workshop, a factory for making money."

"And what does this have to do with the crimes, or the crime?"

"I don't know yet. But now I would like to go upstairs. Come."

The monks were already at work. Silence reigned in the scriptorium, but it was not the silence that comes from the industrious peace of all hearts. Berengar, who had preceded us by only a short time, received us with embarrassment. The other monks looked up from their work. They knew we were there to discover something about Venantius, and the very direction of their gaze drew our attention to a vacant desk, under a window that opened onto the interior, the central octagon.

Although it was a very cold day, the temperature in the scriptorium was rather mild. It was not by chance that it had been situated above the kitchen, whence came adequate heat, especially because the flues of the two ovens below passed inside the columns supporting the two circular staircases in the west and south towers. As for the north tower, on the opposite side of the great room, it had no stair, but a big fireplace that burned and spread a happy warmth. Moreover, the floor had been covered with straw, which muffled our footsteps. In other words, the least-heated corner was that of the east tower, and in fact I noticed that, although there were few places left vacant, given the number of monks at work, all of the monks tended to avoid the desks located in that part. When I later realized that the circular staircase of the east tower was the only one that led, not only down to the refectory, but also up to the library, I asked myself whether a shrewd calculation had not regulated the heating of the room so that the monks would be discouraged from investigating that area and the librarian could more easily control the access to the library.

Poor Venantius's desk had its back to the great fireplace, and it was probably one of the most desired. At that time I had passed very little of my life in a scriptorium, but I spent a great deal of it subsequently and I know what torment it is for the scribe, the rubricator, the scholar to spend the long winter hours at his desk, his fingers numb around the stylus (when even in a normal temperature, after six hours of writing, the fingers are seized by the terrible monk's cramp and the thumb aches as if it had been trodden on). And this explains why we often find in the margins of a manuscript phrases left by the scribe as testimony to his suffering (and his impatience), such as "Thank God it will soon be dark," or "Oh, if I had a good glass of wine," or also "Today it is cold, the light is dim, this vellum is hairy, something is wrong." As an ancient proverb says, three fingers hold the pen, but the whole body works. And aches.

But I was telling about Venantius's desk. It was rather small, like the others set around the octagonal courtyard, since they were meant for scholars, whereas the larger ones under the windows of the outer walls were meant for illuminators and copyists. Venantius also worked with a lectern, because he probably consulted manuscripts on loan to the abbey, of which he made a copy. Under the desk was a low set of shelves piled with unbound sheets, and since they were all in Latin, I deduced they were his most recent translations. They were written hastily and did not represent the pages of a book, for they had yet to be entrusted to a copyist and an illuminator. For this reason they were difficult to read. Among the pages were a few books, in Greek. Another Greek book was open on the lectern, the work on which Venantius had been exercising his skill as translator in the past days. At that time I knew no Greek, but my master read the title and said this was by a certain Lucian and was the story of a man turned into an ass. I recalled then a similar fable by Apuleius, which, as a rule, novices were strongly advised against reading.

"Why was Venantius making this translation?" William asked Berengar, who was at our side.

"The abbey was asked to do it by the lord of Milan, and the abbey will gain from it a preferential right to the wine production of some farms to the east of here." Berengar pointed with his hand toward the distance. But he promptly added, "Not that the abbey performs venal tasks for laymen. But the lord who has given us this commission went to great pains to have this precious Greek manuscript lent us by the Doge of Venice, who received it from the Emperor of Byzantium, and when Venantius had finished his work, we would have made two copies, one for the lord of Milan and one for our library."

"Which therefore does not disdain to add pagan fables to its collection," William said.

"The library is testimony to truth and to error," a voice then said behind us. It was Jorge. Once again I was amazed (but I was to be amazed often in the days that followed) by the old man's way of suddenly, unexpectedly appearing, as if we did not see him and he did see us. I wondered also why on earth a blind man was in the scriptorium, but I realized later that Jorge was omnipresent in all corners of the abbey. And often he was in the scriptorium, seated on a stool by the fireplace, and he seemed to follow everything going on in the room. Once I heard him ask from his place, in a loud voice, "Who is going upstairs?" and he turned to Malachi, who was going toward the library, his steps silenced by the straw. The monks all held him in high esteem and often had recourse to him, reading him passages difficult to understand, consulting him for a gloss, or asking counsel on how to depict an animal or a saint. And he would look into the void with his spent eyes, as if staring at pages vivid in his memory, and he would answer that false prophets are dressed like bishops and frogs come from their mouths, or would say what stones were to adorn the walls of the heavenly Jerusalem, or that the Arimaspi should be depicted on maps near the land of Prester John—urging that their monstrosity not be made excessively seductive, for it

147

sufficed to portray them as emblems, recognizable, but not desirable, or repellent to the point of laughter.

Once I heard him advise a scholiast on how to interpret the recapitulatio in the texts of Tyconius according to the thought of Saint Augustine, so that the Donatist heresy could be avoided. Another time I heard him give advice on how, in making commentary, to distinguish heretics from schismatics. Or again, he told a puzzled scholar what book to seek in the library catalogue, and more or less on what page he would find it listed, assuring him that the librarian would certainly give it to him because it was a work inspired by God. Finally, on another occasion I heard him say that such-and-such a book should not be sought because, though it did indeed exist in the catalogue, it had been ruined by mice fifty years earlier, and by now it would crumble to powder in the fingers of anyone who touched it. He was, in other words, the library's memory and the soul of the scriptorium. At times he admonished monks he heard chatting among themselves: "Hurry, and leave testimony to the truth, for the time is at hand!" He was referring to the coming of the Antichrist.

"The library is testimony to truth and to error," Jorge said.

"Undoubtedly Apuleius and Lucian were reputed to be magicians," William said. "But this fable, beneath the veil of its fictions, contains also a good moral, for it teaches how we pay for our errors, and, furthermore, I believe that the story of the man transformed into an ass refers to the metamorphosis of the soul that falls into sin."

"That may be," Jorge said.

"But now I understand why, during that conversation of which I was told yesterday, Venantius was so interested in the problems of comedy; in fact, fables of this sort can also be considered kin to the comedies of the ancients. Both tell not of men who really existed, as tragedies do; on the contrary, as Isidore says, they are fictions: 'fabulas poetae a *fando* nominaverunt, quia non sunt *res factae* sed tantum loquendo *fictae*. . . .'"

At first I could not understand why William had embarked on this learned discussion, and with a man who seemed to dislike such subjects, but Jorge's reply told me how subtle my master had been.

"That day we were not discussing comedies, but only the licitness of laughter," Jorge said grimly. I remembered very well that when Venantius had referred to that discussion, only the day before, Jorge had claimed not to remember it.

"Ah," William said casually, "I thought you had spoken of poets' lies and shrewd riddles. . . ."

"We talked about laughter," Jorge said sharply. "The comedies were written by the pagans to move spectators to laughter, and they acted wrongly. Our Lord Jesus never told comedies or fables, but only clear parables which allegorically instruct us on how to win paradise, and so be it."

"I wonder," William said, "why you are so opposed to the idea that Jesus may have laughed. I believe laughter is a good medicine, like baths, to treat humors and the other afflictions of the body, melancholy in particular."

"Baths are a good thing," Jorge said, "and Aquinas himself advises them for dispelling sadness, which can be a bad passion when it is not addressed to an evil that can be dispelled through boldness. Baths restore the balance of the humors. Laughter shakes the body, distorts the features of the face, makes man similar to the monkey."

"Monkeys do not laugh; laughter is proper to man, it is a sign of his rationality," William said.

"Speech is also a sign of human rationality, and with speech a man can blaspheme against God. Not everything that is proper to man is necessarily good. He who laughs does not believe in what he laughs at, but neither does he hate it. Therefore, laughing at evil means not preparing oneself to combat it, and laughing at good means denying the power through which good is self-propagating. This is why the Rule says, 'The tenth degree of humility is not to be quick to laughter, as it is written: stultus in risu exaltat vocem suam.' "

"Quintilian," my master interrupted, "says that laughter is to be repressed in the panegyric, for the sake of dignity, but it is to be encouraged in many other cases. Pliny the Younger wrote, 'Sometimes I laugh, I jest, I play, because I am a man.' "

"They were pagans," Jorge replied. "The Rule forbids with stern words these trivialities: 'Scurrilitates vero vel verba otiosa et risum moventia aeterna clausura in omnibus locis damnamus, et ad talia eloquia discipulum aperire os non permittimus.' "

"But once the word of Christ had triumphed on the earth, Synesius of Cyrene said that the divinity could harmoniously combine comic and tragic, and Aelius Spartianus said of the Emperor Hadrian, man of lofty behavior and of naturaliter Christian spirit, that he could mingle moments of gaiety with moments of gravity. And finally Ausonius recommended moderate use of the serious and the jocose."

"But Paulinus of Nola and Clement of Alexandria put us on guard against such foolishness, and Sulpicius Severus said that no one ever saw Saint Martin in the grip of wrath or in the grip of hilarity."

"But he recalled some replies of the saint spiritualiter salsa," William said.

"They were prompt and wise, not ridiculous. Saint Ephraim wrote an exhortation against the laughter of monks, and in the *De habitu et conversatione monachorum* there is a strong warning to avoid obscenity and witticisms as if they were asp venom!"

"But Hildebertus said, 'Admittenda tibi ioca sunt post seria quaedam, sed tamen et dignis ipsa gerenda modis.' And John of Salisbury authorized a discreet hilarity. And finally Ecclesiastes, whom you quoted in the passage to which your Rule refers, where it says that laughter is proper to the fool, permits at least silent laughter, in the serene spirit."

"The spirit is serene only when it contemplates the truth and takes delight in good achieved, and truth and good are not to be laughed at. This is why Christ did not laugh. Laughter foments doubt."

"But sometimes it is right to doubt."

"I cannot see any reason. When you are in doubt, you must turn to an authority, to the words of a father or of a doctor; then all reason for doubt ceases. You seem to me steeped in debatable doctrines, like those of the logicians of Paris. But Saint Bernard knew well how to intervene against the castrate Abelard, who wanted to submit all problems to the cold, lifeless scrutiny of reason not enlightened by Scripture, pronouncing his It-is-so and It-is-not-so. Certainly one who accepts dangerous ideas can also appreciate the jesting of the ignorant man who laughs at the sole truth one should know, which has already been said once and for all. With his laughter the fool says in his heart, 'Deus non est.'"

"Venerable Jorge, you seem to me unjust when you call Abelard a castrate, because you know that he incurred that sad condition through the wickedness of others...."

"For his sins. For the pride of his faith in man's reason. So the faith of the simple was mocked, the mysteries of God were eviscerated (or at least this was tried, fools they who tried), questions concerning the loftiest things were treated recklessly, the fathers were mocked because they had considered that such questions should have been subdued, rather than raised."

"I do not agree, venerable Jorge. Of us God demands that we apply our reason to many obscure things about which Scripture has left us free to decide. And when someone suggests you believe in a proposition, you must first examine it to see whether it is acceptable,

151

because our reason was created by God, and whatever pleases our reason can but please divine reason, of which, for that matter, we know only what we infer from the processes of our own reason by analogy and often by negation. Thus, you see, to undermine the false authority of an absurd proposition that offends reason, laughter can sometimes also be a suitable instrument. And laughter serves to confound the wicked and to make their foolishness evident. It is told of Saint Maurus that when the pagans put him in boiling water, he complained that the bath was too cold; the pagan governor foolishly put his hand in the water to test it, and burned himself. A fine action of that sainted martyr who ridiculed the enemies of the faith."

Jorge sneered. "Even in the episodes the preachers tell, there are many old wives' tales. A saint immersed in boiling water suffers for Christ and restrains his cries, he does not play childish tricks on the pagans!"

"You see?" William said. "This story seems to you offensive to reason and you accuse it of being ridiculous! Though you are controlling your lips, you are tacitly laughing at something, nor do you wish me to take it seriously. You are laughing at laughter, but you are laughing."

Jorge made a gesture of irritation. "Jesting about laughter, you draw me into idle debate. But you know that Christ did not laugh."

"I am not sure of that. When he invites the Pharisees to cast the first stone, when he asks whose image is on the coin to be paid in tribute, when he plays on words and says 'Tu es petrus,' I believe he was making witticisms to confound sinners, to keep up the spirits of his disciples. He speaks with wit also when he says to Caiaphas, 'Thou hast said it.' And you well know that in the most heated moment of the conflict between Cluniacs and Cistercians, the former accused the latter, to make them look ridiculous, of not wearing trousers. And in the *Speculum stultorum* it is narrated of the ass Brunellus that he wonders what would happen if at night the wind lifted the blankets and the monks saw their own pudenda. . . ."

The monks gathered around, laughed, and Jorge became infuriated: "You are drawing these brothers of mine into a feast of fools. I know that among the Franciscans it is the custom to curry the crowd's favor with nonsense of this kind, but of such tricks I will say to you what is said in a verse I heard from one of your preachers: Tum podex carmen extulit horridulum."

The reprimand was a bit too strong. William had been impertinent, but now Jorge was accusing him of breaking wind through the mouth. I wondered if this stern reply did not signify, on the part of the elderly monk, an invitation to leave the scriptorium. But I saw William, so mettlesome a moment earlier, now become meek.

"I beg your pardon, venerable Jorge," he said. "My mouth has betrayed my thoughts. I did not want to show you a lack of respect. Perhaps what you say is correct, and I was mistaken."

Jorge, faced by this act of exquisite humility, emitted a grunt that could express either satisfaction or forgiveness; and he could only go back to his seat, while the monks who had gradually collected during the argument scattered to their places. William knelt again at Venantius's desk and resumed searching through the paper. With his humble reply, William had gained a few seconds of quiet. And what he saw in those few seconds inspired his investigation during the night that was to come.

But they were really only a few seconds. Benno came over at once, pretending he had forgotten his stylus on the desk when he had approached to hear the conversation with Jorge; and he whispered to William that he had to speak with him urgently, fixing a meeting place behind the balneary. He told William to leave first, and he would join him in a short while.

William hesitated a few moments, then called Malachi, who, from his librarian's desk near the catalogue, had followed everything that had happened. William begged him, in view of the injunction received from the abbot (and he heavily emphasized this privilege), to have someone guard Venantius's desk, because William considered it important to his inquiry that no one approach it throughout the day, until he himself could come back. He said this in a loud voice, and so not only committed Malachi to keep watch over the monks, but also set the monks themselves to keep watch over Malachi. The librarian could only consent, and William and I took our leave.

As we were crossing the garden and approaching the balneary, which was next to the infirmary building, William observed, "Many seem to be afraid I might find something that is on or under Venantius's desk."

"What can that be?"

"I have the impression that even those who are afraid do not know."

"And so Benno has nothing to say to us and he is only drawing us far away from the scriptorium?"

"We will soon find out," William said. In fact, a short while later Benno joined us.

SEXT

In which Benno tells a strange tale from which unedifying things about the life of the abbey are learned.

What Benno told us was quite confused. It really seemed that he had drawn us down there only to lure us away from the scriptorium, but it also seemed that, incapable of inventing a plausible pretext, he was telling us fragments of a truth of vaster dimensions than he knew.

He admitted he had been reticent that morning, but now, on sober consideration, he felt William should know the whole truth. During the famous conversation about laughter, Berengar had referred to the "finis Africae." What was it? The library was full of secrets, and especially of books that had never been given to the monks to read. Benno had been struck by William's words on the rational scrutiny of propositions. He considered that a monk-scholar had a right to know everything the library contained, he uttered words of fire against the Council of Soissons, which had condemned Abelard, and while he spoke we realized that this monk was still young, that he delighted in rhetoric, was stirred by yearnings toward freedom, and was

155

having a hard time accepting the limitations the discipline of the abbey set on his intellectual curiosity. I have learned always to distrust such curiosity, but I know well this attitude did not displease my master, and I saw he was sympathizing with Benno and giving him credence. In short, Benno told us he did not know what secrets Adelmo, Venantius, and Berengar had discussed, but he would not be sorry if as a result of this sad story a bit more light were to be cast on the running of the library, and he hoped that my master, however he might unravel the tangle of the inquiry, would have reason to urge the abbot to relax the intellectual discipline that oppressed the monks—some from far places, like himself, he added, who had come for the express purpose of nourishing the mind on the marvels hidden in the vast womb of the library.

I believe Benno was sincere in expecting of the inquiry what he said. Probably, however, as William had foreseen, he wanted at the same time to retain for himself the possibility of rummaging in Venantius's desk first, devoured as he was by curiosity, and in order to keep us away from that desk, he was prepared to give us information in exchange. And here is what it was.

Berengar was consumed, as many of the monks now knew, by an insane passion for Adelmo, the same passion whose evils divine wrath had castigated in Sodom and Gomorrah. So Benno expressed himself, perhaps out of regard for my tender years. But anyone who has spent his adolescence in a monastery, even if he has kept himself chaste, often hears talk of such passions, and at times he has to protect himself from the snares of those enslaved by them. Little novice that I was, had I not already received from an aged monk, at Melk, scrolls with verses that as a rule a layman devotes to a woman? The monkish vows keep us far from that sink of vice that is the female body, but often they bring us close to other errors. Can I finally hide from myself the fact that even today my old age is still stirred by the noonday demon when my eyes, in choir, happen to linger on the beardless face of a novice, pure and fresh as a maiden's?

I say these things not to cast doubt on the choice I made to devote myself to monastic life, but to justify the error of many to whom this holy burden proves heavy. Perhaps to justify Berengar's horrible crime. But, according to Benno, this monk apparently pursued his vice in a yet more ignoble fashion, using the weapon of extortion to obtain from others what virtue and decorum should have advised them against giving.

So for some time the monks had been making sarcastic observations on the tender looks Berengar cast at Adelmo, who, it seems, was of great comeliness. Whereas Adelmo, enamored only of his work, from which he seemed to derive his sole pleasure, paid little attention to Berengar's passion. But perhaps—who knows?—he was unaware that his spirit, secretly, tended toward the same ignominy. The fact is, Benno said, he had overheard a dialogue between Adelmo and Berengar in which Berengar, referring to a secret Adelmo was asking him to reveal, proposed a vile barter, which even the most innocent reader can imagine. And it seems that from Adelmo's lips Benno heard words of consent, spoken as if with relief. As if, Benno ventured, Adelmo at heart desired nothing else, and it sufficed for him to find some excuse other than carnal desire in order to agree. A sign, Benno argued, that Berengar's secret must have concerned arcana of learning, so that Adelmo could harbor the illusion of submitting to a sin of the flesh to satisfy a desire of the intellect. And, Benno added with a smile, how many times had he himself not been stirred by desires of the intellect so violent that to satisfy them he would have consented to complying with others' carnal desires, even against his own inclination.

"Are there not moments," he asked William, "when

you would also do shameful things to get your hands on a book you have been seeking for years?"

"The wise and most virtuous Sylvester II, centuries ago, gave as a gift a most precious armillary sphere in exchange for a manuscript, I believe, of Statius or Lucan," William said. He added then, prudently, "But it was an armillary sphere, not his virtue."

Benno admitted that his enthusiasm had carried him away, and he resumed his story. The night before Adelmo's death, Benno followed the pair, driven by curiosity, and he saw them, after compline, go off together to the dormitory. He waited a long time, holding ajar the door of his cell, not far from theirs, and when silence had fallen over the sleep of the monks, he clearly saw Adelmo slip into Berengar's cell. Benno remained awake, unable to fall asleep, until he heard Berengar's door open again and Adelmo flee, almost running, as his friend tried to hold him back. Berengar followed Adelmo down to the floor below. Cautiously Benno went after them, and at the mouth of the lower corridor he saw Berengar, trembling, huddled in a corner, staring at the door of Jorge's cell. Benno guessed that Adelmo had flung himself at the feet of the venerable brother to confess his sin. And Berengar was trembling, knowing his secret was being revealed, even if under the seal of the sacrament.

Then Adelmo came out, his face pale, thrust away Berengar, who was trying to speak to him, and rushed out of the dormitory, moving behind the apse of the church and entering the choir from the north door (which at night remains open). Probably he wanted to pray. Berengar followed him but did not enter the church; he wandered among the graves in the cemetery, wringing his hands.

Benno was wondering what to do when he realized that a fourth person was moving about the vicinity. This person, too, had followed the pair and certainly had not noticed the presence of Benno, who flattened himself against the trunk of an oak growing at the edge of the cemetery. The fourth man was Venantius. At the sight of him Berengar crouched among the graves, as Venantius also went into the choir. At this point, fearing he would be discovered, Benno returned to the dormitory. The next morning Adelmo's corpse was found at the foot of the cliff. And more than that, Benno did not know.

Dinner hour was now approaching. Benno left us, and my master asked him nothing further. We remained for a little while behind the balneary, then strolled briefly in the garden, meditating on those singular revelations.

"Frangula," William said suddenly, bending over to observe a plant that, on that winter day, he recognized from the bare bush. "A good infusion is made from the bark, for hemorrhoids. And that is arctium lappa; a good cataplasm of fresh roots cicatrizes skin eczemas."

"You are cleverer than Severinus," I said to him, "but now tell me what you think of what we have heard!"

"Dear Adso, you should learn to think with your own head. Benno probably told us the truth. His story fits with what Berengar told us early this morning, for all its hallucinations. Berengar and Adelmo do something very evil together: we had already guessed that. And Berengar must reveal to Adelmo that secret that remains, alas, a secret. Adelmo, after committing his crime against chastity and the law of nature, thinks only of confiding in someone who can absolve him, and he rushes to Jorge. Whose character is very stern, as we know from experience, and he surely attacks Adelmo with distressing reprimands. Perhaps he refuses absolution, perhaps he imposes an impossible penance: we don't know, nor would Jorge ever tell us. The fact remains that Adelmo rushes into church and prostrates himself before the altar, but doesn't quell his remorse. At this point, he is approached by Venantius. We don't know what they say to each other. Perhaps Adelmo confides in Venantius the secret received as a gift (or as payment) from Berengar, which no longer matters to him, since he now has a far more terrible and burning secret. What happens to Venantius? Perhaps, overcome by the same ardent curiosity that today also seized our friend Benno, satisfied with what he has learned, he leaves Adelmo to his remorse. Adelmo sees himself abandoned, determines to kill himself, comes in despair to the cemetery, and there encounters Berengar. He says terrible words to him, flings his responsibilities at him, calls him his master in turpitude. I believe, actually, that Berengar's story, stripped of all hallucination, was exact. Adelmo repeats to him the same words of desperation he must have heard from Jorge. And now Berengar, overcome, goes off in one direction, and Adelmo goes in the other, to kill himself. Then comes the rest, of which we were almost witnesses. All believe Adelmo was murdered, so Venantius has the impression that the secret of the library is more important than he had believed, and he continues the search on his own. Until someone stops him, either before or after he has discovered what he wanted."

"Who killed him? Berengar?"

"Perhaps. Or Malachi, who must guard the Aedificium. Or someone else. Berengar is suspect because he is frightened, and he knew that by then Venantius possessed his secret. Malachi is suspect: guardian of the inviolability of the library, he discovers someone has violated it, and he kills. Jorge knows everything about everyone, possesses Adelmo's secret, does not want me to discover what Venantius may have found.... Many facts would point to him. But tell me how a blind man can kill another man in the fullness of his strength? And how can an old man, even if strong, carry the body to the jar? But finally, why couldn't the murderer be Benno himself? He could have lied to us, impelled by reasons that cannot be confessed. And why limit our suspicions only to those who took part in the discussion of laughter? Perhaps the crime had other motives, which have nothing to do with the library. In any case, we need two things: to know how to get into the library at night, and a lamp. You provide the lamp. Linger in the kitchen at dinner hour, take one...."

"A theft?"

"A loan, to the greater glory of the Lord."

"If that is so, then count on me."

"Good. As for getting into the Aedificium, we saw where Malachi came from last night. Today I will visit the church, and that chapel in particular. In an hour we go to table. Afterward we have a meeting with the abbot. You will bc admitted, because I have asked to bring a secretary to make a note of what we say."

NONES

In which the abbot declares his pride in the wealth of his abbey and his fear of heretics, and eventually Adso wonders whether he has made a mistake in going forth into the world.

We found the abbot in church, at the main altar. He was following the work of some novices who had brought forth from a secret place a number of sacred vessels, chalices, patens, and monstrances, and a crucifix I had not seen during the morning function. I could not repress a cry of wonder at the dazzling beauty of those holy objects. It was noon and the light came in bursts through the choir windows, and even more through those of the façade, creating white cascades that, like mystic streams of divine substance, intersected at various points of the church, engulfing the altar itself.

The vases, the chalices, each piece revealed its precious materials: amid the yellow of the gold, the immaculate white of the ivory, and the transparency of the crystal, I saw gleaming gems of every color and dimension, and I recognized jacinth, topaz, ruby, sapphire, emerald, chrysolite, onyx, carbuncle, and jasper and agate. And at the same time I realized how, that morning, first transported by prayer and then overcome with terror, I had failed to notice many things: the altar frontal and three other panels that flanked it were entirely of gold, and eventually the whole altar seemed of gold, from whatever direction I looked at it.

The abbot smiled at my amazement. "These riches you see," he said, addressing me and my master, "and others you will see later, are the heritage of centuries of piety and devotion, testimony to the power and holiness of this abbey. Princes and potentates of the earth, archbishops and bishops have sacrificed to this altar and to the objects destined for it the rings of their investiture, the gold and precious stones that were the emblem of their greatness, to have them melted down here to the greater glory of the Lord and of this His place. Though today the abbey is distressed by another, sad event, we must not forget, reminded of our fragility, the strength and power of the Almighty. The celebration of the Holy Nativity is approaching, and we are beginning to polish the sacred vessels, so that the Saviour's birth may be celebrated with all the pomp and magnificence it deserves and demands. Everything must appear in its full splendor," he added, looking hard at William, and afterward I understood why he insisted so proudly on justifying his action, "because we believe it useful and fitting not to hide, but on the contrary to proclaim divine generosity."

"Certainly," William said politely, "if Your Sublimity feels that the Lord must be so glorified, your abbey has achieved the greatest excellence in this meed of praise."

"And so it must be," the abbot said. "If it was the custom that amphoras and phials of gold and little gold mortars served, by the will of God or order of the prophets, to collect the blood of goats or calves or of the heifer in the temple of Solomon, then there is all the more reason why vases of gold and precious stones, and the most valuable things created, should be used with constant reverence and complete devotion to receive the blood of Christ! If in a second creation our substance were to be the same as that of the cherubim and the seraphim, the service it could perform for such an ineffable victim would still be unworthy...."

"Amen," I said.

"Many protest that a devoutly inspired mind, a pure heart, a will led by faith should suffice for this sacred function. We are the first to declare explicitly and resolutely that these are the essential things; but we are convinced that homage must also be paid through the exterior ornament of the sacred vessel, because it is profoundly right and fitting that we serve our Saviour in all things, totally. He who has not refused to provide for us, totally and without reservation."

"This has always been the opinion of the great men of your order," William agreed, "and I recall beautiful things written on the ornaments of churches by the very great and venerable abbot Suger."

"True," the abbot said. "You see this crucifix. It is not yet complete...." He took it in his hand with infinite love, gazed at it, his face radiant with bliss. "Some pearls are still missing here, for I have found none the right size. Once Saint Andrew addressed the cross of Golgotha, saying it was adorned with the limbs of Christ as with pearls. And pearls must adorn this humble simulacrum of that great wonder. Still, I have found it proper to set, here, over the very head of the Saviour, the most beautiful diamond you will ever see." His devout hands, his long white fingers, stroked the most precious parts of the sacred wood, or, rather, the sacred ivory, for this noble material had served to form the arms of the cross.

"As I take pleasure in all the beauties of this house of God, when the spell of the many-colored stones has torn me from outside concerns and a worthy meditation has led me to reflect, transferring that which is material to that which is immaterial, on the diversity of the sacred virtues, then I seem to find myself, so to speak, in a strange region of the universe, no longer completely enclosed in the mire of the earth or completely free in the purity of heaven. And it seems to me that, by the grace of God, I can be transported from this lower world to that higher world by anagoge...."

As he spoke, he turned his face to the nave. A shaft of light from above was illuminating his countenance, through a special benevolence of the daystar, and his hands, which he had extended in the form of a cross, caught up as he was in his fervor. "Every creature," he said, "visible or invisible, is a light, brought into being by the father of lights. This ivory, this onyx, but also the stone that surrounds us, are a light, because I perceive that they are good and beautiful, that they exist according to their own rules of proportion, that they differ in genus and species from all other genera and species, that they are defined by their own number, that they are true to their order, that they seek their specific place according to their weight. And the more these things are revealed to me, the more the matter I gaze on is by its nature precious, and the better illuminated is the divine power of creation, for if I must strive to grasp the sublimity of the cause, inaccessible in its fullness, through the sublimity of the effect, how much better am I told of the divine causality by an effect as wondrous as gold and diamond, if even dung or an insect can speak to me of it! And then, when I perceive in these stones such superior things, the soul weeps, moved to joy, and not through terrestrial vanity or love of riches, but through the purest love of the prime, uncaused cause."

"Truly this is the sweetest of theologies," William said, with perfect humility, and I thought he was using that insidious figure of speech that rhetors call irony, which must always be prefaced by the pronunciatio, representing its signal and its justification—something William never did. For which reason the abbot, more inclined to the use of figures of speech, took William literally and added, still in the power of his mystical transport, "It is the most immediate of the paths that put us in touch with the Almighty: theophanic matter."

William coughed politely. "Er...hm..." he said. This is what he did when he wanted to introduce a new subject. He managed to do it gracefully because it was his habit—and I believe this is typical of the men of his country—to begin every remark with long preliminary moans, as if starting the exposition of a completed thought cost him a great mental effort. Whereas, I am now convinced, the more groans he uttered before his declaration, the surer he was of the soundness of the proposition he was expressing.

"Eh...oh..." William continued. "We should talk of the meeting and the debate on poverty."

"Poverty..." the abbot said, still lost in thought, as if having a hard time coming down from that beautiful region of the universe to which his gems had transported him. "Ah, yes, the meeting..."

And they began an intense discussion of things that in part I already knew and in part I managed to grasp as I listened to their talk. As I said at the beginning of this faithful chronicle, it concerned the double quarrel that had set, on the one hand, the Emperor against the Pope, and, on the other, the Pope against the Franciscans, who in the Perugia chapter, though only after many years, had espoused the Spirituals' theories about the poverty of Christ; and it concerned the jumble that had been created as the Franciscans sided with the empire, a triangle of oppositions and alliances that had now been transformed into a square, thanks to the intervention, to me still very obscure, of the abbots of the order of Saint Benedict.

I never clearly grasped the reason why the Benedictine abbots had given refuge and protection to the Spiritual Franciscans, some time before their own order came to share their opinions to a certain extent. Because if the Spirituals preached the renunciation of all worldly goods, the abbots of my order—I had seen that very day the radiant confirmation—followed a path no less virtuous, though exactly the opposite. But I believe the abbots felt that excessive power for the Pope meant excessive power for the bishops and the cities, whereas my order had retained its power intact through the centuries precisely by opposing the secular clergy and the city merchants, setting itself as direct mediator between earth and heaven, and as adviser of sovereigns.

I had often heard repeated the motto according to which the people of God were divided into shepherds (namely, the clerics), dogs (that is, warriors), and sheep (the populace). But I later learned that this sentence can be rephrased in several ways. The Benedictines had often spoken, not of three orders, but of two great divisions, one involving the administration of earthly things and the other the administration of heavenly things. As far as earthly things went, there was a valid division into clergy, lay lords, and populace, but this tripartite division was dominated by the presence of the ordo monachorum, direct link between God's people and heaven, and the monks had no connection with those secular shepherds, the priests and bishops, ignorant and corrupt, now supine before the interests of the cities, where the sheep were no longer the good and faithful peasants but, rather, the merchants and artisans. The Benedictine order was not sorry that the governing of the simple should be entrusted to the secular clerics, provided it was the monks who established the definitive regulation of this government, the monks being in direct contact with the source of all earthly power, the empire, just as they were with the source of all heavenly power. This, I believe, is why many Benedictine abbots, to restore dignity to the empire against the government of the cities (bishops and merchants united), agreed to protect the Spiritual Franciscans, whose ideas they did not share but whose presence was useful to them, since it offered the empire good syllogisms against the overweening power of the Pope.

These were the reasons, I then deduced, why Abo was now preparing to collaborate with William, the Emperor's envoy, and to act as mediator between the Franciscan order and the papal throne. In fact, even in the violence of the dispute that so endangered the unity of the church, Michael of Cesena, several times called to Avignon by Pope John, was ultimately prepared to accept the invitation, because he did not want his order to place itself in irrevocable conflict with the Pontiff. As general of the Franciscans, he wanted at once to see their positions triumph and to obtain papal assent, not least because he surmised that without the Pope's agreement he would not be able to remain for long at the head of the order.

But many had assured him the Pope would be awaiting him in France to ensnare him, charge him with heresy, and bring him to trial. Therefore, they advised that Michael's appearance at Avignon should be preceded by negotiations. Marsilius had had a better idea: to send with Michael an imperial envoy who would present to the Pope the point of view of the Emperor's supporters. Not so much to convince old Cahors but to strengthen the position of Michael, who, as part of an imperial legation, would not then be such easy prey to papal vengeance.

This idea, however, had numerous disadvantages and could not be carried out immediately. Hence the idea of a preliminary meeting between the imperial legation and some envoys of the Pope, to essay their respective positions and to draw up the agreement for a further encounter at which the safety of the Italian visitors would be guaranteed. To organize this first meeting, William of Baskerville had been appointed. Later, he would present the imperial theologians' point of view at Avignon, if he deemed the journey possible without danger. A far-from-simple enterprise, because it was supposed that the Pope, who wanted Michael alone in order to be able to reduce him more readily to obedience, would send to Italy a mission with instructions to make the planned journey of the imperial envoys to his court a failure, as far as possible. William had acted till now with great ability. After long consultations with various Benedictine abbots (this was the reason for the many stops along our journey), he had chosen the abbey where we now were, precisely because the abbot was known to be devoted to the empire and yet, through his great diplomatic skill, not disliked by the papal court. Neutral territory, therefore, this abbey where the two groups could meet.

But the Pope's resistance was not exhausted. He knew that, once his legation was on the abbey's terrain, it would be subject to the abbot's jurisdiction; and since some of his envoys belonged to the secular clergy, he would not accept this control, claiming fears of an imperial plot. He had therefore made the condition that his envoys' safety be entrusted to a company of archers of the King of France, under the command of a person in the Pope's trust. I had vaguely listened as William discussed this with an ambassador of the Pope at Bobbio: it was a matter of defining the formula to prescribe the duties of this company—or, rather, defining what was meant by the guaranteeing of the safety of the papal legates. A formula proposed by the Avignonese had finally been accepted, for it seemed reasonable: the armed men and their officers would have jurisdiction "over all those who in any way made an attempt on the life of members of the papal delegation or tried to influence their behavior or judgment by acts of violence." Then the pact had seemed inspired by purely formal preoccupations. Now, after the recent events at the abbey, the abbot was uneasy, and he revealed his doubts to William. If the legation arrived at the abbey while the author of the two crimes was still unknown (and the following day the abbot's worries were to increase, because the crimes would increase to three), they would have to confess that within those walls someone in circulation was capable of influencing the judgment and behavior of the papal envoys with acts of violence.

Trying to conceal the crimes committed would be of no avail, because if anything further were to happen, the papal envoys would suspect a plot against them. And so there were only two solutions. Either William discovered the murderer before the arrival of the legation (and here the abbot stared hard at him as if silently reproaching him for not having resolved the matter yet) or else the Pope's envoy had to be informed frankly and his collaboration sought, to place the abbey under close surveillance during the course of the discussions. The abbot did not like this second solution, because it meant renouncing a part of his sovereignty and submitting his own monks to French control. But he could run no risks. William and the abbot were both vexed by the turn things were taking; however, they had few choices. They proposed, therefore, to come to a final decision during the next day. Meanwhile, they could only entrust themselves to divine mercy and to William's sagacity.

"I will do everything possible, Your Sublimity," William said. "But, on the other hand, I fail to see how the matter can really compromise the meeting. Even the papal envoy will understand that there is a difference between the act of a madman or a sanguinary, or perhaps only of a lost soul, and the grave problems that upright men will meet to discuss."

"You think so?" the abbot asked, looking hard at William. "Remember: the Avignonese know they are to meet Minorites, and therefore very dangerous persons, close to the Fraticelli and others even more demented than the Fraticelli, dangerous heretics who are stained with crimes"—here the abbot lowered his voice—"compared with which the events that have taken place here, horrible as they are, pale like mist in the sun."

"It is not the same thing!" William cried sharply. "You cannot put the Minorites of the Perugia chapter on the same level as some bands of heretics who have misunderstood the message of the Gospel, transforming the struggle against riches into a series of private vendettas or bloodthirsty follies...."

"It is not many years since, not many miles from here, one of those bands, as you call them, put to fire and the sword the estates of the Bishop of Vercelli and the mountains beyond Novara," the abbot said curtly.

"You speak of Fra Dolcino and the Apostles...."

"The Pseudo Apostles," the abbot corrected him. And once more I heard Fra Dolcino and the Pseudo Apostles mentioned, and once more in a circumspect tone, with almost a hint of terror.

"The Pseudo Apostles," William readily agreed. "But they had no connection with the Minorites...."

"...with whom they shared the same professed reverence for Joachim of Calabria," the abbot persisted, "and you can ask your brother Ubertino."

"I must point out to Your Sublimity that now he is a brother of your own order," William said, with a smile and a kind of bow, as if to compliment the abbot on the gain his order had made by receiving a man of such renown.

"I know, I know." The abbot smiled. "And you know with what fraternal care our order welcomed the Spirituals when they incurred the Pope's wrath. I am not speaking only of Ubertino, but also of many other, more humble brothers, of whom little is known, and of whom perhaps we should know more. Because it has happened that we accepted fugitives who presented themselves garbed in the habit of the Minorites, and afterward I learned that the various vicissitudes of their life had brought them, for a time, quite close to the Dolcinians...."

"Here, too?" William asked.

"Here, too. I am revealing to you something about which, to tell the truth, I know very little, and in any case not enough to pronounce accusations. But inasmuch as you are investigating the life of this abbey, it is best for you to know these things also. I will tell you, further, that on the basis of things I have heard or surmised, I suspect—mind you, only suspect—that there was a very dark moment in the life of our cellarer, who arrived here, in fact, two years ago, following the exodus of the Minorites."

"The cellarer? Remigio of Varagine a Dolcinian? He seems to me the mildest of creatures, and, for that matter, the least interested in Sister Poverty that I have ever seen..." William said.

"I can say nothing against him, and I make use of his good services, for which the whole community is also grateful to him. But I mention this to make you understand how easy it is to find connections between a friar of ours and a Fraticello."

"Once again your magnanimity is misplaced, if I may say so," William interjected. "We were talking about Dolcinians, not Fraticelli. And much can be said about the Dolcinians without anyone's really knowing who is being discussed, because there are many kinds. Still, they cannot be called sanguinary. At most they can be reproached for putting into practice without much consideration things that the Spirituals preached with greater temperance, animated by true love of God, and here I agree the borderline between one group and the other is very fine...."

"But the Fraticelli are heretics!" the abbot interrupted sharply. "They do not confine themselves to sustaining the poverty of Christ and the apostles, a doctrine that—though I cannot bring myself to share it—can be usefully opposed to the haughtiness of Avignon. The Fraticelli derive from that doctrine a practical syllogism: they infer a right to revolution, to looting, to the perversion of behavior."

"But which Fraticelli?"

"All, in general. You know they are stained with unmentionable crimes, they do not recognize matrimony, they deny hell, they commit sodomy, they embrace the Bogomil heresy of the ordo Bulgariae and the ordo Drygonthie...."

"Please," William said, "do not mix things that are separate! You speak as if the Fraticelli, Patarines, Waldensians, Catharists, and within these the Bogomils of Bulgaria and the heretics of Dragovitsa, were all the same thing!"

"They are," the abbot said sharply, "they are because they are heretics, and they are because they jeopardize the very order of the civilized world, as well as the order of the empire you seem to me to favor. A hundred or more years ago the followers of Arnold of Brescia set fire to the houses of the nobles and the cardinals, and these were the fruits of the Lombard heresy of the Patarines."

"Abo," William said, "you live in the isolation of this splendid and holy abbey, far from the wickedness of the world. Life in the cities is far more complex than you believe, and there are degrees, you know, also in error and in evil. Lot was much less a sinner than his fellow citizens who conceived foul thoughts also about the angels sent by God, and the betrayal of Peter was nothing compared with the betrayal of Judas: one, indeed, was forgiven, the other not. You cannot consider Patarines and Catharists the same thing. The Patarines were a movement to reform behavior within the laws of Holy Mother Church. They wanted always to improve the ecclesiastics' behavior."

"Maintaining that the sacraments should not be received from impure priests..."

"And they were mistaken, but it was their only error of doctrine. They never proposed to alter the law of God...."

"But the Patarine preaching of Arnold of Brescia, in

Rome, more than two hundred years ago, drove the mob of rustics to burn the houses of the nobles and the cardinals."

"Arnold tried to draw the magistrates of the city into his reform movement. They did not follow him, and he found support among the crowds of the poor and the outcast. He was not responsible for the violence and the anger with which they responded to his appeals for a less corrupt city."

"The city is always corrupt."

"The city is the place where today live the people of God, of whom you, we, are the shepherds. It is the place of scandal in which the rich prelates preach virtue to poor and hungry people. The Patarine disorders were born of this situation. They are sad, but not incomprehensible. The Catharists are something else. That is an Oriental heresy, outside the doctrine of the church. I don't know whether they really commit or have committed the crimes attributed to them. I know they reject matrimony, they deny hell. I wonder whether many acts they have not committed have been attributed to them only because of the ideas (surely unspeakable) they have upheld."

"And you tell me that the Catharists have not mingled with the Patarines, and that both are not simply two of the faces, the countless faces, of the same demoniacal phenomenon?"

"I say that many of these heresies, independently of the doctrines they assert, encounter success among the simple because they suggest to such people the possibility of a different life. I say that very often the simple do not know much about doctrine. I say that often hordes of simple people have confused Catharist preaching with that of the Patarines, and these together with that of the Spirituals. The life of the simple, Abo, is not illuminated by learning and by the lively sense of distinctions that makes us wise. And it is haunted by illness and poverty, tongue-tied by ignorance. Joining a heretical group, for many of them, is often only another way of shouting their own despair. You may burn a cardinal's house because you want to perfect the life of the clergy, but also because you believe that the hell he preaches does not exist. It is always done because on earth there does exist a hell, where lives the flock whose shepherds we no longer are. But you know very well that, just as they do not distinguish between the Bulgarian church and the followers of the priest Liprando, so often the imperial authorities and their supporters did not distinguish between Spirituals and heretics. Not infrequently, imperial forces, to combat their adversaries, encouraged Catharist tendencies among the populace. In my opinion they acted wrongly. But what I now know is that the same forces often, to rid themselves of these restless and dangerous and too 'simple' adversaries, attributed to one group the heresies of the others, and flung them all on the pyre. I have seen—I swear to you, Abo, I have seen with my own eyes—men of virtuous life, sincere followers of poverty and chastity, but enemies of the bishops, whom the bishops thrust into the hands of the secular arm, whether it was in the service of the empire or of the free cities, accusing these men of sexual promiscuity, sodomy, unspeakable practices— of which others, perhaps, but not they, had been guilty. The simple are meat for slaughter, to be used when they are useful in causing trouble for the opposing power, and to be sacrificed when they are no longer of use."

"Therefore," the abbot said, with obvious maliciousness, "were Fra Dolcino and his madmen, and Gherardo Segarelli and those evil murderers, wicked Catharists or virtuous Fraticelli, sodomite Bogomils or Patarine reformers? Will you tell me, William, you who know so much about heretics that you seem one of them, where the truth lies?"

"Nowhere, at times," William said, sadly.

"You see? You yourself can no longer distinguish

between one heretic and another. I at least have a rule. I know that heretics are those who endanger the order that sustains the people of God. And I defend the empire because it guarantees this order for me. I combat the Pope because he is handing the spiritual power over to the bishops of the cities, who are allied with the merchants and the corporations and will not be able to maintain this order. We have maintained it for centuries. And as for the heretics, I also have a rule, and it is summed up in the reply that Arnald Amalaricus, Bishop of Cîteaux, gave to those who asked him what to do with the citizens of Béziers: Kill them all, God will recognize His own."

William lowered his eyes and remained silent for a while. Then he said, "The city of Béziers was captured and our forces had no regard for dignity of sex or age, and almost twenty thousand people were put to the sword. When the massacre was complete, the city was sacked and burned."

"A holy war is nevertheless a war."

"For this reason perhaps there should not be holy wars. But what am I saying? I am here to defend the rights of Louis, who is also putting Italy to the sword. I, too, find myself caught in a game of strange alliances. Strange the alliance between Spirituals and the empire, and strange that of the empire with Marsilius, who seeks sovereignty for the people. And strange the alliance between the two of us, so different in our ideas and traditions. But we have two tasks in common: the success of the meeting and the discovery of a murderer. Let us try to proceed in peace."

The abbot held out his arms. "Give me the kiss of peace, Brother William. With a man of your knowledge I could argue endlessly about fine points of theology and morals. We must not give way, however, to the pleasure of disputation, as the masters of Paris do. You are right: we have an important task ahead of us, and we must proceed in agreement. But I have spoken of these things because I believe there is a connection. Do you understand? A possible connection—or, rather, a connection others can make—between the crimes that have occurred here and the theses of your brothers. This is why I have warned you, and this is why we must ward off every suspicion or insinuation on the part of the Avignonese."

"Am I not also to suppose Your Sublimity has suggested to me a line for my inquiry? Do you believe that the source of the recent events can be found in some obscure story dating back to the heretical past of one of the monks?"

The abbot was silent for a few moments, looking at William but allowing no expression to be read on his face. Then he said: "In this sad affair you are the inquisitor. It is your task to be suspicious, even to risk unjust suspicion. Here I am only the general father. And, I will add, if I knew that the past of one of my monks lent itself to well-founded suspicion, I would myself already have taken care to uproot the unhealthy plant. What I know, you know. What I do not know should properly be brought to light by your wisdom." He nodded to us and left the church.

"The story is becoming more complicated, dear Adso," William said, frowning. "We pursue a manuscript, we become interested in the diatribes of some overcurious monks and in the actions of other, overlustful ones, and now, more and more insistently, an entirely different trail emerges. The cellarer, then ... And with the cellarer that strange animal Salvatore also arrived here.... But now we must go and rest, because we plan to stay awake during the night."

"Then you still mean to enter the library tonight? You are not going to abandon that first trail?"

"Not at all. Anyway, who says the two trails are separate? And finally, this business of the cellarer could merely be a suspicion of the abbot's."

He started toward the pilgrims' hospice. On reaching the threshold, he stopped and spoke, as if continuing his earlier remarks.

"After all, the abbot asked me to investigate Adelmo's death when he thought that something unhealthy was going on among his young monks. But now that the death of Venantius arouses other suspicions, perhaps the abbot has sensed that the key to the mystery lies in the library, and there he does not wish any investigating. So he offers me the suggestion of the cellarer, to distract my attention from the Aedificium. . . ."

"But why would he not want—"

"Don't ask too many questions. The abbot told me at the beginning that the library was not to be touched. He must have his own good reasons. It could be that he is involved in some matter he thought unrelated to Adelmo's death, and now he realizes the scandal is spreading and could also touch him. And he doesn't want the truth to be discovered, or at least he doesn't want me to be the one who discovers it. . . ."

"Then we are living in a place abandoned by God," I said, disheartened.

"Have you found any places where God would have felt at home?" William asked me, looking down from his great height.

Then he sent me to rest. As I lay on my pallet, I concluded that my father should not have sent me out into the world, which was more complicated than I had thought. I was learning too many things.

"Salva me ab ore leonis," I prayed as I fell asleep.

After Vespers

In which, though the chapter is short, old Alinardo says very interesting things about the labyrinth and about the way to enter it.

I woke when it was almost tolling the hour for the evening meal. I felt dull and somnolent, for daytime sleep is like the sin of the flesh: the more you have the more you want, and yet you feel unhappy, sated and unsated at the same time. William was not in his cell; obviously he had risen much earlier. I found him, after a brief search, coming out of the Aedificium. He told me he had been in the scriptorium, leafing through the catalogue and observing the monks at work, while trying to approach Venantius's desk and resume his inspection. But for one reason or another, each monk seemed bent on keeping him from searching among those papers. First Malachi had come over to him, to show him some precious illuminations. Then Benno had kept him busy on trifling pretexts. Still later, when he had bent over to resume his examination, Berengar had begun hovering around him, offering his collaboration.

Finally, seeing that my master appeared seriously

determined to look into Venantius's things, Malachi told him outright that, before rummaging among the dead man's papers, he ought perhaps to obtain the abbot's authorization; that he himself, even though he was the librarian, had refrained, out of respect and discipline, from looking; and that in any case, as William had requested, no one had approached that desk, and no one would approach it until the abbot gave instructions. William realized it was not worth engaging in a test of strength with Malachi, though all that stir and those fears about Venantius's papers had of course increased his desire to become acquainted with them. But he was so determined to get back in there that night, though he still did not know how, that he decided not to create incidents. He was harboring, however, thoughts of retaliation, which, if they had not been inspired as they were by a thirst for truth, would have seemed very stubborn and perhaps reprehensible.

Before entering the refectory, we took another little walk in the cloister, to dispel the mists of sleep in the cold evening air. Some monks were still walking there in meditation. In the garden opening off the cloister we glimpsed old Alinardo of Grottaferrata, who, by now feeble of body, spent a great part of his day among the trees, when he was not in church praying. He seemed not to feel the cold, and he was sitting in the outer porch.

William spoke a few words of greeting to him, and the old man seemed happy that someone should spend time with him.

"A peaceful day," William said.

"By the grace of God," the old man answered.

"Peaceful in the heavens, but grim on earth. Did you know Venantius well?"

"Venantius who?" the old man said. Then a light flashed in his eyes. "Ah, the dead boy. The beast is roaming about the abbey...."

"What beast?"

"The great beast that comes from the sea...Seven heads and ten horns and upon his horns ten crowns and upon his heads three names of blasphemy. The beast like unto a leopard, with the feet of a bear, and the mouth of a lion...I have seen him."

"Where have you seen him? In the library?"

"Library? Why there? I have not gone to the scriptorium for years and I have never seen the library. No one goes to the library. I knew those who did go up to the library...."

"Who? Malachi? Berengar?"

"Oh, no..." the old man said, chuckling. "Before. The librarian who came before Malachi, many years ago..."

"Who was that?"

"I do not remember; he died when Malachi was still young. And the one who came before Malachi's master, and was a young assistant librarian when I was young ...But I never set foot in the library. Labyrinth..."

"The library is a labyrinth?"

"Hunc mundum tipice labyrinthus denotat ille," the old man recited, absently. "Intranti largus, redeunti sed nimis artus. The library is a great labyrinth, sign of the labyrinth of the world. You enter and you do not know whether you will come out. You must not transgress the pillars of Hercules...."

"So you don't know how one enters the library when the Aedificium doors are closed?"

"Oh, yes." The old man laughed. "Many know. You go by way of the ossarium. You can go through the ossarium, but you do not want to go through the ossarium. The dead monks keep watch."

"Those dead monks who keep watch—they are not those who move at night through the library with a lamp?"

"With a lamp?" The old man seemed amazed. "I have never heard this story. The dead monks stay in the ossarium, the bones drop gradually from the cemetery

181

and collect there, to guard the passage. Have you never seen the altar of the chapel that leads to the ossarium?"

"It is the third on the left, after the transept, is it not?"

"The third? Perhaps. It is the one whose altar stone is carved with a thousand skeletons. The fourth skull on the right: press the eyes...and you are in the ossarium. But do not go there; I have never gone. The abbot does not wish it."

"And the beast? Where did you see the beast?"

"The beast? Ah, the Antichrist...He is about to come, the millennium is past; we await him...."

"But the millennium was three hundred years ago, and he did not come then...."

"The Antichrist does not come after a thousand years have passed. When the thousand years have passed, the reign of the just begins; then comes the Antichrist, to confound the just, and then there will be the final battle...."

"But the just will reign for a thousand years," William said. "Or else they reigned from the death of Christ to the end of the first millennium, and so the Antichrist should have come then; or else the just have not yet reigned, and the Antichrist is still far off."

"The millennium is not calculated from the death of Christ but from the donation of Constantine, three centuries later. Now it is a thousand years...."

"So the reign of the just is ending?"

"I do not know....I do not know any more. I am tired. The calculation is difficult. Beatus of Liébana made it; ask Jorge, he is young, he remembers well.... But the time is ripe. Did you not hear the seven trumpets?"

"Why the seven trumpets?"

"Did you not hear how the other boy died, the illuminator? The first angel sounded the first trumpet, and hail and fire fell mingled with blood. And the second angel sounded the second trumpet, and the third part of the sea became blood....Did the second boy not die in the sea of blood? Watch out for the third trumpet! The third part of the creatures in the sea will die. God punishes us. The world all around the abbey is rank with heresy; they tell me that on the throne of Rome there is a perverse pope who uses hosts for practices of necromancy, and feeds them to his morays.... And in our midst someone has violated the ban, has broken the seals of the labyrinth...."

"Who told you that?"

"I heard it. All were whispering that sin has entered the abbey. Do you have any chickpeas?"

The question, addressed to me, surprised me. "No, I have no chickpeas," I said, confused.

"Next time, bring me some chickpeas. I hold them in my mouth—you see my poor toothless mouth?—until they are soft. They stimulate saliva, aqua fons vitae. Will you bring me some chickpeas tomorrow?"

"Tomorrow I will bring you some chickpeas," I said to him. But he had dozed off. We left him and went to the refectory.

COMPLINE

In which the Aedificium is entered, a mysterious visitor is discovered, a secret message with necromantic signs is found, and also a book is found, but then promptly vanishes, to be sought through many subsequent chapters; nor is the theft of William's precious lenses the last of the vicissitudes.

The supper was joyless and silent. It had been just over twelve hours since the discovery of Venantius's corpse. All the others stole glimpses at his empty place at table. When it was the hour for compline, the procession that marched into the choir seemed a funeral cortège. We followed the office standing in the nave and keeping an eye on the third chapel. The light was scant, and when we saw Malachi emerge from the darkness to reach his stall, we could not tell exactly where he had come from. We moved into the shadows, hiding in the side nave, so that no one would see us stay behind when the office was over. Under my scapular I had the lamp I had purloined in the kitchen during supper. We would light it later at the great bronze tripod that burned all night. I had procured a new wick and ample oil. We would have light for a long time.

I was too excited about our imminent venture to pay attention to the service, which ended almost without my noticing. The monks lowered their cowls over their faces and slowly filed out, to go to their cells. The church remained deserted, illuminated by the glow of the tripod.

"Now," William said, "to work."

We approached the third chapel. The base of the altar was really like an ossarium, a series of skulls with deep hollow eyesockets, which filled those who looked at them with terror, set on a pile of what, in the admirable relief, appeared to be tibias. William repeated in a low voice the words he had heard from Alinardo (fourth skull on the right, press the eyes). He stuck his fingers into the sockets of that fleshless face, and at once we heard a kind of hoarse creak. The altar moved, turning on a hidden pivot, allowing a glimpse of a dark aperture. As I shed light on it with my raised lamp, we made out some damp steps. We decided to go down them, after debating whether to close off the passage again behind us. Better not, William said; we did not know whether we would be able to reopen it afterward. And as for the risk of being discovered, if anyone came at that hour to operate the same mechanism, that meant he knew how to enter, and a closed passage would not deter him.

We descended perhaps a dozen steps and came into a corridor on whose sides there were some horizontal niches, such as I was later to see in many catacombs. But now I was entering an ossarium for the first time, and I was very much afraid. The monks' bones had been collected there over the centuries, dug from the earth and piled in the niches with no attempt to recompose the forms of their bodies. Some niches had only tiny bones, others only skulls, neatly arranged in a kind of pyramid, so that one would not roll over another; and it was a truly terrifying sight, especially in the play of shadows the lamp created as we walked on. In one niche I saw only hands, many hands, now irrevocably interlaced in a tangle of dead fingers. I let out a cry in that place of the dead, for a moment sensing some presence above, a squeaking, a rapid movement in the dark.

"Mice," William said, to reassure me.

"What are mice doing here?"

"Passing through, like us: because the ossarium leads to the Aedificium, and then to the kitchen. And to the tasty books of the library. And now you understand why Malachi's face is so austere. His duties oblige him to come through here twice daily, morning and evening. Truly he has nothing to laugh about."

"But why doesn't the Gospel ever say that Christ laughed?" I asked, for no good reason. "Is Jorge right?"

"Legions of scholars have wondered whether Christ laughed. The question doesn't interest me much. I believe he never laughed, because, omniscient as the son of God had to be, he knew how we Christians would behave. But here we are."

And, in fact, the corridor was ending, thank God; new steps began. After climbing them, we would have only to push an ironclad wooden door and we would find ourselves behind the fireplace of the kitchen, just below the circular staircase leading to the scriptorium. As we went up, we thought we heard a noise above us.

We remained a moment in silence; then I said, "It's impossible. No one came in before us. . . ."

"Assuming this is the only way into the Aedificium. In centuries past this was a fortress, and it must have more secret entrances than we know of. We'll go up slowly. But we have little choice. If we put out the light we can't see where we are going; if we leave it burning we give anyone upstairs the alarm. Our only hope is that if someone really is there, he will be afraid of us."

We reached the scriptorium, emerging from the south tower. Venantius's desk was directly opposite. The room was so vast that, as we moved, we illuminated only a few yards of wall at a time. We hoped no one was in the court, to see the light through the windows. The desk appeared to be in order, but William bent at once to examine the pages on the shelf below, and he cried out in dismay.

"Is something missing?" I asked.

"Today I saw two books here, one of them in Greek. And that's the one missing. Somebody has taken it, and in great haste, because one page fell on the floor here."

"But the desk was watched...."

"Of course. Perhaps somebody grabbed it just a short while ago. Perhaps he's still here." He turned toward the shadows and his voice echoed among the columns: "If you are here, beware!" It seemed to me a good idea: as William had said before, it is always better when the person who frightens us is also afraid of us.

William set down the page he had found under the desk and bent his face toward it. He asked me for more light. I held the lamp closer and saw a page, the first half of it blank, the second covered with tiny characters whose origin I recognized with some difficulty.

"Is it Greek?" I asked.

"Yes, but I don't understand clearly." He took his lenses from his habit and set them firmly astride his nose, then bent his head again.

"It's Greek, written in a very fine hand, and yet in a disorderly way. Even with my lenses I have trouble reading it. I need still more light. Come closer...."

He had picked up the sheet of parchment, holding it to his face; and instead of stepping behind him and holding the lamp high over his head, I foolishly stood directly in front of him. He asked me to move aside, and as I did, I grazed the back of the page with the flame. William pushed me away, asking me whether I wanted to burn the manuscript for him. Then he cried out. I saw clearly that some vague signs, in a yellow-brown color, had appeared on the upper part of the page. William made me give him the lamp and moved it behind the page, holding the flame fairly close to the surface of the parchment, which he heated without setting it afire. Slowly, as if an invisible hand were writing "Mane, Tekel, Peres," I saw some marks emerge one by one on the white side of the sheet as William moved the lamp, and as the smoke that rose from the top of the flame blackened the recto; the marks did not resemble those of any alphabet, except that of necromancers.

"Fantastic!" William said. "More and more interesting!" He looked around. "But it would be better not to expose this discovery to the tricks of our mysterious companion, if he is still here...." He took off his lenses, set them on the desk, then carefully rolled up the parchment and hid it inside his habit. Still amazed by this sequence of events, which were nothing if not miraculous, I was about to ask further explanations when all of a sudden a sharp sound distracted us. It came from the foot of the east stairway, leading to the library.

"Our man is there! After him!" William shouted, and we flung ourselves in that direction, he moving faster, I more slowly, for I was carrying the lamp. I heard the clatter of someone stumbling and falling. I ran, and found William at the foot of the steps, observing a heavy volume, its binding reinforced with metal studs. At that same moment we heard another noise, in the direction from which we had come. "Fool that I am!" William cried. "Hurry! To Venantius's desk!"

I understood: somebody, from the shadows behind us, had thrown the volume to send us far away.

Once again William was faster than I and reached the desk first. Following him, I glimpsed among the columns a fleeing shadow, taking the stairway of the west tower.

Seized with warlike ardor, I thrust the lamp into William's hand and dashed blindly off toward the stairs where the fugitive had descended. At that moment I felt like a soldier of Christ fighting all the legions of hell, and I burned with the desire to lay my hands on the stranger, to turn him over to my master. I tumbled down almost the whole stairway, tripping over the hem of my habit (that was the only moment of my life, I swear, when I regretted having entered a monastic order!); but at that same instant—and it was the thought of an instant—I consoled myself with the idea that my adversary was suffering the same impediment. And, further, if he had taken the book, he would have his hands full. From behind the bread oven I almost dived into the kitchen, and in the starry light that faintly illuminated the vast entrance, I saw the shadow I was pursuing as it slipped past the refectory door, then pulled this shut. I rushed toward the door, I labored a few seconds opening it, entered, looked around, and saw no one. The outside door was still barred. I turned. Shadows and silence. I noticed a glow advancing from the kitchen and I flattened myself against a wall. On the threshold of the passage between the two rooms a figure appeared, illuminated by a lamp. I cried out. It was William.

"Nobody around? I foresaw that. He didn't go out through a door? He didn't take the passage through the ossarium?"

"No, he went out through here, but I don't know where!"

"I told you: there are other passages, and it's useless for us to look for them. Perhaps our man is emerging at some distant spot. And with him my lenses."

"Your lenses?"

"Yes. Our friend could not take the page away from me, but with great presence of mind, as he rushed past, he snatched my glasses from the desk."

"Why?"

"Because he is no fool. He heard me speak of these notes, he realized they were important, he assumed that without my lenses I would be unable to decipher them, and he knows for sure that I would not entrust them to anyone else. In fact, now it's as if I didn't have them."

"But how did he know about your lenses?"

"Come, come. Apart from the fact that we spoke about them yesterday with the master glazier, this morning in the scriptorium I put them on to search among Venantius's papers. So there are many people who could know how valuable those objects are to me. Actually, I could read a normal manuscript, but not this one." And he was again unrolling the mysterious parchment. "The part in Greek is written too fine and the upper part is too hazy...."

He showed me the mysterious signs that had appeared as if by magic in the heat of the flame. "Venantius wanted to conceal an important secret, and he used one of those inks that leave no trace when written but reappear when warmed. Or else he used lemon juice. But since I don't know what substance he used and the signs could disappear again: quickly, you who have good eyes, copy them at once as faithfully as you can, perhaps enlarging them a bit." And so I did, without knowing what I was copying. It was a series of four or five lines, really necromantic, and I will reproduce only the very first signs, to give the reader an idea of the puzzle I had before my eyes:

$$\text{ʒ○ɤ̨℧,○Ʋ⫤☿ ♂ɤ⊙ɤʒ ○̇○̇ɤ̨,ʃ♁○̇○}$$

When I had finished copying, William looked, unfortunately without lenses, holding my tablet at some distance from his nose. "It is unquestionably a secret alphabet that will have to be deciphered," he said. "The signs are badly drawn, and perhaps you copied them worse, but it is certainly a zodiacal alphabet. You see? In the first line we have"—he held the page away from him again and narrowed his eyes with an effort of concentration—"Sagittarius, Sun, Mercury, Scorpio...."

"And what do they mean?"

"If Venantius had been ingenuous he would have used the most common zodiacal alphabet: *A* equals Sun, *B* equals Jupiter.... The first line would then read ... Try transcribing this: RAIQASVL...." He broke off. "No, it means nothing, and Venantius was not ingenuous. He reformulated the alphabet according to another key. I shall have to discover it."

"Is it possible?" I asked, awed.

"Yes, if you know a bit of the learning of the Arabs. The best treatises on cryptography are the work of infidel scholars, and at Oxford I was able to have some read to me. Bacon was right in saying that the conquest of learning is achieved through the knowledge of languages. Abu Bakr Ahmad ben Ali ben Washiyya an-Nabati wrote centuries ago a *Book of the Frenzied Desire of the Devout to Learn the Riddles of Ancient Writings*, and he expounded many rules for composing and deciphering mysterious alphabets, useful for magic practices but also for the correspondence between armies, or between a king and his envoys. I have seen other Arab books that list a series of quite ingenious devices. For example, you can substitute one letter for another, you can write a word backward, you can put the letters in reverse order, using only every other one; and then starting over again, you can, as in this case, replace letters with zodiacal signs, but attributing to the hidden letters their numerical value, and then, according to another alphabet, convert the numbers into other letters...."

"And which of these systems can Venantius have used?"

"We would have to test them all, and others besides. But the first rule in deciphering a message is to guess what it means."

"But then it's unnecessary to decipher it!" I laughed.

"Not exactly. Some hypotheses can be formed on the

possible first words of the message, and then you see whether the rule you infer from them can apply to the rest of the text. For example, here Venantius has certainly noted down the key for penetrating the finis Africae. If I try thinking that the message is about this, then I am suddenly enlightened by a rhythm.... Try looking at the first three words, not considering the letters, but the number of the signs... IIIIIIII IIIII IIIIIII.... Now try dividing them into syllables of at least two signs each, and recite aloud: ta-ta-ta, ta-ta, ta-ta-ta.... Doesn't anything come to your mind?"

"No."

"To mine, yes. 'Secretum finis Africae'... But if this were correct, then the last word should have the same first and sixth letter, and so it does, in fact: the symbol of the Earth is there twice. And the first letter of the first word, the *S*, should be the same as the last of the second: and, sure enough, the sign of the Virgin is repeated. Perhaps this is the right track. But it could also be just a series of coincidences. A rule of correspondence has to be found...."

"Found where?"

"In our heads. Invent it. And then see whether it is the right one. But with one test and another, the game could cost me a whole day. No more than that because—remember this—there is no secret writing that cannot be deciphered with a bit of patience. But now we risk losing time, and we want to visit the library. Especially since, without lenses, I will never be able to read the second part of the message, and you cannot help me because these signs, to your eyes..."

"Graecum est, non legitur," I finished his sentence, humiliated. "It is Greek to me."

"Exactly; and you see that Bacon was right. Study! But we must not lose heart. We'll put away the parchment and your notes, and we'll go up to the library. Because tonight not even ten infernal legions will succeed in keeping us out."

I blessed myself. "But who can he have been, the man who was here ahead of us? Benno?"

"Benno was burning with the desire to know what there was among Venantius's papers, but I can't see him as one with the courage to enter the Aedificium at night."

"Berengar, then? Or Malachi?"

"Berengar seems to me to have the courage to do such things. And, after all, he shares responsibility for the library. He is consumed by remorse at having betrayed some secret of it; he thought Venantius had taken that book, and perhaps he wanted to return it to the place from which it comes. He wasn't able to go upstairs, and now he is hiding the volume somewhere."

"But it could also be Malachi, for the same motives."

"I would say no. Malachi had all the time he wanted to search Venantius's desk when he remained alone to shut up the Aedificium. I knew that very well, but there was no way to avoid it. Now we know he didn't do it. And if you think carefully, we have no reason to think Malachi knows Venantius had entered the library and removed something. Berengar and Benno know this, and you and I know it. After Adelmo's confession, Jorge may know it, but he was surely not the man who was rushing so furiously down the circular staircase. . . ."

"Then either Berengar or Benno . . ."

"And why not Pacificus of Tivoli or another of the monks we saw here today? Or Nicholas the glazier, who knows about my glasses? Or that odd character Salvatore, who they have told us roams around at night on God knows what errands? We must take care not to restrict the field of suspects just because Benno's revelations have oriented us in a single direction; perhaps Benno wanted to mislead us."

"But he seemed sincere to you."

"Certainly. But remember that the first duty of a

good inquisitor is to suspect especially those who seem sincere to him."

"A nasty job, being an inquisitor."

"That's why I gave it up. And as you say, I am forced to resume it. But come now: to the library."

NIGHT

In which the labyrinth is finally broached, and the intruders have strange visions and, as happens in labyrinths, lose their way.

We climbed back up to the scriptorium, this time by the east staircase, which rose also to the forbidden floor. Holding the light high before us, I thought of Alinardo's words about the labyrinth, and I expected frightful things.

I was surprised, as we emerged into the place we should not have entered, at finding myself in a not very large room with seven sides, windowless, where there reigned—as, for that matter, throughout the whole floor—a strong odor of stagnation or mold. Nothing terrifying.

The room, as I said, had seven walls, but only four of them had an opening, a passage flanked by two little columns set in the wall; the opening was fairly wide, surmounted by a round-headed arch. Against the blind walls stood huge cases, laden with books neatly arranged. Each case bore a scroll with a number, and so did each individual shelf; obviously the same numbers we had seen in the catalogue. In the midst of the room was a table, also covered with books. On all the volumes lay a fairly light coat of dust, sign that the books were cleaned with some frequency. Nor was there dirt of any kind on the floor. Above one of the archways, a big scroll, painted on the wall, bore the words "Apocalypsis Iesu Christi." It did not seem faded, even though the lettering was ancient. We noticed afterward, also in the other rooms, that these scrolls were actually carved in the stone, cut fairly deeply, and the depressions had subsequently been filled with color, as painters do in frescoing churches.

We passed through one of the openings. We found ourselves in another room, where there was a window that, in place of glass panes, had slabs of alabaster, with two blind walls and one aperture, like the one we had just come through. It opened into another room, which also had two blind walls, another with a window, and another passage that opened opposite us. In these two rooms, the two scrolls were similar in form to the first we had seen, but with different words. The scroll in the first room said "Super thronos viginti quatuor," and the one in the second room, "Nomen illi mors." For the rest, even though the two rooms were smaller than the one by which we had entered the library (actually, that one was heptagonal, these two rectangular), the furnishing was the same.

We entered the third room. It was bare of books and had no scroll. Under the window, a stone altar. There were three doors: the one by which we had entered; another, leading to the heptagonal room already visited; and a third, which led to a new room, no different from the others except for the scroll, which said "Obscuratus est sol et aer," announcing the growing darkness of sun and air. From here you went into a new room, whose scroll said "Facta est grando et ignis," threatening turmoil and fire. This room was without other apertures: once you reached it, you could proceed no farther and had to turn back.

"Let us think about this," William said. "Five quadrangular or vaguely trapezoidal rooms, each with one window, arranged around a windowless heptagonal room to which the stairway leads. It seems elementary to me. We are in the east tower. From the outside each tower shows five windows and five sides. It works out. The empty room is the one facing east, the same direction as the choir of the church; the dawn sun illuminates the altar, which I find right and pious. The only clever idea, it seems to me, is the use of alabaster slabs. In the daytime they admit a fine light, and at night not even the moon's rays can penetrate. Now let's see where the other two doors of the heptagonal room lead."

My master was mistaken, and the builders of the library had been shrewder than we thought. I cannot explain clearly what happened, but as we left the tower room, the order of the rooms became more confused. Some had two doorways, others three. All had one window each, even those we entered from a windowed room, thinking we were heading toward the interior of the Aedificium. Each had always the same kind of cases and tables; the books arrayed in neat order seemed all the same and certainly did not help us to recognize our location at a glance. We tried to orient ourselves by the scrolls. Once we crossed a room in which was written "In diebus illis," "In those days," and after some roaming we thought we had come back to it. But we remembered that the door opposite the window led into a room whose scroll said "Primogenitus mortuorum," "The firstborn of the dead," whereas now we came upon another that again said "Apocalypsis Iesu Christi," though it was not the heptagonal room from which we had set out. This fact convinced us that sometimes the scrolls repeated the same words in different rooms. We found two rooms with "Apocalypsis" one after the other, and, immediately following them, one with "Cecidit de coelo stella magna," "A great star fell from the heavens."

The source of the phrases on the scrolls was obvious—

they were verses from the Apocalypse of John—but it was not at all clear why they were painted on the walls or what logic was behind their arrangement. To increase our confusion, we discovered that some scrolls, not many, were colored red instead of black.

At a certain point we found ourselves again in the original heptagonal room (easily identified because the stairwell began there), and we resumed moving toward our right, trying to go straight from room to room. We went through three rooms and then found ourselves facing a blank wall. The only opening led into a new room that had only one other aperture, which we went through, and then, after another four rooms, we found ourselves again facing a wall. We returned to the previous room, which had two exits, took the one we had not tried before, went into a new room, and then found ourselves back in the heptagonal room of the outset.

"What was the name of the last room, the one where we began retracing our steps?" William asked.

I strained my memory and I had a vision of a white horse: "Equus albus."

"Good. Let's find it again." And it was easy. From there, if we did not want to turn back as we had before, we could only pass through the room called "Gratia vobis et pax," and from there, on the right, we thought we found a new passage, which did not take us back. Actually we again came upon "In diebus illis" and "Primogenitus mortuorum" (were they the rooms of a few moments earlier?); then finally we came to a room that we did not seem to have visited before: "Tertia pars terrae combusta est." But even when we had learned that a third of the earth had been burned up, we still did not know what our position was with respect to the east tower.

Holding the lamp in front of me, I ventured into the next rooms. A giant of threatening dimensions, a swaying and fluttering form came toward me, like a ghost.

"A devil!" I cried and almost dropped the lamp as I wheeled around and took refuge in William's arms. He seized the lamp from my hands and, thrusting me aside, stepped forward with a decisiveness that to me seemed sublime. He also saw something, because he brusquely stepped back. Then he leaned forward again and raised the lamp. He burst out laughing.

"Really ingenious. A mirror!"

"A mirror?"

"Yes, my bold warrior. You flung yourself so courageously on a real enemy a short while ago in the scriptorium, and now you are frightened by your own image. A mirror that reflects your image, enlarged and distorted."

He took me by the hand and led me up to the wall facing the entrance to the room. On a corrugated sheet of glass, now that the light illuminated it more closely, I saw our two images, grotesquely misshapen, changing form and height as we moved closer or stepped back.

"You must read some treatise on optics," William said, amused, "as the creators of the library surely did. The best ones are by the Arabs. Alhazen wrote a treatise, *De aspectibus,* in which, with precise geometrical demonstrations, he spoke of the power of mirrors, some of which, depending on how their surface is gauged, can enlarge the tiniest things (what else are my lenses?), while others make images appear upside down, or oblique, or show two objects in the place of one, and four in place of two. Still others, like this one, turn a dwarf into a giant or a giant into a dwarf."

"Lord Jesus!" I exclaimed. "Are these, then, the visions some say they have had in the library?"

"Perhaps. A really clever idea." He read the scroll on the wall, over the mirror: "Super thronos viginti quatuor." "'The twenty-four elders upon their seats.' We have seen this inscription before, but it was a room without any mirror. This one, moreover, has no windows, and yet it is not heptagonal. Where are we?" He looked around and went over to a case. "Adso, without those wondrous oculi ad legendum I cannot figure out what is written on these books. Read me some titles."

I picked out a book at random. "Master, it is not written!"

"What do you mean? I can see it is written. What do you read?"

"I am not reading. These are not letters of the alphabet, and it is not Greek. I would recognize it. They look like worms, snakes, fly dung...."

"Ah, it's Arabic. Are there others like it?"

"Yes, several. But here is one in Latin, thank God. Al... Al-Kuwarizmi, *Tabulae*."

"The astronomical tables of Al-Kuwarizmi, translated by Adelard of Bath! A very rare work! Continue."

"Isa ibn-Ali, *De oculis;* Alkindi, *De radiis stellatis*..."

"Now look on the table."

I opened a great volume lying on the table, a *De bestiis*. I happened on a delicately illuminated page where a very beautiful unicorn was depicted.

"Beautifully made," William commented, able to see the illustrations well. "And that?"

I read: *"Liber monstrorum de diversis generibus.* This also has beautiful images, but they seem older to me."

William bent his face to the text. "Illuminated by Irish monks, at least five centuries ago. The unicorn book, on the other hand, is much more recent; it seems to me made in the French fashion." Once again I admired my master's erudition. We entered the next room and crossed the four rooms after it, all with windows, and all filled with volumes in unknown languages, in addition to some texts of occult sciences. Then we came to a wall, which forced us to turn back, because the last five rooms opened one into the other, with no other egress possible.

"To judge by the angles of the walls, I would say we are in the pentagon of another tower," William said, "but there is no central heptagonal room. Perhaps we are mistaken."

"But what about the windows?" I asked. "How can there be so many windows? It is impossible for all the rooms to overlook the outside."

"You're forgetting the central well. Many of the windows we have seen overlook the octagon, the well. If it were day, the difference in light would tell us which are external windows and which internal, and perhaps would even reveal to us a room's position with respect to the sun. But after dusk no difference is perceptible. Let's go back."

We returned to the room with the mirror and headed for the third doorway, which we thought we had not gone through previously. We saw before us a sequence of three or four rooms, and toward the last we noticed a glow.

"Someone's there!" I exclaimed in a stifled voice.

"If so, he has already seen our light," William said, nevertheless shielding the flame with his hand. We hesitated a moment or two. The glow continued to flicker slightly, but without growing stronger or weaker.

"Perhaps it is only a lamp," William said, "set here to convince the monks that the library is inhabited by the souls of the dead. But we must find out. You stay here, and keep covering the light. I'll go ahead cautiously."

Still ashamed at the sorry figure I had cut before the mirror, I wanted to redeem myself in William's eyes. "No, I'll go," I said. "You stay here. I'll proceed cautiously. I am smaller and lighter. As soon as I've made sure there is no risk, I'll call you."

And so I did. I proceeded through three rooms, sticking close to the walls, light as a cat (or as a novice descending into the kitchen to steal cheese from the larder: an enterprise in which I excelled at Melk). I came to the threshold of the room from which the glow, quite faint, was coming. I slipped along the wall to a column that served as the right jamb, and I peered into the room. No one was there. A kind of lamp was set on the table, lighted, and it was smoking, flickering. It was not a lamp like ours: it seemed, rather, an uncovered thurible. It had no flame, but a light ash smoldered, burning something. I plucked up my courage and entered. On the table beside the thurible, a brightly colored book was lying open. I approached and saw four strips of different colors on the page: yellow, cinnabar, turquoise, and burnt sienna. A beast was set there, horrible to see, a great dragon with ten heads, dragging after him the stars of the sky and with his tail making them fall to earth. And suddenly I saw the dragon multiply, and the scales of his hide become a kind of forest of glittering shards that came off the page and took to circling around my head. I flung my head back and I saw the ceiling of the room bend and press down toward me, then I heard something like the hiss of a thousand serpents, but not frightening, almost seductive, and a woman appeared, bathed in light, and put her face to mine, breathing on me. I thrust her away with outstretched hands, and my hands seemed to touch the books in the case opposite, or to grow out of all proportion. I no longer realized where I was, where the earth was, and where the sky. In the center of the room I saw Berengar staring at me with a hateful smile, oozing lust. I covered my face with my hands and my hands seemed the claws of a toad, slimy and webbed. I cried out, I believe; there was an acid taste in my mouth; I plunged into infinite darkness, which seemed to yawn wider and wider beneath me; and then I knew nothing further.

I woke again after a time I thought was centuries, hearing some blows pounding in my head. I was stretched out on the floor and William was slapping me on the cheeks. I was no longer in that room, and before my eyes was a scroll that said "Requiescant a laboribus suis," "May they rest from their labors."

"Come, come, Adso," William was whispering to me. "There's nothing...."

"Everything..." I said, still delirious. "Over there, the beast..."

"No beast. I found you raving underneath a table with a beautiful Mozarabic apocalypse on it, opened to the page of the *mulier amicta sole* confronting the dragon. But I realized from the odor that you had inhaled something dangerous and I carried you away immediately. My head also aches."

"But what did I see?"

"You saw nothing. The fact is that some substances capable of inducing visions were burning there. I recognized the smell: it is an Arab stuff, perhaps the same that the Old Man of the Mountain gave his assassins to breathe before sending them off on their missions. And so we have explained the mystery of the visions. Someone puts magic herbs there during the night to convince importunate visitors that the library is guarded by diabolical presences. What did you experience, by the way?"

In confusion, as best I could recall, I told him of my vision, and William laughed: "For half of it you were developing what you had glimpsed in the book, and for the other half you let your desires and your fears speak out. This is the operation certain herbs set in action. Tomorrow we must talk about it with Severinus; I believe he knows more than he wants us to believe. They are herbs, only herbs, requiring none of those necromantic preparations the glazier talked to us about. Herbs, mirrors...This place of forbidden knowledge is guarded by many and most cunning devices. Knowledge is used to conceal, rather than to enlighten. I don't like it. A perverse mind presides over the holy defense of the library. But this has been a toilsome night; we must leave here for the present. You're distraught and you need water and fresh air. It's useless to try to open these windows: too high, and perhaps closed for decades. How could they think Adelmo had thrown himself down from here?"

Leave, William had said. As if it were easy. We knew the library could be reached only from one tower, the eastern one. But where were we at that moment? We had completely lost our orientation. We wandered, fearing never to emerge from that place again; I, still stumbling, seized with fits of vomiting; and William, somewhat worried about me and irritated by the inadequacy of his learning; but this wandering gave us, or gave him, an idea for the following day. We would come back to the library, assuming we ever got out of it, with a charred firebrand, or some other substance capable of leaving signs on the walls.

"To find the way out of a labyrinth," William recited, "there is only one means. At every new junction, never seen before, the path we have taken will be marked with three signs. If, because of previous signs on some of the paths of the junction, you see that the junction has already been visited, you will make only one mark on the path you have taken. If all the apertures have already been marked, then you must retrace your steps. But if one or two apertures of the junction are still without signs, you will choose any one, making two signs on it. Proceeding through an aperture that bears only one sign, you will make two more, so that now the aperture bears three. All the parts of the labyrinth must have been visited if, arriving at a junction, you never take a passage with three signs, unless none of the other passages is now without signs."

"How do you know that? Are you an expert on labyrinths?"

"No, I am citing an ancient text I once read."

"And by observing this rule you get out?"

"Almost never, as far as I know. But we will try it, all the same. And besides, within the next day or so I will have lenses and time to devote myself more to the books. It may be that where the succession of scrolls confuses us, the arrangement of the books will give us a rule."

"You'll have your lenses? How will you find them again?"

"I said I'll have lenses. I'll have new ones made. I believe the glazier is eager for an opportunity of this kind, to try something new. As long as he has the right tools for grinding the bits of glass. When it comes to bits of glass, he has plenty in his workshop."

As we roamed, seeking the way, suddenly, in the center of one room, I felt an invisible hand stroke my cheek, while a groan, not human and not animal, echoed in both that room and the next, as if a ghost were wandering from one to the other. I should have been prepared for the library's surprises, but once again I was terrified and leaped backward. William must have had an experience similar to mine, because he was touching his cheek as he held up the light and looked around.

He raised one hand, examined the flame, which now seemed brighter, then moistened a finger and held it straight in front of him.

"It's clear," he said then, and showed me two points, on opposite walls, at a man's height. Two narrow slits opened there, and if you put your hand to them you could feel the cold air coming from outside. Putting your ear to them, you could hear a rustling sound, as of a wind blowing outside.

"The library must, of course, have a ventilation system," William said. "Otherwise the atmosphere would be stifling, especially in the summer. Moreover, those slits provide the right amount of humidity, so the parchments will not dry out. But the cleverness of the founders did not stop there. Placing the slits at certain angles, they made sure that on windy nights the gusts penetrating from these openings would encounter other gusts, and swirl inside the sequence of rooms, producing the sounds we have heard. Which, along with the mirrors and the herbs, increase the fear of the foolhardy who come in here, as we have, without knowing the place well. And we ourselves for a moment thought ghosts were breathing on our faces. We've realized it only now because the wind has sprung up only now. So this mystery, too, is solved. But we still don't know how to get out!"

As we spoke, we wandered aimlessly, now bewildered, not bothering to read the scrolls, which seemed all alike. We came into a new heptagonal room, we went through the nearby rooms, we found no exit. We retraced our steps and walked for almost an hour, making no effort to discover where we were. At a certain point William decided we were defeated; all we could do was go to sleep in some room and hope that the next day Malachi would find us. As we bemoaned the miserable end of our bold adventure, we suddenly found again the room from which the stairway descended. We fervently thanked heaven and went down in high spirits.

Once we were in the kitchen, we rushed to the fireplace and entered the corridor of the ossarium, and I swear that the deathly grin of those fleshless heads looked to me like the smiles of dear friends. We re-entered the church and came out through the north door, finally sitting down happily on the tombstones. The beautiful night air seemed a divine balm. The stars shone around us and I felt the visions of the library were far away.

"How beautiful the world is, and how ugly labyrinths are," I said, relieved.

"How beautiful the world would be if there were a procedure for moving through labyrinths," my master replied.

We walked along the left side of the church, passed the great door (I looked away, to avoid seeing the elders of the Apocalypse: "Super thronos viginti quatuor"!), and crossed the cloister to reach the pilgrims' hospice.

At the door of the building stood the abbot, staring

at us sternly. "I have been looking for you all night," he said to William. "I did not find you in your cell, I did not find you in church...."

"We were pursuing a trail..." William said vaguely, with visible embarrassment. The abbot gave him a long look, then said in a slow and severe voice, "I looked for you immediately after compline. Berengar was not in choir."

"What are you telling me?" William said, with a cheerful expression. In fact, it was now clear to him who had been in ambush in the scriptorium.

"He was not in choir at compline," the abbot repeated, "and has not come back to his cell. Matins are about to ring, and we will now see if he reappears. Otherwise I fear some new calamity."

At matins Berengar was absent.

THIRD DAY

From Lauds to Prime

In which a bloodstained cloth is found in the cell of Berengar, who has disappeared; and that is all.

In setting down these words, I feel weary, as I felt that night—or, rather, that morning. What can be said? After matins the abbot sent most of the monks, now in a state of alarm, to seek everywhere; but without any result.

Toward lauds, searching Berengar's cell, a monk found under the pallet a white cloth stained with blood. He showed it to the abbot, who drew the direst omens from it. Jorge was present, and as soon as he was informed, he said, "Blood?" as if the thing seemed improbable to him. They told Alinardo, who shook his head and said, "No, no, at the third trumpet death comes by water...."

William examined the cloth, then said, "Now everything is clear."

"Where is Berengar?" they asked him.

"I don't know," he answered. Aymaro heard him and raised his eyes to heaven, murmuring to Peter of Sant'Albano, "Typically English."

Toward prime, when the sun was already up, servants were sent to explore the foot of the cliff, all around the walls. They came back at terce, having found nothing.

William told me that we could not have done any better. We had to await events. And he went to the forges, to engage in a deep conversation with Nicholas, the master glazier.

I sat in church, near the central door, as the Masses were said. And so I fell devoutly asleep and slept a long time, because young people seem to need sleep more than the old, who have already slept so much and are preparing to sleep for all eternity.

TERCE

In which Adso, in the scriptorium, reflects on the history of his order and on the destiny of books.

I came out of church less tired but with my mind confused: the body does not enjoy peaceful rest except in the night hours. I went up to the scriptorium and, after obtaining Malachi's permission, began to leaf through the catalogue. But as I glanced absently at the pages passing before my eyes, I was really observing the monks.

I was struck by their calm, their serenity. Intent on their work, they seemed to forget that one of their brothers was being anxiously sought throughout the grounds, and that two others had disappeared in frightful circumstances. Here, I said to myself, is the greatness of our order: for centuries and centuries men like these have seen the barbarian hordes burst in, sack their abbeys, plunge kingdoms into chasms of fire, and yet they have gone on cherishing parchments and inks, have continued to read, moving their lips over words that have been handed down through centuries and which they will hand down to the centuries to come.

They went on reading and copying as the millennium approached; why should they not continue to do so now?

The day before, Benno had said he would be prepared to sin in order to procure a rare book. He was not lying and not joking. A monk should surely love his books with humility, wishing their good and not the glory of his own curiosity; but what the temptation of adultery is for laymen and the yearning for riches is for secular ecclesiastics, the seduction of knowledge is for monks.

I leafed through the catalogue, and a feast of mysterious titles danced before my eyes: *Quinti Sereni de medicamentis, Phaenomena, Liber Aesopi de natura animalium, Liber Aethici peronymi de cosmographia, Libri tres quos Arculphus episcopus Adamnano escipiente de locis sanctis ultramarinis designavit conscribendos, Libellus Q. Iulii Hilarionis de origine mundi, Solini Polyhistor de situ orbis terrarum et mirabilibus, Almagesthus....* I was not surprised that the mystery of the crimes should involve the library. For these men devoted to writing, the library was at once the celestial Jerusalem and an underground world on the border between terra incognita and Hades. They were dominated by the library, by its promises and by its prohibitions. They lived with it, for it, and perhaps against it, sinfully hoping one day to violate all its secrets. Why should they not have risked death to satisfy a curiosity of their minds, or have killed to prevent someone from appropriating a jealously guarded secret of their own?

Temptations, to be sure; intellectual pride. Quite different was the scribe-monk imagined by our sainted founder, capable of copying without understanding, surrendered to the will of God, writing as if praying, and praying inasmuch as he was writing. Why was it no longer so? Oh, this was surely not the only degeneration of our order! It had become too powerful, its abbots competed with kings: in Abo did I not perhaps have the example of a monarch who, with monarch's demeanor, tried to settle controversies between monarchs? The very knowledge that the abbeys had accumulated was now used as barter goods, cause for pride, motive for boasting and prestige; just as knights displayed armor and standards, our abbots displayed illuminated manuscripts.... And all the more so now (what madness!), when our monasteries had also lost the leadership in learning: cathedral schools, urban corporations, universities were copying books, perhaps more and better than we, and producing new ones, and this may have been the cause of many misfortunes.

The abbey where I was staying was probably the last to boast of excellence in the production and reproduction of learning. But perhaps for this very reason, the monks were no longer content with the holy work of copying; they wanted also to produce new complements of nature, impelled by the lust for novelty. And they did not realize, as I sensed vaguely at that moment (and know clearly today, now aged in years and experience), that in doing so they sanctioned the destruction of their excellence. Because if this new learning they wanted to produce were to circulate freely outside those walls, then nothing would distinguish that sacred place any longer from a cathedral school or a city university. Remaining isolated, on the other hand, it maintained its prestige and its strength intact, it was not corrupted by disputation, by the quodlibetical conceit that would subject every mystery and every greatness to the scrutiny of the sic et non. There, I said to myself, are the reasons for the silence and the darkness that surround the library: it is the preserve of learning but can maintain this learning unsullied only if it prevents its reaching anyone at all, even the monks themselves. Learning is not like a coin, which remains physically whole even through the most infamous transactions; it is, rather, like a very handsome dress, which is worn out through use and ostentation. Is not a book like that, in fact? Its pages crumble, its ink and gold turn dull, if too many hands touch it. I saw Pacificus of Tivoli, leafing through an ancient volume whose pages had become stuck together because of the humidity. He moistened his thumb and forefinger with his tongue to leaf through his book, and at every touch of his saliva those pages lost vigor; opening them meant folding them, exposing them to the harsh action of air and dust, which would erode the subtle wrinkles of the parchment, and would produce mildew where the saliva had softened but also weakened the corner of the page. As an excess of sweetness makes the warrior flaccid and inept, this excess of possessive and curious love would make the book vulnerable to the disease destined to kill it.

What should be done? Stop reading, and only preserve? Were my fears correct? What would my master have said?

Nearby I saw a rubricator, Magnus of Iona, who had finished scraping his vellum with pumice stone and was now softening it with chalk, soon to smooth the surface with the ruler. Another, next to him, Rabano of Toledo, had fixed the parchment to the desk, pricking the margins with tiny holes on both sides, between which, with a metal stylus, he was now drawing very fine horizontal lines. Soon the two pages would be filled with colors and shapes, the sheet would become a kind of reliquary, glowing with gems studded in what would then be the devout text of the writing. Those two brothers, I said to myself, are living their hours of paradise on earth. They were producing new books, just like those that time would inexorably destroy. . . . Therefore, the library could not be threatened by any earthly force, it was a living thing. . . . But if it was living, why should it not be opened to the risk of knowledge? Was this what Benno wanted and what Venantius perhaps had wanted?

I felt confused, afraid of my own thoughts. Perhaps they were not fitting for a novice, who should only follow the Rule scrupulously and humbly through all the years to come—which is what I subsequently did, without asking myself further questions, while around me the world was sinking deeper and deeper into a storm of blood and madness.

It was the hour of our morning meal. I went to the kitchen, where by now I had become a friend of the cooks, and they gave me some of the best morsels.

SEXT

In which Adso receives the confidences of Salvatore, which cannot be summarized in a few words, but which cause him long and concerned meditation.

As I was eating, I saw Salvatore in one corner, obviously having made his peace with the cook, for he was merrily devouring a mutton pie. He ate as if he had never eaten before in his life, not letting even a crumb fall, and he seemed to be giving thanks to God for this extraordinary event.

He winked at me and said, in that bizarre language of his, that he was eating for all the years when he had fasted. I questioned him. He told me of a very painful childhood in a village where the air was bad, the rains frequent, where the fields rotted while the air was polluted by deathly miasmas. There were floods, or so I understood, season after season, when the fields had no furrows and with a bushel of seed you harvested a sextary, and then the sextary was reduced to nothing. Even the overlords had white faces like the poor, although, Salvatore remarked, the poor died in greater numbers than the gentry did, perhaps (he smiled) because there were more of them.... A sextary cost fifteen pence, a bushel sixty pence, the preachers announced the end of the world, but Salvatore's parents and grandparents remembered the same story in the past as well, so they came to the conclusion that the world was always about to end. And after they had eaten all the bird carcasses and all the unclean animals they could find, there was a rumor in the village that somebody was beginning to dig up the dead. Salvatore explained with great dramatic ability, as if he were an actor, how those "homeni malissimi" behaved, the wicked men who scrabbled with their fingers in the earth of the cemeteries the day after somebody's funeral. "Yum!" he said, and bit into his mutton pie, but I could see on his face the grimace of the desperate man eating the corpse. And then, not content with digging in consecrated ground, some, worse than the others, like highwaymen, crouched in the forest and took travelers by surprise. "Thwack!" Salvatore said, holding his knife to his throat, and "Nyum!" And the worst among the worst accosted boys, offering an egg or an apple, and then devoured them, though, as Salvatore explained to me very gravely, always cooking them first. He told of a man who came to the village selling cooked meat for a few pence, and nobody could understand this great stroke of luck, but then the priest said it was human flesh, and the man was torn to pieces by the infuriated crowd. That same night, however, one man from the village went and dug up the grave of the murdered victim and ate the flesh of the cannibal, whereupon, since he was discovered, the village put him to death, too.

But Salvatore did not tell me only this tale. In broken words, obliging me to recall what little I knew of Provençal and of Italian dialects, he told me the story of his flight from his native village and his roaming about the world. And in his story I recognized many men I had already known or encountered along the road, and I now recognize many more that I have met since, so that after all this time I may even attribute to him adventures and crimes that belonged to others, before him and after him, and which now, in my tired mind, flatten out to form a single image. This, in fact, is the power of the imagination, which, combining the memory of gold with that of the mountain, can compose the idea of a golden mountain.

Often during our journey I heard William mention "the simple," a term by which some of his brothers denoted not only the populace but, at the same time, the unlearned. This expression always seemed to me generic, because in the Italian cities I had met men of trade and artisans who were not clerics but were not unlearned, even if their knowledge was revealed through the use of the vernacular. And, for that matter, some of the tyrants who governed the peninsula at that time were ignorant of theological learning, and medical, and of logic, and ignorant of Latin, but they were surely not simple or benighted. So I believe that even my master, when he spoke of the simple, was using a rather simple concept. But unquestionably Salvatore was simple. He came from a rural land that for centuries had been subjected to famine and the arrogance of the feudal lords. He was simple, but he was not a fool. He yearned for a different world, which, when he fled from his family's house, I gathered, assumed the aspect of the land of Cockaigne, where wheels of cheese and aromatic sausages grow on the trees that ooze honey.

Driven by such a hope, as if refusing to recognize this world as a vale of tears where (as they taught me) even injustice is foreordained by Providence to maintain the balance of things, whose design often eludes us, Salvatore journeyed through various lands, from his native Montferrat toward Liguria, then up through Provence into the lands of the King of France.

Salvatore wandered through the world, begging, pilfering, pretending to be ill, entering the temporary service of some lord, then again taking to the forest or the high road. From the story he told me, I pictured him among those bands of vagrants that in the years that followed I saw more and more often roaming about Europe: false monks, charlatans, swindlers, cheats, tramps and tatterdemalions, lepers and cripples, jugglers, invalid mercenaries, wandering Jews escaped from the infidels with their spirit broken, lunatics, fugitives under banishment, malefactors with an ear cut off, sodomites, and along with them ambulant artisans, weavers, tinkers, chair-menders, knife-grinders, basketweavers, masons, and also rogues of every stripe, forgers, scoundrels, cardsharps, rascals, bullies, reprobates, recreants, frauds, hooligans, simoniacal and embezzling canons and priests, people who lived on the credulity of others, counterfeiters of bulls and papal seals, peddlers of indulgences, false paralytics who lay at church doors, vagrants fleeing from convents, relic-sellers, pardoners, soothsayers and fortunetellers, necromancers, healers, bogus alms-seekers, fornicators of every sort, corruptors of nuns and maidens by deception and violence, simulators of dropsy, epilepsy, hemorrhoids, gout, and sores, as well as melancholy madness. There were those who put plasters on their bodies to imitate incurable ulcerations, others who filled their mouths with a blood-colored substance to feign accesses of consumption, rascals who pretended to be weak in one of their limbs, carrying unnecessary crutches and imitating the falling sickness, scabies, buboes, swellings, while applying bandages, tincture of saffron, carrying irons on their hands, their heads swathed, slipping into the churches stinking, and suddenly fainting in the squares, spitting saliva and popping their eyes, making the nostrils spurt blood concocted of blackberry juice and vermilion, to wrest food or money from the frightened people who recalled the church fathers' exhortations to give alms: Share your bread with the hungry, take the homeless to your hearth, we visit Christ, we house Christ, we clothe Christ, because as water purges fire so charity purges our sins.

Long after the events I am narrating, along the course of the Danube I saw many, and still see some, of these charlatans who had their names and their subdivisions in legions, like the devils.

It was like a mire that flowed over the paths of our world, and with them mingled preachers in good faith, heretics in search of new victims, agitators of discord. It was Pope John—always fearing movements of the simple who might preach and practice poverty—who inveighed against the mendicant preachers, for, he said, they attracted the curious by raising banners with painted figures, preaching, and extorting money. Was the simoniacal and corrupt Pope right in considering the mendicant monks preaching poverty the equivalent of bands of outcasts and robbers? In those days, having journeyed a bit in the Italian peninsula, I no longer had firm opinions on the subject: I had heard of the monks of Altopascio, who, when they preached, threatened excommunications and promised indulgences, absolved those who committed robberies and fratricides, homicides and perjury, for money; they let it be believed that in their hospital every day up to a hundred Masses were said, for which they collected donations, and they said that with their income they supplied dowries for two hundred poor maidens. And I had heard tales of Brother Paolo Zoppo, who in the forest of Rieti lived as a hermit and boasted of having received directly from the Holy Spirit the revelation that the carnal act was not a sin—so he seduced his victims, whom he called sisters, forcing them to submit to the lash on their naked flesh, making five genuflections on the ground in the form of a cross, before he presented them to God and claimed from them what he called the kiss of peace. But was it true? And what link was there between these hermits who were said to be enlightened and the monks of poor life who roamed the roads of the peninsula really doing penance, disliked by the clergy and the bishops, whose vices and thefts they excoriated?

From Salvatore's tale, as it became mingled with the things I already knew from my own experience, these distinctions did not emerge clearly: everything looked the same as everything else. At times he seemed to me one of those crippled beggars of Touraine who, as the story goes, took flight at the approach of the miraculous corpse of Saint Martin, for they feared the saint would heal them and thus deprive them of their source of income, and the saint mercilessly saved them before they reached the border, punishing their wickedness by restoring to them the use of their limbs. At times, however, the monk's ferocious face brightened with a sweet glow as he told me how, when living among those bands, he listened to the word of the Franciscan preachers, as outcast as he was, and he understood that the poor and vagabond life he led should be taken, not as a grim necessity, but as a joyous act of dedication, and he joined penitential sects and groups whose names he could not pronounce properly and whose doctrine he defined in highly unlikely terms. I deduced that he had encountered Patarines and Waldensians, and perhaps Catharists, Arnoldists, and Umiliati, and that, roaming about the world, he had passed from one group to another, gradually assuming as a mission his vagrant state, and doing for the Lord what he had done till then for his belly.

But how, and for how long? As far as I could tell, about thirty years before, he had joined a convent of Minorites in Tuscany, and there he had assumed the habit of Saint Francis, without taking orders. There, I believe, he learned that smattering of Latin he spoke, mixing it with the speech of all the places where he had been as a poor homeless wanderer, and of all the vagabond companions he had encountered, from the mercenaries of my lands to the Bogomils of Dalmatia.

In the convent he had devoted himself to a life of penance, he said (Penitenziagite, he quoted to me, with eyes shining, and I heard again the expression that had aroused William's curiosity), but apparently also the monks he was staying with had confused ideas, because, enraged by the canon of the neighboring church, who was accused of thefts and other wickedness, they invaded his house one day and sent him flying down the steps, and the sinner died; then they looted his house. For which the bishop sent his armed guards, the monks were dispersed, and Salvatore roamed at length in northern Italy with a band of Fraticelli, or mendicant Minorites, at this point without any law or discipline.

From there he took refuge in the Toulouse region and a strange adventure befell him, for he was inflamed by hearing the story of the crusaders' great enterprises. A horde of shepherds and humble folk in great numbers gathered one day to cross the sea and fight against the enemies of the faith. They were called the Pastoureaux, the Shepherds. Actually, they wanted to escape their own wretched land. There were two leaders, who filled their heads with false theories: a priest who had been dismissed from his church because of his conduct, and an apostate monk of the order of Saint Benedict. This pair drove ignorant men so mad that they came running after the two in throngs, even boys of sixteen, against their parents' wishes, carrying only knapsack and stick, all without money, leaving their fields, to follow the leaders like a flock, and they formed a great crowd. At this point they would no longer heed reason or justice, but only power and their own caprice. Gathered together and finally free, with a dim hope of promised lands, they were as if drunk. They stormed through villages and cities, taking everything, and if one of their number was arrested, they would attack the prison and free him. And they killed all the Jews they came upon here and there and stripped them of their possessions.

"Why the Jews?" I asked Salvatore. He answered, "And why not?" He explained to me that all his life preachers had told him the Jews were the enemies of Christianity and accumulated possessions that had been denied the Christian poor. I asked him, however, whether it was not also true that lords and bishops accumulated possessions through tithes, so that the Shepherds were not fighting their true enemies. He replied that when your true enemies are too strong, you have to choose weaker enemies. I reflected that this is why the simple are so called. Only the powerful always know with great clarity who their true enemies are. The lords did not want the Shepherds to jeopardize their possessions, and it was a great good fortune for them that the Shepherds' leaders spread the notion that the greatest wealth belonged to the Jews.

I asked him who had put into the crowd's head the idea of attacking the Jews. Salvatore could not remember. I believe that when such crowds collect, lured by a promise and immediately demanding something, there is never any knowing who among them speaks. I recalled that their leaders had been educated in convents and cathedral schools, and they spoke the language of the lords, even if they translated it into terms that the Shepherds could understand. The Shepherds did not know where the Pope was, but they knew where the Jews were. Anyway, they laid siege to a high and massive tower of the King of France, where the frightened Jews had run in a body to take refuge. And the Jews sallying forth below the walls of the tower defended themselves courageously and pitilessly, hurling wood and stones. But the Shepherds set fire to the gate of the tower, tormenting the barricaded Jews with smoke and flames. And the Jews, unable to defeat their attackers, preferring to kill themselves rather than die at the hand of the uncircumcised, asked one of their number, who seemed the most courageous, to put them all to the sword. He consented, and killed almost five hundred of them. Then he came out of the tower with the children of the Jews, and asked the Shepherds to baptize him. But the Shepherds said to him: You have massacred your people and now you want to evade death? And they tore him to pieces; but they spared the children, whom they baptized. Then they headed for Carcassonne, carrying out many bloody robberies along the way. Then the King of France warned them that they had gone too far and ordered that they be resisted in every city they passed through, and he proclaimed that even the Jews should be defended as if they were the King's men....

Why did the King become so considerate of the Jews at that point? Perhaps because he was beginning to realize what the Shepherds might do throughout the kingdom, and he was concerned because their number was increasing too rapidly. Further, he was moved to tenderness for the Jews, both because the Jews were useful to the trade of the kingdom, and because now it was necessary to destroy the Shepherds, and all good Christians had to have a good reason to weep over their crimes. But many Christians did not obey the King, thinking it wrong to defend the Jews, who had always been enemies of the Christian faith. And in many cities the humble people, who had had to pay usury to the Jews, were happy to see the Shepherds punish them for their wealth. Then the King commanded, under pain of death, that no aid be given the Shepherds. He gathered a considerable army and attacked them, and many of them were killed, while others saved themselves by taking flight and seeking refuge in the forests, but there they died of hardship. Soon all were annihilated. The King's general captured them and hanged them, twenty or thirty at a time, from the highest trees, so the sight of their corpses would serve as an eternal example and no one would dare to disturb the peace of the realm again.

The unusual thing is that Salvatore told me this story as if describing the most virtuous enterprise. And in fact he remained convinced that the horde of so-called Shepherds had aimed to conquer the sepulcher of Christ and free it from the infidels, and it was impossible for me to convince him that this fine conquest had already been achieved, in the days of Peter the Hermit and Saint Bernard, and under the reign of Saint Louis of France. In any case, Salvatore did not reach the infidels, because he had to leave French territory in a hurry. He went into the Novara region, he told me, but he was very vague about what happened at this point. And finally he arrived at Casale, where he was received by the convent of Minorites (and here I believe he met Remigio) at the very time when many of them, persecuted by the Pope, were changing habit and seeking refuge in monasteries of other orders, to avoid being burned at the stake. As, indeed, Ubertino had told us. Thanks to his long familiarity with many manual tasks (which he had performed both for dishonest purposes, when he was roaming freely, and for holy purposes, when he was roaming for the love of Christ), Salvatore was immediately taken on by the cellarer as his personal assistant. And that was why he had been here for many years, with scant interest in the order's pomp, but much in the administration of its cellar and larder, where he was free to eat without stealing and to praise the Lord without being burned.

I looked at him with curiosity, not because of the singularity of his experience, but because what had happened to him seemed to me the splendid epitome of so many events and movements that made the Italy of that time fascinating and incomprehensible.

What had emerged from those tales? The picture of

a man who had led an adventurous life, capable even of killing a fellow man without realizing his own crime. But although at that time one offense to the divine law seemed to me the same as another, I was already beginning to understand some of the phenomena I was hearing discussed, and I saw that it is one thing for a crowd, in an almost ecstatic frenzy, mistaking the laws of the Devil for those of the Lord, to commit a massacre, but it is another thing for an individual to commit a crime in cold blood, with calculation, in silence. And it did not seem to me that Salvatore could have stained his soul with such a crime.

On the other hand, I wanted to discover something about the abbot's insinuations, and I was obsessed by the idea of Fra Dolcino, of whom I knew almost nothing, though his ghost seemed to hover over many conversations I had heard these past few days.

So I asked Salvatore point-blank: "In your journeys did you ever meet Fra Dolcino?"

His reaction was most strange. He widened his eyes, if it were possible to open them wider than they were, he blessed himself repeatedly, murmured some broken phrases in a language that this time I really did not understand. But they seemed to me phrases of denial. Until then he had looked at me with good-natured trust, I would say with friendship. At that moment he looked at me almost with irritation. Then, inventing an excuse, he left.

Now I could no longer resist. Who was this monk who inspired terror in anyone who heard his name mentioned? I decided I could not remain any longer in the grip of my desire to know. An idea crossed my mind. Ubertino! He himself had uttered that name, the first evening we met him; he knew everything of the vicissitudes, open and secret, of monks, friars, and other species of these last years. Where could I find him at this hour? Surely in church, immersed in prayer.

And since I was enjoying a moment of liberty, I went there.

I did not find him; indeed, I did not find him until evening. And so my curiosity stayed with me, for other events were occurring, of which I must now tell.

NONES

In which William speaks to Adso of the great river of heresy, of the function of the simple within the church, of his doubts concerning the possibility of knowing universal laws; and almost parenthetically he tells how he deciphered the necromantic signs left by Venantius.

I found William at the forge, working with Nicholas, both deeply involved in their task. On the counter they had laid out a number of tiny glass discs, perhaps originally intended as parts of a window; with instruments they had reduced some of these to the desired thickness. William was holding them up before his eyes, testing them. Nicholas, for his part, was issuing instructions to the smiths for making the fork in which the correct lenses would be set.

William was grumbling, irritated because so far the most satisfactory lens was an emerald color, and, as he said, he did not want parchments to seem meadows to him. Nicholas went off to supervise the smiths. As William tried out the various discs, I told him of my dialogue with Salvatore.

"The man has had various experiences," he said. "Perhaps he actually was with the Dolcinians. The abbey really is a microcosm, and when we have Pope

John's envoys and Brother Michael here, we'll be complete."

"Master," I said to him, "I understand nothing."

"About what, Adso?"

"First, about the differences among heretical groups. But I'll ask you about that later. Now I am tormented by the problem of difference itself. When you were speaking with Ubertino, I had the impression you were trying to prove to him that all are the same, saints and heretics. But then, speaking with the abbot, you were doing your best to explain to him the difference between one heretic and another, and between the heretical and the orthodox. In other words, you reproached Ubertino for considering different those who were basically the same, and the abbot for considering the same those who were basically different."

William set the lenses on the table for a moment. "My good Adso," he said, "we will try now to make some distinctions, and we may as well use the terms of the school of Paris for our distinguishing. So: they say all men have the same substantial form, am I right?"

"Of course," I said, proud of my knowledge, "men are animals but rational, and the property of man is the capacity for laughing."

"Excellent. But Thomas is different from Bonaventure, Thomas is fat while Bonaventure is thin, and it may even be that Hugh is bad while Francis is good, and Aldemar is phlegmatic while Agilulf is bilious. Or am I mistaken?"

"No, that is the case, beyond any doubt."

"Then this means there is identity in different men as to their substantial form, and diversity as to the accidents, or as to their superficial shape."

"That is so, unquestionably."

"When I say to Ubertino that human nature itself, in the complexity of its operations, governs both the love of good and the love of evil, I am trying to convince

Ubertino of the identity of human nature. When I say to the abbot, however, that there is a difference between a Catharist and a Waldensian, I am insisting on the variety of their accidents. And I insist on it because a Waldensian may be burned after the accidents of a Catharist have been attributed to him, and vice versa. And when you burn a man you burn his individual substance and reduce to pure nothing that which was a concrete act of existing, hence in itself good, at least in the eyes of God, who kept him in existence. Does this seem to you a good reason for insisting on the differences?"

"The trouble is," I said, "I can no longer distinguish the accidental difference among Waldensians, Catharists, the poor of Lyons, the Umiliati, the Beghards, Joachimites, Patarines, Apostles, Poor Lombards, Arnoldists, Williamites, Followers of the Free Spirit, and Luciferines. What am I to do?"

"Oh, poor Adso," William said, laughing and giving me an affectionate slap on the nape, "you're not really wrong! You see, it's as if, over the last two centuries, and even earlier, this world of ours had been struck by storms of intolerance, hope, and despair, all together.... No, that's not a good analogy. Imagine a river, wide and majestic, which flows for miles and miles between strong embankments, where the land is firm. At a certain point, the river, out of weariness, because its flow has taken up too much time and too much space, because it is approaching the sea, which annihilates all rivers in itself, no longer knows what it is, loses its identity. It becomes its own delta. A major branch may remain, but many break off from it in every direction, and some flow together again, into one another, and you can't tell what begets what, and sometimes you can't tell what is still river and what is already sea...."

"If I understand your allegory, the river is the city of God, or the kingdom of the just, which is approaching the millennium, and in this uncertainty it no longer remains secure, false and true prophets are born, and everything flows into the great plain where Armageddon will take place...."

"That isn't exactly what I was thinking. I was trying to explain to you how the body of the church, which for centuries was also the body of all society, the people of God, has become too rich, and wide, and it carries along the dross of all the countries it has passed through, and it has lost its own purity. The branches of the delta are, if you like, so many attempts of the river to flow as quickly as possible to the sea, that is, to the moment of purification. My allegory was meant only to tell you how the branches of heresy and the movements of renewal, when the river is no longer intact, are numerous and become mingled. You can also add to my poor allegory the image of someone who is trying to reconstruct the banks of the river with brute strength, but cannot do so. And some branches of the delta silt up, others are redirected to the river by artificial channels, still others are allowed to flow, because it is impossible to restrain everything and it is better for the river to lose a part of its water and still maintain its course, if it wants to have a recognizable course."

"I understand less and less."

"So do I. I'm not good at speaking in parables. Forget this story of the river. Try instead to understand that many of the movements you mentioned were born at least two hundred years ago and are already dead, yet others are recent...."

"But when heretics are discussed, they are all mentioned together."

"True, and this is one of the ways heresy spreads and one of the ways it is destroyed."

"Again I don't understand."

"God, how difficult it is. Very well. Imagine you are a reformer of morals and you collect some companions on a mountaintop, to live in poverty. And after a while you see that many come to you, even from distant lands, and they consider you a prophet, or a new apostle, and they follow you. Have they really come there for you or for what you say?"

"I don't know. I hope so. Why otherwise?"

"Because from their fathers they have heard stories of other reformers, and legends of more or less perfect communities, and they believe this is that and that is this."

"And so every movement inherits the offspring of others?"

"Of course, because the majority of those who flock after reformers are the simple, who have no subtlety of doctrine. And yet moral reform movements originate in different places and ways and with different doctrines. For example, the Catharists and the Waldensians are often mixed up. But there is a great difference between them. The Waldensians preached a moral reform within the church, the Catharists preached a different church, a different view of God and morality. The Catharists thought the world was divided between the opposing forces of good and evil, and they had built a church in which the perfect were distinguished from simple believers, and they had their sacraments and their rites; they had built a very rigid hierarchy, almost like that of our own Holy Mother, and they didn't for a moment think of destroying every form of power. Which explains to you why men in command, landowners, feudal lords, also joined the Catharists. Nor did they think of reforming the world, because the opposition between good and evil for them can never be settled. The Waldensians, on the contrary (and along with them the Arnoldists, or Poor Lombards), wanted to construct a different world on an ideal of poverty, and this is why they received the outcasts and lived in community with the labor of their hands."

"But why, then, are they confused and spoken of as the same evil weed?"

"I told you: what makes them live is also what makes them die. The movements grow, gathering simple people who have been aroused by other movements and who believe all have the same impulse of revolt and hope; and they are destroyed by the inquisitors, who attribute to one the errors of the other, and if the sectarians of one movement commit a crime, this crime will be attributed to each sectarian of each movement. The inquisitors are mistaken, rationally speaking, because they lump contradictory doctrines together; they are right, according to others' irrationality, because when a movement of, say, Arnoldists springs up in one city, it is swelled by those who would have been or have been Catharists or Waldensians elsewhere. Fra Dolcino's Apostles preached the physical destruction of clerics and lords, and committed many acts of violence; the Waldensians are opposed to violence, and so are the Fraticelli. But I am sure that in Fra Dolcino's day there were many in his group who had previously followed the preachings of the Fraticelli or the Waldensians. The simple cannot choose their personal heresy, Adso; they cling to the man preaching in their land, who passes through their village or stops in their square. This is what their enemies exploit. To present to the eyes of the people a single heresy, which perhaps may suggest at the same time the renunciation of sexual pleasure and the communion of bodies, is good preaching technique: it shows the heretics as one jumble of diabolical contradictions which offend common sense."

"So there is no relationship among them, and it is the Devil's deception that makes a simple man who would like to be a Joachimite or a Spiritual fall into the hands of the Catharists, and vice versa?"

"No, that is not quite it. Let's try again from the beginning, Adso. But I assure you, I am attempting to explain to you something about which I myself am not sure I possess the truth. I think the mistake is to believe that the heresy comes first, and then the simple folk who join it (and damn themselves for it). Actually, first comes the condition of being simple, then the heresy."

"What do you mean?"

"You have a clear conception of the people of God. A great flock—good sheep and bad sheep—kept in order by mastiffs—the warriors, or the temporal power—the Emperor, and the overlords, under the guidance of the shepherds, the clerics, the interpreters of the divine word. The picture is straightforward."

"But false. The shepherds fight with the dogs, because each covets the rights of the other."

"True, and this is exactly what makes the nature of the flock unsure. Concerned as they are with tearing each other apart reciprocally, dogs and shepherds no longer tend the flock. A part of it is left outside."

"What do you mean by outside?"

"On the margin. Peasants: only they are not really peasants, because they have no land, or what land they have does not feed them. And citizens: only they are not citizens, because they do not belong to a guild or a corporation; they are the little people, prey of anyone. Have you sometimes seen groups of lepers in the countryside?"

"Yes, once I saw a hundred together. Misshapen, their flesh decaying and all whitish, hobbling on their crutches, with swollen eyelids, bleeding eyes. They didn't speak or shout; they twittered, like mice."

"For the Christian people they are the others, those who remain on the fringe of the flock. The flock hates them, they hate the flock, who wish all lepers like them would die."

"Yes, I recall a story about King Mark, who had to condemn Isolda the beautiful and was about to have her ascend the stake when the lepers came and said to the King that the stake was a mild punishment and that there was a worse one. And they cried to him: Give us Isolda that she may belong to all of us, our illness enflames our desires, give her to your lepers. Look at our rags, glued to our groaning wounds. She, who at your side enjoyed rich stuffs lined with squirrel fur and jewels, when she sees the courtyard of the lepers, when she has to enter our hovels and lie with us, then she will truly recognize her sin and regret this fine pyre of brambles!"

"I see that for a novice of Saint Benedict you have done some odd reading," William remarked. I blushed, because I knew a novice should not read romances, but they circulated among us young people in the monastery of Melk and we read them at night by candlelight. "But that doesn't matter," William continued, "you have understood what I meant. The outcast lepers would like to drag everything down in their ruin. And they become all the more evil, the more you cast them out; and the more you depict them as a court of lemures who want your ruin, the more they will be outcast. Saint Francis realized this, and his first decision was to go and live among the lepers. The people of God cannot be changed until the outcasts are restored to its body."

"But you were speaking of other outcasts; it isn't lepers who form heretical movements."

"The flock is like a series of concentric circles, from the broadest range of the flock to its immediate surroundings. The lepers are a sign of exclusion in general. Saint Francis understood that. He didn't want only to help the lepers; if he had, his act would have been reduced to quite a poor and impotent act of charity. He wanted to signify something else. Have you been told about his preaching to the birds?"

"Oh, yes, I've heard that beautiful story, and I admired the saint who enjoyed the company of those tender creatures of God," I said with great fervor.

"Well, what they told you was mistaken, or, rather, it's a story the order has revised today. When Francis spoke to the people of the city and its magistrates and saw they didn't understand him, he went out to the cemetery and began preaching to ravens and magpies, to hawks, to raptors feeding on corpses."

"What a horrible thing!" I said. "Then they were not good birds! "

"They were birds of prey, outcast birds, like the lepers. Francis was surely thinking of that verse of the Apocalypse that says: 'I saw an angel standing in the sun; and he cried with a loud voice, saying to all the fowls that fly in the midst of heaven, Come and gather yourselves together at the supper of the great God; that ye may eat the flesh of kings, and the flesh of captains, and the flesh of mighty men, and the flesh of horses, and of them that sit on them, and the flesh of all men, both free and bond, both small and great!' "

"So Francis wanted to incite the outcasts to revolt?"

"No, that was what Fra Dolcino and his followers wanted, if anybody did. Francis wanted to call the outcast, ready to revolt, to be part of the people of God. If the flock was to be gathered again, the outcasts had to be found again. Francis didn't succeed, and I say it with great bitterness. To recover the outcasts he had to act within the church, to act within the church he had to obtain the recognition of his rule, from which an order would emerge, and this order, as it emerged, would recompose the image of a circle, at whose margin the outcasts remain. So now do you understand why there are bands of Fraticelli and Joachimites who again gather the outcasts around themselves?"

"But we weren't talking about Francis; we were talking about how heresy is produced by the simple and the outcast."

"Yes. We were talking about those excluded from the flock of sheep. For centuries, as pope and emperor tore each other apart in their quarrels over power, the excluded went on living on the fringe, like lepers, of whom true lepers are only the illustration ordained by God to make us understand this wondrous parable, so that in saying 'lepers' we would understand 'outcast, poor, simple, excluded, uprooted from the countryside, humiliated in the cities.' But we did not understand; the mystery of leprosy has continued to haunt us because we have not recognized the nature of the sign. Excluded as they were from the flock, all of them were ready to hear, or to produce, every sermon that, harking back to the word of Christ, would condemn the behavior of the dogs and shepherds and would promise their punishment one day. The powerful always realized this. The recovery of the outcasts demanded reduction of the privileges of the powerful, so the excluded who became aware of their exclusion had to be branded as heretics, whatever their doctrine. And for their part, blinded by their exclusion, they were not really interested in any doctrine. This is the illusion of heresy. Everyone is heretical, everyone is orthodox. The faith a movement proclaims doesn't count: what counts is the hope it offers. All heresies are the banner of a reality, an exclusion. Scratch the heresy and you will find the leper. Every battle against heresy wants only this: to keep the leper as he is. As for the lepers, what can you ask of them? That they distinguish in the Trinitarian dogma or in the definition of the Eucharist how much is correct and how much is wrong? Come, Adso, these games are for us men of learning. The simple have other problems. And mind you, they solve them all in the wrong way. This is why they become heretics."

"But why do some people support them?"

"Because it serves their purposes, which concern the faith rarely, and more often the conquest of power."

"Is that why the church of Rome accuses all its adversaries of heresy?"

"That is why, and that is also why it recognizes as orthodoxy any heresy it can bring back under its own control or must accept because the heresy has become too strong. But there is no precise rule: it depends on the individuals, on the circumstances. This holds true also for the secular lords. Sometimes the city magistrates encourage the heretics to translate the Gospel into the vernacular: the vernacular by now is the language of the cities, Latin the language of Rome and the monasteries. And sometimes the magistrates support the Waldensians, because they declare that all, men and women, lowly and mighty, can teach and preach, and the worker who is a disciple after ten days hunts for another whose teacher he can become...."

"And so they eliminate the distinction that makes clerics irreplaceable! But, then, why does it happen that the same city magistrates rebel against the heretics and lend the church a hand in having them burned?"

"Because they realize the heretics' growth could jeopardize also the privileges of the laity who speak in the vernacular. In the Lateran Council of 1179 (you see, these questions date back a hundred fifty years), Walter Map warned against what would happen if credence were given to those foolish and illiterate men the Waldensians. He said, if I recall properly, that they have no fixed dwelling, they go about barefoot and possess nothing, holding everything as common property, following naked the naked Christ; they begin in this very humble way because they are outcasts, but if you give them too much room they will drive out everyone else. This is why the cities favored the mendicant orders, and us Franciscans in particular: we fostered a harmonious balance between the need for penance and the life of the city, between the church and the burghers, concerned for their trade...."

"Was harmony achieved, then, between love of God and love of trade?"

"No, the movements of spiritual renewal were blocked; they were channeled within the bounds of an order recognized by the Pope. But what circulated underneath was not channeled. It flowed, on the one hand, into the movements of the flagellants, who endanger no one, or into the armed bands like Fra Dolcino's, or into the witchcraft rituals of the monks of Montefalco that Ubertino was talking about...."

"But who was right, who is right, who was wrong?" I asked, bewildered.

"They were all right in their way, and all were mistaken."

"And you," I cried, in an access almost of rebellion, "why don't you take a position, why won't you tell me where the truth is?"

William remained silent for a while, holding the lens he was working on up to the light. Then he lowered it to the table and showed me, through the lens, a tool. "Look," he said to me. "What do you see?"

"The tool, a bit larger."

"There: the most we can do is look more closely."

"But the tool remains always the same!"

"The manuscript of Venantius, too, will remain the same when, thanks to this lens, I've been able to read it. But perhaps when I've read the manuscript I'll know a part of the truth better. And perhaps we'll be able to make the life of the abbey better."

"But that isn't enough!"

"I'm saying more than I seem to be, Adso. This isn't the first time I've spoken to you of Roger Bacon. Perhaps he was not the wisest man of all time, but I've always been fascinated by the hope that inspired his love of learning. Bacon believed in the strength, the needs, the spiritual inventions of the simple. He wouldn't have been a good Franciscan if he hadn't thought that the poor, the outcast, idiots and illiterate, often speak with the mouth of our Lord. The simple have something more than do learned doctors, who often become lost in their search for broad, general laws. The simple have a sense of the individual, but this sense, by itself, is not enough. The simple grasp a truth of their own, perhaps truer than that of the doctors of the church, but then they destroy it in unthinking actions. What must be done? Give learning to the simple? Too easy, or too difficult. The Franciscan teachers considered this problem. The great Bonaventure said that the wise must enhance conceptual clarity with the truth implicit in the actions of the simple. . . ."

"Like the chapter of Perugia and the learned memories of Ubertino, which transform into theological decisions the summons of the simple to poverty," I said.

"Yes, but as you have seen, this happens too late, and when it happens, the truth of the simple has already been transformed into the truth of the powerful, more useful for the Emperor Louis than for a Friar of the Poor Life. How are we to remain close to the experience of the simple, maintaining, so to speak, their operative virtue, the capacity of working toward the transformation and betterment of their world? This was the problem for Bacon. 'Quod enim laicali ruditate turgescit non habet effectum nisi fortuito,' he said: The experience of the simple has savage and uncontrollable results. 'Sed opera sapientiae certa lege vallantur et in finem debitum efficaciter diriguntur.' Which is to say that even in the handling of practical things, be they agriculture, mechanics, or the governing of a city, a kind of theology is required. He thought that the new natural science should be the great new enterprise of the learned: to coordinate, through a different knowledge of natural processes, the elementary needs that represented also the heap of expectations, disordered but in its way true and right, of the simple. The new science, the new natural magic. According to Bacon, this enterprise was to be directed by the church, but I believe he said this because in his time the community of clerics was identified with the community of the learned. Today that is no longer the case: learned men grow up outside the monasteries and the cathedrals, even outside the universities. So I think that, since I and my friends today believe that for the management of human affairs it is not the church that should legislate but the assembly of the people, then in the future the community of the learned will have to propose this new and humane theology which is natural philosophy and positive magic."

"A splendid enterprise," I said, "but is it possible?"

"Bacon thought so."

"And you?"

"I think so, too. But to believe in it we must be sure that the simple are right in possessing the sense of the individual, which is the only good kind. However, if the sense of the individual is the only good, how will science succeed in recomposing the universal laws through which, and interpreting which, the good magic will become functional?"

"Yes," I said, "how can it?"

"I no longer know. I have had arguments at Oxford with my friend William of Occam, who is now in Avignon. He has sown doubts in my mind. Because if only the sense of the individual is just, the proposition that identical causes have identical effects is difficult to prove. A single body can be cold or hot, sweet or bitter, wet or dry, in one place—and not in another place. How can I discover the universal bond that orders all things if I cannot lift a finger without creating an infinity of new entities? For with such a movement all the relations of position between my finger and all other objects change. The relations are the ways in which my mind perceives the connections between single entities, but what is the guarantee that this is universal and stable?"

"But you know that a certain thickness of glass corresponds to a certain power of vision, and it is because you know this that now you can make lenses like the ones you have lost: otherwise how could you?"

"An acute reply, Adso. In fact, I have worked out this proposition: equal thickness corresponds necessarily to equal power of vision. I have posited it because on other occasions I have had individual insights of the same type. To be sure, anyone who tests the curative property of herbs knows that individual herbs of the same species have equal effects of the same nature on the patient, and therefore the investigator formulates the proposition that every herb of a given type helps the feverish, or that every lens of such a type magnifies the eye's vision to the same degree. The science Bacon spoke of rests unquestionably on these propositions. You understand, Adso, I must believe that my proposition works, because I learned it by experience; but to believe it I must assume there are universal laws. Yet I cannot speak of them, because the very concept that universal laws and an established order exist would imply that God is their prisoner, whereas God is something absolutely free, so that if He wanted, with a single act of His will He could make the world different."

"And so, if I understand you correctly, you act, and you know why you act, but you don't know why you know that you know what you do?"

I must say with pride that William gave me a look of admiration. "Perhaps that's it. In any case, this tells you why I feel so uncertain of my truth, even if I believe in it."

"You are more mystical than Ubertino!" I said spitefully.

"Perhaps. But as you see, I work on things of nature. And in the investigation we are carrying out, I don't want to know who is good or who is wicked, but who was in the scriptorium last night, who took the eyeglasses, who left traces of a body dragging another body in the snow, and where Berengar is. These are facts. Afterward I'll try to connect them—if it's possible, for it's difficult to say what effect is produced by what cause. An angel's intervention would suffice to change everything, so it isn't surprising that one thing cannot be proved to be the cause of another thing. Even if one must always try, as I am doing."

"Yours is a difficult life," I said.

"But I found Brunellus," William cried, recalling the horse episode of two days before.

"Then there is an order in the world!" I cried, triumphant.

"Then there is a bit of order in this poor head of mine," William answered.

At this point Nicholas came back with an almost finished fork, holding it up victoriously.

"And when this fork is on my poor nose," William said, "perhaps my poor head will be even more orderly."

A novice came to say the abbot wished to see William, and was waiting for him in the garden. As we started off, William slapped his forehead, as if remembering only at this point something he had forgotten.

"By the way," he said, "I've deciphered Venantius's cabalistic signs."

"All of them? When?"

"While you were asleep. And it depends on what you mean by 'all.' I've deciphered the signs that the flame caused to appear, the ones you copied out. The notes in Greek must wait till I have new lenses."

"Well? Was it the secret of the finis Africae?"

"Yes, and the key was fairly easy. At his disposal Venantius had the twelve signs of the zodiac and eight other signs: for the five planets, the two luminaries, and the earth. Twenty signs in all. Enough to associate with them the letters of the Latin alphabet, since you can use the same letter to express the sound of the two initials of 'unum' and 'velut.' The order of the letters, we know. What could be the order of the signs, then? I thought of the order of the heavens, placing the zodiacal quadrant at the far edge. So, then: Earth, Moon, Mercury, Venus, Sun, etc., and, afterward, the signs of the zodiac in their traditional sequence, as Isidore of Seville classifies them, beginning with Aries and the vernal equinox, ending with Pisces. Now, if you try this key, Venantius's message takes on a meaning."

He showed me the parchment, on which he had transcribed the message in big Latin letters: "Secretum finis Africae manus supra idolum age primum et septimum de quatuor."

"Is that clear?" he asked.

"The hand over the idol works on the first and the

seventh of the four..." I repeated, shaking my head. "It isn't clear at all!"

"I know. First of all we have to know what Venantius meant by 'idolum.' An image, a ghost, a figure? And then what can this 'four' be that has a 'first' and a 'seventh'? And what is to be done with them? Move them, push them, pull them?"

"So we know nothing and we are still where we started," I said, with great dismay.

William stopped and looked at me with an expression not entirely benevolent. "My boy," he said, "you have before you a poor Franciscan who, with his modest learning and what little skill he owes to the infinite power of the Lord, has succeeded in a few hours in deciphering a secret code whose author was sure would prove sealed to all save himself... and you, wretched illiterate rogue, dare say we are still where we started?"

I apologized very clumsily. I had wounded my master's vanity, and yet I knew how proud he was of the speed and accuracy of his deductions. William truly had performed a job worthy of admiration, and it was not his fault if the crafty Venantius not only had concealed his discovery behind an obscure zodiacal alphabet, but had further devised an undecipherable riddle.

"No matter, no matter, don't apologize," William interrupted me. "After all, you're right. We still know too little. Come along."

VESPERS

In which the abbot speaks again with the visitors, and William has some astounding ideas for deciphering the riddle of the labyrinth and succeeds in the most rational way. Then William and Adso eat cheese in batter.

The abbot was waiting for us with a grim, worried look. He was holding a paper in his hand.

"I have just received a letter from the abbot of Conques," he said. "He discloses the name of the man to whom John has entrusted the command of the French soldiers and the responsibility for the safety of the legation. He is not a man of arms, he is not a man of the court, and he will be at the same time a member of the legation."

"A rare combination of different qualities," William said uneasily. "Who is it?"

"Bernard Gui, or Bernardo Guidoni, whichever you choose to call him."

William made an ejaculation in his own language that I didn't understand, nor did the abbot understand it, and perhaps it was best for us both, because the word William uttered had an obscene hissing sound.

"I don't like this," he added at once. "For years

Bernard was the scourge of heretics in the Toulouse area, and he has written a *Practica officii inquisitionis heretice pravitatis* for the use of those who must persecute and destroy Waldensians, Beghards, Fraticelli, and Dolcinians."

"I know. I am familiar with the book; remarkably learned."

"Remarkably learned," William conceded. "He's devoted to John, who in recent years has assigned him many missions in Flanders and here in northern Italy. And even when he was named Bishop of Galicia, he was never seen in his diocese but continued his activity as inquisitor. I thought he had now retired to the bishopric of Lodève, but apparently John is recalling him to duty, right here in northern Italy. But why Bernard, of all people, and why with a command of soldiers . . . ?"

"There is an answer," the abbot said, "and it confirms all the fears I expressed to you yesterday. You know well—even if you will not admit it to me—that the positions on the poverty of Christ and of the church sustained by the chapter of Perugia, though supported by an abundance of theological arguments, are the same ones that many heretical movements sustain, much less prudently and in a much less orthodox fashion. It does not take much to demonstrate that the positions of Michael of Cesena, espoused by the Emperor, are the same as those of Ubertino and Angelus Clarenus. And up to this point, the two legations will concur. But Gui could do more, and he has the skill: he will try to insist that the theses of Perugia are the same as those of the Fraticelli, or the Pseudo Apostles."

"This was foreseen. I mean, we knew that things would come to this, even without Bernard's presence. At most Bernard will act more effectively than so many of those inept men of the curia, and the debate with him will necessarily be more subtle."

"Yes," the abbot said, "but at this point we come up

against the question raised yesterday. If by tomorrow we have not discovered the person guilty of two, perhaps three, crimes, I must allow Bernard to exercise control over the abbey's affairs. I cannot conceal from a man invested with the power Bernard will have (and because of our mutual agreement, we must not forget) that here in the abbey inexplicable events have taken place, are still taking place. Otherwise, the moment he finds out, the moment (God forbid) some new mysterious event happens, he will have every right to cry betrayal. . . ."

"True," William murmured, worried. "But there is nothing to be done. Perhaps it will be a good thing: Bernard occupied with the assassin will have less time to participate in the debate."

"Bernard occupied with discovering the murderer will be a thorn in the side of my authority; remember that. This murky business obliges me for the first time to surrender a part of my power within these walls, and it is a new turn in the history not only of this abbey but of the Cluniac order itself. I would do anything to avoid it. Where is Berengar? What has happened to him? What are you doing?"

"I am only a monk who, a long time ago, conducted some effective inquisitorial investigations. You know that the truth is not to be found in two days. And after all, what power have you granted me? May I enter the library? May I ask all the questions I'd like, always supported by your authority?"

"I see no connection between the crimes and the library," the abbot said angrily.

"Adelmo was an illuminator, Venantius a translator, Berengar the assistant librarian . . ." William explained patiently.

"In this sense all sixty monks have something to do with the library, as they have with the church. Why not investigate the church, then? Brother William, you are conducting an inquiry at my behest and within the limits I have established. For the rest, within this girdle of walls I am the only master after God, and by His grace. And this will hold true for Bernard as well. In any event," he added, in a milder tone, "Bernard may not necessarily be coming here specifically for the meeting. The abbot of Conques writes me that the Pope has asked Cardinal Bertrand del Poggetto to come up from Bologna and assume command of the papal legation. Perhaps Bernard is coming here to meet the cardinal."

"Which, in a broader perspective, would be worse. Bertrand is the scourge of heretics in central Italy. This encounter between the two champions of the battle against heretics may herald a vaster offensive in the country, eventually against the whole Franciscan movement. . . ."

"And of this we will promptly inform the Emperor," the abbot said, "but in this case the danger would not be immediate. We will be alert. Good-bye."

William remained silent a moment as the abbot departed. Then he said to me: "First of all, Adso, we must try not to let ourselves be overcome by haste. Things cannot be solved rapidly when so many small, individual experiences have to be put together. I am going back to the laboratory, because in addition to keeping me from reading the manuscript, being without my lenses also makes it pointless for me to return tonight to the library."

At that moment Nicholas of Morimondo came running toward us, bearer of very bad tidings. While he was trying to grind more finely the best lens, the one on which William had based such hope, it had broken. And another, which could perhaps have replaced it, had cracked as he was trying to insert it into the fork. Nicholas, disconsolately, pointed to the sky. It was already the hour of vespers, and darkness was falling. For that day no more work could be done. Another day lost, William acknowledged bitterly, suppressing (as he confessed to me afterward) the temptation to strangle

the master glazier, though Nicholas was already sufficiently humiliated.

We left him to his humiliation and went to inquire
about Berengar. Naturally, no one had found him.

We felt we had reached a dead end. We strolled
awhile in the cloister, uncertain what to do next. But
soon I saw William was lost in thought, staring into the
air, as if he saw nothing. A bit earlier he had taken
from his habit a twig of those herbs that I had seen him
gather weeks before, and he was chewing it as if it gave
him a kind of calm stimulus. In fact, he seemed absent,
but every now and then his eyes brightened as if in the
vacuum of his mind a new idea had kindled; then he
would plunge once more into that singular and active
hebetude of his. All of a sudden he said, "Of course, we
could . . ."

"What?" I asked.

"I was thinking of a way to get our bearings in the
labyrinth. It is not simple, but it would be effective. . . .
After all, the exit is in the east tower: this we know.
Now, suppose that we had a machine that tells us where
north is. What would happen?"

"Naturally, we would have only to turn to our right
and we would be heading east. Or else it would suffice
to go in the opposite direction and we would know we
were going toward the south tower. But, even assuming
such magic existed, the labyrinth is in fact a labyrinth,
and as soon as we headed east we would come upon a
wall that would prevent us from going straight, and we
would lose our way again . . ." I observed.

"Yes, but the machine I am talking about would
always point north, even if we had changed our route,
and at every point it would tell us which way to turn."

"It would be marvelous. But we would have to have
this machine, and it would have to be able to recognize
north at night and indoors, without being able to see
the sun or the stars. . . . And I believe not even your
Bacon possessed such a machine." I laughed.

"But you are wrong," William said, "because a machine of the sort has been constructed, and some navigators have used it. It doesn't need the stars or the sun, because it exploits the power of a marvelous stone, like the one we saw in Severinus's infirmary, the one that attracts iron. And it was studied by Bacon and by a Picard wizard, Pierre of Maricourt, who described its many uses."

"But could you construct it?"

"In itself, that wouldn't be difficult. The stone can be used to produce many wonders, including a machine that moves perpetually without any external power, but the simplest discovery was described also by an Arab, Baylek al-Qabayaki. Take a vessel filled with water and set afloat in it a cork into which you have stuck an iron needle. Then pass the magnetic stone over the surface of the water, until the needle has acquired the same properties as the stone. And at this point the needle— though the stone would also have done it if it had had the capacity to move around a pivot—will turn and point north, and if you move it with the vessel, it will always turn in the direction of the north wind. Obviously, if you bear north in mind and also mark on the edge of the vessel the positions of east, south, and west, you will always know which way to turn in the library to reach the east tower."

"What a marvel!" I exclaimed. "But why does the needle always point north? The stone attracts iron, I saw that, and I imagine that an immense quantity of iron attracts the stone. But then . . . then in the direction of the polestar, at the extreme confines of the globe, there exist great iron mines!"

"Someone, in fact, has suggested such is the case. Except that the needle doesn't point precisely in the direction of the daystar, but toward the intersection of the celestial meridians. A sign that, as has been said, 'hic lapis gerit in se similitudinem coeli,' and the poles of the magnet receive their inclination from the poles of the sky, not from those of the earth. Which is a fine example of movement provoked at a distance, not by direct material causality: a problem that my friend John of Jandun is studying, when the Emperor does not ask him to make Avignon sink into the bowels of the earth...."

"Let's go, then, and take Severinus's stone, and a vessel, and some water, and a cork..." I said, excited.

"Wait a moment," William said. "I do not know why, but I have never seen a machine that, however perfect in the philosophers' description, is perfect in its mechanical functioning. Whereas a peasant's billhook, which no philosopher has ever described, always functions as it should.... I'm afraid that wandering around the labyrinth with a lamp in one hand, a vessel full of water in the other... Wait, though! I have another idea. The machine would point north even if we were outside the labyrinth, would it not?"

"Yes, but at that point it would be of no use to us, because we would have the sun and the stars..." I said.

"I know, I know. But if the machine functions both indoors and outdoors, why should it not be the same with our heads?"

"Our heads? Of course, they also function outside, and in fact, on the outside we know quite well the layout of the Aedificium! But it is when we are inside that we become disoriented!"

"Precisely. But forget the machine for now. Thinking about the machine has led me to think about natural laws and the laws of thought. Here is the point: we must find, from the outside, a way of describing the Aedificium as it is inside...."

"But how?"

"We will use the mathematical sciences. Only in the mathematical sciences, as Averroës says, are things known to us identified with those known absolutely."

"Then you do admit universal notions, you see."

"Mathematical notions are propositions constructed by our intellect in such a way that they function always as truths, either because they are innate or because mathematics was invented before the other sciences. And the library was built by a human mind that thought in a mathematical fashion, because without mathematics you cannot build labyrinths. And therefore we must compare our mathematical propositions with the propositions of the builder, and from this comparison science can be produced, because it is a science of terms upon terms. And, in any case, stop dragging me into discussions of metaphysics. What the Devil has got into you today? Instead, you who have good eyes take a parchment, a tablet, something you can make signs on, and a stylus. . . . Good, you have it? Good for you, Adso. Let's go and take a turn around the Aedificium, while we still have a bit of light."

So we took a long turn around the Aedificium. That is, from the distance we examined the east, south, and west towers, with the walls connecting them. The rest rose over the cliff, though for reasons of symmetry it could not be very different from what we were seeing.

And what we saw, William observed as he made me take precise notes on my tablet, was that each wall had two windows, and each tower five.

"Now, think," my master said to me. "Each room we saw had a window. . . ."

"Except those with seven sides," I said.

"And, naturally, they are the ones in the center of each tower."

"And except some others that we found without windows but that were not heptagonal."

"Forget them. First let us find the rule, then we will try to explain the exceptions. So: we will have on the outside five rooms for each tower and two rooms for each straight wall, each room with a window. But if from a room with a window we proceed toward the interior of the Aedificium, we meet another room with a window. A sign that there are internal windows. Now, what shape is the internal well, as seen from the kitchen and from the scriptorium?"

"Octagonal," I said.

"Excellent. And on each side of the octagon, there could easily be two windows. Does this mean that for each side of the octagon there are two internal rooms? Am I right?"

"Yes, but what about the windowless rooms?"

"There are eight in all. In fact, the internal room of every tower, with seven sides, has five walls that open each into one of the five rooms of the tower. What do the other two walls confine with? Not with rooms set along the outside walls, or there would be windows, and not with rooms along the octagon, for the same reason and because they would then be excessively long rooms. Try to draw a plan of how the library might look from above. You see that in each tower there must be two rooms that confine with the heptagonal room and open into two rooms that confine with the internal octagonal well."

I tried drawing the plan that my master suggested, and I let out a cry of triumph. "But now we know everything! Let me count.... The library has fifty-six rooms, four of them heptagonal and fifty-two more or less square, and of these, there are eight without windows, while twenty-eight look to the outside and sixteen to the interior!"

"And the four towers each have five rooms with four walls and one with seven.... The library is constructed according to a celestial harmony to which various and wonderful meanings can be attributed...."

"A splendid discovery," I said, "but why is it so difficult to get our bearings?"

"Because what does not correspond to any mathematical law is the arrangement of the openings. Some rooms allow you to pass into several others, some into only one, and we must ask ourselves whether there are not rooms that do not allow you to go anywhere else. If you consider this aspect, plus the lack of light or of any clue that might be supplied by the position of the sun (and if you add the visions and the mirrors), you understand how the labyrinth can confuse anyone who goes through it, especially when he is already troubled by a sense of guilt. Remember, too, how desperate we were last night when we could no longer find our way. The maximum of confusion achieved with the maximum of order: it seems a sublime calculation. The builders of the library were great masters."

"How will we orient ourselves, then?"

"At this point it isn't difficult. With the map you've drawn, which should more or less correspond to the plan of the library, as soon as we are in the first heptagonal room we will move immediately to reach one of the blind rooms. Then, always turning right, after two or three rooms we should again be in a tower, which can only be the north tower, until we come to another blind room, on the left, which will confine with the heptagonal room, and on the right will allow us to rediscover a route similar to what I have just described, until we arrive at the west tower."

"Yes, if all the rooms opened into all the other rooms . . ."

"In fact. And for this reason we'll need your map, to mark the blank walls on it, so we'll know what detours we're making. But it won't be difficult."

"But are we sure it will work?" I asked, puzzled; it all seemed too simple to me.

"It will work," William replied. "But unfortunately we don't know everything yet. We have learned how to avoid being lost. Now we must know whether there is a rule governing the distribution of the books among the rooms. And the verses from the Apocalypse tell us very little, not least because many are repeated identically in different rooms...."

"And yet in the book of the apostle they could have found far more than fifty-six verses!"

"Undoubtedly. Therefore only certain verses are good. Strange. As if they had had fewer than fifty: thirty or twenty...Oh, by the beard of Merlin!"

"Of whom?"

"Pay no attention. A magician of my country...They used as many verses as there are letters in the alphabet! Of course, that's it! The text of the verse doesn't count, it's the initial letters that count. Each room is marked by a letter of the alphabet, and all together they make up some text that we must discover!"

"Like a figured poem, in the form of a cross or a fish!"

"More or less, and probably in the period when the library was built, that kind of poem was much in vogue."

"But where does the text begin?"

"With a scroll larger than the others, in the heptagonal room of the entrance tower...or else...Why, of course, with the sentences in red!"

"But there are so many of them!"

"And therefore there must be many texts, or many words. Now make a better and larger copy of your map; while we visit the library, you will mark down with your stylus the rooms we pass through, the positions of the doors and walls (as well as the windows), and also the first letters of the verses that appear there. And like a good illuminator, you will make the letters in red larger."

"But how does it happen," I said with admiration, "that you were able to solve the mystery of the library looking at it from the outside, and you were unable to solve it when you were inside?"

"Thus God knows the world, because He conceived it in His mind, as if from the outside, before it was created, and we do not know its rule, because we live inside it, having found it already made."

"So one can know things by looking at them from the outside!"

"The creations of art, because we retrace in our minds the operations of the artificer. Not the creations of nature, because they are not the work of our minds."

"But for the library this suffices, doesn't it?"

"Yes," William said. "But only for the library. Now let's go and rest. I can do nothing until tomorrow morning, when I will have, I hope, my lenses. We might as well sleep, and rise early. I will try to reflect."

"And supper?"

"Ah, of course, supper. The hour has passed by now. The monks are already at compline. But perhaps the kitchen is still open. Go look for something."

"And steal it?"

"Ask. Ask Salvatore, who is now your friend."

"But he will steal!"

"Are you perhaps your brother's keeper?" William asked, with the words of Cain. But I saw he was joking and meant to say that God is great and merciful. And so I went looking for Salvatore and found him near the horses' stalls.

"A fine animal," I said, nodding at Brunellus, as a way of starting a conversation. "I would like to ride him."

"No se puede. Abbonis est. But you do not need a pulcher horse to ride hard...." He pointed out a sturdy but ill-favored horse. "That one also sufficit.... Vide illuc, tertius equi...."

He wanted to point out to me the third horse. I laughed at his comical Latin. "And what will you do with that one?" I asked him.

And he told me a strange story. He said that any horse, even the oldest and weakest animal, could be made as swift as Brunellus. You had only to mix into his oats an herb called satirion, chopped fine, and then grease his thighs with stag fat. Then you mount the horse, and before spurring him you turn his face eastward and you whisper into his ear, three times, the words: "Nicander, Melchior, and Merchizard." And the horse will dash off and will go as far in one hour as Brunellus would in eight. And if you hang around his neck the teeth of a wolf that the horse himself has trampled and killed, the animal will not even feel the effort.

I asked him whether he had ever tried this. He said to me, coming closer circumspectly and whispering into my ear with his really foul breath, that it was very difficult, because satirion was now cultivated only by bishops and by their lordly friends, who used it to increase their power. Then I put an end to his talk and told him that this evening my master wanted to read certain books in his cell and wished to eat up there.

"I will do," he said, "I will do cheese in batter."

"How is that made?"

"Facilis. You take the cheese before it is too antiquum, without too much salis, and cut in cubes or sicut you like. And postea you put a bit of butierro or lardo to rechauffer over the embers. And in it you put two pieces of cheese, and when it becomes tenero, zucharum et cinnamon supra positurum du bis. And immediately take to table, because it must be ate caldo caldo."

"Cheese in batter it is, then," I said to him. And he vanished toward the kitchen, telling me to wait for him. He arrived half an hour later with a dish covered by a cloth. The aroma was good.

"Here," he said to me, and he also held out a great lamp filled with oil.

"What for?" I asked.

"Sais pas, moi," he said, slyly. "Peut-être your magister wants to go in dark place esta noche."

Salvatore apparently knew more things than I had

suspected. I inquired no further, but took the food to William. We ate, and I withdrew to my cell. Or at least, so I implied. I wanted to find Ubertino again, and stealthily I returned to the church.

AFTER COMPLINE

In which Ubertino tells Adso the story of Fra Dolcino, after which Adso recalls other stories or reads them on his own in the library, and then he has an encounter with a maiden, beautiful and terrible as an army arrayed for battle.

I found Ubertino at the statue of the Virgin. Silently I joined him and for a while pretended (I confess) to pray. Then I made bold to speak to him.

"Holy Father," I said to him, "may I ask enlightenment and counsel of you?"

Ubertino looked at me and, taking me by the hand, rose and led me to a bench, where we both sat. He embraced me tightly, and I could feel his breath on my face.

"Dearest son," he said, "anything this poor sinner can do for your soul will be done joyfully. What is distressing you? Yearnings?" he asked, almost with yearning himself. "The yearnings of the flesh?"

"No," I replied, blushing, "if anything the yearnings of the mind, which wants to know too many things..."

"And that is bad. The Lord knows all things, and we must only adore His knowledge."

"But we must also distinguish good from evil and understand human passions. I am a novice, but I will be monk and priest, and I must learn where evil lies, and what it looks like, in order to recognize it one day and teach others to recognize it."

"This is true, my boy. What do you want to know, then?"

"The tare of heresy, Father," I said with conviction. And then, all in one breath, "I have heard tell of a wicked man who has led others astray: Fra Dolcino."

Ubertino remained silent, then he said: "That is right, you heard Brother William and me refer to him the other evening. But it is a nasty story, and it grieves me to talk about it, because it teaches (yes, in this sense you should know it, to derive a useful lesson from it)—because, I was saying, it teaches how the love of penance and the desire to purify the world can produce bloodshed and slaughter." He shifted his position on the bench, relaxing his grasp of my shoulders but still keeping one hand on my neck, as if to communicate to me his knowledge or (I could not tell) his intensity.

"The story begins before Fra Dolcino," he said, "more than sixty years ago, when I was a child. It was in Parma. There a certain Gherardo Segarelli began preaching, exhorting all to a life of penitence, and he would go along the roads crying 'Penitenziagite!' which was the uneducated man's way of saying 'Penitentiam agite, appropinquabit enim regnum coelorum.' He enjoined his disciples to imitate the apostles, and he chose to call his sect the order of the Apostles, and his men were to go through the world like poor beggars, living only on alms...."

"Like the Fraticelli," I said. "Wasn't this the command of our Lord and of your own Francis?"

"Yes," Ubertino admitted with a slight hesitation in his voice, sighing. "But perhaps Gherardo exaggerated. He and his followers were accused of denying the authority of the priests and the celebration of Mass and confession, and of being idle vagabonds."

"But the Spiritual Franciscans were accused of the same thing. And aren't the Minorites saying today that the authority of the Pope should not be recognized?"

"Yes, but not the authority of priests. We Minorites are ourselves priests. It is difficult, boy, to make distinctions in these things. The line dividing good from evil is so fine.... In some way Gherardo erred and became guilty of heresy.... He asked to be admitted to the order of the Minorites, but our brothers would not receive him. He spent his days in the church of our brothers, and he saw the paintings there of the apostles wearing sandals on their feet and cloaks wrapped around their shoulders, and so he let his hair and beard grow, put sandals on his feet, and wore the rope of the Friars Minor, because anyone who wants to found a new congregation always takes something from the order of the Blessed Francis."

"Then he was in the right...."

"But somewhere he did wrong.... Dressed in a white cloak over a white tunic, with his hair long, he acquired among simple people the reputation for saintliness. He sold a little house of his, and having received the money, he stood on a stone from which in ancient times the magistrates were accustomed to harangue, and he held the little sack of gold pieces in his hand, and he did not scatter them or give them to the poor, but, after summoning some rogues dicing nearby, he flung the money in their midst and said, 'Let him take who will,' and those rogues took the money and went off to gamble it away, and they blasphemed the living God, and he who had given to them heard and did not blush."

"But Francis also stripped himself of everything, and today from William I heard that he went to preach to ravens and hawks, as well as to the lepers—namely, to the dregs that the people who call themselves virtuous had cast out...."

"Yes, but Gherardo somehow erred; Francis never set

himself in conflict with the holy church, and the Gospel says to give to the poor, not to rogues. Gherardo gave and received nothing in return because he had given to bad people, and he had a bad beginning, a bad continuation, and a bad end, because his congregation was disapproved by Pope Gregory the Tenth."

"Perhaps," I said, "he was a less broad-minded pope than the one who approved the Rule of Francis...."

"He was, but Gherardo somehow erred, and Francis, on the contrary, knew well what he was doing. And finally, boy, these keepers of pigs and cows who suddenly because Pseudo Apostles wanted to live blissfully and without sweat off the alms of those whom the Friars Minor had educated with such efforts and such heroic examples of poverty! But that is not the point," he added promptly. "The point is that to resemble the apostles, who had still been Jews, Gherardo Segarelli had himself circumcised, which is contrary to the words of Paul to the Galatians—and you know that many holy persons proclaim that the future Antichrist will come from the race of the circumcised.... But Gherardo did still worse: he went about collecting the simple people and saying, 'Come with me into the vineyard,' and those who did not know him went with him into another's vineyard, believing it his, and they ate another's grapes...."

"Surely the Minorites didn't defend private property," I said impertinently.

Ubertino stared at me severely. "The Minorites ask to be poor, but they have never asked others to be poor. You cannot attack the property of good Christians with impunity; the good Christians will label you a bandit. And so it happened to Gherardo. They said of him finally that to test his strength of will and his continence he slept with women without having carnal knowledge of them; but when his disciples tried to imitate him, the results were quite different.... Oh, these are not things a boy should know: the female is a vessel of the Devil.... And then they began to brawl among themselves over the command of the sect, and evil things happened. And yet many came to Gherardo, not only peasants, but also people of the city, members of the guilds, and Gherardo made them strip themselves so that, naked, they could follow the naked Christ, and he sent them out into the world to preach, but he had a sleeveless tunic made for himself, white, of strong stuff, and in this garb he looked more like a clown than like a religious! They lived in the open air, but sometimes they climbed into the pulpits of the churches, disturbing the assembly of devout folk and driving out their preachers, and once they set a child on the bishop's throne in the Church of Sant'Orso in Ravenna. And they proclaimed themselves heirs of the doctrine of Joachim of Floris...."

"But so do the Franciscans," I said, "and also Gerard of Borgo San Donnino, and you, too!" I cried.

"Calm yourself, boy. Joachim of Floris was a great prophet and he was the first to understand that Francis would begin a renewal of the church. But the Pseudo Apostles used his doctrine to justify their follies. Segarelli took with him a female apostle, one Tripia or Ripia, who claimed to have the gift of prophecy. A woman, you understand?"

"But, Father," I tried to counter, "the other evening you yourself spoke of the saintliness of Clare of Montefalco and Angela of Foligno...."

"They were saints! They lived in humility, recognizing the power of the church; they never claimed the gift of prophecy! But the Pseudo Apostles asserted that women could go preaching from city to city, as many other heretics also said. And they recognized no difference among the wed and the unwed, nor was any vow considered perpetual. In short, not to weary you too much with very sad stories whose subtleties you cannot understand well, Bishop Obizzo of Parma finally decided to put Gherardo in irons. But here a strange thing happened that tells you how weak is human nature, and how insidious the weed of heresy. Because in the end the bishop freed Gherardo and received him at his own table, and laughed at his japes, and kept him as his buffoon."

"But why?"

"I do not know—or, rather, I fear I do know. The bishop was a nobleman and did not like the merchants and craftsmen of the city. Perhaps he did not mind Gherardo's preaching against them with his talk of poverty, or did not care that from begging for alms Gherardo proceeded to robbery. But in the end the Pope intervened, and the bishop resumed his proper severity, and Gherardo ended on the pyre as an impenitent heretic. It was at the beginning of this century."

"And what do these things have to do with Fra Dolcino?"

"They are connected, and this shows you how heresy survives even the destruction of the heretics. This Dolcino was a priest's bastard, living in the Novara diocese, this part of Italy, a bit farther north. He was a youth of sharp mind and he was educated in letters, but he stole from the priest who housed him and fled eastward, to the city of Trent. And there he resumed the preaching of Gherardo, but in a more heretical vein, declaring that he was the only true apostle of God and that everything should be common in love, and that it was licit to lie indiscriminately with all women, whereby no one could be accused of concubinage, even if he went with both a wife and a daughter...."

"Did he truly preach those things, or was he just accused of preaching them? I have heard that the Spirituals, like those monks of Montefalco, were accused of similar crimes...."

"De hoc satis," Ubertino interrupted me sharply. "They were no longer monks. They were heretics. And befouled by Fra Dolcino himself. And, furthermore, listen to me: it is enough to know what Fra Dolcino did afterward to call him a wicked man. How he became familiar with the Pseudo Apostles' teachings, I do not even know. Perhaps he went through Parma as a youth and heard Gherardo. It is known that in the Bologna region he kept in touch with those heretics after Segarelli's death. And it is known for certain that he began his preaching at Trent. There he seduced a very beautiful maiden of noble family, Margaret, or she seduced him, as Héloïse seduced Abelard, because—never forget—it is through woman that the Devil penetrates men's hearts! At that point, the Bishop of Trent drove him from the diocese, but by then Dolcino had gathered more than a thousand followers, and he began a long march, which took him back to the area where he was born. And along the way other deluded folk joined him, seduced by his words, and perhaps he was also joined by many Waldensian heretics who lived in the mountains he passed through, or he himself wanted to join the Waldensians of these lands to the north. When he reached the Novara region, Dolcino found a situation favorable to his revolt, because the vassals governing the town of Gattinara in the name of the Bishop of Vercelli had been driven out by the populace, who then welcomed Dolcino's outlaws as their worthy allies."

"What had the bishop's vassals done?"

"I do not know, and it is not my place to judge. But as you see, heresy in many cases is wed to the revolt against overlords, and this is why the heretic begins by preaching Madonna Poverty and then falls prey to all the temptations of power, war, violence. There was a conflict among certain families in the city of Vercelli, and the Pseudo Apostles took advantage of it, and these families exploited the disorder brought by the Pseudo Apostles. The feudal lords hired mercenaries to rob the citizens, and the citizens sought the protection of the Bishop of Novara."

"What a complicated story. But whose side was Dolcino on?"

"I do not know; he was a faction unto himself; he entered into all these disputes and saw them as an opportunity for preaching the struggle against private ownership in the name of poverty. Dolcino and his followers, who were now three thousand strong, camped on a hill near Novara known as Bald Mountain, and they built hovels and fortifications, and Dolcino ruled over that whole throng of men and women, who lived in the most shameful promiscuity. From there he sent letters to his faithful in which he expounded his heretical doctrine. He said and he wrote that their ideal was poverty and they were not bound by any vow of external obedience, and that he, Dolcino, had been sent by God to break the seals of the prophecies and to understand the writings of the Old and the New Testaments. And he called secular clerics—preachers and Minorites— ministers of the Devil, and he absolved everyone from the duty of obeying them. And he identified four ages in the life of the people of God: The first was that of the Old Testament, the patriarchs and prophets, before the coming of Christ, when marriage was good because God's people had to multiply. The second was the age of Christ and the apostles, and this was the epoch of saintliness and chastity. Then came the third, when the popes had first to accept earthly riches in order to govern the people; but when mankind began to stray from the love of God, Benedict came, and spoke against all temporal possessions. When the monks of Benedict also then went back to accumulating wealth, the monks of Saint Francis and Saint Dominic came, even more stern than Benedict in preaching against earthly power and riches. But finally now, when again the lives of so many prelates were contradicting all those good precepts, we had reached the end of the third age, and it was necessary to follow the teachings of the Apostles."

"Then Dolcino was preaching the things that the Franciscans had preached, and among the Franciscans, the Spirituals in particular, and you yourself, Father!"

"Ah, yes, but he derived a perfidious syllogism from them! He said that to bring to an end this third age of corruption, all the clergy, monks, and friars had to die a very cruel death; he said that all prelates of the church, all clerics, nuns, religious male and female, all those who belong to the preaching orders and the Minorites, the hermits, and even Boniface the Pope had to be exterminated by the Emperor he, Dolcino, had chosen, and this was to be Frederick of Sicily."

"But didn't that same Frederick receive with favor in Sicily the Spirituals expelled from Umbria, and isn't it the Minorites who ask that the Emperor, though he is now Louis, destroy the temporal power of the Pope and the cardinals?"

"It is characteristic of heresy, or of madness, that it transforms the most upright thoughts and aims them at consequences contrary to the law of God and man. The Minorites have never asked the Emperor to kill other priests."

He was mistaken, I know now. Because, a few months later, when the Bavarian established his own order in Rome, Marsilius and other Minorites did to religious who were faithful to the Pope exactly what Dolcino had asked to have done. By this I don't mean that Dolcino was right; if anything, Marsilius was equally wrong. But I was beginning to wonder, especially after that afternoon's conversation with William, if it were possible for the simple people who followed Dolcino to distinguish between the promises of the Spirituals and Dolcino's enactment of them. Was he not perhaps guilty of putting into practice what presumably orthodox men had preached, in a purely mystical fashion? Or was that perhaps where the difference lay? Did holiness consist in waiting for God to give us what His saints had promised, without trying to obtain it through earthly means? Now I know this is the case and I know why Dolcino was in error: the order of things must not be transformed, even if we must fervently hope for its

269

transformation. But that evening I was in the grip of contradictory thoughts.

"Finally," Ubertino was saying to me, "you always find the mark of heresy in pride. In a second letter, in the year 1303, Dolcino appointed himself supreme head of the Apostolic congregation, and named as his lieutenants the perfidious Margaret—a woman—and Longinus of Bergamo, Frederick of Novara, Albert Carentinus, and Walderic of Brescia. And he began raving about a sequence of future popes, two good—the first and the last—and two wicked, the second and the third. The first is Celestine, the second is Boniface the Eighth, of whom the prophets say, 'The pride of your heart has dishonored you, O you who live in the fissures of cliffs.' The third Pope is not named, but of him Jeremiah is supposed to have said, 'There, like a lion.' And—infamy! —Dolcino recognized the lion in Frederick of Sicily. For Dolcino the fourth Pope was still unknown, and he was to be the Sainted Pope, the Angelic Pope of whom the abbot Joachim spoke. He would be chosen by God, and then Dolcino and all his people (who at this point were already four thousand) would receive together the grace of the Holy Spirit, and it would renew the church until the end of the world. But in the three years preceding his coming, all evil would have to be consummated. And this Dolcino tried to do, carrying war everywhere. And the fourth Pope, and here you see how the Devil mocks his familiars, was in fact Clement the Fifth, who proclaimed the crusade against Dolcino. And it was right, because in his letters at this point Dolcino sustained theories that could not be reconciled with orthodoxy. He declared the Roman church a whore, said that obedience is not due priests, that all spiritual power had now passed to the sect of the Apostles, that only the Apostles represented the new church, the Apostles could annul matrimony, no one would be saved unless he was a member of the sect, no pope could absolve sin, tithes should not be paid, a more perfect life was lived without vows than with vows, and a consecrated church was worthless for prayer, no better than a stable, and Christ could be worshiped both in the woods and in the churches."

"Did he really say these things?"

"Of course, this is certain. He wrote them. But unfortunately he did still worse. After he had settled on Bald Mountain, he began sacking the villages in the valley, raiding them to procure provisions—waging outright war, in short, against the nearby towns."

"Were all opposed to him?"

"We do not know. Perhaps he received support from some; I told you that he had involved himself in the snarled knot of local dissensions. Meanwhile winter had come, the winter of the year 1305, one of the harshest in recent decades, and there was great famine all around. Dolcino sent a third letter to his followers, and many more joined him, but on that hill life had become intolerable, and they grew so hungry that they ate the flesh of horses and other animals, and boiled hay. And many died."

"But whom were they fighting against now?"

"The Bishop of Vercelli had appealed to Clement the Fifth, and a crusade had been called against the heretics. A plenary indulgence was granted to anyone taking part in it, and Louis of Savoy, the inquisitors of Lombardy, the Archbishop of Milan were prompt to act. Many took up the cross to aid the people of Vercelli and Novara, even from Savoy, Provence, France; and the Bishop of Vercelli was the supreme commander. There were constant clashes between the vanguards of the two armies, but Dolcino's fortifications were impregnable, and somehow the wicked received help."

"From whom?"

"From other wicked men, I believe, who were happy to foment this disorder. Toward the end of the year 1305, the heresiarch was forced, however, to abandon Bald Mountain, leaving behind the wounded and ill, and he moved into the territory of Trivero, where he entrenched himself on a mountain that was called Zubello at the time and later was known as Rubello or Rebello, because it had become the fortress of the rebels of the church. In any case, I cannot tell you everything that happened. There were terrible massacres, but in the end the rebels were forced to surrender, Dolcino and his people were captured, and they rightly ended up on the pyre."

"The beautiful Margaret, too?"

Ubertino looked at me. "So you remembered she was beautiful? She *was* beautiful, they say, and many local lords tried to make her their bride to save her from the stake. But she would not have it; she died impenitent with her impenitent lover. And let this be a lesson to you: beware of the whore of Babylon, even when she assumes the form of the most exquisite creature."

"But now tell me, Father: I have learned that the cellarer of the convent, and perhaps also Salvatore, met Dolcino and were with him in some way...."

"Be silent! Do not utter rash statements. I found the cellarer in a convent of Minorites. I do not know where Remigio had been before that. I know he was always a good monk, at least from the standpoint of orthodoxy. As for the rest, alas, the flesh is weak...."

"What do you mean?"

"These are not things you should know." He drew me close again, embracing me and pointing to the statue of the Virgin. "You must be introduced to the immaculate love. There is she in whom femininity is sublimated. This is why you may call her beautiful, like the beloved in the Song of Songs. In her," he said, his face carried away by an inner rapture, like the abbot's the day before when he spoke of gems and the gold of his vessels, "in her, even the body's grace is a sign of the beauties of heaven, and this is why the sculptor has portrayed her with all the graces that should adorn a woman." He pointed to the Virgin's slender bust, held high and tight by a cross-laced bodice, which the Child's tiny hands fondled. "You see? As the doctors have said: Beautiful also are the breasts, which protrude slightly, only faintly tumescent, and do not swell licentiously, suppressed but not depressed.... What do you feel before this sweetest of visions?"

I blushed violently, feeling myself stirred as if by an inner fire. Ubertino must have realized it, or perhaps he glimpsed my flushed cheeks, for he promptly added, "But you must learn to distinguish the fire of supernatural love from the raving of the senses. It is difficult even for the saints."

"But how can the good love be recognized?" I asked, trembling.

"What is love? There is nothing in the world, neither man nor Devil nor any thing, that I hold as suspect as love, for it penetrates the soul more than any other thing. Nothing exists that so fills and binds the heart as love does. Therefore, unless you have those weapons that subdue it, the soul plunges through love into an immense abyss. And I believe that without Margaret's seductions Dolcino would not have damned himself, and without the reckless and promiscuous life on Bald Mountain, fewer would have felt the lure of his rebellion. Mind you, I do not say these things to you only about evil love, which of course all must shun as a thing of the Devil; I say this also, and with great fear, of the good love between God and man, between man and his neighbor. It often happens that two or three people, men or women, love one another quite cordially and harbor reciprocal, special fondness, and desire to live always close, and what one party wishes, the other desires. And I confess that I felt something of the kind for most virtuous women, like Angela and Clare. Well, that, too, is blameworthy, even though it is spiritual and conceived in God's name.... Because even the love felt by the soul, if it is not forearmed, if it is felt warmly, then falls, or proceeds in disorder. Oh, love has various

properties: first the soul grows tender, then it sickens
...but then it feels the true warmth of divine love and
cries out and moans and becomes as stone flung in the
forge to melt into lime, and it crackles, licked by the
flame...."

"And this is good love?"

Ubertino stroked my head, and as I looked at him, I
saw his eyes melt with tears. "Yes, this, finally, is good
love." He took his hand from my shoulder. "But how
difficult it is," he added, "how difficult it is to distinguish it from the other. And sometimes when devils
tempt your soul you feel like the man hanged by the
neck who, with his hands tied behind him and his eyes
blindfolded, remains hanging on the gallows and yet
lives, with no help, no support, no remedy, swinging in
the empty air...."

His face was bathed not only with tears but also by a
faint perspiration. "Go now," he said to me quickly. "I
have told you what you wanted to know. On this side
the choir of angels; on that, the gaping maw of hell.
Go, and the Lord be praised." He prostrated himself
again before the Virgin, and I heard him sobbing
softly. He was praying.

I did not leave the church. The talk with Ubertino
had kindled in my spirit, and in my viscera, a strange
fire and an unspeakable restlessness. Perhaps for this
reason, I felt inclined to disobedience and decided to
return to the library alone. I myself didn't know what I
was looking for. I wanted to explore an unknown place
on my own; I was fascinated by the idea of being able
to orient myself there without my master's help. I
climbed the stairs as Dolcino had climbed up Monte
Rubello.

I had the lamp with me (why had I brought it—was I
perhaps already harboring this secret plan?) and I
entered the ossarium almost with my eyes closed. In no
time I was in the scriptorium.

It was a fatal evening, I believe, because as I was wandering among the desks, I glimpsed one on which lay an open manuscript that a monk had been copying: *Historia fratris Dulcini Heresiarche.* I believe it was the desk of Peter of Sant'Albano, who I had been told was writing a monumental history of heresy (after what happened in the abbey, he naturally gave up writing it—but we must not get ahead of the story). So it was therefore normal that the text should be there, and with it others on kindred subjects, on the Patarines and the flagellants. But I took this circumstance as a supernatural sign, whether celestial or diabolical I still cannot say, and I bent eagerly to read the writing. It was not very long, and I found there also what Ubertino had not told me, obviously recounted by one who had seen all and whose imagination was still inflamed by it.

I learned then how, in March of 1307, on Holy Saturday, Dolcino, Margaret, and Longinus, captured at last, were taken into the city of Biella and handed over to the bishop, who was awaiting the decision of the Pope. The Pope, hearing the news, transmitted it to King Philip of France, writing: "We have received most welcome news, rich in joy and exultation, for that pestiferous demon, son of Belial, the most horrendous heresiarch Dolcino, after many dangers, long efforts, massacres, and frequent battles, is finally incarcerated with his followers in our prisons, thanks to our venerated brother Ranier, Bishop of Vercelli, captured on the day of the Lord's holy supper; and numerous people who were with him, infected by the contagion, were killed that same day." The Pope was merciless toward the prisoners and ordered the bishop to put them to death. Then, in July of that same year, the first day of the month, the heretics were handed over to the secular arm. As the bells of the city rang joyously, the heretics were placed in a wagon, surrounded by the executioners, followed by the militia, and carried through the entire city, and at every corner, men with red-hot pincers tore the flesh of the guilty. Margaret was burned first, before Dolcino, who did not move a muscle of his face, just as he had not uttered a moan when the pincers bit into his limbs. Then the wagon continued on its way, while the executioners thrust their irons into pots filled with glowing coals. Dolcino underwent other torments and remained silent, though when they amputated his nose he shrugged a bit, and when they tore off his male member he emitted a long sigh, like a groan. The last things he said sounded impertinent, for he warned that he would rise on the third day. Then he was burned and his ashes were scattered in the wind.

I folded the manuscript with trembling hands. Dolcino had committed many crimes, I had been told, but he had been horribly burned to death. And at the stake he had behaved . . . how? With the steadfastness of martyrs or with the arrogance of the damned? As I staggered up the steps to the library, I realized why I was so upset. I suddenly recalled a scene I had witnessed not many months before, shortly after my arrival in Tuscany. I wondered, indeed, why I had almost forgotten it till then, as if my sick soul had wanted to erase a memory that weighed on me like a nightmare. Or, rather, I had not forgotten it, because every time I heard the Fraticelli discussed, I saw again the scenes of that event, but I immediately thrust them down into the recesses of my spirit, as if witnessing that horror had been a sin.

I had first heard talk of the Fraticelli in the days when, in Florence, I had seen one burned at the stake. It was shortly before I met Brother William in Pisa. He had delayed his arrival in that city, and my father had given me leave to visit Florence, whose churches I had heard praised as most beautiful. I wandered about Tuscany, to learn better the vulgar Italian tongue, and I finally stayed a week in Florence, because I had heard much talk of that city and wished to know it.

And so it was that when I had barely arrived I learned of a great trial that was stirring up the whole city. A heretic Fraticello, accused of crimes against religion and haled before the bishop and other ecclesiastics, was being subjected to severe inquisition at the time. And, following those who told me about it, I went to the place where the trial was taking place, for I heard the people say that this friar, Michael by name, was truly a very pious man who had preached penance and poverty, repeating the words of Saint Francis, and had been brought before the judges because of the spitefulness of certain women who, pretending to confess themselves to him, had then attributed heretical notions to him; and he had indeed been seized by the bishop's men in the house of those same women, a fact that amazed me, because a man of the church should never go to administer the sacraments in such unsuitable places; but this seemed to be a weakness of the Fraticelli, this failure to take propriety into due consideration, and perhaps there was some truth in the popular belief that held them to be not only heretics but also of dubious behavior (as it was always said of the Catharists that they were Bulgars and sodomites).

I came to the Church of San Salvatore, where the inquisition was in progress, but I could not enter, because of the great crowd outside it. However, some had hoisted themselves to the bars of the windows and, clinging there, could see and hear what was going on, and they reported it to those below. The inquisitors were reading to Brother Michael the confession he had made the day before, in which he said that Christ and his apostles "held nothing individually or in common as property," but Michael protested that the notary had now added "many false consequences" and he shouted (this I heard from outside), "You will have to defend yourselves on the day of judgment!" But the inquisitors read the confession as they had drawn it up, and at the end they asked him whether he wanted humbly to follow the opinions of the church and all the people of the city. And I heard Michael shouting in a loud voice that he wanted to follow what he believed, namely that he "wanted to keep Christ poor and crucified, and Pope John XXII was a heretic because he said the opposite." A great debate ensued, in which the inquisitors, many of them Franciscans, sought to make him understand that the Scriptures had not said what he was saying, and he accused them of denying the very Rule of their order, and they assailed him, asking him whether he thought he understood Scripture better than they, who were masters. And Fra Michael, very stubborn indeed, contested them, so that they began provoking him with such assertions as "Then we want you to consider Christ a property owner and Pope John a Catholic and holy man." And Michael, never faltering, said, "No, a heretic." And they said they had never seen anyone so tenacious in his own wickedness. But among the crowd outside the building I heard many compare him to Christ before the Pharisees, and I realized that among the people many believed in the holiness of the friar Michael.

Finally the bishop's men took him back to prison in irons. And that evening I was told that many monks, friends of the bishop, had gone to insult him and enjoin him to retract, but he answered like a man sure of his own truth. And he repeated to each of them that Christ was poor and that Saint Francis and Saint Dominic had said so as well, and that if for professing this upright opinion he had to be condemned to the stake, so much the better, because in a short time he would be able to see what the Scriptures describe, the twenty-four elders of the Apocalypse and Jesus Christ and Saint Francis and the glorious martyrs. And I was told that he said, "If we read with such fervor the doctrine of certain sainted abbots, how much greater should be our fervor and our joy in desiring to be in their midst?" And after words of this sort, the inquisitors left the prison with grim faces, crying out in indignation (and I heard them), "He has a devil in him!"

The next day we learned that the sentence had been pronounced; I went to the bishop's palace, where I could see the parchment, and I copied a part of it onto my tablet.

It began "In nomine Domini amen. Hec est quedam condemnatio corporalis et sententia condemnationis corporalis lata, data et in hiis scriptis sententialiter pronumptiata et promulgata...," etc., and it went on with a stern description of the sins and crimes of the said Michael; among these one seemed to me most foul, even if I do not know (considering the conduct of the trial) whether he really affirmed this, but it was said, in short, that the afore-mentioned Minorite had proclaimed that Saint Thomas Aquinas was not a saint nor did he enjoy eternal salvation, but was, on the contrary, damned and in a state of perdition! And the sentence concluded, establishing the punishment, since the accused would not mend his ways:

Idcirco, dictum Johannem vocatum fratrem Micchaelem hereticum et scismaticum quod ducatur ad locum iustitie consuetum, et ibidem igne et flammis igneis accensis concrementur et comburatur, ita quod penitus moriatur et anima a corpore separetur.

And after the sentence had been made public, more men of the church came to the prison and warned Michael of what would happen, and I heard them say then, "Brother Michael, the miters and copes have already been made, and painted on them are Fraticelli accompanied by devils." To frighten him and force him finally to retract. But Brother Michael knelt down and said, "I believe that beside the pyre there will be our father Francis, and I further believe there will be Jesus and the apostles, and the glorious martyrs Bartholomew and Anthony." Which was a way of refusing for the last time the inquisitors' offers.

The next morning I, too, was on the bridge before

the bishop's palace, where the inquisitors had gathered; Brother Michael, still in irons, was brought to face them. One of his faithful followers knelt before him to receive his benediction, and this follower was seized by the men-at-arms and taken at once to prison. Afterward, the inquisitors again read the sentence to the condemned man and asked him once more whether he wished to repent. At every point where the sentence said he was a heretic Michael replied, "I am no heretic; a sinner, yes, but Catholic," and when the text named "the most venerable and holy Pope John XXII" Michael answered, "No, a heretic." Then the bishop ordered Michael to come and kneel before him, and Michael said no one should kneel before heretics. They forced him to his knees and he murmured, "God will pardon me." And after he had been led out in all his priestly vestments, a ritual began, and one by one his vestments were stripped away until he remained in that little garment that the Florentines call a "cioppa." And as is the custom when a priest is defrocked, they seared the pads of his fingers with a hot iron and they shaved his head. Then he was handed over to the captain and his men, who treated him very harshly and put him in irons, to take him back to prison, as he said to the crowd, "Per Dominum moriemur." He was to be burned, as I found out, only the next day. And on this day they also went to ask him whether he wished to confess himself and receive communion. And he refused, saying it was a sin to accept the sacraments from one in a state of sin. Here, I believe, he was wrong, and he showed he had been corrupted by the heresy of the Patarines.

Finally it was the day of the execution, and a gonfalonier came for him, appearing friendly, for he asked what sort of man Michael was and why he was so stubborn when he had only to affirm what the whole populace affirmed and accept the opinion of Holy Mother Church. But Michael, very harshly, said, "I believe in Christ poor and crucified." And the gonfalonier went away, making a helpless gesture. Then the captain arrived with his men and took Michael into the courtyard, where the bishop's vicar reread the confession and the sentence to him. Michael interrupted again to contest opinions falsely attributed to him; these truly were matters of such subtlety that I do not recall them, and at that time did not understand them clearly. But these were surely what decided the death of Michael and the persecution of the Fraticelli. I did not understand why the men of the church and of the secular arm were so violent against people who wanted to live in poverty and held that Christ had not owned worldly goods. Because, I said to myself, if anything, they should fear men who wish to live in wealth and take money away from others, and lead the church into sin and introduce simoniacal practices into it. And I spoke of this with a man standing near me, for I could not keep silent any more. He smiled mockingly and said to me that a monk who practices poverty sets a bad example for the populace, for then they cannot accept monks who do not practice it. And, he added, the preaching of poverty put the wrong ideas into the heads of the people, who would consider their poverty a source of pride, and pride can lead to many proud acts. And, finally, he said that I should know, thanks to some syllogism which was not clear to him, either, that preaching poverty for monks put you on the side of the Emperor, and this did not please the Pope. All excellent reasons, they seemed to me, even if expounded by a man of scant learning, except that at this point I did not understand why Brother Michael wanted to die so horribly to please the Emperor, or to settle a controversy among religious orders. And in fact some of those present were saying, "He is not a saint, he was sent by Louis to stir up discord among the citizens, and the Fraticelli are Tuscans but behind them are the Emperor's agents." And others said, "He is a madman, he is possessed by the Devil, swollen with pride, and he enjoys martyrdom for his wicked pride; they make these monks read too many lives of the saints, it would be better for them to take a wife!" And still others added, "No, all Christians should be like him, ready to proclaim their faith, as in the time of the pagans." As I listened to those voices, no longer knowing what to think myself, it so happened that I looked straight at the condemned man's face, which at times was hidden by the crowd ahead of me. And I saw the face of a man looking at something that is not of this earth, as I had sometimes seen on statues of saints in ecstatic vision. And I understood that, madman or seer as he might be, he knowingly wanted to die because he believed that in dying he would defeat his enemy, whoever it was. And I understood that his example would lead others to death. And I remain amazed by the possessors of such steadfastness only because I do not know, even today, whether what prevails in them is a proud love of the truth they believe, which leads them to death, or a proud desire for death, which leads them to proclaim their truth, whatever it may be. And I am overwhelmed with admiration and fear.

But let us go back to the execution, for now all were heading for the place where Michael would be put to death.

The captain and his men brought him out of the gate, with his little skirt on him and some of the buttons undone, and as he walked with a broad stride and a bowed head, reciting his office, he seemed one of the martyrs. And the crowd was unbelievably large and many cried, "Do not die!" and he would answer, "I want to die for Christ." "But you are not dying for Christ," they said to him; and he said, "No, for the truth." When they came to a place called the Proconsul's Corner, one man cried to him to pray to God for them all, and he blessed the crowd.

At the Church of the Baptist they shouted to him, "Save your life!" and he answered, "Run for your life from sin!"; at the Old Market they shouted to him, "Live, live!" and he replied, "Save yourselves from hell"; at the New Market they yelled, "Repent, repent," and he replied, "Repent of your usury." And on reaching Santa Croce, he saw the monks of his order on the steps, and he reproached them because they did not follow the Rule of Saint Francis. And some of them shrugged, but others pulled their cowls over their faces to cover them, in shame.

And going toward the Justice Gate, many said to him, "Recant! Recant! Don't insist on dying," and he said, "Christ died for us." And they said, "But you are not Christ, you must not die for us!" And he said, "But I want to die for Him." At the Field of Justice, one said to him he should do as a certain monk, his superior, had done, abjuring; but Michael answered that he would not abjure, and I saw many in the crowd agree and urge Michael to be strong: so I and many others realized those were his followers, and we moved away from them.

Finally we were outside the city and before us the pyre appeared, the "hut," as they called it there, because the wood was arranged in the form of a hut, and there a circle of armed horsemen formed, to keep people from coming too close. And there they bound Brother Michael to the stake. And again I heard someone shout to him, "But what is it you're dying for?" And he answered, "For a truth that dwells in me, which I can proclaim only by death." They set fire to the wood. And Brother Michael, who had chanted the "Credo," afterward chanted the "Te Deum." He sang perhaps eight verses of it, then he bent over as if he had to sneeze, and fell to the ground, because his bonds had burned away. He was already dead: before the body is completely burned it has already died from the great heat, which makes the heart explode, and from the smoke that fills the chest.

Then the hut burned entirely, like a torch, and there

was a great glow, and if it had not been for the poor charred body of Michael, still glimpsed among the glowing coals, I would have said I was standing before the burning bush. And I was close enough to have a view (I recalled as I climbed the steps of the library) that made some words rise spontaneously to my lips, about ecstatic rapture; I had read them in the books of Saint Hildegard: "The flame consists of a splendid clarity, of an unusual vigor, and of an igneous ardor, but possesses the splendid clarity that it may illuminate and the igneous ardor that it may burn."

I remembered some words of Ubertino about love. The image of Michael on the pyre became confused with that of Dolcino, and that of Dolcino with that of the beautiful Margaret. I felt again the restlessness that had seized me in church.

I tried not to think about it and headed straight for the labyrinth.

This was the first time I entered it alone; the long shadows cast by the lamp on the floor terrified me as much as had the visions the previous night. At every moment I feared I would find myself before another mirror, because the magic of mirrors is such that even when you know they are mirrors they still upset you.

On the other hand, I did not try to orient myself, or to avoid the room with the perfumes that induce visions. I proceeded as if in the grip of a fever, nor did I know where I wanted to go. In fact, I did not move far from my starting point, because a short time later I found myself again in the heptagonal room by which I had entered. Here, on a table, some books were laid out that I did not seem to have seen the night before. I guessed they were works that Malachi had withdrawn from the scriptorium and had not yet replaced on their proper shelves. I could not comprehend how far I was from the perfume room, because I felt dazed, which could be the effect of some effluvium that reached even that spot, or else of the things I had been pondering until then. I opened a richly illuminated volume that, by its style, seemed to me to come from the monasteries of Ultima Thule.

On a page where the holy Gospel of the apostle Mark began, I was struck by the image of a lion. I was certain it was a lion, even though I had never seen one in the flesh, and the artist had reproduced its features faithfully, inspired perhaps by the sight of the lions of Hibernia, land of monstrous creatures, and I was convinced that this animal, as for that matter the *Physiologus* says, concentrates in itself all the characteristics of the things at once most horrible and most regal. So that image suggested to me both the image of the Enemy and that of Christ our Lord, nor did I know by what symbolic key I was to read it, and I was trembling all over, out of fear and also because of the wind coming through the fissures in the walls.

The lion I saw had a mouth bristling with teeth, and a finely armored head like a serpent's; the immense body was supported by four paws with sharp, fierce claws, and its coat resembled one of those rugs that later I saw brought from the Orient, with red and emerald scales on which were drawn, yellow as the plague, horrible and sturdy armatures of bone. Also yellow was the tail, which twisted from the rump to the head, ending in a final scroll of black and white tufts.

I was already quite awed by the lion (and more than once I had looked around as if I expected to see an animal of that description suddenly appear) when I decided to look at other pages and my eye fell, at the opening of the Gospel of Matthew, on the image of a man. I do not know why, but it frightened me more than the lion: the face was a man's, but this man was sheathed in a kind of stiff chasuble that covered him to his feet, and this chasuble, or cuirass, was encrusted with red and yellow semiprecious stones. The head, which emerged enigmatically from a castle of rubies and topazes, seemed (how blasphemous terror made me!) that of the mysterious murderer whose impalpable trail we were following. And then I realized why I linked the animal and the armored man so closely with the labyrinth: both illustrations, like all in that book, emerged from a pattern of interlocking labyrinths, whose lines of onyx and emerald, threads of chrysoprase, ribbons of beryl seemed all to refer to the tangle of rooms and corridors where I was. My eye became lost, on the page, along gleaming paths, as my feet were becoming lost in the troublous succession of the rooms of the library, and seeing my own wandering depicted on those parchments filled me with uneasiness and convinced me that each of those books was telling, through mysterious cachinnations, my present story. "De te fabula narratur," I said to myself, and I wondered if those pages did not already contain the story of future events in store for me.

I opened another book, and this seemed of the Hispanic school. The colors were violent, the reds suggested blood or fire. It was the book of Revelation of the apostle, and once again, as the night before, I happened upon the page of the mulier amicta sole. But it was not the same book; the illumination was different. Here the artist had dwelled at greater length on the woman's form. I compared her face, her bosom, her curving thighs with the statue of the Virgin I had seen with Ubertino. The line was different, but this mulier also seemed very beautiful to me. I thought I should not dwell on these notions, and I turned several more pages. I found another woman, but this time it was the whore of Babylon. I was not so much struck by her form as by the thought that she, too, was a woman like the other, and yet this one was the vessel of every vice, whereas the other was the receptacle of every virtue. But the forms were womanly in both cases, and at a certain point I could no longer understand what distinguished them. Again I felt an inner agitation; the image of the Virgin in the church became superimposed on that of the beautiful Margaret. "I am damned!" I said to myself. Or, "I am mad." And I decided I should leave the library.

Luckily I was near the staircase. I rushed down, at the risk of stumbling and extinguishing the lamp. I found myself again under the broad vaults of the scriptorium, but I did not linger even there, and hurled myself down the stairs leading to the refectory.

Here I paused, gasping. The light of the moon came through the windows, very radiant, and I hardly needed the lamp, which would have been indispensable for cells and for passages of the library. Nevertheless, I kept it burning, as if to seek comfort. But I was still breathless, and I decided I should drink some water to calm my tension. Since the kitchen was near, I crossed the refectory and slowly opened one of the doors that led into the second half of the ground floor of the Aedificium.

And at this point my terror, instead of lessening, increased. Because I immediately realized someone else was in the kitchen, near the bread oven—or at least I realized a light was shining in that corner. Filled with fear, I blew mine out. Frightened as I was, I instilled fright, and in fact the other person (or persons) immediately put out their light, too. But in vain, because the moonlight illuminated the kitchen sufficiently to cast before me one or more confused shadows on the floor.

Frozen, I did not dare draw back, or advance. I heard a stammering sound, and I thought I heard, softly, a woman's voice. Then from the shapeless group that could be discerned vaguely near the oven, a dark, squat form broke away and fled toward the outside door, evidently left ajar, closing it after himself.

I remained, on the threshold between refectory and kitchen, and so did a vague something near the oven. A vague and—how to say it?—moaning something. From the shadows, in fact, came a groan, a kind of subdued weeping, rhythmic sobs of fear.

Nothing gives a fearful man more courage than another's fear, but it was not fear that impelled me toward the shadow. Rather, I would say, I was driven by an intoxication not unlike the one that had gripped me when I was having visions. In the kitchen there was something kin to the fumes that had overcome me in the library the night before. It was perhaps not the same substance, but on my overexcited senses it had the same effect. I sniffed a pungent smell of traganth, alum, and tartar, which cooks use to make wine aromatic. Or perhaps, as I learned later, in those days they were brewing beer (which in that northern part of the peninsula was held in some esteem), and it was prepared with the method of my country, with heather, swamp myrtle, and wild rosemary. All spices that intoxicated, more than my nostrils, my mind.

And while my rational instinct was to cry out "Vade retro!" and get away from the moaning thing that was certainly a succubus summoned for me by the Evil One, something in my vis appetitiva urged me forward, as if I wanted to take part in some marvel.

And so I approached the shadow, until, in the moonlight that fell from the high windows, I realized that it was a woman, trembling, clutching to her breast one hand holding a package, and drawing back, weeping, toward the mouth of the oven.

May God, the Blessed Virgin, and all the saints of paradise assist me in telling what then happened. Modesty, the dignity of my position (as an aged monk by now, in this handsome monastery of Melk, a haven of peace and serene meditation), would counsel me to take the most devout precautions. I should simply say that something evil took place and that it would not be meet to tell what it was, and so I would upset neither my reader nor myself.

But I have determined to tell, of those remote events,

the whole truth, and truth is indivisible, it shines with its own transparency and does not allow itself to be diminished by our interests or our shame. The problem is, rather, of telling what happened not as I see it now and remember it—(even if I still remember everything with pitiless vividness, nor do I know whether my subsequent repentance has so fixed in my memory these situations and thoughts, or whether the inadequacy of that same repentance still torments me, resuscitating in my oppressed mind the smallest details of my shame), but as I saw it and felt it then. And I can do so with the fidelity of a chronicler, for if I close my eyes I can repeat not only everything I did but also what I thought in those moments, as if I were copying a parchment written at the time. I must therefore proceed in this way, Saint Michael Archangel protect me, because for the edification of future readers and the flaying of my guilt I want now to tell how a young man can succumb to the snares of the Devil, that they may be known and evident, so anyone encountering them in the future may defeat them.

So, it was a woman. Or, rather, a girl. Having had until then (and since then, God be thanked) little intimacy with creatures of that sex, I cannot say what her age may have been. I know she was young, almost adolescent, perhaps she had passed sixteen or eighteen springs, or perhaps twenty; and I was struck by the impression of human reality that emanated from that form. It was not a vision, and in any case it seemed to me valde bona. Perhaps because she was trembling like a little bird in winter, and was weeping, and was afraid of me.

Thinking that the duty of every good Christian is to succor his neighbor, I approached her with great gentleness and in good Latin told her she should not fear, because I was a friend, in any case not an enemy, certainly not the enemy she perhaps dreaded.

Because of the meekness of my gaze, I imagine, the creature grew calm and came to me. I sensed that she did not understand my Latin and instinctively I addressed her in my German vernacular, and this frightened her greatly, whether because of the harsh sounds, unfamiliar to the people of those parts, or because those sounds reminded her of some other experience with soldiers from my lands, I cannot say which. Then I smiled, considering that the language of gestures and of the face is more universal than that of words, and she was reassured. She smiled at me, too, and said a few words.

I knew her vernacular very slightly; it was different from the bit I had learned in Pisa, but I realized from her tone that she was saying sweet words to me, and she seemed to be saying something like "You are young, you are handsome...." It is rare for a novice who has spent his whole childhood in a monastery to hear declarations of his beauty; indeed, we are regularly admonished that physical beauty is fleeting and must be considered base. But the snares of the Enemy are infinite, and I confess that this reference to my comeliness, though mendacious, fell sweetly on my ears and filled me with an irrepressible emotion. Especially since the girl, in saying this, had extended her hand until the tips of her fingers grazed my cheek, then quite beardless. I felt a kind of delirium, but at that moment I was unable to sense any hint of sin in my heart. Such is the force of the Devil when he wants to try us and dispel from our spirit the signs of grace.

What did I feel? What did I see? I remember only that the emotions of the first moment were bereft of any expression, because my tongue and my mind had not been instructed in how to name sensations of that sort. Until I recalled other inner words, heard in another time and in other places, spoken certainly for other ends, but which seemed wondrously in keeping with my joy in that moment, as if they had been born consubstantially to express it. Words pressed into the caverns of my memory rose to the (dumb) surface of my lips, and I forgot that they had served in Scripture or in the pages of the saints to express quite different, more radiant realities. But was there truly a difference between the delights of which the saints had spoken and those that my agitated spirit was feeling at that moment? At that moment the watchful sense of difference was annihilated in me. And this, it seems to me, is precisely the sign of rapture in the abysses of identity.

Suddenly the girl appeared to me as the black but comely virgin of whom the Song of Songs speaks. She wore a threadbare little dress of rough cloth that opened in a fairly immodest fashion over her bosom, and around her neck was a necklace made of little colored stones, very commonplace, I believe. But her head rose proudly on a neck as white as an ivory tower, her eyes were clear as the pools of Heshbon, her nose was as the tower of Lebanon, her hair like purple. Yes, her tresses seemed to me like a flock of goats, her teeth like flocks of sheep coming up from their bath, all in pairs, so that none preceded its companion. And I could not help murmuring: "Behold, thou art fair, my love; behold, thou art fair. Thy hair is as a flock of goats that lie along the side of Mount Gilead; thy lips are like a thread of scarlet, thy temples are like a piece of a pomegranate, thy neck is like the tower of David whereon there hang a thousand bucklers." And I asked myself, frightened and rapt, who was she who rose before me like the dawn, beautiful as the moon, radiant as the sun, *terribilis ut castorum acies ordinata.*

Then the creature came still closer to me, throwing into a corner the dark package she had till then held pressed to her bosom; and she raised her hand to stroke my face, and repeated the words I had already heard. And while I did not know whether to flee from her or move even closer, while my head was throbbing as if the trumpets of Joshua were about to bring down the walls of Jericho, as I yearned and at once feared to touch her, she smiled with great joy, emitted the stifled moan of a pleased she-goat, and undid the strings that closed her dress over her bosom, slipped the dress from her body like a tunic, and stood before me as Eve must have appeared to Adam in the garden of Eden. "Pulchra sunt ubera quae paululum supereminent et tument modice," I murmured, repeating the words I had heard from Ubertino, because her breasts appeared to me like two fawns that are twins of a roe, feeding among the lilies, her navel was a goblet wherein no mingled wine is wanting, her belly a heap of wheat set about with lilies.

"O sidus clarum pellarum," I cried to her, "o porta clausa, fons hortorum, cella custos unguentorum, cella pigmentaria!" Inadvertently I found myself against her body, feeling its warmth and the sharp perfume of unguents never known before. I remembered, "Sons, when mad love comes, man is powerless!" and I understood that, whether what I felt was a snare of the Enemy or a gift of heaven, I was now powerless against the impulse that moved me, and I cried, "Oh langueo," and, "Causam languoris video nec caveo!," also because a rosy perfume breathed from her lips and her feet were beautiful in sandals, and her legs were like columns and jewels were the joints of her thighs, the work of the hands of a cunning workman. O love, daughter of delights, a king is held captive in your tresses, I murmured to myself, and I was in her arms, and we fell together onto the bare floor of the kitchen, and, whether on my own initiative or through her wiles, I found myself free of my novice's habit and we felt no shame at our bodies and cuncta erant bona.

And she kissed me with the kisses of her mouth, and her loves were more delicious than wine and her ointments had a goodly fragrance, and her neck was beautiful among pearls and her cheeks among earrings, behold thou art fair, my beloved, behold thou art fair; thine eyes are as doves (I said), and let me see thy face, let me hear thy voice, for thy voice is harmonious and thy face enchanting, thou hast ravished my heart, my sister, thou hast ravished my heart with one of thine eyes, with one chain of thy neck, thy lips drop as the honeycomb, honey and milk are under thy tongue, the smell of thy breath is of apples, thy two breasts are clusters of grapes, thy palate a heady wine that goes straight to my love and flows over my lips and teeth.... A fountain sealed, spikenard and saffron, calamus and cinnamon, myrrh and aloes, I have eaten my honeycomb with my honey, I have drunk my wine with my milk. Who was she, who was she who rose like the dawn, fair as the moon, clear as the sun, terrible as an army with banners?

O Lord, when the soul is transported, the only virtue lies in loving what you see (is that not true?), the supreme happiness in having what you have; there blissful life is drunk at its source (has this not been said?), there you savor the true life that we will live after this mortal life among the angels for all eternity.... This is what I was thinking and it seemed to me the prophecies were being fulfilled at last, as the girl lavished indescribable sweetness on me, and it was as if my whole body were an eye, before and behind, and I could suddenly see all surrounding things. And I understood that from it, from love, unity and tenderness are created together, as are good and kiss and fulfillment, as I had already heard, believing I was being told about something else. And only for an instant, as my joy was about to reach its zenith, did I remember that perhaps I was experiencing, and at night, the possession of the noontime Devil, who was condemned finally to reveal himself in his true, diabolical nature to the soul that in ecstasy asks "Who are you?," who knows how to grip the soul and delude the body. But I was immediately convinced that my scruples were indeed devilish, for nothing could be more right and good and holy than what I was experiencing, the sweetness of which grew with every moment. As a little drop of water added to a quantity of wine is completely dispersed and takes on the color and taste of wine, as red-hot iron becomes like molten fire losing its original form, as air when it is inundated with the sun's light is transformed into total splendor and clarity so that it no longer seems illuminated but, rather, seems to be light itself, so I felt myself die of tender liquefaction, and I had only the strength left to murmur the words of the psalm: "Behold my bosom is like new wine, sealed, which bursts new vessels," and suddenly I saw a brilliant light and in it a saffron-colored form which flamed up in a sweet and shining fire, and that splendid light spread through all the shining fire, and this shining fire through that golden form and that brilliant light and that shining fire through the whole form.

As, half fainting, I fell on the body to which I had joined myself, I understood in a last vital spurt that flame consists of a splendid clarity, an unusual vigor, and an igneous ardor, but it possesses the splendid clarity so that it may illuminate and the igneous ardor that it may burn. Then I understood the abyss, and the deeper abysses that it conjured up.

Now that, with a hand that trembles (either in horror at the sin I am recounting or in guilty nostalgia of the event I recall), I write these lines, I realize that to describe my wicked ecstasy of that instant I have used the same words that I used, not many pages before, to describe the fire that burned the martyred body of the Fraticello Michael. Nor is it an accident that my hand, passive agent of the soul, has penned the same expression for two experiences so disparate, because probably I experienced them in the same way both at the time, when I lived through them, and now, as I have tried to bring them back to life on this parchment.

There is a mysterious wisdom by which phenomena among themselves disparate can be called by analogous names, just as divine things can be designated by terrestrial terms, and through equivocal symbols God can be called lion or leopard; and death can be called sword; joy, flame; flame, death; death, abyss; abyss, perdition; perdition, raving; and raving, passion.

Why did I, as a youth, depict the ecstasy of death that had impressed me in the martyr Michael in the words the saint had used for the ecstasy of (divine) life, and yet I could not refrain from depicting in the same words the ecstasy (culpable and fleeting) of earthly pleasure, which immediately afterward had spontaneously appeared to me as a sensation of death and annihilation? I shall try now to reflect both on the way I felt, a few months apart, two experiences at once uplifting and painful, and on the way in which that night in the abbey I consciously remembered the one and felt with my senses the other, a few hours apart, and, further, on the way I have relived them now, penning these lines, and on how in all three instances I recited them to myself with the words of the different experience of that sainted soul annihilated in the divine vision. Have I perhaps blasphemed (then? now?)? What was similar in Michael's desire for death, in the transport I felt at the sight of the flame consuming him, in the desire for carnal union I felt with the girl, in the mystic shame with which I translated it allegorically, and in the desire for joyous annihilation that moved the saint to die in his own love in order to live longer and eternally? Is it possible that things so equivocal can be said in such a univocal way? And this, it seems, is the teaching left us by Saint Thomas, the greatest of all doctors: the more openly it remains a figure of speech, the more it is a dissimilar similitude and not literal, the more a metaphor reveals its truth. But if love of the flame and of the abyss are the metaphor for the love of God, can they be the metaphor for love of death and love of sin? Yes, as the lion and the serpent stand both for Christ and the Devil. The fact is that correct interpretation can be established only on the authority of the fathers, and in the case that torments me, I have no auctoritas to which my obedient mind can refer, and I burn in doubt (and again the image of fire appears to define the void of the truth and the fullness of the error that annihilate me!). What is happening, O Lord, in my spirit, now that I allow myself to be gripped by the vortex of memories and I conflagrate different times at once, as if I were to manipulate the order of the stars and the sequence of their celestial movements? Certainly I am overstepping the boundaries of my sinful and sick intelligence. Now, let us return to the task I had humbly set myself. I was telling about that day and the total bewilderment of the senses into which I sank. There, I have told what I remembered on that occasion, and let my feeble pen, faithful and truthful chronicler, stop there.

I lay, how long I do not know, the girl at my side. With a light motion her hand continued to touch my body, now damp with sweat. I felt an inner exultation, which was not peace, but like the last subdued flicker of a fire taking time to die beneath the embers, when the flame is already dead. I would not hesitate to call blessed a man to whom it was granted to experience something similar in this life (I murmured as if in my sleep), even rarely (and, in fact, I experienced it only that time), and very rapidly, for the space of a single moment. As if one no longer existed, not feeling one's identity at all, or feeling lowered, almost annihilated: if some mortal (I said to myself) could for a single moment and most rapidly enjoy what I have enjoyed, he would immediately look with a baleful eye at this perverse world, would be upset by the bane of daily life, would feel the weight of the body of death. . . . Was this not what I had been taught? That invitation of my whole spirit to lose all memory in bliss was surely (now I understood it) the radiance of the eternal sun; and the joy that it produces opens, extends, enlarges man, and the gaping chasm man bears within himself is no longer sealed so easily, for it is the wound cut by the blow of love's sword, nor is there anything else here below more sweet and terrible. But such is the right of the sun: it riddles the wounded man with its rays and all the wounds widen, the man uncloses and extends, his very veins are laid open, his strength is now incapable of obeying the orders it receives and is moved solely by desire, the spirit burns, sunk into the abyss of what it is now touching, seeing its own desire and its own truth outstripped by the reality it has lived and is living. And one witnesses, dumbfounded, one's own raving.

And in the grip of these sensations of ineffable inner joy, I dozed off.

I reopened my eyes some time later, and the moonlight, perhaps because of a cloud, had grown much fainter. I stretched out my hand at my side and no longer felt the girl's body. I turned my head; she was gone.

The absence of the object that had unleashed my desire and slaked my thirst made me realize suddenly both the vanity of that desire and the perversity of that thirst. Omne animal triste post coitum. I became aware that I had sinned. Now, after years and years, while I still bitterly bemoan my error, I cannot forget how that evening I had felt great pleasure, and I would be doing a wrong to the Almighty, who created all things in goodness and beauty, if I did not admit that also between those two sinners something happened that in itself, naturaliter, was good and beautiful. But perhaps it is my present old age, which makes me feel, culpably, how beautiful and good all my youth was. Just when I should turn my thoughts to death, which is approaching. Then, a young man, I did not think of death, but, hotly and sincerely, I wept for my sin.

I stood up, trembling, also because I had lain a long time on the cold stones of the kitchen and my body was numb. I dressed, almost feverish. I glimpsed then in a corner the package that the girl had abandoned in her flight. I bent to examine the object: it was a kind of bundle, a rolled-up cloth that seemed to come from the kitchen. I unwrapped it, and at first I did not understand what was inside, both because of the scant light and because of the shapeless shape of the contents. Then I understood. Among clots of blood and scraps of flabbier and whitish meat, before my eyes, dead but still throbbing with the gelatinous life of dead viscera, lined by livid nerves: a heart, of great size.

A dark veil descended over my eyes, an acid saliva rose in my mouth, I let out a cry and fell as a dead body falls.

NIGHT

In which Adso, distraught, confesses to William and meditates on the function of woman in the plan of creation, but then he discovers the corpse of a man.

I came around to find someone bathing my face. There, holding a lamp, was Brother William, who had put something under my head.

"What's happened, Adso?" he asked me. "Have you been roaming about at night stealing offal from the kitchen?"

In short, William had awakened, sought me for I forget what reason, and, not finding me, suspected me of going to perform some bit of bravado in the library. Approaching the Aedificium on the kitchen side, he saw a shadow slip from the door toward the vegetable garden (it was the girl, leaving, perhaps because she had heard someone approaching). He tried to figure out who it was and follow her, but she (or, rather, the shadow, as she was for him) went toward the outside wall of the compound and disappeared. Then William—after an exploration of the environs—entered the kitchen and found me lying in a faint.

When, still terrified, I mentioned to him the package

with the heart, blurting out something about another crime, he started laughing: "Adso, what man could have such a big heart? It's the heart of a cow, or an ox; they slaughtered an animal today, in fact. But tell me, how did it come into your hands?"

At that point, overwhelmed with remorse, and still stunned by my great fear, I burst into a flood of tears and asked him to administer to me the sacrament of confession. Which he did, and I told him all, concealing nothing.

Brother William heard me out earnestly, but with a hint of indulgence. When I had finished his face turned grave and he said: "Adso, you have sinned, that is certain, against the commandment that bids you not to fornicate, and also against your duties as a novice. In your defense there is the fact that you found yourself in one of those situations in which even a father in the desert would have damned himself. And of woman as source of temptation the Scriptures have already said enough. Ecclesiastes says of woman that her conversation is like burning fire, and the Proverbs say that she takes possession of man's precious soul and the strongest men are ruined by her. And Ecclesiastes further says: 'And I find more bitter than death the woman, whose heart is snares and nets, and her hands as bands.' And others have said she is the vessel of the Devil. Having affirmed this, dear Adso, I cannot convince myself that God chose to introduce such a foul being into creation without also endowing it with some virtues. And I cannot help reflecting that He granted her many privileges and motives of prestige, three of them very great indeed. In fact, He created man in this base world, and from mud; woman He created later, in paradise and of noble human matter. And he did not mold her from Adam's feet or his viscera, but from the rib. In the second place, the Lord, who is all-powerful, could have become incarnate as a man directly in some miraculous way, but he chose instead to dwell in the womb of a woman, a sign that it was not so foul after all. And when he appeared after the Resurrection, he appeared to a woman. And finally, in the celestial glory no man shall be king of that realm, but the queen will be a woman who has never sinned. If, then, the Lord showed such favor to Eve herself and to her daughters, is it so abnormal that we also should feel drawn by the graces and the nobility of that sex? What I mean to say to you, Adso, is that you must not do it again, of course, but it is not so monstrous that you were tempted to do it. And as far as that goes, for a monk to have, at least once in his life, experience of carnal passion, so that he can one day be indulgent and understanding with the sinners he will counsel and console ... well, dear Adso, it is not a thing to be wished before it happens, but it is not something to vituperate too much once it has happened. So go with God and let us speak of it no more. Indeed, rather than reflect and dwell too much on something best forgotten, if possible"—and it seemed to me at this point that his voice faded as if at some private emotion—"let us ask ourselves the meaning of what happened this night. Who was this girl and whom was she meeting?"

"This I don't know, and I didn't see the man who was with her," I said.

"Very well, but we can deduce who it was from many and certain clues. First of all, the man was old and ugly, one with whom a girl does not go willingly, especially if she is beautiful, as you say, though it seems to me, my dear wolf cub, that you were prepared to find any food delicious."

"Why old and ugly?"

"Because the girl didn't go with him for love, but for a pack of scraps. Certainly she is a girl from the village who, perhaps not for the first time, grants her favors to some lustful monk out of hunger, and receives as recompense something for her and her family to eat."

"A harlot!" I said, horrified.

"A poor peasant girl, Adso. Probably with smaller brothers to feed. Who, if she were able, would give herself for love and not for lucre. As she did last night. In fact, you tell me she found you young and handsome, and gave you gratis and out of love what to others she would have given for an ox heart and some bits of lung. And she felt so virtuous for the free gift she made of herself, and so uplifted, that she ran off without taking anything in exchange. This is why I think the other one, to whom she compared you, was neither young nor handsome."

I confess that, profound as my repentance was, that explanation filled me with a sweet pride; but I kept silent and allowed my master to continue.

"This ugly old man must have the opportunity to go down to the village and deal with the peasants, for some purpose connected with his position. He must know how to get people into the abbey and out of it, and know there would be that offal in the kitchen (perhaps tomorrow it would be said that the door had been left open and a dog had come in and eaten the scraps). And, finally, he must have had a certain sense of economy, and a certain interest in seeing that the kitchen was not deprived of more precious victuals: otherwise he would have given her a steak or some choice cut. And so you see that the picture of our stranger is drawn very clearly and that all these properties, or accidents, are suited to a substance that I would have no fear in defining as our cellarer, Remigio of Varagine. Or, if I am mistaken, our mysterious Salvatore—who, for that matter, since he comes from these parts, can speak easily with the local people and would know how to persuade a girl to do what he would have made her do, if you had not arrived."

"That is certainly all correct," I said, convinced, "but what is the good of knowing it now?"

"None. Or much," William said. "The story may or may not have a connection with the crimes that concern us. On the other hand, if the cellarer was a Dolcinian, that would explain this, and vice versa. And we now know, finally, that this abbey is a place of many, bizarre events at night. And who can say that our cellarer, and Salvatore, who move through it in darkness with such ease, do not know, in any event, more things than what they tell?"

"But will they tell them to us?"

"No, not if we behave in a compassionate manner, ignoring their sins. But if we were really to know something, we would possess a way of persuading them to speak. In other words, if there is need, the cellarer and Salvatore are ours, and may God forgive us this deception, since He forgives so many other things," he said, looking at me slyly; I did not have the heart to make any comment on the licitness of these notions of his.

"And now we should go to bed, because in an hour it is matins. But I see you are still agitated, my poor Adso, still fearful because of your sin.... There is nothing like a good spell in church to calm the spirit. I have absolved you, but one never knows. Go and ask the Lord's confirmation." And he gave me a rather brisk slap on the head, perhaps as a show of paternal and virile affection, perhaps as an indulgent penance. Or perhaps (as I culpably thought at that moment) in a sort of good-natured envy, since he was a man who so thirsted for new and vital experiences.

We headed for the church, taking our usual path, which I followed in haste, closing my eyes, because all those bones reminded me too obviously, that night, of how I was dust and how foolish had been the pride of my flesh.

When we reached the nave we saw a shadowy figure before the main altar. I thought it was again Ubertino, but it was Alinardo, who did not recognize us at first. He said he was unable to sleep and had decided to spend the night praying for that young monk who had disappeared (he could not even remember the name). He prayed for his soul, if he were dead, and for his body, if he were lying ill and alone somewhere.

"Too many dead," he said, "too many dead...But it was written in the book of the apostle. With the first trumpet came the hail, with the second a third part of the sea became blood; and you found one body in the hail, the other in blood....The third trumpet warns that a burning star will fall in the third part of rivers and fountains of waters. So I tell you, our third brother has disappeared. And fear for the fourth, because the third part of the sun will be smitten, and of the moon and the stars, so there will be almost complete darkness...."

As we came out of the transept, William asked himself whether there were not some element of truth in the old man's words.

"But," I pointed out to him, "this would mean assuming that a single diabolical mind, using the Apocalypse as guide, had arranged the three disappearances, also assuming that Berengar is dead. But, on the contrary, we know Adelmo died of his own volition...."

"True," William said, "but the same diabolical or sick mind could have been inspired by Adelmo's death to arrange the other two in a symbolic way. And if this were so, Berengar should be found in a river or a fountain. And there are no rivers or fountains in the abbey, at least not such as someone could drown or be drowned in...."

"There are only the baths," I observed, almost by chance.

"Adso!" William said. "You know, that could be an idea? The balneary!"

"But they must have looked there...."

"I saw the servants this morning when they were making the search; they opened the door of the balneary and took a glance inside, without investigating. They did not expect to find something carefully hidden: they were looking for a corpse lying somewhere theatrically, like Venantius's body in the jar.... Let's go and have a look. It is still dark anyway, and our lamp seems to go on burning merrily."

So we did, and without difficulty we opened the door of the balneary, next to the infirmary.

Separated one from the other by thick curtains were some tubs, I don't recall how many. The monks used them for their ablutions, on the days the Rule established, and Severinus used them for therapeutic reasons, because nothing can restore body and mind better than a bath. A fireplace in one corner allowed the water to be heated easily. We found it dirty with fresh ashes, and before it a great cauldron lay, overturned. The water could be drawn from a font in another corner.

We looked in the first tubs, which were empty. Only the last, concealed by a drawn curtain, was full, and next to it lay a garment, in a heap. At first sight, in the beam of our lamp, the surface of the liquid seemed smooth; but as the light struck it we glimpsed on the bottom, lifeless, a naked human body. We pulled it out slowly: Berengar. And this one, William said, truly had the face of a drowned man. The features were swollen. The body, white and flabby, without hair, seemed a woman's except for the obscene spectacle of the flaccid pudenda. I blushed, then shuddered. I made the sign of the cross as William blessed the corpse.

FOURTH DAY

LAUDS

In which William and Severinus examine Berengar's corpse and discover that the tongue is black, unusual in a drowned man. Then they discuss most painful poisons and a past theft.

I will not go into how we informed the abbot, how the whole abbey woke before the canonical hour, the cries of horror, the fear and grief that could be seen on every face, and how the news spread to all the people of the compound, the servants blessing themselves and uttering formulas against the evil eye. I don't know whether the first office that morning proceeded according to regulations, or who took part in it. I followed William and Severinus, who had Berengar's body wrapped up and ordered it laid out on a table in the infirmary.

When the abbot and the other monks had left, the herbalist and my master studied the corpse at length, with the cold detachment of men of medicine.

"He died by drowning," Severinus said, "there's no doubt. The face is swollen, the belly taut...."

"But he was not drowned by another's hands," William observed, "for in that case he would have reacted against the murderer's violence, whereas everything was neat and clean, as if Berengar had heated the water, filled the bath, and lain in it of his own free will."

"This doesn't surprise me," Severinus said. "Berengar suffered from convulsions, and I myself had often told him that warm baths serve to calm agitation of the body and the spirit. On several occasions he asked me leave to light the balneary fire. So he may have done last night...."

"Night before last," William said, "because this body— as you see—has remained in the water at least one day...."

William informed him of some of the events of that night. He did not tell him we had been in the scriptorium furtively, but, concealing various circumstances, he told him that we had pursued a mysterious figure who had taken a book from us. Severinus realized William was telling him only a part of the truth, but he asked no further questions. He observed that the agitation of Berengar, if he had been the mysterious thief, could have led him then to seek calm in a refreshing bath. Berengar, he said, was of a very sensitive nature, and sometimes a vexation or an emotion brought on his trembling and cold sweats and made his eyes bulge, and he would fall to the ground, spitting out a whitish slime.

"In any case," William said, "before coming here he went somewhere else, because in the balneary I didn't see the book he stole. So he had been somewhere else, and afterward, we'll assume that, to calm his emotion and perhaps to elude our search, he slipped into the balneary and immersed himself in the water. Severinus, do you believe his illness could make him lose consciousness and drown?"

"That's possible," Severinus said, dubiously. For some moments he had been examining the hands of the corpse. "Here's a curious thing..." he said.

"What?"

"The other day I observed Venantius's hands, when

the blood had been washed off, and I noticed a detail to which I attached little importance. The tips of two fingers of Venantius's right hand were dark, as if blackened by some dark substance. Exactly—you see? —like two fingertips of Berengar now. In fact, here we have a trace also on the third finger. At the time I thought that Venantius had handled some inks in the scriptorium...."

"Interesting," William said pensively, taking a closer look at Berengar's fingers. Dawn was breaking, the light indoors was still faint, and my master was obviously suffering the lack of his lenses. "Interesting," he repeated. "But there are fainter traces also on the left hand, at least on the thumb and index."

"If it were only the right hand, they would be the fingers of someone who grasps something small, or long and thin...."

"Like a stylus. Or some food. Or an insect. Or a serpent. Or a monstrance. Or a stick. Too many things. But if there are signs also on the other hand, it could also be a goblet; the right hand holds it firmly and the left helps, exerting less strength...."

Severinus was now gently rubbing the dead man's fingers, but the dark color did not disappear. I noticed he had put on a pair of gloves, which he probably used when he handled poisonous substances. He sniffed, but without receiving any sensation. "I could cite for you many vegetable (and also mineral) substances that leave traces of this sort. Some lethal, others not. The illuminators sometimes have gold dust on their fingers...."

"Adelmo was an illuminator," William said. "I imagine that, shattered as his body was, you didn't think of examining the fingers. But these others may have touched something that had belonged to Adelmo."

"I really don't know," Severinus said. "Two dead men, both with blackened fingers. What do you deduce from that?"

"I deduce nothing: nihil sequitur geminis ex particularibus unquam. Both cases would have to conform to a rule. For example: a substance exists that blackens the fingers of those who touch it...."

Triumphantly, I completed the syllogism: "...Venantius and Berengar have blackened fingers, ergo they touched this substance!"

"Good, Adso," William said, "a pity that your syllogism is not valid, because aut semel aut iterum medium generaliter esto, and in this syllogism the middle term never appears as general. A sign that we haven't chosen the major premise well. I shouldn't have said that all those who touch a certain substance have black fingers, because there could also be people with black fingers who have not touched the substance. I should have said that all those and only all those who have black fingers have certainly touched a given substance. Venantius and Berengar, etc. With which we would have a Darii, an excellent third mode of the first syllogistic figure."

"Then we have the answer," I said, delighted.

"Alas, Adso, you have too much faith in syllogisms! What we have, once again, is simply the question. That is: we have ventured the hypothesis that Venantius and Berengar touched the same thing, an unquestionably reasonable hypothesis. But when we have imagined a substance that, alone among all substances, causes this result (which is still to be established), we still don't know what it is or where they found it, or why they touched it. And, mind you, we don't even know if it's the substance they touched that brought them to their death. Imagine a madman who wants to kill all those who touch gold dust. Would we say it's gold dust that kills?"

I was upset. I had always believed logic was a universal weapon, and now I realized how its validity depended on the way it was employed. Further, since I had been with my master I had become aware, and was to become even more aware in the days that followed, that logic could be especially useful when you entered it but then left it.

Severinus, who was surely not a logician, was meanwhile reflecting on the basis of his own experience. "The universe of poisons is various as the mysteries of nature are various," he said. He pointed to a series of pots and ampoules, which we had already admired, neatly arranged on shelves along the walls, together with many volumes. "As I told you before, many of these herbs, duly compounded and administered in the proper dosage, could be used for lethal beverages and ointments. Over there, datura stramonium, belladonna, hemlock: they can bring on drowsiness, stimulation, or both; taken with due care they are excellent medicines, but in excess doses they bring on death."

"But none of these substances would leave marks on the fingers?"

"None, I believe. Then there are substances that become dangerous only if ingested, whereas others act instead on the skin. And hellebore can cause vomiting in a person who grasps it to uproot it. Dittany and fraxinella, when in flower, bring on intoxication in gardeners who touch them, as if the gardeners had drunk wine. Black hellebore, merely at the touch, provokes diarrhea. Other plants cause palpitations of the heart, others of the head, still others silence the voice. But viper's venom, applied to the skin and not allowed to enter the blood, produces only a slight irritation. . . . And once I was shown a compound that, when applied to the inside of a dog's thighs, near the genitalia, causes the animal to die in a short time in horrible convulsions, as the limbs gradually grow rigid. . . ."

"You know many things about poisons," William said with what sounded like admiration in his voice.

Severinus looked hard into his eyes for a few moments. "I know what a physician, an herbalist, a student of the sciences of human health must know."

William remained thoughtful for some time. Then he asked Severinus to open the corpse's mouth and observe the tongue. Severinus, his curiosity aroused, took a thin spatula, one of the instruments of his medical art, and obeyed. He uttered a cry of amazement: "The tongue is black!"

"So, then," William murmured, "he grasped something with his fingers and ingested it.... This eliminates the poisons you mentioned before, which kill by penetrating the skin. But it doesn't make our deductions any easier. Because now, for him and for Venantius, we must presume a voluntary act. They grasped something and put it in their mouths, knowing what they were doing...."

"Something to eat? To drink?"

"Perhaps. Or perhaps—why not?—a musical instrument, like a flute..."

"Absurd," Severinus said.

"Of course it's absurd. But we mustn't dismiss any hypothesis, no matter how farfetched. Now let's return to the poisonous substance. If someone who knows poisons as you do had broken in here and had used some of these herbs of yours, could he have produced a lethal ointment capable of causing those marks on the fingers and the tongue? Capable of being mixed with food or drink, smeared on a spoon, on something that is put in the mouth?"

"Yes," Severinus admitted, "but who? And besides, even if we accept this hypothesis, how would he have administered the poison to our two poor brothers?"

Frankly, I myself couldn't imagine Venantius or Berengar letting himself be approached by someone who handed him a mysterious substance and being persuaded to eat it or drink it. But William did not seem upset by this unlikelihood. "We will think about that later," he said, "because now I would like you to try to remember some event that perhaps you haven't recalled before. Someone who asked you questions about your herbs, for instance; someone who has easy access to the infirmary..."

"Just a moment," Severinus said. "A long time ago, years it was, on one of those shelves I kept a highly powerful substance, given to me by a brother who had traveled in distant lands. He couldn't tell me what it was made of, herbs for sure, but not all of them familiar. To look at, it was slimy and yellowish; but I was advised not to touch it, because if it only came into contact with my lips it would kill me in a short time. The brother told me that, when ingested even in minimal doses, in the space of a half hour it caused a feeling of great weariness, then a slow paralysis of all the limbs, and finally death. He didn't want to carry it with him, and so he presented it to me. I kept it for a long time, because I meant to examine it somehow. Then one day there was a great storm up here. One of my assistants, a novice, had left the infirmary door open, and the hurricane wrought havoc in this room where we are now. Bottles broken, liquids spilled on the floor, herbs and powders scattered. I worked a whole day putting my things back in order, and I accepted help only in sweeping away the broken vessels and the herbs that could not be recovered. At the end I realized that the very ampoule I mentioned to you was missing. At first I was worried, then I decided it had been broken and become confused with the other rubbish. I had the infirmary floor washed carefully, and the shelves...."

"And you had seen the ampoule a few hours before the storm?"

"Yes...or, rather, no, now that I think about it. It was behind a row of pots, carefully hidden, and I didn't check it every day...."

"Therefore, as far as you know, it could have been stolen quite a while before the storm, without your finding out?"

"Now that I think about it, yes, unquestionably."

"And that novice of yours could have stolen it and

then could have seized the occasion of the storm deliberately to leave the door open and create confusion among your things?"

Severinus seemed very excited. "Yes, of course. Not only that, but as I recall what happened, I was quite surprised that the hurricane, violent though it was, had upset so many things. It could quite well be that someone took advantage of the storm to devastate the room and produce more damage than the wind could have done!"

"Who was the novice?"

"His name was Augustine. But he died last year, a fall from scaffolding as he and other monks and servants were cleaning the sculptures of the façade of the church. Actually, now that I think about it, he swore up and down that he had not left the door open before the storm. I was the one, in my fury, who held him responsible for the accident. Perhaps he really was not guilty."

"And so we have a third person, perhaps far more expert than a novice, who knew about your rare poison. Whom had you told about it?"

"That I really don't remember. The abbot, of course, to ask his permission to keep such a dangerous substance. And a few others, perhaps in the library, because I was looking for some herbaria that might give me information."

"But didn't you tell me you keep here the books that are most useful to your art?"

"Yes, and many of them," he said, pointing to a corner of the room where some shelves held dozens of volumes. "But then I was looking for certain books I couldn't keep here, which Malachi actually was very reluctant to let me see. In fact, I had to ask the abbot's authorization." His voice sank, and he was almost shy about letting me hear his words. "You know, in a secret part of the library, they keep books on necromancy, black magic, and recipes for diabolical philters. I was allowed to consult some of these works, of necessity, and I was hoping to find a description of that poison and its functions. In vain."

"So you spoke about it with Malachi."

"Of course, with him definitely, and perhaps also with Berengar, who was his assistant. But you mustn't jump to conclusions: I don't remember clearly, perhaps other monks were present as I was talking, the scriptorium at times is fairly crowded, you know...."

"I'm not suspecting anyone. I'm only trying to understand what can have happened. In any event, you tell me this took place some years ago, and it's odd that anyone would steal a poison and then not use it until so much later. It would suggest a malignant mind brooding for a long time in darkness over a murderous plan."

Severinus blessed himself, an expression of horror on his face. "God forgive us all!" he said.

There was no further comment to be made. We again covered Berengar's body, which had to be prepared for the funeral.

PRIME

In which William induces first Salvatore and then the cellarer to confess their past, Severinus finds the stolen lenses, Nicholas brings the new ones, and William, now with six eyes, goes to decipher the manuscript of Venantius.

We were coming out as Malachi entered. He seemed very annoyed to find us there and started to leave again. From inside, Severinus saw him and said, "Were you looking for me? Is it for—" He broke off, glancing at us. Malachi signaled to him, imperceptibly, as if to say, "We'll talk about it later. . . ." We were going out as he was entering, and so all three of us were in the doorway.

Malachi said, somewhat redundantly, "I was looking for the brother herbalist. . . . I . . . I have a headache."

"It must be the enclosed air of the library," William said to him, in a tone of considerate sympathy. "You should inhale something."

Malachi's lips twitched as if he wanted to speak again, but then he gave up the idea, bowed his head, and went on inside, as we moved off.

"What is he seeing Severinus for?" I asked.

"Adso," my master said to me impatiently, "learn to

use your head and think." Then he changed the subject: "We must question some people now. At least," he added, as his eyes explored the grounds, "while they're still alive. By the way: from now on we must be careful about what we eat and drink. Always take your food from the common plate, and your beverage from the pitcher the others have filled their cups from. After Berengar we are the ones who know most. Except, naturally, the murderer."

"But whom do you want to question now?"

"Adso," William said, "you will have observed that here the most interesting things happen at night. They die at night, they wander about the scriptorium at night, women are brought at night into the abbey.... We have a daytime abbey and a nighttime abbey, and the nighttime one seems, unhappily, the more interesting. So, every person who roams about at night interests us, including, for example, the man you saw last night with the girl. Perhaps the business of the girl does not have anything to do with the poisonings, and perhaps it has. In any case, I have my ideas about last night's man, and he must be one who knows other things about the nocturnal life of this holy place. And, speak of the Devil, here he is, coming this way."

He pointed to Salvatore, who had also seen us. I noticed a slight hesitation in his step, as if, wishing to avoid us, he was about to turn around. But it was only for a moment. Obviously, he realized he couldn't escape the meeting, and he continued toward us. He greeted us with a broad smile and a fairly unctuous "Benedicite." My master hardly allowed him to finish and spoke to him sharply.

"You know the Inquisition arrives here tomorrow?" he asked him.

Salvatore didn't seem pleased with this news. In a faint voice, he asked, "And me?"

"And you would be wise to tell the truth to me, your

319

friend and a Friar Minor as you once were, rather than have to tell it tomorrow to those whom you know quite well."

Attacked so brusquely, Salvatore seemed to abandon all resistance. With a meek air he looked at William, as if to indicate he was ready to tell whatever he was asked.

"Last night there was a woman in the kitchen. Who was with her?"

"Oh, a female who sells herself like mercandia cannot be bona or have cortesia," Salvatore recited.

"I don't want to know whether the girl is pure. I want to know who was with her!"

"Deu, these evil females are all clever! They think dì e noche about how to trap a man. . . ."

William seized him roughly by the chest." Who was with her, you or the cellarer?"

Salvatore realized he couldn't go on lying. He began to tell a strange story, from which, with great effort, we learned that, to please the cellarer, he procured girls for him in the village, introducing them within the walls at night by paths he would not reveal to us. But he swore he acted out of the sheer goodness of his heart, betraying a comic regret that he could not find a way to enjoy his own pleasure and see that the girl, having satisfied the cellarer, would give something also to him. He said all this with slimy, lubricious smiles and winks, as if to suggest he was speaking to men made of flesh, accustomed to such practices. He stole glances at me, nor could I check him as I would have liked, because I felt myself bound to him by a common secret, his accomplice and companion in sin.

At this point William decided to stake everything. He asked Salvatore abruptly, "Did you know Remigio before or after you were with Dolcino?"

Salvatore knelt at his feet, begging him, between sobs, not to destroy him, to save him from the Inquisition. William solemnly swore not to tell anyone what he would learn, and Salvatore did not hesitate to deliver the cellarer into our hands. The two men had met on Bald Mountain, both in Dolcino's band; Salvatore and the cellarer had fled together and had entered the convent of Casale, and, still together, they had joined the Cluniacs. As he stammered out pleas for forgiveness, it was clear there was nothing further to be learned from him. William decided it was worth taking Remigio by surprise, and he left Salvatore, who ran to seek refuge in the church.

The cellarer was on the opposite side of the abbey, in front of the granaries, bargaining with some peasants from the valley. He looked at us apprehensively and tried to act very busy, but William insisted on speaking with him.

"For reasons connected with your position you are obviously forced to move about the abbey even when the others are asleep, I imagine," William said.

"That depends," Remigio answered. "Sometimes there are little matters to deal with, and I have to sacrifice a few hours' sleep."

"Has nothing happened to you, in these cases, that might indicate there is someone else roaming about, without your justification, between the kitchen and the library?"

"If I had seen anything, I would have told the abbot."

"Of course," William agreed, and abruptly changed the subject: "The village down below is not very rich, is it?"

"Yes and no," Remigio answered. "Some prebenders live there, abbey dependents, and they share our wealth in the good years. For example, on Saint John's Day they received twelve bushels of malt, a horse, seven oxen, a bull, four heifers, five calves, twenty sheep, fifteen pigs, fifty chickens, and seventeen hives. Also twenty smoked pigs, twenty-seven tubs of lard, half a measure of honey, three measures of soap, a fishnet..."

"I understand, I understand," William interrupted

him. "But you must admit that this still tells me nothing of the situation of the village, how many among its inhabitants have prebends, and how much land those who are not prebendaries possess to cultivate on their own...."

"Oh, as far as that goes," Remigio said, "a normal family down there has as much as fifty tablets of land."

"How much is a tablet?"

"Four square trabucchi, of course."

"Square trabucchi? How much are they?"

"Thirty-six square feet is a square trabucco. Or, if you prefer, eight hundred linear trabucchi make a Piedmont mile. And calculate that a family—in the lands to the north—can cultivate olives for at least half a sack of oil."

"Half a sack?"

"Yes, one sack makes five emine, and one emina makes eight cups."

"I see," my master said, disheartened. "Every locality has its own measures. Do you measure wine, for example, by the tankard?"

"Or by the rubbio. Six rubbie make one brenta, and eight brente, a keg. If you like, one rubbio is six pints from two tankards."

"I believe my ideas are clear now," William said, resigned.

"Do you wish to know anything else?" Remigio asked, with a tone that to me seemed defiant.

"Yes, I was asking you about how they live in the valley, because today in the library I was meditating on the sermons to women by Humbert of Romans, and in particular on that chapter 'Ad mulieres pauperes in villulis,' in which he says that they, more than others, are tempted to sins of the flesh because of their poverty, and wisely he says that they commit mortal sin when they sin with a layman, but the mortality of the sin becomes greater when it is committed with a priest, and greatest of all when the sin is with a monk, who is dead to the world. You know better than I that even in holy places such as abbeys the temptations of the noontime Devil are never wanting. I was wondering whether in your contacts with the people of the village you had heard that some monks, God forbid, had induced maidens into fornication."

Although my master said these things in an almost absent tone, my reader can imagine how the words upset the poor cellarer. I cannot say he blanched, but I will say that I was so expecting him to turn pale that I saw him look whiter.

"You ask me about things that I would already have told the abbot if I knew them," he answered humbly. "In any case, if, as I imagine, this information serves for your investigation, I will not keep silent about anything I may learn. Indeed, now that you remind me, with regard to your first question... The night poor Adelmo died, I was stirring about the yard... a question of the hens, you know... I had heard rumors that one of the blacksmiths was stealing from the chicken coops at night.... Yes, that night I did happen to see—from the distance, I couldn't swear to it—Berengar going back into the dormitory, moving along the choir, as if he had come from the Aedificium.... I wasn't surprised; there had been whispering about Berengar among the monks for some time. Perhaps you've heard..."

"No. Tell me."

"Well... how can I say it? Berengar was suspected of harboring passions that... that are not proper for a monk...."

"Are you perhaps trying to tell me he had relations with village girls, as I was asking you?"

The cellarer coughed, embarrassed, and flashed a somewhat obscene smile. "Oh, no... even less proper passions..."

"Then a monk who enjoys carnal satisfaction with a village maid is indulging in passions, on the other hand, that are somehow proper?"

"I didn't say that, but you'll agree that there is a hierarchy of depravity as there is of virtue.... The flesh can be tempted according to nature and ... against nature."

"You're telling me that Berengar was impelled by carnal desires for those of his own sex?"

"I'm saying that such were the whisperings.... I'm informing you of these things as proof of my sincerity and my good will...."

"And I thank you. And I agree with you that the sin of sodomy is far worse than other forms of lust, which, frankly, I am not inclined to investigate...."

"Sad, wretched things, even if they prove to have taken place," the cellarer said philosophically.

"Yes, Remigio. We are all wretched sinners. I would never seek the mote in a brother's eye, since I am so afraid of having a great beam in my own. But I will be grateful to you for any beams you may mention to me in the future. So we will talk great, sturdy trunks of wood and we will allow the motes to swirl in the air. How much did you say a square trabucco was?"

"Thirty-six square feet. But you mustn't waste your time. When you wish to know something specific, come to me. Consider me a faithful friend."

"I do consider you as such," William said warmly. "Ubertino told me that you once belonged to my own order. I would never betray a former brother, especially in these days when we are awaiting the arrival of a papal legation led by a grand inquisitor, famous for having burned many Dolcinians. You said a square trabucco equals thirty-six square feet?"

The cellarer was no fool. He decided it was no longer worthwhile playing at cat and mouse, particularly since he realized he was the mouse.

"Brother William," he said, "I see you know many

more things than I imagined. Help me, and I'll help you. It's true, I am a poor man of flesh, and I succumb to the lures of the flesh. Salvatore told me that you or your novice caught them last night in the kitchen. You have traveled widely, William; you know that not even the cardinals in Avignon are models of virtue. I know you are not questioning me because of these wretched little sins. But I also realize you have learned something of my past. I have had a strange life, like many of us Minorites. Years ago I believed in the ideal of poverty, and I abandoned the community to live as a vagabond. I believed in Dolcino's preaching, as many others like me did. I'm not an educated man; I've been ordained, but I can barely say Mass. I know little of theology. And perhaps I'm not really moved by ideas. You see, I once tried to rebel against the overlords; now I serve them, and for the sake of the lord of these lands I give orders to men like myself. Betray or rebel: we simple folk have little choice."

"Sometimes the simple understand things better than the learned," William said.

"Perhaps," the cellarer said with a shrug. "But I don't even know why I did what I did, then. You see, for Salvatore it was comprehensible: his parents were serfs, he came from a childhood of hardship and illness.... Dolcino represented rebellion, the destruction of the lords. For me it was different: I came from a city family, I wasn't running away from hunger. It was—I don't know how to say it—a feast of fools, a magnificent carnival.... On the mountains with Dolcino, before we were reduced to eating the flesh of our companions killed in battle, before so many died of hardship that we couldn't eat them all, and they were thrown to the birds and the wild animals on the slopes of Rebello...or maybe in those moments, too...there was an atmosphere...can I say of freedom? I didn't know, before, what freedom was; the preachers said to us, 'The truth will make you free.' We felt free, we thought that was the truth. We thought everything we were doing was right...."

"And there you took...to uniting yourself freely with women?" I asked, and I don't even know why, but since the night before, Ubertino's words had been haunting me, along with what I had read in the scriptorium and the events that had befallen me. William looked at me, curious; he had probably not expected me to be so bold and outspoken. The cellarer stared at me as if I were a strange animal.

"On Rebello," he said, "there were people who throughout their childhood had slept, ten or more of them, in a room of a few cubits—brothers and sisters, fathers and daughters. What do you think this new situation meant to them? They did from choice what they had formerly done from necessity. And then, at night, when you fear the arrival of the enemy troops and you cling tight to your neighbor, on the ground, so as not to feel cold... The heretics: you pitiful monks who come from a castle and end up in an abbey think that it's a form of belief, inspired by the Devil. But it's a way of living, and it is...it was...a new experience.... There were no more masters; and God, we were told, was with us. I'm not saying we were right, William, and, in fact, you find me here because I abandoned them before long. But I never really understood our learned disputes about the poverty of Christ and ownership and rights.... I told you, it was a great carnival, and in carnival time everything is done backward. As you grow old, you grow not wise but greedy. And here I am, a glutton.... You can condemn a heretic to death, but would you condemn a glutton?"

"That's enough, Remigio," William said. "I'm not questioning you about what happened then, but about what happened recently. Be frank with me, and I will surely not seek your downfall. I cannot and would not judge you. But you must tell me what you know about events in the abbey. You move about too much, night and day, not to know something. Who killed Venantius?"

"I do not know, I give you my solemn oath. I know when he died, and where."

"When? Where?"

"I'll tell you. That night, an hour after compline, I went into the kitchen...."

"How did you enter, and for what reasons?"

"By the door from the vegetable garden. I have a key I had the smiths make for me long ago. The kitchen door is the only one not barred on the inside. And my reasons...are not important; you said yourself you don't want to condemn me for my weaknesses of the flesh...." He smiled, embarrassed. "But I wouldn't want you to believe I spend my days in fornication, either.... That night I was looking for food to give to the girl Salvatore was to bring into the kitchen...."

"Where from?"

"Oh, the outside walls have other entrances besides the gate. The abbot knows them; I know them.... But that evening the girl didn't come in; I sent her back precisely because of what I discovered, what I'm about to tell you. This is why I tried to have her return last night. If you'd arrived a bit later you would have found me instead of Salvatore; it was he who warned me there were people in the Aedificium. So I went back to my cell. .,"

"Let's return to the night between Sunday and Monday."

"Yes, then. I entered the kitchen, and on the floor I saw Venantius, dead."

"In the kitchen?"

"Yes, near the sink. Perhaps he had just come down from the scriptorium."

"No sign of a struggle?"

"None. Though there was a broken cup beside the body, and traces of water on the ground."

"How do you know it was water?"

"I don't know. I thought it was water. What else might it have been?"

As William pointed out to me later, that cup could mean two different things. Either someone had given Venantius a poisoned potion to drink right there in the kitchen, or else the poor youth had already taken the poison (but where? and when?) and had come down to drink, to soothe a sudden burning, a spasm, a pain that seared his viscera or his tongue (for certainly his must have been black like Berengar's).

In any case, we could learn no more for the moment. Having glanced at the corpse, terrified, Remigio asked himself what he should do and decided he would do nothing. If he sought help, he would have to admit he had been wandering around the Aedificium at night, nor would it do his now lost brother any good. Therefore, he resolved to leave things as they were, waiting for someone else to discover the body in the morning, when the doors were opened. He rushed to head off Salvatore, who was already bringing the girl into the abbey, then he and his accomplice went off to sleep, if their agitated vigil till matins could be called that. And at matins, when the swineherds brought the news to the abbot, Remigio believed the body had been discovered where he had left it, and was aghast to find it in the jar. Who had spirited the corpse out of the kitchen? For this Remigio had no explanation.

"The only one who can move freely about the Aedificium is Malachi," William said.

The cellarer reacted violently: "No, not Malachi. That is, I don't believe...In any case, I didn't say anything to you against Malachi...."

"Rest assured, whatever your debt to Malachi may be. Does he know something about you?"

"Yes." The cellarer blushed. "And he has behaved like a man of discretion. If I were you, I would keep an eye on Benno. He had strange connections with Berengar and Venantius.... But I swear to you, I've seen nothing else. If I learn something, I'll tell you."

"For the present this will do. I'll seek you out again if I need you." The cellarer, obviously relieved, returned to his dealings, sharply reproaching the peasants, who in the meantime had apparently shifted some sacks of seeds.

At that point Severinus joined us. In his hand he was carrying William's lenses—the ones stolen two nights before. "I found them inside Berengar's habit," he said. "I saw them on your nose the other day in the scriptorium. They are yours, aren't they?"

"God be praised," William cried joyously. "We've solved two problems! I have my lenses and I finally know for sure that it was Berengar who robbed us the other night in the scriptorium!"

We had barely finished speaking when Nicholas of Morimondo came running up, even more triumphant than William. In his hands he held a finished pair of lenses, mounted on their fork. "William," he cried, "I did it all by myself. I've finished them! I believe they'll work!" Then he saw that William had other lenses on his nose, and he was stunned. William didn't want to humiliate him: he took off his old lenses and tried on the new ones. "These are better than the others," he said. "So I'll keep the old ones as a spare pair, and will always use yours." Then he turned to me. "Adso, now I shall withdraw to my cell to read those papers you know about. At last! Wait for me somewhere. And thank you, thank all of you, dearest brothers."

Terce was ringing and I went to the choir, to recite with the others the hymn, the psalms, the verses, and the "Kyrie." The others were praying for the soul of the dead Berengar. I was thanking God for having allowed us to find not one but two pairs of lenses.

In that great peace, forgetting all the ugly things I had seen and heard, I dozed off, waking only as the office ended. I realized I hadn't slept that night and I was distressed to think also how I had expended much of my strength. And at this point, coming out into the fresh air, I began to find my thoughts obsessed by the memory of the girl.

Trying to distract myself, I began to stride rapidly over the grounds. I felt a slight dizziness. I clapped my numbed hands together. I stamped my feet on the earth. I was still sleepy, and yet I felt awake and full of life. I could not understand what was happening to me.

TERCE

In which Adso writhes in the torments of love, then William arrives with Venantius's text, which remains undecipherable even after it has been deciphered.

To tell the truth, the other terrible events following my sinful encounter with the girl had caused me almost to forget that occurrence, and once I had confessed to Brother William, my spirit was relieved of the remorse I had felt on waking after my guilty lapse, so it was as if I had handed over to the monk, with my words, the burden itself of which they were the signifying voice. What is the purpose of the holy cleansing of confession, if not to unload the weight of sin, and the remorse it involves, into the very bosom of our Lord, obtaining with absolution a new and airy lightness of soul, such as to make us forget the body tormented by wickedness? But I was not freed of everything. Now, as I walked in the cold, pale sun of that winter morning, surrounded by the fervor of men and animals, I began to remember my experiences in a different way. As if, from everything that had happened, my repentance and the consoling words of the penitential cleansing no longer remained, but only visions of bodies and human limbs.

Into my feverish mind came abruptly the ghost of Berengar, swollen with water, and I shuddered with revulsion and pity. Then, as if to dispel that lemur, my mind turned to other images of which the memory was a fresh receptacle, and I could not avoid seeing, clear before my eyes (the eyes of the soul, but almost as if it appeared before my fleshly eyes), the image of the girl, beautiful and terrible as an army arrayed for battle.

I have vowed (aged amanuensis of a text till now unwritten, though for long decades it has spoken in my mind) to be a faithful chronicler, not only out of love for the truth, or the desire (worthy though it be) to instruct my future readers, but also out of a need to free my memory, dried up and weary of visions that have troubled it for a whole lifetime. Therefore, I must tell everything, decently but without shame. And I must say now, and clearly, what I thought then and almost tried to conceal from myself, walking over the grounds, sometimes breaking into a run so that I might attribute to the motion of my body the sudden pounding of my heart, or stopping to admire the work of the villeins, deluding myself that I was being distracted by such contemplation, breathing the cold air deeply into my lungs, as a man drinks wine to forget fear or sorrow.

In vain. I thought of the girl. My flesh had forgotten the intense pleasure, sinful and fleeting (a base thing), that union with her had given me; but my soul had not forgotten her face, and could not manage to feel that this memory was perverse: rather, it throbbed as if in that face shone all the bliss of creation.

I sensed, in a confused way, and almost denying to myself the truth of what I felt, that the poor, filthy, impudent creature who sold herself (who knows with what stubborn constancy) to other sinners, that daughter of Eve, weak like all her sisters, who had so often bartered her own flesh, was yet something splendid and wondrous. My intellect knew her as an occasion of sin, my sensitive appetite perceived her as the vessel of every grace. It is difficult to say what I felt. I could try to write that, still caught in the snares of sin, I desired, culpably, for her to appear at every moment, and I spied on the labor of the workers to see whether, around the corner of a hut or from the darkness of a barn, that form that had seduced me might emerge. But I would not be writing the truth, or, rather, I would be attempting to draw a veil over the truth to attenuate its force and clarity. Because the truth is that I "saw" the girl, I saw her in the branches of the bare tree that stirred lightly when a benumbed sparrow flew to seek refuge there; I saw her in the eyes of the heifers that came out of the barn, and I heard her in the bleating of the sheep that crossed my erratic path. It was as if all creation spoke to me of her, and I desired to see her again, true, but I was also prepared to accept the idea of never seeing her again, and of never lying again with her, provided that I could savor the joy that filled me that morning, and have her always near even if she were to be, and for eternity, distant. It was, now I am trying to understand, as if—just as the whole universe is surely like a book written by the finger of God, in which everything speaks to us of the immense goodness of its Creator, in which every creature is description and mirror of life and death, in which the humblest rose becomes a gloss of our terrestrial progress —everything, in other words, spoke to me only of the face I had hardly glimpsed in the aromatic shadows of the kitchen. I dwelled on these fantasies because I said to myself (or, rather, did not say: at that moment I did not formulate thoughts translatable into words) that if the whole world is destined to speak to me of the power, goodness, and wisdom of the Creator, and if that morning the whole world spoke to me of the girl, who (sinner though she may have been) was nevertheless a chapter in the great book of creation, a verse of the great psalm chanted by the cosmos—I said to myself (I say now) that if this occurred, it could only be a part of the great theophanic design that sustains the universe, arranged like a lyre, miracle of consonance and harmony. As if intoxicated, I then enjoyed her presence in the things I saw, and, desiring her in them, with the sight of them I was sated.

And yet I felt a kind of sorrow, because at the same time I suffered from an absence, though I was happy with the many ghosts of a presence. It is difficult for me to explain this mystery of contradiction, sign that the human spirit is fragile and never proceeds directly along the paths of divine reason, which has built the world as a perfect syllogism, but instead grasps only isolated and often disjointed propositions of this syllogism, whence derives the ease with which we fall victims to the deceptions of the Evil One. Was it a deception of the Evil One, that morning, that so moved me? I think today that it was, because I was a novice, but I think that the human feeling that stirred me was not bad in itself, but only with regard to my state. Because in itself it was the feeling that moves man toward woman so that the one couples with the other, as the apostle of the Gentiles wants, and that both be flesh of one flesh, and that together they procreate new human beings and succor each other from youth to old age. Only the apostle spoke thus for those who seek a remedy for lust and who do not wish to burn, recalling, however, that the condition of chastity is far preferable, the condition to which as a monk I had consecrated myself. And therefore what I suffered that morning was evil for me, but for others perhaps was good, the sweetest of good things; thus I understand now that my distress was not due to the depravity of my thoughts, in themselves worthy and sweet, but to the depravity of the gap between my thoughts and the vows I had pronounced. And therefore I was doing evil in enjoying something that was good in one situation, bad in another; and my fault lay in trying to reconcile natural appetite and the dictates of the rational soul. Now I know that I was suffering from the conflict between the illicit appetite of the intellect, in which the will's rule should have been displayed, and the illicit appetite of the senses, subject to human passions. In fact, as Aquinas says, the acts of the sensitive appetite are called passions precisely because they involve a bodily change. And my appetitive act was, as it happened, accompanied by a trembling of the whole body, by a physical impulse to cry out and to writhe. The angelic doctor says that the passions in themselves are not evil, but they must be governed by the will led by the rational soul. But my rational soul that morning was dazed by weariness, which kept in check the irascible appetite, addressed to good and evil as terms of conquest, but not the concupiscent appetite, addressed to good and evil as known entities. To justify my irresponsible recklessness of that time, I will say now that I was unquestionably seized by love, which is passion and is cosmic law, because the weight of bodies is actually natural love. And by this passion I was naturally seduced, and I understood why the angelic doctor said that amor est magis cognitivus quam cognitio, that we know things better through love than through knowledge. In fact, I now saw the girl better than I had seen her the previous night, and I understood her intus et in cute because in her I understood myself and in myself her. I now wonder whether what I felt was the love of friendship, in which like loves like and wants only the other's good, or love of concupiscence, in which one wants one's own good and the lacking wants only what completes it. And I believe that the nighttime love had been concupiscent, for I wanted from the girl something I had never had; whereas that morning I wanted nothing from the girl, and I wanted only her good, and I wished her to be saved from the cruel necessity that drove her to barter herself for a bit of food, and I wished her to be happy; nor did I want to ask anything further of her, but only to think of her and see her in sheep, oxen, trees, in the serene light that bathed in happiness the grounds of the abbey.

Now I know that good is cause of love and that which is good is defined by knowledge, and you can only love what you have learned is good, whereas I had, indeed, learned that the girl was the good of the irascible appetite, but the evil of the will. But I was in the grip of so many and such conflicting emotions, because what I felt was like the holiest love just as the doctors describe it: it produced in me that ecstasy in which lover and beloved want the same thing (and by mysterious enlightenment I, in that moment, knew that the girl, wherever she was, wanted the same things I myself wanted), and for her I felt jealousy, but not the evil kind, condemned by Paul in I Corinthians, but that which Dionysius speaks of in *The Divine Names* whereby God also is called jealous because of the great love He feels for all creation (and I loved the girl precisely because she existed, and I was happy, not envious, that she existed). I was jealous in the way in which, for the angelic doctor, jealousy is motus in amatum, the jealousy of friendship, which inspires us to move against all that harms the beloved (and I dreamed, at that moment, only of freeing the girl from the power of him who was buying her flesh and befouling it with his own infamous passions).

Now I know, as the doctor says, that love can harm the lover when it is excessive. And mine was excessive. I have tried to explain what I felt then, not in the least to justify what I felt. I am speaking of what were my sinful ardors of youth. They were bad, but truth obliges me to say that at the time I felt them to be extremely good. And let this serve to instruct anyone who may fall, as I did, into the nets of temptation. Today, an old man, I would know a thousand ways of evading such seductions. And I wonder how proud of them I should be, since I am free of the temptations of the noontime Devil; but not free from others, so that I ask myself whether what

I am now doing is not a sinful succumbing to the terrestrial passion of recollection, a foolish attempt to elude the flow of time, and death.

Then, I saved myself as if by miraculous instinct. The girl appeared to me in nature and in the works of man that surrounded me. I sought then, thanks to a happy intuition of my soul, to lose myself in the relaxed contemplation of those works. I observed the cowherds as they led the oxen out of the stable, the swineherds taking food to the pigs, the shepherds shouting to the dogs to collect the sheep, peasants carrying cracked wheat and millet to the mills and coming out with sacks of good food. I lost myself in the contemplation of nature, trying to forget my thoughts and to look only at beings as they appear, and to forget myself, joyfully, in the sight of them.

How beautiful was the spectacle of nature not yet touched by the often perverse wisdom of man!

I saw the lamb, to which this name was given as if in recognition of its purity and goodness. In fact the noun "agnus" derives from the fact that this animal "agnoscit"; it recognizes its mother, and recognizes her voice in the midst of the flock while the mother, among many lambs of the same form, with the same bleating, recognizes always and only her offspring, and nourishes him. I saw the sheep, which is called "ovis" from "ab oblatione" because from earliest times it served for sacrificial rites; the sheep, which, as is its habit as winter approaches, seeks grass greedily and stuffs itself with forage before the pastures are scared by frost. And the flocks were watched by dogs, called "canes" from the verb "canor" because of their barking. The perfect animal among animals, with superior gifts of perception, the dog recognizes its master and is trained to hunt wild animals in the forests, to guard flocks against wolves; it protects the master's house and his children, and sometimes in its office of defense it is killed. King Garamant, who had been taken away to prison by his enemies, was brought back to his homeland by a pack of two hundred dogs who made their way past the enemy troops; the dog of Jason Licius, after its master's death, persisted in refusing food until it died of starvation; and the dog of King Lysimachus threw himself on his master's funeral pyre, to die with him. The dog has the power to heal wounds by licking them with his tongue, and the tongue of his puppies can heal intestinal lesions. By nature he is accustomed to making second use of the same food, after vomiting it. His sobriety is the symbol of perfection of spirit, as the thaumaturgical power of his tongue is the symbol of the purification of sins through confession and penance. But the dog's returning to his vomit is also a sign that, after confession, we return to the same sins as before, and this moral was very useful to me that morning to admonish my heart, as I admired the wonders of nature.

Meanwhile, my steps were taking me to the oxen's stable, where they were coming out in great number, led by their drovers. They immediately appeared to me as they were and are, symbols of friendship and goodness, because every ox at his work turns to seek his companion at the plow; if by chance the partner is absent at that moment, the ox calls him with affectionate lowing. Oxen learn obediently to go back by themselves to the barn when it rains, and when they take refuge at the manger, they constantly stretch their necks to look out and see whether the bad weather has stopped, because they are eager to resume work. With the oxen at that moment also came from the barn the calves, whose name, "vituli," derives from "viriditas," or from "virgo," because at that age they are still fresh, young, and chaste, and I had done wrong and was still wrong, I said to myself, to see in their graceful movements an image of the girl who was not chaste. I thought of these things, again at peace with the world and with myself, observing the merry toil of that morning hour. And I thought no more of the girl, or, rather, I made an effort to transform the ardor I felt for her into a sense of inner happiness and devout peace.

I said to myself that the world was good and admirable. That the goodness of God is made manifest also in the most horrid beasts, as Honorius Augustoduniensis explains. It is true, there are serpents so huge that they devour stags and swim across the ocean, there is the bestia cenocroca with an ass's body, the horns of an ibex, the chest and maw of a lion, a horse's hoofs but cloven like an ox's, a slit from the mouth that reaches the ears, an almost human voice, and in the place of teeth a single, solid bone. And there is the manticore, with a man's face, triple set of teeth, lion's body, scorpion's tail, glaucous eyes the color of blood, and a voice like the hissing of snakes, greedy for human flesh. And there are monsters with eight toes, wolf's muzzle, hooked talons, sheep's fleece, and dog's back, who in old age turn black instead of white, and who outlive us by many years. And there are creatures with eyes on their shoulders and two holes in the chest instead of nostrils, because they lack a head, and others that dwell along the river Ganges who live only on the odor of a certain apple, and when they go away from it they die. But even all these foul beasts sing in their variety the praises of the Creator and His wisdom, as do the dog and the ox, the sheep and the lamb and the lynx. How great, I said to myself then, repeating the words of Vincent Belovacensis, the humblest beauty of this world, and how pleasing to the eye of reason the consideration of not only the modes and numbers and orders of things, so decorously established for the whole universe, but also the cycle of times that constantly unravel through successions and lapses, marked by the death of what has been born. I confess that, sinner as I am, my soul only for a little while still prisoner of the flesh, I was moved then by spiritual sweetness toward the Creator and the rule of this world, and with joyous veneration I admired the greatness and the stability of creation.

*   *   *

I was in this good frame of mind when my master came upon me. Drawn by my feet and without realizing it, I had almost circled the abbey, and found myself back where we had parted two hours before. There was William, and what he told me jolted me from my thoughts and directed my mind again to the obscure mysteries of the abbey.

William seemed well pleased. In his hand he had Venantius's parchment, which he had finally deciphered. We went to his cell, far from indiscreet ears, and he translated for me what he had read. After the sentence in zodiacal alphabet (Secretum finis Africae manus supra idolum primum et septimum de quatuor), this is what the Greek text said:

> The terrible poison that gives purification...
> The best weapon for destroying the enemy...
> Use humble persons, base and ugly, take pleasure from their defect.... They must not die.... Not in the houses of the noble and the powerful but from the peasants' villages, after abundant meal and libations...Squat bodies, deformed faces.
> They rape virgins and lie with whores, not evil, without fear.
> A different truth, a different image of the truth...
> The venerable figs.
> The shameless stone rolls over the plain.... Before the eyes.
> Deceit is necessary and to surprise in deceit, to say the opposite of what is believed, to say one thing and mean another.
> To them the cicadas will sing from the ground.

That was all. In my opinion too little, almost nothing. The words seemed the ravings of a madman, and I said as much to William.

"Perhaps. And it surely seems even madder thanks to my translation. My knowledge of Greek is rather scanty.

And yet, even if we assume that Venantius was mad or that the author of the book was mad, this would not tell us why so many people, not all of them mad, went to great trouble, first to hide the book and then to recover it. . . ."

"But do the things written here come from the mysterious book?"

"They are unquestionably things written by Venantius. You can see for yourself: this is not an ancient parchment. And these must be notes taken down while he was reading the book; otherwise Venantius would not have written in Greek. He has certainly copied, condensing them, some sentences he found in the book stolen from the finis Africae. He carried it to the scriptorium and began to read it, noting down what seemed to him noteworthy. Then something happened. Either he felt ill, or he heard someone coming up. So he put the book, with his notes, under his desk, probably planning to pick it up again the next evening. In any case, this page is our only possible starting point in re-creating the nature of the mysterious book, and it's only from the nature of that book that we will be able to infer the nature of the murderer. For in every crime committed to possess an object, the nature of the object should give us an idea, however faint, of the nature of the assassin. If someone kills for a handful of gold, he will be a greedy person; if for a book, he will be anxious to keep for himself the secrets of that book. So we must find out what is said in the book we do not have."

"And from these few lines will you be able to understand what that book is?"

"Dear Adso, these seem like the words of a holy text, whose meaning goes beyond the letter. Reading them this morning, after we had spoken with the cellarer, I was struck by the fact that here, too, there are references to the simple folk and to peasants as bearers of a truth different from that of the wise. The cellarer hinted that some strange complicity bound him to

Malachi. Can Malachi have hidden a dangerous heretical text that Remigio had entrusted to him? Then Venantius would have read and annotated some mysterious instructions concerning a community of rough and base men in revolt against everything and everybody. But..."

"But?"

"But two facts work against this hypothesis of mine. The first is that Venantius didn't seem interested in such questions: he was a translator of Greek texts, not a preacher of heresies. The other is that sentences like the ones about the figs and the stone and the cicadas would not be explained by this first hypothesis...."

"Perhaps they are riddles with another meaning," I ventured. "Or do you have another hypothesis?"

"I have, but it is still vague. It seemed to me, as I read this page, that I had read some of these words before, and some phrases that are almost the same, which I have seen elsewhere, return to my mind. It seems to me, indeed, that this page speaks of something there has been talk about during these past days.... But I cannot recall what. I must think it over. Perhaps I'll have to read other books."

"Why? To know what one book says you must read others?"

"At times this can be so. Often books speak of other books. Often a harmless book is like a seed that will blossom into a dangerous book, or it is the other way around: it is the sweet fruit of a bitter stem. In reading Albert, couldn't I learn what Thomas might have said? Or in reading Thomas, know what Averroës said?"

"True," I said, amazed. Until then I had thought each book spoke of the things, human or divine, that lie outside books. Now I realized that not infrequently books speak of books: it is as if they spoke among themselves. In the light of this reflection, the library seemed all the more disturbing to me. It was then the place of a long, centuries-old murmuring, an imperceptible dialogue between one parchment and another, a living thing, a receptacle of powers not to be ruled by a human mind, a treasure of secrets emanated by many minds, surviving the death of those who had produced them or had been their conveyors.

"But then," I said, "what is the use of hiding books, if from the books not hidden you can arrive at the concealed ones?"

"Over the centuries it is no use at all. In a space of years or days it has some use. You see, in fact, how bewildered we are."

"And is a library, then, an instrument not for distributing the truth but for delaying its appearance?" I asked, dumbfounded.

"Not always and not necessarily. In this case it is."

SEXT

In which Adso goes hunting for truffles and sees the Minorites arriving, they confer at length with William and Ubertino, and very sad things are learned about John XXII.

After these considerations my master decided to proceed no further. I have already said that he occasionally had moments of total inactivity, as if the ceaseless cycle of the stars had stopped, and he with it and with them. And so it was that morning. He stretched out on his pallet, staring into the void, his hands folded on his chest, barely moving his lips, as if he were reciting a prayer, but irregularly and without devotion.

I thought he was thinking, and I resolved to respect his meditation. I returned to the courtyard and saw that the sun had grown weaker. Beautiful and clear as it had been, the morning (as the day approached the completion of its first half) was becoming damp and misty. Heavy clouds moved from the north and were invading the top of the mountain, covering it with a light brume. It seemed to be fog, and perhaps fog was also rising from the ground, but at that altitude it was difficult to distinguish the mists that rose from below and those that came down from above. It was becoming hard to discern the bulk of the more distant buildings.

I saw Severinus gaily assembling the swineherds and some of their animals. He told me he was going to descend along the mountain slopes, and into the valley, to hunt for truffles. I wasn't familiar with that choice fruit of the underbrush, which was found in the peninsula and seemed typical especially of the Benedictine domains, whether at Norcia—the black ones—or in these lands—the white and more aromatic. Severinus explained to me what a truffle was, and how tasty, when prepared in the most diverse ways. And he told me it was very difficult to find, because it was hidden underground, more secret than a mushroom, and the only animals capable of unearthing it were pigs, following their smell. But on finding it they wanted to devour it themselves, and they had to be chased off at once, so that you could step in and dig up the truffle. I learned later that many lords did not disdain to join this hunt, following the pigs as if they were noblest hounds, and followed, in turn, by servants with hoes. I remember, indeed, that in later years a lord of my country, knowing I was acquainted with Italy, asked me why, as he had seen down there, some lords went out to pasture their pigs; and I laughed, realizing that, on the contrary, they were going in search of truffles. But when I told him that these lords hoped to find the "truffle" underground, to eat it, he thought I had said they were seeking "der Teufel," the Devil, and he blessed himself devoutly, looking at me in amazement. Then the misunderstanding was cleared up and we both laughed at it. Such is the magic of human languages, that by human accord often the same sounds mean different things.

My curiosity aroused by Severinus's preparations, I decided to follow him, also because I realized he was turning to this hunt in order to forget the sad events that oppressed everyone; and I thought that in helping him to forget his thoughts I would perhaps, if not forget, at least restrain my own. Nor will I deny, since I have determined to write always and only the truth, that I was secretly lured by the idea that, down in the valley, I might perhaps glimpse someone I will not mention. But to myself and almost aloud I declared that, since the two legations were expected to arrive that day, I might perhaps sight one of them.

As we gradually descended the curves of the mountain, the air became clearer. Not that the sun returned, for the upper part of the sky was heavy with clouds, but things stood out sharply, even as the fog remained above our heads. Indeed, when we had gone some distance, I turned to look up at the top of the mountain and could no longer see anything. From the halfway point upward, the summit, the high plain, the Aedificium—everything had disappeared among the clouds.

The morning of our arrival, when we were already among the mountains, at certain bends it was still possible to view the sea, no more than ten miles away, perhaps even less. Our journey had been rich in surprises, because suddenly we would find ourselves on a kind of terrace in the mountain, which fell sharply down to beautiful bays, and then a little later we would enter deep chasms, where mountains rose among mountains, and one blocked from another the sight of the distant shore, while the sun could hardly force its way into the deep valleys. Never before had I seen, as I saw in that part of Italy, such narrow and sudden juttings of sea and mountains, of shores followed by alpine landscapes, and in the wind that whistled among the gorges you could catch the alternate conflict of the marine balms with icy mountain gusts.

That morning, however, all was gray, almost milky white, and there were no horizons even when the gorges opened out toward the distant shores. But I am dwelling on recollections of little interest as far as our story goes, my patient reader. So I will not narrate the ups and downs of our search for "der Teufel," and I will tell, rather, of the legation of Friars Minor, which I was the first to sight. I ran at once to the monastery to inform William.

My master waited till the newcomers had entered and been greeted by the abbot according to the ritual. Then he went to meet the group, and there was a series of fraternal embraces and salutations.

The meal hour had already passed, but a table had been set for the guests, and the abbot thoughtfully left us among them; alone with William, exempted from the obligations of the Rule, they were free to eat and at the same time exchange their impressions. After all, it was, God forgive me the unpleasant simile, like a council of war, to be held as quickly as possible before the enemy host, namely the Avignon legation, could arrive.

Needless to say, the newcomers also promptly met Ubertino, whom all greeted with surprise, joy, veneration inspired not only by his long absence and by the fears surrounding his disappearance, but also by the qualities of that courageous warrior who for decades had fought their same battle.

Of the friars that made up the group I will speak later, when I tell about the next day's meeting. For that matter, I talked very little with them at first, involved as I was in the three-man conference promptly established between William, Ubertino, and Michael of Cesena.

Michael must have been a truly strange man: most ardent in his Franciscan passion (he had at times the gestures, the accents of Ubertino in his moments of mystical transport); very human and jovial in his earthly nature, a man of the Romagna, capable of appreciating a good table and happy to be among his friends. Subtle and evasive, he could abruptly become sly and clever as a fox, elusive as a mole, when problems of relations among the mighty were touched upon; capable of great outbursts of laughter, fervid tensions, eloquent silences, deft in turning his gaze away from his interlocutor if the latter's question required him to conceal, with what seemed absent-mindedness, his refusal to reply.

I have already spoken a bit about him in the preceding pages, and those were things I had heard said, perhaps by persons to whom they had been said. Now, on the other hand, I understood better many of his contradictory attitudes and the sudden changes of political strategy that in recent years had amazed his own friends and followers. Minister general of the order of the Friars Minor, he was in principle the heir of Saint Francis, and actually the heir of his interpreters: he had to compete with the sanctity and wisdom of such a predecessor as Bonaventure of Bagnoregio; he had to assure respect for the Rule and, at the same time, the fortunes of the order, so powerful and vast; he had to keep an eye on the courts and on the city magistrates from whom the order, though in the guise of alms, received gifts and bequests, source of prosperity and wealth; and at the same time he had to make sure that the requirement of penance did not lead the more ardent Spirituals to abandon the order, scattering that splendid community of which he was the head, in a constellation of bands of heretics. He had to please the Pope, the Emperor, the Friars of the Poor Life, and Saint Francis, who was certainly watching over him from heaven, as well as the Christian people, who were watching him from the earth. When John had condemned all Spirituals as heretics, Michael had not hesitated to hand over to him five of the most unruly friars of Provence, allowing the Pontiff to burn them at the stake. But realizing (and Ubertino may have had some share in this) that many in the order sympathized with the followers of evangelical simplicity, Michael had then acted in such a way that the chapter of Perugia, four years later, took up the demands of the burned men, naturally trying to reconcile a need, which could be heretical, with the ways and institutions of the order, and trying to harmonize the desires of the order and those of the Pope. But, as Michael was busy convincing the Pope, without whose consent he would have been unable to proceed, he had been willing also to accept the favors of the Emperor and the imperial theologians. Two years before the day I saw him he had yet enjoined his monks, in the chapter general of Lyons, to speak of the Pope's person only with moderation and respect (and this was just a few months after the Pope, referring to the Minorites, had complained of "their yelping, their errors, their insanities"). But here he was at table, friendly, with persons who spoke of the Pope with less than no respect.

I have already told the rest of the story. John wanted him at Avignon. He himself wanted and did not want to go, and the next day's meeting was to decide on the form and guarantees of a journey that should not appear as an act of submission or as an act of defiance. I don't believe Michael had ever met John personally, at least not as pope. In any event, he hadn't seen him for a long time, and Michael's friends hastened to paint the portrait of that simoniac in the darkest hues.

"One thing you must learn," William said to him, "is never to trust his oaths, which he always maintains to the letter, violating their substance."

"Everyone knows," Ubertino said, "what happened at the time of his election...."

"I wouldn't call it an election, but an imposition!" one man at the table cried, a man I later heard them call Hugh of Newcastle, whose accent was similar to my master's. "For that matter, the death of Clement the Fifth itself was never very clear. The King had never forgiven him for having promised to try Boniface the Eighth posthumously and then doing everything he could to avoid repudiating his predecessor. Nobody really knows how Clement died, at Carpentras. The fact is that when the cardinals met in Carpentras for the conclave, the new Pope didn't materialize, because (quite rightly) the argument shifted to the choice between Avignon and Rome. I don't know exactly what happened at that time—it was a massacre, I'm told—with the cardinals threatened by the nephew of the dead Pope, their servants slaughtered, the palace set afire, the cardinals appealing to the King, who says. he never wanted the Pope to desert Rome and they should be patient and make a good choice.... Then Philip the Fair died, again God only knows how...."

"Or the Devil knows," Ubertino said, blessing himself, in which he was imitated by all the others.

"Or the Devil knows," Hugh agreed, with a sneer. "Anyway, another king succeeds, survives eighteen months, and dies. His newborn heir also dies in a few days' time, and the regent, the King's brother, assumes the throne...."

"And this is Philip the Fifth. The very one who, when he was still Count of Poitiers, stopped the cardinals who were fleeing from Carpentras," Michael said.

"Yes," Hugh went on. "He puts them again into conclave in Lyons, in the Dominicans' convent, swearing he will defend their safety and not keep them prisoner. But once they place themselves in his power, he does not just have them locked up (which is the custom, after all), but every day reduces their food until they come to a decision. And each one promises to support his claim to the throne. When he does assume the throne, the cardinals are so weary of being prisoners after two years, and so afraid of staying there for the rest of their lives, eating badly, that they agree to everything, the gluttons, and on the throne of Peter they put that gnome, who is now over seventy...."

"Gnome, yes, true," Ubertino said, laughing. "And rather consumptive-looking, but stronger and shrewder than anyone thought!"

"Son of a cobbler," one of the legates grumbled.

"Christ was the son of a carpenter," Ubertino reproached him. "That is not the point. He is a cultivated man, he studied law at Montpellier and medicine in Paris, he cultivated his friendships in the ways best suited to win the episcopal seats and the cardinal's hat when it seemed opportune to him, and as counselor of Robert the Wise in Naples he amazed many with his acumen. When Bishop of Avignon, he gave all the right advice (right, that is, for the outcome of that squalid venture) to Philip the Fair about how to ruin the Templars. And after his election he managed to foil a plot of cardinals who wanted to kill him.... But this is not what I meant to talk about: I was speaking of his ability to betray vows without being accused of swearing falsely. To be elected, he promised Cardinal Orsini he would return the papal seat to Rome, and when he was elected he swore on the consecrated host that if he were not to keep his promise, he would never mount a horse or a mule again. Well, you know what that fox did? After he had himself crowned in Lyons (against the will of the King, who wanted the ceremony to take place in Avignon), he traveled from Lyons to Avignon by boat!"

The monks all laughed. The Pope was a perjurer, but there was no denying he had a certain ingeniousness.

"He is without shame," William remarked. "Didn't Hugh say that John made no attempt to conceal his bad faith? Haven't you, Ubertino, told about what he said to Orsini on the day of his arrival in Avignon?"

"To be sure," Ubertino said. "He said to him that the sky of France was so beautiful he could not see why he should set foot in a city full of ruins, like Rome. And inasmuch as the Pope, like Peter, had the power to bind and to loosen, he was now exercising this power: and he decided to remain where he was, where he enjoyed being. And when Orsini tried to remind him that it was his duty to live on the Vatican hill, he recalled him sharply to obedience and broke off the discussion. But I have not finished the story of the oath. On disembarking from the boat, John was to have mounted a white horse, to be followed by the cardinals on black horses, according to tradition. Instead he went to the episcopal palace on foot. Nor have I ever heard of his riding a horse again. And this is the man, Michael, you expect to abide by the guarantees he will give you?"

Michael remained silent for a long time. Then he said, "I can understand the Pope's wish to remain in Avignon, and I will not dispute it. But he cannot dispute our desire for poverty and our interpretation of the example of Christ."

"Don't be ingenuous, Michael," William spoke up, "your wishes, ours, make his appear sinister. You must realize that for centuries a greedier man has never ascended the papal throne. The whore of Babylon against whom our Ubertino used to fulminate, the corrupt popes described by the poets of your country like that Alighieri, were meek lambs and sober compared to John. He is a thieving magpie, a Jewish usurer; in Avignon there is more trafficking than in Florence! I have learned of the ignoble transaction with Clement's nephew, Bertrand of Goth, he of the slaughter of Carpentras (during which, incidentally, the cardinals were relieved of all their jewels). He had laid his hands on his uncle's treasure, which was no trifle, and John had not overlooked anything Bertrand had stolen: in the *Cum venerabiles* John lists precisely the coins, the gold and silver vessels, the books, rugs, precious stones, ornaments.... John, however, pretended not to know that Bertrand had seized more than a million and a half gold florins during the sack of Carpentras; he questioned another thirty thousand florins Bertrand confessed he had received from his uncle for a 'pious cause,' namely for a crusade. It was agreed that Bertrand would keep half the sum for the crusade and donate the other half to the papal throne. Then Bertrand never made the crusade, or at least he has not made it yet, and the Pope has not seen a florin...."

"He is not so clever, then," Michael remarked.

"That was the only time he has been outwitted in a

matter of money," Ubertino said. "You must know well the kind of tradesman you will be dealing with. In every other situation he has displayed a diabolical skill in collecting money. He is a Midas: everything he touches becomes gold and flows into the coffers of Avignon. Whenever I entered his apartments I found bankers, moneychangers, and tables laden with gold, clerics counting florins and piling them neatly one on top of another.... And you will see the palace he has had built for himself, with riches that were once attributed only to the Emperor of Byzantium or the Great Khan of the Tartars. And now you understand why he issued all those bulls against the ideal of poverty. But do you know that he has driven the Dominicans, in their hatred of our order, to carve statues of Christ with a royal crown, a tunic of purple and gold, and sumptuous sandals? In Avignon they display crucifixes where Christ is nailed by a single hand while the other touches a purse hanging from his belt, to indicate that he authorizes the use of money for religious ends...."

"Oh, how shameless!" Michael cried. "But this is outright blasphemy!"

"He has added," William went on, "a third crown to the papal tiara, hasn't he, Ubertino?"

"Certainly. At the beginning of the millennium Pope Hildebrand had assumed one, with the legend 'Corona regni de manu Dei'; the infamous Boniface later added a second, writing on it 'Diadema imperii de manu Petri'; and John has simply perfected the symbol: three crowns, the spiritual power, the temporal, and the ecclesiastical. A symbol worthy of the Persian kings, a pagan symbol..."

There was one monk who till then had remained silent, busily and devoutly consuming the good dishes the abbot had sent to the table. With an absent eye he followed the various discussions, emitting every now and then a sarcastic laugh at the Pope's expense, or a grunt of approval at the other monks' indignant exclamations. But otherwise he was intent on wiping from his chin the juices and bits of meat that escaped his toothless but voracious mouth, and the only times he had spoken a word to one of his neighbors were to praise some delicacy. I learned later that he was Master Jerome, that Bishop of Kaffa whom, a few days before, Ubertino had thought dead. (I must add that the news of his death two years earlier continued to circulate as the truth throughout Christendom for a long time, because I also heard it afterward. Actually, he died a few months after that meeting of ours, and I still think he died of the great anger that filled him at the next day's meeting; I would almost believe he exploded at once, so fragile was he of body and so bilious of humor.)

At this point he intervened in the discussion, speaking with his mouth full: "And then, you know, the villain issued a constitution concerning the taxae sacrae poenitentiariae in which he exploits the sins of religious in order to squeeze out more money. If an ecclesiastic commits a carnal sin, with a nun, with a relative, or even with an ordinary woman (because this also happens!), he can be absolved only by paying sixty-seven gold pieces and twelve pence. And if he commits bestiality, it is more than two hundred pieces, but if he has committed it only with youths or animals, and not with females, the fine is reduced by one hundred. And a nun who has given herself to many men, either all at once or at different times, inside the convent or out, if she then wants to become abbess, must pay one hundred thirty-one gold pieces and fifteen pence...."

"Come, come, Messer Jerome," Ubertino protested, "you know how little I love the Pope, but on this point I must defend him! It is a slander circulated in Avignon. I have never seen this constitution!"

"It exists," Jerome declared vigorously. "I have not seen it, either, but it exists."

Ubertino shook his head, and the others fell silent. I

realized they were accustomed to not paying great heed to Master Jerome, whom William had called a fool the other day. William tried to resume the conversation: "In any case, true or false as it may be, this rumor tells us the moral climate of Avignon, where all, exploited and exploiters, know they are living more in a market than at the court of Christ's vicar. When John ascended the throne there was talk of a treasure of seventy thousand florins and now there are those who say he has amassed more than ten million."

"It is true," Ubertino said. "Ah, Michael, Michael, you have no idea of the shameful things I had to see in Avignon!"

"Let us try to be honest," Michael said. "We know that our own people have also committed excesses. I have been told of Franciscans who made armed attacks on Dominican convents and despoiled their rival monks to impose poverty on them.... This is why I dared not oppose John at the time of the events in Provence.... I want to come to an agreement with him; I will not humiliate his pride, I will only ask him not to humiliate our humility. I will not speak to him of money, I will ask him only to agree to a sound interpretation of Scripture. And this is what we must do with his envoys tomorrow. After all, they are men of theology, and not all will be greedy like John. When some wise men have determined an interpretation of Scripture, he will not be able to—"

"He?" Ubertino interrupted him. "Why, you do not yet know his follies in the field of theology! He really wants to bind everything with his own hand, on earth and in heaven. On earth we have seen what he does. As for heaven ... Well, he has not yet expressed the ideas I cannot divulge to you—not publicly, at least—but I know for certain that he has whispered them to his henchmen. He is planning some mad if not perverse propositions that would change the very substance of doctrine and would deprive our preaching of all power!"

"What are they?" many asked.

"Ask Berengar; he knows, he told me of them."
Ubertino had turned to Berengar Talloni, who over the
past years had been one of the most determined adversaries of the Pope at his own court. Having come from
Avignon, he had joined the group of the other Franciscans
two days earlier and had arrived at the abbey with
them.

"It is a murky and almost incredible story," Berengar
said. "It seems John is planning to declare that the just
will not enjoy the beatific vision until after judgment.
For some time he has been reflecting on the ninth
verse of the sixth chapter of the Apocalypse, where
the opening of the fifth seal is discussed, where under the
altar appear those who were slain for testifying to the
word of God and who ask for justice. To each is given a
white robe, and they are told to be patient a little
longer.... A sign, John argues, that they will not be
able to see God in his essence until the last judgment is
fulfilled."

"To whom has he said these things?" Michael asked,
horrified.

"So far only to a few intimates, but word has spread;
they say he is preparing an open declaration, not
immediately, perhaps in a few years. He is consulting
his theologians...."

"Ha ha!" Jerome sneered as he ate.

"And, more, it seems that he wants to go further and
assert that nor will hell be open before that day ... not
even for the devils!"

"Lord Jesus, assist us!" Jerome cried. "And what will
we tell sinners, then, if we cannot threaten them with
an immediate hell the moment they are dead?"

"We are in the hands of a madman," Ubertino said.
"But I do not understand why he wants to assert these
things...."

"The whole doctrine of indulgences goes up in smoke,"
Jerome complained, "and not even he will be able to

sell any after that. Why should a priest who has committed the sin of bestiality pay so many gold pieces to avoid such a remote punishment?"

"Not so remote," Ubertino said firmly. "The hour is at hand!"

"You know that, dear brother, but the simple do not know it. This is how things stand!" cried Jerome, who no longer seemed to be enjoying his food. "What an evil idea; those preaching friars must have put it into his mind.... Ah!" And he shook his head.

"But why?" Michael of Cesena returned to this question.

"I don't believe there's a reason," William said. "It's a test he allows himself, an act of pride. He wants to be truly the one who decides for heaven and earth. I knew of these whisperings—William of Occam had written me. We shall see in the end whether the Pope has his way or the theologians have theirs, the voice of the whole church, the very wishes of the people of God, the bishops...."

"Oh, on doctrinal matters he can bend even the theologians to his will," Michael said sadly.

"Not necessarily," William replied. "We live in times when those learned in divine things have no fear of proclaiming the Pope a heretic. Those learned in divine things are in their way the voice of the Christian people. And not even the Pope can set himself against them now."

"Worse, still worse," Michael murmured, frightened. "On one side a mad pope, on the other the people of God, who, even if through the words of His theologians, will soon claim to interpret Scripture freely...."

"Why? Was what your people in Perugia did any different?" William asked.

Michael reacted as if stung. "That is why I want to meet the Pope. We can do nothing if he is not in agreement."

"We shall see, we shall see," William said in an enigmatic tone.

My master was truly very sharp. How could he foresee that Michael himself would later decide to support the theologians of the empire and to support the people in condemning the Pope? How could William foresee that, in four years' time, when John was first to pronounce his incredible doctrine, there would be an uprising on the part of all Christianity? If the beatific vision was thus postponed, how could the dead intercede for the living? And what would become of the cult of the saints? It was the Minorites themselves who would open hostilities in condemning the Pope, and William of Occam would be in the front rank, stern and implacable in his arguments. The conflict was to last for three years, until John, close to death, made partial amends. I heard him described, years later, as he appeared in the consistory of December 1334, smaller than he had seemed previously, withered by age, eighty-five years old and dying, his face pale, and he was to say (the fox, so clever in playing on words not only to break his own oaths but also to deny his own stubbornness): "We confess and believe that the souls separated from the body and completely purified are in heaven, in paradise with the angels, and with Jesus Christ, and that they see God in His divine essence, clearly, face to face..." and then, after a pause—it was never known whether this was due to his difficulty in breathing or to his perverse desire to underline the last clause as adversative—"to the extent to which the state and condition of the separated soul allows it." The next morning, a Sunday, he had himself laid on a long chair with reclining back, and he received the cardinals, who kissed his hand, and he died.

But again I digress, and tell things other than those I should tell. Yet, after all, the rest of that conversation at table does not add much to the understanding of the events I am narrating. The Minorites agreed on the stand to be taken the next day. They sized up their adversaries one by one. They commented with concern on the news, announced by William, of the arrival of Bernard Gui. And even more on the fact that Cardinal Bertrand del Poggetto would be presiding over the Avignon legation. Two inquisitors were too many: a sign they planned to use the argument of heresy against the Minorites.

"So much the worse," William said. "We will treat them as heretics."

"No, no," Michael said, "let us proceed cautiously; we must not jeopardize any possible agreement."

"As far as I can see," William said, "though I also worked for the realization of this meeting, and you know it, Michael, I do not believe the Avignonese are coming here to achieve any positive result. John wants you at Avignon alone, and without guarantees. But the meeting will have at least one function: to make you understand that. It would have been worse if you had gone there before having had this experience."

"And so you have worked hard, and for many months, to bring about something you believe futile," Michael said bitterly.

"I was asked to, by the Emperor and by you," William said. "And ultimately it is never a futile thing to know one's enemies better."

At this point they came to tell us that the second delegation was coming inside the walls. The Minorites rose and went out to meet the Pope's men.

NONES

In which Cardinal del Poggetto arrives, with Bernard Gui and the other men of Avignon, and then each one does something different.

Men who had already known one another for some time, men who without knowing one another had each heard the others spoken of, exchanged greetings in the courtyard with apparent meekness. At the abbot's side, Cardinal Bertrand del Poggetto moved like a man accustomed to power, as if he were virtually a second pope himself, and to one and all, especially to the Minorites, he distributed cordial smiles, auguring splendid agreement for the next day's meeting and bearing explicit wishes for peace and good (he used deliberately this expression dear to the Franciscans) from John XXII.

"Excellent," he said to me, when William was kind enough to introduce me as his scribe and pupil. Then he asked me whether I knew Bologna and he praised its beauty to me, its good food and its splendid university, inviting me to visit the city, rather than return one day, as he said, among those German people of mine who were making our lord Pope suffer so much. Then he extended his ring for me to kiss, as he directed his smile at someone else.

For that matter, my attention immediately turned to the person of whom I had heard most talk recently: Bernard Gui, as the French called him, or Bernardo Guidoni or Bernardo Guido, as he was called elsewhere.

He was a Dominican of about seventy, slender and erect. I was struck by his gray eyes, capable of staring without any expression; I was to see them often flash with ambiguous light, shrewd both in concealing thoughts and passions and in deliberately conveying them.

In the general exchange of greetings, he was not affectionate or cordial like the others, but always and just barely polite. When he saw Ubertino, whom he already knew, he was very deferential, but stared at him in a way that gave me an uneasy shudder. When he greeted Michael of Cesena, his smile was hard to decipher, and he murmured without warmth, "You have been awaited there for some time," a sentence in which I was unable to catch either a hint of eagerness or a shadow of irony, either an injunction or, for that matter, a suggestion of interest. He met William, and when he learned who he was, he looked at him with polite hostility: not because his face betrayed his secret feelings, I was sure of that (even while I was unsure that he harbored any feelings at all), but because he certainly wanted William to feel he was hostile. William returned his hostility, smiling at him with exaggerated cordiality and saying, "For some time I have been wanting to meet a man whose fame has been a lesson to me and an admonition for many important decisions that have inspired my life." Certainly words of praise, almost of flattery, for anyone who did not know, as Bernard did know well, that one of the most important decisions in William's life had been to abandon the position of inquisitor. I derived the impression that, if William would gladly have seen Bernard in some imperial dungeon, Bernard certainly would have been pleased to see William suddenly seized by accidental and immediate death; and since Bernard in those days had men-at-arms under his command, I feared for my good master's life.

Bernard must already have been informed by the abbot of the crimes committed in the abbey. In fact, pretending to ignore the venom in William's words, he said to him, "It seems that now, at the abbot's request, and in order to fulfill the mission entrusted to me under the terms of the agreement that has united us all here, I must concern myself with some very sad events in which the pestiferous stink of the Devil is evident. I mention this to you because I know that in remote times, when you would have been closer to me, you fought as did I—and those like me—in that field where the forces of good are arrayed against the forces of evil."

"True," William said calmly, "but then I went over to the other side."

Bernard took the blow well. "Can you tell me anything helpful about these criminal deeds?"

"No, unfortunately," William answered with civility. "I do not have your experience of criminal deeds."

From that moment on I lost track of everyone. William, after another conversation with Michael and Ubertino, withdrew to the scriptorium. He asked Malachi's leave to examine certain books, but I was unable to hear the titles. Malachi looked at him oddly but could not deny permission. Strangely, they did not have to be sought in the library. They were already on Venantius's desk, all of them. My master immersed himself in his reading, and I decided not to disturb him.

I went down into the kitchen. There I saw Bernard Gui. He probably wanted to comprehend the layout of the abbey and was roaming about everywhere. I heard him interrogating the cooks and other servants, speaking the local vernacular after a fashion (I recalled that he had been inquisitor in northern Italy). He seemed to be asking for information about the harvest, the organization of work in the monastery. But even while asking the most innocuous questions, he would look at his companion with penetrating eyes, then would abruptly ask another question, and at this point his victim would blanch and stammer. I concluded that, in some singular way, he was carrying out an inquisition, and was exploiting a formidable weapon that every inquisitor, in the performance of his function, possesses and employs: the fear of others. For every person, when questioned, usually tells the inquisitor, out of fear of being suspected of something, whatever may serve to make somebody else suspect.

For all the rest of the afternoon, as I gradually moved about, I saw Bernard proceed in this fashion, whether by the mills or in the cloister. But he almost never confronted monks: always lay brothers or peasants. The opposite of William's strategy thus far.

Vespers

In which Alinardo seems to give valuable information, and William reveals his method of arriving at a probable truth through a series of unquestionable errors.

Later William descended from the scriptorium in good humor. While we were waiting for suppertime, we came upon Alinardo in the cloister. Remembering his request, I had procured some chickpeas the day before in the kitchen, and I offered them to him. He thanked me, stuffing them into his toothless, drooling mouth. "You see, boy?" he said. "The other corpse also lay where the book announced it would be.... Now wait for the fourth trumpet!"

I asked him why he thought the key to the sequence of crimes lay in the book of Revelation. He looked at me, amazed: "The book of John offers the key to everything!" And he added, with a grimace of bitterness, "I knew it, I've been saying as much for a long time. ...I was the one, you know, to suggest to the abbot...the one we had then...to collect as many commentaries on the Apocalypse as possible. I was to have become librarian.... But then the other one managed to have himself sent to Silos, where he found the finest manuscripts, and he came back with splendid booty.... Oh, he knew where to look; he also spoke the language of the infidels.... And so the library was given into his keeping, and not mine. But God punished him, and sent him into the realm of darkness before his time. Ha ha..." He laughed in a nasty way, that old man who until then, lost in the serenity of his old age, had seemed to me like an innocent child.

"Who was the monk you were speaking of?" William asked.

He looked at us, stunned. "Whom was I speaking of? I cannot remember...it was such a long time ago. But God punishes, God nullifies, God dims even memories. Many acts of pride were committed in the library. Especially after it fell into the hands of foreigners. God punishes still...."

We could get no more out of him, and we left him to his calm, embittered delirium. William declared himself very interested in that exchange: "Alinardo is a man to listen to; each time he speaks he says something interesting."

"What did he say this time?"

"Adso," William said, "solving a mystery is not the same as deducing from first principles. Nor does it amount simply to collecting a number of particular data from which to infer a general law. It means, rather, facing one or two or three particular data apparently with nothing in common, and trying to imagine whether they could represent so many instances of a general law you don't yet know, and which perhaps has never been pronounced. To be sure, if you know, as the philosopher says, that man, the horse, and the mule are all without bile and are all long-lived, you can venture the principle that animals without bile live a long time. But take the case of animals with horns. Why do they have horns? Suddenly you realize that all animals with horns are without teeth in the upper jaw. This would be a fine discovery, if you did not also realize that, alas, there are animals without teeth in the upper jaw who, however, do not have horns: the camel, to name one. And finally you realize that all animals without teeth in the upper jaw have four stomachs. Well, then, you can suppose that one who cannot chew well must need four stomachs to digest food better. But what about the horns? You then try to imagine a material cause for horns—say, the lack of teeth provides the animal with an excess of osseous matter that must emerge somewhere else. But is that sufficient explanation? No, because the camel has no upper teeth, has four stomachs, but does not have horns. And you must also imagine a final cause. The osseous matter emerges in horns only in animals without other means of defense. But the camel has a very tough hide and doesn't need horns. So the law could be..."

"But what have horns to do with anything?" I asked impatiently. "And why are you concerned with animals having horns?"

"I have never concerned myself with them, but the Bishop of Lincoln was greatly interested in them, pursuing an idea of Aristotle. Honestly, I don't know whether his conclusions are the right ones, nor have I ever checked to see where the camel's teeth are or how many stomachs he has. I was trying to tell you that the search for explicative laws in natural facts proceeds in a tortuous fashion. In the face of some inexplicable facts you must try to imagine many general laws, whose connection with your facts escapes you. Then suddenly, in the unexpected connection of a result, a specific situation, and one of those laws, you perceive a line of reasoning that seems more convincing than the others. You try applying it to all similar cases, to use it for making predictions, and you discover that your intuition was right. But until you reach the end you will never know which predicates to introduce into your reasoning and which to omit. And this is what I am doing now. I line up so many disjointed elements and I venture some hypotheses. I have to venture many, and many of them are so absurd that I would be ashamed to tell them to you. You see, in the case of the horse Brunellus, when I saw the clues I guessed many complementary and contradictory hypotheses: it could be a runaway horse, it could be that the abbot had ridden down the slope on that fine horse, it could be that one horse, Brunellus, had left the tracks in the snow and another horse, Favellus, the day before, the traces of mane in the bush, and the branches could have been broken by some men. I didn't know which hypothesis was right until I saw the cellarer and the servants anxiously searching. Then I understood that the Brunellus hypothesis was the only right one, and I tried to prove it true, addressing the monks as I did. I won, but I might also have lost. The others believed me wise because I won, but they didn't know the many instances in which I have been foolish because I lost, and they didn't know that a few seconds before winning I wasn't sure I wouldn't lose. Now, for the events of the abbey I have many fine hypotheses, but there is no evident fact that allows me to say which is best. So, rather than appear foolish afterward, I renounce seeming clever now. Let me think no more, until tomorrow at least."

I understood at that moment my master's method of reasoning, and it seemed to me quite alien to that of the philosopher, who reasons by first principles, so that his intellect almost assumes the ways of the divine intellect. I understood that, when he didn't have an answer, William proposed many to himself, very different one from another. I remained puzzled.

"But then..." I ventured to remark, "you are still far from the solution...."

"I am very close to one," William said, "but I don't know which."

"Therefore you don't have a single answer to your questions?"

"Adso, if I did I would teach theology in Paris."

"In Paris do they always have the true answer?"

"Never," William said, "but they are very sure of their errors."

"And you," I said with childish impertinence, "never commit errors?"

"Often," he answered. "But instead of conceiving only one, I imagine many, so I become the slave of none."

I had the impression that William was not at all interested in the truth, which is nothing but the adjustment between the thing and the intellect. On the contrary, he amused himself by imagining how many possibilities were possible.

At that moment, I confess, I despaired of my master and caught myself thinking, "Good thing the inquisitor has come." I was on the side of that thirst for truth that inspired Bernard Gui.

And in this culpable mood, more torn than Judas on the night of Holy Thursday, I went with William into the refectory to eat my supper.

COMPLINE

In which Salvatore tells of a prodigious spell.

The supper for the legation was superb. The abbot must have known well both human weaknesses and the customs of the papal court (which, I must say, did not displease Brother Michael's Minorites, either). The freshly slaughtered pigs were to have produced blood pudding according to the Monte Cassino recipe, the cook had told us. But Venantius's wretched end had obliged them to throw away all the pigs' blood, though they would eventually slaughter some more pigs. I believe that in those days everyone abhorred the idea of killing the Lord's creatures. Nevertheless, we had a ragout of pigeon, marinaded in the wine of those lands, and roast rabbit, Saint Clare's pasties, rice with the almonds of those hills—the blanc-mange of fast days, that is—and borage tarts, stuffed olives, fried cheese, mutton with a sauce of raw peppers, white broad beans, and exquisite sweets, Saint Bernard's cake, Saint Nicholas's pies, Saint Lucy's dumplings, and wines, and herb liqueurs that put everyone in a good humor, even

Bernard Gui, usually so austere: an elixir of lemon verbena, walnut wine, wine against the gout, and gentian wine. It seemed an assembly of gluttons, except that every sip or every morsel was accompanied by devotional readings.

In the end, all rose very happy, some mentioning vague ailments as an excuse not to go down to compline. But the abbot did not take offense. Not all have the privilege and the obligations we assume on being consecrated in our order.

As the monks departed, my curiosity made me linger in the kitchen, where they were preparing to lock up for the night. I saw Salvatore slip off toward the garden with a bundle under his arm. My curiosity still further aroused, I followed and called him. He tried to evade me, but when I questioned him he replied that in the bundle (which moved as if inhabited by something alive) he was carrying a basilisk.

"Cave basilischium! The rex of serpenti, tant pleno of poison that it all shines dehors! Che dicam, il veleno, even the stink comes dehors and kills you! Poisons you . . . And it has black spots on his back, and a head like a coq, and half goes erect over the terra, and half on the terra like the other serpents. And it kills the bellula. . . ."

"The bellula?"

"Oc! Parvissimum animal, just a bit plus longue than the rat, and also called the musk-rat. And so the serpe and the botta. And when they bite it, the bellula runs to the fenicula or to the cicerbita and chews it, and comes back to the battaglia. And they say it generates through the oculi, but most say they are wrong."

I asked him what he was doing with a basilisk and he said that was his business. Now completely overwhelmed by curiosity, I said that these days, with all the deaths, there could be no more secret matters, and I would tell William. Then Salvatore ardently begged me to remain silent, opened the bundle, and showed me a black cat.

He drew me closer and, with an obscene smile, said that he didn't want the cellarer, who was powerful, or me, young and handsome, to enjoy the love of the village girls any more, when he couldn't because he was ugly and a poor wretch. But he knew a prodigious spell that would make every woman succumb to love. You had to kill a black cat and dig out its eyes, then put them in two eggs of a black hen, one eye in one egg, one eye in the other (and he showed me two eggs that he swore he had taken from appropriate hens). Then you had to let the eggs rot in a pile of horse dung (and he had one ready in a corner of the vegetable garden where nobody ever went), and there a little devil would be born from each egg, and would then be at your service, procuring for you all the delights of this world. But, alas, he told me, for the magic spell to work, the woman whose love he wanted had to spit on the eggs before they were buried in the dung, and that problem tormented him, because he would have to have the woman in question at hand that night, and make her perform the ritual without knowing its purpose.

A sudden heat seized me, in the face, or the viscera, or in my whole body, and I asked in a faint voice whether that night he would bring the same girl within the walls. He laughed, mocking me, and said I was truly gripped by a great lust (I said not, that I was asking out of pure curiosity), and then he said there were plenty of women in the village, and he would bring up another, even more beautiful than the one I liked. I supposed he was lying to me to make me go away. And in any case what could I have done? Follow him all night, when William was awaiting me for quite different enterprises? And again see her (if it was she) toward whom my appetites drove me while my reason drove me away—and whom I should never see again even though I did desire to see her further? Surely not. So I persuaded myself that Salvatore was telling the truth, as far as the woman was concerned. Or perhaps he was lying about everything, and the spell he described was a fantasy of his naïve, superstitious mind, and he would not do anything.

I became irritated with him, treated him roughly, told him that for that night he would do better to go to bed, because archers were patrolling the abbey. He answered that he knew the abbey better than the archers did, and with this fog nobody would see anybody. Indeed, he said to me, I'm going to run off now, and you won't see me any more, even if I were two feet away having my pleasure with the girl you desire. He expressed himself with different words, but this was the meaning of what he said. I left, indignant, because it was unworthy of me, nobleman and novice, to dispute with such rabble.

I joined William and we did what was to be done. That is, we prepared to follow compline at the rear of the nave, so that when the office ended we would be ready to undertake our second (for me, third) journey into the bowels of the labyrinth.

After Compline

In which they visit the labyrinth again, reach the threshold of the finis Africae, but cannot enter because they do not know what the first and seventh of the four are, and, finally, Adso has a recurrence, though a very erudite one, of his love malady.

The visit to the library cost us long hours of work. Described in words, the verification we aimed to carry out was simple, but our progress by lamplight as we read the legends, marked the passages and the blank walls on the map, recorded the initials, followed the various routes that the play of openings and obstacles allowed us, was very long. And tedious.

It was bitter cold. The night was not windy and we did not hear those faint whistlings that had upset us the first evening, but a damp, icy air entered from the arrow slits. We had put on woolen gloves so as to be able to touch the volumes without having our hands become numb. But they were the kind used for writing in winter, the fingertips left bare, and sometimes we had to hold our hands to the flame or put them against our chests or clap them as we hopped about, half frozen.

For this reason we didn't perform the whole task consecutively. We stopped to browse in the cases, and now that William—with his new glasses on his nose—could linger and read the books, at every title he discovered he let out exclamations of happiness, either because he knew the work, or because he had been seeking it for a long time, or finally because he had never heard it mentioned and was highly excited and titillated. In short, for him every book was like a fabulous animal that he was meeting in a strange land. And as he leafed through one manuscript, he ordered me to look for others.

"See what's in that case!"

And I, deciphering and shifting volumes, said, "*Historia anglorum* of Bede... And also by Bede, *De aedificatione templi, De tabernaculo, De temporibus et computo et chronica et circuli Dionysi, Ortographia, De ratione metrorum, Vita Sancti Cuthberti, Ars metrica...*"

"Naturally, the complete works of the Venerable... And look at these! *De rhetorica cognatione, Locorum rhetoricorum distinctio,* and here many grammarians, Priscian, Honoratus, Donatus, Maximus, Victorinus, Eutiches, Phocas, Asper... Odd, I thought at first that here there were authors from Anglia.... Let us look below...."

"*Hisperica...famina.* What is that?"

"A Hibernian poem. Listen:

> *Hoc spumans mundanas obvallat Pelagus oras*
> *terrestres amniosis fluctibus cudit margines.*
> *Saxeas undosis molibus irruit avionias.*
> *Infima bomboso vertice miscet glareas*
> *asprifero spergit spumas sulco,*
> *sonoreis frequenter quatitur flabris....*"

I didn't understand the meaning, but as William read he rolled the words in his mouth so that you seemed to hear the sound of the waves and the sea foam.

"And this? Aldhelm of Malmesbury. Listen to this page: 'Primitus pantorum procerum poematorum pio potissimum paternoque presertim privilegio panegiricum

poemataque passim prosatori sub polo promulgatas.'
... The words all begin with the same letter!"

"The men of my islands are all a bit mad," William
said proudly. "Let us look in the other case."

"Virgil."

"What is he doing here? What Virgil? The *Georgics?*"

"No. *Epitomae.* I've never heard of it."

"But it's Virgil of Toulouse, the rhetorician, six centuries after the birth of our Lord. He was considered a
great sage...."

"Here it says that the arts are poema, rethoria, grama,
leporia, dialecta, geometria.... But what language was
he writing?"

"Latin. A Latin of his own invention, however, which
he considered far more beautiful. Read this; he says
that astronomy studies the signs of the zodiac, which
are mon, man, tonte, piron, dameth, perfellea, belgalic,
margaleth, lutamiron, taminon, and raphalut."

"Was he crazy?"

"I don't know: he didn't come from my islands. And
listen to this; he says there are twelve ways of designat-
ing fire: ignis, coquihabin (quia incocta coquendi habet
dictionem), ardo, calax ex calore, fragon ex fragore
flammae, rusin de rubore, fumaton, ustrax de urendo,
vitius quia pene mortua membra suo vivificat, siluleus,
quod de silice siliat, unde et silex non recte dicitur, nisi
ex qua scintilla silit. And aeneon, de Aenea deo, qui in
eo habitat, sive a quo elementis flatus fertur."

"But there's no one who speaks like that!"

"Happily. But those were times when, to forget an
evil world, grammarians took pleasure in abstruse
questions. I was told that in that period, for fifteen days
and fifteen nights, the rhetoricians Gabundus and
Terentius argued on the vocative of 'ego,' and in the
end they attacked each other, with weapons."

"But this, too. Listen...." I had grasped a book
marvelously illuminated with vegetable labyrinths from

which monkeys and serpents peered out. "Listen to these words: cantamen, collamen, gongelámen, stemiamen, plasmamem, sonerus, alboreus, gaudifluus, glaucicomus. . . ."

"My islands," William said again, with tenderness. "Don't be too harsh with those monks of far-off Hibernia. Perhaps, if this abbey exists and if we still speak of the Holy Roman Empire, we owe it to them. At that time, the rest of Europe was reduced to a heap of ruins; one day they declared invalid all baptisms imparted by certain priests in Gaul because they baptized 'in nomine patris et filiae'—and not because they practiced a new heresy and considered Jesus a woman, but because they no longer knew any Latin."

"Like Salvatore?"

"More or less. Vikings from the Far North came down along the rivers to sack Rome. The pagan temples were falling in ruins, and the Christian ones did not yet exist. It was only the monks of Hibernia in their monasteries who wrote and read, read and wrote, and illuminated, and then jumped into little boats made of animal hide and navigated toward these lands and evangelized them as if you people were infidels, you understand? You have been to Bobbio, which was founded by Saint Columba, one of them. And so never mind if they invented a new Latin, seeing that in Europe no one knew the old Latin any more. They were great men. Saint Brendan reached the Isles of the Blest and sailed along the coasts of hell, where he saw Judas chained to a rock, and one day he landed on an island and went ashore there and found a sea monster. Naturally they were all mad," he repeated contentedly.

"These images are . . . I can hardly believe my eyes! So many colors!" I said, drinking it all in.

"From a land that doesn't have many colors, a bit of blue and much green. But we mustn't stand here discussing Hibernian monks. What I want to know is why they are here with the Anglians and with grammarians of other countries. Look at your chart; where should we be?"

"In the rooms of the west tower. I've copied down the scrolls, too. So, then, leaving the blind room, we enter the heptagonal room, and there is only one passage to a single room of the tower; the letter in red is *H*. Then we go from room to room, moving around the tower, and we return to the blind room. The sequence of the letters spells...you are right! HIBERNI!"

"HIBERNIA, if we come from the blind room back into the heptagonal, which, like all the others, has the letter *A* for Apocalypse. So there are the works of the authors of Ultima Thule, and also the grammarians and rhetoricians, because the men who arranged the library thought that a grammarian should remain with the Hibernian grammarians, even if he came from Toulouse. It is a criterion. You see? We are beginning to understand something."

"But in the rooms of the east tower, where we came in, we read FONS.... What does that mean?"

"Read your map carefully. Keep reading the letters of the rooms that follow, in order of access."

"FONS ADAEU..."

"No, Fons Adae; the *U* is the second east blind room, I remember it; perhaps it fits into another sequence. And what did we find in the Fons Adae, that is, in the earthly paradise (remember that the room with the altar facing the rising sun is there)?"

"There were many Bibles there, and commentaries on the Bible, only books of Holy Scripture."

"And so, you see, the word of God corresponding to the earthly paradise, which as all say is far off to the east. And here, to the west: Hibernia."

"So the plan of the library reproduces the map of the world?"

"That's probable. And the books are arranged according to the country of their origin, or the place where their authors were born, or, as in this instance, the place where they should have been born. The librarians told themselves Virgil the grammarian was born in Toulouse by mistake; he should have been born in the western islands. They corrected the errors of nature."

We resumed our way. We passed through a series of rooms rich in splendid Apocalypses, and one of these was the room where I had had visions. Indeed, we saw the light again from afar. William held his nose and ran to put it out, spitting on the ash. To be on the safe side, we hurried through the room, but I recalled that I had seen there the beautiful, many-colored Apocalypse with the mulier amicta sole and the dragon. We reconstructed the sequence of these rooms, starting from the one we entered last, which had *Y* as its red initial. Reading backward gave us the word YSPANIA, but its final *A* was also the one that concluded HIBERNIA. A sign, William said, that there were some rooms in which works of mixed nature were housed.

In any case, the area denominated YSPANIA seemed to us populated with many codices of the Apocalypse, all splendidly made, which William recognized as Hispanic art. We perceived that the library had perhaps the largest collection of copies of the apostle's book extant in Christendom, and an immense quantity of commentaries on the text. Enormous volumes were devoted to the commentary of the Apocalypse by Beatus of Liébana. The text was more or less always the same, but we found a rich, fantastic variation in the images, and William recognized some of those he considered among the greatest illuminators of the realm of the Asturias: Magius, Facundus, and others.

As we made these and other observations, we arrived at the south tower, which we had already approached the night before. The *S* room of Yspania—windowless— led into an *E* room, and after we gradually went around the five rooms of the tower, we came to the last, without other passages, which bore a red *L*. Again reading backward, we found LEONES.

"Leones: south. On our map we are in Africa, hic sunt leones. And this explains why we have found so many texts by infidel authors."

"And there are more," I said, rummaging in the cases. "*Canon* of Avicenna, and this codex with the beautiful calligraphy I don't recognize..."

"From the decorations I would say it is a Koran, but unfortunately I have no Arabic."

"The Koran, the Bible of the infidels, a perverse book..."

"A book containing a wisdom different from ours. But you understand why they put it here, where the lions, the monsters, are. This is why we saw that book on the monstrous animals, where you also found the unicorn. This area called LEONES contains the books that the creators of the library considered books of falsehood. What's over there?"

"They're in Latin, but from the Arabic. Ayyub al-Ruhawi, a treatise on canine hydrophobia. And this is a book of treasures. And this is *De aspectibus* of Alhazen...."

"You see, among monsters and falsehoods they have also placed works of science from which Christians have much to learn. That was the way they thought in the times when the library was built...."

"But why have they also put a book with the unicorn among the falsehoods?" I asked.

"Obviously the founders of the library had strange ideas. They must have believed that this book which speaks of fantastic animals and beasts living in distant lands was part of the catalogue of falsehoods spread by the infidels...."

"But is the unicorn a falsehood? It's the sweetest of animals and a noble symbol. It stands for Christ, and for chastity; it can be captured only by setting a virgin in the forest, so that the animal, catching her most chaste odor, will go and lay its head in her lap, offering itself as prey to the hunters' snares."

"So it is said, Adso. But many tend to believe that it's a fable, an invention of the pagans."

"What a disappointment," I said. "I would have liked to encounter one, crossing a wood. Otherwise what's the pleasure of crossing a wood?"

"It's not certain the animal doesn't exist. Perhaps it's different from the way it's illustrated in these books. A Venetian traveler went to very distant lands, quite close to the fons paradisi of which maps tell, and he saw unicorns. But he found them rough and clumsy, and very ugly and black. I believe he saw a real animal with one horn on its brow. It was probably the same animal the ancient masters first described faithfully. They were never completely mistaken, and had received from God the opportunity to see things we haven't seen. Then this description, passing from auctoritas to auctoritas, was transformed through successive imaginative exercises, and unicorns became fanciful animals, white and gentle. So if you hear there's a unicorn in a wood, don't go there with a virgin: the animal might resemble more closely the Venetian's account than the description in this book."

"But did the ancient masters happen to receive from God the revelation of the unicorn's true nature?"

"Not the revelation: the experience. They were fortunate enough to be born in lands where unicorns live, or in times when unicorns lived in our own lands."

"But then how can we trust ancient wisdom, whose traces you are always seeking, if it is handed down by lying books that have interpreted it with such license?"

"Books are not made to be believed, but to be subjected to inquiry. When we consider a book, we mustn't ask ourselves what it says but what it means, a precept that the commentators of the holy books had very clearly in mind. The unicorn, as these books speak of him, embodies a moral truth, or allegorical, or analogical, but one that remains true, as the idea that chastity is a noble virtue remains true. But as for the literal truth that sustains the other three truths, we have yet to see what original experience gave birth to the letter. The literal object must be discussed, even if its higher meaning remains good. In a book it is written that diamond can be cut only with a billy goat's blood. My great master Roger Bacon said it was not true, simply because he had tried and had failed. But if the relation between a diamond and goat's blood had had a nobler meaning, that would have remained intact."

"Then higher truths can be expressed while the letter is lying," I said. "Still, it grieves me to think this unicorn doesn't exist, or never existed, or cannot exist one day."

"It is not licit to impose confines on divine omnipotence, and if God so willed, unicorns could also exist. But console yourself, they exist in these books, which, if they do not speak of real existence, speak of possible existence."

"So must we then read books without faith, which is a theological virtue?"

"There are two other theological virtues as well. The hope that the possible is. And charity, toward those who believed in good faith that the possible was."

"But what use is the unicorn to you if your intellect doesn't believe in it?"

"It is of use to me as Venantius's prints in the snow were of use, after he was dragged to the pigs' tub. The unicorn of the books is like a print. If the print exists, there must have existed something whose print it is."

"But different from the print, you say."

"Of course. The print does not always have the same shape as the body that impressed it, and it doesn't always derive from the pressure of a body. At times it reproduces the impression a body has left in our mind: it is the print of an idea. The idea is sign of things, and the image is sign of the idea, sign of a sign. But from the image I reconstruct, if not the body, the idea that others had of it."

"And this is enough for you?"

"No, because true learning must not be content with ideas, which are, in fact, signs, but must discover things in their individual truth. And so I would like to go back from this print of a print to the individual unicorn that stands at the beginning of the chain. As I would like to go back from the vague signs left by Venantius's murderer (signs that could refer to many) to a sole individual, the murderer himself. But it isn't always possible in a short time, and without the help of other signs."

"Then I can always and only speak of something that speaks to me of something else, and so on. But the final something, the true one—does that never exist?"

"Perhaps it does: it is the individual unicorn. And don't worry: one of these days you will encounter it, however black and ugly it may be."

"Unicorns, lions, Arab authors, and Moors in general," I said at that point, "no doubt this is the Africa of which the monks spoke."

"No doubt this is it. And if it is, we should find the African poets mentioned by Pacificus of Tivoli."

And, in fact, when we had retraced our steps and were in room L again, we found in a case a collection of books by Floro, Fronto, Apuleius, Martianus Capella, and Fulgentius.

"So this is where Berengar said the explanations of a certain secret should be," I said.

"Almost here. He used the expression 'finis Africae,' and this was the expression that so infuriated Malachi. The finis could be this last room, unless..." He cried out: "By the seven churches of Clonmacnois! Haven't you noticed something?"

"What?"

"Let's go back to room S, where we started!"

We went back to the first blind room, where the verse

read "Super thronos viginti quatuor." It had four openings. One led to room Y, which had a window on the inner octagon. Another led to room P, which continued, along the outside façade, the YSPANIA sequence. The opening toward the tower led into room E, which we had just come through. Then there was a blank wall, and finally an opening that led into a second blind room with the initial *U*. Room S was the one with the mirror—luckily on the wall immediately to my right, or I would have been seized with fear again.

Looking carefully at my map, I realized the singularity of this room. Like the other blind rooms of the other three towers, it should have led to the central heptagonal room. If it didn't, the entrance to the heptagon would have to be in the adjacent blind room, the *U*. But this room, which through one opening led into a room T with a window on the octagon, and through another was connected to room S, had the other three walls full, occupied with cases. Looking around, we confirmed what was now obvious from the map: for reasons of logic as well as strict symmetry, that tower should have had its heptagonal room, but there was none.

"None," I said. "There's no such room."

"No, that's not it. If there were no heptagon, the other rooms would be larger, whereas they are more or less the shape of those at the other extremes. The room exists, but cannot be reached."

"Is it walled up?"

"Probably. And there is the finis Africae, there is the place that those monks who are now dead were hovering about, in their curiosity. It's walled up, but that does not mean there is no access. Indeed, there surely is one, and Venantius found it, or was given its description by Adelmo, who had it from Berengar. Let's read his notes again."

He took Venantius's paper from his habit and reread it: "The hand over the idol works on the first and the seventh of the four." He looked around. "Why, of course! The 'idolum' is the image in the mirror! Venantius was thinking in Greek, and in that tongue, even more than in ours, 'eidolon' is image as well as ghost, and the mirror reflects our own image, distorted; we ourselves mistook it for a ghost the other night! But what, then, can be the four 'supra idolum'? Something over the reflecting surface? Then we must place ourselves at a certain angle in order to perceive something reflected in the mirror that corresponds to Venantius's description...."

We tried every position, but with no result. Besides our images, the mirror reflected only hazy outlines of the rest of the room, dimly illuminated by the lamp.

"Then," William meditated, "by 'supra idolum' he could mean beyond the mirror...which would oblige us to go into the next room, for surely this mirror is a door...."

The mirror was taller than a normal man, fixed to the wall by a sturdy oak frame. We touched it in every manner, we tried to thrust our fingers into it, our nails between the frame and the wall, but the mirror was as fast as if it were part of the wall, a stone among stones.

"And if not beyond, it could be 'super idolum,' " William murmured, and meanwhile raised his arm, stood on tiptoe, and ran his hand along the upper edge of the frame. He found nothing but dust.

"For that matter," William reflected gloomily, "even if beyond it there were a room, the book we are seeking and the others sought is no longer in that room, because it was taken away, first by Venantius and then, God knows where, by Berengar."

"But perhaps Berengar brought it back here."

"No, that evening we were in the library, and everything suggests he died not long after the theft, that same night, in the balneary. Otherwise we would have seen him again the next morning. No matter...For the present we have established where the finis Africae is and we have almost all the necessary information for perfecting our map of the library. You must admit that many of the labyrinth's mysteries have now been clarified."

We went through other rooms, recording all our discoveries on my map. We came upon rooms devoted solely to writings on mathematics and astronomy, others with works in Aramaic characters which neither of us knew, others in even less recognizable characters, perhaps texts from India. We moved between two overlapping sequences that said IUDAEA and AEGYPTUS. In short, not to bore the reader with the chronicle of our deciphering, when we later perfected the map definitively we were convinced that the library was truly laid out and arranged according to the image of the terraqueous orb. To the north we found ANGLIA and GERMANI, which along the west wall were connected by GALLIA, which turned then, at the extreme west, into HIBERNIA, and toward the south wall ROMA (paradise of Latin classics!) and YSPANIA. Then to the south came the LEONES and AEGYPTUS, which to the east became IUDAEA and FONS ADAE. Between east and north, along the wall, ACAIA, a good synecdoche, as William expressed it, to indicate Greece, and in those four rooms there was, finally, a great hoard of poets and philosophers of pagan antiquity.

The system of words was eccentric. At times it proceeded in a single direction, at other times it went backward, at still others in a circle; often, as I said before, the same letter served to compose two different words (and in these instances the room had one case devoted to one subject and one to another). But obviously there was no point looking for a golden rule in this arrangement. It was purely a mnemonic device to allow the librarian to find a given work. To say of a book that it was found in "quarta Acaiae" meant that it was in the fourth room counting from the one in which the initial *A* appeared, and then, to identify it, presumably the librarian knew by heart the route, circular or straight, that he should follow, as ACAIA was distribut-

ed over four rooms arranged in a square. So we promptly learned the game of the blank walls. For example,
approaching ACAIA from the east, you found none of
the rooms led to the following rooms: the labyrinth at
this point ended, and to reach the north tower you had
to pass through the other three. But naturally the
librarians entered from the FONS, knowing perfectly
well that to go, let us say, into ANGLIA, they had to
pass through AEGYPTUS, YSPANIA, GALLIA, and GERMANI.

With these and other fine discoveries our fruitful exploration in the library ended. But before saying that we
prepared, contentedly, to leave it (only to be involved in
other events I will narrate shortly), I must make a confession to my reader. I said that our exploration was
undertaken, originally, to seek the key to the mysterious place but that, as we lingered along the way in the
rooms we were marking down by subject and arrangement, we leafed through books of various kinds, as if
we were exploring a mysterious continent or a terra
incognita. And usually this second exploration proceeded by common accord, as William and I browsed
through the same books, I pointing out the most curious ones to him, and he explaining to me many things I
was unable to understand.

But at a certain point, and just as we were moving
around the rooms of the south tower, known as LEONES,
my master happened to stop in a room rich in Arabic
works with odd optical drawings; and since we were
that evening provided not with one but with two lamps,
I moved, in my curiosity, into the next room, realizing
that the wisdom and the prudence of the library's
planning had assembled along one of its walls books
that certainly could not be handed out to anyone to
read, because they dealt in various ways with diseases of
body and spirit and were almost always written by
infidel scholars. And my eye fell on a book, not large
but adorned with miniatures far removed (luckily!)

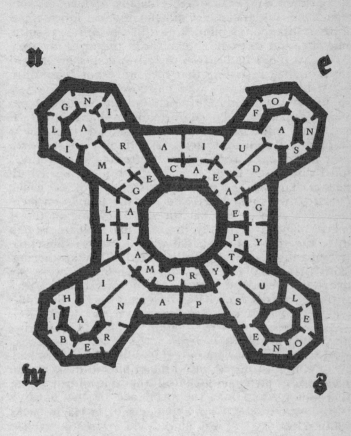

from the subject: flowers, vines, animals in pairs, some medicinal herbs. The title was *Speculum amoris*, by Maximus of Bologna, and it included quotations from many other works, all on the malady of love. As the reader will understand, it did not require much once more to inflame my mind, which had been numb since morning, and to excite it again with the girl's image.

All that day I had driven myself to dispel my morning thoughts, repeating that they were not those of a sober, balanced novice, and moreover, since the day's events had been sufficiently rich and intense to distract me, my appetites had been dormant, so that I thought I had freed myself by now from what had been but a passing restlessness. Instead, I had only to see that book and I was forced to say, "De te fabula narratur," and I discovered I was more sick with love than I had believed. I learned later that, reading books of medicine, you are always convinced you feel the pains of which they speak. So it was that the mere reading of those pages, glanced at hastily in fear that William would enter the room and ask me what I was so diligently investigating, caused me to believe that I was suffering from that very disease, whose symptoms were so splendidly described that if, on the one hand, I was distressed to discover I was sick (and on the infallible evidence of so many auctoritates), on the other I rejoiced to see my own situation depicted so vividly, convincing myself that even if I was ill, my illness was, so to speak, normal, inasmuch as countless others had suffered in the same way, and the quoted authors might have taken me personally as the model for their descriptions.

So I was moved by the pages of Ibn-Hazm, who defines love as a rebel illness whose treatment lies within itself, for the sick person does not want to be healed and he who is ill with it is reluctant to get well (and God knows this was true!). I realized why, that morning, I had been so stirred by everything I saw: it seems that love enters through the eyes, as Basil of Ancira also says, and—unmistakable symptom—he who is seized by such an illness displays an excessive gaiety, while he wishes at the same time to keep to himself and seeks solitude (as I had done that morning), while other phenomena affecting him are a violent restlessness and an awe that makes him speechless.... I was frightened to read that the sincere lover, when denied the sight of the beloved object, must fall into a wasting state that often reaches the point of confining him to bed, and sometimes the malady overpowers the brain, and the subject loses his mind and raves (obviously I had not yet reached that phase, because I had been quite alert in the exploration of the library). But I read with apprehension that if the illness worsens, death can ensue, and I asked myself whether the joy I derived from thinking of the girl was worth this supreme sacrifice of the body, apart from all due consideration of the soul's health.

I learned, further, from some words of Saint Hildegard that the melancholy humor I had felt during the day, which I attributed to a sweet feeling of pain at the girl's absence, was perilously close to the feeling experienced by one who strays from the harmonious and perfect state man experiences in paradise, and this "nigra et amara" melancholy is produced by the breath of the serpent and the influence of the Devil. An idea shared also by infidels of equal wisdom, for my eyes fell on the lines attributed to Abu-Bakr Muhammad ibn-Zakariyya ar-Razi, who in a *Liber continens* identifies amorous melancholy with lycanthropy, which drives its victim to behave like a wolf. His description clutched at my throat: first the lovers seem changed in the external appearance, their eyesight weakens, their eyes become hollow and without tears, their tongue slowly dries up and pustules appear on it, the whole body is parched and they suffer constant thirst; at this point they spend the day lying face down, and on the face and the tibias marks like dog bites appear, and finally the victims roam through the cemeteries at night like wolves.

Finally, I had no more doubts as to the gravity of my situation when I read quotations from the great Avicenna, who defined love as an assiduous thought of a melancholy nature, born as a result of one's thinking again and again of the features, gestures, or behavior of a person of the opposite sex (with what vivid fidelity had Avicenna described my case!): it does not originate as an illness but is transformed into illness when, remaining unsatisfied, it becomes obsessive thought (and why did I feel so obsessed, I who, God forgive me, had been well satisfied? Or was perhaps what had happened the previous night not satisfaction of love? But how is this illness satisfied, then?), and so there is an incessant flutter of the eyelids, irregular respiration; now the victim laughs, now weeps, and the pulse throbs (and indeed mine throbbed, and my breathing stopped as I read those lines!). Avicenna advised an infallible method already proposed by Galen for discovering whether someone is in love: grasp the wrist of the sufferer and utter many names of members of the opposite sex, until you discover which name makes the pulse accelerate. I was afraid my master would enter abruptly, seize my arm, and observe in the throbbing of my veins my secret, of which I would have been greatly ashamed.... Alas, as remedy Avicenna suggested uniting the two lovers in matrimony, which would cure the illness. Truly he was an infidel, though a shrewd one, because he did not consider the condition of the Benedictine novice, thus condemned never to recover—or, rather, consecrated, through his own choice or the wise choice of his relatives, never to fall ill. Luckily Avicenna, though not thinking of the Cluniac order, did consider the case of lovers who cannot be joined, and advised as radical treatment hot baths. (Was Berengar trying to be healed of his lovesickness for the dead Adelmo? But could one suffer lovesickness for a being of one's own sex, or was that only bestial lust? And was the night I had spent perhaps not bestial and lustful? No, of course not, I told myself at once, it was most sweet—and then immediately added: No, you are wrong, Adso, it was an illusion of the Devil, it was most bestial, and if you sinned in being a beast you sin all the more now in refusing to acknowledge it!) But then I read, again in Avicenna, that there were also other remedies: for example, enlisting the help of old and expert women who would spend their time denigrating the beloved—and it seems that old women are more expert than men in this task. Perhaps this was the solution, but I could not find any old women at the abbey (or young ones, actually), and so I would have to ask some monk to speak ill to me of the girl, but who? And besides, could a monk know women as well as an old gossip would know them? The last solution suggested by the Saracen was truly immodest, for it required the unhappy lover to couple with many slave girls, a remedy quite unsuitable for a monk. And so, I asked myself finally, how can a young monk be healed of love? Is there truly no salvation for him? Should I perhaps turn to Severinus and his herbs? I did find a passage in Arnold of Villanova, an author I had heard William mention with great esteem, who had it that lovesickness was born from an excess of humors and pneuma, when the human organism finds itself in an excess of dampness and heat, because the blood (which produces the generative seed), increasing through excess, produces excess of seed, a "complexio venerea," and an intense desire for union in man and woman. There is an estimative virtue situated in the dorsal part of the median ventricle of the encephalus (What is that? I wondered) whose purpose is to perceive the insensitive intentiones perceived by the senses, and when desire for the object perceived by the senses becomes too strong, the estimative faculty is upset, and it feeds only on the phantom of the beloved person; then there is an inflammation of the whole soul and body, as sadness alternates with joy, because heat (which in moments of despair descends into the deepest parts of the body and chills the skin) in moments of joy rises to the surface, inflaming the face. The treatment suggested by Arnold consisted in trying to lose the assurance and the hope of reaching the beloved object, so that the thought would go away.

Why, in that case I am cured, or nearly cured, I said to myself, because I have little or no hope of seeing the object of my thoughts again, and if I saw it, no hope of gaining it, and if I gained it, none of possessing it again, and if I possessed it, of keeping it near me, because of both my monkish state and the duties imposed on me by my family's station.... I am saved, I said to myself, and I closed the book and collected myself, just as William entered the room.

NIGHT

In which Salvatore allows himself to be discovered wretchedly by Bernard Gui, the girl loved by Adso is arrested as a witch, and all go to bed more unhappy and worried than before.

We were coming back down into the refectory when we heard some loud noises and saw some faint flashes of light from the direction of the kitchen. William promptly blew out his lamp. Clinging to the walls, we approached the door to the kitchen; we realized the sound came from outside, but the door was open. Then the voices and lights moved away, and someone slammed the door violently. There was a great tumult, which heralded something unpleasant. Swiftly we went back through the ossarium, re-emerged in the now deserted church, went out by the south door, and glimpsed a flickering of torches in the cloister.

We approached, and in the confusion we must have rushed outside like the many others already on the spot, who had come from either the dormitory or the pilgrims' hospice. We saw archers firmly grasping Salvatore, white as the white of his eyes, and a woman, who was crying. My heart contracted: it was she, the girl of my thoughts. As she saw me, she recognized me and cast me a desperate, imploring look. My impulse was to rush and free her, but William restrained me, whispering some far-from-affectionate reproaches. Monks and guests were now rushing in from all sides.

The abbot arrived, as did Bernard Gui, to whom the captain of the archers made a brief report. This is what had happened.

By the inquisitor's order, they patrolled the whole compound at night, paying special attention to the path that went from the main gate to the church, the gardens, and the façade of the Aedificium. (Why? I wondered. Then I understood: obviously because Bernard had heard from servants or from the cooks rumors about nocturnal movement between the outer walls and the kitchen, perhaps without learning exactly who was responsible; and perhaps the foolish Salvatore, as he had divulged his intentions to me, had already spoken in the kitchen or the barns to some wretch who, intimidated by questioning that afternoon, had thrown this rumor as a sop to Bernard.) Moving cautiously and in darkness through the fog, the archers had finally caught Salvatore in the woman's company, as he was fiddling with the kitchen door.

"A woman in this holy place! And with a monk!" Bernard said sternly, addressing the abbot. "Most magnificent lord," he continued, "if it involved only a violation of the vow of chastity, this man's punishment would be a matter for your jurisdiction. But since we are not yet sure that the traffickings of these two wretches hasn't something to do with the well-being of all the guests, we must first cast light on this mystery. Now, you rogue there!" And from Salvatore's bosom he seized the obvious bundle the poor man was trying to hide. "What's this you have here?"

I already knew: a knife; a black cat, which, once the bundle was unwrapped, fled with a furious yowl; and two eggs, now broken and slimy, which to everyone else looked like blood, or yellow bile, or some such foul substance. Salvatore was about to enter the kitchen, kill the cat, cut out its eyes; and who knows what promises he had used to induce the girl to follow him. I soon learned what promises. The archers searched the girl, with sly laughter and lascivious words, and they found on her a little dead rooster, still to be plucked. Ill-luck would have it that in the night, when all cats are gray, the cock seemed black, like the cat. I was thinking, however, that it took very little to lure her, poor hungry creature, who the night before had abandoned (and for love of me!) her precious ox heart....

"Aha!" Bernard cried, in a tone of great concern. "Black cat and cock...Ah, I know such paraphernalia...." He noticed William among those present. "Do you not also recognize them, Brother William? Were you not inquisitor in Kilkenny three years ago, where that girl had intercourse with a devil who appeared to her in the form of a black cat?"

To me it seemed my master remained silent out of cowardice. I tugged at his sleeve, shook him, whispered to him in despair, "Tell him, tell him it was to eat...."

He freed himself from my grip and spoke politely to Bernard: "I do not believe you need my past experiences to arrive at your conclusions," he said.

"Oh, no, there are far more authoritative witnesses." Bernard smiled. "Stephen of Bourbon, in his treatise on the seven gifts of the Holy Spirit, tells how Saint Dominic, after preaching at Fanjeaux against the heretics, announced to certain women that they would see the master they had served till then. And suddenly into their midst sprang a frightful cat the size of a large dog, with huge blazing eyes, a bloody tongue that came to its navel, a short tail straight in the air so that however the animal turned it displayed the evil of its behind, more fetid than any other, as is proper for that anus which many devotees of Satan, not least the Knights Templar, have always been accustomed to kiss in the course of their meetings. And after moving about the women for an hour, the cat sprang on the bell rope and climbed up it, leaving his stinking waste behind. And is not the cat the animal beloved by the Catharists, who according to Alanus de Insulis are so called from 'catus,' because of this beast whose posterior they kiss, considering it the incarnation of Lucifer? And is this disgusting practice not confirmed also by William of La Verna in the *De legibus*? And does Albertus Magnus not say that cats are potential devils? And does not my venerable brother Jacques Fournier recall that on the deathbed of the inquisitor Geoffrey of Carcassonne two black cats appeared, who were no other than devils come to taunt those remains?"

A horrified murmur ran through the group of monks, many of whom made the sign of the holy cross.

"My lord abbot, my lord abbot," Bernard was saying meanwhile, with a virtuous mien, "perhaps Your Magnificence does not know what sinners are accustomed to do with these instruments! But I know well, God help me! I have seen most wicked men, in the darkest hours of the night, along with others of their stripe, use black cats to achieve wonders that they could never deny: to straddle certain animals and travel immense spaces under cover of night, dragging their slaves, transformed into lustful incubi.... And the Devil shows himself to them, or at least so they strongly believe, in the form of a cock, or some other black animal, and with him—do not ask me how—they even lie together. And I know for certain that not long ago, in Avignon itself, with necromancies of this sort philters and ointments were prepared to make attempts on the life of our lord Pope himself, poisoning his foods. The Pope was able to defend himself and identify the toxin only because he was supplied with prodigious jewels in the form of serpents' tongues, fortified by wondrous emeralds and rubies that through divine power were able to reveal the presence of poison in the foods. The King of France had given him eleven of these most precious tongues, thank heaven, and only thus could our lord Pope elude death! True, the Pontiff's enemies went still further, and everyone knows what was learned about the heretic Bernard Délicieux, arrested ten years ago: books of black magic were found in his house, with notes written on the most wicked pages, containing all the instructions for making wax figures in order to harm enemies. And would you believe it? In his house were also found figures that reproduced, with truly admirable craft, the image of the Pope, with little red circles on the vital parts of the body. And everyone knows that such a figure, hung up by a string, is placed before a mirror, and then the vital parts are pierced with a pin, and . . . Oh, but why do I dwell on these vile, disgusting practices? The Pope himself spoke of them and described and condemned them, just last year, in his constitution *Super illius specula!* And I truly hope you have a copy in this rich library of yours, where it can be properly meditated on. . . ."

"We have it, we have it," the abbot eagerly confirmed, in great distress.

"Very well," Bernard concluded. "Now the case seems clear to me. A monk seduced, a witch, and some ritual, which fortunately did not take place. To what end? That is what we will learn, and I am ready to sacrifice a few hours' sleep to learn it. Will Your Magnificence put at my disposal a place where this man can be confined?"

"We have some cells in the basement of the smithy," the abbot said, "which fortunately are very rarely used and have stood empty for years. . . ."

"Fortunately or unfortunately," Bernard remarked. And he ordered the archers to have someone show them the way and to take the two prisoners to separate cells; and the men were to tie the monk well to some rings set in the wall, so that Bernard could go down shortly and, questioning him, look him in the face. As for the girl, he added, it was clear who she was, and it was not worth questioning her that night. Other trials awaited her before she would be burned as a witch. And if witch she were, she would not speak easily. But the monk might still repent, perhaps (and he glared at the trembling Salvatore, as if to make him understand he was being offered a last chance), telling the truth and, Bernard added, denouncing his accomplices.

The two were dragged off, one silent and destroyed, almost feverish, the other weeping and kicking and screaming like an animal being led to the shambles. But neither Bernard nor the archers nor I myself could understand what she was saying in her peasant tongue. For all her shouting, she was as if mute. There are words that give power, others that make us all the more derelict, and to this latter category belong the vulgar words of the simple, to whom the Lord has not granted the boon of self-expression in the universal tongue of knowledge and power.

Once again I was tempted to follow her; once again William, grim, restrained me. "Be still, fool," he said. "The girl is lost; she is burnt flesh."

As I observed the scene with terror, staring at the girl in a swarm of contradictory thoughts, I felt someone touch my shoulder. I don't know why, but even before I turned I recognized the touch of Ubertino.

"You are looking at the witch, are you not?" he asked me. And I knew he could not know of my story, and therefore he was saying this only because he had caught, with his terrible penetration of human passions, the intensity of my gaze.

"No," I defended myself, "I am not looking at her...or, rather, perhaps I am looking at her, but she isn't a witch....We don't know: perhaps she is innocent...."

"And you look at her because she is beautiful. She is beautiful, is she not?" he asked me with extraordinary warmth, pressing my arm. "If you look at her because she is beautiful, and you are upset by her (but I know you are upset, because the sin of which she is suspected makes her all the more fascinating to you), if you look at her and feel desire, that alone makes her a witch. Be on guard, my son.... The beauty of the body stops at the skin. If men could see what is beneath the skin, as with the lynx of Boeotia, they would shudder at the sight of a woman. All that grace consists of mucus and blood, humors and bile. If you think of what is hidden in the nostrils, in the throat, and in the belly, you will find only filth. And if it revolts you to touch mucus or dung with your fingertip, how could we desire to embrace the sack that contains that dung?"

An access of vomiting seized me. I didn't want to hear any more. My master, who had also heard, came to my rescue. He brusquely approached Ubertino, grasped his arm, and freed it from mine.

"That will do, Ubertino," he said. "That girl will soon be under torture, then on the pyre. She will become exactly as you say, mucus, blood, humors, and bile. But it will be men like us who dig from beneath her skin that which the Lord wanted to be protected and adorned by that skin. And when it comes to prime matter, you are no better than she. Leave the boy alone."

Ubertino was upset. "Perhaps I have sinned," he murmured. "I have surely sinned. What else can a sinner do?"

Now everyone was going back inside, commenting on the event. William remained a little while with Michael and the other Minorites, who were asking him his impressions.

"Bernard now has an argument, ambiguous though it be. In the abbey there are necromancers circulating who do the same things that were done against the Pope in Avignon. It is not, certainly, proof, and, in the first place, it cannot be used to disturb tomorrow's meeting. Tonight he will try to wring from that poor wretch some other clue, which, I'm sure, Bernard will not use immediately tomorrow morning. He will keep it in reserve: it will be of use later, to upset the progress of the discussions if they should ever take a direction unpleasing to him."

"Could he force the monk to say something to be used against us?" Michael of Cesena asked.

William was dubious. "Let's hope not," he said. I realized that, if Salvatore told Bernard what he had told us, about his own past and the cellarer's, and if he hintèd at something about their relationship with Ubertino, fleeting though it may have been, a highly embarrassing situation would be created.

"In any case, let's wait and see what happens," William said with serenity. "For that matter, Michael, everything was already decided beforehand. But you want to try."

"I do," Michael said, "and the Lord will help me. May Saint Francis intercede for all of us."

"Amen," all replied.

"But that is not necessarily possible," was William's irreverent comment. "Saint Francis could be off somewhere waiting for judgment day, without seeing the Lord face to face."

"A curse on that heretic John!" I heard Master Jerome mutter, as each went back to bed. "If he now robs us of the saints' help, what will become of us, poor sinners that we are?"

FIFTH DAY

PRIME

In which there occurs a fraternal debate regarding the poverty of Jesus.

My heart racked by a thousand anxieties after the scene of the night, I woke on the morning of the fifth day when prime was already ringing, as William shook me roughly, warning me that the two legations would be meeting shortly. I looked out of the cell window and saw nothing. The fog of the previous day was now a milky blanket that totally covered the high plain.

When I went outside, I saw the abbey as I had never seen it before. A few of the major buildings— the church, the Aedificium, the chapter house—could be discerned even at a distance, though still vague, shadows among shadows, while the rest of the constructions were visible only at a few paces. Shapes, of things and animals, seemed to rise suddenly from the void; people materialized from the mist, first gray, like ghosts, then gradually though not easily recognizable.

Born in a northern clime, I was not unfamiliar with that element, which at another moment would have pleasantly reminded me of the plains and the castle of my birth. But that morning the condition of the air seemed painfully kin to the condition of my soul, and the sadness with which I had awakened increased as I slowly approached the chapter house.

A few feet from the building, I saw Bernard Gui taking his leave of another person, whom I did not immediately recognize. Then, as he passed me, I realized it was Malachi. He looked around like a man not wishing to be seen while committing some crime.

He did not recognize me and went off. Impelled by curiosity, I followed Bernard and saw that he was glancing through some papers, which perhaps Malachi had delivered to him. At the door of the chapter house, with a gesture, he summoned the captain of the archers, standing nearby, and murmured a few words to him. Then he went in. I followed him still.

It was the first time I had set foot in that place. On the outside it was of modest dimensions and sober design; I realized that it had recently been rebuilt over the remains of a primitive abbatial church, perhaps partly destroyed by fire.

Entering from the outside, you passed beneath a portal in the new fashion, with a pointed arch and no decorations, surmounted by a rose window. But inside you found yourself in a vestibule, built on the traces of an old narthex. Facing you was another doorway, its arch in the old style, and with a half-moon tympanum wondrously carved. It must have been the doorway of the now vanished church.

The sculptures of the tympanum were equally beautiful but not so disturbing as those of the newer church. Here again, the tympanum was dominated by an enthroned Christ; but at his sides, in various poses and with various objects in their hands, were the twelve apostles, who had received from him the mission to go forth and preach among all peoples. Over Christ's head, in an arc divided into twelve panels, and under Christ's feet, in an unbroken procession of figures, the peoples of the world were portrayed, destined to receive the Word. From their dress I could recognize the Hebrews, the Cappadocians, the Arabs, the Indians, the Phrygians, the Byzantines, the Armenians, the Scythians, the Romans. But, along with them, in thirty round frames that made an arc above the arc of twelve panels, were the inhabitants of the unknown worlds, of whom only the *Physiologus* and the vague reports of travelers speak slightly. Many of them were unfamiliar to me, others I identified. For example, brutes with six fingers on each hand; fauns born from the worms that develop between the bark and the pulp of trees; sirens with scaly tails who seduce seamen; Ethiops, their bodies all black, defending themselves against the fire of the sun by digging underground caverns; ass-centaurs, men to the navel and asses below; Cyclopes, each with a single eye the size of a shield; Scylla, with a girl's head and bosom, a she-wolf's belly, and a dolphin's tail; the hairy men of India, who live in swamps and on the river Epigmarides; the cynocephali, who cannot say a word without barking; sciopods, who run swiftly on their single leg and when they want to take shelter from the sun stretch out and hold up their great foot like an umbrella; astomats from Greece, who have no mouth but breathe through their nostrils and live only on air; bearded women of Armenia; Pygmies; blemmyae, born headless, with mouths in their bellies and eyes on their shoulders; the monster women of the Red Sea, twelve feet tall, with hair to the ankles, a cow's tail at the base of the spine, and camel's hoofs; and those whose soles are reversed, so that, following them by their footprints, one arrives always at the place whence they came and never where they are going; and men with three heads, others with eyes that gleam like lamps, and monsters of the island of Circe, human bodies with heads of the most diverse animals...

These and other wonders were carved on that doorway. But none of them caused uneasiness because they did not signify the evils of this earth or the torments of hell but, rather, bore witness that the Word had reached all the known world and was extending to the unknown; thus the doorway was a joyous promise of concord, of unity achieved in the word of Christ, splendid oecumen.

A good augury, I said to myself, for the meeting to take place beyond this threshold, where men who have become one another's enemy through conflicting interpretations of the Gospel will perhaps succeed today in settling their disputes. And I reproached myself, that I was a weak sinner to bewail my personal problems when such important events for the history of Christianity were about to take place. I measured the smallness of my sufferings against the great promise of peace and serenity confirmed in the stone of the tympanum. I asked God's forgiveness for my frailty, and I crossed the threshold with new serenity.

The moment I entered I saw the members of both legations, complete, facing one another on a series of benches arranged in a hemicycle, the two sides separated by a table where the abbot and Cardinal Bertrand were sitting.

William, whom I followed in order to take notes, placed me among the Minorites, where Michael sat with his followers and other Franciscans of the court of Avignon, for the meeting was not meant to seem a duel between Italians and French, but a debate between supporters of the Franciscan Rule and their critics, all united by sound, Catholic loyalty to the papal court.

With Michael of Cesena were Brother Arnold of Aquitaine, Brother Hugh of Newcastle, and Brother William Alnwick, who had taken part in the Perugia chapter, and also the Bishop of Kaffa and Berengar Talloni, Bonagratia of Bergamo, and other Minorites from the Avignon court. On the opposite side sat Lawrence Decoin, bachelor of Avignon, the Bishop of Padua, and Jean d'Anneaux, doctor of theology in

Paris. Next to Bernard Gui, silent and pensive, there was the Dominican Jean de Baune, in Italy called Giovanni Dalbena. Years before, William told me, he had been inquisitor at Narbonne, where he had tried many Beghards; but when he found heresy in a proposition concerning the poverty of Christ, Berengar Talloni, reader in the convent of that city, rose against him and appealed to the Pope. At that time John was still uncertain about this question, so he summoned both men to his court, where they argued without arriving at any conclusion. Thus a short time later the Franciscans took their stand, which I have described, at the Perugia chapter. Finally, there were still others on the side of the Avignonese, including the Bishop of Alborea.

The session was opened by Abo, who deemed it opportune to sum up recent events. He recalled how in the year of our Lord 1322 the general chapter of the Friars Minor, gathered at Perugia under the leadership of Michael of Cesena, had established with mature and diligent deliberation that, to set an example of the perfect life, Christ and, following his teaching, the apostles had never owned anything in common, whether as property or feud, and this truth was a matter of Catholic faith and doctrine, deduced from various passages in the canonical books. Wherefore renunciation of ownership of all things was meritorious and holy, and the early fathers of the church militant had followed this holy rule. The Council of Vienne in 1312 had also subscribed to this truth, and Pope John himself, in 1317, in the constitution regarding the condition of the Friars Minor which begins "Quorundam exigit," had referred to the deliberations of that council as devoutly composed, lucid, sound, and mature. Whence the Perugian chapter, considering that what the apostolic see had always approved as sound doctrine should always be held as accepted, nor should it be strayed from in any way, had merely confirmed that council's decision, with the signature of such masters of sacred theology as Brother William of England, Brother Henry of Germany, Brother Arnold of Aquitaine, provincials and ministers, and also with the seal of Brother Nicholas, minister of France; Brother William Bloc, bachelor; the minister general and the four ministers provincial; Brother Thomas of Bologna; Brother Peter of the province of Saint Francis; Brother Ferdinand of Castello; and Brother Simon of Touraine. However, Abo added, the following year the Pope issued the decretal *Ad conditorem canonum*, against which Brother Bonagratia of Bergamo appealed, considering it contrary to the interests of his order. The Pope then took down that decretal from the doors of the church of Avignon where it had been exposed, and revised it in several places. But he actually made it harsher, as was proved by the fact that, as an immediate consequence, Brother Bonagratia was held in prison for a year. Nor could there be any doubts as to the Pontiff's severity, because that same year he issued the now very well known *Cum inter nonnullos*, in which the theses of the Perugia chapter were definitively condemned.

Politely interrupting Abo at this point, Cardinal Bertrand spoke up, saying we should recall how, to complicate matters and to irritate the Pontiff, in 1324 Louis the Bavarian had intervened with the Declaration of Sachsenhausen, in which for no good reason he confirmed the theses of Perugia (nor was it comprehensible, Bertrand remarked, with a thin smile, that the Emperor should acclaim so enthusiastically a poverty he did not practice in the least), setting himself against the lord Pope, calling him *inimicus pacis* and saying he was bent on fomenting scandal and discord, and finally calling him a heretic, indeed a heresiarch.

"Not exactly," Abo ventured, trying to mediate.

"In substance, yes," Bertrand said sharply. And he added that it was precisely the Emperor's inopportune meddling that had obliged the lord Pope to issue the decretal *Quia quorundam*, and that eventually he had sternly bidden Michael of Cesena to appear before him. Michael had sent letters of excuse, declaring himself ill—something no one doubted—and had sent in his stead Brother John Fidanza and Brother Umile Custodio from Perugia. But it so happened, the cardinal went on, that the Guelphs of Perugia had informed the Pope that, far from being ill, Brother Michael was in communication with Louis of Bavaria. In any case, what was past was past, and now Brother Michael looked well and serene, and so was expected in Avignon. However, it was better, the cardinal admitted, to consider beforehand, as prudent men from both sides were now doing, what Michael would finally say to the Pope, since everyone's aim was still not to exacerbate but, rather, to settle fraternally a dispute that had no reason to exist between a loving father and his devoted sons, and which until then had been kept ablaze only by the interference of secular men, whether emperors or viceroys, who had nothing to do with the questions of Holy Mother Church.

Abo then spoke up and said that, though he was a man of the church and abbot of an order to which the church owed much (a murmur of respect and deference was heard from both sides of the hemicycle), he still did not feel the Emperor should remain aloof from such questions, for the many reasons that Brother William of Baskerville would expound in due course. But, Abo went on, it was nevertheless proper that the first part of the debate should take place between the papal envoys and the representatives of those sons of Saint Francis who, by their very participation in this meeting, showed themselves to be the most devoted sons of the Pope. And then he asked that Brother Michael or his nominee indicate the position he meant to uphold in Avignon.

Michael said that, to his great and joyous emotion, there was in their midst that morning Ubertino of Casale, from whom the Pope himself, in 1322, had asked for a thorough report on the question of poverty. And Ubertino could best sum up, with that lucidity, erudition, and devout faith that all recognized in him, the capital points of those ideas which now, unswervingly, were those of the Franciscan order.

Ubertino rose, and as soon as he began to speak, I understood why he had aroused so much enthusiasm, both as a preacher and as a courtier. Impassioned in his gesticulation, his voice persuasive, his smile fascinating, his reasoning clear and consequential, he held his listeners fast for all the time he spoke. He began a very learned disquisition on the reasons that supported the Perugia theses. He said that, first of all, it had to be recognized that Christ and the apostles were in a double condition, because they were prelates of the church of the New Testament, and in this respect they possessed, as regards the authority of dispensation and distribution, to give to the poor and to the ministers of the church, as is written in the fourth chapter of the Acts of the Apostles, and this point nobody disputes. But secondarily, Christ and the apostles must be considered as individual persons, the base of every religious perfection, and perfect despisers of the world. And on this score two ways of having are posited, one of which is civil and worldly, which the imperial laws define with the words "in bonis nostris," because we call ours those goods of which we have the defense and which, if taken from us, we have the right to claim. Whereby it is one thing to defend in a civil and worldly sense one's own possession against him who would take it, appealing to the imperial judge (to affirm that Christ and the apostles owned things in this sense is heretical, because, as Matthew says in chapter 5, if any man will sue thee at the law, and take away thy coat, let him have thy cloak also; nor does Luke say any differently in chapter 6, where Christ dismisses from himself all power and lordship and imposes the same on his apostles; and consider further Matthew chapter 19, in which Peter says to the Lord that to follow him they have left everything); but in the other way temporal things can yet be held, for the purpose of common fraternal charity, and in this way Christ and his disciples possessed some goods by natural right, which right by some is called ius poli, that is to say the law of heaven, to sustain nature, which without human intervention is consonant with proper reason, whereas ius fori is power that derives from human covenant. Before the first division of things, as far as ownership was concerned, they were like those things today which are not among anyone's possessions and are granted to him who takes them; things were in a certain sense common to all men, whereas it was only after original sin that our progenitors began to divide up ownership of things, and thus began worldly dominion as we now know it. But Christ and the apostles held things in the first way, and so they had clothing and the bread and fishes, and as Paul says in I Timothy: Having food and raiment let us be therewith content. Wherefore Christ and his disciples did not hold these things in possession but in use, their absolute poverty remaining intact. Which had already been recognized by Pope Nicholas II in the decretal *Exiit qui seminat*.

But on the opposite side Jean d'Anneaux rose to say that Ubertino's positions seemed to him contrary both to proper reason and to the proper interpretation of Scripture. Whereas with goods perishable with use, such as bread and foods, a simple right of use cannot be considered, nor can de-facto use be posited, but only abuse; everything the believers held in common in the primitive church, as is deduced from Acts 2 and 3, they held on the basis of the same type of ownership they had had before their conversion; the apostles, after the descent of the Holy Spirit, possessed farms in Judaea; the vow of living without property does not extend to what man needs in order to live, and when Peter said he had left everything he did not mean he had renounced property; Adam had ownership and property of things; the servant who receives money from his master certainly does not just make use or abuse of it; the words of the *Exiit qui seminat* to which the Minorites are always referring and which establish that the Friars Minor have only the use of what serves them, without having control and ownership, must be referring only to goods that are not consumed with use; and in fact if the *Exiit* included perishable goods it would sustain the impossible; de-facto use cannot be distinguished from juridical control; every human right, on the basis of which material goods are owned, is contained in the laws of kings; Christ as a mortal man, from the moment of his conception, was owner of all earthly goods, and as God he received from the Father universal control over everything; he was owner of clothing, food, money for tribute, and offerings of the faithful; and if he was poor, it was not because he had no property, but because he did not receive its fruits; for simple juridical control, separated from the collection of interest, does not enrich the possessor; and finally, even if the *Exiit* had said otherwise, the Roman Pontiff, in everything concerning faith and morals, can revoke the decisions of his predecessors and can even make contrary assertions.

It was at this point that Brother Jerome, Bishop of Kaffa, rose vehemently, his beard shaking with wrath even though he tried to make his words sound conciliatory. He began an argumentation that to me seemed fairly confused. "What I will say to the Holy Father, and myself who will say it, I submit to his correction, because I truly believe John is the vicar of Christ, and for this confession I was seized by the Saracens. And I will refer first to an event recorded by a great doctor, in the dispute that arose one day among monks as to who was the father of Melchizedek. Then the abbot Copes, questioned about this, shook his head and declared: Woe to you, Copes, for you seek only those things that God does not command you to seek and neglect those He does command. There, as is readily deduced from my example, it is so clear that Christ and the Blessed Virgin and the apostles held nothing, individually or in common, that it would be less clear to recognize that Jesus was man and God at the same time, and yet it seems clear to me that anyone denying the evidence of the former must then deny the latter!"

He spoke triumphantly, and I saw William raise his eyes to heaven. I suspect he considered Jerome's syllogism quite defective, and I cannot say he was wrong, but even more defective, it seemed to me, was the infuriated and contrary argumentation of Jean de Baune, who said that he who affirms something about the poverty of Christ affirms what is seen (or not seen) with the eye, whereas to define his simultaneous humanity and divinity, faith intervenes, so that the two propositions cannot be compared.

In reply, Jerome was more acute than his opponent: "Oh, no, dear brother," he said, "I think exactly the opposite is true, because all the Gospels declare Christ was a man and ate and drank, and as his most evident miracles demonstrate, he was also God, and all this is immediately obvious!"

"Magicians and soothsayers also work miracles," de Baune said smugly.

"True," Jerome replied, "but through magic art. Would you compare Christ's miracles to magic art?" The assembly murmured indignantly that they would not consider such a thing. "And finally," Jerome went on, feeling he was now close to victory, "would his lordship the Cardinal del Poggetto want to consider heretical the belief in Christ's poverty, when this proposition is the basis of the Rule of an order such as the Franciscan, whose sons have gone to every realm to preach and shed their blood, from Morocco to India?"

"Holy spirit of Peter of Spain," William muttered, "protect us."

"Most beloved brother," de Baune then cried, taking

a step forward, "speak if you will of the blood of your monks, but do not forget, that same tribute has also been paid by religious of other orders...."

"With all due respect to my lord cardinal," Jerome shouted, "no Dominican ever died among the infidels, whereas in my own time alone, nine Minorites have been martyred!"

The Dominican Bishop of Alborea, red in the face, now stood up. "I can prove that before any Minorites were in Tartary, Pope Innocent sent three Dominicans there!"

"He did?" Jerome said, snickering. "Well, I know that the Minorites have been in Tartary for eighty years, and they have forty churches throughout the country, whereas the Dominicans have only five churches, all along the coast, and perhaps fifteen monks in all. And that settles the question!"

"It does not settle any question at all," the Bishop of Alborea shouted, "because these Minorites, who produce heretics as bitches produce puppies, claim everything for themselves, boast of martyrs, but have fine churches, sumptuous vestments, and buy and sell like all the other religious!"

"No, my lord, no," Jerome interrupted, "they do not buy and sell on their own, but through the procurators of the apostolic see, and the procurators have possession, while the Minorites have only the use!"

"Is that so?" the bishop sneered. "And how many times, then, have you sold without procurators? I know the story of some farms that—"

"If I did so, I was wrong," Jerome hastily interrupted, "not to turn that over to the order may have been a weakness on my part!"

"Venerable brothers," Abo then intervened, "our problem is not whether the Minorites are poor, but whether our Lord was poor...."

"Well, then"—at this point Jerome raised his voice

again—"on that question I have an argument that cuts like a sword...."

"Saint Francis, protect thy sons..." William said, without much confidence.

"The argument," Jerome continued, "is that the Orientals and the Greeks, far more familiar than we with the doctrine of the holy fathers, are convinced of the poverty of Christ. And if those heretics and schismatics so clearly uphold such a clear truth, do we want to be more heretical and schismatical than they, by denying it? These Orientals, if they heard some of our number preaching against this truth, would stone them!"

"What are you saying?" the Bishop of Alborea quipped. "Why, then, do they not stone the Dominicans, who preach precisely against this?"

"Dominicans? Why, no one has ever seen them down there!"

Alborea, his face purple, observed that this monk Jerome had been in Greece perhaps fifteen years, whereas he had been there since his boyhood. Jerome replied that the Dominican Alborea might perhaps have been in Greece, but living a sybaritic life in fine bishops' palaces, whereas he, a Franciscan, had been there not fifteen years, but twenty-two, and had preached before the Emperor in Constantinople. Then Alborea, running short on arguments, started to cross the space that separated him from the Minorites, indicating in a loud voice and with words I dare not repeat his firm intention to pull off the beard of the Bishop of Kaffa, whose masculinity he called into question, and whom he planned to punish, by the logic of an eye for an eye, shoving that beard in a certain place.

The other Minorites rushed to form a barrier and defend their brother; the Avignonese thought it useful to lend the Dominican a hand, and (Lord, have mercy on the best among thy sons!) a brawl ensued, which the abbot and the cardinal tried to quell. In the tumult that followed, Minorites and Dominicans said grave things to one another, as if each were a Christian fighting the Saracens. The only ones who remained in their seats were William, on one side, and Bernard Gui, on the other. William seemed sad, and Bernard happy, if you can call happiness the faint smile that curled the inquisitor's lip.

"Are there no better arguments," I asked my master, as Alborea tugged at the beard of the Bishop of Kaffa, "to prove or refute the poverty of Christ?"

"Why, you can affirm both positions, my good Adso," William said, "and you will never be able to establish on the basis of the Gospels whether, and to what extent, Christ considered as his property the tunic he wore, which he then perhaps threw away when it was worn out. And, if you like, the doctrine of Thomas Aquinas on property is bolder than that of us Minorites. We say: We own nothing and have everything in use. He said: Consider yourselves also owners, provided that, if anyone lacks what you possess, you grant him its use, and out of obligation, not charity. But the question is not whether Christ was poor: it is whether the church must be poor. And 'poor' does not so much mean owning a palace or not; it means, rather, keeping or renouncing the right to legislate on earthly matters."

"Then this," I said, "is why the Emperor is so interested in what the Minorites say about poverty."

"Exactly. The Minorites are playing the Emperor's game against the Pope. But Marsilius and I consider it a two-sided game, and we would like the empire to support our view and serve our idea of human rule."

"And will you say this when you are called on to speak?"

"If I say it I fulfill my mission, which was to expound the opinions of the imperial theologians. But if I say it my mission fails, because I ought to be facilitating a second meeting in Avignon, and I don't believe John would agree to my going there to say these things."

"And so—?"

"And so I am trapped between two opposing forces, like an ass who does not know which of two sacks of hay to eat. The time is not ripe. Marsilius raves of an impossible transformation, immediately; but Louis is no better than his predecessors, even if for the present he remains the only bulwark against a wretch like John. Perhaps I shall have to speak, unless they end up killing one another first. In any case, Adso, write it all down: let at least some trace remain of what is happening today."

As we were speaking—and truly I do not know how we managed to hear each other—the dispute reached its climax. The archers intervened, at a sign from Bernard Gui, to keep the two factions apart. But like besiegers and besieged, on both sides of the walls of a fortress, they hurled insults and rebuttals at one another, which I record here at random, unable to attribute them to specific speakers, and with the premise that the phrases were not uttered in turn, as would happen in a dispute in my country, but in Mediterranean fashion, one overlapping another, like the waves of an angry sea.

"The Gospel says Christ had a purse!"

"Shut up! You people paint that purse even on crucifixes! What do you say, then, of the fact that our Lord, when he entered Jerusalem, went back every night to Bethany?"

"If our Lord chose to go and sleep in Bethany, who are you to question his decision?"

"No, you old ass, our Lord returned to Bethany because he had no money to pay for an inn in Jerusalem!"

"Bonagratia, you're the ass here! What did our Lord eat in Jerusalem?"

"Would you say, then, that a horse who receives oats from his master to keep alive is the owner of the oats?"

417

"You see? You compare Christ to a horse...."

"No, you are the one who compares Christ to a simoniacal prelate of your court, vessel of dung!"

"Really? And how many lawsuits has the holy see had to undertake to protect your property?"

"The property of the church, not ours! We had it in use!"

"In use to spend, to build beautiful churches with gold statues, you hypocrites, whited sepulchers, sinks of iniquity! You know well that charity, not poverty, is the principle of the perfect life!"

"That is what your glutton Thomas said!"

"Mind your words, villain! The man you call 'glutton' is a saint of the holy Roman church!"

"Saint, my foot! Canonized by John to spite the Franciscans! Your Pope can't create saints, because he's a heretic! No, a heresiarch!"

"We've heard that one before! Words spoken by that Bavarian puppet at Sachsenhausen, rehearsed by your Ubertino!"

"Mind how you speak, pig, son of the whore of Babylon and other strumpets as well! You know Ubertino wasn't with the Emperor that year: he was right there in Avignon, in the service of Cardinal Orsini, and the Pope was sending him as a messenger to Aragon!"

"I know, I know, he took his vow of poverty at the cardinal's table, as he now lives in the richest abbey of the peninsula! Ubertino, if you weren't there, who prompted Louis to use your writings?"

"Is it my fault if Louis reads my writings? Surely he cannot read yours, you illiterate!"

"I? Illiterate? Was your Francis a literate, he who spoke with geese?"

"You blaspheme!"

"You're the blasphemer; you know the keg ritual!"

"I have never seen such a thing, and you know it!"

"Yes, you did, you and your little friars, when you slipped into the bed of Clare of Montefalco!"

"May God strike you! I was inquisitor at that time, and Clare had already died in the odor of sanctity!"

"Clare gave off the odor of sanctity, but you were sniffing another odor when you sang matins to the nuns!"

"Go on, go on, the wrath of God will reach you, as it will reach your master, who has given welcome to two heretics like that Ostrogoth Eckhart and that English necromancer you call Branucerton!"

"Venerable brothers, venerable brothers!" Cardinal Bertrand and the abbot shouted.

TERCE

In which Severinus speaks to William of a strange book, and William speaks to the envoys of a strange concept of temporal government.

The quarrel was still raging when one of the novices guarding the door came in, passing through that confusion like someone walking across a field lashed by hail. He approached William, to whisper that Severinus wanted urgently to speak to him. We went out into the narthex, which was crowded with curious monks trying, through the shouts and noise, to catch something of what was going on inside. In the first rank we saw Aymaro of Alessandria, who welcomed us with his usual condescending sneer of commiseration at the foolishness of the universe. "To be sure, since the rise of the mendicant orders Christianity has become more virtuous," he said.

William brushed him aside with a certain roughness and headed for Severinus, awaiting us in a corner. He was distressed and wanted to speak to us in private, but it was impossible to find a calm spot in that confusion. We thought to go outside, but Michael of Cesena looked out through the doorway of the chapter hall, bidding

William to come back in, because, he said, the quarrel was being settled and the series of speeches should be resumed.

William, torn between two bags of hay, urged Severinus to speak, and the herbalist did his best to keep others from overhearing.

"Berengar certainly came to the infirmary before he went to the balneary," he said.

"How do you know?" Some monks approached, their curiosity aroused by our confabulation. Severinus's voice sank still lower, as he looked around.

"You told me that that man . . . must have had something with him. . . . Well, I found something in my laboratory, among the other books . . . a book that is not mine, a strange book. . . ."

"That must be it," William said triumphantly. "Bring it to me at once."

"I can't," Severinus said. "I'll explain to you later. I have discovered . . . I believe I have discovered something interesting. . . . You must come, I have to show you the book . . . cautiously. . . ." He broke off. We realized that, silently as was his custom, Jorge had appeared as if by magic at our side. His hands were extended before him, as if, not used to moving in that place, he were trying to sense his direction. A normal person would not have been able to comprehend Severinus's whispers, but we had learned some time before that Jorge's hearing, like that of all blind men, was especially sharp.

Still, the old man seemed to have heard nothing. He moved, in fact, in the direction away from us, touched one of the monks, and asked him something. The monk took him gently by the arm and led him outside. At that moment Michael reappeared, again summoning William, and my master made a decision. "Please," he said to Severinus, "go back at once to the place from whence you came. Lock yourself inside and wait for me. You"—he said to me—"follow Jorge. Even if he d hear something, I don't believe he will have himself led to the infirmary. In any case, you will tell me where he goes."

As he started to go back into the hall, he noticed (as I also noticed) Aymaro pushing his way through the jostling crowd in order to follow Jorge outside. Here William acted unwisely, because now in a loud voice, from one end of the narthex to the other, he said to Severinus, who was at the outer threshold, "Make sure those papers are safe.... Don't go back to ... where they came from!" Just as I was preparing to follow Jorge, I saw the cellarer leaning against the jamb of the outside door; he had heard William's warnings and was looking from my master to the herbalist, his face tense with fear. He saw Severinus going out and followed him. On the threshold, I was afraid of losing sight of Jorge, who was about to be swallowed up by the fog, but the other two, heading in the opposite direction, were also on the verge of vanishing into the brume. I calculated rapidly what I should do. I had been ordered to follow the blind man, but because it was feared he was going toward the infirmary. Instead, his guide was taking him in another direction: he was crossing the cloister, heading for the church or the Aedificium. The cellarer, on the contrary, was surely following the herbalist, and William was worried about what could happen in the laboratory. So I started following the two men, wondering, among other things, where Aymaro had gone, unless he had come out for reasons quite removed from ours.

Keeping a reasonable distance, I did not lose sight of the cellarer, who was slowing his pace because he had realized I was following him. He couldn't be sure the shadow at his heels was mine, as I couldn't be sure the shadow whose heels I followed belonged to him; but as I had no doubts about him, he had none about me.

Forcing him to keep an eye on me, I prevented him om dogging Severinus too closely. And so when the door of the infirmary appeared in the mist it was closed. Severinus had already gone inside, heaven be thanked. The cellarer turned once again to look at me, while I stood motionless as a tree of the garden; then he seemed to come to a decision and he moved toward the kitchen. I felt I had fulfilled my mission, so I decided to go back and report. Perhaps I made a mistake: if I had remained on guard, many other misfortunes would have been averted. But this I know now; I did not know it then.

I went back into the chapter hall. That busybody, it seemed to me, did not represent a great danger. I approached William again and briefly gave him my report. He nodded his approval, then motioned me to be silent. The confusion was now abating. The legates on both sides were exchanging the kiss of peace. The Bishop of Alborea praised the faith of the Minorites. Jerome exalted the charity of the preachers, all expressed the hope of a church no longer racked by internal conflicts. Some praised the strength of one group, some the temperance of another; all invoked justice and counseled prudence. Never have I seen so many men so sincerely concerned with the triumph of the cardinal and theological virtues.

But now Bertrand del Poggetto was inviting William to expound the theses of the imperial theologians. William rose, reluctantly: he was realizing that the meeting was of no utility, and in any case he was in a hurry to leave, for the mysterious book was now more urgent for him than the results of the meeting. But it was clear he could not evade his duty.

He began speaking then, with many "eh"s and "oh"s, perhaps more than usual and more than proper, as if to make it clear he was absolutely unsure about the things he was going to say, and he opened by affirming that he understood perfectly the viewpoint of those who had spoken before him, and for that matter what others called the "doctrine" of the imperial theologians was no more than some scattered observations that did not claim to be established articles of faith.

He said, further, that, given the immense goodness that God had displayed in creating the race of His sons, loving them all without distinction, recalling those pages of Genesis in which there was yet no mention of priests and kings, considering also that the Lord had given to Adam and to his descendants power over the things of this earth, provided they obeyed the divine laws, we might infer that the Lord also was not averse to the idea that in earthly things the people should be legislator and effective first cause of the law. By the term "people," he said, it would be best to signify all citizens, but since among citizens children must be included, as well as idiots, malefactors, and women, perhaps it would be possible to arrive reasonably at a definition of the people as the better part of the citizens, though he himself at the moment did not consider it opportune to assert who actually belonged to that part.

He cleared his throat, apologized to his listeners, remarking that the atmosphere was certainly very damp, and suggested that the way in which the people could express its will might be an elective general assembly. He said that to him it seemed sensible for such an assembly to be empowered to interpret, change, or suspend the law, because if the law is made by one man alone, he could do harm through ignorance or malice, and William added that it was unnecessary to remind those present of numerous recent instances. I noticed that the listeners, rather puzzled by his previous words, could only assent to these last ones, because each was obviously thinking of a different person, and each considered very bad the person of whom he was thinking.

Well, then, William continued, if one man can make laws badly, will not many men be better? Naturally, he underlined, he was speaking of earthly laws, regarding the management of civil things. God had told Adam not to eat of the tree of good and evil, and that was divine law; but then He had authorized, or, rather, encouraged, Adam to give things names, and on that score He had allowed His terrestrial subject free rein. In fact, though some in our times say that nomina sunt consequentia rerum, the book of Genesis is actually quite explicit on this point: God brought all the animals unto Adam to see what he would call them: and whatsoever Adam called every living creature, that was the name thereof. And though surely the first man had been clever enough to call, in his Adamic language, every thing and animal according to its nature, nevertheless he was exercising a kind of sovereign right in imagining the name that in his opinion best corresponded to that nature. Because, in fact, it is now known that men impose different names to designate concepts, though only the concepts, signs of things, are the same for all. So that surely the word "nomen" comes from "nomos," that is to say "law," since nomina are given by men ad placitum, in other words by free and collective accord.

The listeners did not dare contest this learned demonstration.

Whereby, William concluded, is it clear that legislation over the things of this earth, and therefore over the things of the cities and kingdoms, has nothing to do with the custody and administration of the divine word, an unalienable privilege of the ecclesiastical hierarchy. Unhappy indeed, William said, are the infidels, who have no similar authority to interpret for them the divine word (and all felt sorry for the infidels). But does this perhaps entitle us to say that the infidels do not have the tendency to make laws and administer their affairs through governments, kings, emperors, or sultans, caliphs, or however you chose to call them? And could it be denied that many Roman emperors— Trajan, for instance—had exercised their temporal power with wisdom? And who gave the pagans and the infidels this natural capacity to legislate and live in political communities? Was it perhaps their false divinities, who necessarily do not exist (or do not exist necessarily, however you understand the negation of this modality)? Certainly not. It could only have been conferred by the God of hosts, the God of Israel, Father of our Lord Jesus Christ.... Wondrous proof of the divine goodness that conferred the capacity for judging political things also on those who deny the authority of the Roman Pontiff and do not profess the same sacred, sweet, and terrible mysteries of the Christian people! But what finer demonstration than this of the fact that temporal rule and secular jurisdiction have nothing to do with the church and with the law of Jesus Christ and were ordained by God beyond all ecclesiastical confirmation and even before our holy religion was founded?

He coughed again, but this time he was not alone. Many of those present were wriggling on their benches and clearing their throats. I saw the cardinal run his tongue over his lips and make a gesture, anxious but polite, to urge William to get to the point. And William now grappled with what seemed to all, even to those who did not share them, the perhaps unpleasant conclusions of his incontrovertible reasoning. William said that his deductions seemed to him supported by the very example of Christ, who did not come into this world to command, but to be subject to the conditions he found in the world, at least as far as the laws of Caesar were concerned. He did not want the apostles to have command and dominion, and therefore it seemed a wise thing that the successors of the apostles should be relieved of any worldly or coercive power. If the pope, the bishops, and the priests were not subject to the worldly and coercive power of the prince, the authority of the prince would be challenged, and thus, with it, an order would be challenged that, as had been demonstrated previously, had been decreed by God. To be sure, some delicate cases must be considered—William said—like those of the heretics, on whose heresy only the church, custodian of the truth, can pronounce, though only the secular arm can act. When the church identifies some heretics she must surely point them out to the prince, who must rightly be informed of the conditions of his citizens. But what should the prince do with a heretic? Condemn him in the name of that divine truth of which he is not the custodian? The prince can and must condemn the heretic if his action harms the community, that is, if the heretic, in declaring his heresy, kills or impedes those who do not share it. But at that point the power of the prince ends, because no one on this earth can be forced through torture to follow the precepts of the Gospel: otherwise what would become of that free will on the exercising of which each of us will be judged in the next world? The church can and must warn the heretic that he is abandoning the community of the faithful, but she cannot judge him on earth and force him against his will. If Christ had wanted his priests to obtain coercive power, he would have laid down specific precepts as Moses did in the ancient law. He did not do it; therefore he did not wish it. Or does someone want to suggest the idea that he did wish it but lacked the time or the ability to say so in three years of preaching? But it was right that he should not wish it, because if he had wished it, then the pope would be able to impose his will on the king, and Christianity would no longer be a law of freedom, but one of intolerable slavery.

All this, William added with a cheerful expression, is no limitation of the powers of the supreme Pontiff, but, rather, an exaltation of his mission: because the servant of the servants of God is on this earth to serve and not to be served. And, finally, it would be odd, to say the least, if the Pope had jurisdiction over the things of the Roman Empire but not over the other kingdoms of the earth. As everyone knows, what the Pope says on divine questions is as valid for the subjects of the King of

427

France as it is for those of the King of England, but it must be valid also for the subjects of the Great Khan or the Sultan of the infidels, who are called infidels precisely because they are not faithful to this beautiful truth. And so if the Pope were to assume he had temporal jurisdiction—as pope—only over the affairs of the empire, that might justify the suspicion that, identifying temporal jurisdiction with the spiritual, by that same token he would have no spiritual jurisdiction over not only the Saracens or the Tartars, but also over the French and the English—which would be a criminal blasphemy. And this was the reason, my master concluded, why it seemed right to him to suggest that the church of Avignon was injuring all mankind by asserting the right to approve or suspend him who had been elected emperor of the Romans. The Pope does not have greater rights over the empire than over other kingdoms, and since neither the King of France nor the Sultan is subject to the Pope's approval, there seems to be no good reason why the Emperor of the Germans and Italians should be subject to it. Such subjection is not a matter of divine right, because Scripture does not speak of it. Nor is it sanctioned by the rights of peoples, for the reasons already expounded. As for the connection with the dispute about poverty, William added, his own humble opinions, developed in the form of conversational suggestions by him and by some others such as Marsilius of Padua and John of Jandun, led to the following conclusions: if the Franciscans wanted to remain poor, the Pope could not and should not oppose such a virtuous wish. To be sure, if the hypothesis of Christ's poverty were to be proved, this would not only help the Minorites but also strengthen the idea that Jesus had not wished any earthly jurisdiction. But that morning he, William, had heard very wise people assert that it could not be proved that Christ had been poor. Whence it seemed to him more fitting to reverse the demonstration. Since nobody had asserted, or could assert, that Jesus had sought any earthly jurisdiction for himself or for his disciples, this detachment of Jesus from temporal things seemed sufficient evidence to suggest the belief, without sinning, that Jesus, on the contrary, preferred poverty.

William had spoken in such a meek tone, he had expressed his certainties in such a hesitant way, that none of those present was able to stand up and rebut. This does not mean that all were convinced of what he had said. The Avignonese were now writhing, frowning, and muttering comments among themselves, and even the abbot seemed unfavorably impressed by those words, as if he were thinking this was not the relationship he had desired between his order and the empire. And as for the Minorites, Michael of Cesena was puzzled, Jerome aghast, Ubertino pensive.

The silence was broken by Cardinal del Poggetto, still smiling and relaxed as he politely asked William whether he would go to Avignon to say these same things to the lord Pope. William asked the opinion of the cardinal, who said that the Pope had heard many debatable opinions uttered during his life and was a most loving father toward all his sons, but surely these propositions would grieve him very much.

Bernard Gui, who until then had not opened his mouth, now spoke up: "I would be very happy if Brother William, so skilled and eloquent in expounding his own ideas, were to submit them to the judgment of the Pontiff...."

"You have convinced me, my lord Bernard," William said. "I will not come." Then, addressing the cardinal, in an apologetic tone: "You know, this fluxion that is affecting my chest dissuades me from undertaking such a long journey in this season...."

"Then why did you speak at such length?" the cardinal asked.

"To bear witness to the truth," William said humbly. "The truth shall make us free."

"Ah, no!" Jean de Baune exploded at this point. "Here we are not talking about the truth that makes us free, but about excessive freedom that wants to set itself up as truth!"

"That is also possible," William admitted sweetly.

My intuition suddenly warned me that another tempest of hearts and tongues was about to burst, far more furious than the earlier one. But nothing happened. While de Baune was still speaking, the captain of the archers entered and went to whisper something into Bernard's ear. Bernard rose abruptly and held up his hand to speak.

"Brothers," he said, "it is possible this profitable discussion may be resumed, but for the moment an event of tremendous gravity obliges us to suspend our session, with the abbot's permission. Something has happened there...." He pointed vaguely outside, then strode through the hall and went out. Many followed him, William among the first, and I with him.

My master looked at me and said, "I fear something has happened to Severinus."

SEXT

In which Severinus is found murdered but the book that he had found is to be found no longer.

We crossed the grounds with a rapid step, in anguish. The captain of the archers led us toward the infirmary, and as we arrived there we glimpsed in the thick grayness a stirring of shadows: monks and servants were rushing about, archers were standing outside the door to prevent access.

"Those guards were sent by me, to seek a man who could shed light on many mysteries," Bernard said.

"The brother herbalist?" the abbot asked, dumbfounded.

"No. You will see now," Bernard said, making his way inside.

We entered Severinus's laboratory, and here a painful sight greeted our eyes. The unfortunate herbalist lay, a corpse, in a pool of blood, his head bashed in. On every side the shelves seemed to have been devastated by a storm: pots, bottles, books, documents lay all around in great disorder, ruined. Beside the body was an armillary sphere at least twice the size of a man's head, of finely worked metal, surmounted by a gold cross, and set on a short, decorated tripod. On other occasions I had noticed it on the table to the left of the front door.

At the other end of the room two archers were holding the cellarer fast, though he wriggled and proclaimed his innocence, increasing his noise when he saw the abbot enter. "My lord!" he cried out. "Appearances are against me! Severinus was already dead when I came in, and they found me staring at this massacre, speechless!"

The archers' captain went over to Bernard, and with his permission made a report, in front of everyone. The archers had been ordered to find the cellarer and arrest him, and for over two hours they had searched for him throughout the abbey. This, I thought, must have been the command Bernard had given before entering the hall; and the soldiers, foreigners in this place, had probably pursued their search in the wrong places, without realizing that the cellarer, unaware of his fate, was with the others in the narthex; the fog had also made their hunt more difficult. In any case, from the captain's words it emerged that Remigio, after I left him, went toward the kitchen, where someone saw him and informed the archers, who reached the Aedificium after Remigio had left it again, missing them only by a moment. In the kitchen was Jorge, who declared he had just finished speaking with the cellarer. The archers then explored the grounds in the direction of the gardens, and there, emerging from the mist like a ghost, they found old Alinardo, who seemed lost. It was Alinardo who said he had seen the cellarer, a short while before, going into the infirmary. The archers went there and found the door open. Once inside, they discovered Severinus lifeless and the cellarer furiously rummaging over the shelves, flinging everything on the floor, as if he were hunting for something. It was easy to see what had happened, the captain concluded. Remigio had entered, had attacked the herbalist and killed him, and then was seeking the thing for which he had killed.

An archer picked the armillary sphere up from the floor and handed it to Bernard. The elegant architecture of brass and silver circles, held together by a stronger frame of bronze rings grasped by the stem of the tripod, had been brought down heavily on the victim's skull, and at the impact many of the finer circles had shattered or bent to one side. This side was the one brought down on Severinus's head, as was revealed by traces of blood and even tufts of hair and horrible gobbets of cerebral matter.

William bent over Severinus to verify his death. The poor man's eyes, veiled by the streams of blood from his head, were fixed, and I wondered if it were ever possible to read in the stiffened pupil, as it has been said in some cases, the image of the murderer, the last vestige of the victim's perception. I saw that William sought the dead man's hands, to see if he had black stains on his fingers, even though, this time, the cause of death was obviously quite different: but Severinus was wearing the same leather gloves with which I had occasionally seen him handling dangerous herbs, lizards, unfamiliar insects.

Meanwhile, Bernard Gui was addressing the cellarer: "Remigio of Varagine—that is your name, is it not? I had sent my men after you on the basis of other accusations and to confirm other suspicions. Now I see that I acted properly, although, to my regret, too slowly. My lord," he said to the abbot, "I hold myself virtually responsible for this last crime, because I have known since this morning that this man should be taken into custody, after I heard the revelations of that other wretch, arrested last night. But as you saw for yourself, during the morning I was occupied with other duties, and my men did their best...."

He spoke in a loud voice so that all those present could hear (and the room had meanwhile filled u people crowding into every corner, looking at the things scattered and destroyed, pointing to the corpse and commenting in low voices on the crime), and, as he spoke, I glimpsed Malachi in the little crowd, grimly observing the scene. The cellarer, about to be dragged away, also glimpsed him. He wrested himself from the archer's grasp and flung himself on his brother, grabbing him by the habit and speaking to him briefly and desperately, his face close to the other man's, until the archers seized him again. But, as he was being led off roughly, he turned again toward Malachi and shouted at him, "You swear, and I swear!"

Malachi did not answer at once, as if he were seeking the most suitable words. Then, as the cellarer was being pulled across the threshold, he said, "I will do nothing to harm you."

William and I looked at each other, wondering what was the meaning of this scene. Bernard had also observed it, but did not appear upset by it; rather, he smiled at Malachi, as if to approve his words and to seal with him a sinister bargain. Then he announced that immediately after our meal a first court would meet in the chapter hall to open this investigation publicly. And he went out, ordering the cellarer to be taken to the forges, but not allowed to speak with Salvatore.

At that moment we heard Benno calling us, at our back. "I came in right after you," he said in a whisper, "when the room was still half empty, and Malachi was not here."

"He must have entered afterward," William said.

"No," Benno insisted, "I was near the door, I saw the people come in. I tell you, Malachi was already inside . . . before."

"Before what?"

"Before the cellarer entered. I cannot swear it, but I believe he came from behind that curtain, when there were already many of us in here." And he nodded ׁoward an ample hanging that concealed the bed where

Severinus had usually made anyone who had been given some medication lie down and rest.

"Are you insinuating he killed Severinus and hid there when the cellarer came in?" William asked.

"Or else from behind the curtain he witnessed what happened out here. Why, otherwise, would the cellarer have implored him not to harm him, promising in return not to do him harm, either?"

"That is possible," William said. "In any case, there was a book here and it should still be here, because both the cellarer and Malachi went out empty-handed." William knew from my report that Benno knew; and at that moment he needed help. He went over to the abbot, who was sadly observing Severinus's corpse; William asked him to make everyone leave, because he wanted to examine the place more closely. The abbot consented and then left, not without giving William a skeptical look, as if reproaching him for always arriving too late. Malachi tried to remain, inventing various reasons, all quite vague; William pointed out that this was not the library, and that here Malachi could claim no rights. William was polite but inflexible, and he got his revenge for the time when Malachi had not allowed him to examine Venantius's desk.

When only three of us were left, William cleared the rubble and papers away from one of the tables and told me to hand him, one after another, the books in Severinus's collection. A small collection, compared with the immense one of the labyrinth, but still there were dozens and dozens of volumes, of various sizes, which had formerly stood neatly on the shelves and now lay in disorder on the ground among other objects, already disturbed by the cellarer's frantic hands, some even torn, as if he were seeking not a book but something that could be placed between the pages of a book. Some had been ripped violently, separated from their binding. To collect them, rapidly ascertain their subject, and pile them up on the table was no easy undertaking; and everything had to be done in haste, because the abbot had given us little time: the monks had to come in and lay out Severinus's battered body and prepare it for burial. We also had to move about, search under the tables, behind the shelves, in the cupboards, to see whether anything had escaped the first inspection. William would not let Benno help me and allowed him only to stand guard at the door. Despite the abbot's orders, many were pressing to enter: servants terrified by the news, monks mourning their brother, novices carrying clean cloths and basins of water to wash and enshroud the corpse....

So we had to act fast. I grabbed the books and handed them to William, who examined them and set them on the table. Then we realized it was a long job, and we proceeded together: I would pick up a book, smooth it out if it was ruffled, read its title, and set it down. In many cases there were only scattered pages.

"*De plantis libri tres.* Damnation, that's not it," William said, slamming the book on the table.

"*Thesaurus herbarum,*" I said, and William snapped, "Drop it; we're looking for a Greek book!"

"This?" I asked, showing him a work whose pages were covered with abstruse letters. And William said, "No, that's Arabic, idiot! Bacon was right: the scholar's first duty is to learn languages!"

"But you don't know Arabic, either!" I replied, irked, to which William answered, "At least I understand when it *is* Arabic!" And I blushed, because I could hear Benno snickering behind my back.

There were many books, and even more notes, scrolls with drawings of the heavenly vault, catalogues of strange plants, written on scattered pages, probably by the dead man. We worked a long time, exploring every corner of the laboratory. William, with great coldness, even shifted the corpse to see whether there was anything beneath it, and he rummaged inside the habit. Nothing.

"It has to be done," he said. "Severinus locked himself in here with a book. The cellarer didn't have it...."

"Can he have hidden it inside his habit?" I asked.

"No, the book I saw the other morning under Venantius's desk was big, and we would have noticed."

"How was it bound?" I asked.

"I don't know. It was lying open, and I saw it only for a few seconds, just long enough to realize it was in Greek, but I remember nothing else. Let us continue; the cellarer didn't take it, nor, I believe, did Malachi."

"Absolutely not," Benno confirmed. "When the cellarer grabbed him by the chest, it was obvious he could have nothing under his scapular."

"Good. Or, rather, bad. If the book is not in this room, obviously someone else, besides Malachi and the cellarer, had come in here before."

"A third person, then, who killed Severinus?"

"Too many people," William said.

"But anyway," I asked, "who could have known the book was here?"

"Jorge, for example, if he overheard us."

"Yes," I said, "but Jorge couldn't have killed a strong man like Severinus, and with such violence."

"No, certainly not. Besides, you saw him going toward the Aedificium, and the archers found him in the kitchen shortly before they found the cellarer. So he wouldn't have had time to come here and then go back to the kitchen."

"Let me think with my own head," I said, aiming at emulating my master. "Alinardo was moving around in the vicinity, but he, too, can hardly stand, and he couldn't have overpowered Severinus. The cellarer was here, but the time between his leaving the kitchen and the arrival of the archers was so short that I think it would have been difficult for him to make Severinus open the door, to attack and kill him, and then to make all this mess. Malachi could have come before them all: Jorge hears us in the narthex, he goes to the scriptorium to tell Malachi that a book from the library is in Severinus's laboratory, Malachi comes here, persuades Severinus to open the door, and kills him, God knows why. But if he was looking for the book, he should have recognized it, without all this ransacking, because he's the librarian! So who's left?"

"Benno," William said.

Benno shook his head, in vigorous denial. "No, Brother William, you know I was consumed with curiosity. But if I had come in here and had been able to leave with the book, I would not be here now keeping you company; I would be examining my treasure somewhere else...."

"An almost convincing argument," William said, smiling. "However, you don't know what the book looks like, either. You could have killed and now you would be here trying to identify the book."

Benno blushed violently. "I am not a murderer!" he protested.

"No one is, until he commits his first crime," William said philosophically. "Anyway, the book is missing, and this is sufficient proof that you didn't leave it here."

Then he turned to contemplate the corpse. He seemed only at that point to take in his friend's death. "Poor Severinus," he said, "I had suspected even you and your poisons. And you were expecting some trick with poison; otherwise you wouldn't have worn those gloves. You feared a danger of the earth and instead it came to you from the heavenly vault...." He picked up the sphere again, observing it with attention. "I wonder why they used this particular weapon...."

"It was within reach."

"Perhaps. But there were other things, pots, garden-

438

ing tools.... It is a fine example of the craft of metals and of astronomical science. It is ruined and...Good heavens!" he cried.

"What is it?"

"And the third part of the sun was smitten and the third part of the moon and the third part of the stars..." he quoted.

I knew all too well the text of John the apostle. "The fourth trumpet," I exclaimed.

"In fact. First hail, then blood, then water, and now the stars... If this is the case, then everything must be re-examined; the murderer did not strike at random, he was following a plan....But is it possible to imagine a mind so evil that he kills only when he can do so while following the dictates of the book of the Apocalypse?"

"What will happen with the fifth trumpet?" I asked, terrified. I tried to recall: "And I saw a star fallen from heaven unto the earth and to him was given the key of the bottomless pit.... Will somebody die by drowning in the well?"

"The fifth trumpet also promises many other things," William said. "From the pit will come the smoke of a great furnace, then locusts will come from it to torment mankind with a sting similar to a scorpion's. And the shape of the locusts will resemble that of horses, with gold crowns on their heads and lions' teeth.... Our man could have various means at his disposal to carry out the words of the book.... But we must not pursue fantasies. Let us try, rather, to remember what Severinus said to us when he informed us he had found the book...."

"You told him to bring it to you and he said he couldn't...."

"So he did, and then we were interrupted. Why couldn't he? A book can be carried. And why did he put on gloves? Is there something in the book's binding connected with the poison that killed Berengar and Venantius? A mysterious trap, a poisoned tip..."

"A snake!" I said.

"Why not a whale? No, we are indulging in fantasies again. The poison, as we have seen, had to enter the mouth. Besides, Severinus didn't actually say he couldn't carry the book. He said he preferred to show it to me here. And then he put on his gloves....So we know this book must be handled with gloves. And that goes for you, too, Benno, if you find it, as you hope to. And since you're being so helpful, you can help me further. Go up to the scriptorium again and keep an eye on Malachi. Don't let him out of your sight."

"I will!" Benno said, and he went out, happy at his mission, it seemed to us.

We could restrain the other monks no longer, and the room was invaded. Mealtime was now past, and Bernard was probably assembling his tribunal in the chapter house.

"There is nothing more to be done here," William said.

With the infirmary, we abandoned my poor hypothesis, and as we were crossing the vegetable garden I asked William whether he really trusted Benno. "Not entirely," William said, "but we told him nothing he didn't already know, and we have made him fear the book. And, finally, in setting him to watch Malachi, we are also setting Malachi to watch him, and Malachi is obviously looking for the book on his own."

"What did the cellarer want, then?"

"We'll soon know. Certainly he wanted something, and he wanted it quickly, to avert some danger that was terrifying him. This something must be known to Malachi: otherwise there would be no explanation of Remigio's desperate plea to him...."

"Anyway, the book has vanished...."

"This is the most unlikely thing," William said, as we

ing tools....It is a fine example of the craft of metals and of astronomical science. It is ruined and...Good heavens!" he cried.

"What is it?"

"And the third part of the sun was smitten and the third part of the moon and the third part of the stars..." he quoted.

I knew all too well the text of John the apostle. "The fourth trumpet," I exclaimed.

"In fact. First hail, then blood, then water, and now the stars...If this is the case, then everything must be re-examined; the murderer did not strike at random, he was following a plan....But is it possible to imagine a mind so evil that he kills only when he can do so while following the dictates of the book of the Apocalypse?"

"What will happen with the fifth trumpet?" I asked, terrified. I tried to recall: "And I saw a star fallen from heaven unto the earth and to him was given the key of the bottomless pit....Will somebody die by drowning in the well?"

"The fifth trumpet also promises many other things," William said. "From the pit will come the smoke of a great furnace, then locusts will come from it to torment mankind with a sting similar to a scorpion's. And the shape of the locusts will resemble that of horses, with gold crowns on their heads and lions' teeth....Our man could have various means at his disposal to carry out the words of the book....But we must not pursue fantasies. Let us try, rather, to remember what Severinus said to us when he informed us he had found the book...."

"You told him to bring it to you and he said he couldn't...."

"So he did, and then we were interrupted. Why couldn't he? A book can be carried. And why did he put on gloves? Is there something in the book's binding connected with the poison that killed Berengar and Venantius? A mysterious trap, a poisoned tip..."

"A snake!" I said.

"Why not a whale? No, we are indulging in fantasies again. The poison, as we have seen, had to enter the mouth. Besides, Severinus didn't actually say he couldn't carry the book. He said he preferred to show it to me here. And then he put on his gloves....So we know this book must be handled with gloves. And that goes for you, too, Benno, if you find it, as you hope to. And since you're being so helpful, you can help me further. Go up to the scriptorium again and keep an eye on Malachi. Don't let him out of your sight."

"I will!" Benno said, and he went out, happy at his mission, it seemed to us.

We could restrain the other monks no longer, and the room was invaded. Mealtime was now past, and Bernard was probably assembling his tribunal in the chapter house.

"There is nothing more to be done here," William said.

With the infirmary, we abandoned my poor hypothesis, and as we were crossing the vegetable garden I asked William whether he really trusted Benno. "Not entirely," William said, "but we told him nothing he didn't already know, and we have made him fear the book. And, finally, in setting him to watch Malachi, we are also setting Malachi to watch him, and Malachi is obviously looking for the book on his own."

"What did the cellarer want, then?"

"We'll soon know. Certainly he wanted something, and he wanted it quickly, to avert some danger that was terrifying him. This something must be known to Malachi: otherwise there would be no explanation of Remigio's desperate plea to him...."

"Anyway, the book has vanished...."

"This is the most unlikely thing," William said, as we

arrived at the chapter house. "If it was there, as Severinus told us it was, either it's been taken away or it's there still."

"And since it isn't there, someone has taken it away," I concluded.

"It is also possible that the argument should proceed from another minor premise. Since everything confirms the fact that nobody can have taken it away..."

"Then it should be there still. But it is not there."

"Just a moment. We say it isn't there because we didn't find it. But perhaps we didn't find it because we haven't seen it where it was."

"But we looked everywhere!"

"We looked, but did not see. Or else saw, but did not recognize.... Adso, how did Severinus describe that book to us? What words did he use?"

"He said he had found a book that was not one of his, in Greek...."

"No! Now I remember. He said a *strange* book. Severinus was a man of learning, and for a man of learning a book in Greek is not strange; even if that scholar doesn't know Greek, he would at least recognize the alphabet. And a scholar wouldn't call a book in Arabic strange, either, even if he doesn't know Arabic...." He broke off. "And what was an Arabic book doing in Severinus's laboratory?"

"But why should he have called an Arabic book strange?"

"This is the problem. If he called it strange it was because it had an unusual appearance, unusual at least for him, who was an herbalist and not a librarian.... And in libraries it can happen that several ancient manuscripts are bound together, collecting in one volume various and curious texts, one in Greek, one in Aramaic..."

"...and one in Arabic!" I cried, dazzled by the illumination.

William roughly dragged me out of the narthex and sent me running toward the infirmary. "You Teuton animal, you turnip! You ignoramus! You looked only at the first pages and not at the rest!"

"But, master," I gasped, "you're the one who looked at the pages I showed you and said it was Arabic and not Greek!"

"That's true, Adso, that's true: I'm the animal. Now hurry! Run!"

We went back to the laboratory, but we had trouble entering, because the novices were carrying out the corpse. Other curious visitors were roaming about the room. William rushed to the table and picked up the volumes, seeking the fatal one, flinging away one after another before the amazed eyes of those present, then opening and reopening them all again. Alas, the Arabic manuscript was no longer there. I remembered it vaguely because of its old cover, not strong, quite worn, with light metal bands.

"Who came in here after I left?" William asked a monk. The monk shrugged: it was clear that everyone and no one had come in.

We tried to consider the possibilities. Malachi? It was possible; he knew what he wanted, had perhaps spied on us, had seen us go out empty-handed, and had come back, sure of himself. Benno? I remembered that when William and I had gibed at each other over the Arabic text, he had laughed. At the time I believed he was laughing at my ignorance, but perhaps he had been laughing at William's ingenuousness: he knew very well the various guises in which an ancient manuscript could appear, and perhaps he had thought what we did not think immediately but should have thought—namely, that Severinus knew no Arabic, and so it was odd that he should keep among his books one he was unable to read. Or was there a third person?

William was deeply humiliated. I tried to comfort

him; I told him that for three days he had been looking for a text in Greek and it was natural in the course of his examination for him to discard all books not in Greek. And he answered that it is certainly human to make mistakes, but there are some human beings who make more than others, and they are called fools, and he was one of them, and he wondered whether it was worth the effort to study in Paris and Oxford if one was then incapable of thinking that manuscripts are also bound in groups, a fact even novices know, except stupid ones like me, and a pair of clowns like the two of us would be a great success at fairs, and that was what we should do instead of trying to solve mysteries, especially when we were up against people far more clever than we.

"But there's no use weeping," he concluded. "If Malachi took it, he has already replaced it in the library. And we would find it only if we knew how to enter the finis Africae. If Benno took it, he must have assumed that sooner or later I would have the suspicion I did have and would return to the laboratory, or he wouldn't have acted in such haste. And so he must be hiding, and the one place where he has not hidden surely is the one where we would look for him immediately: namely, his cell. Therefore, let's go back to the chapter house and see if during the interrogation the cellarer says anything useful. Because, after all, I still don't see Bernard's plan clearly; he was seeking his man before the death of Severinus, and for other reasons."

We went back to the chapter. We would have done better to go to Benno's cell, because, as we were to learn later, our young friend did not have such a high opinion of William and had not thought he would go back to the laboratory so quickly; so, thinking he was not being sought from that quarter, he had gone straight to his cell to hide the book.

But I will tell of this later. In the meantime dramatic

443

and disturbing events took place, enough to make anyone forget about the mysterious book. And though we did not forget it, we were engaged by other urgent tasks, connected with the mission that William, after all, was supposed to fulfill.

NONES

In which justice is meted out, and there is the embarrassing impression that everyone is wrong.

Bernard Gui took his place at the center of the great walnut table in the chapter hall. Beside him a Dominican performed the function of notary, and two prelates of the papal legation sat flanking him, as judges. The cellarer was standing before the table, between two archers.

The abbot turned to William and whispered: "I do not know whether this procedure is legitimate. The Lateran Council of 1215 decreed in its Canon Thirty-seven that a person cannot be summoned to appear before judges whose seat is more than two days' march from his domicile. Here the situation is perhaps different; it is the judge who has come from a great distance, but..."

"The inquisitor is exempt from all normal jurisdiction," William said, "and does not have to follow the precepts of ordinary law. He enjoys a special privilege and is not even bound to hear lawyers."

I looked at the cellarer. Remigio was in wretched

445

shape. He looked around like a frightened animal, as if he recognized the movements and gestures of a liturgy he feared. Now I know he was afraid for two reasons, equally terrifying: one, that he had been caught, to all appearances, in flagrant crime; the other, that the day before, when Bernard had begun his inquiry, collecting rumors and insinuations, Remigio had already been afraid his past would come to light; and his alarm had grown when he saw them arrest Salvatore.

If the hapless Remigio was in the grip of his own fear, Bernard Gui, for his part, knew how to transform his victims' fear into terror. He did not speak: while all were now expecting him to begin the interrogation, he kept his hands on the papers he had before him, pretending to arrange them, but absently. His gaze was really fixed on the accused, and it was a gaze in which hypocritical indulgence (as if to say: Never fear, you are in the hands of a fraternal assembly that can only want your good) mixed with icy irony (as if to say: You do not yet know what your good is, and I will shortly tell you) and merciless severity (as if to say: But in any case I am your judge here, and you are in my power). All things that the cellarer already knew, but which the judge's silence and delay served to make him feel more deeply, so that, as he became more and more humiliated, his uneasiness would be transformed into desperation instead of relaxation, and he would belong entirely to the judge, soft wax in his hands.

Finally Bernard broke the silence. He uttered some ritual formulas, told the judges they would now proceed to the interrogation of the defendant with regard to two equally odious crimes, one of which was obvious to all but less deplorable than the other, because the defendant had been surprised in the act of murder when he was actually being sought for the crime of heresy.

It was said. The cellarer hid his face in his hands,

which he could move only with difficulty because they were bound in chains. Bernard began the questioning.

"Who are you?" he asked.

"Remigio of Varagine. I was born fifty-two years ago, and while still a boy, I entered the convent of the Minorites in Varagine."

"And how does it happen that today you are found in the order of Saint Benedict?"

"Years ago, when the Pope issued the bull *Sancta Romana*, because I was afraid of being infected by the heresy of the Fraticelli...though I had never shared their notions...I thought it was better for my sinning soul to escape an atmosphere filled with seductions, and I applied and was received among the monks of this abbey, where for more than eight years I have served as cellarer."

"You escaped the seductions of heresy," Bernard mocked, "or, rather, you escaped the investigation of those who had determined to discover the heresy and uproot it, and the good Cluniac monks believed they were performing an act of charity in receiving you and those like you. But changing habit is not enough to erase from the soul the evil of heretical depravity, and so we are here now to find out what lurks in the recesses of your impenitent soul and what you did before arriving at this holy place."

"My soul is innocent and I do not know what you mean when you speak of heretical depravity," the cellarer said cautiously.

"You see?" Bernard cried, addressing the other judges. "They're all alike! When one of them is arrested, he faces judgment as if his conscience were at peace and without remorse. And they do not realize this is the most obvious sign of their guilt, because a righteous man on trial is uneasy! Ask him whether he knows the reason why I had ordered his arrest. Do you know it, Remigio?"

"My lord," the cellarer replied, "I would be happy to learn it from your lips."

I was surprised, because it seemed to me the cellarer was answering the ritual questions with equally ritual words, as if he were well versed in the rules of the investigation and its pitfalls and had long been trained to face such an eventuality.

"There," Bernard cried, "the typical reply of the impenitent heretic! They cover trails like foxes and it is very difficult to catch them out, because their beliefs grant them the right to lie in order to evade due punishment. They recur to tortuous answers, trying to trap the inquisitor, who already has to endure contact with such loathsome people. So then, Remigio, you have never had anything to do with the so-called Fraticelli or Friars of the Poor Life, or the Beghards?"

"I experienced the vicissitudes of the Minorites when there was long debate about poverty, but I have never belonged to the sect of the Beghards!"

"You see?" Bernard said. "He denies ever having been a Beghard, because the Beghards, though they share the heresy of the Fraticelli, consider the latter a dead branch of the Franciscan order and consider themselves more pure and perfect. But much of the behavior of one group is like that of the others. Can you deny, Remigio, that you have been seen in church, huddled down with your face against the wall, or prostrate with your hood over your head, instead of kneeling with folded hands like other men?"

"Also in the order of Saint Benedict the monks prostrate themselves, at the proper times. . . ."

"I am not asking what you did at the proper times, but at the improper ones! So do not deny that you assumed one posture or the other, typical of the Beghards! But you are not a Beghard, you say. . . . Tell me, then: what do you believe?"

"My lord, I believe everything a good Christian should. . . ."

"A holy reply! And what does a good Christian believe?"

"What the holy church teaches."

"And which holy church? The church that is so considered by those believers who call themselves perfect, the Pseudo Apostles, the heretical Fraticelli, or the church they compare to the whore of Babylon, in which all of us devoutly believe?"

"My lord," the cellarer said, bewildered, "tell me which you believe is the true church...."

"I believe it is the Roman church, one, holy, and apostolic, governed by the Pope and his bishops."

"So I believe," the cellarer said.

"Admirable shrewdness!" the inquisitor cried. "Admirable cleverness de dicto! You all heard him: he means to say he believes that I believe in this church, and he evades the requirement of saying what he believes in! But we know well these weasel tricks! Let us come to the point. Do you believe that the sacraments were instituted by our Lord, that to do true penance you must confess to the servants of God, that the Roman church has the power to loosen and to bind on this earth that which will be bound and loosened in heaven?"

"Should I not believe that?"

"I did not ask what you should believe, but what you do believe!"

"I believe everything that you and the other good doctors command me to believe," the frightened cellarer said.

"Ah! But are not the good doctors you mention perhaps those who command your sect? Is this what you meant when you spoke of the good doctors? Are these perverse liars the men you follow in recognizing your articles of faith? You imply that if I believe what they believe, then you will believe me; otherwise you will believe only them!"

"I did not say that, my lord," the cellarer stammered. "You are making me say it. I believe you, if you teach me what is good."

"Oh, what impudence!" Bernard shouted, slamming his fist on the table. "You repeat from memory with grim obstinacy the formula they teach in your sect. You say you will believe me only if I preach what your sect considers good. Thus the Pseudo Apostles have always answered and thus you answer now, perhaps without realizing it, because from your lips again the words emerge that you were once trained for deceiving inquisitors. And so you are accusing yourself with your own words, and I would fall into your trap only if I had not had a long experience of inquisition. . . . But let us come to the real question, perverse man! Have you ever heard of Gherardo Segarelli of Parma?"

"I have heard him spoken of," the cellarer said, turning pale, if one could still speak of pallor on that destroyed face.

"Have you ever heard of Fra Dolcino of Novara?"

"I have heard him spoken of."

"Have you ever seen him in person and had conversation with him?"

The cellarer remained silent for a few moments, as if to gauge how far he should go in telling a part of the truth. Then he made up his mind and said, in a faint voice, "I have seen him and spoken with him."

"Louder!" Bernard shouted. "Let a word of truth finally be heard escaping your lips! When did you speak with him?"

"My lord," the cellarer said, "I was a monk in a convent near Novara when Dolcino's people gathered in those parts, and they even went past my convent, and at first no one knew clearly who they were. . . ."

"You lie! How could a Franciscan of Varagine be in a convent in the Novara region? You were not in a convent, you were already a member of a band of Fraticelli roaming around those lands and living on alms, and then you joined the Dolcinians!"

"How can you assert that, sir?" the cellarer asked, trembling.

"I will tell you how I can, indeed I must, assert it," Bernard said, and he ordered Salvatore to be brought in.

The sight of the wretch, who had certainly spent the night under his own interrogation, not public and more severe than this one, moved me to pity. Salvatore's face, as I have said, was horrible normally, but that morning it was more bestial than ever. And though it showed no signs of violence, the way his chained body moved, the limbs disjointed, almost incapable of walking, the way he was dragged by the archers like a monkey tied to a rope, revealed very clearly how his ghastly questioning must have proceeded.

"Bernard has tortured him..." I murmured to William.

"Not at all," William answered. "An inquisitor never tortures. The custody of the defendant's body is always entrusted to the secular arm."

"But it's the same thing!" I said.

"Not in the least. It isn't the same thing for the inquisitor, whose hands remain clean, or for the accused, who, when the inquisitor arrives, suddenly finds support in him, an easing of his sufferings, and so he opens his heart."

I looked at my master. "You're jesting," I said, aghast.

"Do these seem things to jest about?" William replied.

Bernard was now questioning Salvatore, and my pen cannot transcribe the man's broken words—if it were possible, more Babelish than ever, as he answered, unmanned, reduced to the state of a baboon, while all understood him only with difficulty. Guided by Bernard, who asked the questions in such a way that he could reply only yes or no, Salvatore was unable to tell any lies. And what Salvatore said my reader can easily imagine. He told, or confirmed that he had told during the night, a part of that story I had already pieced together: his wanderings as a Fraticello, Shepherd, and Pseudo Apostle; and how in the days of Fra Dolcino he met Remigio among the Dolcinians and escaped with him, following the Battle of Monte Rebello, taking refuge after various ups and downs in the Casale convent. Further, he added that the heresiarch Dolcino, near defeat and capture, had entrusted to Remigio certain letters, to be carried he did not know where or to whom. And Remigio always carried those letters with him, never daring to deliver them, and on his arrival at the abbey, afraid of keeping them on his person but not wanting to destroy them, he entrusted them to the librarian, yes, to Malachi, who was to hide them somewhere in the recesses of the Aedificium.

As Salvatore spoke, the cellarer was looking at him with hatred, and at a certain point he could not restrain himself from shouting, "Snake, lascivious monkey, I was your father, friend, shield, and this is how you repay me!"

Salvatore looked at his protector, now in need of protection, and answered, with an effort, "Lord Remigio, while I could be, I was your man. And you were to me dilectissimo. But you know the chief constable's family. Qui non habet caballum vadat cum pede...."

"Madman!" Remigio shouted at him again. "Are you hoping to save yourself? You, too, will die as a heretic, you know? Say that you spoke under torture; say you invented it all!"

"What do I know, lord, what all these heresias are called....Patarini, gazzesi, leoniste, arnaldiste, speroniste, circoncisi...I am not homo literatus. I sinned with no malicia, and Signor Bernardo Magnificentissimo knows it, and I am hoping in his indulgencia in nomine patre et filio et spiritis sanctis..."

"We shall be indulgent insofar as our office allows," the inquisitor said, "and we shall consider with paternal benevolence the good will with which you have opened your spirit. Go now, go and meditate further in your cell, and trust in the mercy of the Lord. Now we must debate a question of quite different import. So, then, Remigio, you were carrying with you some letters from

Dolcino, and you gave them to your brother monk who is responsible for the library...."

"That is not true, not true!" the cellarer cried, as if such a defense could still be effective. And, rightly, Bernard interrupted him: "But you are not the one who must confirm this: it is Malachi of Hildesheim."

He had the librarian called, but Malachi was not among those present. I knew he was either in the scriptorium or near the infirmary, seeking Benno and the book. They went to fetch him, and when he appeared, distraught, trying to look no one in the face, William muttered with dismay, "And now Benno is free to do what he pleases." But he was mistaken, because I saw Benno's face peep up over the shoulders of the other monks crowding around the door of the hall, to follow the interrogation. I pointed him out to William. We thought that Benno's curiosity about what was happening was even stronger than his curiosity about the book. Later we learned that, by then, he had already concluded an ignoble bargain of his own.

Malachi appeared before the judges, his eyes never meeting those of the cellarer.

"Malachi," Bernard said, "this morning, after Salvatore's confession during the night, I asked you whether you had received from the defendant here present any letters...."

"Malachi!" the cellarer cried. "You swore you would do nothing to harm me!"

Malachi shifted slightly toward the defendant, to whom his back was turned, and said in a low voice, which I could barely hear, "I did not swear falsely. If I could have done anything to harm you, it was done already. The letters were handed over to Lord Bernard this morning, before you killed Severinus...."

"But you know, you must know. I didn't kill Severinus! You know because you were there before me!"

"I?" Malachi asked. "I went in there after they discovered you."

"Be that as it may," Bernard interrupted, "what were you looking for in Severinus's laboratory, Remigio?"

The cellarer turned to William with dazed eyes, then looked at Malachi, then at Bernard again. "But this morning I... I heard Brother William here present tell Severinus to guard certain papers...and since last night, since Salvatore was captured, I have been afraid those letters—"

"Then you know something about those letters!" Bernard cried triumphantly. The cellarer at this point was trapped. He was caught between two necessities: to clear himself of the accusation of heresy, and to dispel the suspicion of murder. He must have decided to face the second accusation—instinctively, because by now he was acting by no rule, and without counsel. "I will talk about the letters later.... I will explain... I will tell how they came into my possession.... But let me tell what happened this morning. I thought there would be talk of those letters when I saw Salvatore fall into the hands of Lord Bernard; for years the memory of those letters has been tormenting my heart... Then when I heard William and Severinus speaking of some papers... I cannot say... overcome with fear, I thought Malachi had got rid of them and given them to Severinus.... I wanted to destroy them and so I went to Severinus.... The door was open and Severinus was already dead, I started searching through his things for the letters.... I was just afraid...."

William whispered into my ear, "Poor fool, fearing one danger, he has plunged headlong into another...."

"Let us assume that you are telling almost—I say, almost—the truth," Bernard intervened. "You thought Severinus had the letters and you looked for them in his laboratory. And why did you think he had them? Why did you first kill the other brothers? Did you perhaps think those letters had for some time been passing through many hands? Is it perhaps customary in this abbey to gather relics of burned heretics?"

I saw the abbot start. Nothing could be more insidious than an accusation of collecting relics of heretics, and Bernard was very sly in mixing the murders with heresy, and everything with the life of the abbey. I was interrupted in my reflections by the cellarer, who was shouting that he had nothing to do with the other crimes. Bernard indulgently calmed him: this, for the moment, was not the question they were discussing, Remigio was being interrogated for a crime of heresy, and he should not attempt (and here Bernard's voice became stern) to draw attention away from his heretical past by speaking of Severinus or trying to cast suspicion on Malachi. So he should therefore return to the letters.

"Malachi of Hildesheim," he said, addressing the witness. "You are not here as a defendant. This morning you answered my questions and my request with no attempt to hide anything. Now you will repeat here what you said to me this morning, and you will have nothing to fear."

"I repeat what I said this morning," Malachi said. "A short time after Remigio arrived up here, he began to take charge of the kitchen, and we met frequently for reasons connected with our duties—as librarian, I am charged with shutting up the whole Aedificium at night, and therefore also the kitchen. I have no reason to deny that we became close friends, nor had I any reason to harbor suspicions of this man. He told me that he had with him some documents of a secret nature, entrusted to him in confession, which should not fall into profane hands and which he dared not keep himself. Since I was in charge of the only part of the monastery forbidden to all the others, he asked me to keep those papers, far from any curious gaze, and I consented, never suspecting the documents were of a heretical nature, nor did I even read them as I placed them ... I placed them in the most inaccessible of the secret rooms of the library, and after that I forgot this matter, until this morning, when the lord inquisitor mentioned the papers to me, and then I fetched them and handed them over to him...."

The abbot, frowning, took the floor. "Why did you not inform me of this agreement of yours with the cellarer? The library is not intended to house things belonging to the monks!" The abbot had made it clear that the abbey had no connection with this business.

"My lord," Malachi answered, confused, "it seemed to me a thing of scarce importance. I sinned without malice."

"Of course, of course," Bernard said, in a cordial tone, "we are all convinced the librarian acted in good faith, and his frankness in collaborating with this court is proof. I fraternally beg Your Magnificence not to chastise him for this imprudent act of the past. We believe Malachi. And we ask him only to confirm now, under oath, that the papers I will now show him are those he gave me this morning and are those that Remigio of Varagine consigned to him years ago, after his arrival at the abbey." He displayed two parchments among the papers lying on the table. Malachi looked at them and said in a firm voice, "I swear by God the Father Almighty, by the most holy Virgin, and by all the saints that so it is and so it was."

"That is enough for me," Bernard said. "You may go, Malachi of Hildesheim."

Just before Malachi reached the door, his head bowed, a voice was heard from the curious crowd packed at the rear of the hall: "You hid his letters and he showed you the novices' asses in the kitchen!" There was some scattered laughter, and Malachi hurried out, pushing others aside left and right. I could have sworn the voice was Aymaro's, but the words had been shouted in falsetto. The abbot, his face purple, shouted for silence and threatened terrible punishments for all, commanding the monks to clear the hall. Bernard smiled treacherously; Cardinal Bertrand, at one side of the hall, bent to the ear of Jean d'Anneaux and said something to him. The other man reacted by covering his mouth with his hand and bowing his head as if he were coughing. William said to me, "The cellarer was not only a carnal sinner for his own purposes; he also acted as procurer. But Bernard cares nothing about that, except that it embarrasses Abo, the imperial mediator...."

He was interrupted by Bernard, who now spoke straight to him. "I would also be interested to know from you, Brother William, what papers you were talking about this morning with Severinus, when the cellarer overheard you and misunderstood."

William returned his gaze. "He did misunderstand me, in fact. We were referring to a copy of the treatise on canine hydrophobia by Ayyub al-Ruhawi, a remarkably erudite book that you must surely know of by reputation, and which must often have been of great use to you. Hydrophobia, Ayyub says, may be recognized by twenty-five evident signs...."

Bernard, who belonged to the order of the Dominicans, the Domini canes, the Lord's dogs, did not consider it opportune to start another battle. "So the matters were extraneous to the case under discussion," he said rapidly. And the trial continued.

"Let us come back to you, Brother Remigio, Minorite, far more dangerous than a hydrophobic dog. If Brother William in these past few days had paid more attention to the drool of heretics than to that of dogs, perhaps he would also have discovered what a viper was nesting in the abbey. Let us go back to these letters. Now, we know for certain that they were in your hands and that you took care to hide them as if they were a most poisonous thing, and that you actually killed"— with a gesture he forestalled an attempt at denial— "and of the killing we will speak later ... that you killed, I was saying, so that I would never have them. So you recognize these papers as your possessions?"

The cellarer did not answer, but his silence was

sufficiently eloquent. So Bernard insisted: "And what are these papers? They are two pages written in the hand of the heresiarch Dolcino, a few days before his capture. He entrusted them to a disciple who would take them to others of his sect still scattered about Italy. I could read you everything said in them, how Dolcino, fearing his imminent end, entrusts a message of hope— he says to his brethren—in the Devil! He consoles them, and though the dates he announces here do not coincide with those of his previous letters, when for the year 1305 he promised the complete destruction of all priests at the hand of the Emperor Frederick, still, he declares, this destruction was not far off. Once again the heresiarch was lying, because twenty and more years have gone by since that day and none of his sinful predictions has come true. But it is not the ridiculous presumption of these prophecies that we must discuss but, rather, the fact that Remigio was their bearer. Can you still deny, heretical and impenitent monk, that you had traffic and cohabitation with the sect of the Pseudo Apostles?"

The cellarer at this point could deny no longer. "My lord," he said, "my youth was filled with the direst errors. When I learned of the preaching of Dolcino, already seduced as I was by the Friars of the Poor Life, I believed in his words and I joined his band. Yes, it is true, I was with them in the regions of Brescia and Bergamo, I was with them at Como and in Valsesia, with them I took refuge on Bald Mountain and in the Rassa Valley, and finally on Monte Rebello. But I never took part in any evil deed, and when they began their sacking and their violence, I still maintained within me the spirit of meekness that was the quality of the sons of Francis, and on Monte Rebello itself I told Dolcino I no longer felt capable of participating in their battle, and he gave me permission to leave, because, he said, he did not want cowards with him, and he asked me only to take those letters for him to Bologna...."

"To whom?" Cardinal Bertrand asked.

"To some sectarians of his, whose names I believe I can remember, and when I remember them, I will tell them to you, my lord," Remigio hastily affirmed. And he uttered the names of some men that Cardinal Bertrand seemed to know, because he smiled with a contented look, exchanging a nod of approval with Bernard.

"Very well," Bernard said, and he made a note of those names. Then he asked Remigio, "And why are you now handing your friends over to us?"

"They are not friends of mine, my lord, and the proof is that I never delivered the letters. Indeed, I went further, and I will say it now after having tried to forget it for so many years: in order to leave that place without being seized by the Bishop of Vercelli's army, which was awaiting us on the plain, I managed to get in touch with some of his men, and in exchange for a safe-conduct I told them the passages that were good for attacking Dolcino's fortifications, so that the success of the church's troops was in part due to my collaboration...."

"Very interesting. This tells us that you were not only a heretic, but also a coward and a traitor. Which does not alter your situation. Just as today you tried to save yourself by accusing Malachi, who had done you a favor, so, then, to save yourself you handed your companions in sin over to the forces of law. But you betrayed their bodies, never their teachings, and you kept those letters as relics, hoping one day to have the courage, and the opportunity without running any risks, to deliver them, to win again the favor of the Pseudo Apostles."

"No, my lord, no," the cellarer said, covered with sweat, his hands shaking. "No, I swear to you that..."

"An oath!" Bernard said. "Here is another proof of your guile! You want to swear because you know that I know how Waldensian heretics are prepared to use any duplicity, and even to suffer death, rather than swear!

And if fear overcomes them, they pretend to swear and mutter false oaths! But I am well aware you do not belong to the sect of the Poor of Lyons, you wicked fox, and you are trying to convince me you are not what you are not so I will not say you are what you are! You swear, do you? You swear, hoping to be absolved, but I tell you this: a single oath is not enough for me! I can require one, two, three, a hundred, as many as I choose. I know very well that you Pseudo Apostles grant dispensations to those who swear false oaths rather than betray the sect. And so every oath will be further proof of your guilt!"

"But what must I do, then?" the cellarer shouted, falling to his knees.

"Do not prostrate yourself like a Beghard! You must do nothing. At this point, only I know what must be done," Bernard said, with a terrible smile. "You must only confess. And you will be damned and condemned if you confess, and damned and condemned if you do not confess, because you will be punished as a perjurer! So confess, then, if only to shorten this most painful interrogation, which distresses our consciences and our sense of meekness and compassion!"

"But what must I confess?"

"Two orders of sins: That you were in the sect of Dolcino, that you shared its heretical notions, and its actions and its offenses to the dignity of the bishops and the city magistrates, that you impenitently continue in those lies and illusions, even though the heresiarch is dead and the sect has been dispersed, though not entirely extirpated and destroyed. And that, corrupted in your innermost spirit by the practices learned among the foul sect, you are guilty of the disorders against God and man perpetrated in this abbey, for reasons that still elude me but which need not even be totally clarified, once it has been luminously demonstrated (as we are doing) that the heresy of those who preached and preach poverty, against the teachings of the lord Pope and his bulls, can only lead to criminal acts. This is what the faithful must learn, and this will be enough for me. Confess."

What Bernard wanted was clear. Without the slightest interest in knowing who had killed the other monks, he wanted only to show that Remigio somehow shared the ideas propounded by the Emperor's theologians. And once he had shown the connection between those ideas, which were also those of the chapter of Perugia, and the ideas of the Fraticelli and the Dolcinians, and had shown that one man in that abbey subscribed to all those heresies and had been the author of many crimes, he would thus have dealt a truly mortal blow to his adversaries. I looked at William and saw that he had understood but could do nothing, even though he had foreseen it all. I looked at the abbot and saw his face was grim: he was realizing, belatedly, that he, too, had been drawn into a trap, and that his own authority as mediator was crumbling, now that he was going to appear to be lord of a place where all the evils of the century had chosen to assemble. As for the cellarer, by now he no longer knew of what crime he might still try to proclaim his innocence. But perhaps at that moment he was incapable of any calculation; the cry that escaped his throat was the cry of his soul, and in it and with it he was releasing years of long and secret remorse. Or, rather, after a life of uncertainties, enthusiasms, and disappointments, cowardice and betrayal, faced with the ineluctability of his ruin, he decided to profess the faith of his youth, no longer asking himself whether it was right or wrong, but as if to prove to himself that he was capable of some faith.

"Yes, it is true," he shouted, "I was with Dolcino, and I shared in his crimes, his license; perhaps I was mad, I confused the love of our Lord Jesus Christ with the need for freedom and with hatred of bishops. It is true

461

that I have sinned, but I am innocent of everything that has happened in the abbey, I swear!"

"For the present we have achieved something," Bernard said, "since you admit having practiced the heresy of the Dolcinians, the witch Margaret, and her companions. Do you admit being with them near Trivero, when they hanged many faithful Christians, including an innocent child of ten? And when they hanged other men in the presence of their wives and parents because they would not submit to the whim of those dogs? Because, by then, blinded by your fury and pride, you thought no one could be saved unless he belonged to your community? Speak!"

"Yes, I believed those things and did those things!"

"And you were present when they captured some followers of the bishops and starved some to death in prison, and they cut off the arm and the hand of a woman with child, leaving her then to give birth to a baby who immediately died, unbaptized? And you were with them when they set fire and razed to the ground the villages of Mosso, Trivero, Cossila, and Clecchia, and many other localities in the zone of Crepacorio, and many houses of Mortiliano and Quorino, and they burned the church in Trivero after befouling the sacred images, tearing tombstones from the altars, breaking an arm of the statue of the Virgin, looting the chalices and vessels and books, destroying the spire, shattering the bells, seizing all the vessels of the confraternity and the possessions of the priest?"

"Yes, yes, I was there, and none of us knew what we were doing by then, we wanted to herald the moment of punishment, we were the vanguard of the Emperor sent by heaven and the holy Pope, we were to hasten the descent of the angel of Philadelphia, when all would receive the grace of the Holy Spirit and the church would be renewed, and after the destruction of all the perverse, only the perfect would reign!"

The cellarer seemed at once possessed and illuminated, the dam of silence and simulation now seemed broken, his past was returning not only in words but also in images, and he was feeling again the emotions that at one time had exalted him.

"So," Bernard resumed, "you confess that you have revered Gherardo Segarelli as a martyr, that you have denied all power to the Roman church and declared that neither the Pope nor any authority could ordain for you a life different from the one your people led, that no one had the right to excommunicate you, that since the time of Saint Sylvester all the prelates of the church had been prevaricators and seducers except Peter of Morrone, that laymen are not required to pay tithes to priests who do not practice a condition of absolute perfection and poverty as the first apostles practiced, that tithes therefore should be paid to your sect alone, who are the only apostles and paupers of Christ, that to pray to God in a stable or in a consecrated church is the same thing; you also confess that you went through villages and seduced people crying 'Penitenziagite,' that you treacherously sang the 'Salve Regina' to draw crowds, and you passed yourselves off as penitents leading a perfect life before the eyes of the world and then allowed yourselves every license and every lustfulness because you did not believe in the sacrament of matrimony or in any other sacrament, and, deeming yourselves purer than anyone else, you could allow yourselves every filthiness and every offense to your bodies and the bodies of others? Speak!"

"Yes, yes, I confess the true faith which I then believed with my whole soul, I confess that we took off our garments in sign of renunciation, that we renounced all our belongings while you, race of dogs, will never renounce anything; and from that time on we never accepted money from anyone or carried any about our persons, and we lived on alms and we saved nothing for the morrow, and when they received us and set a table for us, we ate and went away, leaving on the table anything that remained...."

"And you burned and looted to seize the possessions of good Christians!"

"And we burned and looted because we had proclaimed poverty the universal law, and we had the right to appropriate the illegitimate riches of others, and we wanted to strike at the heart of the network of greed that extended from parish to parish, but we never looted in order to possess, or killed in order to loot; we killed to punish, to purify the impure through blood. Perhaps we were driven by an overweening desire for justice: a man can sin also through overweening love of God, through superabundance of perfection. We were the true spiritual congregation sent by the Lord and destined for the glory of the last days; we sought our reward in paradise, hastening the time of your destruction. We alone were the apostles of Christ, all the others had betrayed him, and Gherardo Segarelli had been a divine plant, planta Dei pullulans in radice fidei; our Rule came to us directly from God. We had to kill the innocent as well, in order to kill all of you more quickly. We wanted a better world, of peace and sweetness and happiness for all, we wanted to kill the war that you brought on with your greed, because you reproached us when, to establish justice and happiness, we had to shed a little blood.... The fact is ... the fact is that it did not take much, the hastening, and it was worth turning the waters of the Carnasco red that day at Stavello, there was our own blood, too, we did not spare ourselves, our blood and your blood, much of it, at once, immediately, the times of Dolcino's prophecy were at hand, we had to hasten the course of events...."

His whole body trembling, he rubbed his hands over his habit as if he wanted to cleanse them of the blood he was recalling. "The glutton has become pure again," William said to me.

"But is this purity?" I asked, horrified.

"There must be some other kind as well," William said, "but, however it is, it always frightens me."

"What terrifies you most in purity?" I asked.

"Haste," William answered.

"Enough, enough," Bernard was saying now. "We sought a confession from you, not a summons to massacre. Very well, not only have you been a heretic: you are one still. Not only have you been a murderer: you have murdered again. Now tell us how you killed your brothers in this abbey, and why."

The cellarer stopped trembling, looked around as if he were coming out of a dream. "No," he said, "I have nothing to do with the crimes in the abbey. I have confessed everything I did: do not make me confess what I have not done. . . ."

"But what remains that you cannot have done? Do you now say you are innocent? O lamb, O model of meekness! You have heard him: he once had his hands steeped in blood and now he is innocent! Perhaps we were mistaken, Remigio of Varagine is a paragon of virtue, a loyal son of the church, an enemy of the enemies of Christ, he has always respected the order that the hand of the church has toiled to impose on villages and cities, the peace of trade, the craftsmen's shops, the treasures of the churches. He is innocent, he has committed nothing. Here, come to my arms, Brother Remigio, that I may console you for the accusations that evil men have brought against you!" And as Remigio looked at him with dazed eyes, as if he were all of a sudden believing in a final absolution, Bernard resumed his demeanor and addressed the captain of the archers in a tone of command:

"It revolts me to have recourse to measures the church has always criticized when they are employed by the secular arm. But there is a law that governs and directs even my personal feelings. Ask the abbot to provide a place where the instruments of torture can be installed. But do not proceed at once. For three days let him remain in a cell, with his hands and feet in irons. Then have the instruments shown him. Only shown. And then, on the fourth day, proceed. Justice is not inspired by haste, as the Pseudo Apostles believe, and the justice of God has centuries at its disposal. Proceed slowly, and by degrees. And, above all, remember what has been said again and again: avoid mutilations and the risk of death. One of the benefits this procedure grants the criminal is precisely that death be savored and expected, but it must not come before confession is full, and voluntary, and purifying."

The archers bent to lift the cellarer, but he planted his feet on the ground and put up resistance, indicating he wanted to speak. Given leave, he spoke, but the words could hardly come from his mouth, and his speech was like a drunkard's mumbling, and there was something obscene about it. Only gradually did he regain that kind of savage energy that had marked his confession a moment before.

"No, my lord. No, not torture. I am a cowardly man. I betrayed then, I denied for eleven years in this monastery my past faith, collecting tithes from vine-dressers and peasants, inspecting stables and sties so that they would flourish and enrich the abbot; I have collaborated readily in the management of this estate of the Antichrist. And I was well off, I had forgotten my days of revolt, I wallowed in the pleasures of the palate and in others as well. I am a coward. Today I sold my former brothers of Bologna, then I sold Dolcino. And as a coward, disguised as one of the men of the crusade, I witnessed the capture of Dolcino and Margaret, when on Holy Saturday they were taken in the castle of Bugello. I wandered around Vercelli for three months until Pope Clement's letter arrived with the death sentence. And I saw Margaret cut to pieces before Dolcino's eyes, and she screamed, disemboweled as she was, poor body that I, too, had touched one night....

And as her lacerated body was burning, they fell on Dolcino and pulled off his nose and his testicles with burning tongs, and it is not true what they said afterward, that he did not utter even a moan. Dolcino was tall and strong, he had a great devil's beard and red hair that fell in curls to his shoulder blades, he was handsome and powerful when he led us, in his broad-brimmed hat with a plume, with his sword girded over his habit. Dolcino made men fear and women cry out with pleasure.... But when they tortured him he, too, cried, in pain, like a woman, like a calf, he was bleeding from all his wounds as they carried him from one corner to another, and they continued to wound him slightly, to show how long an emissary of the Devil could live, and he wanted to die, he asked them to finish him, but he died too late, after he reached the pyre and was only a mass of bleeding flesh. I followed him and I congratulated myself on having escaped that trial, I was proud of my cleverness, and that rogue Salvatore was with me, and he said to me: How wise we were, Brother Remigio, to act like sensible men, there is nothing nastier than torture! I would have foresworn a thousand religions that day. And for years, many years, I have told myself how base I was, and how happy I was to be base, and yet I was always hoping that I could demonstrate to myself that I was not such a coward. Today you have given me this strength, Lord Bernard; you have been for me what the pagan emperors were for the most cowardly of the martyrs. You have given me the courage to confess what I believe in my soul, as my body falls away from it. But do not demand too much courage of me, more than this mortal frame can bear. No, not torture. I will say whatever you want. Better the stake at once: you die of suffocation before you burn. Not torture, like Dolcino's. No. You want a corpse, and to have it you need me to assume the guilt for other corpses. I will be a corpse soon in any case. And so I will give you what you want. I killed Adelmo of

Otranto out of hatred for his youth and for his wit in taunting monsters like me, old, fat, squat, and ignorant. I killed Venantius of Salvemec because he was too learned and read books I did not understand. I killed Berengar of Arundel out of hatred of his library, I, who studied theology by clubbing priests that were too fat. I killed Severinus of Sankt Wendel . . . why? Because he gathered herbs, I, who was on Monte Rebello, where we ate herbs and grasses without wondering about their properties. In truth, I could also kill the others, including our abbot: with the Pope or with the empire, he still belongs to my enemies, and I have always hated him, even when he fed me because I fed him. Is that enough for you? Ah, no, you also want to know *how* I killed all those people. . . . Why, I killed them . . . let me see . . . by calling up the infernal powers, with the help of a thousand legions brought under my command by the art that Salvatore taught me. To kill someone it is not necessary to strike: the Devil does it for you, if you know how to command the Devil."

He gave the onlookers a sly glance, laughing. But by now it was the laughter of a madman, even if, as William pointed out to me afterward, this madman was clever enough to drag Salvatore down with him also, to avenge his betrayal.

"And how could you command the Devil?" Bernard insisted, taking this delirium as a legitimate confession.

"You yourself know: it is impossible to traffic for so many years with the possessed and not wear their habit! You yourself know, butcher of apostles! You take a black cat—isn't that it?—that does not have even one white hair (you know this), and you bind his four paws, and then you take him at midnight to a crossroads and you cry in a loud voice: O great Lucifer, Emperor of Hell, I call you and I introduce you into the body of my enemy just as I now hold prisoner this cat, and if you will bring my enemy to death, then the following night at midnight, in this same place, I will offer you this cat in sacrifice, and you will do what I command of you by the powers of the magic I now exercise according to the secret book of Saint Cyprian, in the name of all the captains of the great legions of hell, Adramelch, Alastor, and Azazel, to whom now I pray, with all their brothers...." His lip trembled, his eyes seemed to bulge from their sockets, and he began to pray—or, rather, he seemed to be praying, but he addressed his implorations to all the chiefs of the infernal legions: "Abigor, pecca pro nobis...Amon, miserere nobis... Samael, libera nos a bono...Belial eleison...Focalor, in corruptionem meam intende...Haborym, damnamus dominum...Zaebos, anum meum aperies...Leonard, asperge me spermate tuo et inquinabor...."

"Stop, stop!" everyone in the hall cried, making the sign of the cross. "O Lord, have mercy on us all!"

The cellarer was now silent. When he had uttered the names of all these devils, he fell face down, a whitish saliva drooling from his twisted mouth and the clenched rows of his teeth. His hands, though tormented by his chains, opened and closed convulsively, his feet kicked the air in irregular fits. Seeing me gripped by a trembling of horror, William put his hand on my head and clasped me almost at the nape, pressing it, which calmed me again. "You see?" he said to me. "Under torture or the threat of torture, a man says not only what he has done but what he would have liked to do even if he didn't know it. Remigio now wants death with all his soul."

The archers led the cellarer away, still in convulsions. Bernard gathered his papers. Then he looked hard at those present, motionless, but in great agitation.

"The interrogation is over. The accused, guilty by his own confession, will be taken to Avignon, where the final trial will be held, as a scrupulous safeguard of truth and justice, and only after that formal trial will he be burned. He no longer belongs to you, Abo, nor does he belong any longer to me, who am only the humble instrument of the truth. The fulfillment of justice will take place elsewhere; the shepherds have done their duty, now the dogs must separate the infected sheep from the flock and purify it with fire. The wretched episode that has seen this man commit such ferocious crimes is ended. Now may the abbey live in peace. But the world"—here he raised his voice and addressed the group of envoys—"the world has still not found peace. The world is riven by heresy, which finds refuge even in the halls of imperial palaces! Let my brothers remember this: a cingulum diaboli binds Dolcino's perverse sectarians to the honored masters of the chapter of Perugia. We must not forget: in the eyes of God the ravings of the wretch we have just handed over to justice are no different from those of the masters who feast at the table of the excommunicated German of Bavaria. The source of the heretics' wickedness springs from many preachings, even respected, still unpunished. Hard passion and humble Calvary are the lot of him who has been called by God, like my own sinful person, to distinguish the viper of heresy wherever it may nest. But in carrying out this holy task, we learn that he who openly practices heresy is not the only kind of heretic. Heresy's supporters can be distinguished by five indicators. First, there are those who visit heretics secretly when they are in prison; second, those who lament their capture and have been their intimate friends (it is, in fact, unlikely that one who has spent much time with a heretic remains ignorant of his activity); third, those who declare the heretics have been unjustly condemned, even when their guilt has been proved; fourth, those who look askance and criticize those who persecute heretics and preach against them successfully, and this can be discovered from the eyes, nose, the expression they try to conceal, showing hatred toward those for whom they feel bitterness and love toward those whose misfortune so grieves them; the fifth sign, finally, is the fact that they collect the charred bones of burned heretics and make them an object of veneration. . . . But I attach great value also to a sixth sign, and I consider open friends of heretics the authors of those books where (even if they do not openly offend orthodoxy) the heretics have found the premises with which to syllogize in their perverse way."

As he spoke, he was looking at Ubertino. The whole French legation understood exactly what Bernard meant. By now the meeting had failed, and no one would dare repeat the discussion of that morning, knowing that every word would be weighed in the light of these latest, disastrous events. If Bernard had been sent by the Pope to prevent a reconciliation between the two groups, he had succeeded.

Vespers

In which Ubertino takes flight, Benno begins to observe the laws, and William makes some reflections on the various types of lust encountered that day.

As the monks slowly emerged from the chapter house, Michael came over to William, and then both of them were joined by Ubertino. Together we all went out into the open, to confer in the cloister under cover of the fog, which showed no sign of thinning out. Indeed, it was made even thicker by the shadows.

"I don't think it necessary to comment on what has happened," William said. "Bernard has defeated us. Don't ask me whether that imbecile Dolcinian is really guilty of all those crimes. As far as I can tell, he isn't, not at all. The fact is, we are back where we started. John wants you alone in Avignon, Michael, and this meeting hasn't given you the guarantees we were looking for. On the contrary, it has given you an idea of how every word of yours, up there, could be distorted. Whence we must deduce, it seems to me, that you should not go."

Michael shook his head. "I will go, on the contrary. I do not want a schism. You, William, spoke very clearly

472

today, and you said what you would like. Well, that is not what I want, and I realize that the decisions of the Perugia chapter have been used by the imperial theologians beyond our intentions. I want the Franciscan order to be accepted by the Pope with its ideal of poverty. And the Pope must understand that unless the order confirms the ideal of poverty, it will never be possible for it to recover the heretical offshoots. I will go to Avignon, and if necessary I will make an act of submission to John. I will compromise on everything except the principle of poverty."

Ubertino spoke up. "You know you are risking your life?"

"So be it," Michael answered. "Better than risking my soul."

He did seriously risk his life, and if John was right (as I still do not believe), Michael also lost his soul. As everyone knows by now, Michael went to the Pope a week after the events I am narrating. He held out against him for four months, until in April of the following year John convened a consistory in which he called Michael a madman, a reckless, stubborn, tyrannical fomentor of heresy, a viper nourished in the very bosom of the church. And one might think that, according to his way of seeing things, John was right, because during those four months Michael had become a friend of my master's friend, the other William, the one from Occam, and had come to share his ideas—more extreme, but not very different from those my master shared with Marsilius and had expounded that morning. The life of these dissidents became precarious in Avignon, and at the end of May, Michael, William of Occam, Bonagratia of Bergamo, Francis of Ascoli, and Henri de Talheim took flight, pursued by the Pope's men to Nice, then Toulon, Marseilles, and Aigues-Mortes, where they were overtaken by Cardinal Pierre de Arrablay, who tried to persuade them to go back but was unable to overcome their resistance, their hatred of the Pontiff, their fear. In June they reached Pisa, where they were received in triumph by the imperial forces, and in the following months Michael was to denounce John publicly. Too late, by then. The Emperor's fortunes were ebbing; from Avignon John was plotting to give the Minorites a new superior general, and he finally achieved victory. Michael would have done better not to decide that day to go to the Pope: he could have led the Minorites' resistance more closely, without wasting so many months in his enemy's power, weakening his own position.... But perhaps divine omnipotence had so ordained things— nor do I know now who among them all was in the right. After so many years even the fire of passion dies, and with it what was believed the light of the truth. Who of us is able to say now whether Hector or Achilles was right, Agamemnon or Priam, when they fought over the beauty of a woman who is now dust and ashes?

But I am straying into melancholy digressions. I must tell instead of the end of that sad conversation. Michael had made up his mind, and there was no way of convincing him to desist. But another problem arose, and William announced it without mincing words: Ubertino himself was no longer safe. The words Bernard had addressed to him, the hatred the Pope now felt toward him, the fact that, whereas Michael still represented a power with which to negotiate, Ubertino was a party unto himself at this point...

"John wants Michael at court and Ubertino in hell. If I know Bernard, before tomorrow is over, with the complicity of the fog, Ubertino will have been killed. And if anyone asks who did it, the abbey can easily bear another crime, and they will say it was done by devils summoned by Remigio and his black cats, or by some surviving Dolcinian still lurking inside these walls...."

Ubertino was worried. "Then—?" he asked.

"Then," William said, "go and speak with the abbot.

Ask him for a mount, some provisions, and a letter to some distant abbey, beyond the Alps. And take advantage of the darkness and the fog to leave at once."

"But are the archers not still guarding the gates?"

"The abbey has other exits, and the abbot knows them. A servant has only to be waiting for you at one of the lower curves with a horse; and after slipping through some passage in the walls, you will have only to go through a stretch of woods. You must act immediately, before Bernard recovers from the ecstasy of his triumph. I must concern myself with something else. I had two missions: one has failed, at least the other must succeed. I want to get my hands on a book, and on a man. If all goes well, you will be out of here before I seek you again. So farewell, then." He opened his arms. Moved, Ubertino held him in a close embrace: "Farewell, William. You are a mad and arrogant Englishman, but you have a great heart. Will we meet again?"

"We will meet again," William assured him. "God will wish it."

God, however, did not wish it. As I have already said, Ubertino died, mysteriously killed, two years later. A hard and adventurous life, the life of this mettlesome and ardent old man. Perhaps he was not a saint, but I hope God rewarded his adamantine certainty of being one. The older I grow and the more I abandon myself to God's will, the less I value intelligence that wants to know and will that wants to do; and as the only element of salvation I recognize faith, which can wait patiently, without asking too many questions. And Ubertino surely had great faith in the blood and agony of our Lord Crucified.

Perhaps I was thinking these things even then, and the old mystic realized it, or guessed that I would think them one day. He smiled at me sweetly and embraced me, without the intensity with which he had sometimes gripped me in the preceding days. He embraced me as

475

a grandfather embraces his grandson, and in the same spirit I returned the embrace. Then he went off with Michael to seek the abbot.

"And now?" I asked William.

"And now, back to our crimes."

"Master," I said, "today many things happened, grave things for Christianity, and our mission has failed. And yet you seem more interested in solving this mystery than in the conflict between the Pope and the Emperor."

"Madmen and children always speak the truth, Adso. It may be that, as imperial adviser, my friend Marsilius is better than I, but as inquisitor I am better. Even better than Bernard Gui, God forgive me. Because Bernard is interested, not in discovering the guilty, but in burning the accused. And I, on the contrary, find the most joyful delight in unraveling a nice, complicated knot. And it must also be because, at a time when as philosopher I doubt the world has an order, I am consoled to discover, if not an order, at least a series of connections in small areas of the world's affairs. Finally, there is probably another reason: in this story things greater and more important than the battle between John and Louis may be at stake...."

"But it is a story of theft and vengeance among monks of scant virtue!" I cried, dubiously.

"Because of a forbidden book, Adso. A forbidden book!" William replied.

By now the monks were heading for supper. Our meal was half over when Michael of Cesena sat down beside us and told us Ubertino had left. William heaved a sigh of relief.

At the end of the meal, we avoided the abbot, who was conversing with Bernard, and noted Benno, who greeted us with a half smile as he tried to gain the door. William overtook him and forced him to follow us to a corner of the kitchen.

"Benno," William asked him, "where is the book?"

"What book?"

"Benno, neither of us is a fool. I am speaking of the book we were hunting for today in Severinus's laboratory, which I did not recognize. But you recognized it very well and went back to get it. . . ."

"What makes you think I took it?"

"I think you did, and you think the same. Where is it?"

"I cannot tell."

"Benno, if you refuse to tell me, I will speak with the abbot."

"I cannot tell by order of the abbot," Benno said, with a virtuous air. "Today, after we saw each other, something happened that you should know about. On Berengar's death there was no assistant librarian. This afternoon Malachi proposed me for the position. Just half an hour ago the abbot agreed, and tomorrow morning, I hope, I will be initiated into the secrets of the library. True, I did take the book this morning, and I hid it in the pallet in my cell without even looking at it, because I knew Malachi was keeping an eye on me. Eventually Malachi made me the proposal I told you. And then I did what an assistant librarian must do: I handed the book over to him."

I could not refrain from speaking out, and violently.

"But, Benno, yesterday and the day before you . . . you said you were burning with the curiosity to know, you didn't want the library to conceal mysteries any longer, you said a scholar must know. . . ."

Benno was silent, blushing; but William stopped me: "Adso, a few hours ago Benno joined the other side. Now he is the guardian of those secrets he wanted to know, and while he guards them he will have all the time he wants to learn them."

"But the others?" I asked. "Benno was speaking also in the name of all men of learning!"

"Before," William said. And he drew me away, leaving Benno the prey of confusion.

"Benno," William then said to me, "is the victim of a great lust, which is not that of Berengar or that of the cellarer. Like many scholars, he has a lust for knowledge. Knowledge for its own sake. Barred from a part of this knowledge, he wanted to seize it. Now he has it. Malachi knew his man: he used the best means to recover the book and seal Benno's lips. You will ask me what is the good of controlling such a hoard of learning if one has agreed not to put it at the disposal of everyone else. But this is exactly why I speak of lust. Roger Bacon's thirst for knowledge was not lust: he wanted to employ his learning to make God's people happier, and so he did not seek knowledge for its own sake. Benno's is merely insatiable curiosity, intellectual pride, another way for a monk to transform and allay the desires of his loins, or the ardor that makes another man a warrior of the faith or of heresy. There is lust not only of the flesh. Bernard Gui is lustful; his is a distorted lust for justice that becomes identified with a lust for power. Our holy and no longer Roman Pontiff lusts for riches. And the cellarer as a youth had a lust to testify and transform and do penance, and then a lust for death. And Benno's lust is for books. Like all lusts, including that of Onan, who spilled his seed on the ground, it is sterile and has nothing to do with love, not even carnal love...."

"I know," I murmured, despite myself. William pretended not to hear. Continuing his observations, he said, "True love wants the good of the beloved."

"Can it be that Benno wants the good of his books (and now they are also his) and thinks their good lies in their being kept far from grasping hands?" I asked.

"The good of a book lies in its being read. A book is made up of signs that speak of other signs, which in their turn speak of things. Without an eye to read them, a book contains signs that produce no concepts; therefore it is dumb. This library was perhaps born to save the books it houses, but now it lives to bury them.

This is why it has become a sink of iniquity. The cellarer says he betrayed. So has Benno. He has betrayed. Oh, what a nasty day, my good Adso! Full of blood and ruination. I have had enough of this day. Let us also go to compline, and then to bed."

Coming out of the kitchen, we encountered Aymaro. He asked us whether the rumor going around was true, that Malachi had proposed Benno as his assistant. We could only confirm it.

"Our Malachi has accomplished many fine things today," Aymaro said, with his usual sneer of contempt and indulgence. "If justice existed, the Devil would come and take him this very night."

COMPLINE

In which a sermon is heard about the coming of the Antichrist, and Adso discovers the power of proper names.

Vespers had been sung in a confused fashion while the interrogation of the cellarer was still under way, with the curious novices escaping their master's control to observe through windows and cracks what was going on in the chapter hall. Now the whole community was to pray for the good soul of Severinus. Everyone expected the abbot to speak, and wondered what he would say. But instead, after the ritual homily of Saint Gregory, the responsory, and the three prescribed psalms, the abbot did step into the pulpit, but only to say he would remain silent this evening. Too many calamities had befallen the abbey, he said, to allow even the spiritual father to speak in a tone of reproach and admonition. Everyone, with no exceptions, should now make a strict examination of conscience. But since it was necessary for someone to speak, he suggested the admonition should come from the oldest of their number, now close to death, the brother who was the least involved of all in the terrestrial passions that had generated so many evils. By right of age Alinardo of Grottaferrata should speak, but all knew the fragile condition of the venerable brother's health. Immediately after Alinardo, in the order established by the inevitable progress of time, came Jorge. And the abbot now called upon him.

We heard a murmuring from the section of the stalls where Aymaro and the other Italians usually sat. I suspected the abbot had entrusted the sermon to Jorge without discussing the matter with Alinardo. My master pointed out to me, in a whisper, that the abbot's decision not to speak had been wise, because whatever he might have said would have been judged by Bernard and the other Avignonese present. Old Jorge, on the other hand, would confine himself to his usual mystical prophecies, and the Avignonese would not attach much importance to them. "But I will," William added, "because I don't believe Jorge agreed, and perhaps asked, to speak without a very precise purpose."

Jorge climbed into the pulpit, with someone's help. His face was illuminated by the tripod, which alone lighted the nave. The glow of the flame underlined the darkness shrouding his eyes, which seemed two black holes.

"Most beloved brothers," he began, "and all of our guests, most dear to us. If you care to listen to this poor old man...The four deaths that have afflicted our abbey—not to mention the sins, remote and recent, of the most abject among the living—are not, as you know, to be attributed to the severity of nature, which, implacable in its rhythms, ordains our earthly day, from cradle to grave. All of you no doubt believe that, though you have been overwhelmed with grief, these sad events have not involved your soul, because all of you, save one, are innocent, and when this one has been punished, while you will, to be sure, continue to mourn the absence of those who have gone, you will not have to clear yourselves of any charge before the tribunal of God. So you believe. Madmen!" he shouted in an awful voice. "Madmen and presumptuous fools that you are! He who has killed will bear before God the burden of his guilt, but only because he agreed to become the vehicle of the decrees of God. Just as it was necessary for someone to betray Jesus in order for the mystery of redemption to be accomplished, yet the Lord sanctioned damnation and vituperation for the one who betrayed him. Thus someone has sinned in these days, bringing death and ruination, but I say to you that this ruination was, if not desired, at least permitted by God for the humbling of our pride!"

He was silent, and turned his blank gaze on the solemn assembly as if his eyes could perceive its emotions, as in fact with his ear he savored the silence and consternation.

"In this community," he went on, "for some time the serpent of pride has been coiled. But what pride? The pride of power, in a monastery isolated from the world? No, certainly not. The pride of wealth? My brothers, before the known world echoed with long debates about poverty and ownership, from the days of our founder, we, even when we had everything, have never had anything, our one true wealth being the observation of the Rule, prayer, and work. But of our work, the work of our order and in particular the work of this monastery, a part—indeed, the substance—is study, and the preservation of knowledge. Preservation of, I say, not search for, because the property of knowledge, as a divine thing, is that it is complete and has been defined since the beginning, in the perfection of the Word which expresses itself to itself. Preservation, I say, and not search, because it is a property of knowledge, as a human thing, that it has been defined and completed over the course of the centuries, from the preaching of the prophets to the interpretation of the fathers of the church. There is no progress, no revolution of ages, in the history of knowledge, but at most a continuous and sublime recapitulation. Human history proceeds with a motion that cannot be arrested, from the creation through the redemption, toward the return of Christ triumphant, who will appear seated on a cloud to judge the quick and the dead; but human and divine knowledge does not follow this path: steady as a fort that does not cede, it allows us, when we are humble and alert to its voice, to follow, to predict this path, but it is not touched by the path. I am He who is, said the God of the Jews. I am the way, the truth, and the life, said our Lord. There you have it: knowledge is nothing but the awed comment on these two truths. Everything else that has been said was uttered by the prophets, by the evangelists, by the fathers and the doctors, to make these two sayings clearer. And sometimes an apposite comment came also from the pagans, who were ignorant of them, and their words have been taken into the Christian tradition. But beyond that there is nothing further to say. There is only to continue meditation, to gloss, preserve. This was and should be the office of our abbey with its splendid library—nothing else. It is said that an Oriental caliph one day set fire to the library of a famous and glorious and proud city, and that, as those thousands of volumes were burning, he said that they could and should disappear: either they were repeating what the Koran already said, and therefore they were useless, or else they contradicted that book sacred to the infidels, and therefore they were harmful. The doctors of the church, and we along with them, did not reason in this way. Everything that involves commentary and clarification of Scripture must be preserved, because it enhances the glory of the divine writings; what contradicts must not be destroyed, because only if we preserve it can it be contradicted in its turn by those who can do so and are so charged, in the ways and times that the Lord chooses. Hence the responsibility of our order through the centuries, and the burden of our abbey today: proud of the truth we proclaim, humble and prudent in preserving those words hostile to the truth, without allowing ourselves to be soiled by them. Now, my brothers, what is the sin of pride that can tempt a scholar-monk? That of considering as his task not preserving but seeking some information not yet vouchsafed mankind, as if the last word had not already resounded in the words of the last angel who speaks in the last book of Scripture: 'For I testify unto every man that heareth the words of the prophecy of this book. If any man shall add unto these things, God shall add unto him the plagues that are written in this book: and if any man shall take away from the words of the book of this prophecy, God shall take away his part out of the book of life, and out of the holy city, and from the things which are written in this book.' There ... does it not seem to you, my unfortunate brothers, that these words only adumbrate what has recently happened within these walls, whereas what has happened within these walls adumbrates only the same vicissitude as that afflicting the century in which we live, determined in word and in deed, in cities as in castles, in proud universities and cathedral churches, to seek anxiously to discover new codicils to the words of the truth, distorting the meaning of that truth already rich in all the scholia, and requiring only fearless defense and not foolish increment? This is the pride that lurked and is still lurking within these walls: and I say to him who has labored and labors to break the seals of the books that are not his to see, that it is this pride the Lord wanted to punish and will continue to punish if it is not brought down and does not humble itself, for the Lord has no difficulty in finding, always and still, thanks to our fragility, the instruments of His vengeance."

"Did you hear that, Adso?" William murmured to me. "The old man knows more than he is saying. Whether or not he had a hand in this business, he knows, and is warning, that if certain curious monks continue violating the library, the abbey will not regain its peace."

Jorge, after a long pause, now resumed speaking.

"But who, finally, is the very symbol of this pride, of whom the proud are the illustration and messengers, the accomplices and standard-bearers? Who in truth has acted and is perhaps acting also inside these walls, so as to warn us that the time is at hand—and to console us, because if the time is at hand, the sufferings will surely be intolerable, but not infinite, since the great cycle of this universe is about to be fulfilled? Oh, you have all understood very well, and you fear to utter the name, for it is also yours and you are afraid of it, but though you have fear, I shall have none, and I will say this name in a loud voice so that your viscera may twist in fright and your teeth chatter and cut off your tongue, and the chill that forms in your blood make a dark veil descend over your eyes. . . . He is the foul beast, he is the Antichrist!"

He paused for a long time. The listeners seemed dead. The only moving thing in the whole church was the flame in the tripod, but even the shadows it formed seemed to have frozen. The only sound, faint, was Jorge's gasping, as he wiped the sweat from his brow. Then Jorge went on.

"You would perhaps like to say to me: No, he has not yet come; where are the signs of his coming? Fool who says this! Why, we have them before our eyes, day after day, in the great amphitheater of the world and in the narrower image of the abbey, the premonitory catastrophes. . . . It has been said that when the moment is near, a foreign king will rise in the West, lord of immense deceits, atheist, killer of men, fraudulent, thirsting for gold, skilled in tricks, wicked, enemy and persecutor of the faithful, and in his time he will not hold silver dear but will esteem only gold! I know well, you who listen to me hasten now to make your calculations to see whether he of whom I speak resembles the Pope or the Emperor or the King of France or whomever you will, so that you will be able to say: He is my enemy and I am on the right side! But I am not so ingenuous; I will not single out one man for you. The Antichrist, when he comes, comes in all and for all, and each is a part of him. He will be in the bands of brigands who sack cities and countryside, he will be in unforeseen signs in the heavens whereby suddenly rainbows will appear, horns and fires, while the moaning of voices will be heard and the sea will boil. It has been said that men and animals will generate monsters, but this means that hearts will conceive hatred and discord. Do not look around you for a glimpse of the animals of the illuminations you so enjoy on parchments! It has been said that young wives not long wed will give birth to babes already able to speak perfectly, who will bring word that the time is at hand and will ask to be killed. But do not search the villages down below us, the too-wise babes have already been killed inside these very walls! And like those babes of the prophecies, they had the appearance of men already old, and in the prophecy they were the quadruped children, and the ghosts, and the embryos that were to prophesy in the mothers' wombs uttering magic spells. And all has been written, do you know that? It has been written that many will be the agitations among those of rank, and among the peoples, the churches; that wicked shepherds will rise up, perverse, disdainful, greedy, pleasure-seeking, lovers of gain, enjoyers of idle speech, boastful, proud, avid, arrogant, plunged in lewdness, seekers of vainglory, enemies of the Gospel, ready to repudiate the strait gate, to despise the true word; and they will hate every path of piety, they will not repent their sins, and therefore will spread among all peoples disbelief, fraternal hatred, wickedness, hardness of heart, envy, indifference, robbery, drunkenness, intemperance, lasciviousness, carnal pleasure, fornication, and all the other vices. Affliction will vanish, and humility, love of peace, poverty, compassion, the gift of tears. . . . Come, do you not recognize yourselves, all of you here present, monks of this abbey and mighty visitors from the outside world?"

In the pause that followed a rustling was heard. It was Cardinal Bertrand wriggling on his bench. After all, I thought, Jorge was behaving like a great preacher, and as he lashed his brothers he was not sparing the guests, either. I would have given anything to know what was going through Bernard's mind at that moment, or the minds of the fat Avignonese.

"And it will be at this point, precisely this," Jorge thundered, "that the Antichrist will have his blasphemous apparition, ape as he wants to be of our Lord. In those times (which are these) all kingdoms will be swept away, there will be famine and poverty, and poor harvests, and winters of exceptional severity. And the children of that time (which is this) will no longer have anyone to administer their goods and preserve food in their storerooms, and they will be harassed in the markets of buying and selling. Blessed, then, are those who will no longer live, or who, living, will be able to survive! Then will come the son of perdition, the enemy who boasts and swells up, displaying many virtues to deceive the whole earth and to prevail over the just. Syria will fall and mourn her sons. Cilicia will raise her head until he who is called to judge her shall appear. The daughter of Babylon will rise from the throne of her splendor to drink from the cup of bitterness. Cappadocia, Lycia, and Lycaonia will bow down, for whole throngs will be destroyed in the corruption of their iniquity. Barbarian camps and war chariots will appear on all sides to occupy the lands. In Armenia, in Pontus, and in Bithynia youths will die by the sword, girl children will be taken prisoner, sons and daughters will commit incest. Pisidia, who boasts in her glory, will be laid prostrate, the sword will pass through the midst of Phoenicia, Judaea will be garbed in mourning and will prepare for the day of perdition brought on by her impurity. On every side will appear abomination and desolation, the Antichrist will defeat the West and will destroy the trade routes; in his hand he will have sword and raging fire, and in violent fury the flame will burn: his strength will be blasphemy, his hand treachery, the right hand will be ruin, the left the bearer of darkness. These are the features that will mark him: his head will be of burning fire, his right eye will be bloodshot, his left eye a feline green with two pupils, and his eyebrows will be white, his lower lip swollen, his ankle weak, his feet big, his thumb crushed and elongated!"

"It seems his own portrait," William whispered, chuckling. It was a very wicked remark, but I was grateful to him for it, because my hair was beginning to stand on end. I could barely stifle a laugh, my cheeks swelling as my clenched lips let out a puff. A sound that, in the silence following the old man's words, was clearly audible, but fortunately everyone thought someone was coughing, or weeping, or shuddering; and all of them were right.

"It is the moment," Jorge was now saying, "when everything will fall into lawlessness, sons will raise their hands against fathers, wives will plot against husbands, husbands will bring wives to law, masters will be inhuman to servants and servants will disobey their masters, there will be no more respect for the old, the young will demand to rule, work will seem a useless chore to all, everywhere songs will rise praising license, vice, dissolute liberty of behavior. And after that, rape, adultery, perjury, sins against nature will follow in a great wave, and disease, and soothsaying, and spells, and flying bodies will appear in the heavens, in the midst of the good Christians false prophets will rise, false apostles, corrupters, impostors, wizards, rapists, usurers, perjurers and falsifiers; the shepherds will turn into wolves, priests will lie, monks will desire things of this world, the poor will not hasten to the aid of their lords, the powerful will be without mercy, the just will bear witness to injustice. All cities will be shaken by earthquakes, there will be pestilence in every land, storm winds will uproot the earth, the fields will be contaminated, the sea will secrete black humors, new and strange wonders will take place upon the moon, the stars will abandon their courses, other stars—unknown—will furrow the sky, it will snow in summer, and in winter the heat will be intense. And the times of the end will have come, and the end of time.... On the first day at the third hour in the firmament a great and powerful voice will be raised, a purple cloud will advance from the north, thunder and lightning will follow it, and on the earth a rain of blood will fall. On the second day the earth will be uprooted from its seat and the smoke of a great fire will pass through the gates of the sky. On the third day the abysses of the earth will rumble from the four corners of the cosmos. The pinnacles of the firmament will open, the air will be filled with columns of smoke, and there will be the stench of sulphur until the tenth hour. On the fourth day, early in the morning, the abyss will liquefy and emit explosions, and buildings will collapse. On the fifth day at the sixth hour the powers of light and the wheel of the sun will be destroyed, and there will be darkness over the earth till evening, and the stars and the moon will cease their office. On the sixth day at the fourth hour the firmament will split from east to west and the angels will be able to look down on the earth through the crack in the heavens and all those on earth will be able to see the angels looking down from heaven. Then all men will hide on the mountains to escape the gaze of the just angels. And on the seventh day Christ will arrive in the light of his Father. And there will then be the judgment of the just and their ascent, in the eternal bliss of bodies and souls. But this is not the object of your meditation this evening, proud brothers! It is not sinners who will see the dawn of the eighth day, when a sweet and tender voice will rise from the east, in the midst of the heavens, and that angel will be seen who commands all the other holy angels, and all the angels will advance together with him, seated on a chariot of clouds, filled with joy, speeding through the air, to set free the blessed who have believed, and all together they will rejoice because the destruction of this world will have been consummated! But this is not to make us rejoice proudly this evening! We will meditate instead on the words the Lord will utter to drive from him those who have not earned salvation: Far from me, ye accursed, into the eternal fire that has been prepared for you by the Devil and his ministers! You yourselves have earned it, and now enjoy it! Go ye from me, descending into the eternal darkness and into the unquenchable fire! I made you and you became followers of another! You became servants of another lord, go and dwell with him in the darkness, with him, the serpent who never rests, amid the gnashing of teeth! I gave you ears to hear the Scripture and you listened to the words of pagans! I formed a mouth for you to glorify God, and you used it for the lies of poets and the riddles of buffoons! I gave you eyes to see the light of my precepts, and you used them to peer into the darkness! I am a humane judge, but a just one. To each I shall give what he deserves. I would have mercy on you, but I find no oil in your jars. I would be impelled to take pity, but your lamps are not cleaned. Go from me.... Thus will speak the Lord. And they... and perhaps we... will descend into the eternal torment. In the name of the Father, of the Son, and of the Holy Ghost."

"Amen," all replied, with one voice.

In a line, without a murmur, the monks went off to their pallets. Feeling no desire to speak with one another, the Minorites and the Pope's men disappeared, longing for solitude and rest. My heart was heavy.

"To bed, Adso," William said to me, climbing the

stairs of the pilgrims' hospice. "This is not a night for roaming about. Bernard Gui might have the idea of heralding the end of the world by beginning with our carcasses. Tomorrow we must try to be present at matins, because immediately afterward Michael and the other Minorites will leave."

"Will Bernard leave, too, with his prisoners?" I asked in a faint voice.

"Surely he has nothing more to do here. He will want to precede Michael to Avignon, but in such a way that Michael's arrival coincides with the trial of the cellarer, a Minorite, heretic, and murderer. The pyre of the cellarer will illuminate, like a propitiatory torch, Michael's first meeting with the Pope."

"And what will become of Salvatore and . . . the girl?"

"Salvatore will go with the cellarer, because he will have to testify at the trial. Perhaps in exchange for this service Bernard will grant him his life. He may allow him to escape and then have him killed, or he may really let him go, because a man like Salvatore is of no interest to a man like Bernard. Who knows? Perhaps Salvatore will end up a cutthroat bandit in some forest of Languedoc. . . ."

"And the girl?"

"I told you: she is burnt flesh. But she will be burned beforehand, along the way, to the edification of some Catharist village along the coast. I have heard it said that Bernard is to meet his colleague Jacques Fournier (remember that name: for the present he is burning Albigensians, but he has higher ambitions), and a beautiful witch to throw on the fire will increase the prestige and the fame of both. . . ."

"But can nothing be done to save them?" I cried. "Can't the abbot intervene?"

"For whom? For the cellarer, a confessed criminal? For a wretch like Salvatore? Or are you thinking of the girl?"

"What if I were?" I made bold to say. "After all, of the three she is the only truly innocent one: you know she is not a witch...."

"And do you believe that the abbot, after what has happened, wants to risk for a witch what little prestige he has left?"

"But he assumed the responsibility for Ubertino's escape!"

"Ubertino was one of his monks and was not accused of anything. Besides, what nonsense are you saying? Ubertino is an important man; Bernard could have struck him only from behind."

"So the cellarer was right: the simple folk always pay for all, even for those who speak in their favor, even for those like Ubertino and Michael, who with their words of penance have driven the simple to rebel!" I was in such despair that I did not consider that the girl was not even a Fraticello, seduced by Ubertino's mystical vision, but a peasant, paying for something that did not concern her.

"So it is," William answered me sadly. "And if you are really seeking a glimmer of justice, I will tell you that one day the big dogs, the Pope and the Emperor, in order to make peace, will pass over the corpses of the smaller dogs who bit one another in their service. And Michael or Ubertino will be treated as your girl is being treated today."

Now I know that William was prophesying—or, rather, syllogizing—on the basis of principles of natural philosophy. But at that moment his prophecies and his syllogisms did not console me in the least. The only sure thing was that the girl would be burned. And I felt responsible, because it was as if she would also expiate on the pyre the sin I had committed with her.

I burst shamefully into sobs and fled to my cell, where all through the night I chewed my pallet and moaned helplessly, for I was not even allowed—as they did in the romances of chivalry I had read with my companions at Melk—to lament and call out the beloved's name.

This was the only earthly love of my life, and I could not, then or ever after, call that love by name.

SIXTH DAY

Matins

In which the princes sederunt, and Malachi slumps to the ground.

We went down to matins. That last part of the night, virtually the first part of the imminent new day, was still foggy. As I crossed the cloister the dampness penetrated to my bones, aching after my uneasy sleep. Although the church was cold, I knelt under those vaults with a sigh of relief, sheltered from the elements, comforted by the warmth of other bodies, and by prayer.

The chanting of the psalms had just begun when William pointed to the stalls opposite us: there was an empty place in between Jorge and Pacificus of Tivoli. It was the place of Malachi, who always sat beside the blind man. Nor were we the only ones who had noticed the absence. On one side I caught a worried glance from the abbot, all too well aware, surely, that those vacancies always heralded grim news. And on the other I noticed that old Jorge was unusually agitated. His face, as a rule so inscrutable because of those white, blank eyes, was plunged almost entirely in darkness;

but his hands were nervous and restless. In fact, more than once he groped at the seat beside him, as if to see whether it was occupied. He repeated that gesture again and again, at regular intervals, as if hoping that the absent man would appear at any moment but fearing not to find him.

"Where can the librarian be?" I whispered to William.

"Malachi," William answered, "is by now the sole possessor of the book. If he is not guilty of the crimes, then he may not know the dangers that book involves...."

There was nothing further to be said. We could only wait. And we waited: William and I, the abbot, who continued to stare at the empty place, and Jorge, who never stopped questioning the darkness with his hands.

When we reached the end of the office, the abbot reminded monks and novices that it was necessary to prepare for the Christmas High Mass; therefore, as was the custom, the time before lauds would be spent assaying the accord of the whole community in the performance of some chants prescribed for the occasion. That assembly of devout men was in effect trained as a single body, a single harmonious voice; through a process that had gone on for years, they acknowledged their unification, into a single soul, in their singing.

The abbot invited them to chant the "Sederunt":

> *Sederunt principes*
> *et adversus me*
> *loquebantur, iniqui*
> *persecuti sunt me.*
> *Adiuva me, Domine*
> *Deus meus, salvum me*
> *fac propter magnam misericordiam tuam.*

I asked myself whether the abbot had not chosen deliberately that gradual to be chanted on that particular night, the cry to God of the persecuted, imploring help against wicked princes. And there, the princes' envoys were still present at the service, to be reminded of how for centuries our order had been prompt to resist the persecution of the powerful, thanks to its special bond with the Lord, God of hosts. And indeed the beginning of the chant created an impression of great power.

On the first syllable, a slow and solemn chorus began, dozens and dozens of voices, whose bass sound filled the naves and floated over our heads and yet seemed to rise from the heart of the earth. Nor did it break off, because as other voices began to weave, over that deep and continuing line, a series of vocalises and melismas, it—telluric—continued to dominate and did not cease for the whole time that it took a speaker to repeat twelve "Ave Maria"s in a slow and cadenced voice. And as if released from every fear by the confidence that the prolonged syllable, allegory of the duration of eternity, gave to those praying, the other voices (and especially the novices') on that rock-solid base raised cusps, columns, pinnacles of liquescent and underscored neumae. And as my heart was dazed with sweetness at the vibration of a climacus or a porrectus, a torculus or a salicus, those voices seemed to say to me that the soul (of those praying, and my own as I listened to them), unable to bear the exuberance of feeling, was lacerated through them to express joy, grief, praise, love, in an impetus of sweet sounds. Meanwhile, the obstinate insistence of the chthonian voices did not let up, as if the threatening presence of enemies, of the powerful who persecuted the people of the Lord, remained unresolved. Until that Neptunian roiling of a single note seemed overcome, or at least convinced and enfolded, by the rejoicing hallelujahs of those who opposed it, and all dissolved on a majestic and perfect chord and on a resupine neuma.

Once the "sederunt" had been uttered with a kind of stubborn difficulty, the "principes" rose in the air with grand and seraphic calm. I no longer asked myself who were the mighty who spoke against me (against us); the shadow of that seated, menacing ghost had dissolved, had disappeared.

And other ghosts, I also believed, dissolved at that point, because on looking again at Malachi's stall, after my attention had been absorbed by the chant, I saw the figure of the librarian among the others in prayer, as if he had never been missing. I looked at William and saw a hint of relief in his eyes, the same relief that I noted from the distance in the eyes of the abbot. As for Jorge, he had once more extended his hands and, encountering his neighbor's body, had withdrawn them promptly. But I could not say what feelings stirred him.

Now the choir was festively chanting the "Adiuva me," whose bright *a* swelled happily through the church, and even the *u* did not seem grim as that in "sederunt," but full of holy vigor. The monks and the novices sang, as the rule of chant requires, with body erect, throat free, head looking up, the book almost at shoulder height so they could read without having to lower their heads and thus causing the breath to come from the chest with less force. But it was still night, and though the trumpets of rejoicing blared, the haze of sleep trapped many of the singers, who, lost perhaps in the production of a long note, trusting the very wave of the chant, nodded at times, drawn by sleepiness. Then the wakers, even in that situation, explored the faces with a light, one by one, to bring them back to wakefulness of body and of soul.

So it was a waker who first noticed Malachi sway in a curious fashion, as if he had suddenly plunged back into the Cimmerian fog of a sleep that he had probably not enjoyed during the night. The waker went over to him with the lamp, illuminating his face and so attracting my attention. The librarian had no reaction. The man touched him, and Malachi slumped forward heavily. The waker barely had time to catch him before he fell.

The chanting slowed down, the voices died, there was

brief bewilderment. William had jumped immediately
from his seat and rushed to the place where Pacificus
of Tivoli and the waker were now laying Malachi on the
ground, unconscious.

We reached them almost at the same time as the
abbot, and in the light of the lamp we saw the poor
man's face. I have already described Malachi's countenance, but that night, in that glow, it was the very image
of death: the sharp nose, the hollow eyes, the sunken
temples, the white, wrinkled ears with lobes turned
outward, the skin of the face now rigid, taut, and dry,
the color of the cheeks yellowish and suffused with a
dark shadow. The eyes were still open and a labored
breathing escaped those parched lips. He opened his
mouth, and as I stooped behind William, who had bent
over him, I saw a now blackish tongue stir within the
cloister of his teeth. William, his arm around Malachi's
shoulders, raised him, wiping away with his free hand a
film of sweat that blanched his brow. Malachi felt a
touch, a presence; he stared straight ahead, surely not
seeing, certainly not recognizing who was before him.
He raised a trembling hand, grasped William by the
chest, drawing his face down until they almost touched,
then faintly and hoarsely he uttered some words: "He
told me . . . truly. . . . It had the power of a thousand
scorpions. . . ."

"Who told you?" William asked him. "Who?"

Malachi tried again to speak. But he was seized by a
great trembling and his head fell backward. His face
lost all color, all semblance of life. He was dead.

. William stood up. He noticed the abbot beside him,
but did not say a word to him. Then, behind the abbot,
he saw Bernard Gui.

"My lord Bernard," William asked, "who killed this
man, after you so cleverly found and confined the
murderers?"

"Do not ask me," Bernard said. "I have never said I
had consigned to the law all the criminals loose in this

abbey. I would have done so gladly, had I been able."
He looked at William. "But the others I now leave to
the severity . . . or the excessive indulgence of my lord
abbot." The abbot blanched and remained silent. Then
Bernard left.

At that moment we heard a kind of whimpering, a
choked sob. It was Jorge, on his kneeling bench,
supported by a monk who must have described to him
what had happened.

"It will never end . . ." he said in a broken voice. "O
Lord, forgive us all!"

William bent over the corpse for another moment.
He grasped the wrists, turned the palms of the hands
toward the light. The pads of the first three fingers of
the right hand were darkened.

LAUDS

In which a new cellarer is chosen, but not a new librarian.

Was it time for lauds already? Was it earlier or later? From that point on I lost all temporal sense. Perhaps hours went by, perhaps less, in which Malachi's body was laid out in church on a catafalque, while the brothers formed a semicircle around it. The abbot issued instructions for a prompt funeral. I heard him summon Benno and Nicholas of Morimondo. In less than a day, he said, the abbey had been deprived of its librarian and its cellarer. "You," he said to Nicholas, "will take over the duties of Remigio. You know the jobs of many here in the abbey. Name someone to take your place in charge of the forges, and provide for today's immediate necessities in the kitchen, the refectory. You are excused from offices. Go." Then to Benno he said, "Only yesterday evening you were named Malachi's assistant. Provide for the opening of the scriptorium and make sure no one goes up into the library alone." Shyly, Benno pointed out that he had not yet been initiated into the secrets of that place. The abbot glared at him sternly. "No one has said you will be. You see that work goes on and is offered as a prayer for our dead brothers...and for those who will yet die. Each monk will work only on the books already given him. Those who wish may consult the catalogue. Nothing else. You are excused from vespers, because at that hour you will lock up everything."

"But how will I come out?" Benno asked.

"Good question. I will lock the lower doors after supper. Go."

He went out with them, avoiding William, who wanted to talk to him. In the choir, a little group remained: Alinardo, Pacificus of Tivoli, Aymaro of Alessandria, and Peter of Sant'Albano. Aymaro was sneering.

"Let us thank the Lord," he said. "With the German dead, there was the risk of having a new librarian even more barbarous."

"Who do you think will be named in his place?" William asked.

Peter of Sant'Albano smiled enigmatically. "After everything that has happened these past few days, the problem is no longer the librarian, but the abbot...."

"Hush," Pacificus said to him. And Alinardo, with his usual pensive look, said, "They will commit another injustice...as in my day. They must be stopped."

"Who?" William asked. Pacificus took him confidentially by the arm and led him a distance from the old man, toward the door.

"Alinardo...as you know...we love him very much. For us he represents the old tradition and the finest days of the abbey....But sometimes he speaks without knowing what he says. We are all worried about the new librarian. The man must be worthy, and mature, and wise....That is all there is to it."

"Must he know Greek?" William asked.

"And Arabic, as tradition has it: his office requires it.

But there are many among us with these gifts. I, if I may say so, and Peter, and Aymaro..."

"Benno knows Greek."

"Benno is too young. I do not know why Malachi chose him as his assistant yesterday, but..."

"Did Adelmo know Greek?"

"I believe not. No, surely not."

"But Venantius knew it. And Berengar. Very well, I thank you."

We left, to go and get something in the kitchen.

"Why did you want to find out who knew Greek?" I asked.

"Because all those who die with blackened fingers know Greek. Therefore it would be well to expect the next corpse among those who know Greek. Including me. You are safe."

"And what do you think of Malachi's last words?"

"You heard them. Scorpions. The fifth trumpet announces, among other things, the coming of locusts that will torment men with a sting like a scorpion's. And Malachi informed us that someone had forewarned him."

"The sixth trumpet," I said, "announces horses with lions' heads from whose mouths come smoke and fire and brimstone, ridden by men covered with breastplates the color of fire, jacinth, and brimstone."

"Too many things. But the next crime might take place near the horse barn. We must keep an eye on it. And we must prepare ourselves for the seventh blast. Two more victims still. Who are the most likely candidates? If the objective is the secret of the finis Africae, those who know it. And as far as I can tell, that means only the abbot. Unless the plot is something else. You heard them just now, scheming to depose the abbot, but Alinardo spoke in the plural...."

"The abbot must be warned," I said.

"Of what? That they will kill him? I have no convincing evidence. I proceed as if the murderer and I think alike. But if he were pursuing another design? And if, especially, there were not *a* murderer?"

"What do you mean?"

"I don't know exactly. But as I said to you, we must imagine all possible orders, and all disorders."

Prime

In which Nicholas tells many things as the crypt of the treasure is visited.

Nicholas of Morimondo, in his new position as cellarer, was giving orders to the cooks, and they were supplying him with information about the operation of the kitchen. William wanted to speak with him, but Nicholas asked us to wait a few moments, until he had to go down into the crypt of the treasure to supervise the polishing of the glass cases, which was still his responsibility; there he would have more time for conversation.

A little later, he did in fact ask us to follow him. He entered the church, went behind the main altar (while the monks were setting up a catafalque in the nave, to keep vigil over Malachi's corpse), and led us down a little ladder. At its foot we found ourselves in a room with a very low vaulted ceiling supported by thick rough-stone columns. We were in the crypt where the riches of the abbey were stored, a place of which the abbot was very jealous and which he allowed to be opened only under exceptional circumstances and for very important visitors.

On every side were cases of different dimensions; in them, objects of wondrous beauty shone in the glow of the torches (lighted by two of Nicholas's trusted assistants). Gold vestments, golden crowns studded with gems, coffers of various metals engraved with figures, works in niello and ivory. In ecstasy, Nicholas showed us an evangeliarium whose binding displayed amazing enamel plaques composing a variegated unity of graduated compartments, outlined in gold filigree and fixed by precious stones in the guise of nails. He showed us a delicate aedicula with two columns of lapis lazuli and gold which framed an Entombment of Christ in fine silver bas-relief surmounted by a golden cross set with thirteen diamonds against a background of grainy onyx, while the little pediment was scalloped with agate and rubies. Then I saw a chryselephantine diptych divided into five sections, with five scenes from the life of Christ, and in the center a mystical lamp composed of cells of gilded silver with glass paste, a single polychrome image on a ground of waxen whiteness.

Nicholas's face and gestures, as he illustrated these things for us, were radiant with pride. William praised the objects he had seen, then asked Nicholas what sort of man Malachi had been.

Nicholas moistened one finger and rubbed it over a crystal surface imperfectly polished, then answered with a half smile, not looking William in the face: "As many said, Malachi seemed quite thoughtful, but on the contrary he was a very simple man. According to Alinardo, he was a fool."

"Alinardo bears a grudge against someone for a remote event, when he was denied the honor of being librarian."

"I, too, have heard talk of that, but it is an old story, dating back at least fifty years. When I arrived here the librarian was Robert of Bobbio, and the old monks muttered about an injustice committed against Alinardo. Robert had an assistant, who later died, and Malachi, still very young, was appointed in his place. Many said that Malachi was without merit, that though he claimed to know Greek and Arabic it was not true, he was only good at aping, copying manuscripts in those languages in fine calligraphy, without understanding what he was copying. Alinardo insinuated that Malachi had been put in that position to favor the schemes of his, Alinardo's, enemy. But I did not understand whom he meant. That is the whole story. There have always been whispers that Malachi protected the library like a guard dog, but with no knowledge of what he was guarding. For that matter, there was also whispering against Berengar, when Malachi chose him as assistant. They said that the young man was no cleverer than his master, that he was only an intriguer. They also said—but you must have heard these rumors yourself by now—that there was a strange relationship between him and Malachi.... Old gossip. Then, as you know, there was talk about Berengar and Adelmo, and the young scribes said that Malachi silently suffered horrible jealousy.... And then there was also murmuring about the ties between Malachi and Jorge. No, not in the sense you might believe—no one has ever murmured against Jorge's virtue!—but Malachi, as librarian, by tradition should have chosen the abbot as his confessor, whereas all the other monks go to Jorge for confession (or to Alinardo, but the old man is by now almost mindless).... Well, they said that in spite of this, the librarian conferred too often with Jorge, as if the abbot directed Malachi's soul but Jorge ruled his body, his actions, his work. Indeed, as you know yourself and have probably seen, if anyone wanted to know the location of an ancient, forgotten book, he did not ask Malachi, but Jorge. Malachi kept the catalogue and went up into the library, but Jorge knew what each title meant. . . ."

"Why did Jorge know so many things about the library?"

"He is the oldest, after Alinardo; he has been here

since his youth. Jorge must be over eighty, and they say he has been blind at least forty years, perhaps longer...."

"How did he become so learned, before his blindness?"

"Oh, there are legends about him. It seems that when he was only a boy he was already blessed by divine grace, and in his native Castile he read the books of the Arabs and the Greek doctors while still a child. And then even after his blindness, even now, he sits for long hours in the library, he has others recite the catalogue to him and bring him books, and a novice reads aloud to him for hours and hours."

"Now that Malachi and Berengar are dead, who is left who possesses the secrets of the library?"

"The abbot, and the abbot must now hand them on to Benno...if he chooses...."

"Why do you say 'if he chooses'?"

"Because Benno is young, and he was named assistant while Malachi was still alive; being assistant librarian is different from being librarian. By tradition, the librarian later becomes abbot...."

"Ah, so that is it.... That is why the post of librarian is so coveted. But then Abo was once librarian?"

"No, not Abo. His appointment took place before I arrived here; it must be thirty years ago now. Before that, Paul of Rimini was abbot, a curious man about whom they tell strange stories. It seems he was a most voracious reader, he knew by heart all the books in the library, but he had a strange infirmity: he was unable to write. They called him Abbas agraphicus.... He became abbot when very young; it was said he had the support of Algirdas of Cluny.... But this is old monkish gossip. Anyway, Paul became abbot, and Robert of Bobbio took his place in the library, but he wasted away as an illness consumed him; they knew he would never be able to govern the abbey, and when Paul of Rimini disappeared..."

"He died?"

"No, he disappeared, I do not know how. One day he

went off on a journey and never came back; perhaps he was killed by thieves in the course of his travels.... Anyway, when Paul disappeared, Robert could not take his place, and there were obscure plots. Abo—it is said—was the natural son of the lord of this district. He grew up in the abbey of Fossanova; it was said that as a youth he had tended Saint Thomas when he died there and had been in charge of carrying that great body down the stairs of a tower where the corpse could not pass.... That was his moment of glory, the malicious here murmured.... The fact is, he was elected abbot, even though he had not been librarian, and he was instructed by someone, Robert I believe, in the mysteries of the library. Now you understand why I do not know whether the abbot will want to instruct Benno: it would be like naming him his successor, a heedless youth, a half-barbarian grammarian from the Far North, what could he know about this country, the abbey, its relations with the lords of the area?"

"But Malachi was not Italian, either, or Berengar, and yet both of them were appointed to the library."

"There is a mysterious thing for you. The monks grumble that for the past half century or more the abbey has been forsaking its traditions.... This is why, over fifty years ago, perhaps earlier, Alinardo aspired to the position of librarian. The librarian had always been Italian—there is no scarcity of great minds in this land. And besides, you see..." Here Nicholas hesitated, as if reluctant to say what he was about to say. "...you see, Malachi and Berengar died, perhaps so that they would not become abbot."

He stirred, waved his hand before his face as if to dispel thoughts less than honest, then made the sign of the cross. "Whatever am I saying? You see, in this country shameful things have been happening for many years, even in the monasteries, in the papal court, in the churches.... Conflicts to gain power, accusations of heresy to take a prebend from someone... How ugly! I am losing faith in the human race; I see plots and palace conspiracies on every side. That our abbey should come to this, a nest of vipers risen through occult magic in what had been a triumph of sainted members. Look: the past of this monastery!"

He pointed to the treasures scattered all around, and, leaving the crosses and other vessels, he took us to see the reliquaries, which represented the glory of this place.

"Look," he said, "this is the tip of the spear that pierced the side of the Saviour!" We saw a golden box with a crystal lid, containing a purple cushion on which lay a piece of iron, triangular in shape, once corroded by rust but now restored to vivid splendor by long application of oils and waxes. But this was still nothing. For in another box, of silver studded with amethysts, its front panel transparent, I saw a piece of the venerated wood of the holy cross, brought to this abbey by Queen Helena herself, mother of the Emperor Constantine, after she had gone as a pilgrim to the holy places, excavated the hill of Golgotha and the holy sepulcher, and constructed a cathedral over it.

Then Nicholas showed us other things, and I could not describe them all, in their number and their rarity. There was, in a case of aquamarine, a nail of the cross. In an ampoule, lying on a cushion of little withered roses, there was a portion of the crown of thorns; and in another box, again on a blanket of dried flowers, a yellowed shred of the tablecloth from the last supper. And then there was the purse of Saint Matthew, of silver links; and in a cylinder, bound by a violet ribbon eaten by time and sealed with gold, a bone from Saint Anne's arm. I saw, wonder of wonders, under a glass bell, on a red cushion embroidered with pearls, a piece of the manger of Bethlehem, and a hand's length of the purple tunic of Saint John the Evangelist, two links of the chains that bound the ankles of the apostle Peter in Rome, the skull of Saint Adalbert, the sword of Saint

Stephen, a tibia of Saint Margaret, a finger of Saint Vitalis, a rib of Saint Sophia, the chin of Saint Eobanus, the upper part of Saint Chrysostom's shoulder blade, the engagement ring of Saint Joseph, a tooth of the Baptist, Moses's rod, a tattered scrap of very fine lace from the Virgin Mary's wedding dress.

And then other things that were not relics but still bore perennial witness to wonders and wondrous beings from distant lands, brought to the abbey by monks who had traveled to the farthest ends of the world: a stuffed basilisk and hydra, a unicorn's horn, an egg that a hermit had found inside another egg, a piece of the manna that had fed the Hebrews in the desert, a whale's tooth, a coconut, the scapula of an animal from before the Flood, an elephant's ivory tusk, the rib of a dolphin. And then more relics that I did not identify, whose reliquaries were perhaps more precious than they, and some (judging by the craftsmanship of their containers, of blackened silver) very ancient: an endless series of fragments, bone, cloth, wood, metal, glass. And phials with dark powders, one of which, I learned, contained the charred remains of the city of Sodom, and another some mortar from the walls of Jericho. All things, even the humblest, for which an emperor would have given more than a castle, and which represented a hoard not only of immense prestige but also of actual material wealth for the abbey that preserved them.

I continued wandering about, dumbfounded, for Nicholas had now stopped explaining the objects, each of which was described by a scroll anyway; and now I was free to roam virtually at random amid that display of priceless wonders, at times admiring things in full light, at times glimpsing them in semidarkness, as Nicholas's helpers moved to another part of the crypt with their torches. I was fascinated by those yellowed bits of cartilage, mystical and revolting at the same time, transparent and mysterious; by those shreds of clothing from some immemorial age, faded, threadbare, sometimes rolled up in a phial like a faded manuscript; by those crumbled materials mingling with the fabric that was their bed, holy jetsam of a life once animal (and rational) and now, imprisoned in constructions of crystal or of metal that in their minuscule size mimed the boldness of stone cathedrals with towers and turrets, all seemed transformed into mineral substance as well. Is this, then, how the bodies of the saints, buried, await the resurrection of the flesh? From these shards would there be reconstructed those organisms that in the splendor of the beatific vision, regaining their every natural sensitivity, would sense, as Pipernus wrote, even the minimas differentias odorum?

William stirred me from my meditations as he touched my shoulder. "I am going," he said. "I'm going up to the scriptorium. I have yet something to consult. . . ."

"But it will be impossible to have any books," I said. "Benno was given orders. . . ."

"I have to re-examine only the books I was reading the other day; all are still in the scriptorium, on Venantius's desk. You stay here, if you like. This crypt is a beautiful epitome of the debates on poverty you have been following these past few days. And now you know why your brothers make mincemeat of one another as they aspire to the position of abbot."

"But do you believe what Nicholas implied? Are the crimes connected with a conflict over the investiture?"

"I've already told you that for the present I don't want to put hypotheses into words. Nicholas said many things. And some interested me. But now I am going to follow yet another trail. Or perhaps the same, but from a different direction. And don't succumb too much to the spell of these cases. I have seen many other fragments of the cross, in other churches. If all were genuine, our Lord's torment could not have been on a couple of planks nailed together, but on an entire forest."

"Master!" I said, shocked.

"So it is, Adso. And there are even richer treasuries. Some time ago, in the cathedral of Cologne, I saw the skull of John the Baptist at the age of twelve."

"Really?" I exclaimed, amazed. Then, seized by doubt, I added, "But the Baptist was executed at a more advanced age!"

"The other skull must be in another treasury," William said, with a grave face. I never understood when he was jesting. In my country, when you joke you say something and then you laugh very noisily, so everyone shares in the joke. But William laughed only when he said serious things, and remained very serious when he was presumably joking.

TERCE

In which Adso, listening to the "Dies irae," has a dream, or vision, howsoever you may choose to define it.

William took his leave of Nicholas and went up to the scriptorium. By now I had seen my fill of the treasure and decided to go into the church and pray for Malachi's soul. I had never loved that man, who frightened me; and I will not deny that for a long time I believed him guilty of all the crimes. But now I had learned that he was perhaps a poor wretch, oppressed by unfulfilled passions, an earthenware vessel among vessels of iron, surly because bewildered, silent and evasive because conscious he had nothing to say. I felt a certain remorse toward him, and I thought that praying for his supernatural destiny might allay my feelings of guilt.

The church was now illuminated by a faint and livid glow, dominated by the poor man's corpse, and inhabited by the monotone murmur of the monks reciting the office of the dead.

In the monastery of Melk I had several times witnessed a brother's decease. It was not what I could call a happy occasion, but still it seemed to me serene, governed by calm and by a sense of rightness. The monks took turns in the dying man's cell, comforting him with good words, and each in his heart considered how the dying man was fortunate, because he was about to conclude a virtuous life and would soon join the choir of angels in that bliss without end. And a part of this serenity, the odor of that pious envy, was conveyed to the dying man, who in the end died serenely. How different the deaths of the past few days! Finally I had seen at close hand how a victim of the diabolical scorpions of the finis Africae died, and certainly Venantius and Berengar had also died like that, seeking relief in water, their faces already wasted as Malachi's had been.

I sat at the back of the church, huddled down to combat the chill. As I felt a bit of warmth, I moved my lips to join the chorus of the praying brothers. I followed them almost without being aware of what my lips were saying, while my head nodded and my eyes wanted to close. Long minutes went by; I believe I fell asleep and woke up at least three or four times. Then the choir began to chant the "Dies irae." . . . The chanting affected me like a narcotic. I went completely to sleep. Or perhaps, rather than slumber, I fell into an exhausted, agitated doze, bent double, like an infant still in its mother's womb. And in that fog of the soul, finding myself as if in a region not of this world, I had a vision, or dream, if you prefer to call it that.

I was descending some narrow steps into a low passage, as if I were entering the treasure crypt, but, continuing to descend, I arrived in a broader crypt, which was the kitchen of the Aedificium. It was certainly the kitchen, but there was a bustle among not only ovens and pots, but also bellows and hammers, as if Nicholas's smiths had assembled there as well. Everything glowed red from the stoves and cauldrons, and boiling pots gave off steam while huge bubbles rose to their surfaces and popped suddenly with a dull, repeated sound. The cooks turned spits in the air, as the novices, who had all

517

gathered, leaped up to snatch the chickens and the other fowl impaled on those red-hot irons. But nearby the smiths hammered so powerfully that the whole air was deafened, and clouds of sparks rose from the anvils, mingling with those belching from the two ovens.

I could not understand whether I was in hell or in such a paradise as Salvatore might have conceived, dripping with juices and throbbing with sausages. But I had no time to wonder where I was, because in rushed a swarm of little men, dwarfs with huge pot-shaped heads; sweeping me away, they thrust me to the threshold of the refectory, forcing me to enter.

The hall was bedecked for a feast. Great tapestries and banners hung on the walls, but the images adorning them were not those usually displayed for the edification of the faithful or the celebration of the glories of kings. They seemed inspired, on the contrary, by Adelmo's marginalia, and they reproduced his less awful and more comical images: hares dancing around the tree of plenty, rivers filled with fish that flung themselves spontaneously into frying pans held out by monkeys dressed as cook-bishops, monsters with fat bellies skipping around steaming kettles.

In the center of the table was the abbot, in feast-day dress, with a great vestment of embroidered purple, holding his fork like a scepter. Beside him, Jorge drank from a great mug of wine, and Remigio, dressed like Bernard Gui, held a book shaped like a scorpion, virtuously reading the lives of the saints and passages from the Gospels, but they were stories about Jesus joking with the apostle, reminding him that he was a stone and on that shameless stone that rolled over the plain he would build his church, or the story of Saint Jerome commenting on the Bible and saying that God wanted to bare Jerusalem's behind. And at every sentence the cellarer read, Jorge laughed, pounded his fist on the table, and shouted, "You shall be the next abbot, by God's belly!" Those were his very words, may the Lord forgive me.

At a merry signal from the abbot, the procession of virgins entered. It was a radiant line of richly dressed females, in whose midst I thought at first I could discern my mother; then I realized my error, because it was certainly the maiden terrible as an army with banners. Except that she wore a crown of white pearls on her head, a double strand, and two cascades of pearls fell on either side of her face, mingling with two other rows which hung on her bosom, and from each pearl hung a diamond as big as a plum. Further, from both ears descended rows of blue pearls, which joined to become a choker at the base of her neck, white and erect as a tower of Lebanon. The cloak was murex-colored, and in her hand she had a diamond-studded golden goblet in which I knew, I cannot say how, was contained the lethal unguent one day stolen from Severinus. This woman, fair as the dawn, was followed by other female forms. One was clothed in a white embroidered mantle over a dark dress adorned with a double stole of gold embroidered in wild flowers; the second wore a cloak of yellow damask on a pale-pink dress dotted with green leaves, and with two great spun squares in the form of a dark labyrinth; and the third had an emerald dress interwoven with little red animals, and she bore in her hands a white embroidered stole; I did not observe the clothing of the others, because I was trying to understand who they were, to be accompanying the maiden, who now resembled the Virgin Mary; and as if each bore in her hand a scroll, or as if a scroll came from each woman's mouth, I knew they were Ruth, Sarah, Susanna, and other women of Scripture.

At this point the abbot cried, "Come on in, you whoresons!" and into the refectory came another array of sacred personages, in austere and splendid dress, whom I recognized clearly; and in the center of the group was one seated on a throne who was our Lord but at the same time He was Adam, dressed in a purple cloak with a great diadem, red and white with rubies and pearls, holding the cloak on His shoulders, and on His head a crown similar to the maiden's, in His hand a larger goblet, brimming with pig's blood. Other most holy personages of whom I will speak, all familiar to me, surrounded him, along with a host of the King of France's archers, dressed either in green or in red, with a pale-emerald shield on which the monogram of Christ stood out. The chief of this band went to pay homage to the abbot, extending the goblet to him. At which point the abbot said, "Age primum et septimum de quatuor," and all chanted, "In finibus Africae, amen." Then all sederunt.

When the two facing hosts had thus dispersed, at an order from Abbot Solomon the tables began to be laid, James and Andrew brought a bale of hay, Adam settled himself in the center, Eve lay down on a leaf, Cain entered dragging a plow, Abel came with a pail to milk Brunellus, Noah made a triumphal entry rowing the ark, Abraham sat under a tree, Isaac lay on the gold altar of the church, Moses crouched on a stone, Daniel appeared on a catafalque in Malachi's arms, Tobias stretched out on a bed, Joseph threw himself on a bushel, Benjamin reclined on a sack, and there were others still, but here the vision grew confused. David stood on a mound, John on the floor, Pharaoh on the sand (naturally, I said to myself, but why?), Lazarus on the table, Jesus on the edge of the well, Zaccheus on the boughs of a tree, Matthew on a stool, Raab on stubble, Ruth on straw, Thecla on the window sill (from outside, Adelmo's pale face appeared, as he warned her it was possible to fall down, down the cliff), Susanna in the garden, Judas among the graves, Peter on the throne, James on a net, Elias on a saddle, Rachel on a bundle. And Paul the apostle, putting down his sword, listened to Esau complain, while Job moaned on the dungheap and Rebecca rushed to his aid with a garment and Judith with a blanket, Hagar with a shroud, and some novices carried a large steaming pot from which leaped Venantius of Salvemec, all red, as he began to distribute pig's-blood puddings.

The refectory was now becoming more and more crowded, and all were eating at full tilt; Jonas brought some gourds to the table, Isaiah some vegetables, Ezekiel blackberries, Zaccheus sycamore flowers, Adam lemons, Daniel lupins, Pharaoh peppers, Cain cardoons, Eve figs, Rachel apples, Ananias some plums as big as diamonds, Leah onions, Aaron olives, Joseph an egg, Noah grapes, Simeon peach pits, while Jesus was singing the "Dies irae" and gaily poured over all the dishes some vinegar that he squeezed from a little sponge he had taken from the spear of one of the King of France's archers.

At this point Jorge, having removed his vitra ad legendum, lighted a burning bush; Sarah had provided kindling for it, Jephtha had brought it, Isaac had unloaded it, Joseph had carved it, and while Jacob opened the well and Daniel sat down beside the lake, the servants brought water, Noah wine, Hagar a wineskin, Abraham a calf that Raab tied to a stake while Jesus held out the rope and Elijah bound its feet. Then Absalom hung him by his hair, Peter held out his sword, Cain killed him, Herod shed his blood, Shem threw away his giblets and dung, Jacob added the oil, Molessadon the salt; Antiochus put him on the fire, Rebecca cooked him, and Eve first tasted him and was taken sick, but Adam said not to give it a thought and slapped Severinus on the back as he suggested adding aromatic herbs. Then Jesus broke the bread and passed around some fishes, Jacob shouted because Esau had eaten all the pottage, Isaac was devouring a roast kid, and Jonah a boiled whale, and Jesus fasted for forty days and forty nights.

Meanwhile, all came in and out bringing choice game

of every shape and color, of which Benjamin always kept the biggest share and Mary the choicest morsel, while Martha complained of always having to wash the dishes. Then they divided up the calf, which had meanwhile grown very big, and John was given the head, Abessalom the brain, Aaron the tongue, Sampson the jaw, Peter the ear, Holofernes the head, Leah the rump, Saul the neck, Jonah the belly, Tobias the gall, Eve the rib, Mary the breast, Elizabeth the vulva, Moses the tail, Lot the legs, and Ezekiel the bones. All the while, Jesus was devouring a donkey, Saint Francis a wolf, Abel a lamb, Eve a moray, the Baptist a locust, Pharaoh an octopus (naturally, I said to myself, but why?), and David was eating Spanish fly, flinging himself on the maiden nigra sed formosa while Sampson bit into a lion's behind and Thecla fled screaming, pursued by a hairy black spider.

All were obviously drunk by now, and some slipped on the wine, some fell into the jars with only their legs sticking out, crossed like two stakes, and all of Jesus's fingers were black as he handed out pages of books saying: Take this and eat, these are the riddles of Synphosius, including the one about the fish that is the son of God and your Saviour.

Sprawled on his back, Adam gulped, and the wine came from his rib, Noah cursed Ham in his sleep, Holofernes snored, all unsuspecting, Jonah slept soundly, Peter kept watch till cockcrow, and Jesus woke with a start, hearing Bernard Gui and Bertrand del Poggetto plotting to burn the maiden; and he shouted: Father, if it be thy will, let this chalice pass from me! And some poured badly and some drank well, some died laughing and some laughed dying, some bore vases and some drank from another's cup. Susanna shouted that she would never grant her beautiful white body to the cellarer and to Salvatore for a miserable beef heart, Pilate wandered around the refectory like a lost soul asking for water to wash his hands, and Fra Dolcino, with his plumed hat, brought the water, then opened his garment, snickering, and displayed his pudenda red with blood, while Cain taunted him and embraced the beautiful Margaret of Trent: and Dolcino fell to weeping and went to rest his head on the shoulder of Bernard Gui, calling him Angelic Pope, Ubertino consoled him with a tree of life, Michael of Cesena with a gold purse, the Marys sprinkled him with unguents, and Adam convinced him to bite into a freshly plucked apple.

And then the vaults of the Aedificium opened and from the heavens descended Roger Bacon on a flying machine, *unico homine regente.* Then David played his lyre, Salome danced with her seven veils, and at the fall of each veil she blew one of the seven trumpets and showed one of the seven seals, until only the *amicta sole* remained. Everyone said there had never been such a jolly abbey, and Berengar pulled up everyone's habit, man and woman, kissing them all on the anus.

Then it was that the abbot flew into a rage, because, he said, he had organized such a lovely feast and nobody was giving him anything; so they all outdid one another in bringing him gifts and treasures, a bull, a lamb, a lion, a camel, a stag, a calf, a mare, a chariot of the sun, the chin of Saint Eubanus, the tail of Saint Ubertina, the uterus of Saint Venantia, the neck of Saint Burgosina engraved like a goblet at the age of twelve, and a copy of the *Pentagonum Salomonis*. But the abbot started yelling that they were trying to distract his attention with their behavior, and in fact they were looting the treasure crypt, where we all were, and a most precious book had been stolen which spoke of scorpions and the seven trumpets, and he called the King of France's archers to search all the suspects. And, to everyone's shame, the archers found a multicolored cloth on Hagar, a gold seal on Rachel, a silver mirror in Thecla's bosom, a siphon under Benjamin's arm, a silk coverlet among Judith's clothes, a spear in Longinus's hand, and a neighbor's wife in the arms of Abimelech. But the worst was when they found a black rooster on the girl, black and beautiful she was, like a cat of the same color, and they called her a witch and a Pseudo Apostle, so all flung themselves on her, to punish her. The Baptist decapitated her, Abel cut her open, Adam drove her out, Nebuchadnezzar wrote zodiacal signs on her breast with a fiery hand, Elijah carried her off in a fiery chariot, Noah plunged her in water, Lot changed her into a pillar of salt, Susanna accused her of lust, Joseph betrayed her with another woman, Ananias stuck her into a furnace, Sampson chained her up, Paul flagellated her, Peter crucified her head down, Stephen stoned her, Lawrence burned her on a grate, Bartholomew skinned her, Judas denounced her, the cellarer burned her, and Peter denied everything. Then they all were on that body, flinging excrement on her, farting in her face, urinating on her head, vomiting on her bosom, tearing out her hair, whipping her buttocks with glowing torches. The girl's body, once so beautiful and sweet, was now lacerated, torn into fragments that were scattered among the glass cases and gold-and-crystal reliquaries of the crypt. Or, rather, it was not the body of the girl that went to fill the crypt, it was the fragments of the crypt that, whirling, gradually composed to form the girl's body, now something mineral, and then again decomposed and scattered, sacred dust of segments accumulated by insane blasphemy. It was now as if a single immense body had, in the course of millennia, dissolved into its parts, and these parts had been arranged to occupy the whole crypt, more splendid than the ossarium of the dead monks but not unlike it, and as if the substantial form of man's very body, the masterpiece of creation, had shattered into plural and separate accidental forms, thus becoming the image of its own opposite, form no longer ideal but earthly, of dust and stinking fragments, capable of signifying only death and destruction. . . .

Now I could no longer find the banqueters or the gifts they had brought, it was as if all the guests of the symposium were now in the crypt, each mummified in its own residue, each the diaphanous synecdoche of itself, Rachel as a bone, Daniel as a tooth, Sampson as a jaw, Jesus as a shred of purple garment. As if, at the end of the banquet, the feast transformed into the girl's slaughter, it had become the universal slaughter, and here I was seeing its final result, the bodies (no, the whole terrestrial and sublunar body of those ravenous and thirsting feasters) transformed into a single dead body, lacerated and tormented like Dolcino's body after his torture, transformed into a loathsome and resplendent treasure, stretched out to its full extent like the hide of a skinned and hung animal, which still contained, however, petrified, the leather sinews, the viscera, and all the organs, and even the features of the face. The skin with each of its folds, wrinkles, and scars, with its velvety plains, its forest of hairs, the dermis, the bosom, the pudenda, having become a sumptuous damask, and the breasts, the nails, the horny formations under the heel, the threads of the lashes, the watery substance of the eyes, the flesh of the lips, the thin spine of the back, the architecture of the bones, everything reduced to sandy powder, though nothing had lost its own form or respective placement, the legs emptied and limp as a boot, their flesh lying flat like a chasuble with all the scarlet embroidery of the veins, the engraved pile of the viscera, the intense and mucous ruby of the heart, the pearly file of even teeth arranged like a necklace, with the tongue as a pink-and-blue pendant, the fingers in a row like tapers, the seal of the navel reknotting the threads of the unrolled carpet of the belly...From every corner of the crypt, now I was grinned at, whispered to, bidden to death by this macrobody divided among glass cases and reliquaries and yet reconstructed in its vast and irrational whole, and it was the same body that at the supper had eaten and tumbled obscenely but here, instead, appeared to me fixed in the intangibility of its deaf and blind ruin. And Ubertino, seizing me by the arm, digging his nails into my flesh, whispered to me: "You see, it is the same thing, what first triumphed in its folly and took delight in its jesting now is here, punished and rewarded, liberated from the seduction of the passions, rigidified by eternity, consigned to the eternal frost that is to preserve and purify it, saved from corruption through the triumph of corruption, because nothing more can reduce to dust that which is already dust and mineral substance, mors est quies viatoris, finis est omnis laboris. . . ."

But suddenly Salvatore entered the crypt, glowing like a devil, and cried, "Fool! Can't you see this is the great Lyotard? What are you afraid of, my little master? Here is the cheese in batter!" And suddenly the crypt was bright with reddish flashes and it was again the kitchen, but not so much a kitchen as the inside of a great womb, mucous and viscid, and in the center an animal black as a raven and with a thousand hands was chained to a huge grate, and it extended those limbs to snatch everybody around it, and as the peasant when thirsty squeezes a bunch of grapes, so that great beast squeezed those it had snatched so that its hands broke them all, the legs of some, the heads of others, and then it sated itself, belching a fire that seemed to stink more than sulphur. But, wondrous mystery, that scene no longer instilled fear in me, and I was surprised to see that I could watch easily that "good devil" (so I thought) who after all was none other than Salvatore, because now I knew all about the mortal human body, its sufferings and its corruption, and I feared nothing any more. In fact, in the light of that flame, which now seemed mild and convivial, I saw again all the guests of the supper, now restored to their original forms, singing and declaring that everything was beginning again, and among them was the maiden, whole and most beautiful, who said to me, "It is nothing, it is nothing, you will see: I shall be even more beautiful than before; just let me go for a moment and burn on the pyre, then we shall meet again here!" And she displayed to me, God have mercy on me, her vulva, into which I entered, and I found myself in a beautiful cave, which seemed the happy valley of the golden age, dewy with waters and fruits and trees that bore cheeses in batter. And all were thanking the abbot for the lovely feast, and they showed him their affection and good humor by pushing him, kicking him, tearing his clothes, laying him on the ground, striking his rod with rods, as he laughed and begged them to stop tickling him. And, riding mounts whose nostrils emitted clouds of brimstone, the Friars of the Poor Life entered, carrying at their belts purses full of gold with which they transformed wolves into lambs and lambs into wolves and crowned them emperor with the approval of the assembly of the people, who sang praises of God's infinite omnipotence. "Ut cachinnis dissolvatur, torqueatur rictibus!" Jesus shouted, waving his crown of thorns. Pope John came in, cursing the confusion and saying, "At this rate I don't know where it all will end!" But everyone mocked him and, led by the abbot, went out with the pigs to hunt truffles in the forest. I was about to follow them when in a corner I saw William, emerging from the labyrinth and carrying in his hand the magnet, which pulled him rapidly northward. "Do not leave me, master!" I shouted. "I, too, want to see what is in the finis Africae!"

"You have already seen it!" William answered, far away by now. And I woke up as the last words of the funeral chant were ending in the church:

> *Lacrimosa dies illa*
> *qua resurget ex favilla*
> *iudicandus homo reus:*

huic ergo parce deus!
Pie Iesu domine
dona eis requiem.

A sign that my vision, rapid like all visions, if it had not lasted the space of an "amen," as the saying goes, had lasted almost the length of a "Dies irae."

After Terce

In which William explains Adso's dream to him.

Dazed, I came out through the main door and discovered a little crowd there. The Franciscans were leaving, and William had come down to say good-bye to them.

I joined in the farewells, the fraternal embraces. Then I asked William when the others would be leaving, with the prisoners. He told me they had already left, half an hour before, while we were in the treasure crypt, or perhaps, I thought, when I was dreaming.

For a moment I was aghast, then I recovered myself. Better so. I would not have been able to bear the sight of the condemned (I meant the poor wretched cellarer and Salvatore...and, of course, I also meant the girl) being dragged off, far away and forever. And besides, I was still so upset by my dream that my feelings seemed numb.

As the caravan of Minorites headed for the gate, to leave the abbey, William and I remained in front of the church, both melancholy, though for different reasons.

Then I decided to tell my master my dream. Though the vision had been multiform and illogical, I remembered it with amazing clarity, image by image, action by action, word by word. And so I narrated it, omitting nothing, because I knew that dreams are often mysterious messages in which learned people can read distinct prophecies.

William listened to me in silence, then asked me, "Do you know what you have dreamed?"

"Exactly what I told you . . ." I replied, at a loss.

"Of course, I realize that. But do you know that to a great extent what you tell me has already been written? You have added people and events of these past few days to a picture already familiar to you, because you have read the story of your dream somewhere, or it was told you as a boy, in school, in the convent. It is the *Coena Cypriani*."

I remained puzzled briefly. Then I remembered. He was right! Perhaps I had forgotten the title, but what adult monk or unruly young novice has not smiled or laughed over the various visions, in prose or rhyme, of this story, which belongs to the tradition of the paschal season and the ioca monachorum? Though the work is banned or execrated by the more austere among novice masters, there is still not a convent in which the monks have not whispered it to one another, variously condensed and revised, while some piously copied it, declaring that behind a veil of mirth it concealed secret moral lessons, and others encouraged its circulation because, they said, through its jesting, the young could more easily commit to memory certain episodes of sacred history. A verse version had been written for Pope John VIII, with the inscription "I loved to jest; accept me, dear Pope John, in my jesting. And, if you wish, you can also laugh." And it was said that Charles the Bald himself had staged it, in the guise of a comic sacred mystery, in a rhymed version to entertain his dignitaries at supper.

And how many scoldings had I received from my masters when, with my companions, I recited passages from it! I remembered an old friar at Melk who used to say that a virtuous man like Cyprian could not have written such an indecent thing, such a sacrilegious parody of Scripture, worthier of an infidel and a buffoon than of a holy martyr.... For years I had forgotten those childish jokes. Why on this day had the *Coena* reappeared so vividly in my dream? I had always thought that dreams were divine messages, or at worst absurd stammerings of the sleeping memory about things that had happened during the day. I was now realizing that one can also dream books, and therefore dream of dreams.

"I should like to be Artemidorus to interpret your dream correctly," William said. "But it seems to me that even without Artemidorus's learning it is easy to understand what happened. In these past days, my poor boy, you have experienced a series of events in which every upright rule seems to have been destroyed. And this morning, in your sleeping mind, there returned the memory of a kind of comedy in which, albeit with other intentions, the world is described upside down. You inserted into that work your most recent memories, your anxieties, your fears. From the marginalia of Adelmo you went on to relive a great carnival where everything seems to proceed in the wrong direction, and yet, as in the *Coena*, each does what he really did in life. And finally you asked yourself, in the dream, which world is the false one, and what it means to walk head down. Your dream no longer distinguished what is down and what is up, where life is and where death. Your dream cast doubt on the teachings you have received."

"My dream," I said virtuously, "not I. But dreams are not divine messages, then; they are diabolical ravings, and they contain no truth!"

"I don't know, Adso," William said. "We already have so many truths in our possession that if the day came

531

when someone insisted on deriving a truth even from our dreams, then the day of the Antichrist would truly be at hand. And yet, the more I think of your dream, the more revealing it seems to me. Perhaps not to you, but to me. Forgive me if I use your dream in order to work out my hypotheses; I know, it is a base action, it should not be done.... But I believe that your sleeping soul understood more things than I have in six days, and awake...."

"Truly?"

"Truly. Or perhaps not. I find your dream revealing because it coincides with one of my hypotheses. But you have given me great help. Thank you."

"But what was there in my dream that interests you so much? It made no sense, like all dreams!"

"It had another sense like all dreams, and visions. It must be read as an allegory, or an analogy...."

"Like Scripture?"

"A dream is a scripture, and many scriptures are nothing but dreams."

Sext

In which the succession of librarians is reconstructed, and there is further information about the mysterious book.

William decided to go back up to the scriptorium, from which he had just come. He asked Benno's leave to consult the catalogue, and he leafed through it rapidly. "It must be around here," he said, "I saw it just an hour ago...." He stopped at one page. "Here," he said, "read this title."

As a single entry there was a group of four titles, indicating that one volume contained several texts. I read:

I.   ar. de dictis cuiusdam stulti
II. syr. libellus alchemicus aegypt.
III. Expositio Magistri Alcofribae de coena beati Cypriani Cartaginensis Episcopi
IV. Liber acephalus de stupris virginum et meretricum amoribus

"What is it?" I asked.

"It is our book," William whispered to me. "This is

why your dream reminded me of something. Now I am sure this is it. And in fact"—he glanced quickly at the pages immediately preceding and following—"in fact, here are the books I was thinking about, all together. But this isn't what I wanted to check. See here. Do you have your tablet? Good. We must make a calculation, and try to remember clearly what Alinardo told us the other day as well as what we heard this morning from Nicholas. Now, Nicholas told us he arrived here about thirty years ago, and Abo had already been named abbot. The abbot before him was Paul of Rimini. Is that right? Let's say this succession took place around 1290, more or less, it doesn't matter. Nicholas also told us that, when he arrived, Robert of Bobbio was already librarian. Correct? Then Robert died, and the post was given to Malachi, let's say at the beginning of this century. Write this down. There is a period, however, before Nicholas came, when Paul of Rimini was librarian. How long was he in that post? We weren't told. We could examine the abbey ledgers, but I imagine the abbot has them, and for the moment I would prefer not to ask him for them. Let's suppose Paul was appointed librarian sixty years ago. Write that. Why does Alinardo complain of the fact that, about fifty years ago, he should have been given the post of librarian and instead it went to another? Was he referring to Paul of Rimini?"

"Or to Robert of Bobbio!" I said.

"So it would seem. But now look at this catalogue. As you know, the titles are recorded in the order of acquisition. And who writes them in this ledger? The librarian. Therefore, by the changes of handwriting in these pages we can establish the succession of librarians. Now we will look at the catalogue from the end; the last handwriting is Malachi's, you see. And it fills only a few pages. The abbey has not acquired many books in these last thirty years. Then, as we work backward, a series of pages begins in a shaky hand. I clearly read the presence of Robert of Bobbio, who was ill. Robert probably did not occupy the position long. And then what do we find? Pages and pages in another hand, straight and confident, a whole series of acquisitions (including the group of books I was examining a moment ago), truly impressive. Paul of Rimini must have worked hard! Too hard, if you recall that Nicholas told us he became abbot while still a young man. But let's assume that in a few years this voracious reader enriched the abbey with so many books. Weren't we told he was called Abbas agraphicus because of that strange defect, or illness, which made him unable to write? Then who wrote these pages? His assistant librarian, I would say. But if by chance this assistant librarian were then named librarian, he would then have continued writing, and we would have figured out why there are so many pages here in the same hand. So, then, between Paul and Robert we would have another librarian, chosen about fifty years ago, who was the mysterious rival of Alinardo, who was hoping, as an older man, to succeed Paul. Then this man died, and somehow, contrary to Alinardo's expectations and the expectations of others, Robert was named in his place."

"But why are you so sure this is the right scansion? Even granting that this handwriting is the nameless librarian's, why couldn't Paul also have written the titles of the still earlier pages?"

"Because among the acquisitions they recorded all bulls and decretals, and these are precisely dated. I mean, if you find here, as you do, the *Firma cautela* of Boniface the Seventh, dated 1296, you know that text did not arrive before that year, and you can assume it didn't arrive much later. I have these milestones, so to speak, placed along the years, so if I grant that Paul of Rimini became librarian in 1265 and abbot in 1275, and I find that his hand, or the hand of someone else who is not Robert of Bobbio, lasts from 1265 to 1285, then I discover a discrepancy of ten years."

My master was truly very sharp. "But what conclusions do you draw from this discrepancy?" I asked.

"None," he answered. "Only some premises."

Then he got up and went to talk with Benno, who was staunchly at his post, but with a very unsure air. He was still behind his old desk and had not dared take over Malachi's, by the catalogue. William addressed him with some coolness. We had not forgotten the unpleasant scene of the previous evening.

"Even in your new and powerful position, Brother Librarian, I trust you will answer a question. That morning when Adelmo and the others were talking here about witty riddles, and Berengar made the first reference to the finis Africae, did anybody mention the *Coena Cypriani*?"

"Yes," Benno said, "didn't I tell you? Before they talked about the riddles of Symphosius, Venantius himself mentioned the *Coena*, and Malachi became furious, saying it was an ignoble work and reminding us that the abbot had forbidden anyone to read it...."

"The abbot?" William said. "Very interesting. Thank you, Benno."

"Wait," Benno said, "I want to talk with you." He motioned us to follow him out of the scriptorium, onto the stairs going down to the kitchen, so the others could not hear him. His lips were trembling.

"I'm frightened, William," he said. "They've killed Malachi. Now I am the one who knows too many things. Besides, the group of Italians hate me.... They do not want another foreign librarian.... I believe the others were murdered for this very reason.... I've never told you about Alinardo's hatred for Malachi, his bitterness."

"Who was it who took the post from him, years ago?"

"That I don't know: he always talks about it vaguely, and anyway it's ancient history. They must all be dead now. But the group of Italians around Alinardo speaks often ... spoke often of Malachi as a straw man ... put

here by someone else, with the complicity of the abbot....
Not realizing it, I...I have become involved in the
conflict of the two hostile factions....I became aware
of it only this morning....Italy is a land of conspiracies:
they poison popes here, so just imagine a poor boy like
me....Yesterday I hadn't understood, I believed that
book was responsible for everything, but now I'm no
longer sure. That was the pretext: you've seen that the
book was found but Malachi died all the same....I
must...I want to...I would like to run away. What do
you advise me to do?"

"Stay calm. Now you ask advice, do you? Yesterday
evening you seemed ruler of the world. Silly youth, if
you had helped me yesterday we would have prevented
this last crime. You are the one who gave Malachi the
book that brought him to his death. But tell me one
thing at least. Did you have that book in your hands,
did you touch it, read it? Then why are you not dead?"

"I don't know. I swear I didn't touch it; or, rather, I
touched it when I took it in the laboratory but without
opening it; I hid it inside my habit, then went and put
it under the pallet in my cell. I knew Malachi was
watching me, so I came back at once to the scriptorium.
And afterward, when Malachi offered to make me his
assistant, I gave him the book. That's the whole story."

"Don't tell me you didn't even open it."

"Yes, I did open it before hiding it, to make sure it
really was the one you were also looking for. It began
with an Arabic manuscript, then I believe one in Syriac,
then there was a Latin text, and finally one in Greek...."

I remembered the abbreviations we had seen in the
catalogue. The first two titles were listed as "ar." and
"syr." It was *the book!* But William persisted: "You touched
it and you are not dead. So touching it does not kill.
And what can you tell me about the Greek text? Did
you look at it?"

"Very briefly. Just long enough to realize it had no
title; it began as if a part were missing...."

"Liber acephalus..." William murmured.

"I tried to read the first page, but the truth is that my Greek is very poor. And then my curiosity was aroused by another detail, connected with those same pages in Greek. I did not leaf through all of them, because I was unable to. The pages were—how can I explain?—damp, stuck together. It was hard to separate one from the other. Because the parchment was odd...softer than other parchments, and the first page was rotten, and almost crumbling. It was...well, strange."

"'Strange': the very word Severinus used," William said.

"The parchment did not seem like parchment....It seemed like cloth, but very fine..." Benno went on.

"Charta lintea, or linen paper," William said. "Had you never seen it?"

"I had heard of it, but I don't believe I ever saw it before. It is said to be very costly, and delicate. That's why it is rarely used. The Arabs make it, don't they?"

"They were the first. But it is also made here in Italy, at Fabriano. And also...Why, of course, naturally!" William's eyes shone. "What a beautiful and interesting revelation! Good for you, Benno! I thank you! Yes, I imagine that here in the library charta lintea must be rare, because no very recent manuscripts have arrived. And besides, many are afraid linen paper will not survive through the centuries like parchment, and perhaps that is true. Let us imagine, if they wanted something here that was not more perennial than bronze ...Charta lintea, then? Very well. Good-bye. And don't worry. You're in no danger."

We went away from the scriptorium, leaving Benno calmer, if not totally reassured.

The abbot was in the refectory. William went to him and asked to speak with him. Abo, unable to temporize, agreed to meet us in a short while at his house.

Nones

In which the abbot refuses to listen to William, discourses on the language of gems, and expresses a wish that there be no further investigation of the recent unhappy events.

The abbot's apartments were over the chapter hall, and from the window of the large and sumptuous main room, where he received us, you could see, on that clear and windy day, beyond the roof of the abbatial church, the massive Aedificium.

The abbot, standing at the window, was in fact contemplating it, and he pointed it out to us with a solemn gesture.

"An admirable fortress," he said, "whose proportions sum up the golden rule that governed the construction of the ark. Divided into three stories, because three is the number of the Trinity, three were the angels who visited Abraham, the days Jonah spent in the belly of the great fish, and the days Jesus and Lazarus passed in the sepulcher; three times Christ asked the Father to let the bitter chalice pass from him, and three times he hid himself to pray with the apostles. Three times Peter denied him, and three times Christ appeared to his disciples after the Resurrection. The theological virtues are three, and three are the holy languages, the parts of the soul, the classes of intellectual creatures, angels, men, and devils; there are three kinds of sound—vox, flatus, pulsus—and three epochs of human history, before, during, and after the law."

"A wondrous harmony of mystical relations," William agreed.

"But the square shape also," the abbot continued, "is rich in spiritual lessons. The cardinal points are four, and the seasons, the elements, and heat, cold, wet, and dry; birth, growth, maturity, and old age; the species of animals, celestial, terrestrial, aerial, and aquatic; the colors forming the rainbow; and the number of years required to make a leap year."

"Oh, to be sure," William said, "and three plus four is seven, a superlatively mystical number, whereas three multiplied by four makes twelve, like the apostles, and twelve by twelve makes one hundred forty-four, which is the number of the elect." And to this last display of mystical knowledge of the ideal world of numbers, the abbot had nothing further to add. Thus William could come to the point.

"We must talk about the latest events, on which I have reflected at length," he said.

The abbot turned his back to the window and looked straight at William with a stern face. "At too-great length, perhaps. I must confess, Brother William, that I expected more of you. Almost six days have passed since you arrived here; four monks have died besides Adelmo, two have been arrested by the Inquisition—it was justice, to be sure, but we could have avoided this shame if the inquisitor had not been obliged to concern himself with the previous crimes—and finally the meeting over which I presided has—precisely because of all these wicked deeds—had a pitiful outcome...."

William remained silent, embarrassed. Without question, the abbot was right.

"That is true," he admitted. "I have not lived up to your expectations, but I will explain why, Your Sublimity. These crimes do not stem from a brawl or from some vendetta among the monks, but from deeds that, in their turn, originate in the remote history of the abbey...."

The abbot looked at him uneasily. "What do you mean? I myself realize that the key is not that miserable affair of the cellarer, which has intersected another story. But the other, that other which I may know but cannot discuss... I hoped it was clear, and that you would speak to me about it...."

"Your Sublimity is thinking of some deed he learned about in confession...." The abbot looked away, and William continued: "If Your Magnificence wants to know whether I know, without having learned it from Your Magnificence, that there were illicit relations between Berengar and Adelmo, and between Berengar and Malachi, well, yes, everyone in the abbey knows this...."

The abbot blushed violently. "I do not believe it useful to speak of such things in the presence of this novice. And I do not believe, now that the meeting is over, that you need him any longer as scribe. Go, boy," he said to me imperiously. Humiliated, I went. But in my curiosity I crouched outside the door of the hall, which I left ajar, so that I could follow the dialogue.

William resumed speaking: "So, then, these illicit relations, if they did take place, had scant influence on the painful events. The key is elsewhere, as I thought you imagined. Everything turns on the theft and possession of a book, which was concealed in the finis Africae, and which is now there again thanks to Malachi's intervention, though, as you have seen, the sequence of crimes was not thereby arrested."

A long silence followed; then the abbot resumed speaking, in a broken, hesitant voice, like someone taken aback by unexpected revelations. "This is impossible... you... How do you know about the finis

Africae? Have you violated my ban and entered the library?"

William ought to have told the truth, but the abbot's rage would have known no bounds. Yet, obviously my master did not want to lie. He chose to answer the question with another question: "Did Your Magnificence not say to me, at our first meeting, that a man like me, who had described Brunellus so well without ever having seen him, would have no difficulty picturing places to which he did not have access?"

"So that is it," Abo said. "But why do you think what you think?"

"How I arrived at my conclusion is too long a story. But a series of crimes was committed to prevent many from discovering something that it was considered undesirable for them to discover. Now all those who knew something of the library's secrets, whether rightly or through trickery, are dead. Only one person remains: yourself."

"Do you wish to insinuate . . . you wish to insinuate . . ." the abbot said.

"Do not misunderstand me," said William, who probably had indeed wished to insinuate. "I say there is someone who knows and wants no one else to know. As the last to know, you could be the next victim. Unless you tell me what you know about that forbidden book, and, especially, who in the abbey might know what you know, and perhaps more, about the library."

"It is cold in here," the abbot said. "Let us go out."

I moved rapidly away from the door and waited for them at the head of the stairs. The abbot saw me and smiled at me.

"How many upsetting things this young monk must have heard in the past few days! Come, boy, do not allow yourself to be too distressed. It seems to me that more plots have been imagined than really exist. . . ."

He raised one hand and allowed the daylight to illuminate a splendid ring he wore on his fourth finger, the emblem of his power. The ring sparkled with all the brilliance of its stones.

"You recognize it, do you not?" he said to me. "The symbol of my authority, but also of my burden. It is not an ornament: it is a splendid syllogy of the divine word whose guardian I am." With his fingers he touched the stone—or, rather, the arrangement of variegated stones composing that admirable masterpiece of human art and nature. "This is amethyst," he said, "which is the mirror of humility and reminds us of the ingenuousness and sweetness of Saint Matthew; this is chalcedony, mark of charity, symbol of the piety of Joseph and Saint James the Greater; this is jasper, which bespeaks faith and is associated with Saint Peter; and sardonyx, sign of martyrdom, which recalls Saint Bartholomew; this is sapphire, hope and contemplation, the stone of Saint Andrew and Saint Paul; and beryl, sound doctrine, learning, and longanimity, the virtues of Saint Thomas…. How splendid the language of gems is," he went on, lost in his mystical vision, "which the lapidaries of tradition have translated from the reasoning of Aaron and the description of the heavenly Jerusalem in the book of the apostle. For that matter, the walls of Zion were decked with the same jewels that decorated the pectoral of Moses's brother, except for carbuncle, agate, and onyx, which, mentioned in Exodus, are replaced in the Apocalypse by chalcedony, sardonyx, chrysoprase, and jacinth."

He moved the ring and dazzled my eyes with its sparkling, as if he wanted to stun me. "Marvelous language, is it not? For other fathers stones signify still other things. For Pope Innocent the Third the ruby announced calm and patience; the garnet, charity. For Saint Bruno aquamarine concentrates theological learning in the virtue of its purest rays. Turquoise signifies joy; sardonyx suggests the seraphim; topaz, the cherubim; jasper, thrones; chrysolite, dominions; sapphire, the virtues; onyx, the powers; beryl, principalities; ruby, archangels; and emerald, angels. The language of gems is multiform; each expresses several truths, according to the sense of the selected interpretation, according to the context in which they appear. And who decides what is the level of interpretation and what is the proper context? You know, my boy, for they have taught you: it is authority, the most reliable commentator of all and the most invested with prestige, and therefore with sanctity. Otherwise how to interpret the multiple signs that the world sets before our sinner's eyes, how to avoid the misunderstandings into which the Devil lures us? Mind you: it is extraordinary how the Devil hates the language of gems, as Saint Hildegard testifies. The foul beast sees in it a message illuminated by different meanings or levels of knowledge, and he would like to destroy it because he, the Enemy, senses in the splendor of stones the echo of the marvels in his possession before his fall, and he understands that this radiance is produced by fire, which is his torment." He held out the ring for me to kiss, and I knelt. He stroked my head. "And so, boy, you must forget the things, no doubt erroneous, that you have heard these days. You have entered the noblest, the greatest order of all; of this order I am an abbot, and you are under my jurisdiction. Hear my command: forget, and may your lips be sealed forever. Swear."

Moved, subjugated, I would certainly have sworn. And you, my good reader, would not be able now to read this faithful chronicle of mine. But at this point William intervened, not perhaps to prevent me from swearing, but in an instinctive reaction, out of irritation, to interrupt the abbot, to break that spell he had surely cast.

"What does the boy have to do with it? I asked you a question, I warned you of a danger, I asked you to tell me a name.... Do you now wish me, too, to kiss the ring and swear to forget what I have learned or what I suspect?"

"Ah, you..." the abbot said sadly, "I do not expect a mendicant friar to understand the beauty of our traditions, or respect the reticence, the secrets, the mysteries of charity... yes, charity, and the sense of honor, and the vow of silence on which our greatness is based.... You have spoken to me of a strange story, an incredible story. About a banned book that has caused a chain of murders, about someone who knows what only I should know... Tales, meaningless accusations. Speak of it, if you wish: no one will believe you. And even if some element of your fanciful reconstruction were true ...well, now everything is once more under my control, my jurisdiction. I will look into this, I have the means, I have the authority. At the very beginning I made a mistake, asking an outsider, however wise, however worthy of trust, to investigate things that are my responsibility alone. But you understood, as you have told me; I believed at the outset that it involved a violation of the vow of chastity, and (imprudent as I was) I wanted someone else to tell me what I had heard in confession. Well, now you have told me. I am very grateful to you for what you have done or have tried to do. The meeting of the legations has taken place, your mission here is over. I imagine you are anxiously awaited at the imperial court; one does not deprive oneself at length of a man like you. I give you permission to leave the abbey. Today it is perhaps late: I do not want you to travel after sunset, for the roads are not safe. You will leave tomorrow morning, early. Oh, do not thank me, it has been a joy to have you here, a brother among brothers, honoring you with our hospitality. You may withdraw now with your novice to prepare your baggage. I will say good-bye to you again tomorrow at dawn. I thank you, with all my heart. Naturally, it is not necessary for you to continue your investigations. Do not disturb the monks further. You may go."

It was more than a dismissal, it was an expulsion. William said good-bye and we went down the stairs.

"What does this mean?" I asked. I no longer understood anything.

"Try to formulate a hypothesis. You must have learned how it is done."

"Actually, I have learned I must formulate at least two, one in opposition to the other, and both incredible. Very well, then..." I gulped: formulating hypotheses made me nervous. "First hypothesis: the abbot knew everything already and imagined you would discover nothing. Second hypothesis: the abbot never suspected anything (about what I don't know, because I don't know what's in your mind). But, anyhow, he went on thinking it was all because of a quarrel between...between sodomite monks.... Now, however, you have opened his eyes, he has suddenly understood something terrible, has thought of a name, has a precise idea about who is responsible for the crimes. But at this point he wants to resolve the matter by himself and wants to be rid of you, in order to save the honor of the abbey."

"Good work. You are beginning to reason well. But you see already that in both cases our abbot is concerned for the good name of his monastery. Murderer or next victim as he may be, he does not want defamatory news about this holy community to travel beyond these mountains. Kill his monks, but do not touch the honor of his abbey. Ah, by..." William was now becoming infuriated. "That bastard of a feudal lord, that peacock who gained fame for having been the Aquinas's gravedigger, that inflated wineskin who exists only because he wears a ring as big as the bottom of a glass! Proud, proud, all of you Cluniacs, worse than princes, more baronial than barons!"

"Master..." I ventured, hurt, in a reproachful tone.

"You be quiet, you are made of the same stuff. Your band are not simple men, or sons of the simple. If a peasant comes along you may receive him, but as I saw yesterday, you do not hesitate to hand him over to the secular arm. But not one of your own, no; he must be shielded. Abo is capable of identifying the wretch, stabbing him in the treasure crypt, and passing out his kidneys among the reliquaries, provided the honor of the abbey is saved.... Have a Franciscan, a plebeian Minorite, discover the rat's nest of this holy house? Ah, no, this is something Abo cannot allow at any price. Thank you, Brother William, the Emperor needs you, you see what a beautiful ring I have, good-bye. But now the challenge is not just a matter between me and Abo, it is between me and the whole business: I am not leaving these walls until I have found out. He wants me to leave tomorrow morning, does he? Very well, it's his house; but by tomorrow morning I must know. I must."

"You must? Who obliges you now?"

"No one ever obliges us to know, Adso. We must, that is all, even if we comprehend imperfectly."

I was still confused and humiliated by William's words against my order and its abbots. And I tried to justify Abo in part, formulating a third hypothesis, exercising a skill at which, it seemed to me, I was becoming very dextrous. "You have not considered a third possibility, master," I said. "We had noticed these past days, and this morning it seemed quite clear to us after Nicholas's confidences and the rumors we heard in church, that there is a group of Italian monks reluctant to tolerate the succession of foreign librarians; they accuse the abbot of not respecting tradition, and, as I understand it, they hide behind old Alinardo, thrusting him forward like a standard, to ask for a different government of the abbey. So perhaps the abbot fears our revelations could give his enemies a weapon, and he wants to settle the question with great prudence...."

"That is possible. But he is still an inflated wineskin, and he will get himself killed."

We were in the cloister. The wind was growing angrier all the time, the light dimmer, even if it was just past nones. The day was approaching its sunset, and we had very little time left.

"It is late," William said, "and when a man has little time, he must take care to maintain his calm. We must act as if we had eternity before us. I have a problem to solve: how to penetrate the finis Africae, because the final answer must be there. Then we must save some person, I have not yet determined which. Finally, we should expect something from the direction of the stables, which you will keep an eye on.... Look at all the bustle...."

In fact, the space between the Aedificium and the cloister was unusually animated. A moment before, a novice, coming from the abbot's house, had run toward the Aedificium. Now Nicholas was coming out of it, heading for the dormitories. In one corner, that morning's group, Pacificus, Aymaro, and Peter, were deep in discussion with Alinardo, as if trying to convince him of something.

Then they seemed to reach a decision. Aymaro supported the still-reluctant Alinardo, and went with him toward the abbatial residence. They were just entering as Nicholas came out of the dormitory, leading Jorge in the same direction. Seeing the two Italians enter, he whispered something into Jorge's ear, and the old man shook his head. They continued, however, toward the chapter house.

"The abbot is taking the situation in hand..." William murmured skeptically. From the Aedificium were emerging more monks, who belonged in the scriptorium, and they were immediately followed by Benno, who came toward us, more worried than ever.

"There is unrest in the scriptorium," he told us. "Nobody is working, they are all talking among themselves.... What is happening?"

"What's happening is that the people who until this morning seemed the most suspect are all dead. Until yesterday everyone was on guard against Berengar, foolish and treacherous and lascivious, then the cellarer, a suspect heretic, and finally Malachi, so generally disliked. . . . Now they don't know whom to be on guard against, and they urgently need to find an enemy, or a scapegoat. And each suspects the others; some are afraid, like you; others have decided to frighten someone else. You are all too agitated. Adso, take a look at the stables every now and then. I am going to get some rest."

I should have been amazed: to go and rest when he had only a few hours left did not seem the wisest decision. But by now I knew my master. The more relaxed his body, the more ebullient his mind.

BETWEEN VESPERS AND COMPLINE

In which long hours of bewilderment are briefly narrated.

It is difficult for me to narrate what happened in the hours that followed, between vespers and compline.

William was absent. I roamed around the stables but noticed nothing abnormal. The grooms were bringing in the animals, made nervous by the wind; otherwise all was calm.

I entered the church. Everyone was already in his place among the stalls, but the abbot noticed Jorge was absent. With a gesture he delayed the beginning of the office. He called for Benno, to dispatch him to look for the old man, but Benno was not there. Someone pointed out that he was probably making the scriptorium ready for its evening closing. The abbot, annoyed, said it had been decided that Benno would close nothing because he did not know the rules. Aymaro of Alessandria rose from his stall: "If Your Paternity agrees, I will go and summon him...."

"No one asked anything of you," the abbot said curtly, and Aymaro sat back down in his place, not without casting an inscrutable glance at Pacificus of Tivoli. The abbot called for Nicholas, who was not present. Someone reminded him that Nicholas was preparing supper, and the abbot made a gesture of annoyance, as if he were displeased to reveal to all that he was upset.

"I want Jorge here," he cried. "Find him! You go!" he ordered the master of novices.

Another pointed out to him that Alinardo was also missing. "I know," the abbot said, "he is not well." I was near Peter of Sant'Albano and heard him say to his neighbor, Gunzo of Nola, in a vulgar dialect from central Italy which I partly understood, "I should think so. Today, when he came out after the colloquy, the poor old man was distraught. Abo behaves like the whore of Avignon!"

The novices were bewildered; with their innocent, boyish sensitivity they felt the tension reigning in choir, as I felt it. Long moments of silence and embarrassment ensued. The abbot ordered some psalms to be recited and he picked at random three that were not prescribed for vespers by the Rule. All looked at one another, then began praying in low voices. The novice master came back, followed by Benno, who took his seat, his head bowed. Jorge was not in the scriptorium or in his cell. The abbot commanded that the office begin.

When it was over, before everyone headed for supper, I went to call William. He was stretched out on his pallet, dressed, motionless. He said he had not realized it was so late. I told him briefly what had happened. He shook his head.

At the door of the refectory we saw Nicholas, who a few hours earlier had been accompanying Jorge. William asked him whether the old man had gone in immediately to see the abbot. Nicholas said Jorge had had to wait a long time outside the door, because Alinardo and Aymaro of Alessandria were in the hall. After Jorge was received, he remained inside for some time, while Nicholas waited for him. Then he came out and asked Nicholas to accompany him to the church, still deserted an hour before vespers.

The abbot saw us talking with the cellarer. "Brother William," he admonished, "are you still investigating?" He bade William sit at his table, as usual. For Benedictines hospitality is sacred.

The supper was more silent than usual, and sad. The abbot ate listlessly, oppressed by grim thoughts. At the end he told the monks to hurry to compline.

Alinardo and Jorge were still absent. The monks pointed to the blind man's empty place and whispered. When the office was finished, the abbot asked all to say a special prayer for the health of Jorge of Burgos. It was not clear whether he meant physical health or eternal health. All understood that a new calamity was about to befall the community. Then the abbot ordered each monk to hurry, with greater alacrity than usual, to his own pallet. He commanded that no one, and he emphasized the words "no one," should remain in circulation outside the dormitory. The frightened novices were the first to leave, cowls over their faces, heads bowed, without exchanging the remarks, the nudges, the flashing smiles, the sly and concealed trippings with which they usually provoked one another (for novices, though young monks, are still boys, and the reproaches of their master are of little avail in preventing them all from behaving like boys, as their tender age demands).

When the adults filed out, I fell into line, unobtrusively, behind the group that by now had been characterized to me as "the Italians." Pacificus was murmuring to Aymaro, "Do you really believe Abo doesn't know where Jorge is?" And Aymaro answered, "He might know, and know that from where Jorge is he will never return. Perhaps the old man wanted too much, and Abo no longer wants him...."

As William and I pretended to retire to the pilgrims'

hospice, we glimpsed the abbot re-entering the Aedificium through the still-open door of the refectory. William advised waiting a while; once the grounds were empty of every presence, he told me to follow him. We rapidly crossed the empty area and entered the church.

AFTER COMPLINE

*In which, almost by chance, William discovers
the secret of entering the finis Africae.*

Like a pair of assassins, we lurked near the entrance,
behind a column, whence we could observe the chapel
with the skulls.

"Abo has gone to close the Aedificium," William said.
"When he has barred the doors from the inside, he can
only come out through the ossarium."

"And then?"

"And then we will see what he does."

We did not discover what he did. An hour went by
and he still had not reappeared. He's gone into the
finis Africae, I said. Perhaps, William answered. Eager
to formulate more hypotheses, I added: Perhaps he
came out again through the refectory and has gone to
look for Jorge. And William answered: That is also
possible. Perhaps Jorge is already dead, I imagined
further. Perhaps he is in the Aedificium and is killing
the abbot. Perhaps they are both in some other place
and some other person is lying in wait for them. What
did "the Italians" want? And why was Benno so

frightened? Was it perhaps only a mask he had assumed, to mislead us? Why had he lingered in the scriptorium during vespers, if he didn't know how to close the scriptorium or how to get out? Did he want to essay the passages of the labyrinth?

"All is possible," William said. "But only one thing is happening, or has happened, or is about to happen. And at last divine Providence is endowing us with a radiant certitude."

"What is that?" I asked, full of hope.

"That Brother William of Baskerville, who now has the impression of having understood everything, does not know how to enter the finis Africae. To the stables, Adso, to the stables."

"And what if the abbot finds us?"

"We will pretend to be a pair of ghosts."

To me this did not seem a practical solution, but I kept silent. William was growing uneasy. We came out of the north door and crossed the cemetery, while the wind was whistling loudly and I begged the Lord not to make us encounter two ghosts, for the abbey, on that night, did not lack for souls in torment. We reached the stables and heard the horses, more nervous than ever because of the fury of the elements. The main door of the building had, at the level of a man's chest, a broad metal grating, through which the interior could be seen. In the darkness we discerned the forms of the horses. I recognized Brunellus, the first on the left. To his right, the third animal in line raised his head, sensing our presence, and whinnied. I smiled. "Tertius equi," I said.

"What?" William asked.

"Nothing. I was remembering poor Salvatore. He wanted to perform God knows what magic with that horse, and with his Latin he called him 'tertius equi.' Which would be the *u*."

"The *u*?" asked William, who had heard my prattle without paying much attention to it.

"Yes, because 'tertius equi' does not mean the third horse, but the third of the horse, and the third letter of the word 'equus' is *u*. But this is all nonsense...."

William looked at me, and in the darkness I seemed to see his face transformed. "God bless you, Adso!" he said to me. "Why, of course, suppositio materialis, the discourse is presumed de dicto and not de re.... What a fool I am!" He gave himself such a great blow on the forehead that I heard a clap, and I believe he hurt himself. "My boy, this is the second time today that wisdom has spoken through your mouth, first in dream and now waking! Run, run to your cell and fetch the lamp, or, rather, both the lamps we hid. Let no one see you, and join me in church at once! Ask no questions! Go!"

I asked no questions and went. The lamps were under my bed, already filled with oil, and I had taken care to trim them in advance. I had the flint in my habit. With the two precious instruments clutched to my chest, I ran into the church.

William was under the tripod and was rereading the parchment with Venantius's notes.

"Adso," he said to me, " 'primum et septimum de quatuor' does not mean the first and seventh of four, but of *the* four, the word 'four'!" For a moment I still did not understand, but then I was enlightened: "Super thronos viginti quatuor! The writing! The verse! The words are carved over the mirror!"

"Come," William said, "perhaps we are still in time to save a life!"

"Whose?" I asked, as he was manipulating the skulls and opening the passage to the ossarium.

"The life of someone who does not deserve it," he said. We were already in the underground passage, our lamps alight, moving toward the door that led to the kitchen.

I said before that at this point you pushed a wooden door and found yourself in the kitchen, behind the fireplace, at the foot of the circular staircase that led to the scriptorium. And just as we were pushing that door, we heard to our left some muffled sounds within the wall. They came from the wall beside the door, where the row of niches with skulls and bones ended. Instead of a last niche, there was a stretch of blank wall of large squared blocks of stone, with an old plaque in the center that had some worn monograms carved on it. The sounds came, it seemed, from behind the plaque, or else from above the plaque, partly beyond the wall, and partly almost over our heads.

If something of the sort had happened the first night, I would immediately have thought of dead monks. But by now I tended to expect worse from living monks. "Who can that be?" I asked.

William opened the door and emerged behind the fireplace. The blows were heard also along the wall that flanked the stairs, as if someone were prisoner inside the wall, or else in that thickness (truly vast) that presumably existed between the inner wall of the kitchen and the outer wall of the south tower.

"Someone is shut up inside there," William said. "I have wondered all along whether there were not another access to the finis Africae, in this Aedificium so full of passages. Obviously there is. From the ossarium, before you come up into the kitchen, a stretch of wall opens, and you climb up a staircase parallel to this, concealed in the wall, which leads right to the blind room."

"But who is in there?"

"The second person. One is in the finis Africae, another has tried to reach him, but the one above must have blocked the mechanism that controls the entrances. So the visitor is trapped. And he is making a great stir because, I imagine, there cannot be much air in that narrow space."

"Who is it? We must save him!"

"We shall soon know who it is. And as for saving him,

that can only be done by releasing the mechanism from above: we don't know the secret at this end. Let's hurry upstairs."

So we went up to the scriptorium, and from there to the labyrinth, and we quickly reached the south tower. Twice I had to curb my haste, because the wind that came through the slits that night created currents that, penetrating those passages, blew moaning through the rooms, rustling the scattered pages on the desks, so that I had to shield the flame with my hand.

Soon we were in the mirror room, this time prepared for the game of distortion awaiting us. We raised the lamps to illuminate the verse that surmounted the frame. Super thronos viginti quatuor . . . At this point the secret was quite clear: the word "quatuor" has seven letters, and we had to press on the *q* and the *r*. I thought, in my excitement, to do it myself: I rapidly set the lamp down on the table in the center of the room. But I did this nervously, and the flame began to lick the binding of a book also set there.

"Watch out, idiot!" William cried, and with a puff blew out the flame. "You want to set fire to the library?"

I apologized and started to light the lamp again. "It doesn't matter," William said, "mine is enough. Take it and give me light, because the legend is too high and you couldn't reach it. We must hurry."

"And what if there is somebody armed in there?" I asked, as William, almost groping, sought the fatal letters, standing on tiptoe, tall as he was, to touch the apocalyptic verse.

"Give me light, by the Devil, and never fear: God is with us!" he answered me, somewhat incoherently. His fingers were touching the *q* of "quatuor," and, standing a few paces back, I saw better than he what he was doing. I have already said that the letters of the verses seemed carved or incised in the wall: apparently those of the word "quatuor" were metal outlines, behind which a wondrous mechanism had been placed and walled up. When it was pushed forward, the *q* made a kind of sharp click, and the same thing happened when William pressed on the *r*. The whole frame of the mirror seemed to shudder, and the glass surface snapped back. The mirror was a door, hinged on its left side. William slipped his hand into the opening now created between the right edge and the wall, and pulled toward himself. Creaking, the door opened out, in our direction. William slipped through the opening and I scuttled behind him, the lamp high over my head.

Two hours after compline, at the end of the sixth day, in the heart of the night that was giving birth to the seventh day, we entered the finis Africae.

SEVENTH DAY

NIGHT

In which, if it were to summarize the prodigious revelations of which it speaks, the title would have to be as long as the chapter itself, contrary to usage.

We found ourselves on the threshold of a room similar in shape to the other three heptagonal blind rooms, dominated by a strong musty odor, as of mildewed books. The lamp, which I held up high, first illuminated the vault; then, as I moved my arm downward, to right and left, the flame cast a vague light on the distant shelves along the walls. Finally, in the center, we saw a table covered with papers, and behind the table a seated figure, who seemed to be waiting for us in the darkness, immobile, if he was still alive. Even before the light revealed his face, William spoke.

"Happy night, venerable Jorge," he said. "Were you waiting for us?"

The lamp now, once we had taken a few steps forward, illuminated the face of the old man, looking at us as if he could see.

"Is that you, William of Baskerville?" he asked. "I have been waiting for you since this afternoon before

563

vespers, when I came and closed myself in here. I knew you would arrive."

"And the abbot?" William asked. "Is he the one making that noise in the secret stairway?"

Jorge hesitated for a moment. "Is he still alive?" he asked. "I thought he would already have suffocated."

"Before we start talking," William said, "I would like to save him. You can open from this side."

"No," Jorge said wearily, "not any longer. The mechanism is controlled from below, by pressing on the plaque, and up here a lever snaps, which opens a door back there, behind that case." He nodded over his shoulder. "Next to the case you could see a wheel with some counterweights, which controls the mechanism from up here. But when I heard the wheel turning, a sign that Abo had entered down below, I yanked at the rope that holds the weights, and the rope broke. Now the passage is closed on both sides, and you could never repair that device. The abbot is dead."

"Why did you kill him?"

"Today, when he sent for me, he told me that thanks to you he had discovered everything. He did not yet know what I had been trying to protect—he has never precisely understood the treasures and the ends of the library. He asked me to explain what he did not know. He wanted the finis Africae to be opened. The Italians had asked him to put an end to what they call the mystery kept alive by me and my predecessors. They are driven by the lust for new things...."

"And you no doubt promised him you would come here and put an end to your life as you had put an end to the lives of the others, in such a way that the abbey's honor would be saved and no one would know anything. Then you told him the way to come, later, and check. But instead you waited for him, to kill him. Didn't you think he might enter through the mirror?"

"No, Abo is too short; he would never have been able to reach the verse by himself. I told him about the other passage, which I alone still knew. It is the one I used for so many years, because it was simpler in the darkness. I had only to reach the chapel, then follow the bones of the dead to the end of the passage."

"So you had him come here, knowing you would kill him...."

"I could no longer trust him. He was frightened. He had become famous because at Fossanova he managed to get a body down some circular stairs. Undeserved glory. Now he is dead because he was unable to climb his own stairway."

"You have been using it for forty years. When you realized you were going blind and would no longer be able to control the library, you acted shrewdly. You had a man you could trust elected abbot; and as librarian you first had him name Robert of Bobbio, whom you could direct as you liked, and then Malachi, who needed your help and never took a step without consulting you. For forty years you have been master of this abbey. This is what the Italian group realized, this is what Alinardo kept repeating, but no one would listen to him because they considered him mad by now. Am I right? But you were still awaiting me, and you couldn't block the mirror entrance, because the mechanism is set in the wall. Why were you waiting for me? How could you be sure I would arrive?" William asked, but from his tone it was clear he had already guessed the answer and was expecting it as a reward for his own skill.

"From the first day I realized you would understand. From your voice, from the way you drew me to debate on a subject I did not want mentioned. You were better than the others: you would have arrived at the solution no matter what. You know that it suffices to think and to reconstruct in one's own mind the thoughts of the other. And then I heard you were asking the other monks questions, all of them the right ones. But you never asked questions about the library, as if you already knew its every secret. One night I came and knocked at your cell, and you were not in. You had to be here. Two lamps had disappeared from the kitchen, I heard a servant say. And finally, when Severinus came to talk to you about a book the other day in the narthex, I was sure you were on my trail."

"But you managed to get the book away from me. You went to Malachi, who had had no idea of the situation. In his jealousy, the fool was still obsessed with the idea that Adelmo had stolen his beloved Berengar, who by then craved younger flesh. Malachi didn't understand what Venantius had to do with this business, and you confused his thinking even further. You probably told him Berengar had been intimate with Severinus, and as a reward Severinus had given him a book from the finis Africae; I don't know exactly what you told him. Crazed with jealousy, Malachi went to Severinus and killed him. Then he didn't have time to hunt for the book you had described to him, because the cellarer arrived. Is that what happened?"

"More or less."

"But you didn't want Malachi to die. He had probably never looked at the books of the finis Africae, for he trusted you, respected your prohibitions. He confined himself to arranging the herbs at evening to frighten any intruders. Severinus supplied him with them. This is why Severinus let Malachi enter the infirmary the other day: it was his regular visit to collect the fresh herbs he prepared daily, by the abbot's order. Have I guessed?"

"You have guessed. I did not want Malachi to die. I told him to find the book again, by whatever means, and bring it back here without opening it. I told him it had the power of a thousand scorpions. But for the first time the madman chose to act on his own initiative. I did not want him to die: he was a faithful agent. But do not repeat to me what you know: I know that you know. I do not want to feed your pride; you already see to that on your own. I heard you this morning in the scriptorium questioning Benno about the *Coena Cypriani*. You were very close to the truth. I do not know how you discovered the secret of the mirror, but when I learned from the abbot that you had mentioned the finis Africae, I was sure you would come shortly. This is why I was waiting for you. So, now, what do you want?"

"I want," William said, "to see the last manuscript of the bound volume that contains an Arabic text, a Syriac one, and an interpretation or a transcription of the *Coena Cypriani*. I want to see that copy in Greek, made perhaps by an Arab, or by a Spaniard, that you found when, as assistant to Paul of Rimini, you arranged to be sent back to your country to collect the finest manuscripts of the Apocalypse in León and Castile, a booty that made you famous and respected here in the abbey and caused you to win the post of librarian, which rightfully belonged to Alinardo, ten years your senior. I want to see that Greek copy written on linen paper, which was then very rare and was manufactured in Silos, near Burgos, your home. I want to see the book you stole there after reading it, to keep others from reading it, and you hid it here, protecting it cleverly, and you did not destroy it because a man like you does not destroy a book, but simply guards it and makes sure no one touches it. I want to see the second book of the *Poetics* of Aristotle, the book everyone has believed lost or never written, and of which you hold perhaps the only copy."

"What a magnificent librarian you would have been, William," Jorge said, with a tone at once admiring and regretful. "So you know everything. Come, I believe there is a stool on your side of the table. Sit. Here is your prize."

William sat and put down the lamp, which I had handed him, illuminating Jorge's face from below. The old man took a volume that lay before him and passed it to William. I recognized the binding: it was the book I had opened in the infirmary, thinking it an Arabic manuscript.

"Read it, then, leaf through it, William," Jorge said. "You have won."

William looked at the volume but did not touch it. From his habit he took a pair of gloves, not his usual mitts with the fingertips exposed, but the ones Severinus was wearing when we found him dead. Slowly he opened the worn and fragile binding. I came closer and bent over his shoulder. Jorge, with his sensitive hearing, caught the noise I made. "Are you here, too, boy?" he said. "I will show it to you, too...afterward."

William rapidly glanced over the first pages. "It is an Arabic manuscript on the sayings of some fool, according to the catalogue," he said. "What is it?"

"Oh, silly legends of the infidels, which hold that fools utter clever remarks that amaze even their priests and delight their caliphs..."

"The second is a Syriac manuscript, but according to the catalogue it is the translation of a little Egyptian book on alchemy. How does it happen to be in this collection?"

"It is an Egyptian work from the third century of our era. Coherent with the work that follows, but less dangerous. No one would lend an ear to the ravings of an African alchemist. He attributes the creation of the world to divine laughter...." He raised his face and recited, with the prodigious memory of a reader who for forty years now had been repeating to himself things read when he still had the gift of sight: "'The moment God laughed seven gods were born who governed the world, the moment he burst out laughing light appeared, at his second laugh appeared water, and on the seventh day of his laughing appeared the soul....' Folly. Likewise the work that comes after, by one of the countless idiots who set themselves to glossing the *Coena*...But these are not what interest you."

William, in fact, had rapidly passed over the pages and had come to the Greek text. I saw immediately that the pages were of a different, softer material, the first almost worn away, with a part of the margin consumed, spattered with pale stains, such as time and dampness usually produce on other books. William read the opening lines, first in Greek, then translating into Latin, and then he continued in this language so that I, too, could learn how the fatal book began:

In the first book we dealt with tragedy and saw how, by arousing pity and fear, it produces catharsis, the purification of those feelings. As we promised, we will now deal with comedy (as well as with satire and mime) and see how, in inspiring the pleasure of the ridiculous, it arrives at the purification of that passion. That such passion is most worthy of consideration we have already said in the book on the soul, inasmuch as—alone among the animals—man is capable of laughter. We will then define the type of actions of which comedy is the mimesis, then we will examine the means by which comedy excites laughter, and these means are actions and speech. We will show how the ridiculousness of actions is born from the likening of the best to the worst and vice versa, from arousing surprise through deceit, from the impossible, from violation of the laws of nature, from the irrelevant and the inconsequent, from the debasing of the characters, from the use of comical and vulgar pantomime, from disharmony, from the choice of the least worthy things. We will then show how the ridiculousness of speech is born from the misunderstandings of similar words for different things and different words for similar things, from garrulity and repetition, from play on words, from diminutives, from errors of pronunciation, and from barbarisms.

William translated with some difficulty, seeking the right words, pausing now and then. As he translated he smiled, as if he recognized things he was expecting to find. He read the first page aloud, then stopped, as if he were not interested in knowing more, and rapidly leafed through the following pages. But after a few pages he encountered resistance, because near the upper corner of the side edge, and along the top, some pages had stuck together, as happens when the damp and deteriorating papery substance forms a kind of sticky paste. Jorge realized that the rustle of pages had ceased, and he urged William on.

"Go on, read it, leaf through it. It is yours, you have earned it."

William laughed, seeming rather amused. "Then it is not true that you consider me so clever, Jorge! You cannot see: I have gloves on. With my fingers made clumsy like this, I cannot detach one page from the next. I should proceed with bare hands, moistening my fingers with my tongue, as I happened to do this morning while reading in the scriptorium, so that suddenly that mystery also became clear to me. And I should go on leafing like that until a good portion of the poison had passed to my mouth. I am speaking of the poison that you, one day long ago, took from the laboratory of Severinus. Perhaps you were already worried then, because you had heard someone in the scriptorium display curiosity, either about the finis Africae or about the lost book of Aristotle, or about both. I believe you kept the ampoule for a long time, planning to use it the moment you sensed danger. And you sensed that days ago, when Venantius came too close to the subject of this book, and at the same time Berengar, heedless, vain, trying to impress Adelmo, showed he was less secretive than you had hoped. So you came and set your trap. Just in time, because a few nights later Venantius got in, stole the book, and avidly leafed through it, with an almost physical voracity. He soon felt ill and ran to seek help in the kitchen. Where he died. Am I mistaken?"

"No. Go on."

"The rest is simple. Berengar finds Venantius's body in the kitchen, fears there will be an inquiry, because, after all, Venantius got into the Aedificium at night thanks to Berengar's prior revelation to Adelmo. He doesn't know what to do; he loads the body on his shoulders and flings it into the jar of blood, thinking everyone will be convinced Venantius drowned."

"And how do you know that was what happened?"

"You know it as well. I saw how you reacted when they found a cloth stained with Berengar's blood. With that cloth the foolhardy man had wiped his hands after putting Venantius in the jar. But since Berengar had disappeared, he could only have disappeared with the book, which by this point had aroused his curiosity, too. And you were expecting him to be found somewhere, not bloodstained but poisoned. The rest is clear. Severinus finds the book, because Berengar went first to the infirmary to read it, safe from indiscreet eyes. Malachi, at your instigation, kills Severinus, then dies himself when he comes back here to discover what was so forbidden about the object that had made him a murderer. And thus we have an explanation for all the corpses. . . . What a fool . . ."

"Who?"

"I. Because of a remark of Alinardo's, I was convinced the series of crimes followed the sequence of the seven trumpets of the Apocalypse. Hail for Adelmo, and his death was a suicide. Blood for Venantius, and there it had been a bizarre notion of Berengar's; water for Berengar himself, and it had been a random act; the third part of the sky for Severinus, and Malachi had struck him with the armillary sphere because it was the only thing he found handy. And finally scorpions for Malachi . . . Why did you tell him that the book had the power of a thousand scorpions?"

"Because of you. Alinardo had told me about his idea, and then I heard from someone that you, too, found it persuasive. . . . I became convinced that a divine plan was directing these deaths, for which I was not responsible. And I told Malachi that if he were to become curious he would perish in accordance with the same divine plan; and, so he did."

"So, then . . . I conceived a false pattern to interpret the moves of the guilty man, and the guilty man fell in with it. And it was this same false pattern that put me on your trail. Everyone nowadays is obsessed with the book of John, but you seemed to me the one who pondered it most, and not so much because of your speculations about the Antichrist as because you came from the country that has produced the most splendid Apocalypses. One day somebody told me it was you who had brought the most beautiful codices of this book to the library. Then, another day, Alinardo was raving about a mysterious enemy who had been sent to seek books in Silos (my curiosity was piqued when he said this enemy had returned prematurely into the realm of darkness: at first it might have seemed the man he was speaking of had died young, but he was referring to your blindness). Silos is near Burgos, and this morning, in the catalogue, I found a series of acquisitions, all of them Spanish Apocalypses, from the period when you had succeeded or were about to succeed Paul of Rimini. And in that group of acquisitions there was this book also. But I couldn't be positive of my reconstruction until I learned that the stolen book was on linen paper. Then I remembered Silos, and I was sure. Naturally, as the idea of this book and its venomous power gradually began to take shape, the idea of an apocalyptic pattern began to collapse, though I couldn't understand how both the book and the sequence of the trumpets pointed to you. But I understood the story of the book better because, directed by the apocalyptic pattern, I was forced more and more to think of you, and your debates about laughter. So that this evening, when I no longer believed in the apocalyptic pattern, I insisted on watching the stables, and in the stables, by pure chance, Adso gave me the key to entering the finis Africae."

"I cannot follow you," Jorge said. "You are proud to show me how, following the dictates of your reason, you arrived at me, and yet you have shown me you arrived here by following a false reasoning. What do you mean to say to me?"

"To you, nothing. I am disconcerted, that is all. But it is of no matter. I am here."

"The Lord was sounding the seven trumpets. And you, even in your error, heard a confused echo of that sound."

"You said this yesterday evening in your sermon. You are trying to convince yourself that this whole story proceeded according to a divine plan, in order to conceal from yourself the fact that you are a murderer."

"I have killed no one. Each died according to his destiny because of his sins. I was only an instrument."

"Yesterday you said that Judas also was an instrument. That does not prevent him from being damned."

"I accept the risk of damnation. The Lord will absolve me, because He knows I acted for His glory. My duty was to protect the library."

"A few minutes ago you were ready to kill me, too, and also this boy. . . ."

"You are subtler, but no better than the others."

"And now what will happen, now that I have eluded the trap?"

"We shall see," Jorge answered. "I do not necessarily want your death; perhaps I will succeed in convincing you. But first tell me: how did you guess it was the second book of Aristotle?"

"Your anathemas against laughter would surely not have been enough for me, or what little I learned about your argument with the others. At first I didn't understand their significance. But there were references to a shameless stone that rolls over the plain, and to cicadas that will sing from the ground, to venerable fig trees. I had already read something of the sort: I verified it during these past few days. These are examples that Aristotle used in the first book of the *Poetics*, and in the *Rhetoric*. Then I remembered that Isidore of Seville defines comedy as something that tells of *stupra virginum et amores meretricum*—how shall I put it?—of less than virtuous loves.... Gradually this second book took shape in my mind as it had to be. I could tell you almost all of it, without reading the pages that were meant to poison me. Comedy is born from the *komai*—that is, from the peasant villages—as a joyous celebration after a meal or a feast. Comedy does not tell of famous and powerful men, but of base and ridiculous creatures, though not wicked; and it does not end with the death of the protagonists. It achieves the effect of the ridiculous by showing the defects and vices of ordinary men. Here Aristotle sees the tendency to laughter as a force for good, which can also have an instructive value: through witty riddles and unexpected metaphors, though it tells us things differently from the way they are, as if it were lying, it actually obliges us to examine them more closely, and it makes us say: Ah, this is just how things are, and I didn't know it. Truth reached by depicting men and the world as worse than they are or than we believe them to be, worse in any case than the epics, the tragedies, lives of the saints have shown them to us. Is that it?"

"Fairly close. You reconstructed it by reading other books?"

"Many of which Venantius was working on. I believe Venantius had been hunting for this book for some time. He must have read in the catalogue the indications I also read, and must have been convinced this was the book he was seeking. But he didn't know how to enter the finis Africae. When he heard Berengar speak of it with Adelmo, then he was off like a dog on the track of a hare."

"That is what happened. I understood at once. I realized the moment had come when I would have to defend the library tooth and nail...."

"And you spread the ointment. It must have been a hard task...in the dark...."

"By now my hands see more than your eyes. I had taken a brush from Severinus, and I also used gloves. It was a good idea, was it not? It took you a long time to arrive at it...."

"Yes. I was thinking of a more complex device, a poisoned pin or something of the sort. I must say that your solution was exemplary: the victim poisoned himself when he was alone, and only to the extent that he wanted to read...."

I realized, with a shudder, that at this moment these two men, arrayed in a mortal conflict, were admiring each other, as if each had acted only to win the other's applause. The thought crossed my mind that the artifices Berengar used to seduce Adelmo, and the simple and natural acts with which the girl had aroused my passion and my desire, were nothing compared with the cleverness and mad skill each used to conquer the other, nothing compared with the act of seduction going on before my eyes at that moment, which had unfolded over seven days, each of the two interlocutors making, as it were, mysterious appointments with the other, each secretly aspiring to the other's approbation, each fearing and hating the other.

"But now tell me," William was saying, "why? Why did you want to shield this book more than so many others? Why did you hide—though not at the price of crime—treatises on necromancy, pages that may have blasphemed against the name of God, while for these pages you damned your brothers and have damned yourself? There are many other books that speak of comedy, many others that praise laughter. Why did this one fill you with such fear?"

"Because it was by the Philosopher. Every book by

that man has destroyed a part of the learning that Christianity had accumulated over the centuries. The fathers had said everything that needed to be known about the power of the Word, but then Boethius had only to gloss the Philosopher and the divine mystery of the Word was transformed into a human parody of categories and syllogism. The book of Genesis says what has to be known about the composition of the cosmos, but it sufficed to rediscover the *Physics* of the Philosopher to have the universe reconceived in terms of dull and slimy matter, and the Arab Averroës almost convinced everyone of the eternity of the world. We knew everything about the divine names, and the Dominican buried by Abo—seduced by the Philosopher— renamed them, following the proud paths of natural reason. And so the cosmos, which for the Areopagite revealed itself to those who knew how to look up at the luminous cascade of the exemplary first cause, has become a preserve of terrestrial evidence for which they refer to an abstract agent. Before, we used to look to heaven, deigning only a frowning glance at the mire of matter; now we look at the earth, and we believe in the heavens because of earthly testimony. Every word of the Philosopher, by whom now even saints and prophets swear, has overturned the image of the world. But he had not succeeded in overturning the image of God. If this book were to become . . . had become an object for open interpretation, we would have crossed the last boundary."

"But what frightened you in this discussion of laughter? You cannot eliminate laughter by eliminating the book."

"No, to be sure. But laughter is weakness, corruption, the foolishness of our flesh. It is the peasant's entertainment, the drunkard's license; even the church in her wisdom has granted the moment of feast, carnival, fair, this diurnal pollution that releases humors and distracts from other desires and other ambitions. . . . Still, laughter remains base, a defense for the simple, a mystery desecrated for the plebeians. The apostle also said as much: it is better to marry than to burn. Rather than rebel against God's established order, laugh and enjoy your foul parodies of order, at the end of the meal, after you have drained jugs and flasks. Elect the king of fools, lose yourselves in the liturgy of the ass and the pig, play at performing your saturnalia head down.... But here, here"—now Jorge struck the table with his finger, near the book William was holding open—"here the function of laughter is reversed, it is elevated to art, the doors of the world of the learned are opened to it, it becomes the object of philosophy, and of perfidious theology.... You saw yesterday how the simple can conceive and carry out the most lurid heresies, disavowing the laws of God and the laws of nature. But the church can deal with the heresy of the simple, who condemn themselves on their own, destroyed by their ignorance. The ignorant madness of Dolcino and his like will never cause a crisis in the divine order. He will preach violence and will die of violence, will leave no trace, will be consumed as carnival is consumed, and it does not matter whether during the feast the epiphany of the world upside down will be produced on earth for a brief time. Provided the act is not transformed into plan, provided this vulgar tongue does not find a Latin that translates it. Laughter frees the villein from fear of the Devil, because in the feast of fools the Devil also appears poor and foolish, and therefore controllable. But this book could teach that freeing oneself of the fear of the Devil is wisdom. When he laughs, as the wine gurgles in his throat, the villein feels he is master, because he has overturned his position with respect to his lord; but this book could teach learned men the clever and, from that moment, illustrious artifices that could legitimatize the reversal. Then what in the villein is still, fortunately, an operation of the belly would be transformed into an operation of the brain. That laughter is proper to man is a sign of our limitation, sinners that we are. But from this book many corrupt minds like yours would draw the extreme syllogism, whereby laughter is man's end! Laughter, for a few moments, distracts the villein from fear. But law is imposed by fear, whose true name is fear of God. This book could strike the Luciferine spark that would set a new fire to the whole world, and laughter would be defined as the new art, unknown even to Prometheus, for canceling fear. To the villein who laughs, at that moment, dying does not matter: but then, when the license is past, the liturgy again imposes on him, according to the divine plan, the fear of death. And from this book there could be born the new destructive aim to destroy death through redemption from fear. And what would we be, we sinful creatures, without fear, perhaps the most foresighted, the most loving of the divine gifts? For centuries the doctors and the fathers have secreted perfumed essences of holy learning to redeem, through the thought of that which is lofty, the wretchedness and temptation of that which is base. And this book—considering comedy a wondrous medicine, with its satire and mime, which would produce the purification of the passions through the enactment of defect, fault, weakness—would induce false scholars to try to redeem the lofty with a diabolical reversal: through the acceptance of the base. This book could prompt the idea that man can wish to have on earth (as your Bacon suggested with regard to natural magic) the abundance of the land of Cockaigne. But this is what we cannot and must not have. Look at the young monks who shamelessly read the parodizing buffoonery of the *Coena Cypriani*. What a diabolical transfiguration of the Holy Scripture! And yet as they read it they know it is evil. But on the day when the Philosopher's word would justify the marginal jests of the debauched imagination, or when what has been marginal would leap to the center, every trace of the center would be lost. The people of God would be

transformed into an assembly of monsters belched forth
from the abysses of the terra incognita, and at that
moment the edge of the known world would become
the heart of the Christian empire, the Arimaspi on the
throne of Peter, Blemmyes in the monasteries, dwarfs
with huge bellies and immense heads in charge of the
library! Servants laying down the law, we (but you, too,
then) obeying, in the absence of any law. A Greek
philosopher (whom your Aristotle quotes here, an accomplice and foul auctoritas) said that the seriousness
of opponents must be dispelled with laughter, and
laughter opposed with seriousness. The prudence of
our fathers made its choice: if laughter is the delight of
the plebeians, the license of the plebeians must be
restrained and humiliated, and intimidated by sternness.
And the plebeians have no weapons for refining their
laughter until they have made it an instrument against
the seriousness of the spiritual shepherds who must
lead them to eternal life and rescue them from the
seductions of belly, pudenda, food, their sordid desires.
But if one day somebody, brandishing the words of the
Philosopher and therefore speaking as a philosopher,
were to raise the weapon of laughter to the condition of
subtle weapon, if the rhetoric of conviction were replaced
by the rhetoric of mockery, if the topics of the patient
construction of the images of redemption were to be
replaced by the topics of the impatient dismantling and
upsetting of every holy and venerable image—oh, that
day even you, William, and all your knowledge, would
be swept away!"

"Why? I would match my wit with the wit of others.
It would be a better world than the one where the fire
and red-hot iron of Bernard Gui humiliate the fire and
red-hot iron of Dolcino."

"You yourself would by then be caught in the Devil's
plot. You would fight on the other side at the field of
Armageddon, where the final conflict must take place.
But by that day the church must be able to impose once

again its rule on the conflict. Blasphemy does not frighten us, because even in the cursing of God we recognize the deformed image of the wrath of Jehovah, who curses the rebellious angels. We are not afraid of the violence of those who kill the shepherds in the name of some fantasy of renewal, because it is the same violence as that of the princes who tried to destroy the people of Israel. We are not afraid of the severity of the Donatists, the mad suicide of the Circumcellions, the lust of the Bogomils, the proud purity of the Albigensians, the flagellants' need for blood, the evil madness of the Brothers of the Free Spirit: we know them all and we know the root of their sins, which is also the root of our holiness. We are not afraid, and, above all, we know how to destroy them—better, how to allow them to destroy themselves, arrogantly carrying to its zenith the will to die that is born from their own nadir. Indeed, I would say their presence is precious to us, it is inscribed in the plan of God, because their sin prompts our virtue, their cursing encourages our hymn of praise, their undisciplined penance regulates our taste for sacrifice, their impiety makes our piety shine, just as the Prince of Darkness was necessary, with his rebellion and his desperation, to make the glory of God shine more radiantly, the beginning and end of all hope. But if one day—and no longer as plebeian exception, but as ascesis of the learned, devoted to the indestructible testimony of Scripture—the art of mockery were to be made acceptable, and to seem noble and liberal and no longer mechanical; if one day someone could say (and be heard), 'I laugh at the Incarnation,' then we would have no weapons to combat that blasphemy, because it would summon the dark powers of corporal matter, those that are affirmed in the fart and the belch, and the fart and the belch would claim the right that is only of the spirit, to breathe where they list!"

"Lycurgus had a statue erected to laughter."

"You read that in the libellus of Cloritian, who tried

to absolve mimes of the sin of impiety, and tells how a sick man was healed by a doctor who helped him laugh. What need was there to heal him, if God had established that his earthly day had reached its end?"

"I don't believe the doctor cured him. He taught him to laugh at his illness."

"Illness is not exorcised. It is destroyed."

"With the body of the sick man."

"If necessary."

"You are the Devil," William said then.

Jorge seemed not to understand. If he had been able to see, I would say he stared at his interlocutor with a dazed look. "I?" he said.

"Yes. They lied to you. The Devil is not the Prince of Matter; the Devil is the arrogance of the spirit, faith without smile, truth that is never seized by doubt. The Devil is grim because he knows where he is going, and, in moving, he always returns whence he came. You are the Devil, and like the Devil you live in darkness. If you wanted to convince me, you have failed. I hate you, Jorge, and if I could, I would lead you downstairs, across the ground, naked, with fowl's feathers stuck in your asshole and your face painted like a juggler and a buffoon, so the whole monastery would laugh at you and be afraid no longer. I would like to smear honey all over you and then roll you in feathers, and take you on a leash to fairs, to say to all: He was announcing the truth to you and telling you that the truth has the taste of death, and you believed, not in his words, but in his grimness. And now I say to you that, in the infinite whirl of possible things, God allows you also to imagine a world where the presumed interpreter of the truth is nothing but a clumsy raven, who repeats words learned long ago."

"You are worse than the Devil, Minorite," Jorge said. "You are a clown, like the saint who gave birth to you all. You are like your Francis, who de toto corpore fecerat linguam, who preached sermons giving a performance like a mountebank's, who confounded the miser by putting gold pieces in his hand, who humiliated the nuns' devotion by reciting the 'Miserere' instead of the sermon, who begged in French, and imitated with a piece of wood the movements of a violin player, who disguised himself as a tramp to confound the gluttonous monks, who flung himself naked in the snow, spoke with animals and plants, transformed the very mystery of the Nativity into a village spectacle, called the lamb of Bethlehem by imitating the bleat of a sheep.... It was a good school. Was that Friar Diotisalvi of Florence not a Minorite?"

"Yes." William smiled. "The one who went to the convent of the preachers and said he would not accept food if first they did not give him a piece of Brother John's tunic to preserve as a relic, and when he was given it he wiped his behind and threw it in the dung-heap and with a stick rolled it around in the dung, shouting: Alas, help me, brothers, because I dropped the saint's relic in the latrine!"

"This story amuses you, apparently. Perhaps you would like to tell me also the one about that other Minorite Friar Paul Millemosche, who one day fell full length on the ice; when his fellow citizens mocked him and one asked him whether he would not like to lie on something better, he said to the man: Yes, your wife... That is how you and your brothers seek the truth."

"That is how Francis taught people to look at things from another direction."

"But we have disciplined them. You saw them yesterday, your brothers. They have rejoined our ranks, they no longer speak like the simple. The simple must not speak. This book would have justified the idea that the tongue of the simple is the vehicle of wisdom. This had to be prevented, which I have done. You say I am the Devil, but it is not true: I have been the hand of God."

"The hand of God creates; it does not conceal."

"There are boundaries beyond which it is not permitted to go. God decreed that certain papers should bear the words 'hic sunt leones.'"

"God created the monsters, too. And you. And He wants everything to be spoken of."

Jorge reached out his shaking hands and drew the book to him. He held it open but turned it around, so that William could still see it in the right position. "Then why," he said, "did He allow this text to be lost over the course of the centuries, and only one copy to be saved, and the copy of that copy, which had ended up God knows where, to remain buried for years in the hands of an infidel who knew no Greek, and then to lie abandoned in the secrecy of an old library, where I, not you, was called by Providence to find it and to hide it for more years still? I know, I know as if I saw it written in adamantine letters, with my eyes, which see things you do not see, I know that this was the will of the Lord, and I acted, interpreting it. In the name of the Father, of the Son, and of the Holy Ghost."

Night

In which the ecpyrosis takes place, and because of excess virtue the forces of hell prevail.

The old man was silent. He held both hands open on the book, as if caressing its pages, flattening them the better to read them, or as if he wanted to protect the book from a raptor's talons.

"All of this, in any case, has been to no avail," William said to him. "Now it is over. I have found you, I have found the book, and the others died in vain."

"Not in vain," Jorge said. "Perhaps there were too many of them. And if you needed proof that this book is accursed, you have had it. And to ensure they have not died in vain, one more death will not be too many."

He spoke, and with his fleshless, diaphanous hands he began slowly tearing to strips and shreds the limp pages of the manuscript, stuffing them into his mouth, slowly swallowing as if he were consuming the host and he wanted to make it flesh of his flesh.

William looked at him, fascinated, and seemed not to grasp what was happening. Then he recovered himself and leaned forward, shouting, "What are you doing?"

584

Jorge smiled, baring his bloodless gums, as a yellowish slime trickled from his pale lips over the sparse white hairs on his chin.

"You were awaiting the sound of the seventh trumpet, were you not? Now listen to what the voice says: Seal what the seven thunders have said and do not write it, take and devour it, it will make bitter your belly but to your lips it will be sweet as honey. You see? Now I seal that which was not to be said, in the grave I become."

He laughed, he, Jorge. For the first time I heard him laugh. . . . He laughed with his throat, though his lips did not assume the shape of gaiety, and he seemed almost to be weeping. "You did not expect it, William, not this conclusion, did you? This old man, by the grace of God, wins once more, does he not?" And as William tried to take the book away from him, Jorge, who sensed the movement, feeling the vibration of the air, drew back, clasping the volume to his chest with his left hand while his right went on tearing the pages and cramming them into his mouth.

He was on the other side of the table, and William, who could not reach him, tried abruptly to move around the obstacle. But he knocked over his stool, catching his habit in it, so that Jorge was able to perceive the disturbance. The old man laughed again, louder this time, and with unexpected rapidity thrust out his right hand, groping for the lamp. Guided by the heat, he reached the flame and pressed his hand over it, unafraid of pain, and the light went out. The room was plunged into darkness, and for the last time we heard the laughter of Jorge, who said, "Find me now! Now I am the one who sees best!" Then he was silent and did not make another sound, moving with those silent footsteps that always made his appearances so unexpected; and we heard only, from time to time, in different parts of the room, the sound of the tearing paper.

"Adso!" William cried. "Stay by the door. Don't let him go out!"

But he had spoken too late, because I, who for some moments had been yearning to fling myself on the old man, had jumped forward when the darkness fell, trying to circle the table on the side opposite the one around which my master had moved. Too late I realized I had enabled Jorge to gain the door, because the old man could move in the dark with extraordinary confidence. We heard a sound of tearing paper behind us—somewhat muffled, because it came from the next room. And at the same time we heard another sound, a harsh, progressive creaking, the groan of hinges.

"The mirror!" William cried. "He is shutting us inside!" Led by the sound, we both rushed toward the entrance; I stumbled over a stool and bruised my leg but paid no heed, because in a flash I realized that if Jorge shut us in we would never get out: in the darkness we would never find the way to open the door, not knowing what had to be maneuvered on this side, or how.

I believe William moved with the same desperation as I did, because I felt him beside me as both of us, reaching the threshold, pressed ourselves against the back of the mirror, which was closing toward us. We arrived in time; the door stopped, then gave way and reopened. Obviously Jorge, sensing the conflict was unequal, had left. We came out of the accursed room, but now we had no idea where the old man was heading, and the darkness was still complete.

All of a sudden I remembered: "Master! I have the flint with me!"

"What are you waiting for, then?" William cried. "Find the lamp and light it!" I rushed back in the darkness, into the finis Africae, groping for the lamp. I found it at once, by divine miracle, then dug inside my scapular and pulled out the flint. My hands were trembling, and two or three times I failed before I was able to light it, as William gasped at the door, "Hurry, hurry!" Finally I made a light.

"Hurry!" William urged me again. "Otherwise the old man will eat up all of Aristotle!"

"And die!" I cried in anguish, overtaking him and joining in the search.

"I don't care whether he dies, damn the monster!" William cried, peering in every direction, moving at random. "With what he has eaten, his fate is already sealed. But I want the book!"

Then he stopped and added, more calmly, "Wait. If we continue like this, we'll never find him. Hush: we'll remain still for a moment." We stiffened, in silence. And in the silence we heard, not far away, the sound of a body bumping into a case, and the racket of some falling books. "That way!" we shouted, together.

We ran in the direction of the noise, but soon realized we would have to slow our pace. In fact, outside the finis Africae, the library was filled that evening with gusts of air that hissed and moaned, in proportion to the strong wind outside. Heightened by our speed, they threatened to put out our light, so painfully recovered. Since we could not move faster, we would have to make Jorge move more slowly. But William had just the opposite idea and shouted, "We've caught you, old man; now we have light!" And it was a wise decision, because the revelation probably upset Jorge, who moved faster, compromising his magic sensibility, his gift for seeing in the darkness. Soon we heard another noise, and, following it, when we entered room Y of YSPANIA, we saw him lying on the floor, the book still in his hands, as he attempted to pull himself to his feet among the books that had spilled from the table he had struck and overturned. He was trying to stand, but he went on tearing the pages, determined to devour his prey as quickly as possible.

By the time we overtook him he was on his feet; sensing our presence, he confronted us, moving backward. His face, in the reddish glow of the lamp, now seemed horrible to us: the features were distorted, a malignant sweat streaked his brow and cheeks, his eyes, usually a deathly white, were bloodshot, from his mouth came scraps of parchment, and he looked like a ravening beast who had stuffed himself and could no longer swallow his food. Disfigured by anxiety, by the menace of the poison now flowing abundantly through his veins, by his desperate and diabolical determination, the venerable figure of the old man now seemed disgusting and grotesque. At other moments he might have inspired laughter, but we, too, were reduced to the condition of animals, dogs stalking their quarry.

We could have taken him calmly, but we fell on him with violence; he writhed, clasped his hands on his chest to defend the volume; I grasped him with my left hand while with my right I tried to hold the lamp high, but I grazed his face with the flame, he sensed the heat, let out a muffled cry, almost a roar, as bits of paper spilled from his mouth, and his right hand let go of the volume, darted toward the lamp, and abruptly tore it from me, flinging it away....

The lamp fell right on the pile of books that had been knocked from the table all in a heap, lying open. The oil spilled out, the fire immediately seized a fragile parchment, which blazed up like a bundle of dry twigs. Everything happened in a few moments, as if for centuries those ancient pages had been yearning for arson and were rejoicing in the sudden satisfaction of an immemorial thirst for ecpyrosis. William realized what was happening and let go of the old man, who, feeling himself free, stepped back a few paces. William hesitated an instant, most likely too long, uncertain whether to seize Jorge again or to hasten to put out the little pyre. One book, older than the others, burned almost immediately, sending up a tongue of flame.

The fine gusts of the wind, which might have extinguished a weak flicker, encouraged the stronger, livelier flame, and even carried sparks flying from it.

"Put out that fire! Quickly!" William cried. "Everything will burn up!"

I rushed toward the blaze, then stopped, because I was unsure what to do. William again moved after me, to come to my aid. We held out our hands as our eyes sought something to smother the fire. I had a flash of inspiration: I slipped my habit over my head and tried to throw it on the heart of the fire. But the flames by now were too high; they consumed my garment and were nourished by it. Snatching back my scorched hands, I turned toward William and saw Jorge, who had approached again, directly behind him. The heat was now so strong that the old man could feel it very easily, so he knew with absolute certainty where the fire was; he flung the Aristotle into it.

In an explosion of ire, William gave the old man a violent push. Jorge slammed into a case, banging his head against one corner. He fell to the ground.... But William, whom I believe I heard utter a horrible curse, paid no heed to him. He turned to the books. Too late. The Aristotle, or what had remained of it after the old man's meal, was already burning.

Meanwhile, some sparks had flown toward the walls, and already the volumes of another bookcase were crumpling in the fury of the fire. By now, not one but two fires were burning in the room.

William, realizing we would not be able to put them out with our hands, decided to use books to save books. He seized a volume that seemed to him more stoutly bound than the others, more compact, and he tried to use it as a weapon to stifle the hostile element. But, slamming the studded binding on the pyre of glowing books, he merely stirred more sparks. Though he tried to scatter them with his feet, he achieved the opposite effect: fluttering scraps of parchment, half burned, rose and hovered like bats, while the air, allied with its airy fellow element, sent them to kindle the terrestrial matter of further pages.

As misfortune would have it, this was one of the most untidy rooms of the labyrinth. Rolled-up manuscripts hung from the shelves; other books, falling apart, let pages slip from their covers, as from gaping mouths, tongues of vellum dried up by the years; and the table must have held a great number of writings that Malachi (by then unassisted for some days) had neglected to put back in their places. So the room, after the spill Jorge caused, was invaded by parchments waiting only to be transformed into another element.

In no time the place was a brazier, a burning bush. The bookcases themselves also joined in this sacrifice and were beginning to crackle. I realized the whole labyrinth was nothing but an immense sacrificial pyre, all prepared for the first spark.

"Water. We need water!" William was saying, but then he added, "But where can any water be found in this inferno?"

"In the kitchen, down in the kitchen!" I cried.

William looked at me, puzzled, his face flushed by that raging glow. "Yes, but by the time we've gone down and come back up... The Devil take it!" he then cried. "This room is lost, in any case, and perhaps the next one as well. Let's go down at once. I'll find water, and you rush out to give the alarm. We need a lot of people!"

We found the way toward the stairs: the conflagration lighted the subsequent rooms as well, but more and more faintly, so we crossed the last two almost groping again. Below, the moon dimly illuminated the scriptorium, and from there we went down to the refectory. William rushed into the kitchen; I to the refectory door, fumbling to open it from the inside. I succeeded after a fair amount of labor, for my agitation made me clumsy and inept. I stepped out onto the grass, ran toward the dormitory, then realized I could not wake the monks one by one. I had an inspiration: I went into the church, hunting for the access to the bell tower. When I found it, I grabbed all the ropes, ringing the alarm. I pulled hard, and the central bell rope, as it rose, drew me up with it. In the library the backs of my hands had been burned. My palms were still unhurt, but now I burned them, too, letting them slip along the ropes until they bled and I had to let go.

By then, however, I had made enough noise. I rushed outside in time to see the first monks coming from the dormitory, as I heard in the distance the voices of the servants, who were appearing at the doors of their lodgings. I could not explain myself clearly, because I was unable to formulate words, and the first that came to my lips were in my mother tongue. With bleeding hand I pointed to the windows of the south wing of the Aedificium, at whose alabaster panes there was an abnormal glow. I realized, from the intensity of the light, that the fire had spread to other rooms while I had come down and rung the bells. All the windows of Africa and the whole façade between it and the east tower now flickered with irregular flashes.

"Water! Fetch water!" I shouted.

At first no one understood. The monks were so used to considering the library a sacred and inaccessible place that they could not understand it was threatened by the sort of banal accident that might have befallen a peasant hut. The first who looked up at the windows blessed themselves, murmuring words of fear, and I realized they were thinking of further apparitions. I grabbed their clothing and begged them to understand, until someone finally translated my sobs into human words.

It was Nicholas of Morimondo, who said, "The library is on fire!"

"It is, indeed," I whispered, sinking to the ground, exhausted.

Nicholas displayed great energy, shouted orders to the servants, gave advice to the monks surrounding him, sent some to open the other doors of the Aedificium, others to seek water and vessels of every kind. He directed those present toward the wells and the water tanks of the abbey. He ordered the cowherds to use the mules and asses to transport jars.... If a man invested with authority had given these orders, he would have been obeyed at once. But the servants were accustomed to taking orders from Remigio, the scribes from Malachi, all of them from the abbot. And, alas, none of those three was present. The monks looked around for the abbot, to ask instructions and solace, and did not find him; only I knew that he was dead, or dying, at that moment, shut up in an airless passage that was now turning into an oven, a bull of Phalaris.

Nicholas shoved the cowherds in one direction, but some other monks, with the best of intentions, pushed them in another. Some of the brothers had obviously lost their heads, others were still dazed with sleep. I tried to explain, now that I had recovered the power of speech, but it must be remembered that I was almost naked, having thrown my habit on the flames, and the sight of a boy, as I was then, bleeding, his face smudged by soot, his body indecently hairless, numbed now by the cold, surely did not inspire much confidence.

Finally Nicholas managed to drag a few brothers and some other men into the kitchen, which in the meantime someone had opened. Another monk had the good sense to bring some torches. We found the place in great disorder, and I realized William must have turned it upside down, seeking water and vessels to carry it.

At that point I saw William himself appear from the door of the refectory, his face singed, his habit smoking. He was carrying a large pot in his hand, and I felt pity for him, pathetic allegory of helplessness. I realized that even if he had succeeded in carrying a pan of water to the second floor without spilling it, and even if he had done so more than once, he could have achieved very little. I recalled the story of Saint Augustine, when he saw a boy trying to scoop up the water of the sea with a spoon: the boy was an angel and did this to make fun of a saint who wanted to understand the mysteries of the divine nature. And, like the angel, William spoke to me, leaning in exhaustion against the door jamb: "It is impossible, we will never do it, not even with all the monks of the abbey. The library is lost." Unlike the angel, William wept.

I hugged him, as he tore a cloth from a table and tried to cover me. We stopped and, finally defeated, observed what was going on around us.

There was a confused bustle, people going up the spiral staircase bare-handed and encountering others, bare-handed, who had been driven upstairs by their curiosity and were now coming down to look for vessels. Others, cleverer, had immediately started hunting for pans and basins, only to realize there was not sufficient water in the kitchen. Suddenly the great room was invaded by mules, bearing huge jars, and the cowherds driving the animals unloaded them and started to carry up the water. But they did not know how to climb to the scriptorium, and it was a while before some of the scribes told them, and when they went up they bumped into others rushing down, terrified. Jars broke and the water spread over the ground, though other jars were passed up the stairs by willing hands. I followed the group and found myself in the scriptorium. Thick smoke came from the access to the library; the last men who had tried to go up to the east tower were already coming down, coughing, red-eyed, and they announced it was no longer possible to penetrate that hell.

Then I saw Benno. His face distorted, he was coming up from the lower floor with an enormous vessel. He heard what those coming down were saying and he attacked them: "Hell will swallow you all, cowards!" He turned, as if seeking help, and saw me. "Adso," he cried, "the library...the library..." He did not await my answer, but ran to the foot of the stairs and boldly plunged into the smoke. That was the last time I saw him.

I heard a creaking sound from above. Bits of stone mixed with mortar were falling from the ceiling of the scriptorium. The keystone of a vault, carved in the shape of a flower, came loose and almost landed on my head. The floor of the labyrinth was giving way.

I rushed downstairs and out into the open air. Some willing servants had brought ladders, with which they were trying to reach the windows of the upper floors, to take water up that way. But the highest ladders barely extended to the windows of the scriptorium, and those who had climbed up were unable to open them from the outside. They sent word down to have them opened from within, but at this point nobody dared try to go up there.

Meanwhile, I was looking at the windows of the top floor. The whole library by now must have become a single smoking brazier as the fire raced from room to room, spreading rapidly among the thousands of dry pages. All the windows were alight, a black smoke came from the roof: the fire had already spread to the beams. The Aedificium, which had seemed so solid and tetragonous, revealed in these circumstances its weakness, its cracks, the walls corroded from within, the crumbling stones allowing the flames to reach the wooden elements wherever they were.

Suddenly some windows shattered as if pressed by an inner force, the sparks flew out into the open air, dotting with fluttering glints the darkness of the night. The strong wind had become lighter: a misfortune, because, strong, it might have blown out the sparks, but light, it carried them, stimulating them, and with them made scraps of parchment swirl in the air, the delicate fragments of an inner torch. At that point an explosion was heard: the floor of the labyrinth had given way at some point and its blazing beams must have plunged to the floor below. Now I saw tongues of flame rise from the scriptorium, which was also tenanted by books and cases, and by loose papers, spread on the desks, ready to provoke the sparks. I heard cries of woe from a group of scribes who tore their hair and still thought of climbing up heroically, to recover their beloved parchments. In vain: the kitchen and refectory were now a crossroads of lost souls, rushing in all directions, each hindering the others. People bumped into one another, fell down; those carrying vessels spilled their redemptive contents; the mules brought into the kitchen had sensed the presence of fire and, with a clatter of hoofs, dashed toward the exits, knocking down the human beings and even their own terrified grooms. It was obvious, in any case, that this horde of villeins and of devout, wise, but unskilled men, with no one in command, was blocking even what aid might still have arrived.

The whole abbey was in the grip of disorder, but this was only the beginning of the tragedy. Pouring from the windows and the roof, the triumphant cloud of sparks, fostered by the wind, was now descending on all sides, touching the roof of the church. Everyone knows how the most splendid cathedrals are vulnerable to the sting of fire: the house of God appears beautiful and well defended as the heavenly Jerusalem itself thanks to the stone it proudly displays, but the walls and ceilings are supported by a fragile, if admirable, architecture of wood, and if the church of stone recalls the most venerable forests with its columns rising high, bold as oaks, to the vaults of the ceilings, these columns often have cores of oak—and many of the trappings are also of wood: the altars, the choirs, the painted panels, the benches, the stalls, the candelabra. And so it was with the abbatial church, whose beautiful door had so fascinated me on the first day. The church caught fire in no time. The monks and the whole population of the place then understood that the very survival of the abbey was at stake, and all began rushing even more earnestly, and in even greater confusion, to deal with the new danger.

To be sure, the church was more accessible, more easily defended than the library. The library had been doomed by its own impenetrability, by the mystery that protected it, by its few entrances. The church, maternally open to all in the hour of prayer, was open to all in the hour of succor. But there was no more water, or at least very little could be found stored, and the wells supplied it with natural parsimony and at a slow pace that did not correspond to the urgency of the need. All the monks would have liked to put out the fire of the church, but nobody knew how at this point. Moreover, the fire was spreading from above, and it was difficult to hoist men up to beat on the flames or smother them with dirt or rags. And when the flames arrived from below, it was futile by then to throw earth or sand on them, for the ceiling was crashing down on the firefighters, striking more, than a few of them.

And so the cries of regret for the many riches burned were now joined by the cries of pain at seared faces, crushed limbs, bodies buried under a sudden collapse of the high vaults.

The wind had become furious again, and more furiously helped spread the fire. Immediately after the church, the barns and stables caught fire. The terrified animals broke their halters, kicked down the doors, scattered over the grounds, neighing, mooing, bleating, grunting horribly. Sparks caught the manes of many horses, and there were infernal creatures racing across the grass, flaming steeds that trampled everything in their path, without goal or respite. I saw old Alinardo wandering around, not understanding what was happening, knocked down by the magnificent Brunellus, haloed by fire; the old man was dragged in the dust, then abandoned there, a poor shapeless object. But I had neither means nor time to succor him, or to bemoan his end, because similar scenes were taking place everywhere.

The horses in flames had carried the fire to places where the wind had not yet brought it: now the forges were burning, and the novices' house. Hordes of people were running from one end of the compound to another, for no purpose or for illusory purposes. I saw Nicholas, his head wounded, his habit in shreds, now defeated, kneeling in the path from the gate, cursing the divine curse. I saw Pacificus of Tivoli, who, abandoning all notion of help, was trying to seize a crazed mule as it passed; when he succeeded, he shouted to me to do the same and to flee, to escape that horrid replica of Armageddon.

I wondered where William was, fearing he had been trapped under some collapsing wall. I found him, after a long search, near the cloister. In his hand he had his traveling sack: when the fire was already spreading to the pilgrims' hospice, he had gone up to his cell to save at least his most precious belongings. He had collected my sack, too, and in it I found something to put on. We paused, breathless, to watch what was happening around us.

By now the abbey was doomed. Almost all its buildings, some more, some less, had been reached by the fire. Those still intact would not remain so for long, because everything, from the natural elements to the confused work of the rescuers, was now contributing to the spread of the fire. Only the parts without buildings remained safe; the vegetable patch, the garden outside the cloister.... Nothing more could be done to save the buildings; abandoning the idea of saving them, we were able to observe everything without danger, standing in an open space.

We looked at the church, now burning slowly, for it is characteristic of these great constructions to blaze up quickly in their wooden parts and then to agonize for hours, sometimes for days. The conflagration of the

Aedificium was different. Here inflammable material was much more abundant, and the fire, having spread all through the scriptorium, had invaded the kitchen floor. As for the top floor, where once, and for hundreds of years, there had been the labyrinth, it was now virtually destroyed.

"It was the greatest library in Christendom," William said. "Now," he added, "the Antichrist is truly at hand, because no learning will hinder him any more. For that matter, we have seen his face tonight."

"Whose face?" I asked, dazed.

"Jorge, I mean. In that face, deformed by hatred of philosophy, I saw for the first time the portrait of the Antichrist, who does not come from the tribe of Judas, as his heralds have it, or from a far country. The Antichrist can be born from piety itself, from excessive love of God or of the truth, as the heretic is born from the saint and the possessed from the seer. Fear prophets, Adso, and those prepared to die for the truth, for as a rule they make many others die with them, often before them, at times instead of them. Jorge did a diabolical thing because he loved his truth so lewdly that he dared anything in order to destroy falsehood. Jorge feared the second book of Aristotle because it perhaps really did teach how to distort the face of every truth, so that we would not become slaves of our ghosts. Perhaps the mission of those who love mankind is to make people laugh at the truth, *to make truth laugh,* because the only truth lies in learning to free ourselves from insane passion for the truth."

"But, master," I ventured, sorrowfully, "you speak like this now because you are wounded in the depths of your spirit. There is one truth, however, that you discovered tonight, the one you reached by interpreting the clues you read over the past few days. Jorge has won, but you have defeated Jorge because you exposed his plot...."

"There was no plot," William said, "and I discovered it by mistake."

The assertion was self-contradictory, and I couldn't decide whether William really wanted it to be. "But it was true that the tracks in the snow led to Brunellus," I said, "it was true that Adelmo committed suicide, it was true that Venantius did not drown in the jar, it was true that the labyrinth was laid out the way you imagined it, it was true that one entered the finis Africae by touching the word 'quatuor,' it was true that the mysterious book was by Aristotle.... I could go on listing all the true things you discovered with the help of your learning...."

"I have never doubted the truth of signs, Adso; they are the only things man has with which to orient himself in the world. What I did not understand was the relation among signs. I arrived at Jorge through an apocalyptic pattern that seemed to underlie all the crimes, and yet it was accidental. I arrived at Jorge seeking one criminal for all the crimes and we discovered that each crime was committed by a different person, or by no one. I arrived at Jorge pursuing the plan of a perverse and rational mind, and there was no plan, or, rather, Jorge himself was overcome by his own initial design and there began a sequence of causes, and concauses, and of causes contradicting one another, which proceeded on their own, creating relations that did not stem from any plan. Where is all my wisdom, then? I behaved stubbornly, pursuing a semblance of order, when I should have known well that there is no order in the universe."

"But in imagining an erroneous order you still found something...."

"What you say is very fine, Adso, and I thank you. The order that our mind imagines is like a net, or like a ladder, built to attain something. But afterward you must throw the ladder away, because you discover that,

even if it was useful, it was meaningless. Er muoz
gelîchesame die leiter abewerfen, sô er an ir ufgestigen.
. . . Is that how you say it?"

"That is how it is said in my language. Who told you
that?"

"A mystic from your land. He wrote it somewhere, I
forget where. And it is not necessary for somebody one
day to find that manuscript again. The only truths that
are useful are instruments to be thrown away."

"You have no reason to reproach yourself: you did
your best."

"A human best, which is very little. It's hard to accept
the idea that there cannot be an order in the universe
because it would offend the free will of God and His
omnipotence. So the freedom of God is our condemnation, or at least the condemnation of our pride."

I dared, for the first and last time in my life, to
express a theological conclusion: "But how can a necessary being exist totally polluted with the possible? What
difference is there, then, between God and primigenial
chaos? Isn't affirming God's absolute omnipotence and
His absolute freedom with regard to His own choices
tantamount to demonstrating that God does not
exist?"

William looked at me without betraying any feeling
in his features, and he said, "How could a learned man
go on communicating his learning if he answered yes to
your question?"

I did not understand the meaning of his words. "Do
you mean," I asked, "that there would be no possible
and communicable learning any more if the very criterion of truth were lacking, or do you mean you
could no longer communicate what you know because
others would not allow you to?"

At that moment a section of the dormitory roof
collapsed with a huge din, blowing a cloud of sparks
into the sky. Some of the sheep and the goats wander-

ing through the grounds went past us, bleating horribly. A group of servants also went by us, shouting, nearly knocking us down.

"There is too much confusion here," William said. "Non in commotione, non in commotione Dominus."

LAST PAGE

7

The Abbey burned for three days and three nights, and the last efforts were of no avail. As early as that morning of the seventh day of our sojourn in that place, when the survivors were fully aware that no building could be saved, when the finest constructions showed only their ruined outer walls, and the church, as if drawing into itself, swallowed its tower—even at that point everyone's will to combat the divine chastisement failed. The rush for the last few buckets of water grew more and more listless, while the chapter house and the superb apartments of the abbot were still burning. By the time the fire reached the far side of the various workshops, the servants had long since saved as many objects as they could, and had chosen to beat the countryside to recapture at least some of the livestock, which had fled beyond the walls in the confusion of the night.

I saw some of the servants venture into what remained of the church: I presumed they were trying to get into

605

the crypt to seize some precious object before running away. I do not know whether they succeeded, whether the crypt had not already collapsed, whether the louts did not sink into the bowels of the earth in their attempt to reach the treasure.

Meanwhile, men were coming up from the village to lend a hand or to try to snatch some further booty. The dead for the most part remained among the ruins, which were still red-hot. On the third day, when the wounded had been treated and the corpses found outside had been buried, the monks and all the others collected their belongings and abandoned the still-smoking abbey, as a place accursed. They scattered, I do not know whereto.

William and I left those parts on two horses we found astray in the wood; we considered them res nullius by now. We headed east. When we reached Bobbio again, we began to receive bad news of the Emperor. On arriving in Rome, he had been crowned by the people. Considering any agreement with John now impossible, he had chosen an antipope, Nicholas V. Marsilius had been named spiritual vicar of Rome, but through his fault, or his weakness, things very sad to report were taking place in that city. Priests loyal to the Pope and unwilling to say Mass were tortured, an Augustinian prior had been thrown into the lions' pit on the Capitoline. Marsilius and John of Jandun had declared John a heretic, and Louis had had him sentenced to death. But the Emperor's misrule was antagonizing the local lords and depleting public funds. Gradually, as we heard this news, we delayed our descent to Rome, and I realized that William did not want to find himself witnessing events that would dash his hopes.

When we came to Pomposa, we learned that Rome had rebelled against Louis, who had moved back up toward Pisa, while John's legates were triumphantly entering the papal city.

Meanwhile, Michael of Cesena had realized that his

presence in Avignon was producing no results—indeed, he feared for his life—so he had fled, joining Louis in Pisa.

Soon, foreseeing events and learning that the Bavarian would move on to Munich, we reversed our route and decided to proceed there, also because William sensed that Italy was becoming unsafe for him. In the ensuing months and years, Louis saw the alliance of his supporters, the Ghibelline lords, dissolve; and the following year the Antipope Nicholas was to surrender to John, presenting himself with a rope around his neck.

When we came to Munich, I had to take leave of my good master, amid many tears. His destiny was uncertain, and my family preferred for me to return to Melk. After that tragic night when William revealed to me his dismay before the ruins of the abbey, as if by tacit agreement we had not spoken again of that story. Nor did we mention it in the course of our sorrowful farewell.

My master gave me much good advice about my future studies, and presented me with the glasses Nicholas had made for him, since he had his own back again. I was still young, he said to me, but one day they would come in handy (and, truly, I am wearing them on my nose now, as I write these lines). Then he embraced me with a father's tenderness and dismissed me.

I never saw him again. I learned much later that he had died during the great plague that raged through Europe toward the middle of this century. I pray always that God received his soul and forgave him the many acts of pride that his intellectual vanity had made him commit.

Years later, as a grown man, I had occasion to make a journey to Italy, sent by my abbot. I could not resist temptation, and on my return I went far out of my way to revisit what remained of the abbey.

The two villages on the slopes of the mountain were

deserted, the lands around them uncultivated. When I climbed up to the top, a spectacle of desolation and death appeared before my eyes, which moistened with tears.

Of the great and magnificent constructions that once adorned that place, only scattered ruins remained, as had happened before with the monuments of the ancient pagans in the city of Rome. Ivy covered the shreds of walls, columns, the few architraves still intact. Weeds invaded the ground on all sides, and there was no telling where the vegetables and the flowers had once grown. Only the location of the cemetery was recognizable, because of some graves that still rose above the level of the terrain. Sole sign of life, some birds of prey hunted lizards and serpents that, like basilisks, slithered among the stones or crawled over the walls. Of the church door only a few traces remained, eroded by mold. Half of the tympanum survived, and I still glimpsed there, dilated by the elements and dulled by lichens, the left eye of the enthroned Christ, and something of the lion's face.

The Aedificium, except for the south wall, which was in ruins, seemed yet to stand and defy the course of time. The two outer towers, over the cliff, appeared almost untouched, but all the windows were empty sockets whose slimy tears were rotting vines. Inside, the work of art, destroyed, became confused with the work of nature, and across vast stretches of the kitchen the eye ran to the open heavens through the breach of the upper floors and the roof, fallen like fallen angels. Everything that was not green with moss was still black from the smoke of so many decades ago.

Poking about in the rubble, I found at times scraps of parchment that had drifted down from the scriptorium and the library and had survived like treasures buried in the earth; I began to collect them, as if I were going to piece together the torn pages of a book. Then I noticed that in one of the towers there rose, tottering but still intact, a circular staircase to the scriptorium, and from there, by climbing a sloping bit of the ruin, I could reach the level of the library: which, however, was only a sort of gallery next to the outside walls, looking down into the void at every point.

Along one stretch of wall I found a bookcase, still miraculously erect, having come through the fire I cannot say how; it was rotted by water and consumed by termites. In it there were still a few pages. Other remnants I found by rummaging in the ruins below. Mine was a poor harvest, but I spent a whole day reaping it, as if from those disiecta membra of the library a message might reach me. Some fragments of parchment had faded, others permitted the glimpse of an image's shadow, or the ghost of one or more words. At times I found pages where whole sentences were legible; more often, intact bindings, protected by what had once been metal studs.... Ghosts of books, apparently intact on the outside but consumed within; yet sometimes a half page had been saved, an incipit was discernible, a title.

I collected every relic I could find, filling two traveling sacks with them, abandoning things useful to me in order to save that miserable hoard.

Along the return journey and afterward at Melk, I spent many, many hours trying to decipher those remains. Often from a word or a surviving image I could recognize what the work had been. When I found, in time, other copies of those books, I studied them with love, as if destiny had left me this bequest, as if having identified the destroyed copy were a clear sign from heaven that said to me: Tolle et lege. At the end of my patient reconstruction, I had before me a kind of lesser library, a symbol of the greater, vanished one: a library made up of fragments, quotations, unfinished sentences, amputated stumps of books.

*   *   *

The more I reread this list the more I am convinced it is the result of chance and contains no message. But these incomplete pages have accompanied me through all the life that has been left me to live since then; I have often consulted them like an oracle, and I have almost had the impression that what I have written on these pages, which you will now read, unknown reader, is only a cento, a figured hymn, an immense acrostic that says and repeats nothing but what those fragments have suggested to me, nor do I know whether thus far I have been speaking of them or they have spoken through my mouth. But whichever of the two possibilities may be correct, the more I repeat to myself the story that has emerged from them, the less I manage to understand whether in it there is a design that goes beyond the natural sequence of the events and the times that connect them. And it is a hard thing for this old monk, on the threshold of death, not to know whether the letter he has written contains some hidden meaning, or more than one, or many, or none at all.

But this inability of mine to see is perhaps the effect of the shadow that the great darkness, as it approaches, is casting on the aged world.

Est ubi gloria nunc Babyloniae? Where are the snows of yesteryear? The earth is dancing the dance of Macabré; at times it seems to me that the Danube is crowded with ships loaded with fools going toward a dark place.

All I can do now is be silent. O quam salubre, quam iucundum et suave est sedere in solitudine et tacere et loqui cum Deo! Soon I shall be joined with my beginning, and I no longer believe that it is the God of glory of whom the abbots of my order spoke to me, or of joy, as the Minorites believed in those days, perhaps not even of piety. Gott ist ein lauter Nichts, ihn rührt kein Nun noch Hier. . . . I shall soon enter this broad desert, perfectly level and boundless, where the truly pious heart succumbs in bliss. I shall sink into the divine shadow, in a dumb silence and an ineffable union, and in this sinking all equality and all inequality shall be lost, and in that abyss my spirit will lose itself, and will not know the equal or the unequal, or anything else: and all differences will be forgotten. I shall be in the simple foundation, in the silent desert where diversity is never seen, in the privacy where no one finds himself in his proper place. I shall fall into the silent and uninhabited divinity where there is no work and no image.

It is cold in the scriptorium, my thumb aches. I leave this manuscript, I do not know for whom; I no longer know what it is about: stat rosa pristina nomine, nomina nuda tenemus.